Barbara J. Wright

THE SCRIBNER TREASURY

22 Classic Tales

by

MARY RAYMOND SHIPMAN ANDREWS

SIR JAMES BARRIE

HENRY CUYLER BUNNER

GEORGE W. CABLE

JAMES BRENDAN CONNOLLY

RICHARD HARDING DAVIS

CARL EWALD

JOHN FOX, JR.

JOHN GALSWORTHY

JOEL CHANDLER HARRIS

ROBERT HERRICK

RING LARDNER

THOMAS NELSON PAGE

ERNEST THOMPSON SETON

ANNIE TRUMBULL SLOSSON

FRANK R. STOCKTON

HENRY VAN DYKE

EDITH WHARTON

INTRODUCTION AND NOTES
by J. G. E. HOPKINS

CHARLES SCRIBNER'S SONS

New York 1953

PRINTED IN THE UNITED STATES OF AMERICA BY
KINGSPORT PRESS, INC., KINGSPORT, TENNESSEE

TABLE OF CONTENTS

INTRODUCTION

Of the twenty-two stories offered in this volume, eleven made their earliest appearance in *Scribner's Magazine,* and all were published by Charles Scribner's Sons as individual volumes. *Free Joe,* by Harris, Page's *The Burial of the Guns,* and Stockton's *The Lady, or the Tiger?* shared covers, on publication, with other short fiction by the same author, but the popularity of the story which we have included in *The Scribner Treasury* gave it authority as the title-story and established the reputation of the original book. We trust that the many persons who have read these tales singly over the years will enjoy them anew in association with one another, and that America's latest generation of readers will be pleased to make their acquaintance.

The Scribner Treasury is presented modestly as an entertainment. It has no thesis. The stories have, indeed, but one point of unity (excluding the fact of original publication by a single house), yet that is an important one. For all their diversity of form, of place of origin, of theme, of technique, of literary merit—these tales won immediate public favor at the time of their publication, and the demand for them thereafter has never ceased. This book is no mere stirring of dry bones, even though its professed intention is to recall to its readers the very real excellence of fiction written under influences of an earlier time.

The earliest work included dates from 1881. It is *Madame Delphine,* George Cable's masterpiece, wherein a New Orleans which was fading into history even in the author's day flowered again in pages wonderfully evocative of warm southern scents and Gallic romance. The latest of the stories appeared first in 1932—an eerie winter's tale of a lovely Scottish ghost—the memorable *Farewell Miss Julie Logan* by Sir James Barrie. Fourteen of the writers here represented were Americans; one was a Scot, one an Englishman, one a Canadian, one a Dane.

The Scribner Treasury does not set out to prove anything, but it does in fact tell us a good deal about popular taste—at least up to the 1930's. Although superficial manners and conventions vary from story to story, an ethical pattern is implicit in each. The context of life within which these writers observed and wrote was clearly delimited. They—and the readers who enjoyed their work—believed firmly in standards of behavior, in right and wrong, in law and its opposite, disorder. They might differ in particulars, but the great ends of living were common in their thinking; and they were assured that literature, to have meaning, must offer not only a slice of life but a criticism of it. Also, along with yesterday's demand that even popular entertainers must have something to say, went the imperative that it be said with the finest economy of means; in consequence, all these stories are craftily put together. They are tales in the classic style, written with a professional skill which transcends changing literary fashion. Each has its beginning, its middle and its logical end. The range of emotion runs a gamut—from the disciplined restraint of *The Apple Tree* to the frank, heart-on-sleeve sentiment of *The Perfect Tribute*; from the pulpit tone of *Fishin' Jimmy* to the deliberate understatement of *Madame de Treymes*.

A brief note on the author and a little about the publishing history of the book will be found on the page preliminary to each tale.

J. G. E. Hopkins

GEORGE W. CABLE

Madame Delphine

George W. Cable (1844–1925)

on his tour of the southern states in 1873, in search of material for articles on the "New South," commissioned by Scribner's Magazine, Edward King met George Cable, admired his work, and was responsible for the magazine publication of the stories later to become celebrated in collected form as Old Creole Days (1879)—stories which stand at the head of American regional fiction as much in quality as in point of time.

In Cable's own words, he was then "drifting into literature," although he still had a sheet-anchor ready in his regular employment as cashier-bookkeeper for a firm of cotton-brokers at New Orleans. After magazine publication of his earliest stories, and their successful debut as a book in 1879, Cable could abandon commerce. Old Creole Days was followed by The Grandissimes (1880) and by Madame Delphine (1881), but this last was the high point of Cable's career as a writer. Thereafter, his interest in reform movements, his lecture engagements and other concerns blunted his sense for the one moment in time and the one place which were his by right of mastery.

Shortly after Madame Delphine appeared in 1881, Lafcadio Hearn commented on Cable's genius for recreation of a past era: "The author must have made many a pilgrimage . . . to study the wrinkled faces of the houses, or perhaps to read the queer names upon the signs—as Balzac loved to do in old-fashioned Paris." Hearn here put his finger on the two factors which influenced Cable's writing in the greatest degree; French literary models and an antiquarian bent.

Cable had grown up in New Orleans. The old Creole city fascinated him and stirred his imagination, whereas the "American" side of Canal Street left him cold. The narrow lanes and dreaming, high-walled old houses of French and Spanish colonial days provided the inspiration; he peopled them thereafter with characters fitted to them. He did not make the blunder of attempting to recreate old New Orleans by piling up antiquarian fact, but by his own imaginative understanding he entered into the very life of the past, lived within it himself, and so was able to make his readers share the experience.

Cable's success as an artist was a triumph of manner and feeling, for he is no model of the mathematical virtues of plot. His stories "grow" by a slow but continuing recognition in the reader's mind of the absolute rightness of the episodes and scenes, the descriptions and the atmosphere—a belief in the story which has nothing to do with logical conviction. His use of words exhibits a similar exactness and sureness. His manner is impressionistic, elliptical; he does his reader the honor of supposing him mature and literate, emotionally as well as intellectually.

MADAME DELPHINE

I

AN OLD HOUSE

A FEW steps from the St. Charles Hotel, in New Orleans, brings you to and across Canal Street, the central avenue of the city, and to that corner where the flower-women sit at the inner and outer edges of the arcaded sidewalk, and make the air sweet with their fragrant merchandise. The crowd—and if it is near the time of the carnival it will be great—will follow Canal Street.

But you turn, instead, into the quiet, narrow way which a lover of Creole antiquity, in fondness for a romantic past, is still prone to call the Rue Royale. You will pass a few restaurants, a few auction-rooms, a few furniture warehouses, and will hardly realize that you have left behind you the activity and clatter of a city of merchants before you find yourself in a region of architectural decrepitude, where an ancient and foreign-seeming domestic life, in second stories, overhangs the ruins of a former commercial prosperity, and upon every thing has settled down a long sabbath of decay. The vehicles in the street are few in number, and are merely passing through; the stores are shrunken into shops; you see here and there, like a patch of bright mould, the stall of that significant fungus, the Chinaman. Many great doors are shut and clamped and grown gray with cobweb; many street windows are nailed up; half the balconies are begrimed and rust-eaten, and many of the humid arches and alleys which characterize the older Franco-Spanish piles of stuccoed brick betray a squalor almost oriental.

Yet beauty lingers here. To say nothing of the picturesque, sometimes you get sight of comfort, sometimes of opulence, through the unlatched wicket in some *porte-cochère*—red-painted brick pavement, foliage of dark palm or pale banana, marble or granite masonry and blooming parterres; or through a chink between some pair of heavy batten window-shutters, opened with an almost reptile wariness, your eye gets a glimpse of lace and brocade upholstery, silver and bronze, and much similar rich antiquity.

The faces of the inmates are in keeping; of the passengers in the street a sad proportion are dingy and shabby; but just when these are putting you off your guard, there will pass you a woman—more likely two or three—of patrician beauty.

Now, if you will go far enough down this old street, you will see, as you approach its intersection with ——. Names in that region elude one like ghosts.

However, as you begin to find the way a trifle more open, you will not fail to notice on the right-hand side, about midway of the square, a small, low, brick house of a story and a half, set out upon the sidewalk, as weather-beaten and mute as an aged beggar fallen asleep. Its corrugated roof of dull red tiles, sloping down toward you with an inward curve, is overgrown with weeds, and in the fall of the year is gay with the yellow plumes of the golden-rod. You can almost touch with your cane the low edge of the broad, overhanging eaves. The batten shutters at door and window, with hinges like those of a postern, are shut with a grip that makes one's knuckles and nails feel lacerated. Save in the brick-work itself there is not a cranny. You would say the house has the lockjaw. There are two doors, and to each a single chipped and battered marble step. Continuing on down the sidewalk, on a line with the house, is a garden masked from view by a high, close board-fence. You may see the tops of its fruit-trees—pomegranate, peach, banana, fig, pear, and particularly one large orange, close by the fence, that must be very old.

The residents over the narrow way, who live in a three-story house, originally of much pretension, but from whose front door hard times have removed almost all vestiges of paint, will tell you:

"Yass, de 'ouse is in'abit; 'tis live in."

And this is likely to be all the information you get—not that they would not tell, but they cannot grasp the idea that you wish to know—until, possibly, just as you are turning to depart, your informant, in a single word and with the most evident non-appreciation of its value, drops the simple key to the whole matter:

"Dey's quadroons."

He may then be aroused to mention the better appearance of the place in former years, when the houses of this region generally stood farther apart, and that garden comprised the whole square.

Here dwelt, sixty years ago and more, one Delphine Carraze; or, as she was commonly designated by the few who knew her, Madame Delphine. That she owned her home, and that it had been given her by the then deceased companion of her days of beauty, were facts so generally admitted as to be, even as far back as that sixty years ago, no longer a subject of gossip. She was never pointed out by the denizens of the quarter as a character, nor her house as a "feature." It would have passed all Creole powers of guessing to divine what you could find worthy of inquiry concerning a retired quadroon woman; and not the least puzzled of all would have been the timid and restive Madame Delphine herself.

II

MADAME DELPHINE

During the first quarter of the present century, the free quadroon caste of New Orleans was in its golden age. Earlier generations—sprung, upon the one hand, from the merry gallants of a French colonial military service which had grown gross by affiliation with Spanish-American frontier life, and, upon the other hand, from comely Ethiopians culled out of the less negroidal types of African live goods, and bought at the ship's side with vestiges of quills and cowries and copper wire still in their head-dresses,—these earlier generations, with scars of battle or private rencontre still on the fathers, and of servitude on the manumitted mothers, afforded a mere hint of the splendor that was to result from a survival of the fairest through seventy-five years devoted to the elimination of the black pigment and the cultivation of hyperian excellence and nymphean grace and beauty. Nor, if we turn to the present, is the evidence much stronger which is offered by the *gens de couleur* whom you may see in the quadroon quarter this afternoon, with "Ichabod" legible on their murky foreheads through a vain smearing of toilet powder, dragging their chairs down to the narrow gateway of their close-fenced gardens, and staring shrinkingly at you as you pass, like a nest of yellow kittens.

But as the present century was in its second and third decades, the *quadroones* (for we must contrive a feminine spelling to define the strict limits of the caste as then established) came forth in splendor. Old travellers spare no terms to tell their praises, their faultlessness of feature, their perfection of form, their varied styles of beauty,—for there were even pure Caucasian blondes among them, —their fascinating manners, their sparkling vivacity, their chaste and pretty wit, their grace in the dance, their modest propriety, their taste and elegance in dress. In the gentlest and most poetic sense they were indeed the sirens of this land, where it seemed "always afternoon"—a momentary triumph of an Arcadian over a Christian civilization, so beautiful and so seductive that it became the subject of special chapters by writers of the day more original than correct as social philosophers.

The balls that were got up for them by the male *sang-pur* were to that day what the carnival is to the present. Society balls given the same nights proved failures through the coincidence. The magnates of government,—municipal, state, federal,—those of the army, of the learned professions and of the clubs,—in short, the white male aristocracy in every thing save the ecclesiastical desk,—were there. Tickets were high-priced to insure the exclusion of the vulgar. No distinguished stranger was allowed to miss them. They were beautiful! They were clad in silken extenuations from the throat to the feet, and wore, withal, a pathos in their charm that gave them a family likeness to innocence.

Madame Delphine, were you not a stranger, could have told you all about it; though hardly, I suppose, without tears.

But at the time of which we would speak (1821–22) her day of splendor was set, and her husband—let us call him so for her sake—was long dead. He was an American, and, if we take her word for it, a man of noble heart and extremely handsome; but this is knowledge which we can do without.

Even in those days the house was always shut, and Madame Delphine's chief occupation and end in life seemed to be to keep well locked up in-doors. She was an excellent person, the neighbors said, —a very worthy person; and they were, maybe, nearer correct than they knew. They rarely saw her save when she went to or returned from church; a small, rather tired-looking, dark quadroone of very good features and a gentle thoughtfulness of expression which would take long to describe: call it a widow's look.

In speaking of Madame Delphine's house, mention should have been made of a gate in the fence on the Royal-street sidewalk. It is gone now, and was out of use then, being fastened once for all by an iron staple clasping the cross-bar and driven into the post.

Which leads us to speak of another person.

III

CAPITAINE LEMAITRE

He was one of those men that might be any age,—thirty, forty, forty-five; there was no telling from his face what was years and what was only weather. His countenance was of a grave and quiet, but also luminous, sort, which was instantly admired and ever afterward remembered, as was also the fineness of his hair and the blueness of his eyes. Those pronounced him youngest who scrutinized his face the closest. But waiving the discussion of age, he was odd, though not with the oddness that he who had reared him had striven to produce.

He had not been brought up by mother or father. He had lost both in infancy, and had fallen to the care of a rugged old military grandpa of the colonial school, whose unceasing endeavor had been to make "his boy" as savage and ferocious a holder of unimpeachable social rank as it became a pure-blooded French Creole to be who would trace his pedigree back to the god Mars.

"Remember, my boy," was the adjuration received by him as regularly as his waking cup of black coffee, "that none of your family line ever kept the laws of any government or creed." And if it was well that he should bear this in mind, it was well to reiterate it persistently, for, from the nurse's arms, the boy wore a look, not of docility so much as of gentle, *judicial* benevolence. The domestics of the old man's house used to shed tears of laughter to see that look on the face of a babe. His rude guardian addressed himself to the modification of this facial expression; it had not enough of majesty in it, for instance, or of large dare-deviltry; but with care these could be made to come.

And, true enough, at twenty-one (in Ursin Lemaitre), the labors of his grandfather were an apparent success. He was not rugged, nor was he loud-spoken, as his venerable trainer would have liked to present him to society; but he was as serenely terrible as a well-aimed rifle, and the old man looked upon his results with pride. He had cultivated him up to that pitch where he scorned to practise any vice, or any virtue, that did not include the principle of self-assertion. A few touches only were wanting here and there to achieve perfection, when suddenly the old man died. Yet it was his proud satisfaction, before he finally lay down, to see Ursin a favored companion and the peer, both in courtesy and pride, of those polished gentlemen famous in history, the brothers Lafitte.

The two Lafittes were, at the time young Lemaitre reached his majority (say 1808 or 1812), only merchant-blacksmiths, so to speak, a term intended to convey the idea of blacksmiths who never soiled their hands, who were men of capital, stood a little higher than the clergy, and moved in society among its autocrats. But they were full of possibilities, men of action, and men, too, of thought, with already a pronounced disbelief in the custom-house. In these days of big carnivals they would have been patented as the dukes of Little Manchac and Barataria.

Young Ursin Lemaitre (in full the name was Lemaitre-Vignevielle) had not only the hearty friendship of these good people, but also a natural turn for accounts; and as his two friends were looking about them with an enterprising eye, it easily resulted that he presently connected himself with the blacksmithing profession. Not exactly at the forge in the Lafittes' famous smithy, among the African Samsons, who, with their shining black bodies bared to the waist, made the Rue St. Pierre ring with the stroke of their hammers; but as a—there was no occasion to mince the word in those days—smuggler.

Smuggler—patriot—where was the difference? Beyond the ken of a community to which the enforcement of the revenue laws had long been merely so much out of every man's pocket and dish, into the all-devouring treasury of Spain. At this date they had come under a kinder yoke, and to a treasury that at least echoed when the customs were dropped into it; but the change was still new. What could a man be more than Capitaine Lemaitre was—the soul of honor, the pink of courtesy, with the courage of the lion, and the magnanimity of the elephant; frank—the very exchequer of truth! Nay, go higher still: his paper was good in Toulouse Street. To the gossips in the gaming-clubs he was the culminating proof that smuggling was one of the sublimer virtues.

Years went by. Events transpired which have their place in history. Under a government which the community by and by saw was conducted in their interest, smuggling began to lose its respectability and to grow disreputable, hazardous, and debased. In certain onslaughts made upon them by officers of the law, some of the smugglers became murderers. The business became unprofitable for a time until the enterprising Lafittes—thinkers—bethought them of a corrective—"privateering."

Thereupon the United States Government set a price upon their heads. Later yet it became known that these outlawed pirates had been offered money and rank by Great Britain if they would join her standard, then hovering about the water-approaches to their native city, and that they had spurned the bribe; wherefore their heads were ruled out of the market, and, meeting and treating with Andrew Jackson, they were received as lovers of their country, and as compatriots fought in the battle of New Orleans at the head of their fearless men, and—here tradition takes up the tale—were never seen afterward.

Capitaine Lemaitre was not among the killed or wounded, but he was among the missing.

IV

THREE FRIENDS

The roundest and happiest-looking priest in the city of New Orleans was a little man fondly known among his people as Père Jerome. He was a Creole and a member of one of the city's leading families. His dwelling was a little frame cottage, standing on high pillars just inside a tall, close fence, and reached by a narrow out-door stair from the green batten gate. It was well surrounded by crape myrtles, and communicated behind by a descending stair and a plank-walk with the rear entrance of the chapel over whose worshippers he daily spread his hands in benediction. The name of the street—ah! there is where light is wanting. Save the Cathedral and the Ursulines, there is very little of record concerning churches at that time, though they were springing up here and there. All there is certainty of is that Père Jerome's frame chapel was some little new-born "down-town" thing, that may have survived the passage of years, or may have escaped "Paxton's Directory" "so as by fire." His parlor was dingy and carpetless; one could smell distinctly there the vow of poverty. His bed-chamber was bare and clean, and the bed in it narrow and hard; but between the two was a dining-room that would tempt a laugh to the lips of any who looked in. The table was small, but stout, and all the furniture of the room substantial, made of fine wood, and carved just enough to give the notion of wrinkling pleasantry. His mother's and sister's doing, Père Jerome would explain; they would not permit this apartment—or department—to suffer. Therein, as well as in the parlor, there was odor, but of a more epicurean sort, that explained interestingly the Père Jerome's rotundity and rosy smile.

In this room, and about this miniature round table, used sometimes to sit with Père Jerome two friends to whom he was deeply attached—one, Evariste Varrillat, a playmate from early childhood, now his brother-in-law; the other, Jean Thompson, a companion from youngest manhood, and both, like the little priest himself, the regretful rememberers of a fourth comrade who was a comrade no more. Like Père Jerome, they had come, through years, to the thick of life's conflicts,—the priest's brother-in-law a physician, the other an attorney, and brother-in-law to the lonely wanderer,—yet they loved to huddle around this small board, and be boys again in heart while men in mind. Neither one nor another was leader. In earlier days they had always yielded to him who no longer met with them a certain chieftainship, and they still thought of him and talked of him, and, in their conjectures, groped after him, as one of whom they continued to expect greater things than of themselves.

They sat one day drawn thus close together, sipping and theorizing, speculating upon the nature of things in an easy, bold, sophomoric way, the conversation for the most part being in French, the native tongue of the doctor and the priest, and spoken with facility by Jean Thompson the lawyer, who was half Américain; but running sometimes into English and sometimes into mild laughter. Mention had been made of the absentee.

Père Jerome advanced an idea something like this:

"It is impossible for any finite mind to fix the degree of criminality of any human act or of any human life. The Infinite One alone can know how much of our sin is chargeable to us, and how much to our brothers or our fathers. We all participate in one another's sins. There is a community of responsibility attaching to every misdeed. No human since Adam—nay, nor Adam himself—ever sinned entirely to himself. And so I never am called upon to contemplate a crime or a criminal but I feel my conscience pointing at me as one of the accessories."

"In a word," said Evariste Varrillat, the physician, "you think we are partly to blame for the omission of many of your Paternosters, eh?"

Father Jerome smiled.

"No; a man cannot plead so in his own defence; our first father tried that, but the plea was not allowed. But, now, there is our absent friend. I tell you truly this whole community ought to be recognized as partners in his moral errors. Among another people, reared under wiser care and with better companions, how different might he not have been! How can *we* speak of him as a law-breaker who might have saved him from that name?" Here the speaker turned to Jean Thompson, and changed his speech to English. "A lady sez to me today: 'Père Jerome, ow dat is a dreadfool dat 'e gone at de coas' of Cuba to be one corsair! Ain't it?' 'Ah, madame,' I sez, ''tis a terrible! I 'ope de good God will fo'give me an' you fo' dat!' "

Jean Thompson answered quickly:

"You should not have let her say that."

"*Mais*, fo' w'y?"

"Why, because, if you are partly responsible, you ought so much the more to do what you can to shield his reputation. You should have said,"—the attorney changed to French,—" 'He is no pirate; he has merely taken out letters of marque and reprisal under the flag of the republic of Carthagena!' "

"*Ah, bah!*" exclaimed Doctor Varrillat, and both he and his brother-in-law, the priest, laughed.

"Why not?" demanded Thompson.

"Oh!" said the physician, with a shrug, "say id thad way iv you wand."

Then, suddenly becoming serious, he was about to add something else, when Père Jerome spoke.

"I will tell you what I could have said. I could have said: 'Madame, yes; 'tis a terrible fo' him. He stum'le in de dark; but dat good God will mek it a *mo' terrible* fo' dat man oohever he is, w'at put 'at light out!' "

"But how do you know he is a pirate?" demanded Thompson, aggressively.

"How do we know?" said the little priest, returning to French. "Ah! there is no other explanation of the ninety-and-nine stories that come to us, from every port where ships arrive from the north coast of Cuba, of a commander of pirates there who is a marvel of courtesy and gentility"—[1]

"And whose name is Lafitte," said the obstinate attorney.

"And who, nevertheless, is not Lafitte," insisted Père Jerome.

"Daz troo, Jean," said Doctor Varrillat. "We hall know daz troo."

Père Jerome leaned forward over the board and spoke, with an air of secrecy, in French.

"You have heard of the ship which came into port here last Mon-

[1] See gazettes of the period.

day. You have heard that she was boarded by pirates, and that the captain of the ship himself drove them off."

"An incredible story," said Thompson.

"But not so incredible as the truth. I have it from a passenger. There was on the ship a young girl who was very beautiful. She came on deck, where the corsair stood, about to issue his orders, and, more beautiful than ever in the desperation of the moment, confronted him with a small missal spread open, and her finger on the Apostles' Creed, commanded him to read. He read it, uncovering his head as he read, then stood gazing on her face, which did not quail; and then with a low bow, said: 'Give me this book and I will do your bidding.' She gave him the book and bade him leave the ship, and he left it unmolested."

Père Jerome looked from the physician to the attorney and back again, once or twice, with his dimpled smile.

"But he speaks English, they say," said Jean Thompson.

"He has, no doubt, learned it since he left us," said the priest.

"But this ship-master, too, says his men called him Lafitte."

"Lafitte? No. Do you not see? It is your brother-in-law, Jean Thompson! It is your wife's brother! Not Lafitte, but" (softly) "Lemaitre! Lemaitre! Capitaine Ursin Lemaitre!"

The two guests looked at each other with a growing drollery on either face, and presently broke into a laugh.

"Ah!" said the doctor, as the three rose up, "you juz kip dad cogan'-bull fo' you' negs summon."

Père Jerome's eyes lighted up—

"I goin' to do it!"

"I tell you," said Evariste, turning upon him with sudden gravity, "iv dad is troo, I tell you w'ad is sure-sure! Ursin Lemaitre din kyare nut'n fo' doze creed; *he fall in love!*"

Then, with a smile, turning to Jean Thompson, and back again to Père Jerome:

"But any'ow you tell it in dad summon dad 'e kyare fo' dad creed."

Père Jerome sat up late that night, writing a letter. The remarkable effects upon a certain mind, effects which we shall presently find him attributing solely to the influences of surrounding nature, may find for some a more sufficient explanation in the fact that this letter was but one of a series, and that in the rover of doubted identity and incredible eccentricity Père Jerome had a regular correspondent.

V

THE CAP FITS

About two months after the conversation just given and therefore somewhere about the Christmas holidays of the year 1821, Père Jerome delighted the congregation of his little chapel with the announcement that he had appointed to preach a sermon in French on the following sabbath—not there, but in the cathedral.

He was much beloved. Notwithstanding that among the clergy there were two or three who shook their heads and raised their eyebrows, and said he would be at least as orthodox if he did not make quite so much of the Bible and quite so little of the dogmas, yet "the common people heard him gladly." When told, one day, of the unfavorable whispers, he smiled a little and answered his informant,—whom he knew to be one of the whisperers himself,—laying a hand kindly upon his shoulder:

"Father Murphy,"—or whatever the name was,—"your words comfort me."

"How is that?"

"Because—'*Vae quum benedixerint mihi homines!*' "[1]

The appointed morning, when it came, was one of those exquisite days in which there is such a universal harmony, that worship rises from the heart like a spring.

"Truly," said Père Jerome to the companion who was to assist him in the mass, "this is a sabbath day which we do not have to make holy, but only to *keep* so."

Maybe it was one of the secrets of Père Jerome's success as a preacher, that he took more thought as to how he should feel, than as to what he should say.

The cathedral of those days was called a very plain old pile, boast-

1 "Woe unto me when all men speak well of me!"

ing neither beauty nor riches; but to Père Jerome it was very lovely; and before its homely altar, not homely to him, in the performance of those solemn offices, symbols of heaven's mightiest truths, in the hearing of the organ's harmonies, and the yet more eloquent inter-union of human voices in the choir, in overlooking the worshipping throng which knelt under the soft, chromatic lights, and in breathing the sacrificial odors of the chancel, he found a deep and solemn joy; and yet I guess the finest thought of his soul the while was one that came thrice and again:

"Be not deceived, Père Jerome, because saintliness of feeling is easy here; you are the same priest who overslept this morning, and over-ate yesterday, and will, in some way, easily go wrong to-morrow and the day after."

He took it with him when—the *Veni Creator* sung—he went into the pulpit. Of the sermon he preached, tradition has preserved for us only a few brief sayings, but they are strong and sweet.

"My friends," he said,—this was near the beginning,—"the angry words of God's book are very merciful—they are meant to drive us home; but the tender words, my friends, they are sometimes terrible! Notice these, the tenderest words of the tenderest prayer that ever came from the lips of a blessed martyr—the dying words of the holy Saint Stephen, 'Lord, lay not this sin to their charge.' Is there nothing dreadful in that? Read it thus: 'Lord, lay not this sin to *their* charge.' Not to the charge of them who stoned him? To whose charge then? Go ask the holy Saint Paul. Three years afterward, praying in the temple at Jerusalem, he answered that question: 'I stood by and consented.' He answered for himself only; but the Day must come when all that wicked council that sent Saint Stephen away to be stoned, and all that city of Jerusalem, must hold up the hand and say: 'We, also, Lord—we stood by.' Ah! friends, under the simpler meaning of that dying saint's prayer for the pardon of his murderers is hidden the terrible truth that we all have a share in one another's sins."

Thus Père Jerome touched his key-note. All that time has spared us beside may be given in a few sentences.

"Ah!" he cried once, "if it were merely my own sins that I had to answer for, I might hold up my head before the rest of mankind;

but no, no, my friends—we cannot look each other in the face, for each has helped the other to sin. Oh, where is there any room, in this world of common disgrace, for pride? Even if we had no common hope, a common despair ought to bind us together and forever silence the voice of scorn!"

And again, this:

"Even in the promise to Noë, not again to destroy the race with a flood, there is a whisper of solemn warning. The moral account of the antediluvians was closed off and the balance brought down in the year of the deluge; but the account of those who come after runs on and on, and the blessed bow of promise itself warns us that God will not stop it till the Judgment Day! O God, I thank thee that that day must come at last, when thou wilt destroy the world, and stop the interest on my account!"

It was about at this point that Père Jerome noticed, more particularly than he had done before, sitting among the worshippers near him, a small, sad-faced woman, of pleasing features, but dark and faded, who gave him profound attention. With her was another in better dress, seemingly a girl still in her teens, though her face and neck were scrupulously concealed by a heavy veil, and her hands, which were small, by gloves.

"Quadroones," thought he, with a stir of deep pity.

Once, as he uttered some stirring word, he saw the mother and daughter (if such they were), while they still bent their gaze upon him, clasp each other's hand fervently in the daughter's lap. It was at these words:

"My friends, there are thousands of people in this city of New Orleans to whom society gives the ten commandments of God with all the *nots* rubbed out! Ah! good gentlemen! if God sends the poor weakling to purgatory for leaving the right path, where ought some of you to go who strew it with thorns and briers!"

The movement of the pair was only seen because he watched for it. He glanced that way again as he said:

"O God, be very gentle with those children who would be nearer heaven this day had they never had a father and mother, but had got their religious training from such a sky and earth as we have in

Louisiana this holy morning! Ah! my friends, nature is a big-print catechism!"

The mother and daughter leaned a little farther forward, and exchanged the same spasmodic hand-pressure as before. The mother's eyes were full of tears.

"I once knew a man," continued the little priest, glancing to a side aisle where he had noticed Evariste and Jean sitting against each other, "who was carefully taught, from infancy to manhood, this single only principle of life: defiance. Not justice, not righteousness, not even gain; but defiance: defiance to God, defiance to man, defiance to nature, defiance to reason; defiance and defiance and defiance."

"He is going to tell it!" murmured Evariste to Jean.

"This man," continued Père Jerome, "became a smuggler and at last a pirate in the Gulf of Mexico. Lord, lay not that sin to his charge alone! But a strange thing followed. Being in command of men of a sort that to control required to be kept at the austerest distance, he now found himself separated from the human world and thrown into the solemn companionship with the sea, with the air, with the storm, the calm, the heavens by day, the heavens by night. My friends, that was the first time in his life that he ever found himself in really good company.

"Now, this man had a great aptness for accounts. He had kept them—had rendered them. There was beauty, to him, in a correct, balanced, and closed account. An account unsatisfied was a deformity. The result is plain. That man, looking out night after night upon the grand and holy spectacle of the starry deep above and the watery deep below, was sure to find himself, sooner or later, mastered by the conviction that the great Author of this majestic creation keeps account of it; and one night there came to him, like a spirit walking on the sea, the awful, silent question: 'My account with God—how does it stand?' Ah! friends, that is a question which the book of nature does not answer.

"Did I say the book of nature is a catechism? Yes. But, after it answers the first question with 'God,' nothing but questions follow; and so, one day, this man gave a ship full of merchandise for one little book which answered those questions. God help him to understand it! and God help you, monsieur, and you, madame, sitting here in your *smuggled clothes,* to beat upon the breast with me and cry, 'I, too, Lord—I, too, stood by and consented.'"

Père Jerome had not intended these for his closing words; but just there, straight away before his sight and almost at the farthest door, a man rose slowly from his seat and regarded him steadily with a kind, bronzed, sedate face, and the sermon, as if by a sign of command, was ended. While the *Credo* was being chanted he was still there; but when, a moment after its close, the eye of Père Jerome returned in that direction, his place was empty.

As the little priest, his labor done and his vestments changed, was turning into the Rue Royale and leaving the cathedral out of sight, he just had time to understand that two women were purposely allowing him to overtake them, when the one nearer him spoke in the Creole *patois,* saying, with some timid haste:

"Good-morning, Père—Père Jerome; Père Jerome, we thank the good God for that sermon."

"Then, so do I," said the little man. They were the same two that he had noticed when he was preaching. The younger one bowed silently; she was a beautiful figure, but the slight effort of Père Jerome's kind eyes to see through the veil was vain. He would presently have passed on, but the one who had spoken before said:

"I thought you lived in the Rue des Ursulines."

"Yes; I am going this way to see a sick person."

The woman looked up at him with an expression of mingled confidence and timidity.

"It must be a blessed thing to be so useful as to be needed by the good God," she said.

Père Jerome smiled:

"God does not need me to look after his sick; but he allows me to do it, just as you let your little boy in frocks carry in chips." He might have added that he loved to do it, quite as much.

It was plain the woman had somewhat to ask, and was trying to get courage to ask it.

"You have a little boy?" asked the priest.

"No, I have only my daughter;" she indicated the girl at her side. Then she began to say something else, stopped, and with much nervousness asked:

"Père Jerome, what was the name of that man?"

"His name?" said the priest. "You wish to know his name?"

"Yes, Monsieur" (or *Miché,* as she spoke it); "it was such a beautiful story." The speaker's companion looked another way.

"His name," said Father Jerome,—"some say one name and some another. Some think it was Jean Lafitte, the famous; you have heard of him? And do you go to my church, Madame ——?"

"No, Miché; not in the past; but from this time, yes. My name"—she choked a little, and yet it evidently gave her pleasure to offer this mark of confidence—"is Madame Delphine—Delphine Carraze."

VI

A CRY OF DISTRESS

Père Jerome's smile and exclamation, as some days later he entered his parlor in response to the announcement of a visitor, were indicative of hearty greeting rather than surprise.

"Madame Delphine!"

Yet surprise could hardly have been altogether absent, for though another Sunday had not yet come around, the slim, smallish figure sitting in a corner, looking very much alone, and clad in dark attire, which seemed to have been washed a trifle too often, was Delphine Carraze on her second visit. And this, he was confident, was over and above an attendance in the confessional, where he was sure he had recognized her voice.

She rose bashfully and gave her hand, then looked to the floor, and began a faltering speech, with a swallowing motion in the throat, smiled weakly and commenced again, speaking, as before, in a gentle, low note, frequently lifting up and casting down her eyes, while shadows of anxiety and smiles of apology chased each other rapidly across her face. She was trying to ask his advice.

"Sit down," said he; and when they had taken seats she resumed, with downcast eyes:

"You know,—probably I should have said this in the confessional, but"—

"No matter, Madame Delphine; I understand; you did not want an oracle, perhaps; you want a friend."

She lifted her eyes, shining with tears, and dropped them again.

"I"—she ceased. "I have done a"—she dropped her head and shook it despondingly—"a cruel thing." The tears rolled from her eyes as she turned away her face.

Père Jerome remained silent, and presently she turned again, with the evident intention of speaking at length.

"It began nineteen years ago—by"—her eyes, which she had lifted, fell lower than ever, her brow and neck were suffused with blushes, and she murmured—"I fell in love."

She said no more, and by and by Père Jerome replied:

"Well, Madame Delphine, to love is the right of every soul. I believe in love. If your love was pure and lawful I am sure your angel guardian smiled upon you; and if it was not, I cannot say you have nothing to answer for, and yet I think God may have said: 'She is a quadroone; all the rights of her womanhood trampled in the mire, sin made easy to her—almost compulsory,—charge it to account of whom it may concern.' "

"No, no!" said Madame Delphine, looking up quickly, "some of it might fall upon"— Her eyes fell, and she commenced biting her lips and nervously pinching little folds in her skirt. "He was good—as good as the law would let him be—better, indeed, for he left me property, which really the strict law does not allow. He loved our little daughter very much. He wrote to his mother and sisters, owning all his error and asking them to take the child and bring her up. I sent her to them when he died, which was soon after, and did not see my child for sixteen years. But we wrote to each other all the time, and she loved me. And then—at last"—Madame Delphine ceased speaking, but went on diligently with her agitated fingers, turning down foolish hems lengthwise of her lap.

"At last your mother-heart conquered," said Père Jerome.

She nodded.

"The sisters married, the mother died; I saw that even where she was she did not escape the reproach of her birth and blood, and when she asked me to let her come"— The speaker's brimming eyes rose an instant. "I know it was wicked, but—I said, come."

The tears dripped through her hands upon her dress.

"Was it she who was with you last Sunday?"

"Yes."

"And now you do not know what to do with her?"

"*Ah! c'est ça oui!*—that is it."

"Does she look like you, Madame Delphine?"

"Oh, thank God, no! you would never believe she was my daughter; she is white and beautiful."

"You thank God for that which is your main difficulty, Madame Delphine."

"Alas! yes."

Père Jerome laid his palms tightly across his knees with his arms bowed out, and fixed his eyes upon the ground, pondering.

"I suppose she is a sweet, good daughter?" said he, glancing at Madame Delphine, without changing his attitude.

Her answer was to raise her eyes rapturously.

"Which gives us the dilemma in its fullest force," said the priest, speaking as if to the floor. "She has no more place than if she had dropped upon a strange planet." He suddenly looked up with a brightness which almost as quickly passed away, and then he looked down again. His happy thought was the cloister; but he instantly said to himself: "They cannot have overlooked that choice, except intentionally—which they have a right to do." He could do nothing but shake his head.

"And suppose you should suddenly die," he said; he wanted to get at once to the worst.

The woman made a quick gesture, and buried her head in her handkerchief, with the stifled cry:

"Oh, Olive, my daughter!"

"Well, Madame Delphine," said Père Jerome, more buoyantly, "one thing is sure: we *must* find a way out of this trouble."

"Ah!" she exclaimed, looking heavenward, "if it might be!"

"But it must be!" said the priest.

"But how shall it be?" asked the desponding woman.

"Ah!" said Père Jerome, with a shrug, "God knows."

"Yes," said the quadroone, with a quick sparkle in her gentle eye; "and I know, if God would tell anybody, He would tell you!"

The priest smiled and rose.

"Do you think so? Well, leave me to think of it. I will ask Him."

"And He will tell you!" she replied. "And He will bless you!" She rose and gave her hand. As she withdrew it she smiled. "I had such a strange dream," she said, backing toward the door.

"Yes?"

"Yes. I got my troubles all mixed up with your sermon. I dreamed I made that pirate the guardian of my daughter."

Père Jerome smiled also, and shrugged.

"To you, Madame Delphine, as you are placed, every white man in this country, on land or on water, is a pirate, and of all pirates, I think that one is, without doubt, the best."

"Without doubt," echoed Madame Delphine, wearily, still withdrawing backward. Père Jerome stepped forward and opened the door.

The shadow of some one approaching it from without fell upon the threshold, and a man entered, dressed in dark blue cottonade, lifting from his head a fine Panama hat, and from a broad, smooth brow, fair where the hat had covered it, and dark below, gently stroking back his very soft, brown locks. Madame Delphine slightly started aside, while Père Jerome reached silently, but eagerly, forward, grasped a larger hand than his own, and motioned its owner to a seat. Madame Delphine's eyes ventured no higher than to discover that the shoes of the visitor were of white duck.

"Well, Père Jerome," she said, in a hurried undertone, "I am just going to say Hail Marys all the time till you find that out for me!"

"Well, I hope that will be soon, Madame Carraze. Good-day, Madame Carraze."

And as she departed, the priest turned to the newcomer and extended both hands, saying, in the same familiar dialect in which he had been addressing the quadroone:

"Well-a-day, old playmate! After so many years!"

They sat down side by side, like husband and wife, the priest playing with the other's hand, and talked of times and seasons past, often mentioning Evariste and often Jean.

Madame Delphine stopped short half-way home and returned to Père Jerome's. His entry door was wide open and the parlor door ajar. She passed through the one and with downcast eyes was standing at the other, her hand lifted to knock, when the door was drawn open and the white duck shoes passed out. She saw, besides, this time the blue cottonade suit.

"Yes," the voice of Père Jerome was saying, as his face appeared in the door—"Ah! Madame"—

"I lef' my para*sol,*" said Madame Delphine, in English.

There was this quiet evidence of a defiant spirit hidden somewhere down under her general timidity, that, against a fierce conventional prohibition, she wore a bonnet instead of the turban of her caste, and carried a parasol.

Père Jerome turned and brought it.

He made a motion in the direction in which the late visitor had disappeared.

"Madame Delphine, you saw dat man?"

"Not his face."

"You couldn' billieve me iv I tell you w'at dat man pur*pose* to do!"

"Is dad so, Père Jerome?"

"He's goin' to hopen a bank!"

"Ah!" said Madame Delphine, seeing she was expected to be astonished.

Père Jerome evidently longed to tell something that was best kept secret; he repressed the impulse, but his heart had to say something. He threw forward one hand and looking pleasantly at Madame Delphine, with his lips dropped apart, clenched his extended hand and thrusting it toward the ground, said in a solemn undertone:

"He is God's own banker, Madame Delphine."

VII

MICHE VIGNEVIELLE

Madame Delphine sold one of the corner lots of her property. She had almost no revenue, and now and then a piece had to go. As a consequence of the sale, she had a few large bank-notes sewed up in her petticoat, and one day—maybe a fortnight after her tearful interview with Père Jerome—she found it necessary to get one of these changed into small money. She was in the Rue Toulouse, looking from one side to the other for a bank which was not in that street at all, when she noticed a small sign hanging above a door, bearing the name "Vignevielle." She looked in. Père Jerome had told her (when she had gone to him to ask where she should apply for change) that if she could only wait a few days, there would be a new concern opened in Toulouse Street,—it really seemed as if Vignevielle was the name, if she could judge; it looked to be, and it was, a private banker's,—"U. L. Vignevielle's," according to a larger inscription which met her eyes as she ventured in. Behind the counter, exchanging some last words with a busy-mannered man outside, who, in withdrawing, seemed bent on running over Madame Delphine, stood the man in blue cottonade, whom she had met in Père Jerome's doorway. Now, for the first time, she saw his face, its strong, grave, human kindness shining softly on each and every bronzed feature. The recognition was mutual. He took pains to speak first, saying, in a re-assuring tone, and in the language he had last heard her use:

"'Ow I kin serve you, Madame?"

"Iv you pliz, to mague dad bill change, Miché."

She pulled from her pocket a wad of dark cotton handkerchief, from which she began to untie the imprisoned note. Madame Delphine had an uncommonly sweet voice, and it seemed so to strike Monsieur Vignevielle. He spoke to her once or twice more, as he waited on her, each time in English, as though he enjoyed the humble melody of its tone, and presently, as she turned to go, he said:

"Madame Carraze!"

She started a little, but bethought herself instantly that he had heard her name in Père Jerome's parlor. The good father might even have said a few words about her after her first departure; he had such an overflowing heart. "Madame Carraze," said Monsieur Vignevielle, "doze kine of note wad you *'an'* me juz now is bein' contrefit. You muz tek kyah from doze kine of note. You see"— He drew from his cash-drawer a note resembling the one he had just changed for her, and proceeded to point out certain tests of genuineness. The counterfeit, he said, was so and so.

"Bud," she exclaimed, with much dismay, "dad was de manner of my bill! Id muz be—led me see dad bill wad I give you,—if you pliz, Miché."

Monsieur Vignevielle turned to engage in conversation with an employé and a new visitor, and gave no sign of hearing Madame Delphine's voice. She asked a second time, with like result, lingered timidly, and as he turned to give his attention to a third visitor, reiterated.

"Miché Vignevielle, I wizh you pliz led"—

"Madame Carraze," he said, turning so suddenly as to make the frightened little woman start, but extending his palm with a show of frankness, and assuming a look of benignant patience, "'ow I kin fine doze note now, mongs' all de rez? Iv you pliz nod to mague me doze troub'."

The dimmest shadow of a smile seemed only to give his words a more kindly authoritative import, and as he turned away again with a manner suggestive of finality, Madame Delphine found no choice but to depart. But she went away loving the ground beneath the feet of Monsieur U. L. Vignevielle.

"Oh, Père Jerome!" she exclaimed in the corrupt French of her caste, meeting the little father on the street a few days later, "you told the truth that day in your parlor. *Mo conné li à c't heure.* I know him now; he is just what you called him."

"Why do you not make him *your* banker, also, Madame Delphine?"

"I have done so this very day!" she replied, with more happiness in her eyes than Père Jerome had ever before seen there.

"Madame Delphine," he said, his own eyes sparkling, "make *him* your daughter's guardian; for myself, being a priest, it would not be best; but ask him; I believe he will not refuse you."

Madame Delphine's face grew still brighter as he spoke.

"It was in my mind," she said.

Yet to the timorous Madame Delphine many trifles became, one after another, an impediment to the making of this proposal, and many weeks elapsed before further delay was positively without excuse. But at length, one day in May, 1822, in a small private office behind Monsieur Vignevielle's banking-room,—he sitting beside a table, and she, more timid and demure than ever, having just taken a chair by the door,—she said, trying, with a little bashful laugh, to make the matter seem unimportant, and yet with some tremor of voice:

"Miché Vignevielle, I bin maguing my will." (Having commenced their acquaintance in English, they spoke nothing else.)

"'Tis a good idy," responded the banker.

"I kin mague you de troub' to kib dad will fo' me, Miché Vignevielle?"

"Yez."

She looked up with grateful re-assurance; but her eyes dropped again as she said:

"Miché Vignevielle"— Here she choked, and began her peculiar motion of laying folds in the skirt of her dress, with trembling fingers. She lifted her eyes, and as they met the look of deep and placid kindness that was in his face, some courage returned, and she said:

"Miché."

"Wad you wand?" asked he, gently.

"If it arrive to me to die"—

"Yez?"

Her words were scarcely audible:

"I wand you teg kyah my lill' girl."

"You 'ave one lill' gal, Madame Carraze?"

She nodded with her face down.

"An' you godd some mo' chillen?"

"No."

"I nevva know dad, Madame Carraze. She's a lill' small gal?"

Mothers forget their daughters' stature. Madame Delphine said: "Yez."

For a few moments neither spoke, and then Monsieur Vignevielle said:

"I will do dad."

"Lag she been you' h-own?" asked the mother, suffering from her own boldness.

"She's a good lill' chile, eh?"

"Miché, she's a lill' hangel!" exclaimed Madame Delphine, with a look of distress.

"Yez; I teg kyah 'v 'er, lag my h-own. I mague you dad promise."

"But"— There was something still in the way, Madame Delphine seemed to think.

The banker waited in silence.

"I suppose you will want to see my lill' girl?"

He smiled; for she looked at him as if she would implore him to decline.

"Oh, I tek you' word fo' hall dad, Madame Carraze. It mague no differend wad she loog lag; I don' wan see 'er."

Madame Delphine's parting smile—she went very shortly—was gratitude beyond speech.

Monsieur Vignevielle returned to the seat he had left, and resumed a newspaper,—the *Louisiana Gazette* in all probability,—which he had laid down upon Madame Delphine's entrance. His eyes fell upon a paragraph which had previously escaped his notice. There they rested. Either he read it over and over unwearyingly, or he was lost in thought. Jean Thompson entered.

"Now," said Mr. Thompson, in a suppressed tone, bending a little across the table, and laying one palm upon a package of papers which lay in the other, "it is completed. You could retire from your business any day inside of six hours without loss to anybody." (Both here and elsewhere, let it be understood that where good English is given the words were spoken in good French.)

Monsieur Vignevielle raised his eyes and extended the newspaper to the attorney, who received it, and read the paragraph. Its substance was that a certain vessel of the navy had returned from a cruise in the

Gulf of Mexico and Straits of Florida, where she had done valuable service against the pirates—having, for instance, destroyed in one fortnight in January last twelve pirate vessels afloat, two on the stocks, and three establishments ashore.

"United States brig *Porpoise*," repeated Jean Thompson. "Do you know her?"

"We are acquainted," said Monsieur Vignevielle.

VIII

SHE

A quiet footstep, a grave new presence on financial sidewalks, a neat garb slightly out of date, a gently strong and kindly pensive face, a silent bow, a new sign in the Rue Toulouse, a lone figure with a cane, walking in meditation in the evening light under the willows of Canal Marigny, a long-darkened window re-lighted in the Rue Conti—these were all; a fall of dew would scarce have been more quiet than was the return of Ursin Lemaitre-Vignevielle to the precincts of his birth and early life.

But we hardly give the event its right name. It was Capitaine Lemaitre who had disappeared; it was Monsieur Vignevielle who had come back. The pleasures, the haunts, the companions, that had once held out their charms to the impetuous youth, offered no enticements to Madame Delphine's banker. There is this to be said even for the pride his grandfather had taught him, that it had always held him above low indulgencies; and though he had dallied with kings, queens, and knaves through all the mazes of Faro, Rondeau, and Craps, he had done it loftily; but now he maintained a peaceful estrangement from all. Evariste and Jean, themselves, found him only by seeking.

"It is the right way," he said to Père Jerome, the day we saw him there. "Ursin Lemaitre is dead. I have buried him. He left a will. I am his executor."

"He is crazy," said his lawyer brother-in-law, impatiently.

"On the contr-y," replied the little priest, "'e 'as come ad hisse'f."

Evariste spoke.

"Look at his face, Jean. Men with that kind of face are the last to go crazy."

"You have not proved that," replied Jean, with an attorney's obstinacy. "You should have heard him talk the other day about that newspaper paragraph. 'I have taken Ursin Lemaitre's head; I have it with me; I claim the reward, but I desire to commute it to citizenship.' He is crazy."

Of course Jean Thompson did not believe what he said; but he said it, and, in his vexation, repeated it, on the *banquettes* and at the clubs; and presently it took the shape of a sly rumor, that the returned rover was a trifle snarled in his top-hamper.

This whisper was helped into circulation by many trivial eccentricities of manner, and by the unaccountable oddness of some of his transactions in business.

"My dear sir!" cried his astounded lawyer, one day, "you are not running a charitable institution!"

"How do you know?" said Monsieur Vignevielle. There the conversation ceased.

"Why do you not found hospitals and asylums at once," asked the attorney, at another time, with a vexed laugh, "and get the credit of it?"

"And make the end worse than the beginning," said the banker, with a gentle smile, turning away to a desk of books.

"Bah!" muttered Jean Thompson.

Monsieur Vignevielle betrayed one very bad symptom. Wherever he went he seemed looking for somebody. It may have been perceptible only to those who were sufficiently interested in him to study his movements; but those who saw it once saw it always. He never passed an open door or gate but he glanced in; and often, where it stood but slightly ajar, you might see him give it a gentle push with his hand or cane. It was very singular.

He walked much alone after dark. The *guichinangoes* (garroters, we might say), at those times the city's particular terror by night, never crossed his path. He was one of those men for whom danger appears to stand aside.

One beautiful summer night, when all nature seemed hushed in ecstasy, the last blush gone that told of the sun's parting, Monsieur Vignevielle, in the course of one of those contemplative, uncompanioned walks which it was his habit to take, came slowly along the more open portion of the Rue Royale, with a step which was soft without intention, occasionally touching the end of his stout cane gently to the ground and looking upward among his old acquaintances, the stars.

It was one of those southern nights under whose spell all the sterner energies of the mind cloak themselves and lie down in bivouac, and the fancy and the imagination, that cannot sleep, slip their fetters and escape, beckoned away from behind every flowering bush and sweet-smelling tree, and every stretch of lonely, half-lighted walk, by the genius of poetry. The air stirred softly now and then, and was still again, as if the breezes lifted their expectant pinions and lowered them once more, awaiting the rising of the moon in a silence which fell upon the fields, the roads, the gardens, the walls, and the suburban and half-suburban streets, like a pause in worship. And anon she rose.

Monsieur Vignevielle's steps were bent toward the more central part of the town, and he was presently passing along a high, close, board-fence, on the right-hand side of the way, when, just within this enclosure, and almost overhead, in the dark boughs of a large orange-tree, a mocking-bird began the first low flute-notes of his all-night song. It may have been only the nearness of the songster that attracted the passer's attention, but he paused and looked up.

And then he remarked something more,—that the air where he had stopped was filled with the overpowering sweetness of the night-jasmine. He looked around; it could only be inside the fence. There was a gate just there. Would he push it, as his wont was? The grass was growing about it in a thick turf, as though the entrance had not been used for years. An iron staple clasped the cross-bar, and was driven deep into the gate-post. But now an eye that had been in the blacksmithing business—an eye which had later received high training as an eye for fastenings—fell upon that staple, and saw at a glance that the wood had shrunk from it, and it had sprung from its hold, though without falling out. The strange habit asserted itself; he laid his large hand upon the cross-bar; the turf at the base yielded, and the tall gate was drawn partly open.

At that moment, as at the moment whenever he drew or pushed a door or gate, or looked in at a window, he was thinking of one, the image of whose face and form had never left his inner vision since the day it had met him in his life's path and turned him face about from the way of destruction.

The bird ceased. The cause of the interruption, standing within the opening, saw before him, much obscured by its own numerous shadows, a broad, ill-kept, many-flowered garden, among whose untrimmed rose-trees and tangled vines, and often, also, in its old walks of pounded shell, the coco-grass and crab-grass had spread riotously, and sturdy weeds stood up in bloom. He stepped in and drew the gate to after him. There, very near by, was the clump of jasmine, whose ravishing odor had tempted him. It stood just beyond a brightly moonlit path, which turned from him in a curve toward the residence, a little distance to the right, and escaped the view at a point where it seemed more than likely a door of the house might open upon it. While he still looked, there fell upon his ear, from around that curve, a light footstep on the broken shells—one only, and then all was for a moment still again. Had he mistaken? No. The same soft click was repeated nearer by, a pale glimpse of robes came through the tangle, and then, plainly to view, appeared an outline—a presence—a form—a spirit—a girl!

From throat to instep she was as white as Cynthia. Something above the medium height, slender, lithe, her abundant hair rolling in dark, rich waves back from her brows and down from her crown, and falling in two heavy plaits beyond her round, broadly girt waist and full to her knees, a few escaping locks eddying lightly on her graceful neck and her temples,—her arms, half hid in a snowy mist of sleeve, let down to guide her spotless skirts free from the dewy touch of the grass,—straight down the path she came!

Will she stop? Will she turn aside? Will she espy the dark form in the deep shade of the orange, and, with one piercing scream, wheel and vanish? She draws near. She approaches the jasmine; she raises her arms, the sleeves falling like a vapor down to the shoulders; rises upon tiptoe, and plucks a spray. O Memory! Can it be? *Can it be?* Is this his quest, or is it lunacy? The ground seems to Monsieur Vignevielle the unsteady sea, and he to stand once more on a deck. And she? As she is now, if she but turn toward the orange, the whole glory of the moon will shine upon her face. His heart stands still; he is waiting for her to do that. She reaches up again; this time a bunch for her mother. That neck and throat! Now she fastens a spray in her hair. The mocking-bird cannot withhold; he breaks into song—she turns—she turns her face—it is she, it is she! Madame Delphine's daughter is the girl he met on the ship.

IX
OLIVE

She was just passing seventeen—that beautiful year when the heart of the maiden still beats quickly with the surprise of her new dominion, while with gentle dignity her brow accepts the holy coronation of womanhood. The forehead and temples beneath her loosely bound hair were fair without paleness, and meek without languor. She had the soft, lack-lustre beauty of the South; no ruddiness of coral, no waxen white, no pink of shell; no heavenly blue in the glance; but a face that seemed, in all its other beauties, only a tender accompaniment for the large, brown, melting eyes, where the openness of child-nature mingled dreamily with the sweet mysteries of maiden thought. We say no color of shell on face or throat; but this was no deficiency, that which took its place being the warm, transparent tint of sculptured ivory.

This side doorway which led from Madame Delphine's house into her garden was over-arched partly by an old remnant of vine-covered lattice, and partly by a crape-myrtle, against whose small, polished trunk leaned a rustic seat. Here Madame Delphine and Olive loved to sit when the twilights were balmy or the moon was bright.

"*Chérie,*" said Madame Delphine on one of those evenings, "why do you dream so much?"

She spoke in the *patois* most natural to her, and which her daughter had easily learned.

The girl turned her face to her mother, and smiled, then dropped her glance to the hands in her own lap, which were listlessly handling the end of a ribbon. The mother looked at her with fond solicitude. Her dress was white again; this was but one night since that in which Monsieur Vignevielle had seen her at the bush of night-jasmine. He had not been discovered, but had gone away, shutting the gate, and leaving it as he had found it.

Her head was uncovered. Its plaited masses, quite black in the moonlight, hung down and coiled upon the bench, by her side. Her chaste drapery was of that revived classic order which the world of fashion was again laying aside to re-assume the mediaeval bondage of the staylace; for New Orleans was behind the fashionable world, and Madame Delphine and her daughter were behind New Orleans. A delicate scarf, pale blue, of lightly netted worsted, fell from either shoulder down beside her hands. The look that was bent upon her changed perforce to one of gentle admiration. She seemed the goddess of the garden.

Olive glanced up. Madame Delphine was not prepared for the movement, and on that account repeated her question:

"What are you thinking about?"

The dreamer took the hand that was laid upon hers between her own palms, bowed her head, and gave the hand a soft kiss.

The mother submitted. Wherefore, in the silence which followed, a daughter's conscience felt the burden of having withheld an answer, and Olive presently said, as the pair sat looking up into the sky:

"I was thinking of Père Jerome's sermon."

Madame Delphine had feared so. Olive had lived on it ever since the day it was preached. The poor mother was almost ready to repent having ever afforded her the opportunity of hearing it. Meat and drink had become of secondary value to her daughter; she fed upon the sermon.

Olive felt her mother's thought and knew that her mother knew her own; but now that she had confessed, she would ask a question:

"Do you think, *maman,* that Père Jerome knows it was I who gave that missal?"

"No," said Madame Delphine, "I am sure he does not."

Another question came more timidly:

"Do—do you think he knows *him?*"

"Yes, I do. He said in his sermon he did."

Both remained for a long time very still, watching the moon gliding in and through and among the small dark-and-white clouds. At last the daughter spoke again.

"I wish I was Père—I wish I was as good as Père Jerome."

"My child," said Madame Delphine, her tone betraying a painful summoning of strength to say what she had lacked the courage to utter,—"my child, I pray the good God you will not let your heart go after one whom you may never see in this world!"

The maiden turned her glance, and their eyes met. She cast her arms about her mother's neck, laid her cheek upon it for a moment, and then, feeling the maternal tear, lifted her lips, and, kissing her, said:

"I will not! I will not!"

But the voice was one, not of willing consent, but of desperate resolution.

"It would be useless, anyhow," said the mother, laying her arm around her daughter's waist.

Olive repeated the kiss, prolonging it passionately.

"I have nobody but you," murmured the girl; "I am a poor quadroone!"

She threw back her plaited hair for a third embrace, when a sound in the shrubbery startled them.

"*Qui ci ça?*" called Madame Delphine, in a frightened voice, as the two stood up, holding to each other.

No answer.

"It was only the dropping of a twig," she whispered, after a long holding of the breath. But they went into the house and barred it everywhere.

It was no longer pleasant to sit up. They retired, and in course of time, but not soon, they fell asleep, holding each other very tight, and fearing, even in their dreams, to hear another twig fall.

X

BIRDS

Monsieur Vignevielle looked in at no more doors or windows; but if the disappearance of this symptom was a favorable sign, others came to notice which were especially bad,—for instance, wakefulness. At well-nigh any hour of the night, the city guard, which itself dared not patrol singly, would meet him on his slow, unmolested, sky-gazing walk.

"Seems to enjoy it," said Jean Thompson; "the worst sort of evidence. If he showed distress of mind, it would not be so bad; but his calmness,—ugly feature."

The attorney had held his ground so long that he began really to believe it was tenable.

By day, it is true, Monsieur Vignevielle was at his post in his quiet "bank." Yet here, day by day, he was the source of more and more vivid astonishment to those who held preconceived notions of a banker's calling. As a banker, at least, he was certainly out of balance; while as a promenader, it seemed to those who watched him that his ruling idea had now veered about, and that of late he was ever on the quiet alert, not to find, but to evade, somebody.

"Olive, my child," whispered Madame Delphine one morning, as the pair were kneeling side by side on the tiled floor of the church, "yonder is Miché Vignevielle! If you will only look at once—he is just passing a little in— Ah, much too slow again; he stepped out by the side door."

The mother thought it a strange providence that Monsieur Vignevielle should always be disappearing whenever Olive was with her.

One early dawn, Madame Delphine, with a small empty basket on her arm, stepped out upon the *banquette* in front of her house, shut and fastened the door very softly, and stole out in the direction whence you could faintly catch, in the stillness of the daybreak, the songs of the Gascon butchers and the pounding of their meat-axes on the stalls of the distant market-house. She was going to see if she could find some birds for Olive,—the child's appetite was so poor;

and, as she was out, she would drop an early prayer at the cathedral. Faith and works.

"One must venture something, sometimes, in the cause of religion," thought she, as she started timorously on her way. But she had not gone a dozen steps before she repented her temerity. There was some one behind her.

There should not be any thing terrible in a footstep merely because it is masculine; but Madame Delphine's mind was not prepared to consider that. A terrible secret was haunting her. Yesterday morning she had found a shoe-track in the garden. She had not disclosed the discovery to Olive, but she had hardly closed her eyes the whole night.

The step behind her now might be the fall of that very shoe. She quickened her pace, but did not leave the sound behind. She hurried forward almost at a run; yet it was still there—no farther, no nearer. Two frights were upon her at once—one for herself, another for Olive, left alone in the house; but she had but the one prayer—"God protect my child!" After a fearful time she reached a place of safety, the cathedral. There, panting, she knelt long enough to know the pursuit was, at least, suspended, and then arose, hoping and praying all the saints that she might find the way clear for her return in all haste to Olive.

She approached a different door from that by which she had entered, her eyes in all directions and her heart in her throat.

"Madame Carraze."

She started wildly and almost screamed, though the voice was soft and mild. Monsieur Vignevielle came slowly forward from the shade of the wall. They met beside a bench, upon which she dropped her basket.

"Ah, Miché Vignevielle, I thang de good God to mid you!"

"Is dad so, Madame Carraze? Fo' w'y dad is?"

"A man was chase me all dad way since my 'ouse!"

"Yes, Madame, I sawed him."

"You sawed 'im? Oo it was?"

"'Twas only one man wad is a foolizh. De people say he's crezzie. *Mais*, he don' goin' to meg you no 'arm."

"But I was scare' fo' my lill' girl."

"Noboddie don' goin' trouble you' lill' gal, Madame Carraze."

Madame Delphine looked up into the speaker's strangely kind and patient eyes, and drew sweet re-assurance from them.

"Madame," said Monsieur Vignevielle, "wad pud you hout so hearly dis morning?"

She told him her errand. She asked if he thought she would find any thing.

"Yez," he said, "it was possible—a few lill' *bécassines-de-mer*, ou somezin' ligue. But fo' w'y you lill' gal lose doze hapetide?"

"Ah, Miché,"—Madame Delphine might have tried a thousand times again without ever succeeding half so well in lifting the curtain upon the whole, sweet, tender, old, old-fashioned truth,—"Ah, Miché, she wone tell me!"

"Bud, anny'ow, Madame, wad you thing?"

"Miché," she replied, looking up again with a tear standing in either eye, and then looking down once more as she began to speak, "I thing—I thing she's lonesome."

"You thing?"

She nodded.

"Ah! Madame Carraze," he said, partly extending his hand, "you see? 'Tis impossible to mague you' owze shud so tighd to priv-en dad. Madame, I med one mizteg."

"Ah, *non*, Miché!"

"Yez. There har nod one poss'bil'ty fo' me to be dad guardian of you' daughteh!"

Madame Delphine started with surprise and alarm.

"There is ondly one wad can be," he continued.

"But oo, Miché?"

"God."

"Ah, Miché Vignevielle"—She looked at him appealingly.

"I don' goin' to dizzerd you, Madame Carraze," he said.

She lifted her eyes. They filled. She shook her head, a tear fell, she bit her lip, smiled, and suddenly dropped her face into both hands, sat down upon the bench and wept until she shook.

"You dunno wad I mean, Madame Carraze?"

She did not know.

"I mean dad guardian of you' daughteh godd to fine 'er now one 'uzban'; an' noboddie are hable to do dad egceb de good God 'imsev. But, Madame, I tell you wad I do."

She rose up. He continued:

"Go h-open you' owze; I fin' you' daughteh dad uzban'."

Madame Delphine was a helpless, timid thing; but her eyes showed she was about to resent this offer. Monsieur Vignevielle put forth his hand—it touched her shoulder—and said, kindly still, and without eagerness:

"One w'ite man, Madame: 'tis prattycabble. I *know* 'tis prattycabble. One w'ite jantleman, Madame. You can truz me. I goin' fedge 'im. H-ondly you go h-open you' owze."

Madame Delphine looked down, twining her handkerchief among her fingers.

He repeated his proposition.

"You will come firz by you'se'f?" she asked.

"Iv you wand."

She lifted up once more her eye of faith. That was her answer.

"Come," he said, gently, "I wan' sen' some bird ad you' lill' gal."

And they went away, Madame Delphine's spirit grown so exaltedly bold that she said as they went, though a violent blush followed her words:

"Miché Vignevielle, I thing Père Jerome mighd be ab'e to tell you someboddie."

XI

FACE TO FACE

Madame Delphine found her house neither burned nor rifled.

"*Ah! ma piti sans popa!* Ah! my little fatherless one!" Her faded bonnet fell back between her shoulders, hanging on by the strings, and her dropped basket, with its "few lill' *bécassines-de-mer*" dangling from the handle, rolled out its okra and soup-joint upon the floor. "*Ma piti!* kiss!—kiss!—kiss!"

"But is it good news you have, or bad?" cried the girl, a fourth or fifth time.

"*Dieu sait, ma cère; mo pas conné!*"—God knows, my darling; I cannot tell!

The mother dropped into a chair, covered her face with her apron, and burst into tears, then looked up with an effort to smile, and wept afresh.

"What have you been doing?" asked the daughter, in a long-drawn, fondling tone. She leaned forward and unfastened her mother's bonnet-strings. "Why do you cry?"

"For nothing at all, my darling; for nothing—I am such a fool."

The girl's eyes filled. The mother looked up into her face and said:

"No, it is nothing, nothing, only that"—turning her head from side to side with a slow, emotional emphasis, "Miché Vignevielle is the best—*best* man on the good Lord's earth!"

Olive drew a chair close to her mother, sat down and took the little yellow hands into her own white lap, and looked tenderly into her eyes. Madame Delphine felt herself yielding; she must make a show of telling something:

"He sent you those birds!"

The girl drew her face back a little. The little woman turned away, trying in vain to hide her tearful smile, and they laughed together, Olive mingling a daughter's fond kiss with her laughter.

"There is something else," she said, "and you shall tell me."

"Yes," replied Madame Delphine, "only let me get composed."

But she did not get so. Later in the morning she came to Olive with the timid yet startling proposal that they would do what they could to brighten up the long-neglected front room. Olive was mystified and troubled, but consented, and thereupon the mother's spirits rose.

The work began, and presently ensued all the thumping, the trundling, the lifting and letting down, the raising and swallowing of dust, and the smells of turpentine, brass, pumice and woollen rags that go to characterize a housekeeper's *émeute*; and still, as the work progressed, Madame Delphine's heart grew light, and her little black eyes sparkled.

"We like a clean parlor, my daughter, even though no one is ever coming to see us, eh?" she said, as entering the apartment she at last sat down, late in the afternoon. She had put on her best attire.

Olive was not there to reply. The mother called but got no answer. She rose with an uneasy heart, and met her a few steps beyond the door that opened into the garden, in a path which came up from an old latticed bower. Olive was approaching slowly, her face pale and wild. There was an agony of hostile dismay in the look, and the trembling and appealing tone with which, taking the frightened mother's cheeks between her palms, she said:

"*Ah! ma mère, qui vini 'ci ce soir?*"—Who is coming here this evening?

"Why, my dear child, I was just saying, we like a clean"—

But the daughter was desperate:

"Oh, tell me, my mother, *who* is coming?"

"My darling, it is our blessed friend, Miché Vignevielle!"

"To see me?" cried the girl.

"Yes."

"Oh, my mother, what have you done?"

"Why, Olive, my child," exclaimed the little mother, bursting into tears, "do you forget it is Miché Vignevielle who has promised to protect you when I die?"

The daughter had turned away, and entered the door; but she faced around again, and extending her arms toward her mother, cried:

"How can—he is a white man—I am a poor"—

"Ah! *chérie,*" replied Madame Delphine, seizing the outstretched hands, "it is there—it is there that he shows himself the best man alive! He sees that difficulty; he proposes to meet it; he says he will find you a suitor!"

Olive freed her hands violently, motioned her mother back, and stood proudly drawn up, flashing an indignation too great for speech; but the next moment she had uttered a cry, and was sobbing on the floor.

The mother knelt beside her and threw an arm about her shoulders.

"Oh, my sweet daughter, you must not cry! I did not want to tell you at all! I did not want to tell you! It isn't fair for you to cry so hard. Miché Vignevielle says you shall have the one you wish, or none at all, Olive, or none at all."

"None at all! none at all! None, none, none!"

"No, no, Olive," said the mother, "none at all. He brings none with him to-night, and shall bring none with him hereafter."

Olive rose suddenly, silently declined her mother's aid, and went alone to their chamber in the half-story.

Madame Delphine wandered drearily from door to window, from window to door, and presently into the newly-furnished front room which now seemed dismal beyond degree. There was a great Argand lamp in one corner. How she had labored that day to prepare it for evening illumination! A little beyond it, on the wall, hung a crucifix. She knelt under it, with her eyes fixed upon it, and thus silently remained until its outline was indistinguishable in the deepening shadows of evening.

She arose. A few minutes later, as she was trying to light the lamp, an approaching step on the sidewalk seemed to pause. Her heart stood still. She softly laid the phosphorus-box out of her hands. A shoe grated softly on the stone step, and Madame Delphine, her heart beating in great thuds, without waiting for a knock, opened the door, bowed low, and exclaimed in a soft perturbed voice:

"Miché Vignevielle!"

He entered, hat in hand, and with that almost noiseless tread which we have noticed. She gave him a chair and closed the door; then hastened, with words of apology, back to her task of lighting the lamp. But her hands paused in their work again,—Olive's step was on the stairs; then it came off the stairs; then it was in the next room, and then there was the whisper of soft robes, a breath of gentle perfume, and a snowy figure in the door. She was dressed for the evening.

"Maman?"

Madame Delphine was struggling desperately with the lamp, and at that moment it responded with a tiny bead of light.

"I am here, my daughter."

She hastened to the door, and Olive, all unaware of a third presence, lifted her white arms, laid them about her mother's neck, and, ignoring her effort to speak, wrested a fervent kiss from her lips. The crystal of the lamp sent out a faint gleam; it grew; it spread on every side; the ceiling, the walls lighted up; the crucifix, the furniture of the room came back into shape.

"Maman!" cried Olive, with a tremor of consternation.

"It is Miché Vignevielle, my daughter"—

The gloom melted swiftly away before the eyes of the startled maiden, a dark form stood out against the farther wall, and the light, expanding to the full, shone clearly upon the unmoving figure and quiet face of Capitaine Lemaitre.

XII

THE MOTHER BIRD

One afternoon, some three weeks after Capitaine Lemaitre had called on Madame Delphine, the priest started to make a pastoral call and had hardly left the gate of his cottage, when a person, overtaking him, plucked his gown:

"Père Jerome"—

He turned.

The face that met his was so changed with excitement and distress that for an instant he did not recognize it.

"Why, Madame Delphine"—

"Oh, Père Jerome! I wan' see you so bad, so bad! *Mo oulé dit quiç'ose,*—I godd some' to tell you."

The two languages might be more successful than one, she seemed to think.

"We had better go back to my parlor," said the priest, in their native tongue.

They returned.

Madame Delphine's very step was altered,—nervous and inelastic.

She swung one arm as she walked, and brandished a turkey-tail fan.

"I was glad, yass, to kedge you," she said, as they mounted the front, outdoor stair; following her speech with a slight, unmusical laugh, and fanning herself with unconscious fury.

"*Fé chaud,*" she remarked again, taking the chair he offered and continuing to ply the fan.

Père Jerome laid his hat upon a chest of drawers, sat down opposite her, and said, as he wiped his kindly face:

"Well, Madame Carraze?"

Gentle as the tone was, she started, ceased fanning, lowered the fan to her knee, and commenced smoothing its feathers.

"Père Jerome"—She gnawed her lip and shook her head.

"Well?"

She burst into tears.

The priest rose and loosed the curtain of one of the windows. He did it slowly—as slowly as he could, and, as he came back, she lifted her face with sudden energy, and exclaimed:

"Oh, Père Jerome, de law is brogue! de law is brogue! I brogue it! 'Twas me! 'Twas me!"

The tears gushed out again, but she shut her lips very tight, and dumbly turned away her face. Père Jerome waited a little before replying; then he said, very gently:

"I suppose dad muss 'ave been by accyden', Madame Delphine?"

The little father felt a wish—one which he often had when weeping women were before him—that he were an angel instead of a man, long enough to press the tearful cheek upon his breast, and assure the weeper God would not let the lawyers and judges hurt her. He allowed a few moments more to pass, and then asked:

"*N'est-ce-pas,* Madame Delphine? Daz ze way, ain't it?"

"No, Père Jerome, no. My daughter—oh, Père Jerome, I bethroath my lill' girl—to a w'ite man!" And immediately Madame Delphine commenced savagely drawing a thread in the fabric of her skirt with one trembling hand, while she drove the fan with the other. "Dey goin' git marry."

On the priest's face came a look of pained surprise. He slowly said:

"Is dad possib', Madame Delphine?"

"Yass," she replied, at first without lifting her eyes; and then again, "Yass," looking full upon him through her tears, "yass, 'tis tru'."

He rose and walked once across the room, returned, and said, in the Creole dialect:

"Is he a good man—without doubt?"

"De bez in God's world!" replied Madame Delphine, with a rapturous smile.

"My poor, dear friend," said the priest, "I am afraid you are being deceived by somebody."

There was the pride of an unswerving faith in the triumphant tone and smile with which she replied, raising and slowly shaking her head:

"Ah-h, no-o-o, Miché! Ah-h, no, no! Not by Ursin Lemaitre-Vignevielle!"

Père Jerome was confounded. He turned again, and, with his hands at his back and his eyes cast down, slowly paced the floor.

"He *is* a good man," he said, by and by, as if he thought aloud. At length he halted before the woman.

"Madame Delphine"—

The distressed glance with which she had been following his steps was lifted to his eyes.

"Suppose dad should be true w'at doze peop' say 'bout Ursin."

"*Qui ci ça?* What is that?" asked the quadroone, stopping her fan.

"Some peop' say Ursin is crezzie."

"Ah, Père Jerome!" She leaped to her feet as if he had smitten her, and putting his words away with an outstretched arm and wide-open palm, suddenly lifted hands and eyes to heaven, and cried: "I wizh to God—*I wizh to God*—de whole worl' was crezzie dad same way!" She sank, trembling, into her chair. "Oh, no, no," she continued, shaking her head, "'tis not Miché Vignevielle w'at's crezzie." Her eyes lighted with sudden fierceness. "'Tis dad *law!* Dad *law* is crezzie! Dad law is a fool!"

A priest of less heart-wisdom might have replied that the law is—the law; but Père Jerome saw that Madame Delphine was expecting this very response. Wherefore he said, with gentleness:

"Madame Delphine, a priest is not a bailiff, but a physician. How can I help you?"

A grateful light shone a moment in her eyes, yet there remained a piteous hostility in the tone in which she demanded:

"Mais, pou'quoi yé fé cette méchanique là?"—What business had they to make that contraption?

His answer was a shrug with his palms extended and a short, disclamatory "Ah." He started to resume his walk, but turned to her again and said:

"Why did they make that law? Well, they made it to keep the two races separate."

Madame Delphine startled the speaker with a loud, harsh, angry laugh. Fire came from her eyes and her lip curled with scorn.

"Then they made a lie, Pére Jerome! Separate! No-o-o! They do not want to keep us separated; no, no! But they *do* want to keep us despised!" She laid her hand on her heart, and frowned upward with physical pain. "But, very well! from which race do they want to keep my daughter separate? She is seven parts white! The law did not stop her from being that; and now, when she wants to be a white man's good and honest wife, shall that law stop her? Oh, no!" She rose up. "No; I will tell you what that law is made for. It is made to—punish—my—child—for—not—choosing—her—father! Père Jerome—my God, what a law!" She dropped back into her seat. The tears came in a flood, which she made no attempt to restrain.

"No," she began again—and here she broke into English—"fo' me I don' kyare; but, Père Jerome,—'tis fo' dat I came to tell you,—dey *shall not* punizh my daughter!" She was on her feet again, smiting her heaving bosom with the fan. "She shall marrie oo she want!"

Père Jerome had heard her out, not interrupting by so much as a motion of the hand. Now his decision was made, and he touched her softly with the ends of his fingers.

"Madame Delphine, I want you to go at 'ome. Go at 'ome."

"Wad you goin' mague?" she asked.

"Nottin'. But go at 'ome. Kip quite; don' put you'se'f sig. I goin' see Ursin. We trah to figs dat law fo' you."

"You kin figs dad!" she cried, with a gleam of joy.

"We goin' to try, Madame Delphine. Adieu!"

He offered his hand. She seized and kissed it thrice, covering it with tears, at the same time lifting up her eyes to his and murmuring:

"De bez man God evva mague!"

At the door she turned to offer a more conventional good-by; but he was following her out, bareheaded. At the gate they paused an instant, and then parted with a simple adieu, she going home and he returning for his hat, and starting again upon his interrupted business.

Before he came back to his own house, he stopped at the lodgings of Monsieur Vignevielle, but did not find him in.

"Indeed," the servant at the door said, "he said he might not return for some days or weeks."

So Père Jerome, much wondering, made a second detour toward the residence of one of Monsieur Vignevielle's employés.

"Yes," said the clerk, "his instructions are to hold the business, as far as practicable, in suspense, during his absence. Every thing is in another name." And then he whispered:

"Officers of the Government looking for him. Information got from some of the prisoners taken months ago by the United States brig *Porpoise*. But"—a still softer whisper—"have no fear; they will never find him: Jean Thompson and Evariste Varrillat have hid him away too well for that."

XIII

TRIBULATION

The Saturday following was a very beautiful day. In the morning a light fall of rain had passed across the town, and all the afternoon you could see signs, here and there upon the horizon, of other showers. The ground was dry again, while the breeze was cool and sweet, smelling of wet foliage and bringing sunshine and shade in frequent and very pleasing alternation.

There was a walk in Père Jerome's little garden, of which we have not spoken, off on the right side of the cottage, with his chamber window at one end, a few old and twisted, but blossom-laden, crape-myrtles on either hand, now and then a rose of some unpretending variety and some bunches of rue, and at the other end a shrine, in whose blue niche stood a small figure of Mary, with folded hands and uplifted eyes. No other window looked down upon the spot, and its seclusion was often a great comfort to Père Jerome.

Up and down this path, but a few steps in its entire length, the priest was walking, taking the air for a few moments after a prolonged sitting in the confessional. Penitents had been numerous this afternoon. He was thinking of Ursin. The officers of the Government had not found him, nor had Père Jerome seen him; yet he believed they had, in a certain indirect way, devised a simple project by which they could at any time "figs dad law," providing only that these Government officials would give over their search; for, though he had not seen the fugitive, Madame Delphine had seen him, and had been the vehicle of communication between them. There was an orange-tree, where a mocking-bird was wont to sing and a girl in white to walk, that the detectives wot not of. The law was to be "figs" by the departure of the three frequenters of the jasmine-scented garden in one ship to France, where the law offered no obstacles.

It seemed moderately certain to those in search of Monsieur Vignevielle (and it was true) that Jean and Evariste were his harborers; but for all that the hunt, even for clews, was vain. The little banking establishment had not been disturbed. Jean Thompson had told the searchers certain facts about it, and about its gentle proprietor as well, that persuaded them to make no move against the concern, if the same relations did not even induce a relaxation of their efforts for his personal discovery.

Père Jerome was walking to and fro, with his hands behind him, pondering these matters. He had paused a moment at the end of the walk farthest from his window, and was looking around upon the sky, when, turning, he beheld a closely veiled female figure standing at the other end, and knew instantly that it was Olive.

She came forward quickly and with evident eagerness.

"I came to confession," she said, breathing hurriedly, the excitement in her eyes shining through her veil, "but I find I am too late."

"There is no too late or too early for that; I am always ready," said the priest. "But how is your mother?"

"Ah!"—

Her voice failed.

"More trouble?"

"Ah, sir, I have *made* trouble. Oh, Père Jerome, I am bringing so much trouble upon my poor mother!"

Père Jerome moved slowly toward the house, with his eyes cast down, the veiled girl at his side.

"It is not your fault," he presently said. And after another pause: "I thought it was all arranged."

He looked up and could see, even through the veil, her crimson blush.

"Oh, no," she replied, in a low, despairing voice, dropping her face.

"What is the difficulty?" asked the priest, stopping in the angle of the path, where it turned toward the front of the house.

She averted her face, and began picking the thin scales of bark from a crape-myrtle.

"Madame Thompson and her husband were at our house this morning. *He* had told Monsieur Thompson all about it. They were very kind to me at first, but they tried"— She was weeping.

"What did they try to do?" asked the priest.

"They tried to make me believe he is insane."

She succeeded in passing her handkerchief up under her veil.

"And I suppose then your poor mother grew angry, eh?"

"Yes; and they became much more so, and said if we did not write, or send a writing, to *him*, within twenty-four hours, breaking the"—

"Engagement," said Père Jerome.

"They would give him up to the Government. Oh, Père Jerome, what shall I do? It is killing my mother!"

She bowed her head and sobbed.

"Where is your mother now?"

"She has gone to see Monsieur Jean Thompson. She says she has a plan that will match them all. I do not know what it is. I begged her not to go; but oh, sir, *she is* crazy,—and I am no better."

"My poor child," said Père Jerome, "what you seem to want is not absolution, but relief from persecution."

"Oh, father, I have committed mortal sin,—I am guilty of pride and anger."

"Nevertheless," said the priest, starting toward his front gate, "we will put off your confession. Let it go until to-morrow morning; you will find me in my box just before mass; I will hear you then. My child, I know that in your heart, now, you begrudge the time it would take; and that is right. There are moments when we are not in place even on penitential knees. It is so with you now. We must find your mother. Go you at once to your house; if she is there, comfort her as best you can, and *keep her in, if possible,* until I come. If she is not there, stay; leave me to find her; one of you, at least, must be where I can get word to you promptly. God comfort and uphold you. I hope you may find her at home; tell her, for me, not to fear,"—he lifted the gate-latch,—"that she and her daughter are of more value than many sparrows; that God's priest sends her that word from Him. Tell her to fix her trust in the great Husband of the Church, and she shall yet see her child receiving the grace-giving sacrament of matrimony. Go; I shall, in a few minutes, be on my way to Jean Thompson's, and shall find her, either there or wherever she is. Go; they shall not oppress you. Adieu!"

A moment or two later he was in the street himself.

XIV

BY AN OATH

Père Jerome, pausing on a street-corner in the last hour of sunlight, had wiped his brow and taken his cane down from under his arm to start again, when somebody, coming noiselessly from he knew not where, asked, so suddenly as to startle him:

"*Miché, commin yé pellé la rie ici?*—how do they call this street here?"

It was by the bonnet and dress, disordered though they were, rather than by the haggard face which looked distractedly around, that he recognized the woman to whom he replied in her own *patois*:

"It is the Rue Burgundy. Where are you going, Madame Delphine?"

She almost leaped from the ground.

"Oh, Père Jerome! *mo pas conné,*—I dunno. You know w'ere's dad 'ouse of Miché Jean Tomkin? *Mo courri 'ci, mo courri là,—mo pas capabe li trouvé.* I go (run) here—there—I cannot find it," she gesticulated.

"I am going there myself," said he; "but why do you want to see Jean Thompson, Madame Delphine?"

"I *'blige'* to see 'im!" she replied, jerking herself half around away, one foot planted forward with an air of excited pre-occupation; "I godd some' to tell 'im wad I *'blige'* to tell 'im!"

"Madame Delphine"—

"Oh! Père Jerome, fo' de love of de good God, show me dad way to de 'ouse of Jean Tomkin!"

Her distressed smile implored pardon for her rudeness.

"What are you going to tell him?" asked the priest.

"Oh, Père Jerome,"—in the Creole *patois* again,—"I am going to put an end to all this trouble—only I pray you do not ask me about it now; every minute is precious!"

He could not withstand her look of entreaty.

"Come," he said, and they went.

Jean Thompson and Doctor Varrillat lived opposite each other on the Bayou road, a little way beyond the town limits as then prescribed. Each had his large, white-columned, four-sided house among the magnolias,—his huge live-oak overshadowing either corner of the darkly shaded garden, his broad, brick walk leading down to the tall, brick-pillared gate, his square of bright, red pavement on the turf-covered sidewalk, and his railed platform spanning the draining-ditch, with a pair of green benches, one on each edge, facing each other crosswise of the gutter. There, any sunset hour, you were sure to find the householder sitting beside his cool-robed matron, two or three slave nurses in white turbans standing at hand, and an excited throng of fair children, nearly all of a size.

Sometimes, at a beckon or call, the parents on one side of the way would join those on the other, and the children and nurses of both families would be given the liberty of the opposite platform and an ice-cream fund! Generally the parents chose the Thompson platform, its outlook being more toward the sunset.

Such happened to be the arrangement this afternoon. The two husbands sat on one bench and their wives on the other, both pairs very quiet, waiting respectfully for the day to die, and exchanging only occasional comments on matters of light moment as they passed through the memory. During one term of silence Madame Varrillat, a pale, thin-faced, but cheerful-looking lady, touched Madame Thompson, a person of two and a half times her weight, on her extensive and snowy bare elbow, directing her attention obliquely up and across the road.

About a hundred yards distant, in the direction of the river, was a long, pleasantly shaded green strip of turf, destined in time for a sidewalk. It had a deep ditch on the nearer side, and a fence of rough cypress palisades on the farther, and these were overhung, on the one hand, by a row of bitter-orange-trees inside the enclosure, and, on the other, by a line of slanting china-trees along the outer edge of the ditch. Down this cool avenue two figures were approaching side by side. They had first attracted Madame Varrillat's notice by the bright play of sunbeams which, as they walked, fell upon them in soft, golden flashes through the chinks between the palisades.

Madame Thompson elevated a pair of glasses which were no detraction from her very good looks, and remarked, with the serenity of a reconnoitring general:

"Père Jerome et cette milatraise."

All eyes were bent toward them.

"She walks like a man," said Madame Varrillat, in the language with which the conversation had opened.

"No," said the physician, "like a woman in a state of high nervous excitement."

Jean Thompson kept his eyes on the woman, and said:

"She must not forget to walk like a woman in the State of Louisiana,"—as near as the pun can be translated. The company laughed. Jean Thompson looked at his wife, whose applause he prized, and she answered by an asseverative toss of the head, leaning back and contriving, with some effort, to get her arms folded. Her laugh was musical and low, but enough to make the folded arms shake gently up and down.

"Père Jerome is talking to her," said one. The priest was at that moment endeavoring, in the interest of peace, to say a good word for the four people who sat watching his approach. It was in the old strain:

"Blame them one part, Madame Delphine, and their fathers, mothers, brothers, and fellow-citizens the other ninety-nine."

But to every thing she had the one amiable answer which Père Jerome ignored:

"I am going to arrange it to satisfy everybody, all together. *Tout à fait.*"

"They are coming here," said Madame Varrillat, half articulately.

"Well, of course," murmured another; and the four rose up, smiling courteously, the doctor and attorney advancing and shaking hands with the priest.

No—Père Jerome thanked them—he could not sit down.

"This, I believe you know, Jean, is Madame Delphine"—

The quadroone courtesied.

"A friend of mine," he added, smiling kindly upon her, and

turning, with something imperative in his eye, to the group. "She says she has an important private matter to communicate."

"To me?" asked Jean Thompson.

"To all of you; so I will— Good-evening." He responded nothing to the expressions of regret, but turned to Madame Delphine. She murmured something.

"Ah! yes, certainly." He addressed the company: "She wishes me to speak for her veracity; it is unimpeachable. Well, good-evening." He shook hands and departed.

The four resumed their seats, and turned their eyes upon the standing figure.

"Have you something to say to us?" asked Jean Thompson, frowning at her law-defying bonnet.

"*Oui*," replied the woman, shrinking to one side, and laying hold of one of the benches, "*mo oulé di' tou' ç'ose*"—I want to tell every thing. "*Miché Vignevielle la plis bon homme di moune*"—the best man in the world; "*mo pas capabe li fé tracas*"—I cannot give him trouble. "*Mo pas capabe, non; m'olé di' tous ç'ose.*" She attempted to fan herself, her face turned away from the attorney, and her eyes rested on the ground.

"Take a seat," said Doctor Varrillat, with some suddenness, starting from his place and gently guiding her sinking form into the corner of the bench. The ladies rose up; somebody had to stand; the two races could not both sit down at once—at least not in that public manner.

"Your salts," said the physician to his wife. She handed the vial. Madame Delphine stood up again.

"We will all go inside," said Madame Thompson, and they passed through the gate and up the walk, mounted the steps, and entered the deep, cool drawing-room.

Madame Thompson herself bade the quadroone be seated.

"Well?" said Jean Thompson, as the rest took chairs.

"*C'est drole*"—it's funny—said Madame Delphine, with a piteous effort to smile, "that nobody thought of it. It is so plain. You have only to look and see. I mean about Olive." She loosed a button in the front of her dress and passed her hand into her bosom. "And yet, Olive herself never thought of it. She does not know a word."

The hand came out holding a miniature. Madame Varrillat passed it to Jean Thompson.

"*Ouala so popa,*" said Madame Delphine. "That is her father."

It went from one to another, exciting admiration and murmured praise.

"She is the image of him," said Madame Thompson, in an austere undertone, returning it to her husband.

Doctor Varrillat was watching Madame Delphine. She was very pale. She had passed a trembling hand into a pocket of her skirt, and now drew out another picture, in a case the counterpart of the first. He reached out for it, and she handed it to him. He looked at it a moment, when his eyes suddenly lighted up and he passed it to the attorney.

"*Et là*"—Madame Delphine's utterance failed—"*et là ouala sa moman.* That is her mother."

The three others instantly gathered around Jean Thompson's chair. They were much impressed.

"It is true beyond a doubt!" muttered Madame Thompson.

Madame Varrillat looked at her with astonishment.

"The proof is right there in the faces," said Madame Thompson.

"Yes! yes!" said Madame Delphine, excitedly; "the proof is there! You do not want any better! I am willing to swear to it! But you want no better proof! That is all anybody could want! My God! you cannot help but see it!"

Her manner was wild.

Jean Thompson looked at her sternly.

"Nevertheless you say you are willing to take your solemn oath to this."

"Certainly"—

"You will have to do it."

"Certainly, Miché Thompson, *of course* I shall; you will make out the paper and I will swear before God that it is true! Only"—turning to the ladies—"do not tell Olive; she will never believe it. It will break her heart! It"—

A servant came and spoke privately to Madame Thompson, who rose quickly and went to the hall. Madame Delphine continued, rising unconsciously:

"You see, I have had her with me from a baby. She knows no better. He brought her to me only two months old. Her mother had died in the ship, coming out here. He did not come straight from home here. His people never knew he was married!"

The speaker looked around suddenly with a startled glance. There was a noise of excited speaking in the hall.

"It is not true, Madame Thompson!" cried a girl's voice.

Madame Delphine's look became one of wildest distress and alarm, and she opened her lips in a vain attempt to utter some request, when Olive appeared a moment in the door, and then flew into her arms.

"My mother! my mother! my mother!"

Madame Thompson, with tears in her eyes, tenderly drew them apart and let Madame Delphine down into her chair, while Olive threw herself upon her knees, continuing to cry:

"Oh, my mother! Say you are my mother!"

Madame Delphine looked an instant into the upturned face, and then turned her own away, with a long, low cry of pain, looked again, and laying both hands upon the suppliant's head, said:

"Oh, chére piti à moin, to pa' ma fie!"—Oh, my darling little one, you are not my daughter!—Her eyes closed, and her head sank back; the two gentlemen sprang to her assistance, and laid her upon a sofa unconscious.

When they brought her to herself, Olive was kneeling at her head silently weeping.

"Maman, chère maman!" said the girl softly, kissing her lips.

"Ma courri c'ez moin"—I will go home—said the mother, drearily.

"You will go home with me," said Madame Varrillat, with great kindness of manner—"just across the street here; I will take care of you till you feel better. And Olive will stay here with Madame Thompson. You will be only the width of the street apart."

But Madame Delphine would go nowhere but to her home. Olive she would not allow to go with her. Then they wanted to send a servant or two to sleep in the house with her for aid and protection; but all she would accept was the transient service of a messenger to invite two of her kinspeople—man and wife—to come and make their dwelling with her.

In course of time these two—a poor, timid, helpless pair—fell heir to the premises. Their children had it after them; but, whether in those hands or these, the house had its habits and continued in them; and to this day the neighbors, as has already been said, rightly explain its close-sealed, uninhabited look by the all-sufficient statement that the inmates "is quadroons."

XV

KYRIE ELEISON

The second Saturday afternoon following was hot and calm. The lamp burning before the tabernacle in Père Jerome's little church might have hung with as motionless a flame in the window behind. The lilies of St. Joseph's wand, shining in one of the half opened panes, were not more completely at rest than the leaves on tree and vine without, suspended in the slumbering air. Almost as still, down under the organ-gallery, with a single band of light falling athwart his box from a small door which stood ajar, sat the little priest, behind the lattice of the confessional, silently wiping away the sweat that beaded on his brow and rolled down his face. At distant intervals the shadow of some one entering softly through the door would obscure, for a moment, the band of light, and an aged crone, or a little boy, or some gentle presence that the listening confessor had known only by the voice of many years, would kneel a few moments beside his waiting ear, in prayer for blessing and in review of those slips and errors which prove us all akin.

The day had been long and fatiguing. First, early mass; a hasty meal; then a business call upon the archbishop in the interest of some projected charity; then back to his cottage, and so to the banking-house of "Vignevielle," in the Rue Toulouse. There all was open, bright, and re-assured, its master virtually, though not actually, present. The search was over and the seekers gone, personally wiser than they would tell, and officially reporting that (to the best of their knowledge and belief, based on evidence, and especially on the assurances of an unexceptionable eye-witness, to wit, Monsieur Vignevielle, banker) Capitaine Lemaitre was dead and buried. At noon there had been a wedding in the little church. Its scenes lingered before Père Jerome's vision now—the kneeling pair: the bridegroom, rich in all the excellences of man, strength and kindness slumbering interlocked in every part and feature; the bride, a saintly weariness on her pale face, her awesome eyes lifted in adoration upon the image of the Saviour; the small knots of friends behind: Madame Thompson, large, fair, self-contained; Jean Thompson, with the affidavit of Madame Delphine showing through his tightly buttoned coat; the physician and his wife, sharing one expression of amiable consent; and last—yet first—one small, shrinking female figure, here at one side, in faded robes and dingy bonnet. She sat as motionless as stone, yet wore a look of apprehension, and in the small, restless black eyes which peered out from the pinched and wasted face, betrayed the peacelessness of a harrowed mind; and neither the recollection of bride, nor of groom, nor of potential friends behind, nor the occupation of the present hour, could shut out from the tired priest the image of that woman, or the sound of his own low words of invitation to her, given as the company left the church—"Come to confession this afternoon."

By and by a long time passed without the approach of any step, or any glancing of light or shadow, save for the occasional progress from station to station of some one over on the right who was noiselessly going the way of the cross. Yet Père Jerome tarried.

"She will surely come," he said to himself; "she promised she would come."

A moment later, his sense, quickened by the prolonged silence, caught a subtle evidence or two of approach, and the next moment a penitent knelt noiselessly at the window of his box, and the whisper came tremblingly, in the voice he had waited to hear:

"*Bénissez-moin, mo' Père, pa'ce que mo péché.*" (Bless me, father, for I have sinned.)

He gave his blessing.

"*Ainsi soit-il*—Amen," murmured the penitent, and then, in the soft accents of the Creole *patois,* continued:

"'I confess to Almighty God, to the blessed Mary, ever Virgin, to blessed Michael the Archangel, to blessed John the Baptist, to the holy Apostles Peter and Paul, and to all the saints, that I have sinned exceedingly in thought, word, and deed, *through my fault, through my fault, through my most grievous fault.*' I confessed on Saturday, three weeks ago, and received absolution, and I have performed the penance enjoined. Since then"— There she stopped.

There was a soft stir, as if she sank slowly down, and another as if she rose up again, and in a moment she said:

"Olive *is* my child. The picture I showed to Jean Thompson is the half-sister of my daughter's father, dead before my child was born. She is the image of her and of him; but, O God! Thou knowest! Oh, Olive, my own daughter!"

She ceased, and was still. Père Jerome waited, but no sound came. He looked through the window. She was kneeling, with her forehead resting on her arms—motionless.

He repeated the words of absolution. Still she did not stir.

"My daughter," he said, "go to thy home in peace." But she did not move.

He rose hastily, stepped from the box, raised her in his arms, and called her by name:

"Madame Delphine!" Her head fell back in his elbow; for an instant there was life in the eyes—it glimmered—it vanished, and tears gushed from his own and fell upon the gentle face of the dead, as he looked up to heaven and cried:

"Lord, lay not this sin to her charge!"

FRANK R. STOCKTON

The Lady, or the Tiger?

Frank R. Stockton (1834–1902)

THE SUCCESS OF The Lady, or the Tiger?, and the public's *unhappy disposition to read into an ingenious yarn all manner of moral and psychological implications—and, what was worse, to write to the author about them—was one of the few crosses Frank Stockton was called on to bear; yet it was a sufficient one. His reputation survives for most readers only in this story and the national sensation it caused; and never was a charming and versatile humorist more foully served. By including the story in* The Scribner Treasury, *we are aggravating the situation, of course; but we could not very well leave* The Lady *out of any collection of our representative fiction.*

Even in his earliest writings, prentice work, done while he followed his trade of engraver on wood, Stockton employed the grotesque, wry, fanciful humor which sets off his stories like a hallmark. Most of his stories are elaborate fairy-tales; his humor is that best of humors, not verbal but rising out of situation, out of the unexpected act. His Rudder Grange *(1879) could have been a mildly funny account of life on an old canal-boat, occupied by a pair of newlyweds and their fantastic maidservant, Pomona. But the difference between these sketches and the conventional sort of domestic-difficulties comedy lay precisely in Pomona, whose habit of expressing the commonest domestic affairs in the language of the cheap, romantic fiction she devoured, was a typically Stocktonian invention.*

Stockton has been too much neglected of late. Even his professedly juvenile tales are meat for men. His ghosts are among the most amiable and literate ghosts in literature—sweetly reasonable, sufficiently spectral, splendidly funny. He could delineate the Negro character excellently, as in The Late Mrs. Null *(1886); and the Yankee female's capability has never been so pleasantly satirized as in* The Casting Away of Mrs. Lecks and Mrs. Aleshine *(1886–1888), a tale of desert islands and castaways and the triumph of common sense.*

THE LADY, OR THE TIGER?

IN THE very olden time, there lived a semi-barbaric king, whose ideas, though somewhat polished and sharpened by the progressiveness of distant Latin neighbors, were still large, florid, and untrammelled, as became the half of him which was barbaric. He was a man of exuberant fancy, and, withal, of an authority so irresistible that, at his will, he turned his varied fancies into facts. He was greatly given to self-communing; and, when he and himself agreed upon any thing, the thing was done. When every member of his domestic and political systems moved smoothly in its appointed course, his nature was bland and genial; but whenever there was a little hitch, and some of his orbs got out of their orbits, he was blander and more genial still, for nothing pleased him so much as to make the crooked straight, and crush down uneven places.

Among the borrowed notions by which his barbarism had become semified was that of the public arena, in which, by exhibitions of manly and beastly valor, the minds of his subjects were refined and cultured.

But even here the exuberant and barbaric fancy asserted itself. The arena of the king was built, not to give the people an opportunity of hearing the rhapsodies of dying gladiators, nor to enable them to view the inevitable conclusion of a conflict between religious opinions and hungry jaws, but for purposes far better adapted to widen and develop the mental energies of the people. This vast amphitheatre, with its encircling galleries, its mysterious vaults, and its unseen passages, was an agent of poetic justice, in which crime was punished, or virtue rewarded, by the decrees of an impartial and incorruptible chance.

When a subject was accused of a crime of sufficient importance to interest the king, public notice was given that on an appointed day the fate of the accused person would be decided in the king's arena,—a structure which well deserved its name; for, although its form and plan were borrowed from afar, its purpose emanated solely from the brain of this man, who, every barleycorn a king, knew no tradition to which he owed more allegiance than pleased his fancy, and who ingrafted on every adopted form of human thought and action the rich growth of his barbaric idealism.

When all the people had assembled in the galleries, and the king, surrounded by his court, sat high up on his throne of royal state on one side of the arena, he gave a signal, a door beneath him opened, and the accused subject stepped out into the amphitheatre. Directly opposite him, on the other side of the enclosed space, were two doors, exactly alike and side by side. It was the duty and the privilege of the person on trial, to walk directly to these doors and open one of them. He could open either door he pleased: he was subject to no guidance or influence but that of the aforementioned impartial and incorruptible chance. If he opened the one, there came out of it a hungry tiger, the fiercest and most cruel that could be procured, which immediately sprang upon him, and tore him to pieces, as a punishment for his guilt. The moment that the case of the criminal was thus decided, doleful iron bells were clanged, great wails went up from the hired mourners posted on the outer rim of the arena, and the vast audience, with bowed heads and downcast hearts, wended slowly their homeward way, mourning greatly that one so young and fair, or so old and respected, should have merited so dire a fate.

But, if the accused person opened the other door, there came forth from it a lady, the most suitable to his years and station that his majesty could select among his fair subjects; and to this lady he was immediately married, as a reward of his innocence. It mattered not that he might already possess a wife and family, or that his affections might be engaged upon an object of his own selection: the king allowed no such subordinate arrangements to interfere with his great scheme of retribution and reward. The exercises, as in the other instance, took place immediately, and in the arena. Another door opened beneath the king, and a priest, followed by a band of choristers, and dancing maidens blowing joyous airs on golden horns and treading an epithalamic measure, advanced to where the pair stood, side by side; and the wedding was promptly and cheerily solemnized. Then the gay brass bells rang forth their merry peals, the people shouted glad hurrahs, and the innocent man, preceded by children strewing flowers on his path, led his bride to his home.

This was the king's semi-barbaric method of administering justice. Its perfect fairness is obvious. The criminal could not know out of which door would come the lady: he opened either he pleased, without having the slightest idea whether, in the next instant, he was to be devoured or married. On some occasions the tiger came out of one door, and on some out of the other. The decisions of this tribunal were not only fair, they were positively determinate: the accused person was instantly punished if he found himself guilty; and, if innocent, he was rewarded on the spot, whether he liked it or not. There was no escape from the judgments of the king's arena.

The institution was a very popular one. When the people gathered together on one of the great trial days, they never knew whether they were to witness a bloody slaughter or a hilarious wedding. This element of uncertainty lent an interest to the occasion which it could not otherwise have attained. Thus, the masses were entertained and pleased, and the thinking part of the community could bring no charge of unfairness against this plan; for did not the accused person have the whole matter in his own hands?

This semi-barbaric king had a daughter as blooming as his most florid fancies, and with a soul as fervent and imperious as his own. As is usual in such cases, she was the apple of his eye, and was loved by him above all humanity. Among his courtiers was a young man of that fineness of blood and lowness of station common to the conventional heroes of romance who love royal maidens. This royal maiden was well satisfied with her lover, for he was handsome and brave to a degree unsurpassed in all this kingdom; and she loved him with an ardor that had enough of barbarism in it to make it exceedingly warm and strong. This love affair moved on happily for many months, until one day the king happened to discover its existence. He did not hesitate nor waver in regard to his duty in the premises. The youth was immediately cast into prison, and a day was appointed for his trial in the king's arena. This, of course, was an especially important occasion; and his majesty, as well as all the people, was greatly interested in the workings and development of this trial.

Never before had such a case occurred; never before had a subject dared to love the daughter of a king. In after-years such things became commonplace enough; but then they were, in no slight degree, novel and startling.

The tiger-cages of the kingdom were searched for the most savage and relentless beasts, from which the fiercest monster might be selected for the arena; and the ranks of maiden youth and beauty throughout the land were carefully surveyed by competent judges, in order that the young man might have a fitting bride in case fate did not determine for him a different destiny. Of course, everybody knew that the deed with which the accused was charged had been done. He had loved the princess, and neither he, she, nor any one else thought of denying the fact; but the king would not think of allowing any fact of this kind to interfere with the workings of the tribunal, in which he took such great delight and satisfaction. No matter how the affair turned out, the youth would be disposed of; and the king would take an aesthetic pleasure in watching the course of events, which would determine whether or not the young man had done wrong in allowing himself to love the princess.

The appointed day arrived. From far and near the people gathered, and thronged the great galleries of the arena; and crowds, unable to gain admittance, massed themselves against its outside walls. The king and his court were in their places, opposite the twin doors,—those fateful portals, so terrible in their similarity.

All was ready. The signal was given. A door beneath the royal party opened, and the lover of the princess walked into the arena. Tall, beautiful, fair, his appearance was greeted with a low hum of admiration and anxiety. Half the audience had not known so grand a youth had lived among them. No wonder the princess loved him! What a terrible thing for him to be there!

As the youth advanced into the arena, he turned, as the custom was, to bow to the king: but he did not think at all of that royal personage; his eyes were fixed upon the princess, who sat to the right of her father. Had it not been for the moiety of barbarism in her nature, it is probable that lady would not have been there; but her intense and fervid soul would not allow her to be absent on an occasion in which she was so terribly interested. From the moment that the decree had gone forth, that her lover should decide his fate in the king's arena, she had thought of nothing, night or day, but this great event and the various subjects connected with it. Possessed of more power, influence, and force of character than any one who had ever before been interested in such a case, she had done what no other person had done,—she had possessed herself of the secret of the doors. She knew in which of the two rooms, that lay behind those doors, stood the cage of the tiger, with its open front, and in which waited the lady. Through these thick doors, heavily curtained with skins on the inside, it was impossible that any noise or suggestion should come from within to the person who should approach to raise the latch of one of them; but gold, and the power of a woman's will, had brought the secret to the princess.

And not only did she know in which room stood the lady ready to emerge, all blushing and radiant, should her door be opened, but she knew who the lady was. It was one of the fairest and loveliest of the damsels of the court who had been selected as the reward of the accused youth, should he be proved innocent of the crime of aspiring to one so far above him; and the princess hated her. Often had she seen, or imagined that she had seen, this fair creature throwing glances of admiration upon the person of her lover, and sometimes she thought these glances were perceived and even returned. Now and then she had seen them talking together; it was but for a moment or two, but much can be said in a brief space; it may have been on most unimportant topics, but how could she know that? The girl was lovely, but she had dared to raise her eyes to the loved one of the princess; and, with all the intensity of the savage blood transmitted to her through long lines of wholly barbaric ancestors, she hated the woman who blushed and trembled behind that silent door.

When her lover turned and looked at her, and his eye met hers as she sat there paler and whiter than any one in the vast ocean of anxious faces about her, he saw, by that power of quick perception which is given to those whose souls are one, that she knew behind which door crouched the tiger, and behind which stood the lady. He had expected her to know it. He understood her nature, and his soul was assured that she would never rest until she had made plain to herself this thing, hidden to all other lookers-on, even to the king. The only hope for the youth in which there was any element of certainty was based upon the success of the princess in discovering this mystery; and the moment he looked upon her, he saw she had succeeded, as in his soul he knew she would succeed.

Then it was that his quick and anxious glance asked the question: "Which?" It was as plain to her as if he shouted it from where he stood. There was not an instant to be lost. The question was asked in a flash; it must be answered in another.

Her right arm lay on the cushioned parapet before her. She raised her hand, and made a slight, quick movement toward the right. No one but her lover saw her. Every eye but his was fixed on the man in the arena.

He turned, and with a firm and rapid step he walked across the empty space. Every heart stopped beating, every breath was held, every eye was fixed immovably upon that man. Without the slightest hesitation, he went to the door on the right, and opened it.

Now, the point of the story is this: Did the tiger come out of that door, or did the lady?

The more we reflect upon this question, the harder it is to answer. It involves a study of the human heart which leads us through devious mazes of passion, out of which it is difficult to find our way. Think of it, fair reader, not as if the decision of the question depended upon yourself, but upon that hot-blooded, semi-barbaric princess, her soul at a white heat beneath the combined fires of despair and jealousy. She had lost him, but who should have him?

How often, in her waking hours and in her dreams, had she started in wild horror, and covered her face with her hands, as she thought of her lover opening the door on the other side of which waited the cruel fangs of the tiger!

But how much oftener had she seen him at the other door! How in her grievous reveries had she gnashed her teeth, and torn her hair, when she saw his start of rapturous delight as he opened the door of the lady! How her soul had burned in agony when she had seen him rush to meet that woman, with her flushing cheek and sparkling eye of triumph; when she had seen him lead her forth, his whole frame kindled with the joy of recovered life; when she had heard the glad shouts from the multitude, and the wild ringing of the happy bells; when she had seen the priest, with his joyous followers, advance to the couple, and make them man and wife before her very eyes; and when she had seen them walk away together upon their path of flowers, followed by the tremendous shouts of the hilarious multitude, in which her one despairing shriek was lost and drowned!

Would it not be better for him to die at once, and go to wait for her in the blessed regions of semi-barbaric futurity?

And yet, that awful tiger, those shrieks, that blood!

Her decision had been indicated in an instant, but it had been made after days and nights of anguished deliberation. She had known she would be asked, she had decided what she would answer, and, without the slightest hesitation, she had moved her hand to the right.

The question of her decision is one not to be lightly considered, and it is not for me to presume to set myself up as the one person able to answer it. And so I leave it with all ow you: Which came out of the opened door,—the lady, or the tiger?

HENRY CUYLER BUNNER

The Story of a New York House

HENRY CUYLER BUNNER (1855–1896)

BUNNER CONSTRUCTED *his stories in conscious discipleship to French writers, and in particular to de Maupassant; yet the American's basic moods of humor and pity soften what is stark and repellent in the work of his master. His austerity of method steeled him against the temptations to sentimentality in the taste of his time, although it led him too often in his shorter stories into over-contrivance and superficiality of character development. Fiction was his avocation. In his day, he was a working journalist—an editor of the humorous weekly,* Puck, *a political satirist, and a steady contributor of witty parody and light verse to the magazines.*

New York City and its people constitute Bunner's principal theme in fiction. Few writers have succeeded as he did in expressing the romantic character of the city in the 80's—from the gaslit, aspiring, brownstone avenues to backwaters like the area south of Washington Square, where young, ambitious Americans set up a sedate Bohemia among vociferous Latin immigrants who lived there not by choice but for its cheapness. The "Village" was the scene of Bunner's first successful novelette, The Midge *(1886), but he is represented in* The Scribner Treasury *by a book of ampler scope.* The Story of a New York House *describes the rise and fall of two New York families in terms of the house old Jacob Dolph built "out of town" on Bleecker Street. It is a masterfully simple statement of the wear of eighty years on the characters and the community in which they live; its effortless movement and deft touch in handling character betray none of the labor which must have gone into the compression of events and background detail.*

THE STORY OF A NEW YORK HOUSE

I

"I HEAR," said Mrs. Abram Van Riper, seated at her breakfast-table, and watching the morning sunlight dance on the front of the great Burrell house on the opposite side of Pine Street, "that the Dolphs are going to build a prodigious fine house out of town—somewhere up near the Rynders's place."

"And I hear," said Abram Van Riper, laying down last night's *Evening Post*, "that Jacob Dolph is going to give up business. And if he does, it's a disgrace to the town."

It was in the summer of 1807, and Abram Van Riper was getting well over what he considered the meridian line of sixty years. He was hale and hearty; his business was flourishing; his boy was turning out all that should have been expected of one of the Van Riper stock; the refracted sunlight from the walls of the stately house occupied by the Cashier of the Bank of the United States lit with a subdued secondary glimmer the Van Riper silver on the breakfast-table—the squat teapot and slop-bowl, the milk-pitcher, that held a quart, and the apostle-spoon in the broken loaf-sugar on the Delft plate. Abram Van Riper was decorously happy, as a New York merchant should be. In all other respects, he was pleased to think, he was what a New York merchant should be, and the word of the law and the prophets was fulfilled with him and in his house.

"I'm sure," Mrs. Van Riper began again, somewhat querulously, "I can't see why Jacob Dolph shouldn't give up business, if he's so minded. He's a monstrous fortune, from all I hear—a good hundred thousand dollars."

"A hundred thousand dollars!" repeated her husband, scornfully. "Ay, and twice twenty thousand pounds on the top of that. He's done well, has Dolph. All the more reason he should stick to his trade; and not go to lolling in the sun, like a runner at the Custom-House door. He's not within ten years of me, and here he must build his country house, and set up for the fine gentleman. Jacob Dolph! Did I go on his note, when he came back from France, brave as my master, in '94, or did I not? And where 'ud he have raised twenty thousand in this town, if I hadn't? What's got into folks nowadays? Damn me if I can see!"

His wife protested in wifely fashion. "I'm sure, Van Riper," she began, "you've no need to fly in such a huff if I so much as speak of folks who have some conceit of being genteel. It's only proper pride of Mr. Dolph to have a country house, and——" (her voice faltering a little, timorously) "ride in and—and out——"

"*Ride!*" snorted Mr. Van Riper. "In a carriage, maybe?"

"In a carriage, Van Riper. You may think to ride in a carriage is like being the Pope of Rome; but there's some that knows better. And if you'd set up your carriage," went on the undaunted Mrs. Van Riper, "and gone over to Greenwich Street two years ago, as I'd have had you, and made yourself friendly with those people there, I'd have been on the Orphan Asylum Board at this very minute; and *you* would——"

Mr. Van Riper knew all that speech by heart, in all its variations. He knew perfectly well what it would end in, this time, although he was not a man of quick perception: "He would have been a member of the new Historical Society."

"Yes," he thought to himself, as he found his hat and shuffled out into Pine Street; "and John Pintard would have had my good check in his pocket for his tuppenny society. Pine Street is fine enough for me."

Mr. Van Riper had more cause for his petulancy than he would have acknowledged even to himself. He was a man who had kept his shop open all through Clinton's occupancy and who had had no trouble with the British. And when they had gone he had had to do enough to clear his skirts of any smirch of Toryism, and to implant in his own breast a settled feeling of militant Americanism. He did not like it that the order of things should change—and the order of things was changing. The town was growing out of all knowledge of itself. Here they had their Orphan Asylum, and their Botanical Garden, and their Historical Society; and the Jews were having it all their own way; and now people were talking of free schools, and of laying out a map for the upper end of the town to grow on, in the "system" of straight streets and avenues. To the devil with systems and avenues! said he. That was all the doing of those cursed Frenchmen. He knew how it would be when they brought their plaguy frigate here in the first fever year—'93—and the fools marched up from Peck's Slip after a red nightcap, and howled their cut-throat song all night long.

It began to hum itself in his head as he walked toward Water Street—*Ça ira—ça ira—les aristocrats à la lanterne.* A whiff of the wind that blew through Paris streets in the terrible times had come across the Atlantic and tickled his dull old Dutch nostrils.

But something worse than this vexed the conservative spirit of Abram Van Riper. He could forgive John Pintard—whose inspiration, I think, foreran the twentieth century—his fancy for free schools and historical societies, as he had forgiven him for his sidewalk-building fifteen years before; he could proudly overlook the fact that the women were busying themselves with all manner of wild charities; he could be contented though he knew that the Hebrew Hart was president of that merchants' club at Baker's, of which he himself would fain have been a member. But there was something in the air that he could neither forgive nor overlook, nor be contented with.

There was a change coming over the town—a change which he could not clearly define, even in his own mind. There was a great keeping of carriages, he knew. A dozen men had bought carriages, or were likely to buy them at any time. The women were forming societies for the improvement of this and that. And he, who had moved up-town from Dock Street, was now in an old-fashioned quarter. All this he knew, but the something which made him uneasy was more subtile.

Within the last few years he had observed an introduction of certain strange distinctions in the social code of the town. It had been vaguely intimated to him—perhaps by his wife, he could not remember—that there was a difference between his trade and Jacob Dolph's trade. He was a ship-chandler. Jacob Dolph sold timber. Their shops were side by side; Jacob Dolph's rafts lay in the river in front of Abram Van Riper's shop, and Abram Van Riper had gone on Jacob

Dolph's note, only a few years ago. Yet, it seemed that it was *genteel* of Jacob Dolph to sell timber, and it was not genteel of Abram Van Riper to be a ship-chandler. There was, then, a difference between Jacob Dolph and Abram Van Riper—a difference which, in forty years, Abram Van Riper had never conceived of. There were folks who held thus. For himself, he could not understand it. What difference there was between selling the wood to make a ship, and selling the stores to go inside of her, he could not understand.

The town was changing for the worse; he saw that. He did not wish—God forbid!—that his son John should go running about to pleasure-gardens. But it would be no more than neighborly if these young bucks who went out every night should ask him to go with them. Were William Irving's boys and Harry Brevoort and those young Kembles too fine to be friends with his boy? Not that he'd go with them a-rollicking—no, not that—but 'twould be neighborly. It was all wrong, he thought; they were going whither they knew not, and wherefore they knew not; and with that he cursed their airs and their graces, and pounded down to the Tontine, to put his name at the head of the list of those who subscribed for a testimonial service of plate, to be presented to our esteemed fellow-citizen and valued associate, Jacob Dolph, on his retirement from active business.

. . . .

Jacob Dolph at this moment was setting forth from his house in State Street, whose pillared balcony, rising from the second floor to the roof, caught a side glance of the morning sun, that loved the Battery far better than Pine Street. He had his little boy by the hand —young Jacob, his miniature, his heir, and the last and only living one of his eight children. Mr. Dolph walked with his stock thrust out and the lower end of his waistcoat drawn in—he was Colonel Dolph, if he had cared to keep the title; and had come back from Monmouth with a hole in his hip that gave him a bit of a limp, even now in eighteen-hundred-and-seven. He and the boy marched forth like an army with a small but enthusiastic left wing, into the poplar-studded Battery. The wind blew fresh off the bay; the waves beat up against the sea-wall, and swirled with a chuckle under Castle Garden bridge.

A large brig was coming up before the wind, all her sails set, as though she were afraid—and she was—of British frigates outside the Hook. Two or three fat little boats, cat-rigged, after the good old New York fashion, were beating down toward Staten Island, to hunt for the earliest blue-fish.

The two Dolphs crossed the Battery, where the elder bowed to his friends among the merchants who lounged about the city's pleasure-ground, lazily chatting over their business affairs. Then they turned up past Bowling Green into Broadway, where Mr. Dolph kept on bowing, for half the town was out, taking the fresh morning for marketing and all manner of shopping. Everybody knew Jacob Dolph afar off by his blue coat with the silver buttons, his nankeen waistcoat, and his red-checked Indian silk neckcloth. He made it a sort of uniform. Captain Beare had brought him a bolt of nankeen and a silk kerchief every year since 1793, when Mr. Dolph gave him credit for the timber of which the *Ursa Minor* was built.

And everybody seemed willing to make acquaintance with young Jacob's London-made kerseymere breeches, of a bright canary color, and with his lavender silk coat, and with his little *chapeau de Paris*. Indeed, young Jacob was quite the most prominent moving spectacle on Broadway, until they came to John Street, and saw something rolling down the street that quite cut the yellow kerseymeres out of all popular attention.

This was a carriage, the body of which was shaped like a huge section of a cheese, set up on its small end upon broad, swinging straps between two pairs of wheels. It was not unlike a piece of cheese in color, for it was of a dull and faded grayish-green, like mould, relieved by pale-yellow panels and gilt ornaments. It was truly an interesting structure, and it attracted nearly as much notice on Broadway in 1807 as it might to-day. But it was received with far more reverence, for it was a court coach, and it belonged to the Des Anges family, the rich Huguenots of New Rochelle. It had been built in France, thirty years before, and had been sent over as a present to his brother from the Count Des Anges, who had himself neglected to make use of his opportunities to embrace the Protestant religion.

When the white-haired old lady who sat in this coach, with a very little girl by her side, saw Mr. Dolph and his son, she leaned out of the window and signalled to the old periwigged driver to stop, and he drew up close to the sidewalk. And then Mr. Dolph and his son came up to the window and took off their hats, and made a great low bow and a small low bow to the old lady and the little girl.

"Madam Des Anges," said Mr. Dolph, with an idiom which he had learned when he was presented at the court of Louis the Sixteenth, "has surely not driven down from New Rochelle this morning? That would tax even her powers."

Madam Des Anges did not smile—she had no taste for smiling—but she bridled amiably.

"No, Mr. Dolph," she replied; "I have been staying with my daughter-in-law, at her house at King's Bridge, and I have come to town to put my little granddaughter to school. She is to have the privilege of being a pupil of Mme. Dumesnil."

Madam Des Anges indicated the little girl with a slight movement, as though she did not wish to allow the child more consideration than a child deserved. The little girl turned a great pair of awed eyes, first on her grandmother, and then on the gentlemen, and spoke no word. Young Jacob Dolph stared hard at her, and then contemplated his kerseymeres with lazy satisfaction. He had no time for girls. And a boy who had his breeches made in London was a boy of consequence, and need not concern himself about every one he saw.

"And this is your son, I make no doubt," went on Madam Des Anges; "you must bring him to see us at King's Bridge, while we are so near you. These young people should know each other."

Mr. Dolph said he would, and showed a becoming sense of the honor of the invitation; and he made young Jacob say a little speech of thanks, which he did with a doubtful grace; and then Mr. Dolph sent his compliments to Madam Des Anges' daughter-in-law, and Madam Des Anges sent her compliments to Mrs. Dolph, and there was more stately bowing, and the carriage lumbered on, with the little girl looking timorously out of the window, her great eyes fixed on the yellow kerseymeres, as they twinkled up the street.

"Papa," said young Jacob, as they turned the corner of Ann Street, "when may I go to a boys' school? I'm monstrous big to be at Mrs. Kilmaster's. And I don't like to be a girl-boy."

"Are you a girl-boy?" inquired his father, smiling.

"Aleck Cameron called me one yesterday. He said I was a girl-boy because I went to dame-school. He called me Missy, too!" the boy went on, with his breast swelling.

"We'll see about it," said Mr. Dolph, smiling again; and they walked on in silence to Mrs. Kilmaster's door, where he struck the knocker, and a neat mulatto girl opened the narrow door. Then he patted his boy on the head and bade him good-by for the morning, and told him to be a good boy at school. He took a step or two and looked back. Young Jacob lingered on the step, as if he had a further communication to make. He paused.

"I thumped him," said young Jacob, and the narrow door swallowed him up.

Mr. Dolph continued on his walk up Broadway. As he passed the upper end of the Common he looked with interest at the piles of red sandstone among the piles of white marble, where they were building the new City Hall. The Council had ordered that the rear or northward end of the edifice should be constructed of red stone; because red stone was cheap, and none but a few suburbans would ever look down on it from above Chambers Street. Mr. Dolph shook his head. He thought he knew better. He had watched the growth of trade; he knew the room for further growth; he had noticed the long converging lines of river-front, with their unbounded accommodation for wharves and slips. He believed that the day would come—and his own boy might see it—when the business of the city would crowd the dwelling-houses from the river side, east and west, as far, maybe, as Chambers Street. He had no doubt that the boy might find himself, forty years from then, in a populous and genteel neighborhood. Perhaps he foresaw too much; but he had a jealous yearning for a house that should be a home for him, and for his child, and for his grandchildren. He wanted a place where his wife might have a garden; a place which the boy would grow up to love and cherish, where the boy might bring a wife some day. And even if it were a little out of town—why, his wife did not want a rout every night; and it was likely his old friends would come out and see him once in a while, and smoke a pipe in his garden and eat a dish of strawberries, perhaps.

As he thought it all over for the hundredth time, weighing for and against in his gentle and deliberative mind, he strolled far out of town. There was a house here and there on the road—a house with a trim, stiff little garden, full of pink and white and blue flowers in orderly, clam-shell-bordered beds. But it was certainly, he had to admit, as he looked about him, very *countrified* indeed. It seemed that the city must lose itself if it wandered up here among these rolling meadows and wooded hills. Yet even up here, half way to Greenwich Village, there were little outposts of the town—clumps of neighborly houses, mostly of the poorer class, huddling together to form small nuclei for sporadic growth. There was one on his right, near the head of Collect Street. Perhaps that quizzical little old German was right, who had told him that King's Bridge property was a rational investment.

He went across the hill where Grand Street crosses Broadway, and up past what was then North and is to-day Houston Street, and then turned down a straggling road that ran east and west. He walked toward the Hudson, and passed a farmhouse or two, and came to a bare place where there were no trees, and only a few tangled bushes and ground-vines.

Here a man was sitting on a stone, awaiting him. As he came near, the man arose.

"Ah, it's you, Weeks? And have you the plan?"

"Yes, Colonel—Mr. Dolph. I've put the window where you want it—that is, my brother Levi did—though I don't see as you're going to have much trouble in looking over anything that's likely to come between you and the river."

Mr. Dolph took the crisp roll of parchment and studied it with loving interest. It had gone back to Ezra Weeks, the builder, and his brother Levi, the architect, for the twentieth time, perhaps. Was there ever an architect's plan put in the hands of a happy nest-builder where the windows did not go up and down from day to day, and the doors did not crawl all around the house, and the veranda did not contract and expand like a sensitive plant; or where the rooms and closets and corridors did not march backward and forward and in and out at the bidding of every fond, untutored whim?

"It's a monstrous great big place for a country-house, Mr. Dolph," said Ezra Weeks, as he looked over Jacob Dolph's shoulder at the drawings of the house, and shook his head with a sort of pitying admiration for the projector's audacity.

They talked for a while, and looked at the site as if they might see more in it than they saw yesterday, and then Weeks set off for the city, pledged to hire laborers and to begin the work on the morrow.

"I think I can get you some of that stone that's going into the back of the City Hall, if you say so, Mr. Dolph. That stone was bought cheap, you know—bought for the city."

"See what you can do, Weeks," said Mr. Dolph; and Mr. Weeks went whistling down the road.

Jacob Dolph walked around his prospective domain. He kicked a wild blackberry bush aside, to look at the head of a stake, and tried to realize that that would be the corner of his house. He went to where the parlor fireplace would be, and stared at the grass and stones, wondering what it would be like to watch the fire flickering on the new hearth. Then he looked over toward the Hudson, and saw the green woods on Union Hill and the top of a white sail over the high riverbank. He hoped that no one would build a large house between him and the river.

He lingered so long that the smoke of midday dinners was arising from Greenwich Village when he turned back toward town. When he reached the Common on his homeward way he came across a knot of idlers who were wasting the hour of the noontide meal in gaping at the unfinished municipal building.

They were admiringly critical. One man was vociferously enthusiastic.

"It's a marvellous fine building, say I, sir! Worthy of the classic shades of antiquity. If Europe can show a finer than that will be when she's done, then, in *my* opinion, sir, Europe is doing well."

"You admire the architecture, Mr. Huggins?" asked Mr. Dolph, coming up behind him. Mr. Huggins turned around, slightly disconcerted, and assumed an amiability of manner such as can only be a professional acquirement among us poor creatures of human nature.

"Ah, Mr. Dolph—Colonel, I should say! I have purposed to do myself the honor of presenting myself at your house this afternoon, Colonel Dolph, to inquire if you did not desire to have your peruke *frisée*. For I had taken the liberty of observing you in conversation with Madam Des Anges this morning, in her equipage, and it had occurred to me that possibly the madam might be a-staying with you."

"Madam Des Anges does not honor my house this time, Huggins," returned Mr. Dolph, with an indulgent little laugh; "and my poor old peruke will do very well for to-day."

There was a perceptible diminution in Mr. Huggins's ardor; but he was still suave.

"I hope the madam is in good health," he remarked.

"She is, I believe," said Mr. Dolph.

"And your good lady, sir? I have not had the pleasure of treating Mrs. Dolph professionally for some time, sir, I——"

Mr. Dolph was wary. "I don't think Mrs. Dolph is fond of the latest modes, Huggins. But here comes Mr. Van Riper. Perhaps he will have his peruke *frisée*."

Mr. Huggins got out of a dancing-master's pose with intelligent alacrity, bade Mr. Dolph a hasty "Good-afternoon!" and hurried off toward his shop, one door above Wall Street. Mr. Van Riper did not like "John Richard Desborus Huggins, Knight of the Comb."

There was something else that Mr. Van Riper did not like.

"Hullo, Dolph!" he hailed his friend. "What's this I hear about you building a preposterous tomfool of a town-house out by Greenwich? Why don't you hire that house that Burr had, up near Lispenard's cow-pasture, and be done with it?"

Mr. Dolph seized his chance.

"It's not so preposterous as all that. By the way, talking of Burr, I hear from Richmond that he'll positively be tried next week. Did you know that young Irving—William's son, the youngest, the lad that writes squibs—has gone to Richmond for the defence?"

"William Irving's son might be in better business," grunted Mr.

Van Riper, for a moment diverted. "If we'd got at that devil when he murdered poor Hamilton—'fore gad, we'd have saved the trouble of trying him. Do you remember when we was for going to Philadelphia after him, and there the sly scamp was at home all the time up in his fine house, a-sitting in a tub of water, reading French stuff, as cool as a cowcumber, with the whole town hunting for him?" Then he came back. "But that house of yours. You haven't got this crazy notion that New York's going to turn into London while you smoke your pipe, have you? You're keeping some of your seven business senses, ain't you?"

"I don't know," Mr. Dolph mildly defended his hobby; "there is a great potentiality of growth in this city. Here's an estimate that John Pintard made the other day——"

"John Pintard! He's another like *you*!" said Mr. Van Riper.

"Well, look at it for yourself," pleaded the believer in New York's future.

Mr. Van Riper took the neatly written paper, and simply snorted and gasped as he read this:

Statistical.

By the numeration of the inhabitants of this city, recently published, the progress of population for the last 5 years appears to be at the rate of 25 per cent. Should our city continue to increase in the same proportion during the present century, the aggregate number at its close will far exceed that of any other city in the Old World, Pekin not excepted, as will appear from the following table. Progress of population in the city of New York, computed at the rate of 25 per cent. every 5 years:

Year	Population	Year	Population
1805	75,770	1855	705,650
1810	95,715	1860	882,062
1815	110,390	1865	1,102,577
1820	147,987	1870	1,378,221
1825	184,923	1875	1,722,776
1830	231,228	1880	2,153,470
1835	289,035	1885	2,691,837
1840	361,293	1890	3,364,796
1845	451,616	1895	4,205,995
1850	564,520	1900	5,257,493

When he had read it through he was a-quivering, crimson with that rage of Conservative indignation which is even more fervent than the flames of Radical enthusiasm.

"Yes," he said, "there's seventy-five thousand people in this town, and there'll be seventy-five thousand bankrupts if this lunacy goes on. And there's seventy-five thousand maggots in your brain, and seventy-five thousand in John Pintard's; and if you two live to see nineteen hundred, you'll have twice five million two hundred and fifty-seven thousand four hundred and ninety-three—whatever that may be!" And he thrust the paper back at Jacob Dolph, and made for the Tontine and the society of sensible men.

. . . .

The house was built, in spite of Abram Van Riper's remonstrance. It had a stone front, almost flush with the road, and brick gable-ends, in each one of which high up near the roof, stood an arched window, to lift an eyebrow to the sun, morning and evening. But it was only a country-house, after all; and the Dolphs set up their carriage and drove out and in, from June to September.

There was a garden at the side, where Mrs. Dolph could have the flowers her heart had yearned after ever since Jacob Dolph brought her from her home at Rondout, when she was seventeen.

. . . .

Strengthened by the country air—so they said—young Jacob grew clean out of his dame-school days and into and out of Columbia College, and was sent abroad, a sturdy youth, to have a year's holiday. It was to the new house that he came back the next summer, with a wonderful stock of fine clothes and of finer manners, and with a pair of mustaches that scandalized everybody but Madam Des Anges, who had seen the like in France when she visited her brother. And a very fine young buck was young Jacob, altogether, with his knowledge of French and his ignorance of Dutch, and a way he had with the women, and another way he had with the men, and his heirship to old Jacob Dolph's money and his two houses.

For they stayed in the old house until 1822.

. . . .

It was a close, hot night in the early summer; there was a thick, warm mist that turned now and then into a soft rain; yet every window in the Dolphs' house on State Street was closed.

It had been a hideous day for New York. From early morning until long after dark had set in, the streets had been filled with frightened, disordered crowds. The city was again stricken with the old, inevitable, ever-recurring scourge of yellow fever, and the people had lost their heads. In every house, in every office and shop, there was hasty packing, mad confusion, and wild flight. It was only a question of getting out of town as best one might. Wagons and carts creaked and rumbled and rattled through every street, piled high with household chattels, up-heaped in blind haste. Women rode on the swaying loads, or walked beside with the smaller children in their arms. Men bore heavy burdens, and children helped according to their strength. There was only one idea, and that was flight—from a pestilence whose coming might have been prevented, and whose course could have been stayed. To most of these poor creatures the only haven seemed to be Greenwich Village; but some sought the scattered settlements above; some crossed to Hoboken; some to Bushwick; while others made a long journey to Staten Island, across the bay. And when they reached their goals, it was to beg or buy lodgings anywhere and anyhow; to sleep in cellars and garrets, in barns and stables.

The panic was not only among the poor and ignorant. Merchants were moving their offices, and even the Post Office and the Custom House were to be transferred to Greenwich. There were some who remained faithful throughout all, and who labored for the stricken, and whose names are not even written in the memory of their fellow-men. But the city had been so often ravaged before, that at the first sight there was one mere animal impulse of flight that seized upon all alike.

At one o'clock, when some of the better streets had once more taken on their natural quiet, an oxcart stood before the door of the Dolphs' old house. A little behind it stood the family carriage, its lamps unlit. The horses stirred uneasily, but the oxen waited in dull, indifferent patience. Presently the door opened, and two men came out and awkwardly bore a plain coffin to the cart. Then they mounted to the front of the cart, hiding between them a muffled lantern. They wore cloths over the lower part of their faces, and felt hats drawn low over their eyes. Something in their gait showed them to be seafaring men, or the like.

Then out of the open door came Jacob Dolph, moving with a feeble shuffle between his son and his old negro coachman—this man and his wife the only faithful of all the servants. The young man put his father in the carriage, and the negro went back and locked the doors and brought the keys to his young master. He mounted to the box, and through the darkness could be seen a white towel tied around his arm—the old badge of servitude's mourning.

The oxen were started up, and the two vehicles moved up into Broadway. They travelled with painful slowness; the horses had to be held in to keep them behind the cart, for the oxen could be only guided by the whip, and not by word of mouth. The old man moaned a little at the pace, and quivered when he heard the distant sound of hammers.

"What is it?" he asked, nervously.

"They are boarding up some of the streets," said his son; "do not fear, father. Everything is prepared; and if we make no noise, we shall not be troubled."

"If we can only keep her out of the Potter's Field—the Potter's Field!" cried the father; "I'll thank God—I'll ask no more—I'll ask no more!"

And then he broke down and cried a little, feebly.

It was nearly two when they came to St. Paul's and turned the corner to the gate. It was dark below, but some frenzied fools were burning tar-barrels far down Ann Street, and the light flickered on the top of the church spire. They crossed the churchyard to where a shallow grave had been dug, half way down the hill. The men lowered the body into it; the old negro gave them a little *rouleau* of coin, and they went hurriedly away into the night.

The clergyman came out by and by, with the sexton behind him. He stood high up above the grave, and drew his long cloak about him and lifted an old pomander-box to his face. He was not more foolish than his fellows; in that evil hour men took to charms and to saying of spells. Below the grave and apart, for the curse rested upon them, too, stood Jacob Dolph and his son, the old man leaning on the arm of the younger. Then the clergyman began to read the service for the burial of the dead, over the departed sister—and wife and mother. He spoke low; but his voice seemed to echo in the stillness. He came forward with a certain shrinking, and cast the handful of dust and ashes into the grave. When it was done, the sexton stepped forward and rapidly threw in the earth until he had filled the little hollow even with the ground. Then, with fearful precaution, he laid down the carefully cut sods, and smoothed them until there was no sign of what had been done. The clergyman turned to the two mourners, without moving nearer to them, and lifted up his hands. The old man tried to kneel; but his son held him up, for he was too feeble, and they bent their heads for a moment of silence. The clergyman went away as he had come; and Jacob Dolph and his son went back to the carriage. When his father was seated, young Jacob said to the coachman: "To the new house."

The heavy coach swung into Broadway, and climbed up the hill out into the open country. There were lights still burning in the farmhouses, bright gleams to east and west, but the silence of the damp summer night hung over the sparse suburbs, and the darkness seemed to grow more intense as they drove away from the city. The trees by the roadside were almost black in the gray mist; the raw, moist smell of the night, the damp air, chilly upon the high land, came in through the carriage windows. Young Jacob looked out and noted their progress by familiar landmarks on the road, but the old man sat with his head bent on his new black stock.

It was almost three, and the east was beginning to look dark, as though a storm were settling there in the grayness, when they turned down the straggling street and drew up before the great dark mass that was the new house. The carriage-wheels gritted against the loose stones at the edge of the roadway, and the great door of the house swung open. The light of one wavering candleflame, held high above her head, fell on the black face of old Chloe, the coachman's wife. There were no candles burning on the high-pitched stairway; all was dark behind her in the empty house.

Young Jacob Dolph helped his father to the ground, and between the young man and the negro old Jacob Dolph wearily climbed the steps. Chloe lifted her apron to her face, and turned to lead them up the stair. Her husband went out to his horses, shutting the door softly after him, between Jacob Dolph's old life and the new life that was to begin in the new house.

II

When young Jacob Dolph came down to breakfast the next morning he found his father waiting for him in the breakfast-room. The meal was upon the table. Old Chloe stood with her black hands folded upon her white apron, and her pathetic negro eyes following the old gentleman as he moved wistfully about the room.

Father and son shook hands in silence, and turned to the table. There were three chairs in their accustomed places. They hesitated a half-second, looking at the third great armchair, as though they waited for the mistress of the house to take her place. Then they sat down. It was six years before any one took that third chair, but every morning Jacob Dolph the elder made that little pause before he put himself at the foot of the table.

On this first morning there was very little said and very little eaten. But when they had made an end of sitting at the table old Jacob Dolph said, with something almost like testiness in his husky voice.

"Jacob, I want to sell the house."

"Father!"

"The old house, I mean; I shall never go back there."

His son looked at him with a further inquiry. He felt a sudden new apprehension. The father sat back in his easy-chair, drumming on the arms with nervous fingers.

"I shall never go back there," he said again.

"Of course you know best, sir," said young Jacob, gently; "but would it be well to be precipitate? It is possible that you may feel differently some time——"

"There is no 'some time' for me!" broke in the old man, gripping the chair-arms, fiercely; "my time's done—done, sir!"

Then his voice broke and became plaintively kind.

"There, there! Forgive me, Jacob, boy. But it's true, my boy, true. The world's done, for me; but there's a world ahead for you, my son, thank God! I'll be patient—I'll be patient. God has been good to me, and I haven't many years to wait, in the course of nature."

He looked vacantly out of the window, trying to see the unforeseen with his mental sight.

"While I'm here, Jacob, let the old man have his way. It's a whimsey; I doubt 'tis hardly rational. But I have no heart to go home. Let me learn to live my life here. 'Twill be easier."

"But do you think it necessary to sell, sir? Could you not hold the house? Are you certain that you would like to have a stranger living there?"

"I care not a pin who lives within those four walls now, sir!" cried the elder, with a momentary return of his vehemence. "It's no house to me now. Sell it, sir, sell it!—if there's any one will give money for it at a time like this. Bring every stick of furniture and every stitch of carpet up here; and let me have my way, Jacob—it won't be for long."

He got up and went blindly out of the room, and his son heard him muttering, "Not for long—not for long, now," as he wandered about the house and went aimlessly into room after room.

Old Jacob Dolph had always been an indulgent parent, and none kinder ever lived. But we should hardly call him indulgent to-day. Good as he was to his boy, it had always been with the goodness of a superior. It was the way of his time. A half-century ago the child's position was equivocal. He lived by the grace of God and his parents, and their duty to him was rather a duty to society, born of an abstract morality. Love was given him, not as a right, but as an indulgence. And young Jacob Dolph, in all his grief and anxiety, was guiltily conscious of a secret thrill of pleasure—natural enough, poor boy—in his sudden elevation to the full dignity of manhood, and his father's abdication of the headship of the house.

A little later in the day, urged again by the old gentleman, he put on his hat and went to see Abram Van Riper. Mr. Van Riper was now, despite his objections to the pernicious institution of country-houses, a near neighbor of the Dolphs. He had yielded, not to fashion, but to yellow fever, and at the very first of the outbreak had bought a house on the outskirts of Greenwich Village, and had moved there in unseemly haste. He had also registered an unnecessarily profane oath that he would never again live within the city limits.

When young Jacob Dolph came in front of the low, hip-roofed house, whose lower story of undressed stone shone with fresh white-wash, Mr. Van Riper stood on his stoop and checked his guest at the front gate, a dozen yards away. From this distance he jabbed his big gold-headed cane toward the young man, as though to keep him off.

"Stay there, sir—you, sir, you Jacob Dolph!" he roared, brandishing the big stick. "Stand back, I tell you! Don't come in, sir! Good-day, sir—good-day, good-day, good-day!" (This hurried excursus was in deference to a sense of social duty.) "Keep away, confound you, keep away—consume your body, sir, stay where you are!"

"I'm not coming any nearer, Mr. Van Riper," said Jacob Dolph, with a smile which he could not help.

"I can't have you in here, sir," went on Mr. Van Riper, with no abatement of his agitation. "I don't want to be inhospitable; but I've got a wife and a son, sir, and you're infectious—damn it, sir, you're infectious!"

"I'll stay where I am, Mr. Van Riper," said young Jacob, smiling again. "I only came with a message from my father."

"With a what?" screamed Mr. Van Riper. "I can't have—oh, ay, a message! Well, say it then and be off, like a sensible youngster. Consume it, man, can't you talk farther out in the street?"

When Mr. Van Riper learned his visitor's message, he flung his stick on the white pebbles of the clam-shell-bordered path, and swore that he, Van Riper, was the only sane man in a city of lunatics, and that if Jacob Dolph tried to carry out his plan he should be shipped straightway to Bloomingdale.

But young Jacob had something of his father's patience, and, despite the publicity of the interview, he contrived to make Mr. Van Riper understand how matters stood. To tell the truth, Van Riper grew quite sober and manageable when he realized that his extravagant imputation of insanity was not so wide of the mark as it might have seemed, and that there was a possibility that his old friend's mind might be growing weak. He even ventured a little way down the path and permitted Jacob to come to the gate while they discussed the situation.

"Poor old Dolph—poor old Jacob!" he groaned. "We must keep him out of the hands of the sharks, that we must!" He did not see young Jacob's irrepressible smile at this singular extension of metaphor. "He mustn't be allowed to sell that house in open market—never, sir! Confound it, I'll buy it myself before I'll see him fleeced!"

In the end he agreed, on certain strict conditions of precaution, to see young Jacob the next day and discuss ways and means to save the property.

"Come here, sir, at ten, and I'll see you in the sitting-room, and we'll find out what we can do for your father—curse it, it makes me feel bad; by gad, it does! Ten to-morrow, then—and come fumigated, young man, don't you forget that—come fumigated, sir!"

It was Van Riper who bought the property at last. He paid eighteen thousand dollars for it. This was much less than its value; but it was more than any one else would have given just at that time, and it was all that Van Riper could afford. The transaction weighed on the purchaser's mind, however. He had bought the house solely out of kindness, at some momentary inconvenience to himself; and yet it looked as though he were taking advantage of his friend's weakness. Abram Van Riper was a man who cultivated a clear conscience, of a plain, old-fashioned sort, and the necessity for self-examination was novel and disagreeable to him.

. . . .

Life lived itself out at Jacob Dolph's new house whether he liked it or not. The furniture came up-town, and was somewhat awkwardly disposed about its new quarters; and in this unhomelike combination of two homes old Mr. Dolph sat himself down to finish his stint of life. He awoke each morning and found that twenty-four hours of sleep and waking lay before him, to be got through in their regular order, just as they were lived through by men who had an interest in living. He went to bed every night, and crossed off one from a tale of days of which he could not know the length.

Of course his son, in some measure, saved his existence from emptiness. He was proud of young Jacob—fond and proud. He looked upon him as a prince of men, which he was, indeed. He trusted absolutely in the young man, and his trust was well placed. And he knew that his boy loved him. But he had an old man's sad consciousness that he was not necessary to Jacob—that he was an adjunct, at the best, not an integral part of this younger existence. He saw Jacob the younger gradually recovering from his grief for the mother who had left them; and he knew that even so would Jacob some day recover from grief when his father should have gone.

He saw this; but it is doubtful if he felt it acutely. Nature was gradually dulling his sensibilities with that wonderful anaesthetic of hers, which is so much kinder to the patient than it is to his watching friends. After the first wild freak of selling the house, he showed, for a long time, no marked signs of mental impairment, beyond his lack of interest in the things which he had once cared about—even in the growth of the city he loved. And in a lonely and unoccupied man, sixty-five years of age, this was not unnatural. It was not unnatural, even, if now and then he was whimsical, and took odd fancies and prejudices. But nevertheless the work was going on within his brain, little by little, day by day.

He settled his life into an almost mechanical routine, of which the most active part was his daily walk down into the city. At first he would not go beyond St. Paul's churchyard; but after a while he began to take timorous strolls among the old business streets where his life had been passed. He would drop into the offices of his old friends, and would read the market reports with a pretence of great interest, and then he would fold up his spectacles and put them in their worn leather case, and walk slowly out. He was always pleased when one of the younger clerks bowed to him and said, "Good-day, Mr. Dolph!"

It was in the fourth year of his widowhood that he bethought himself of young Jacob's need of a more liberal social life than he had been leading. The boy went about enough; he was a good deal of a beau, so his father heard; and there was no desirable house in the town that did not welcome handsome, amiable young Dolph. But he showed no signs of taking a wife unto himself, and in those days the bachelor had only a provisional status in society. He was expected to wed, and the whole circle of his friends chorused yearly a deeper regret for the lost sheep, as time made that detestable thing, an "old bachelor," of him.

Young Jacob was receiving many courtesies and was making no adequate return. He felt it himself, but he was too tender of his father's changeless grief to urge him to open the great empty house to their friends. The father, however, felt that it was his duty to sacrifice his own desire for solitude, and, when the winter of 1825 brought home the city's wandering children—there were not so many of the wandering sort in 1825—he insisted that young Jacob should give a dinner to his friends among the gay young bachelors. That would be a beginning; and if all went went well they would have an old maiden aunt from Philadelphia to spend the winter with them, and help them to give the dinner parties which do not encourage bachelorhood, but rather convert and reform the coy celibate.

The news went rapidly through the town. The Dolph hospitality had been famous, and this was taken for a signal that the Dolph doors were to open again. There was great excitement in Hudson Street and St. John's Park. Maidens, bending over their tambour-frames, working secret hopes and aspirations in with their blossoming silks and worsted, blushed, with faint speculative smiles, as they thought of the vast social possibilities of the mistress of the grand Dolph house. Young bachelors, and old bachelors, too, rolled memories of the Dolph Madeira over longing tongues.

The Dolph cellar, too, had been famous, and just at that period New Yorkers had a fine and fanciful taste in wine, if they had any self-respect whatever.

I think it must have been about then that Mr. Dominick Lynch began his missionary labors among the smokers and drinkers of this city; he who bought a vineyard in France and the Vuelta Abajo plantations in Cuba, solely to teach the people of his beloved New York what was the positively proper thing in wines and cigars. If it was not then, it could not have been much later that Mr. Dolph had got accustomed to receiving, every now and then, an unordered and unexpected consignment of wines or Havana cigars, sent up from Little Dock Street—or what we call Water Street now, the lower end of it. And I am sure that he paid Mr. Lynch's bill with glowing pride; for Mr. Lynch extended the evangelizing hand of culture to none but those of pre-eminent social position.

It was to be quite a large dinner; but it was noticeable that none of the young men who were invited had engagements of regrettable priority.

Jacob Dolph the elder looked more interested in life than he had looked in four years when he stood on the hearthrug in the drawing-room and received his son's guests. He was a bold figure among all the young men, not only because he was tall and white-haired, and for the moment erect, and of a noble and gracious cast of countenance, but because he clung to his old style of dress—his knee-breeches and silk stockings, and his long coat, black, for this great occasion, but of the "shadbelly" pattern. He wore his high black stock, too, and his snow-white hair was gathered behind into a loose peruke.

The young men wore trousers, or pantaloons, as they mostly called them, strapped under their varnished boots. Their coats were cut like our dress-coats, if you can fancy them with a wild amplitude of collar and lapel. They wore large cravats and gaudy waistcoats, and two or three of them who had been too much in England came with shawls or rugs around their shoulders.

They were a fashionable lot of people, and this was a late dinner, so they sat down at six o'clock in the great dining-room—not the little breakfast-room—with old Jacob Dolph at one end of the table and young Jacob Dolph at the other.

It was a pleasant dinner, and the wine was good, and the company duly appreciative, although individually critical.

Old Jacob Dolph had on his right an agreeable French count, just arrived in New York, who was creating a *furor*; and on his left was Mr. Philip Waters, the oldest of the young men, who, being thirty-five, had a certain consideration for old age. But old Jacob Dolph was not quite at his ease. He did not understand the remarkable decorum of the young men. He himself belonged to the age of "bumpers and no heel-taps," and nobody at his board to-night seemed to care about drinking bumpers, even out of the poor, little, new-fangled claret-glasses, that held only a thimbleful apiece. He had never known a lot of gentlemen, all by themselves, to be so discreet. Before the evening was over he became aware of the fact that he was the only man who was proposing toasts, and then he proposed no more.

Things had changed since he was a young buck, and gave bachelor parties. Why, he could remember seeing his own good father—an irreproachable gentleman, surely—lock the door of his dining-room on the inside—ay, at just such a dinner as this—and swear that no guest of his should go out of that room sober. And his word had been kept. Times were changing. He thought, somehow, that these young men needed more good port in their veins.

Toward the end of the festivities he grew silent. He gave no more toasts, and drank no more bumpers, although he might safely have put another bottle or two under his broad waistcoat. But he leaned back in his chair, and rested one hand on the table, playing with his wineglass in an absent-minded way. There was a vague smile on his face; but every now and then he knit his heavy gray brows as if he were trying to work out some problem of memory. Mr. Philip Waters and the French count were talking across him; he had been in the conversation, but he had dropped out some time before. At last he rose, with his brows knit, and pulled out his huge watch, and looked at its face. Everybody turned toward him, and, at the other end of the table, his son half rose to his feet. He put the watch back in his pocket, and said, in his clear, deep voice: "Gentlemen, I think we will rejoin the ladies."

There was a little impulsive stir around the table, and then he seemed to understand that he had wandered, and a frightened look came over his face. He tottered backward, and swayed from side to side. Mr. Philip Waters and the Frenchman had their arms behind him before he could fall, and in a second or two he had straightened himself up. He made a stately, tremulous apology for what he called his "infelicitous absence of mind," and then he marched off to bed by himself, suffering no one to go with him.

A little while later in the evening, Mr. Philip Waters, walking down Broadway (which thoroughfare was getting to have a fairly suburban look), informed the French count that in his, Mr. Waters's, opinion, young Jacob Dolph would own that house before long.

Young Jacob Dolph's father insisted on repetitions of the bachelor dinner, but he never again appeared in the great dining-room. When there was a stag-party he took his own simple dinner at five o'clock and went to bed early, and lay awake until his son had dismissed the last mild reveller, and he could hear the light, firm, young footstep mounting the stairs to the bedroom door opposite his own.

. . . .

That was practically the end of it for old Jacob Dolph. The maiden aunt, who had been invited, was notified that she could not come, for Mr. Dolph was not well enough to open his house that winter. But it was delicately intimated to her that if he grew worse she might still be sent for, and that alleviated her natural disappointment. She liked to give parties; but there is also a chastened joy for some people in being at the head of a house of mourning.

Old Mr. Dolph grew no worse physically, except that he was inclined to make his daily walks shorter, and that he grew fonder of sitting at home in the little breakfast-room, where the sun shone almost all day long, and where Mrs. Dolph had once been fond of coming to sew. Her little square work-table of mahogany stood there still. There the old gentleman liked to dine, and often he dined alone. Young Jacob was in great demand all over town, and his father knew that he ought to go out and amuse himself. And the young man, although he was kind and loving, and never negligent in any office of respect or affection, had that strong youth in him which makes it impossible to sit every day of the week opposite an old man whose world had slipped by him, who knew nothing of youth except to love it and wonder at it.

In the morning, before he went out for his daily tramp into town, old Jacob would say to young Jacob:

"I suppose I shall see you at dinner, my boy?"

And young Jacob would say, "Yes, sir," or "No, sir, I think not. Mrs. Des Anges was in town yesterday, and she asked me to ride up there to-day and dine. And Diana" (Diana was his big black mare) "needs a little work; she's getting badly out of condition. So, if it doesn't matter to you, sir, I'll just run up there and get back before the moon sets."

And the father would answer that it didn't matter, and would send his best respects, through Mrs. Des Anges at King's Bridge, to Madam Des Anges at New Rochelle; and at night he would sit down alone to his dinner in the breakfast-room, served by old Chloe, who did her humble best to tempt his appetite, which was likely to be feeble when Master Jacob was away.

Master Jacob had taken to riding to King's Bridge of late. Sometimes he would start out early in the morning, just about the time when young Van Riper was plodding by on his way to the shop. Young Van Riper liked to be at the shop an hour earlier than his father. Old Mr. Dolph was always up, on these occasions, to see his son start off. He loved to look at the boy, in his English riding-boots and breeches, astride of black Diana, who pranced and curvetted up the unpaved road. Young Jacob had her well in hand, but he gave her her head and let her play until they reached Broadway, where he made her strike a rattling regular pace until they got well up the road; and then she might walk up Bloomingdale way or across to Hickory Lane.

If he went up by the east he was likely to dismount at a place which you can see now, a little west and south of McComb's Dam Bridge, where there is a bit of rocky hollow, and a sort of horizontal cleft in the rocks that had been called a cave, and a water-washed stone above, whose oddly shaped depression is called an Indian's foot-print. He would stop there, because right in that hollow, as I can tell you myself, grew, in his time as in mine, the first of the spring flowers. It was full of violets once, carpeted fairly with the pale, delicate petals.

And up toward the west, on a bridle-path between the hills and the river, as you came toward Fort Washington, going to Tubby Hook—we are refined nowadays, and Tubby Hook is "Inwood"—Heaven help it!—there were wonderful flowers in the woods. The wind-flowers came there early, nestling under the gray rocks that sparkled with garnets; and there bloomed great bunches of Dutchman's-breeches—not the thin sprays that come in the late New England spring, but huge clumps that two men could not enclose with linked hands; great masses of scarlet and purple, and—mostly—of a waxy white, with something deathlike in their translucent beauty. There, also, he would wade into the swamps around a certain little creek, lured by a hope of the jack-in-the-pulpit, to find only the odorous and disappointing skunk-cabbage. And there the woods were full of the aroma of sassafras, and of birch tapped by the earliest woodpecker, whose drumming throbbed through the young man's deep and tender musing.

And—strange enough for a young man who rides only to exercise his black mare—he never came out of those woods without an armful of columbine or the like. And—strange enough for any young man in this world of strange things—when he sat down at the table of Mrs. Des Anges, in her pleasant house near Harlem Creek, Miss Aline Des Anges wore a bunch of these columbines at her throat. Miss Aline Des Anges was a slim girl, not very tall, with great dark eyes that followed some people with a patient wistfulness.

. . . . . .

One afternoon, in May of 1827, young Jacob found his father in the breakfast-room, and said to him:

"Father, I am going to marry Aline Des Anges."

His father, who had been dozing in the sun by the south window, raised his eyes to his son's face with a kindly, blank look, and said, thoughtfully:

"Des Anges. That's a good family, Jacob, and a wonderful woman, Madam Des Anges. Is she alive yet?"

. . . . . .

When Madam Des Anges, eighty years old, and strong and well, heard of this, she said:

"It is the etiquette of France that one family should make the proposition to the other family. Under the circumstances *I* will be the family that proposes. I will make a precedent. The Des Anges make precedents."

And she rode down to the Dolph house in the family carriage —the last time it ever went out—and made her "proposition" to Jacob Dolph the elder, and he brightened up most wonderfully, until you would have thought him quite his old self, and he told her what an honor he esteemed the alliance, and paid her compliments a hundred words long.

And in May of the next year, King's Bridge being out of the question, and etiquette being waived at the universal demand of society, the young couple stood up in the drawing-room of the Dolph house to be wed.

The ceremony was fashionably late—seven o'clock in the evening. And after it was over, and the young couple had digested what St. Paul had to say about the ordinance of wedlock, and had inaudibly promised to do and be whatever the dominie required of them, they were led by the half-dozen groomsmen to the long glass between the front windows, and made to stand up there, with their faces toward the company, and to receive the congratulations of a mighty procession of friends, who all used the same formulas, except the very old ones, who were delicately indelicate.

The bridegroom wore a blue coat and trousers, and a white satin waistcoat embroidered with silver-thread roses and lilies-of-the-valley. The coat was lined with cream-colored satin, quilted in a most elaborate pattern; and his necktie was of satin, too, with embroidered ends. His shirt was a miracle of fine linen. As to the bride, she was in white satin and lace, and at her throat she wore a little bunch of late white columbines, for which Mr. Jacob Dolph the younger had scoured the woods near Fort Washington.

There was to be a grand supper, later; and the time of waiting was filled up with fashionable conversation.

That dear old doctor, who was then a dear young doctor, and whose fine snow-crowned face stood in later years as an outward and visible sign of all that was brave, kindly, self-sacrificing, and benevolent in the art of healing, was seated by Madam Des Anges, and was telling her, in stately phrase, suited to his auditor, of a certain case of heroism with which he had met in the course of his practice. Mr. Blank, it appeared, had been bitten by a dog that was supposed to be possessed by the rabies. For months he had suffered the agonies of mental suspense and of repeated cauterizing of the flesh, and during those months had concealed his case from his wife, that he might spare her pain—suffering in silence enough to unnerve most men.

"It was heroic," said Dr. F.

Madam Des Anges bowed her gray head approvingly.

"I think," she said, "his conduct shows him to be a man of taste. Had he informed his wife of his condition, she might have experienced the most annoying solicitude; and I am informed that she is a person of feeble character."

The doctor looked at her, and then down at the floor; and then he asked her if she did not hope that Almaviva Lynch would bring Garcia back again, with that marvellous Italian opera, which, as he justly observed, captivated the eye, charmed the ear, and awakened the profoundest emotions of the heart.

And at that Madam Des Anges showed some animation, and responded that she had listened to some pleasing operas in Paris; but she did not know that they were of Italian origin.

But if Madam Des Anges was surprised to learn that any good thing could come out of any other country than France, there was another surprise in store for her, and it did not long impend.

It was only a little while after this that her grandson-in-law, finding her on his right and Abram Van Riper on his left—he had served out his time as a statue in front of the mirror—thought it proper to introduce to Madam Des Anges his father's old friend, Mr. Van Riper. Mr. Van Riper bowed as low as his waistcoat would allow, and courteously observed that the honor then accorded him he had enjoyed earlier in the evening through the kind offices of Mr. Jacob Dolph, senior.

Madam Des Anges dandled her quizzing-glass as though she meant to put it up to her eye, and said, in a weary way:

"Mr.—ah—Van Riper must pardon me. I have not the power of

remembering faces that some people appear to have; and my eyes —my eyes are not strong."

Old Van Riper stared at her, and he turned a turkey-cock purple all over his face, down to the double chin that hung over his white neckerchief.

"If your ladyship has to buy spectacles," he sputtered, "it needn't be on my account."

And he stamped off to the sideboard and tried to cool his red-hot rage with potations of Jamaica rum. There his wife found him. She had drawn near when she saw him talking with the great Madam Des Anges, and she had heard, as she stood hard by and smiled unobtrusively, the end of that brief conversation. Her face, too, was flushed—a more fiery red than her flame-colored satin dress. She attacked him in a vehement whisper.

"Van Riper, what are you doing? I'd almost believe you'd had too much liquor, if I didn't know you hadn't had a drop. Will you ever learn what gentility is? D'ye want us to live and die like toads in a hole? Here you are with your ill manners, offending Madam Des Anges, that everybody knows is the best of the best, and there's an end of all likelihood of ever seeing her and her folks, and two nieces unmarried and as good girls as ever was, and such a connection for your son, who hasn't been out of the house it's now twelve months—except to this very wedding here, and you've no thought of your family when once you lose that mighty fine temper of yours, that you're so prodigious proud of; and where you'll end us, Van Riper, is more than I know, I vow."

But all she could get out of Van Riper was:

"The old harridan! She'll remember my name this year or two to come, I'll warrant ye!"

. . . .

It was all over at last, and old black Julius, who had been acting as a combination of link-boy and major-domo at the foot of the front steps, extinguished his lantern, and went to bed, some time before a little white figure stole up the stairs and slipped into a door that Chloe—black Chloe—held open.

And the next day Jacob Dolph the elder handed the young bride into the new travelling-carriage with his stateliest grace, and Mr. and Mrs. Jacob Dolph, junior, rolled proudly up the road, through Bloomingdale, and across King's Bridge—stopping for luncheon at the Des Anges house—over to New Rochelle, where the feminine head of the house of Des Anges received them at her broad front door, and where they had the largest room in her large, old-fashioned house, for one night. Madam Des Anges wished to keep them longer, and was authoritative about it. But young Jacob settled the question of supremacy then and there, with the utmost courtesy, and Madam Des Anges, being great enough to know that she was beaten, sent off the victor on the morrow, with his trembling accomplice by his side, and wished them *bon voyage* as heartily as she possibly could.

So they started afresh on their bridal tour, and very soon the travelling carriage struck the old Queen Anne's Road, and reached Yonkers. And there, and from there up to Fishkill, they passed from one country-house to another, bright particular stars at this dinner and at that supper, staying a day here and a night there, and having just the sort of sociable, public, restless, rattling good time that neither of them wanted.

At every country-house where they stayed a day they were pressed to stay a week, and always the whole neighborhood was routed out to pay them social tribute. The neighbors came in by all manner of conveyances. One family of aristocrats started at six o'clock in the morning, and travelled fourteen miles down the river in an ox-cart, the ladies sitting bolt upright, with their hair elaborately dressed for the evening's entertainment. And once a regular assembly ball was given in their honor, at a town-hall, the use of which was granted for the purpose specified by unanimous vote of the town council. Of course, they had a very good time; but then there are various sorts of good times. Perhaps they might have selected another sort for themselves.

There is a story that, on their way back, they put up for several days at a poor little hostelry under the hills below Peekskill, and spent their time in wandering through the woods and picking wild-flowers; but it lacks confirmation, and I should be sorry to believe that two well-brought-up young people would prefer their own society to the unlimited hospitality of their friends in the country.

Old Jacob Dolph, at home, had the great house all to himself; and, although black Chloe took excellent care of his material comforts, he was restless and troubled. He took most pleasure in a London almanac, on whose smudgy pages he checked off the days. Letters came as often as the steamboat arrived from Albany, and he read them, after his fashion. It took him half the week to get through one missive, and by that time another had arrived. But I fear he did not make much out of them. Still, they gave him one pleasure. He endorsed them carefully with the name of the writer, and the date of receipt, and then he laid them away in his desk, as neatly as he had filed his business letters in his old days of active life.

Every night he had a candle alight in the hallway; and if there were a far-off rumble of carriage-wheels late at night, he would rise from his bed—he was a light sleeper, in his age—and steal out into the corridor, hugging his dressing-robe about him, to peer anxiously down over the balusters till the last sound and the last faint hope of his son's return had died away.

And, indeed, it was late in July when the travelling-carriage once more drew up in front of the Dolph house, and old Julius opened the door, and old Mr. Dolph welcomed them, and told them that he had been very lonely in their absence, and that their mother—and then he remembered that their mother was dead, and went into the house with his head bowed low.

III

St. John's Park and Hudson Street and all well-bred New York, for that matter, had its fill of the Dolph hospitality the next winter. It was dinner and ball and rout and merry-making of one sort or another, the season through. The great family sleighs and the little bachelor sleighs whirred and jingled up to the Dolph door surely two, and sometimes four, evenings in every week, and whirred and jingled away again at intensely fashionable hours, such as plain folk used for sleeping.

They woke up Abram Van Riper, did the revellers northward bound to country houses on the river-side, and, lying deep in his featherbed, he directed his rumbling imprecations at the panes of glass, that sparkled with frost in the mild moonlight.

"Oh, come, maidens, come, o'er the blue, rolling wave,
The lovely should still be the care of the brave—
Trancadillo, trancadillo, trancadillo, dillo, dillo, dillo!"

sang the misguided slaves of fashion, as they sped out of hearing.

"Trancadillo!" rumbled Mr. Van Riper. "I'd like to trancadillo them, consume 'em!" and then he cursed his old friend's social circle for a parcel of trumpery fools and Mrs. Van Riper, lying by his side, sighed softly with chastened regret and hopeless aspiration.

But everybody else—everybody who was anybody—blessed the Dolphs and the Dolphs' cellar, and their man-servant and their maid-servant, and their roasted ox and their saddle of venison, and the distinguished stranger who was within their gates; and young Mrs. Dolph was made as welcome as she made others.

For the little girl with the great dark eyes took to all this giddiness as naturally as possible—after her quiet fashion. The dark eyes sparkled with subdued pleasure that had no mean pride in it when she sat at the head of her great mahogany table, and smiled at the double row of bright faces that hemmed in the gorgeous display of the Dolph silver and china and fine linen. And it was wonderful how charming were the famous Des Anges manners, when they were softened and sweetened by so much grace and beauty.

"Who would have thought she had it in her?" said the young ladies down in St. John's Park. "You remember her, don't you, what a shy little slip of a thing she was when we were at old Dumesnil's together? Who was it used to say that she had had the life grandmothered out of her?"

"Fine little creature, that wife of Dolph's," said the young men as they strolled about in Niblo's Garden. "Dolph wouldn't have had the road all to himself if that old dragon of a grandmother had given the girl half a chance. 'Gad, she's an old grenadier! They say that Dolph had to put her through her facings the day after he was married, and that he did it in uncommon fine style, too."

"He's a lucky devil, that Dolph," the younger ones would sigh. "Nothing to do, all the money he wants, pretty wife, and the best wine in New York! I wish *my* old man would cut the shop and try to get an education in wine."

Their devotion to the frivolities of fashion notwithstanding, the young Dolphs were a loving, and, in a way, a domestic couple. Of course, everybody they knew had to give them a dinner or a ball, or pay them some such social tribute, and there were a myriad calls to be received and returned; but they found time for retired communings, even for long drives in the sleigh which, many a time in young Jacob Dolph's bachelor days, had borne the young man and a female companion—not always the same companion, either—up the Bloomingdale Road. And in the confidences of those early days young Jacob learned what his gentle little wife told him—without herself realizing the pathos of it—the story of her crushed, unchildlike youth, loveless till he came, her prince, her deliverer. Dolph understood it; he had known, of course, that she could not have been happy under the *régime* of Madam Des Anges; but when he heard the simple tale in all its monotonous detail, and saw spread out before him this poor young life, with its thousand little disappointments, submissions, abnegations, and undeserved punishments and needless restrictions, a generous rage glowed in his heart, and perhaps sprang once in a while to his indiscreet lips; and out of this grew a deeper and maturer tenderness than his honeymoon love for the sweet little soul that he had at first sought only for the dark eyes through which it looked out upon its joyless world.

It is unwise to speak in profane language, it is injudicious to speak disrespectfully of old age, yet the Recording Angel, if he did not see fit to let a tear fall upon the page, perchance found it convenient to be mending his pen when young Jacob Dolph once uttered certain words that made his wife cry out:

"Oh, Jacob, don't, *please* don't. She didn't mean it!"

This is only a supposition. Perhaps Madam Des Anges really had meant well. But oh, how much happier this world would be if all the people who "mean well" and do ill would only take to meaning ill and doing well!

Jacob Dolph the elder took but a doubtful part in all the festivities. The cloud that had hung dimly over him had begun to show little rifts; but the dark masses between the rifts were thicker and heavier than ever. It was the last brief convulsive struggle of the patient against the power of the anaesthetic, when the nervous hand goes up to put the cloth away from the mouth, just before the work is done and consciousness slips utterly away, and life is no more for the sufferer, though his heart beat and the breath be warm between his lips.

When he was bright he was almost like his old self, and these delusive periods came oftenest when he met some old friend, or in quiet morning hours when his daughter—so he always called her—sat at his feet in the sunny breakfast-room, and sewed and listened, or perhaps read to him from Scott's latest novel.

He may have had some faint sub-consciousness of his condition, for although he took the deepest interest in the balls and the dinners, he would never appear before his son's guests except when he was at his best and brightest. But he loved to sit, withdrawn in a corner, watching the young life that fluttered through the great rooms, smiling to himself, and gently pleased if some old crony sought him out and talked of old times—the older the times were, the better he remembered them. Indeed, he now recalled some things that he had not thought of since his far-off boyhood.

In truth, the younger Dolphs often had small heart in their festal doings. But the medical science of the day, positive, self-satisfied, and blinded by all manner of tradition, gave them, through its ministers, cruelly false hopes of the old man's ultimate recovery. Besides, they could not well order things otherwise. The extravagant hospitality of the day demanded such ceremonial, and to have abated any part of it would only have served to grieve and to alarm the object of their care.

The whole business was a constant pride and joy to old Mr. Jacob Dolph. When there was a dinner to be given, he would follow Aline as she went about the house superintending the preparations of her servants, in her flowered apron of black silk, with her bunch of keys—honest keys, those, a good four inches long, with tongues as big as a domino—jingling at her side. He would himself overlook the making ready of the wines, and give oft-repeated instructions as to the proper temperature for the port, and see that the champagne was put on ice in the huge octagonal cellaret in the dining-room corner. And when all was ready, as like as not he would kiss Aline on the forehead, and say:

"I have a headache to-night, my dear, and I think I shall take my dinner in my room."

And he would go feebly up stairs, and when old Julius, who always waited upon him, brought up his tray, he would ask:

"Is it a fine dinner, Julius? Did everybody come?"

And Julius would invariably reply, with profound African dignity: "Mons'us gran' dinneh, seh! 'E fines' dinneh I eveh witness', seh! I have stood behin' you' chai', seh, this thutty y'ah, an' I neveh see no such a gran' dinneh, Misteh Do'ph, seh!"

"Except the dinner we gave Mr. Hamilton, in State Street, Julius," the old man would put in.

"Excep' that, seh," Julius would gravely reply: "*that* was a pol-litical dinneh, seh; an' *of* co'se, a pol'litical dinneh—" an expressive pause—"but this he' is sho'ly a mons'us fine dinneh, seh."

. . . .

His bodily vigor was unimpaired, however, and except that his times of entire mental clearness grew fewer and briefer as the months went on, there was little change in the old gentleman when the spring of 1829 came. He was not insane, he was not idiotic, even at the worst. It seemed to be simply a premature old age that clouded his faculties. He forgot many things, he was weakly absent-minded, often he did not recognize a familiar face, and he seemed ever more and more disinclined to think and to talk. He liked best to sit in silence, seemingly unconscious of the world about him; and if he was aroused from his dreamy trance, his wandering speech would show that his last thought—and it might have entered his mind hours before, at the suggestion of some special event—was so far back in the past that it dealt with matters beyond his son's knowledge.

He was allowed to do as he pleased, for in the common affairs of daily life he seemed to be able to care for himself, and he plaintively resented anything that looked like guardianship. So he kept up his custom of walking down into the city, at least as far as St. Paul's. It was thought to be safe enough, for he was a familiar figure in the town, and had friends at every turn.

But one afternoon he did not return in time for dinner. Young Jacob was out for his afternoon ride, which that day had taken him in the direction of the good doctor's house. And when he had reached the house, he found the doctor likewise mounted for a ride. The doctor was going up to Bond Street—the Dolphs' quarter was growing fashionable already—to look at a house near Broadway that he had some thoughts of buying, for he was to be married the coming winter. So they had ridden back together, and after a long examination of the house, young Jacob had ridden off for a gallop through the country lanes; and it was five o'clock, and dinner was on the table, when he came to his father's house and learned from tearful Aline that his father was missing.

The horse was at the stable door when young Jacob mounted him once more and galloped off to Bond Street, where he found the doctor just ready to turn down the Bowery; and they joined forces and hurried back, and down Broadway, inquiring of the people who sat on their front stoops—it was a late spring evening, warm and fair —if they had seen old Mr. Dolph that day.

Many had seen him as he went down; but no one could remember that the old gentleman had come back over his accustomed path. At St. Paul's the sexton thought that Mr. Dolph had prolonged his walk down the street. Further on, some boys had seen him, still going southward. The searchers stopped at one or two of the houses where he might have called; but there was no trace of him. It was long since old Jacob Dolph had made a formal call.

But at Bowling Green they were hailed by Mr. Philip Waters, who came toward them with more excitement in his mien than a young man of good society often exhibited.

"I was going for a carriage, Dolph," he said: "your father is down there in the Battery Park, and I'm afraid—I'm afraid he's had a stroke of paralysis."

They hurried down, and found him lying on the grass, his head on the lap of a dark-skinned earringed Spanish sailor. He had been seen to fall from the bench near by, another maritime man in the crowd about him explained.

"It was only a minit or two ago," said the honest seafarer, swelled with the importance that belongs to the narrator of a tale of accident and disaster. "He was a-settin' there, had been for two hours 'most, just a-starin' at them houses over there, and all of a sudden chuck forward he went, right on his face. And then a man come along that knowed him, and said he'd go for a kerridge, or I'd 'a' took him on my sloop—she's a-layin' here now, with onions from Weathersfield—and treated him well; I see he wa'n't no disrespectable character. Here, Pedro, them's the old man's folks—let 'em take him. A-settin' there nigh on two hours, he was, just a-studyin' them houses. B'long near here?"

Young Jacob had no words for the Connecticut captain. Waters had arrived, with somebody's carriage, confiscated on the highway, and they gently lifted up the old gentleman and set off homeward. They were just in time, for Waters had been the earliest of the evening promenaders to reach the Battery. It was dinner hour—or supper hour for many—and the park was given up to the lounging sailors from the river-side streets.

The doctor's face was dark.

"No, it is not paralysis," he said. "Let us proceed at once to your own home, Mr. Dolph. In view of what I am now inclined to consider his condition, I think it would be the most advisable course."

He was as precise and exact in his speech even then, as he was later on, when years had given an innocent, genial pomposity to his delivery of his rounded sentences.

They put old Jacob Dolph to bed in the room which he had always occupied, in his married as in his widowed days. He never spoke again; that day, indeed, he hardly moved. But on the next he stirred uneasily, as though he were striving to change his position. The doctor bled him, and they shifted him as best they could, but he seemed no more comfortable. So the doctor bled him again; and even that did no good.

About sunset, Aline, who had watched over him with hardly a

moment's rest, left the room for a quarter of an hour, to listen to what the doctors had to say—there were four of them in the drawing-room below. When she and her husband entered the sick-room again, the old man had moved in his bed. He was lying on his side, his face to the windows that looked southward, and he had raised himself a little on his arm. There was a troubled gaze in his eyes, as of one who strains to see something that is unaccountably missing from his sight. He turned his head a little, as though to listen. Thus gazing, with an inward and spiritual vision only, at the bay that his eyes might never again see, and listening to the waves whose cadence he should hear no more, the troubled look faded into one of inscrutable peace, and he sank back into the hollow of his son's arm and passed away.

. . . .

The next time that the doctor was in the house it was of a snowy night a few days after New Year's Day. It was half-past two o'clock in the morning, and Jacob Dolph—no longer Jacob Dolph the younger—had been pacing furiously up and down the long dining-room—that being the longest room in the house—when the doctor came down stairs, and addressed him with his usual unruffled precision:

"I will request of you, Dolph, a large glass of port. I need not suggest to you that it is unnecessary to stint the measure, for the hospitality of this house is——"

"How is she, doctor? For God's sake, tell me—is she—is she——"

"The hospitality of this house is prover—" the precise doctor recommenced.

"Damn the hospitality!" cried Jacob Dolph: "I mean—oh, doctor—tell me—is anything wrong?"

"Should I request of you the cup of amity and geniality, Mr. Dolph, were there cause for anything save rejoicing in this house?" demanded the physician, with amiable severity. "I had thought that my words would have conveyed——"

"It's all over?"

"And bravely over!" And the doctor nodded his head with a dignified cheerfulness.

"And may I go to her?"

"You may, sir, after you have given me my glass of port. But remember, sir——"

Dolph turned to the sideboard, grasped a bottle and a glass, and thrust them into the doctor's hand, and started for the door.

"But remember, sir," went on the unperturbed physician, "you must not agitate or excite her. A gentle step, a tranquil tone, and a cheerful and encouraging address, brief and affectionate, will be all that is permitted."

Dolph listened in mad impatience, and was over the threshold before the doctor's peremptory call brought him back.

"What is it now?" he demanded, impatiently.

The doctor looked at him with a gaze of wonder and reproach.

"It is a male child, sir," he said.

Jacob Dolph crept up the stairs on tiptoe. As he paused for a moment in front of a door at the head, he heard the weak, spasmodic wail of another Dolph.

. . . .

"There's no help for it—I've got to do it," said Jacob Dolph.

It was another wintry morning, just after breakfast. The snow was on the ground, and the sleigh-bells up in Broadway sent down a faint jingling. Ten winters had come and gone, and Mr. Dolph was as comfortably stout as a man should be who is well fed and forty. He stood with his back to the fire, pulling at his whiskers—which formed what was earlier known as a Newgate collar—with his right thumb and forefinger. His left thumb was stuck in the armhole of his flowered satin waistcoat, black and shiny.

Opposite him sat a man of his own age, clean-shaven and sharp-featured. He had calm, somewhat cold, gray eyes, a deliberate, self-contained manner of speaking, and a pallid, dry complexion that suited with his thin features. His dress was plain, although it was thoroughly neat. He had no flowered satin waistcoat; but something in his bearing told you that he was a man who had no anxiety about the narrow things of the counting-room; who had no need to ask himself how much money was coming in to-morrow. And at the same time you felt that every cent of whatever might be to-morrow's dues would find its way to his hands as surely as the representative figures stood on his ledger's page. It was young Mr. Van Riper—but he, too, had lost his right to that title, not only because of his years, but because, in the garret of the house in Greenwich Village, a cobweb stretched from one of the low beams to the head of old Abram Van Riper's great walking-stick, which stood in the corner where it had been placed, with other rubbish, the day after Abram Van Riper's funeral.

"I should not advise it, Dolph, if it can be helped," Mr. Van Riper observed, thoughtfully.

"It can't be helped."

"I can give you your price, of course," Van Riper went on, with deliberation; "but equally of course, it won't be anything like what the property will bring in the course of a few years."

Dolph kicked at the hearthrug, as he answered, somewhat testily:

"I'm not making a speculation of it."

Mr. Van Riper was unmoved.

"And I'm not making a speculation of you, either," he said, calmly; "I am speaking only for your own benefit, Dolph."

Mr. Dolph put his hands in his pockets, strode to the window and back again, and then said, with an uneasy little laugh:

"I beg your pardon, Van Riper; you're quite right, of course. The fact is, I've got to do it. I must have the money, and I must have it now."

Mr. Van Riper stroked his sharp chin.

"Is it necessary to raise the money in that particular way? You are temporarily embarrassed—I don't wish to be obtrusive—but why not borrow what you need, and give me a mortgage on the house?"

Ten years had given Jacob Dolph a certain floridity; but at this he blushed a hot red.

"Mortgage on the house? No, sir," he said, with emphasis.

"Well, any other security, then," was Van Riper's indifferent amendment.

Again Jacob Dolph strode to the window and back again, staring hard at the carpet, and knitting his brows.

Mr. Van Riper waited in undisturbed calm until his friend spoke once more.

"I might as well tell you the truth, Van Riper," he said, at last; "I've made a fool of myself. I've lost money, and I've got to pocket the loss. As to borrowing, I've borrowed all I ought to borrow. I *won't* mortgage the house. This sale simply represents the hole in my capital."

Something like a look of surprise came into Mr. Van Riper's wintry eyes.

"It's none of my business, of course," he observed; "but if you haven't any objection to telling me——"

"What did it? What does for everybody nowadays? Western lands and Wall Street—that's about the whole story. Oh, yes, I know —I ought to have kept out of it. But I didn't. I was nothing better than a fool at such business. I'm properly punished."

He sighed as he stood on the hearthrug, his hands under his coat-tails, and his head hanging down. He looked as though many other thoughts were going through his mind than those which he expressed.

"I wish," he began again, "that my poor old father had brought me up to business ways. I might have kept out of it all. College is a good thing for a man, of course; but college doesn't teach you how to buy lots in western cities—especially when the western cities aren't built."

"College teaches you a good many other things, though," said Van Riper, frowning slightly, as he put the tips of his long fingers together; "I wish I'd had your chance, Dolph. *My* boy shall go to Columbia, that's certain."

"*Your* boy?" queried Dolph, raising his eyebrows.

Van Riper smiled.

"Yes," he said, "my boy. You didn't know I had a boy, did you? He's nearly a year old."

This made Mr. Jacob Dolph kick at the rug once more, and scowl a little.

"I'm afraid I haven't been very neighborly, Van Riper—" he began; but the other interrupted him, smiling good-naturedly.

"You and I go different ways, Dolph," he said. "We're plain folks over in Greenwich Village, and you—you're a man of fashion."

Jacob Dolph smiled—not very mirthfully. Van Riper's gaze travelled around the room, quietly curious.

"It costs money to be a man of fashion, doesn't it?"

"Yes," said Dolph, "it does."

There was silence for a minute, which Van Riper broke.

"If you've got to sell, Dolph, why, it's a pity; but I'll take it. I'll see Ogden to-day, and we can finish the business whenever you wish. But in my opinion, you'd do better to borrow."

Dolph shook his head.

"I've been quite enough of a fool," he replied.

"Well," said Mr. Van Riper, rising, "I must get to the office. You'll hear from Ogden to-morrow. I'm sorry you've got into such a snarl; but—" his lips stretched into something like a smile—"I suppose you'll know better next time. Good-day."

. . . .

After Mr. Dolph had bowed his guest to the door, Mrs. Dolph slipped down the stairs and into the drawing-room.

"Did he take it?" she asked.

"Of course he took it," Dolph answered, bitterly, "at that price."

"Did he say anything," she inquired again, "about its being hard for us to—to sell it?"

"He said we had better not sell it now—that it would bring more a few years hence."

"He doesn't understand," said Mrs. Dolph.

"He *couldn't* understand," said Mr. Dolph.

Then she went over to him and kissed him.

"It's only selling the garden, after all," she said; "it isn't like selling our home."

He put his arm around her waist, and they walked into the breakfast-room, and looked out on the garden which to-morrow would be theirs no longer, and in a few months would not be a garden at all.

High walls hemmed it in—the walls of the houses which had grown up around them. A few stalks stood up out of the snow, the stalks of old-fashioned flowers—hollyhock and larkspur and Job's-tears and the like—and the lines of the beds were defined by the tiny hedges of box, with the white snow-powder sifted into their dark, shiny green. The bare rose-bushes were there, with their spikes of thorns, and little mounds of snow showed where the glories of the poppy-bed had bloomed.

Jacob Dolph, looking out, saw the clear summer sunlight lying where the snow lay now. He saw his mother moving about the path, cutting a flower here and a bud there. He saw himself, a little boy in brave breeches, following her about, and looking for the harmless toads, and working each into one of the wonderful legends which he had heard from the old German gardener across the way. He saw his father, too, pacing those paths of summer evenings, when the hollyhocks nodded their pink heads, and glancing up, from time to time, at his mother as she sat knitting at that very window. And, last of all in the line, yet first in his mind, he saw his wife tripping out in the fresh morning, to smile on the flowers she loved, to linger lovingly over the beds of verbena, and to pick the little nosegay that stood by the side of the tall coffee-urn at every summer-morning breakfast.

And the wife, looking out by his side, saw that splendid boy of theirs running over path and bed, glad of the flowers and the air and the freedom, full of young life and boyish sprightliness, his long hair floating behind him, the light of hope and youth in his bright face.

And to-morrow it would be Van Riper's; and very soon there would be houses there, to close up the friendly window which had seen so much, which had let so much innocent joy and gladness into the old breakfast-room; and there would be an end of flower-bordered paths and nodding hollyhocks. She put her face upon her husband's shoulder, and cried a little, though he pretended not to know it. When she lifted it, somehow she had got her eyes dry, though they were painfully bright and large.

"It isn't like selling our house," she said.

IV

Jacob Dolph got out of the Broadway stage at Bowling Green, followed by Eustace Dolph. Eustace Dolph at twenty-two was no more like his father than his patrician name was like simple and scriptural Jacob. The elder Dolph was a personable man, certainly; a handsome man, even, who looked to be nearer forty than fifty-two; and he was well dressed—perhaps a trifle out of the mode—and carried himself with a certain genial dignity, and with the lightness of a man who has not forgotten that he has been a buck in his time. But Eustace was distinctly and unmistakably a dandy. There are superficial differences, of course, between the dandy of 1852 and the dandy of 1887; but the structural foundation of all types of dandy is the same through all ages. Back of the clothes—back of the ruffles, or the bright neck-cloth, or the high pickardil—which may vary with the time or the individual, you will ever find clearly displayed to your eyes the obvious and unmistakable spiritual reason for and cause of the dandy—and it is always self-assertion pushed beyond the bounds of self-respect.

Now, as a matter of fact, young Eustace's garments were not really worse than many a man has worn from simple, honest bad taste. To be sure, the checked pattern of his trousers was for size like the design of a prison grating; he had a coat so blue that it shimmered in the sunlight; his necktie was of purple satin, and fearfully and wonderfully made and fringed, and decked with gems fastened by little gold chains to other inferior guardian gems; and his waistcoat was confected of satin and velvet and damask all at once; yet you might have put all these things on his father, and, although the effect would not have been pleasant, you would never have called the elder gentleman a dandy. In other words, it was Why young Eustace wore his raiment that made it dandified, and not the inherent gorgeousness of the raiment itself.

The exchange of attire might readily have been made, so far as the size of the two men was concerned. But only in size were they alike. There was nothing of the Dolph in Eustace's face. He bore, indeed, a strong resemblance to his maternal great-grandmother, now many years put away where she could no longer trouble the wicked, and where she had to let the weary be at rest. (And how poor little Aline had wept and wailed over that death, and lamented that she had not been more dutiful as a child!) But his face was not strong, as the face of Madam Des Anges had been. Some strain of a weaker ancestry reappeared in it, and, so to speak, changed the key of the expression. What had been pride in the old lady bordered on superciliousness in the young man. What had been sternness became a mere haughtiness. Yet it was a handsome face, and pleasant, too, when the young smile came across it, and you saw the white, small teeth and the bright, intelligent light in the dark eyes.

The two men strolled through the Battery, and then up South Street, and so around through Old Slip. They were on business; but this was also a pleasure trip to the elder. He walked doubly in spirit through those old streets—a boy by his father's side, a father with his son at his elbow. He had not been often in the region of late years. You remember, he was a man of pleasure. He was one of the first-fruits of metropolitan growth and social culture. His father had made an idler and *dilettante* of him. It was only half a life at best, he thought, happy as he had been; blessed as he was in wife and child. He was going to make a business man of his own boy. After all, it was through the workers that great cities grew. Perhaps we were not ripe yet for that European institution, the idler. He himself had certain accomplishments that other Americans had not. He could *flâner*, for instance. But to have to *flâner* through fifty or sixty or seventy years palled on the spirit, he found. And one thing was certain, if any Dolph was ever to be an accomplished *flâneur*, and to devote his whole life to that occupation, the Dolph fortune must be vastly increased. Old Jacob Dolph had miscalculated. The sum he had left in 1829 might have done very well for the time, but it was no fortune to idle on among the fashionables of 1852.

Something of this Mr. Dolph told his son; but the young man, although he listened with respectful attention, appeared not to take a deep interest in his father's reminiscences. Jacob Dolph fancied even that Eustace did not care to be reminded of the city's day of small things. Perhaps he had something of the feeling of the successful struggler who tries to forget the shabbiness of the past. If this were the case, his pride must have been chafed, for his father was eloquent in displaying the powers of an uncommonly fine memory; and he had to hear all about the slips, and the Fly Market, and the gradual extension of the water-front, and the piles on which the old Tontine was built, and the cucumber-wood pipes of the old water-company, still lying under their feet. Once, at least, he showed a genuine enjoyment of his father's discourse, and that was when it ran on the great retinue of servants in which Jacob Dolph the elder had indulged himself. I think he was actually pleased when he heard that his grandfather had at one time kept slaves.

Wandering in this way, to the running accompaniment of Mr. Dolph's lecture, they came to Water Street, and here, as though he were reminded of the object of their trip, the father summed up his reminiscences in shape for a neat moral.

"The city grows, you see, my boy, and we've got to grow with it. I've stood still; but you shan't."

"Well, governor," said the younger man, "I'll be frank with you. I don't like the prospect."

"You will—you will, my boy. You'll live to thank me."

"Very likely you're right, sir; I don't deny it; but, as I say, I don't like the prospect. I don't see—with all due respect, sir—how any gentleman can *like* trade. It may be necessary, and of course I don't think it's lowering, or any of that nonsense, you know; but it can't be *pleasant*. Of course, if *your* governor had to do it, it was all right; but I don't believe he liked it any better than I should, or he wouldn't have been so anxious to keep you out of it."

"My poor father made a great mistake, Eustace. He would admit it now, I'm sure, if he were alive."

"Well, sir, I'm going to try it, of course. I'll give it a fair trial. But when the two years are up, sir, as we agreed, I hope you won't say anything against my going into the law, or—well, yes—" he colored a little—"trying what I can do on the Street. I know what you think about it, sir," he went on, hastily; "but there are two sides to the question, and it's my opinion that, for an intelligent man, there's more money to be made up there in Wall Street in one year than can be got out of haggling over merchandise for a lifetime."

Jacob Dolph grew red in the face and shook his head vigorously.

"Don't speak of it, sir, don't speak of it!" he said, vehemently. "It's the curse of the country. If you have any such infernal opinions, don't vent them in my presence, sir. I know what I am talking about. Keep clear of Wall Street, sir. It is the straight road to perdition."

They entered one of a row of broad-fronted buildings of notable severity and simplicity of architecture. Four square stone columns upheld its brick front, and on one of these faded gilt letters, on a ground of dingy black, said simply:

ABRAM VAN RIPER'S SON.

There was no further announcement of Abram Van Riper's Son's character, or of the nature of his business. It was assumed that all people knew who Abram Van Riper's Son was, and that his (Abram Van Riper's) ship-chandlery trade had long before grown into a great "commission merchant's" business.

It was full summer, and there were no doors between the pillars to bar entrance to the gloomy cavern behind them, which stretched in semi-darkness the whole length and width of the building, save for a narrow strip at the rear, where, behind a windowed partition, clerks were writing at high desks, and where there was an inner and more secluded pen for Abram Van Riper's son.

In the front of the cave, to one side, was a hoistway, where bales and boxes were drawn up from the cellar or swung twisting and twirling to the lofts above. Amidships the place was strewn with small tubs, matting-covered bales and boxes, coils of bright new rope, and odd-looking packages of a hundred sorts, all of them with gaping wounds in their envelopes, or otherwise having their pristine integrity wounded. From this it was not difficult to guess that these were samples of merchandise. Most of them gave forth odors upon the air, odors ranging from the purely aromatic, suggestive of Oriental fancies or tropic dreams of spice, to the positively offensive—the latter varieties predominating.

But certain objects upon a long table were so peculiar in appearance that the visitors could not pass them by with a mere glance of wonder. They looked like small leather pies, badly warped in the baking. A clerk in his shirt sleeves, with his straw hat on one side of his head, whistled as he cut into these, revealing a livid interior, the color of half-cooked veal, which he inspected with care. Eustace was moved to positive curiosity.

"What are they?" he inquired of the clerk, pride mingling with disgust in his tone, as he caught a smell like unto the smell which might arise from raw smoked salmon that had lain three days in the sun.

"Central American," responded the clerk, with brevity, and resumed his whistling of

"My name is Jake Keyser, I was born in Spring Garden;
To make me a preacher my father did try."

"Central American *what*?" pursued the inquirer.

"*Rubber!*" said the clerk, with a scorn so deep and far beyond expression that the combined pride of the Dolphs and the Des Anges wilted into silence for the moment. As they went on toward the rear office, while the clerk gayly whistled the notes of

"It's no use a-blowing, for I am a hard 'un—
I'm bound to be a butcher, by heavens, or die!"

Eustace recovered sufficiently to demand of his father:

"I say, sir, shall I have to handle that damned stuff?"

"Hush!" said his senior; "here's Mr. Van Riper."

Mr. Van Riper came to the office door to welcome them, with his thin face set in the form of a smile.

"Ah!" he said, "here's the young man, is he? Fine big fellow, Dolph. Well, sir, so you are going to embrace a mercantile career, are you? That's what they call it these fine days, Dolph."

"I am going to try to, sir," replied the young man.

"He will, Van Riper," put in his father, hastily; "he'll like it as soon as he gets used to it—I know he will."

"Well," returned Mr. Van Riper, with an attempt at facetious geniality, "we'll try to get his nose down to the grindstone, we will. Come into my office with me, Dolph, and I'll hand this young gentleman over to old Mr. Daw. Mr. Daw will feel his teeth—eh, Mr. Daw?—see what he *doesn't* know—how's that—Mr. Daw? You remember Mr. Daw, Dolph—used to be with your father before he went out of business—been with us ever since. Let's see, how long is that, Daw? Most fifty years, ain't it?"

Mr. Daw, who looked as though he might have been one hundred years at the business, wheeled around and descended with stiff deliberation from his high stool, holding his pen in his mouth as he solemnly shook hands with Jacob Dolph, and peered into his face. Then he took the pen from his mouth.

"Looks like his father," was Mr. Daw's comment. "Forty-five years the twenty-ninth of this month, sir. You was a little shaver then. I remember you comin' into the store and whittlin' timber with your little jack-knife. I was only eleven years with your father, sir—eleven years and six months—went to him when I was fourteen years old. That's fifty-six years and six months in the service of two of the best houses that ever was in New York—an' I can do my work with any two young shavers in the town—ain't missed a day in nineteen years now. Your father hadn't never ought to have gone out of business, Mr. Dolph. He did a great business for those days, and he had the makin' of a big house. Goin' to bring your boy up like a good New York merchant, hey? Come along with me, young man, and I'll see if you're half the man your grandfather was. He hadn't never ought to have given up business, Mr. Dolph. But he was all for pleasurin', an' the playhouses, an' havin' fine times. Come along, young man. What's your name?"

"Eustace Dolph."

"Hm! Jacob's better."

And he led the neophyte away.

"Curious old case," said Mr. Van Riper, dryly. "Best accountant in New York. See that high stool of his?—can't get him off it. Five years ago I gave him a low desk and an armchair. In one week he was back again, roosting up there. Said he didn't feel comfortable with his feet on the ground. He thought that sort of thing might do for aged people, but *he* wasn't made of cotton-batting."

Thus began Eustace Dolph's apprenticeship to business, and mightily ill he liked it.

. . . .

There came a day, a winter day in 1854, when there was a great agitation among what were then called the real old families of New York. I cannot use the term "fashionable society," because that is more comprehensive, and would include many wealthy and ambitious families from New England, who were decidedly not of the Dolphs' set. And then, the Dolphs could hardly be reckoned among the leaders of fashion. To live on or near the boundaries of fashion's domain is to lower your social status below the absolute pitch of perfection, and fashion in 1854 drew the line pretty sharply at Bleecker Street. Above Bleecker Street the cream of the cream rose to the surface; below, you were ranked as skim milk. The social world was spreading up into the wastes sacred to the circus and the market-garden, although, if Admiral Farragut had stood on his sea-legs where he stands now, he might have had a fairly clear view of Chelsea Village, and seen Alonzo Cushman II., or Alonzo Cushman III., perhaps, going around and collecting his rents.

But the old families still fought the tide of trade, many of them neck-deep and very uncomfortable. They would not go from St. John's Park, nor from North Moore and Grand Streets. They had not the *bourgeois* conservatism of the Greenwich Villagers, which has held them in a solid phalanx almost to this very day; but still, in a way, they resented the up-town movement, and resisted it. So that when they did have to buy lots in the high-numbered streets they had to pay a fine price for them.

It was this social party that was stirred by a bit of scandal about the Dolphs. I do not know why I should call it scandal; yet I am sure society so held it. For did not society whisper it, and nod and wink over it, and tell it in dark corners, and chuckle, and lift its multitudinous hands and its myriad eyebrows, and say in innumerable keys: "Well, *upon* my word!" and "Well, I *should* think——!" and "Who would *ever* have thought of such a thing?" and the like? Did not society make very funny jokes about it, and did not society's professional gossips get many an invitation to dinner because they professed to have authentic details of the way Mr. and Mrs. Dolph looked when they spoke about it, and just what they had to say for themselves?

And yet it was nothing more than this, that Mr. Dolph, being fifty-four, and his wife but a few years younger, were about to give to the world another Dolph. It was odd, I admit; it was unusual; if I must go so far, it was, I suppose, unconventional. But I don't see that it was necessary for Mr. Philip Waters to make an epigram about it. It was a very clever epigram; but if you had seen dear old Mrs. Dolph, with her rosy cheeks and the gray in her hair, knitting baby-clothes with hands which were still white and plump and comely, while great dark eyes looked timorously into the doubtful, fear-clouded future, I think you would have been ashamed that you had even listened to that epigram.

The expected event was of special and personal interest to only three people—for, after all, when you think of it, it was not exactly society's business—and it affected them in widely different ways.

Jacob Dolph was all tenderness to his wife, and all sympathy with her fears, with her nervous apprehensions, even with her morbid forebodings of impossible ills. He did not repine at the seclusion which the situation forced upon them, although his life for years had been given up to society's demands, until pleasure-seeking and pleasure-giving had grown into a routine, which occupied his whole mind. His wife saw him more than she had for many years. Clubs and card-parties had few temptations for him now; he sat at home and read to her and talked to her, and did his best to follow the injunctions of the doctor, and "create and preserve in her a spirit of cheerful and hopeful tranquillity, free of unnecessary apprehension."

But when he *did* go to the club, when he was in male society, his breast expanded, and if he had to answer a polite inquiry as to Mrs. Dolph's health, I am afraid that he responded: "Mrs. Dolph is extremely well, sir, extremely well!" with a pride which the moralists will tell you is baseless, unworthy, and unreasonable.

As for Aline herself, no one may know what timorous hopes stirred in her bosom and charmed the years away, and brought back to her a lovely youth that was almost girlish in its innocent, half-frightened gladness. Outside, this great, wise, eminently proper world that she lived in girded at the old woman who was to bear a child, and laughed behind tasselled fans, and made wondrous merry over Nature's work; but within the old house she sat, and sewed upon the baby-clothes, or, wandering from cupboard to cupboard, found the yellowing garments, laid away more than a score of years before—the poor little lace-decked trifles that her first boy had worn; and she thanked heaven, in her humble way, that twenty-four years had not taken the love and joy of a wife and a mother out of her heart.

She could not find all her boy's dresses and toys, for she was open-handed, and had given many of them away to people who needed them. This brought about an odd encounter. The third person who had a special interest in the prospect of the birth of a Dolph was young Eustace, and he found nothing in it wherewith to be pleased. For Eustace Dolph was of the ultra-fashionables. He cared less for old family than for new ideas, and he did not let himself fall behind in the march of social progress, even though he was, as he admitted with humility born of pride, only a poor devil of a down-town clerk. If his days were occupied, he had his nights to himself, and he lengthened them to suit himself. At first this caused his mother to fret a little; but poor Aline had come into her present world from the conventional seclusion of King's Bridge, and her only authority on questions of masculine license was her husband. He, being appealed to, had to admit that his own hours in youth had been late, and that he supposed the hours of a newer generation should properly be later still. Mr. Dolph forgot, perhaps, that while his early potations had been vinous, those of the later age were distinctly spirituous; and that the early morning cocktail and the midnight brandy-and-soda were abominations unknown to his own well-bred youth. With port and sherry and good Bordeaux he had been familiar all his life; a dash of *liqueur* after dinner did not trouble his digestion; he found a bottle of champagne a pleasant appetizer and a gentle stimulant; but whiskey and gin were to him the drinks of the vulgar; and rum and brandy stood on his sideboard only to please fiercer tastes than his own. Perhaps, also, he was ignorant of the temptations that assail a young man in a great city, he who had grown up in such a little one that he had at one time known every one who was worth knowing in it.

However this may have been, Eustace Dolph ruled for himself his going out and his coming in. He went further, and chose his own associates, not always from among the scions of the "old families." He found those excellent young men "slow," and he selected for his own private circle a set which was mixed as to origin and unanimously frivolous as to tendency. The foreign element was strongly represented. Bright young Irishmen of excellent families, and mysterious French and Italian counts and marquises, borrowed many of the good gold dollars of the Dolphs, and forgot to return an equivalent in the local currency of the O'Reagans of Castle Reagan, or the D'Arcy de Montmorenci, or the Montescudi di Bajocchi. Among this set there was much merrymaking when the news from the Dolph household sifted down to them from the gossip-sieve of the best society. They could not very well chaff young Dolph openly, for he was muscular and high-tempered, and, under the most agreeable conditions, needed a fight of some sort every six months or so, and liked a bit of trouble in between fights. But a good deal of low and malicious humor came his way, from one source or another, and he, with the hot and concentrated egotism of youth, thought that he was in a ridiculous and trying position, and chafed over it.

There had been innuendos and hints and glancing allusions, but no one had dared to make any direct assault of wit, until one evening young Haskins came into the club "a little flushed with wine." (The "wine" was brandy.) It seems that young Haskins had found at home an ivory rattle which had belonged to Eustace twenty years before, and which Mrs. Dolph had given to Mrs. Haskins when Eustace enlarged his horizon in the matter of toys.

Haskins being, as I have said, somewhat flushed with brandy, came up to young Dolph, who was smoking in the window, and meditating with frowning brows, and said to him:

"Here, Dolph, I've done with this. You'd better take it back—it may be wanted down your way."

There was a scene. Fortunately, two men were standing just behind Dolph, who were able to throw their arms about him, and hold him back for a few seconds. There would have been further consequences, however, if it had not been that Eustace was in the act of throwing the rattle back at Haskins when the two men caught him. Thus the toy went wide of its mark, and fell in the lap of Philip Waters, who, old as he was, generally chose to be in the company of the young men at the club; and then Philip Waters did something that almost atones, I think, for the epigram.

He looked at the date on the rattle, and then he rose up and went between the two young men, and spoke to Haskins.

"Young man," he said, "when Mrs. Jacob Dolph gave your mother this thing, your father had just failed for the second time in three years. He had come to New York about five years before from Hartford, or Providence, or—Succotash, or whatever his confounded town was. Mr. Jacob Dolph got Mr. Van Riper to give your father an extension on his note, or he would have gone to the debtors' prison down by the City Hall. As it was, he had to sell his house, and the coat off his back, for all I know. If it hadn't been for the Dolphs, devil the rattle you'd have had, and you wouldn't have been living in Bond Street to-day."

After which Mr. Philip Waters sat down and read the evening paper; and when young Haskins was able to speak he asked young Dolph's pardon, and got it—at least, a formal assurance that he had it.

The baby was born in the spring, and everybody said she was the image of her mother.

. . . .

There will come a day, it may be, when advancing civilization will civilize sleighing out of existence, as far as New York is concerned. Year after year the days grow fewer that will let a cutter slip up beyond the farthest of the "roadhouses" and cross the line into Westchester. People say that the climate is changing; but close observers recognize a sympathy between the decrease of snow-storms and the increase of refinement—that is, a sympathy in inverse ratio; a balanced progress in opposite directions. As we grow further and further beyond even old-world standards of polite convention, as we formalize and super-formalize our codes, and steadily eliminate every element of amusement from our amusements, Nature in strict conformity represses her joyous exuberance. The snow-storm of the past is gone, because the great public sleigh that held twenty-odd merry-makers in a shell like a circus band-wagon has gone out of fashion among all classes. Now we have, during severe winters, just enough snow from time to time to bear the light sleigh of the young man who, being in good society, is also horsy. When *he* finds the road vulgar, the poor plebeian souls who go sleighing for the sport of it may sell their red and blue vehicles, for Nature, the sycophant of fashion, will snow no more.

But they had "good old-fashioned" snow-storms eighty years after the Declaration of Independence, and one had fallen upon New York that tempted Mrs. Jacob Dolph to leave her baby, ten months old, in the nurse's charge, and go out with her husband in the great family sleigh for what might be the last ride of the season.

They had been far up the road—to Arcularius's, maybe, there swinging around and whirling back. They had flown down the long country road, and back into the city, to meet—it was early in the day—the great procession of sleighing folk streaming northward up Broadway. It was one of New York's great, irregular, chance-set carnivals, and every sleigh was out, from the "exquisite's" gilded chariot, a shell hardly larger than a fair-sized easy-chair, to the square, low-hung red sledge of the butcher-boy, who braved it with the fashionables, his *Schneider*-made clothes on his burly form, and his girl by his side, in her best Bowery bonnet. Everybody was a-sleighing. The jingle of countless bells fell on the crisp air in a sort of broken rhythm—a rude *tempo rubato*. It was fashionable then. But we—we amuse ourselves less boisterously.

They drew up at the door of the Dolph house, and Jacob Dolph lifted his wife out of the sleigh, and carried her up the steps into the breakfast-room, and set her down in her easy-chair. He was bending over her to ask her if her ride had done her good, when a servant entered and handed him a letter marked "Immediate."

He read it, and all the color of the winter's day faded out of his face.

"I've got to go down to Van Riper's," he said, "at once; he wants me."

"Has anything happened to—to Eustace?" his wife cried out.

"He doesn't say so—I suppose—I suppose it's only business of some sort," her husband said. His face was white. "Don't detain me, dear. I'll come back as soon as—as soon as I can get through."

He kissed her, and was gone. Half an hour later he sat in the office of Abram Van Riper's Son.

There was no doubting it, no denying it, no palliating it even. The curse had come upon the house of Jacob Dolph, and his son was a thief and a fugitive.

It was an old story and a simple story. It was the story of the Haskins's million and the Dolphs' hundred thousand; it was the story of the boy with a hundred thousand in prospect trying to spend money against the boy with a million in sight. It was the story of cards, speculation—another name for that sort of gambling which is worse than any on the green cloth—and what is euphemistically known as wine.

There was enough oral and documentary evidence to make the whole story hideously clear to Jacob Dolph, as he sat in that dark little pen of Van Riper's and had the history of his son's fall spelled out to him, word by word. The boy had proved himself apt and clever in his office work. His education had given him an advantage over all the other clerks, and he had learned his duties with wonderful ease. And when, six months before, old Mr. Daw had let himself down from his stool for the last time, and had muffled up his thin old throat in his great green worsted scarf, and had gone home to die, young Dolph had been put temporarily in his place. In those six months he had done his bad work. Even Van Riper admitted that it must have been a sudden temptation. But—he had yielded. In those six months fifty thousand dollars of Abram Van Riper's money had gone into the gulf that yawned in Wall Street; fifty thousand dollars, not acquired by falsifying the books, but filched outright from the private safe to which he had access; fifty thousand dollars, in securities which he had turned into money, acting as the confidential man of the house.

When Jacob Dolph, looking like a man of eighty, left the private office of Mr. Van Riper he had two things to do. One was to tell his wife, the other was to assign enough property to Van Riper to cover the amount of the defalcation. Both had been done before night.

V

It is to be said for society that there was very little chuckling and smiling when this fresh piece of news about the Dolphs came out. Nor did the news pass from house to house like wildfire. It rather leaked out here and there, percolating through barriers of friendly silence, slipping from discreet lips and repeated in anxious confidence, with all manner of qualifications and hopeful suppositions and suggestions. As a matter of fact, people never really knew just what Eustace Dolph had done, or how far his wrongdoing had carried him. All that was ever positively known was that the boy had got into trouble down-town, and had gone to Europe. The exact nature of the trouble could only be conjectured. The very brokers who had been the instruments of young Dolph's ruin were not able to separate his authorized speculations from those which were illegitimate. They could do no more than guess, from what they knew of Van Riper's conservative method of investment, that the young man's unfortunate purchases were made for himself, and they figured these at fifty-five thousand odd hundred dollars.

Somebody, who looked up the deed which Jacob Dolph executed that winter day, found that he had transferred to Van Riper real estate of more than that value.

No word ever came from the cold lips of Abram Van Riper's son; and his office was a piece of all but perfect machinery, which dared not creak when he commanded silence. And no one save Van Riper and Dolph, and their two lawyers, knew the whole truth. Dolph never spoke about it to his wife, after that first night. It was these five people only who knew that Mr. Jacob Dolph had parted with the last bit of real estate that he owned, outside of his own home, and they knew that his other property was of a doubtful sort, that could yield at the best only a very limited income—hardly enough for a man who lived in so great a house, and whose doors were open to all his friends nine months in the year.

Yet he stayed there, and grew old with an age which the years have not among their gifts. When his little girl was large enough to sit upon his knee, her small hands clutched at a snowy-white mustache, and she complained that his great, dark, hollow eyes never would look "right into hers, away down deep." Yet he loved her, and talked more to her perhaps than to any one else, not even excepting Aline.

But he never spoke to her of the elder brother whom she could not remember. It was her mother who whispered something of the story to her, and told her not to let papa know that she knew of it, for it would grieve him. Aline herself knew nothing about the boy save that he lived, and lived a criminal. Jacob himself could only have told her that their son was a wandering adventurer, known as a blackleg and sharper in every town in Europe.

The doors of the great house were closed to all the world, or opened only for some old friend, who went away very soon out of the presence of a sadness beyond all solace of words, or kindly look, or hand-clasp. And so, in something that only the grace of their gentle lives relieved from absolute poverty, those three dwelt in the old house, and let the world slip by them.

. . . .

There was no sleep for any one of the little household in the great house on the night of the 14th of July, 1863. Doors and blinds were closed; only a light shone through the half-open slats at a second-story window, and in that room Aline lay sick, almost unto death, her white hair loosed from its usual dainty neatness, her dark eyes turning with an unmeaning gaze from the face of the little girl at her side to the face of her husband at the foot of her bed. Her hands, wrinkled and small, groped over the coverlet, with nervous twitchings, as every now and then the howls or the pistol-shots of the mob in the streets below them fell on her ear. And at every such movement the lips of the girl by her pillow twitched in piteous sympathy. About half-past twelve there was sharp firing in volleys to the southward of them, that threw the half-conscious sufferer into an agony of supersensitive disturbance. Then there came a silence that seemed unnaturally deep, yet it was only the silence of a summer night in the deserted city streets.

Through it they heard, sharp and sudden, with something inexplicably fearful about it, the patter of running feet. They had heard that sound often enough that night and the night before; but these feet stopped at their own door, and came up the steps, and the runner beat and pounded on the heavy panels.

Father and child looked in each other's eyes, and then Jacob Dolph left his post at the foot of the bed, and, passing out of the room, went down the stairs with deliberate tread, and opened the door.

A negro's face, almost gray in its mad fear, stared into his with a desperate appeal which the lips could not utter. Dolph drew the man in, and shut the door behind him. The negro leaned, trembling and exhausted, against the wall.

"I knowed you'd take me in, Mist' Dolph," he panted; "I'm feared they seen me, though—they was mighty clost behind."

They were close behind him, indeed. In half a minute the roar of the mob filled the street with one terrible howl and shriek of animal rage, heard high above the tramp of half a thousand feet; and the beasts of disorder, gathered from all the city's holes and dens of crime, wild for rapine and outrage, burst upon them, sweeping up the steps, hammering at the great door, crying for the blood of the helpless and the innocent.

Foreign faces, almost all; Irish, mostly; but there were heavy, ignorant German types of feature uplifted under the gas-light, sallow, black-mustached Magyar faces; thin, acute, French faces—all with the stamp of old-world ignorance and vice upon them.

The door opened, and the white-haired old gentleman, erect,

haughty, with brightening eyes, faced the leader of the mob—a great fellow, black-bearded, who had a space to himself on the stoop, and swung his broad shoulders from side to side.

"Have you got a nigger here?" he began, and then stopped short, for Jacob Dolph was looking upon the face of his son.

Vagabond and outcast, he had the vagabond's quick wit, this leader of infuriate crime, and some one good impulse stirred in him of his forfeited gentlehood. He turned savagely upon his follower.

"He ain't here!" he roared. "I told you so—I saw him turn the corner."

"Shtap an' burrn the bondholder's house!" yelled a man behind. Eustace Dolph turned round with a furious, threatening gesture.

"You damned fool!" he thundered; "he's no bondholder—he's one of us. Go on, I tell you! Will you let that nigger get away?"

He half drove them down the steps. The old man stepped out, his face aflame under his white hair, his whole frame quivering.

"You lie, sir!" he cried; but his voice was drowned in the howl of the mob as it swept around the corner, forgetting all things else in the madness of its hideous chase.

When Jacob Dolph returned to his wife's chamber, her feeble gaze was lifted to the ceiling. At the sound of his footsteps she let it fall dimly upon his face. He was thankful that, in that last moment of doubtful quickening, she could not read his eyes; and she passed away, smiling sweetly, one of her white old hands in his, and one in her child's.

. . . .

Age takes small account of the immediate flight of time. To the young, a year is a mighty span. Be it a happy or an unhappy year that youth looks forward to, it is a vista that stretches far into the future. And when it is done, this interminable year, and youth, just twelve months older, looks back to the first of it, what a long way off it is! What tremendous progress we have made! How much more we know! How insufficient are the standards by which we measured the world a poor three hundred and sixty-five days back!

But age has grown habituated to the flight of time. Years? We have seen so many of them that they make no great impression upon us. What! is it ten years since young Midas first came to the counting room, asking humbly for an entry-clerk's place—he who is now the head of the firm? Bless us! it seems like yesterday. Is it ten years since we first put on that coat? Why, it must be clean out of the fashion by this time.

But age does not carry out the thought, and ask if itself be out of fashion. Age knows better. A few wrinkles, a stoop in the back, a certain slowness of pace, do not make a man old at sixty—nor at seventy, neither; for now you come to think of it, the ten years we were speaking of is gone, and it is seventy now, and not sixty. Seventy! Why, 'tis not to be thought of as old age—save when it may be necessary to rebuke the easy arrogance of youth.

The time had come to Jacob Dolph when he could not feel that he was growing old. He was old, of course, in one sense. He was sixty-one when the war broke out; and they had not allowed him to form a regiment and go to the front at its head. But what was old for a soldier in active service was not old for a well-preserved civilian. True, he could never be the same man again, now that poor Aline was gone. True, he was growing more and more disinclined for active exercise, and he regretted he had led so sedentary a life. But though '64 piled itself up on '63, and '65 on top of that, these arbitrary divisions of time seemed to him but trivial.

Edith was growing old, perhaps; getting to be a great girl, taller than her mother and fairer of complexion, yet not unlike her, he sometimes thought, as she began to manage the affairs of the house, and to go about the great shabby mansion with her mother's keys jingling at her girdle. For the years went on crawling one over the other, and soon it was 1873, and Edith was eighteen years old.

One rainy day in this year found Jacob Dolph in Wall Street. Although he himself did not think so, he was an old man to others, and kindly hands such as were to be found even in that infuriate crowd, had helped him up the marble steps of the Sub-Treasury and had given him lodgment on one of the great blocks of marble that dominate the street. From where he stood he could see Wall Street, east and west, and the broad plaza of Broad Street to the south, filled with a compact mass of men, half hidden by a myriad of umbrellas, rain-soaked, black, glinting in the dim light. So might a Roman legion have looked, when each man raised his targum above his head and came shoulder to shoulder with his neighbor for the assault.

There was a confused, ant-like movement in the vast crowd, and a dull murmur came from it, rising, in places, into excited shouts. Here and there the fringe of the mass swelled up and swept against the steps of some building, forcing, or trying to force, an entry. Sometimes a narrow stream of men trickled into the half-open doorway; sometimes the great portals closed, and then there was a mad outcry and a low groan, and the foremost on the steps suddenly turned back, and in some strange way slipped through the throng and sped in all directions to bear to hushed or clamorous offices the news that this house or that bank had "suspended payment." "Busted," the panting messengers said to white-faced merchants; and in the slang of the street was conveyed the message of doom. The great panic of 1873 was upon the town—the outcome of long years of unwarranted self-confidence, of selfish extravagance, of conscienceless speculation—and, as hour after hour passed by, fortunes were lost in the twinkling of an eye, and the bread was taken out of the mouths of the helpless.

After Jacob Dolph had stood for some time, looking down upon the tossing sea of black umbrellas, he saw a narrow lane made through the crowd in the wake of a little party of clerks and porters, bearing aid perhaps to some stricken bank. Slipping down, he followed close behind them. Perhaps the jostling hundreds on the sidewalk were gentle with him, seeing that he was an old man; perhaps the strength of excitement nerved him, for he made his way down the street to the flight of steps leading to the door of a tall white building, and he crowded himself up among the pack that was striving to enter. He had even got so far that he could see the line pouring in above his head, when there was a sudden cessation of motion in the press, and one leaf of the outer iron doors swung forward, meeting the other, already closed to bar the crush, and two green-painted panels stood, impassable, between him and the last of the Dolph fortune.

One howl and roar, and the crowd turned back on itself, and swept him with it. In five minutes a thousand offices knew of the greatest failure of the day; and Jacob Dolph was leaning—weak, gasping, dazed—against the side wall of a hallway in William Street, with two stray office-boys staring at him out of their small, round, unsympathetic eyes.

Let us not ask what wild temptation led the old man back again to risk all he owned in that hellish game that is played in the narrow street. We may remember this: that he saw his daughter growing to womanhood in that silent and almost deserted house, shouldered now by low tenements and wretched shops and vile drinking-places; that he may have pictured for her a brighter life in that world that had long ago left him behind it in his bereaved and disgraced loneliness; that he had had some vision of her young beauty fulfilling its destiny amid sweeter and fairer surroundings. And let us not forget that he knew no other means than these to win the money for which he cared little; which he found absolutely needful.

After Jacob Dolph had yielded for the last time to the temptation that had conquered him once before, and had ruined his son's soul; after that final disastrous battle with the gamblers of Wall Street, wherein he lost the last poor remnant of the great Dolph fortune, giving up with it his father's home forever, certain old bread of his father's casting came back to him upon strange waters.

Abram Van Riper came to the daughter of the house of Dolph, a little before it became certain that the house must be sold, and told her, in his dry way, that he had to make a business communication to her, for he feared that her father was hardly capable of understanding such matters any longer. She winced a little; but he took a load off her heart when he made his slow, precise explanation. The fact was, he said, that the business transactions between her father and himself, consequent upon the defalcation of her brother Eustace, had never been closed, in all these seventeen years. (Edith Dolph trembled.) It was known at the time that the property transferred by her father rather more than covered the amount of her brother's—peculation. But her father's extreme sensitiveness had led him to avoid a precise adjustment, and as the property transferred was subject to certain long leases, he, Mr. Van Riper, had thought it best to wait until the property was sold and the account closed, to settle the matter with Mr. Dolph. This had lately been done, and Mr. Van Riper found that, deducting charges, and interest on his money at seven per cent., he had made by the transaction six thousand three hundred and seventy dollars. This sum, he thought, properly belonged to Mr. Dolph. And if Miss Dolph would take the counsel of an old friend of her father's, she would leave the sum in charge of the house of Abram Van Riper's Son. The house would invest it at ten per cent.—he stopped and looked at Edith, but she only answered him with innocent eyes of attention—and would pay her six hundred and thirty-seven dollars annually in quarterly payments. It might be of assistance to Mr. Dolph in his present situation.

It was of assistance. They lived on it, father and daughter, with such aid as Decorative Art—just introduced to this country—gave in semi-remunerative employment for her deft fingers.

Abram Van Riper, when he left the weeping, grateful girl, marched out into the street, turned his face toward what was once Greenwich Village, and said to his soul:

"I think that will balance any obligation my father may have put himself under in buying that State Street house too cheap. Now then, old gentleman, you can lie easy in your grave. The Van Ripers ain't beholden to the Dolphs, that's sure."

. . . . .

A few years ago—shall we say as many as ten?—there were two small rooms up in a quiet street in Harlem, tenanted by an old gentleman and a young gentlewoman; and in the front room, which was the young woman's room by night, but a sort of parlor or sitting-room in the daytime, the old gentleman stood up, four times a year, to have his collar pulled up, and his necktie set right, and his coat dusted off by a pair of small white hands, so that he might be presentable when he went down town to collect certain moneys due him.

They were small rooms, but they were bright and cheerful, being decorated with sketches and studies of an artistic sort, which may have been somewhat crude and uncertain as to treatment, but were certainly pleasant and feminine. Yet few saw them save the young woman and the old man. The most frequent visitor was a young artist from the West, who often escorted Miss Dolph to and from the Art League rooms. His name was Rand; he had studied in Munich; he had a future before him, and was making money on his prospects. He might just as well have lived in luxurious bachelor quarters in the lower part of the city; but, for reasons of his own, he preferred to live in Harlem.

Old Mr. Dolph insisted on going regularly every quarter-day to the office of the Van Riper Estate, "to collect," as he said, "the interest due him." Four times a year he went down town on the Eighth Avenue cars, where the conductors soon learned to know him by his shiny black broadcloth coat and his snow-white hair. His daughter was always uneasy about these trips; but her father could not be dissuaded from them. To him they were his one hold on active life—the all-important events of the year. It would have broken his tender old heart to tell him that he could not go to collect his "interest." And so she set his necktie right, and he went.

When he got out of the car at Abingdon Square he tottered, in his slow, old way, to a neat structure which combined modern jauntiness with old-time solidity, and which was labelled simply: "Office of the Van Riper Estate," and there he told the smilingly indulgent clerk that he thought he would "take it in cash, this time," and, taking it in cash, went forth.

And then he walked down through Greenwich Village into New York city, and into the street where stood the house that his father had built. Thus he had gone to view it four times a year, during every year save the first, since he had given it up.

He had seen it go through one stage of decadence after another. First it was rented, by its new owner, to the Jewish pawnbroker, with his numerous family. Good, honest folk they were, who tried to make the house look fine, and the five daughters made the front stoop resplendent of summer evenings. But they had long ago moved uptown. Then it was a cheap boarding-house, and vulgar and flashy men and women swarmed out in the morning and in at eventide. Then it was a lodging-house, and shabby people let themselves out and in at all hours of the day and night. And last of all it had become a tenement-house, and had fallen into line with its neighbors to left and right, and the window-panes were broken, and the curse of misery and poverty and utter degradation had fallen upon it.

But still it lifted its grand stone front, still it stood, broad and great, among all the houses in the street. And it was the old man's custom, after he had stood on the opposite sidewalk and gazed at it for a while, to go to a little French *café* a block to the eastward, and there to take a glass of *vermouth gommé*—it was a mild drink, and pleasing to an old man. Sometimes he chanced to find some one in this place who would listen to his talk about the old house—he was very grand; but they were decent people who went to that *café*, and perhaps would go back with him a block and look at it. We would not have talked to chance people in an east-side French *café*. But then we have never owned such a house, and lost it—and everything else.

. . . .

Late one hot summer afternoon young Rand sat in his studio, working enthusiastically on a "composition." A new school of art had invaded New York, and compositions were everything, for the moment, whether they composed anything or nothing. He heard a nervous rattling at his door-knob, and he opened the door. A young woman lifted a sweet, flushed, frightened face to his.

"Oh, John," she cried, "father hasn't come home yet, and it's five o'clock, and he left home at nine."

John Rand threw off his flannel jacket, and got into his coat.

"We'll find him; don't worry, dear," he said.

They found him within an hour. The great city, having no further use for the old Dolph house, was crowding it out of existence. With the crashing of falling bricks, and the creaking of the tackle that swung the great beams downward, the old house was crumbling into a gap between two high walls. Already you could see through to where the bright new bricks were piled at the back to build the huge eight-story factory that was to take its place. But it was not to see this demolition that the crowd was gathered, filling the narrow street. It stood, dense, ugly, vulgar, stolidly intent, gazing at the windows of the house opposite—a poor tenement house.

As they went up the steps they met the young hospital surgeon, going back to his ambulance.

"You his folks?" he inquired. "Sorry to tell you so, but I can't do any good. Sunstroke, I suppose—may have been something else—but it's collapse now, and no mistake. You take charge, sir?" he finished, addressing Rand.

Jacob Dolph was lying on his back in the bare front room on the first floor. His daughter fell on her knees by his side, and made as though she would throw her arms around him; but, looking in his face, she saw death quietly coming upon him, and she only bent down and kissed him, while her tears wet his brow.

Meanwhile a tall Southerner, with hair half way down his neck, and kindly eyes that moved in unison with his broad gestures, was talking to Rand.

"I met the ol' gentleman in the French *café*, neah heah," he said, "and he was jus' honing to have me come up and see his house, seh—house he used to have. Well, I came right along, an' when we got here, sure 'nough, they's taihin' down that house. Neveh felt so bad in all my life, seh. He wasn't expectin' of it, and I 'lowed 'twuz his old home like, and he was right hahd hit, fo' a fact. He said to me, 'Good-day, seh,' sezee; 'good-day, seh,' he says to me, an' then he starts across the street, an' first thing I know, he falls down flat on his face, seh. Saw that theah brick an' mortar comin' down, an' fell flat on his face. This hyeh pill-man 'lowed 'twuz sunstroke; but a Southern man like I am don't need to be told what a gentleman's feelings are when he sees his house a-torn down—no, seh. If you ever down oweh way, seh, I'd be right glad——"

But Rand had lifted Edith from the floor, for her father would know her no more, and had passed out of this world, unconscious of all the squalor and ruin about him; and the poor girl was sobbing on his shoulder.

He was very tender with her, very sorry for her—but he had never known the walls that fell across the way; he was a young man, an artist, with a great future before him, and the world was young to him, and she was to be his wife.

Still, looking down, he saw that sweetly calm, listening look, that makes beautiful the faces of the dead, come over the face of Jacob Dolph, as though he, lying there, heard the hammers of the workmen breaking down his father's house, brick by brick—and yet the sound could no longer jar upon his ear or grieve his gentle spirit.

JOEL CHANDLER HARRIS

Free Joe and the Rest of the World

Joel Chandler Harris (1848–1908)

THE AUTHOR OF Uncle Remus was apprenticed to a printer at fourteen years of age. His school and his university were a unique country newspaper called the Countryman, published on a plantation some nine miles from Eatonton, Georgia, and edited in the best traditions of the eighteenth century by Joseph Addison Turner, the master of "Turnwold" as the plantation was called. At the type-case, and in attendance on the old Washington #2 press, Harris learned his trade; and from the sympathetic teaching of his employer, he got a better education than formal schools would have furnished him.

By the time one wing of Sherman's army swept over Turnwold in the fall of 1864, young Harris had had ample opportunity to study the old, patriarchal plantation life, and to meet and understand the plantation Negro. He had listened eagerly to the lore of the quarters, in which African memories blended queerly with the cosmogonies and animal fables of the Indian tribes who were once masters of the Georgia backwoods; and had stored up in his mind much of the materials out of which, years afterward, he was to make his own stories.

After the war, Harris followed his newsman's trade in New Orleans for a short space, but grew homesick for Georgia and returned there, settling down at last as a member of the staff of the Atlanta Constitution.

Harris's professedly literary work was never his first concern; the paper came first, and indeed his distinctive dialect tales grew out of an assignment to write humorous, dialect "locals." His earliest legends of the animals and their very human foibles soon were copied around the country, and were gathered into Uncle Remus, His Songs and His Sayings (1880). The charm of his boyhood memories, and the fidelity with which he rendered the speech of the Negroes of his section, won him immediate fame and a permanent place in American literature. Whereas, in the work of Thomas Nelson Page and other southern writers of the period, the Negro is an accessory or agent whereby the virtues of his master are highlighted, and his own are seen as reflections of the dominant code, Harris lets the Negro live as a man—as the whole story. Uncle Remus is no Uncle Tom. Likewise, in Harris's sketches of the "cracker" character, the backwoods white man, is found the same deep understanding and sympathy—the same refusal to condescend. Because in the title-story to Free Joe, and Other Georgian Sketches we feel that all the characteristics of this author are displayed in their finest form—his intuitive democracy, honesty, and pity for the weak and friendless, and also the simple objective force of his narrative method, we have chosen it to represent him in The Scribner Treasury.

FREE JOE
AND THE REST OF THE WORLD

THE name of Free Joe strikes humorously upon the ear of memory. It is impossible to say why, for he was the humblest, the simplest, and the most serious of all God's living creatures, sadly lacking in all those elements that suggest the humorous. It is certain, moreover, that in 1850 the sober-minded citizens of the little Georgian village of Hillsborough were not inclined to take a humorous view of Free Joe, and neither his name nor his presence provoked a smile. He was a black atom, drifting hither and thither without an owner, blown about by all the winds of circumstance, and given over to shiftlessness.

The problems of one generation are the paradoxes of a succeeding one, particularly if war, or some such incident, intervenes to clarify the atmosphere and strengthen the understanding. Thus, in 1850, Free Joe represented not only a problem of large concern, but, in the watchful eyes of Hillsborough, he was the embodiment of that vague and mysterious danger that seemed to be forever lurking on the outskirts of slavery, ready to sound a shrill and ghostly signal in the impenetrable swamps, and steal forth under the midnight stars to murder, rapine, and pillage,—a danger always threatening, and yet never assuming shape; intangible, and yet real; impossible, and yet not improbable. Across the serene and smiling front of safety, the pale outlines of the awful shadow of insurrection sometimes fell. With this invisible panorama as a background, it was natural that the figure of Free Joe, simple and humble as it was, should assume undue proportions. Go where he would, do what he might, he could not escape the finger of observation and the kindling eye of suspicion. His lightest words were noted, his slightest actions marked.

Under all the circumstances it was natural that his peculiar condition should reflect itself in his habits and manners. The slaves laughed loudly day by day, but Free Joe rarely laughed. The slaves sang at their work and danced at their frolics, but no one ever heard Free Joe sing or saw him dance. There was something painfully plain-tive and appealing in his attitude, something touching in his anxiety to please. He was of the friendliest nature, and seemed to be delighted when he could amuse the little children who had made a playground of the public square. At times he would please them by making his little dog Dan perform all sorts of curious tricks, or he would tell them quaint stories of the beasts of the field and birds of the air; and frequently he was coaxed into relating the story of his own freedom. That story was brief, but tragical.

In the year of our Lord 1840, when a negro-speculator of a sportive turn of mind reached the little village of Hillsborough on his way to the Mississippi region, with a caravan of likely negroes of both sexes, he found much to interest him. In that day and at that time there were a number of young men in the village who had not bound themselves over to repentance for the various misdeeds of the flesh. To these young men the negro-speculator (Major Frampton was his name) proceeded to address himself. He was a Virginian, he declared; and, to prove the statement, he referred all the festively inclined young men of Hillsborough to a barrel of peach-brandy in one of his covered wagons. In the minds of these young men there was less doubt in regard to the age and quality of the brandy than there was in regard to the negro-trader's birthplace. Major Frampton might or might not have been born in the Old Dominion,—that was a matter for consideration and inquiry,—but there could be no question as to the mellow pungency of the peach-brandy.

In his own estimation, Major Frampton was one of the most accomplished of men. He had summered at the Virginia Springs; he had been to Philadelphia, to Washington, to Richmond, to Lynchburg, and to Charleston, and had accumulated a great deal of experience which he found useful. Hillsborough was hid in the woods of Middle Georgia, and its general aspect of innocence impressed him. He looked on the young men who had shown their readiness to test his peach-brandy, as overgrown country boys who needed to be introduced to some of the arts and sciences he had at his command. Thereupon the major pitched his tents, figuratively speaking, and became, for the time being, a part and parcel of the innocence that characterized Hillsborough. A wiser man would doubtless have made the same mistake.

The little village possessed advantages that seemed to be providentially arranged to fit the various enterprises that Major Frampton had in view. There was the auction-block in front of the stuccoed court-house, if he desired to dispose of a few of his negroes; there was a quarter-track, laid out to his hand and in excellent order, if he chose to enjoy the pleasures of horse-racing; there were secluded pine thickets within easy reach, if he desired to indulge in the exciting pastime of cock-fighting; and various lonely and unoccupied rooms in the second story of the tavern, if he cared to challenge the chances of dice or cards.

Major Frampton tried them all with varying luck, until he began his famous game of poker with Judge Alfred Wellington, a stately gentleman with a flowing white beard and mild blue eyes that gave him the appearance of a benevolent patriarch. The history of the game in which Major Frampton and Judge Alfred Wellington took part is something more than a tradition in Hillsborough, for there are still living three or four men who sat around the table and watched its progress. It is said that at various stages of the game Major Frampton would destroy the cards with which they were playing, and send for a new pack, but the result was always the same. The mild blue eyes of Judge Wellington, with few exceptions, continued to overlook "hands" that were invincible—a habit they had acquired during a long and arduous course of training from Saratoga to New Orleans. Major Frampton lost his money, his horses, his wagons, and all his negroes but one, his body-servant. When his misfortune had reached this limit, the major adjourned the game. The sun was shining brightly, and all nature was cheerful. It is said that the major also seemed to be cheerful. However this may be, he visited the court-house, and executed the papers that gave his body-servant his freedom. This being done, Major Frampton sauntered into a convenient pine thicket, and blew out his brains.

The negro thus freed came to be known as Free Joe. Compelled, under the law, to choose a guardian, he chose Judge Wellington, chiefly because his wife Lucinda was among the negroes won from Major Frampton. For several years Free Joe had what may be called a jovial time. His wife Lucinda was well provided for, and he found it a comparatively easy matter to provide for himself; so that, taking all the circumstances into consideration, it is not matter for astonishment that he became somewhat shiftless.

When Judge Wellington died, Free Joe's troubles began. The judge's negroes, including Lucinda, went to his half-brother, a man named Calderwood, who was a hard master and a rough customer generally,—a man of many eccentricities of mind and character. His neighbors had a habit of alluding to him as "Old Spite"; and the name seemed to fit him so completely, that he was known far and near as "Spite" Calderwood. He probably enjoyed the distinction the name gave him, at any rate, he never resented it, and it was not often that he missed an opportunity to show that he deserved it. Calderwood's place was two or three miles from the village of Hillsborough, and Free Joe visited his wife twice a week, Wednesday and Saturday nights.

One Sunday he was sitting in front of Lucinda's cabin, when Calderwood happened to pass that way.

"Howdy, marster?" said Free Joe, taking off his hat.

"Who are you?" exclaimed Calderwood abruptly, halting and staring at the negro.

"I'm name' Joe, marster. I'm Lucindy's ole man."

"Who do you belong to?"

"Marse John Evans is my gyardeen, marster."

"Big name—gyardeen. Show your pass."

Free Joe produced that document, and Calderwood read it aloud slowly, as if he found it difficult to get at the meaning:—

"To whom it may concern: This is to certify that the boy Joe Frampton has my permission to visit his wife Lucinda."

This was dated at Hillsborough, and signed "*John W. Evans.*"

Calderwood read it twice, and then looked at Free Joe, elevating his eyebrows, and showing his discolored teeth.

"Some mighty big words in that there. Evans owns this place, I reckon. When's he comin' down to take hold?"

Free Joe fumbled with his hat. He was badly frightened. "Lucindy say she speck you wouldn't min' my comin', long ez I behave, marster."

Calderwood tore the pass in pieces and flung it away.

"Don't want no free niggers 'round here," he exclaimed: "There's the big road. It'll carry you to town. Don't let me catch you here no more. Now, mind what I tell you."

Free Joe presented a shabby spectacle as he moved off with his little dog Dan slinking at his heels. It should be said in behalf of Dan, however, that his bristles were up, and that he looked back and growled. It may be that the dog had the advantage of insignificance, but it is difficult to conceive how a dog bold enough to raise his bristles under Calderwood's very eyes could be as insignificant as Free Joe. But both the negro and his little dog seemed to give a new and more dismal aspect to forlornness as they turned into the road and went toward Hillsborough.

After this incident Free Joe appeared to have clearer ideas concerning his peculiar condition. He realized the fact that though he was free he was more helpless than any slave. Having no owner, every man was his master. He knew that he was the object of suspicion, and therefore all his slender resources (ah! how pitifully slender they were!) were devoted to winning, not kindness and appreciation, but toleration; all his efforts were in the direction of mitigating the circumstances that tended to make his condition so much worse than that of the negroes around him,—negroes who had friends because they had masters.

So far as his own race was concerned, Free Joe was an exile. If the slaves secretly envied him his freedom (which is to be doubted, considering his miserable condition), they openly despised him, and lost no opportunity to treat him with contumely. Perhaps this was in some measure the result of the attitude which Free Joe chose to maintain toward them. No doubt his instinct taught him that to hold himself aloof from the slaves would be to invite from the whites the toleration which he coveted, and without which even his miserable condition would be rendered more miserable still.

His greatest trouble was the fact that he was not allowed to visit his wife; but he soon found a way out of this difficulty. After he had been ordered away from the Calderwood place, he was in the habit of wandering as far in that direction as prudence would permit. Near the Calderwood place, but not on Calderwood's land, lived an old man named Micajah Staley and his sister Becky Staley. These people were old and very poor. Old Micajah had a palsied arm and hand; but, in spite of this, he managed to earn a precarious living with his turning-lathe.

When he was a slave Free Joe would have scorned these representatives of a class known as poor white trash, but now he found them sympathetic and helpful in various ways. From the back door of their cabin he could hear the Calderwood negroes singing at night, and he sometimes fancied he could distinguish Lucinda's shrill treble rising above the other voices. A large poplar grew in the woods some distance from the Staley cabin, and at the foot of this tree Free Joe would sit for hours with his face turned toward Calderwood's. His little dog Dan would curl up in the leaves near by, and the two seemed to be as comfortable as possible.

One Saturday afternoon Free Joe, sitting at the foot of this friendly poplar, fell asleep. How long he slept, he could not tell; but when he awoke little Dan was licking his face, the moon was shining brightly, and Lucinda his wife stood before him laughing. The dog, seeing that Free Joe was asleep, had grown somewhat impatient, and he concluded to make an excursion to the Calderwood place on his own account. Lucinda was inclined to give the incident a twist in the direction of superstition.

"I 'uz settin' down front er de fireplace," she said, "cookin' me some meat, w'en all of a sudden I year sumpin at de do'—scratch, scratch. I tuck'n tu'n de meat over, en make out I aint year it. Bimeby it come dar 'gin—scratch, scratch. I up en open de do', I did, en, bless the Lord! dar wuz little Dan, en it look like ter me dat his ribs done grow tergeer. I gin 'im some bread, en den, w'en he start out, I tuck'n foller 'im, kaze, I say ter myse'f, maybe my nigger man mought be some'rs 'roun'. Dat ar little dog got sense, mon."

Free Joe laughed and dropped his hand lightly on Dan's head.

For a long time after that he had no difficulty in seeing his wife. He had only to sit by the poplar-tree until little Dan could run and fetch her. But after a while the other negroes discovered that Lucinda was meeting Free Joe in the woods, and information of the fact soon reached Calderwood's ears. Calderwood was what is called a man of action. He said nothing; but one day he put Lucinda in his buggy, and carried her to Macon, sixty miles away. He carried her to Macon, and came back without her; and nobody in or around Hillsborough, or in that section, ever saw her again.

For many a night after that Free Joe sat in the woods and waited. Little Dan would run merrily off and be gone a long time, but he always came back without Lucinda. This happened over and over again. The "willis-whistlers" would call and call, like phantom huntsmen wandering on a far-off shore; the screech-owl would shake and shiver in the depths of the woods; the night-hawks, sweeping by on noiseless wings, would snap their beaks as though they enjoyed the huge joke of which Free Joe and little Dan were the victims; and the whip-poor-wills would cry to each other through the gloom. Each night seemed to be lonelier than the preceding, but Free Joe's patience was proof against loneliness. There came a time, however, when little Dan refused to go after Lucinda. When Free Joe motioned him in the direction of the Calderwood place, he would simply move about uneasily and whine; then he would curl up in the leaves and make himself comfortable.

One night, instead of going to the poplar-tree to wait for Lucinda, Free Joe went to the Staley cabin, and, in order to make his welcome good, as he expressed it, he carried with him an armful of fat-pine splinters. Miss Becky Staley had a great reputation in those parts as a fortune-teller, and the schoolgirls, as well as older people, often tested her powers in this direction, some in jest and some in earnest. Free Joe placed his humble offering of light-wood in the chimney-corner, and then seated himself on the steps, dropping his hat on the ground outside.

"Miss Becky," he said presently, "whar in de name er gracious you reckon Lucindy is?"

"Well, the Lord he'p the nigger!" exclaimed Miss Becky, in a tone that seemed to reproduce, by some curious agreement of sight with sound, her general aspect of peakedness. "Well, the Lord he'p the nigger! haint you been a-seein' her all this blessed time? She's over at old Spite Calderwood's, if she's anywheres, I reckon."

"No'm, dat I aint, Miss Becky. I aint seen Lucindy in now gwine on mighty nigh a mont'."

"Well, it haint a-gwine to hurt you," said Miss Becky, somewhat sharply. "In my day an' time it wuz allers took to be a bad sign when niggers got to honeyin' 'roun' an' gwine on."

"Yessum," said Free Joe, cheerfully assenting to the proposition—"yessum, dat's so, but me an' my ole 'oman, we 'uz raise tergeer, en dey aint bin many days w'en we 'uz' 'way fum one 'n'er like we is now."

"Maybe she's up an' took up wi' some un else," said Micajah Staley from the corner. "You know what the sayin' is, 'New Master, new nigger.' "

"Dat's so, dat's de sayin', but tain't wid my ole 'oman like 'tis wid yuther niggers. Me en her wuz des natally raise up tergeer. Dey's lots likelier niggers dan w'at I is," said Free Joe, viewing his shabbiness with a critical eye, "but I knows Lucindy mos' good ez I does little Dan dar—dat I does."

There was no reply to this, and Free Joe continued,—

"Miss Becky, I wish you please, ma'am, take en run yo' kyards en see sump'n n'er 'bout Lucindy; kaze ef she sick, I'm gwine dar. Dey ken take en take me up en gimme a stroppin', but I'm gwine dar."

Miss Becky got her cards, but first she picked up a cup, in the bottom of which were some coffee-grounds. These she whirled slowly round and round, ending finally by turning the cup upside down on the hearth and allowing it to remain in that position.

"I'll turn the cup first," said Miss Becky, "an' then I'll run the cards and see what they say."

As she shuffled the cards the fire on the hearth burned low, and in its fitful light the gray-haired, thin-featured woman seemed to deserve the weird reputation which rumor and gossip had given her. She shuffled the cards for some moments, gazing intently in the dying fire; then, throwing a piece of pine on the coals, she made three divisions of the pack, disposing them about in her lap. Then she took the first pile, ran the cards slowly through her fingers, and studied them carefully. To the first she added the second pile. The study of these was evidently not satisfactory. She said nothing, but frowned heavily; and the frown deepened as she added the rest of the cards until the entire fifty-two had passed in review before her. Though she frowned, she seemed to be deeply interested. Without changing the relative position of the cards, she ran them all over again. Then she threw a larger piece of pine on the fire, shuffled the cards afresh, divided them into three piles, and subjected them to the same careful and critical examination.

"I can't tell the day when I've seed the cards run this a-way," she said after a while. "What is an' what aint, I'll never tell you; but I know what the cards sez."

"W'at does dey say, Miss Becky?" the negro inquired, in a tone the solemnity of which was heightened by its eagerness.

"They er runnin' quare. These here that I'm a-lookin' at," said Miss Becky, "they stan' for the past. Them there, they er the present; and the t'others, they er the future. Here's a bundle,"—tapping the ace of clubs with her thumb,—"an' here's a journey as plain as the nose on a man's face. Here's Lucinda"—

"Whar she, Miss Becky?"

"Here she is—the queen of spades."

Free Joe grinned. The idea seemed to please him immensely.

"Well, well, well!" he exclaimed. "Ef dat don't beat my time! De queen er spades! W'en Lucindy year dat hit'll tickle 'er, sho'!"

Miss Becky continued to run the cards back and forth through her fingers.

"Here's a bundle an' a journey, and here's Lucinda. An' here's ole Spite Calderwood."

She held the cards toward the negro and touched the king of clubs.

"De Lord he'p my soul!" exclaimed Free Joe with a chuckle. "De faver's dar. Yesser, dat's him! W'at de matter 'long wid all un um, Miss Becky?"

The old woman added the second pile of cards to the first, and then the third, still running them through her fingers slowly and critically. By this time the piece of pine in the fireplace had wrapped itself in a mantle of flame, illuminating the cabin and throwing into strange relief the figure of Miss Becky as she sat studying the cards. She frowned ominously at the cards and mumbled a few words to herself. Then she dropped her hands in her lap and gazed once more into the fire. Her shadow danced and capered on the wall and floor behind her, as if, looking over her shoulder into the future, it could behold a rare spectacle. After a while she picked up the cup that had been turned on the hearth. The coffee-grounds, shaken around, presented what seemed to be a most intricate map.

"Here's the journey," said Miss Becky, presently; "here's the big road, here's rivers to cross, here's the bundle to tote." She paused and sighed. "They haint no names writ here, an' what it all means I'll never tell you. Cajy, I wish you'd be so good as to han' me my pipe."

"I haint no hand wi' the kyards," said Cajy, as he handed the pipe, "but I reckon I can patch out your misinformation, Becky, bekaze the other day, whiles I was a-finishin' up Mizzers Perdue's rollin'-pin, I hearn a rattlin' in the road. I looked out, an' Spite Calderwood was a-drivin' by in his buggy, an' thar sot Lucinda by him. It'd in-about drapt out er my min'."

Free Joe sat on the door-sill and fumbled at his hat, flinging it from one hand to the other.

"You aint see um gwine back, is you, Mars Cajy?" he asked after a while.

"Ef they went back by this road," said Mr. Staley, with the air of one who is accustomed to weigh well his words, "it must 'a' bin endurin' of the time whiles I was asleep, bekaze I haint bin no furder from my shop than to yon bed."

"Well, sir!" exclaimed Free Joe in an awed tone, which Mr. Staley seemed to regard as a tribute to his extraordinary powers of statement.

"Ef it's my beliefs you want," continued the old man, "I'll pitch 'em at you fair and free. My beliefs is that Spite Calderwood is gone an' took Lucindy outen the county. Bless your heart and soul! when

Spite Calderwood meets the Old Boy in the road they'll be a turrible scuffle. You mark what I tell you."

Free Joe, still fumbling with his hat, rose and leaned against the door-facing. He seemed to be embarrassed. Presently he said,—

"I speck I better be gittin' 'long. Nex' time I see Lucindy, I'm gwine tell 'er w'at Miss Becky say 'bout de queen er spades—dat I is. Ef dat don't tickle 'er, dey ain't no nigger 'oman never bin tickle'."

He paused a moment, as though waiting for some remark or comment, some confirmation of misfortune, or, at the very least, some indorsement of his suggestion that Lucinda would be greatly pleased to know that she had figured as the queen of spades; but neither Miss Becky nor her brother said any thing.

"One minnit ridin' in the buggy 'longside er Mars Spite, en de nex' highfalutin' 'roun' playin' de queen er spades. Mon, deze yer nigger gals gittin' up in de pictur's; dey sholy is."

With a brief "Good-night, Miss Becky, Mars Cajy," Free Joe went out into the darkness, followed by little Dan. He made his way to the poplar, where Lucinda had been in the habit of meeting him, and sat down. He sat there a long time; he sat there until little Dan, growing restless, trotted off in the direction of the Calderwood place. Dozing against the poplar, in the gray dawn of the morning, Free Joe heard Spite Calderwood's fox-hounds in full cry a mile away.

"Shoo!" he exclaimed, scratching his head, and laughing to himself, "dem ar dogs is des a-warmin' dat old fox up."

But it was Dan the hounds were after, and the little dog came back no more. Free Joe waited and waited, until he grew tired of waiting. He went back the next night and waited, and for many nights thereafter. His waiting was in vain, and yet he never regarded it as in vain. Careless and shabby as he was, Free Joe was thoughtful enough to have his theory. He was convinced that little Dan had found Lucinda, and that some night when the moon was shining brightly through the trees, the dog would rouse him from his dreams as he sat sleeping at the foot of the poplar-tree, and he would open his eyes and behold Lucinda standing over him, laughing merrily as of old; and then he thought what fun they would have about the queen of spades.

How many long nights Free Joe waited at the foot of the poplar-tree for Lucinda and little Dan, no one can ever know. He kept no account of them, and they were not recorded by Micajah Staley nor by Miss Becky. The season ran into summer and then into fall. One night he went to the Staley cabin, cut the two old people an armful of wood, and seated himself on the door-steps, where he rested. He was always thankful—and proud, as it seemed—when Miss Becky gave him a cup of coffee, which she was sometimes thoughtful enough to do. He was especially thankful on this particular night.

"You er still layin' off for to strike up wi' Lucindy out thar in the woods, I reckon," said Micajah Staley, smiling grimly. The situation was not without its humorous aspects.

"Oh, dey er comin', Mars Cajy, dey er comin', sho," Free Joe replied. "I boun' you dey'll come; en w'en dey does come, I'll des take en fetch um yer, whar you kin see um wid you own eyes, you en Miss Becky."

"No," said Mr. Staley, with a quick and emphatic gesture of disapproval. "Don't! don't fetch 'em anywheres. Stay right wi' 'em as long as may be."

Free Joe chuckled, and slipped away into the night, while the two old people sat gazing in the fire. Finally Micajah spoke.

"Look at that nigger; look at 'im. He's pine-blank as happy now as a killdee by a mill-race. You can't 'faze 'em. I'd in-about give up my t'other hand ef I could stan' flat-footed, an' grin at trouble like that there nigger."

"Niggers is niggers," said Miss Becky, smiling grimly, "an' you can't rub it out; yit I lay I've seed a heap of white people lots meaner'n Free Joe. He grins,—an' that's nigger,—but I've ketched his under jaw a-trimblin' when Lucindy's name uz brung up. An' I tell you," she went on, bridling up a little, and speaking with almost fierce emphasis, "the Old Boy's done sharpened his claws for Spite Calderwood. You'll see it."

"Me, Rebecca?" said Mr. Staley, hugging his palsied arm; "me? I hope not."

"Well, you'll know it then," said Miss Becky, laughing heartily at her brother's look of alarm.

The next morning Micajah Staley had occasion to go into the woods after a piece of timber. He saw Free Joe sitting at the foot of the poplar, and the sight vexed him somewhat.

"Git up from there," he cried, "an' go an' arn your livin'. A mighty purty pass it's come to, when great big buck niggers can lie a-snorin' in the woods all day, when t'other folks is got to be up an' a-gwine. Git up from there!"

Receiving no response, Mr. Staley went to Free Joe, and shook him by the shoulder; but the negro made no response. He was dead. His hat was off, his head was bent, and a smile was on his face. It was if he had bowed and smiled when death stood before him, humble to the last. His clothes were ragged; his hands were rough and callous; his shoes were literally tied together with strings; he was shabby in the extreme. A passer-by, glancing at him, could have no idea that such a humble creature had been summoned as a witness before the Lord God of Hosts.

The next morning Micajah Staley had occasion to go into the woods after a piece of timber. He saw Free Joe sitting at the foot of the poplar, and the sight vexed him somewhat.

"Git up from there," he cried, "an' go an' earn your livin'. A mighty purty pass it's come to, when great big buck niggers can lie a-snorin' in the woods all day, when t'other folks is got to be up an' a-gwine. Git up from there!"

Receiving no response, Mr. Staley went to Free Joe and shook him by the shoulder; but the negro made no response. He was dead. His hat was off, his head was bent, and a smile was on his face. It was as if he had bowed and smiled when death stood before him, humble to the last. His clothes were ragged; his hands were rough and callous; his shoes were literally tied together with strings; he was shabby in the extreme. A passer-by, glancing at him, could have no idea that such a humble creature had been summoned as a witness before the Lord God of Hosts.

THOMAS NELSON PAGE

The Burial of the Guns

Thomas Nelson Page (1853–1922)

A NOTICING CHILD reared in the old Virginia plantation society, kin to Carters, Randolphs and Pendletons, would naturally find post-bellum life something of a vulgar anti-climax, no matter how successful he might be. Throughout a long writing career Page's imagination drew on recollection of his boyhood days at Oakland plantation in Hanover County; he peopled his remembered paradise with gallant men, lovely women and loyal slaves, all moving in an atmosphere of grace and romance which is today incredible.

His dialect sketches of life "befo' de wa' " seemed bold innovations to the readers of the '80's. The first of them, "Marse Chan," was published by the Century magazine in 1884, and, when it was gathered with subsequent stories in In Ole Virginia (1887), Page rose high in reputation among the leaders of the emerging "local color" school of American writers. His lecturing and writing, at first secondary to his practice of the law, became in time his entire occupation.

Page's attitude toward his characters differs markedly, however, from that of other regional writers, particularly Cable and Harris. So far as in them lay, these latter two were realistic in their view of the manners of a vanished society, but the modern reader of Page's sketches is bound to ask himself: Was all this ever true, or only a boy's fancy given reality by a man's technical skill? For skill he did have; sureness of touch, a power of concentrating his forces so as to produce a single effect, a certain ear for the cadences and turns of Negro speech. And another characteristic of Page operates against him today—his frank, patrician acceptance of caste—of the inevitable differences between man and man. It is not to be found in the work of Cable or Harris.

Rarely in his later work was Page the artist of In Ole Virginia. His novels tended to break down in their plots, and become little more than special pleading for a section and its state of mind. In one later story, however, The Burial of the Guns, we have something which is at least the equal of any of the better-known sketches. The old Colonel and his batterymen, standing firm in the breach as the Confederacy crumbles around them—the fierce loyalty of the born soldier to his mates and his unit—these are truly observed and common experience, much to be preferred to dreams.

THE BURIAL OF THE GUNS

LEE surrendered the remnant of his army at Appomattox, April 9, 1865, and yet a couple of days later the old Colonel's battery lay intrenched right in the mountain-pass where it had halted three days before. Two weeks previously it had been detailed with a light division sent to meet and repel a force which it was understood was coming in by way of the southwest valley to strike Lee in the rear of his long line from Richmond to Petersburg. It had done its work. The mountain-pass had been seized and held, and the Federal force had not gotten by that road within the blue rampart which guarded on that side the heart of Virginia. This pass, which was the key to the main line of passage over the mountains, had been assigned by the commander of the division to the old Colonel and his old battery, and they had held it. The position taken by the battery had been chosen with a soldier's eye. A better place could not have been selected to hold the pass. It was its highest point, just where the road crawled over the shoulder of the mountain along the limestone cliff, a hundred feet sheer above the deep river, where its waters had cut their way in ages past, and now lay deep and silent, as if resting after their arduous toil before they began to boil over the great bowlders which filled the bed a hundred or more yards below.

The little plateau at the top guarded the descending road on either side for nearly a mile, and the mountain on the other side of the river was the centre of a clump of rocky, heavily timbered spurs, so inaccessible that no feet but those of wild animals or of the hardiest hunter had ever climbed it. On the side of the river on which the road lay, the only path out over the mountain except the road itself was a charcoal-burner's track, dwindling at times to a footway known only to the mountain-folk, which a picket at the top could hold against an army. The position, well defended, was impregnable, and it was well defended. This the general of the division knew when he detailed the old Colonel and gave him his order to hold the pass until relieved, and not let his guns fall into the hands of the enemy. He knew both the Colonel and his battery. The battery was one of the oldest in the army. It had been in the service since April, 1861, and its commander had come to be known as "The Wheel Horse of his division." He was, perhaps, the oldest officer of his rank in his branch of the service. Although he had bitterly opposed secession, and was many years past the age of service when the war came on, yet as soon as the President called on the State for her quota of troops to coerce South Carolina, he had raised and uniformed an artillery company, and offered it, not to the President of the United States, but to the Governor of Virginia.

It is just at this point that he suddenly looms up to me as a soldier; the relation he never wholly lost to me afterward, though I knew him for many, many years of peace. His gray coat with the red facing and the bars on the collar; his military cap; his gray flannel shirt—it was the first time I ever saw him wear anything but immaculate linen—his high boots; his horse caparisoned with a black, high-peaked saddle, with crupper and breast-girth, instead of the light English hunting-saddle to which I had been accustomed, all come before me now as if it were but the other day. I remember but little beyond it, yet I remember, as if it were yesterday, his leaving home, and the scenes which immediately preceded it; the excitement created by the news of the President's call for troops; the unanimous judgment that it meant war; the immediate determination of the old Colonel, who had hitherto opposed secession, that it must be met; the suppressed agitation on the plantation, attendant upon the tender of his services and the Governor's acceptance of them. The prompt and continuous work incident to the enlistment of the men, the bustle of preparation, and all the scenes of that time, come before me now. It turned the calm current of the life of an old and placid country neighborhood, far from any city or centre, and stirred it into a boiling torrent, strong enough, or fierce enough to cut its way and join the general torrent which was bearing down and sweeping everything before it. It seemed but a minute before the quiet old plantation in which the harvest, the corn-shucking, and the Christmas holidays alone marked the passage of the quiet seasons, and where a strange carriage or a single horseman coming down the big road was an event in life, was turned into a depot of war-supplies, and the neighborhood became a parade-ground. The old Colonel, not a colonel yet, nor even a captain, except by brevet, was on his horse by daybreak and off on his rounds through the plantations and the pines enlisting his company. The office in the yard, heretofore one in name only, became one now in reality, and a table was set out piled with papers, pens, ink, books of tactics and regulation, at which men were accepted and enrolled. Soldiers seemed to spring from the ground, as they did from the sowing of the dragon's teeth in the days of Cadmus. Men came up the high road or down the paths across the fields, sometimes singly, but oftener in little parties of two or three, and, asking for the Captain, entered the office as private citizens and came out soldiers enlisted for the war. There was nothing heard of on the plantation except fighting; white and black, all were at work, and all were eager; the servants contended for the honor of going with their master; the women flocked to the house to assist in the work of preparation, cutting out and making under-clothes, knitting socks, picking lint, preparing bandages, and sewing on uniforms; for many of the men who had enlisted were of the poorest class, far too poor to furnish anything themselves, and their equipment had to be contributed mainly by wealthier neighbors. The work was carried on at night as well as by day, for the occasion was urgent. Meantime the men were being drilled by the Captain and his lieutenants, who had been militia officers of old. We were carried to see the drill at the cross-roads, and a brave sight it seemed to us: the lines marching and countermarching in the field, with the horses galloping as they wheeled amid clouds of dust, at the hoarse commands of the excited officers, and the roadside lined with spectators of every age and condition. I recall the arrival of the messenger one night, with the telegraphic order to the Captain to report with his company at "Camp Lee" immediately; the hush in the parlor that attended its reading; then the forced beginning of the conversation afterwards in a somewhat strained and unnatural key, and the Captain's quick and decisive outline of his plans.

Within the hour a dozen messengers were on their way in various directions to notify the members of the command of the summons, and to deliver the order for their attendance at a given point next day. It seemed that a sudden and great change had come. It was the actual appearance of what had hitherto only been theoretical—war. The next morning the Captain, in full uniform, took leave of the assembled plantation, with a few solemn words commending all he left behind to God, and galloped away up the big road to join and lead his battery to the war, and to be gone just four years.

Within a month he was on "the Peninsula" with Magruder, guarding Virginia on the east against the first attack. His camp was first at Yorktown and then on Jamestown Island, the honor having been assigned his battery of guarding the oldest cradle of the race on this continent. It was at "Little Bethel" that his guns were first trained on the enemy, and that the battery first saw what they had to do, and from this time until the middle of April, 1865, they were in service, and no battery saw more service or suffered more in it. Its story was a part of the story of the Southern Army in Virginia. The Captain was a rigid disciplinarian, and his company had more work to do than most new companies. A pious churchman, of the old puritanical type not uncommon to Virginia, he looked after the spiritual as well as the physical welfare of his men, and his chaplain or he read prayers at the head of his company every morning during the war. At first he was not popular with the men, he made the duties of camp life so onerous to them; it was "nothing but drilling and praying all the time," they said. But he had not commanded very long before they came to know the stuff that was in him. He had not been in service a year before he had had four horses shot under him, and when later on he was offered the command of a battalion, the old company petitioned to be one of his batteries, and still remained under his command. Before the first year was out the battery had, through its own elements, and the discipline of the Captain, become a cohesive force, and a distinct integer in the Army of Northern Virginia. Young farmer recruits knew of its prestige and expressed preference for it of many batteries of rapidly growing or grown reputation. Owing to its high stand, the old and clumsy guns with which it had started out were taken from it, and in their place was presented a battery of four fine, brass, twelve-pound Napoleons of the newest and most approved kind, and two three-inch Parrotts, all captured. The men were as pleased with them as children with new toys. The care and attention needed to keep them in prime order broke the monotony of camp life. They soon had abundant opportunities to test their power. They worked admirably, carried far, and were extraordinarily accurate in their aim. The men from admiration of their guns grew to have first a pride in, and then an affection for, them, and gave them nicknames as they did their comrades; the four Napoleons being dubbed, "The Evangelists," and the two rifles being "The Eagle," because of its scream and force, and "The Cat," because when it became hot from rapid firing "It jumped," they said, "like a cat." From many a hill-top in Virginia, Maryland, and Pennsylvania "The Evangelists" spoke their hoarse message of battle and death, "The Eagle" screamed her terrible note, and "The Cat" jumped as she spat her deadly shot from her hot throat. In the Valley of Virginia; on the levels of Henrico and Hanover; on the slopes of Manassas; in the woods of Chancellorsville; on the heights of Fredericksburg; at Antietam and Gettysburg; in the Spottsylvania wilderness, and again on the Hanover levels and on the lines before Petersburg, the old guns through nearly four years roared from fiery throats their deadly messages. The history of the battery was bound up with the history of Lee's army. A rivalry sprang up among the detachments of the different guns, and their several records were jealously kept. The number of duels each gun was in was carefully counted, every scar got in battle was treasured, and the men around their camp-fires, at their scanty messes, or on the march, bragged of them among themselves and avouched them as witnesses. New recruits coming in to fill the gaps made by the killed and disabled, readily fell in with the common mood and caught the spirit like a contagion. It was not an uncommon thing for a wheel to be smashed in by a shell, but if it happened to one gun oftener than to another there was envy. Two of the Evangelists seemed to be especially favored in this line, while the Cat was so exempt as to become the subject of some derision. The men stood by the guns till they were knocked to pieces, and when the fortune of the day went against them, had with their own hands oftener than once saved them after most of their horses were killed.

This had happened in turn to every gun, the men at times working like beavers in mud up to their thighs and under a murderous fire to get their guns out. Many a man had been killed tugging at trail or wheel when the day was against them; but not a gun had ever been lost. At last the evil day arrived. At Winchester a sudden and impetuous charge for a while swept everything before it, and carried the knoll where the old battery was posted; but all the guns were got out by the toiling and rapidly dropping men, except the Cat, which was captured with its entire detachment working at it until they were surrounded and knocked from the piece by cavalrymen. Most of the men who were not killed were retaken before the day was over, with many guns; but the Cat was lost. She remained in the enemy's hands and probably was being turned against her old comrades and lovers. The company was inconsolable. The death of comrades was too natural and common a thing to depress the men beyond what such occurrences necessarily did; but to lose a gun! It was like losing the old Colonel; it was worse: a gun was ranked as a brigadier; and the Cat was equal to a major-general. The other guns seemed lost without her; the Eagle especially, which generally went next to her, appeared to the men to have a lonely and subdued air. The battery was no longer the same: it seemed broken and depleted, shrunken to a mere section. It was worse than Cold Harbor, where over half the men were killed or wounded. The old Captain, now Colonel of the battalion, appreciated the loss and apprehended its effect on the men as much as they themselves did, and application was made for a gun to take the place of the lost piece; but there was none to be had, as the men said they had known all along. It was added—perhaps by a department clerk—that if they wanted a gun to take the place of the one they had lost, they had better capture it. "By ——, we will," they said—adding epithets, intended for the department clerk in his "bomb-proof," not to be printed in this record—and they did. For some time afterwards in every engagement into which they got there used to be speculation among them as to whether the Cat were not there on the other side; some of the men swearing they could tell her report, and even going to the rash length of offering bets on her presence.

By one of those curious coincidences, as strange as anything in fiction, a new general had, in 1864, come down across the Rapidan to take Richmond, and the old battery had found a hill-top in the line in which Lee's army lay stretched across "the Wilderness" country to stop him. The day, though early in May, was a hot one, and the old battery, like most others, had suffered fearfully. Two of the guns had had wheels cut down by shells and the men had been badly cut up; but the fortune of the day had been with Lee, and a little before nightfall, after a terrible fight, there was a rapid advance, Lee's infantry sweeping everything before it, and the artillery, after opening the way for the charge, pushing along with it; now unlimbering as some vantage-point was gained, and using canister with deadly effect; now driving ahead again so rapidly that it was mixed up with the muskets when the long line of breastworks was carried with a rush, and a line of guns were caught still hot from their rapid work. As the old battery, with lathered horses and smoke-grimed men, swung up the crest and unlimbered on the captured breastwork, a cheer went up which was heard even above the long general yell of the advancing line, and for a moment half the men in the battery crowded together around some object on the edge of the redoubt, yelling like madmen. The next instant they divided, and there was the Cat, smoke-grimed and blood-stained and still sweating hot from her last fire, being dragged from her muddy ditch by as many men as could get hold of trail-rope or wheel, and rushed into her old place beside the Eagle, in time to be double-shotted with canister to the muzzle, and to pour it from among her old comrades into her now retiring former masters. Still, she had a new carriage, and her record was lost, while those of the other guns had been faithfully kept by the men. This made a difference in her position for which even the bullets in her wheels did not wholly atone; even Harris, the sergeant of her detachment, felt that.

It was only a few days later, however, that abundant atonement was made. The new general did not retire across the Rapidan after his first defeat, and a new battle had to be fought: a battle, if anything, more furious, more terrible than the first, when the dead filled the trenches and covered the fields. He simply marched by the left flank, and Lee marching by the right flank to head him, flung himself upon him again at Spottsylvania Court-House. That day the Cat, standing in her place behind the new and temporary breastwork thrown up when the battery was posted, had the felloes of her wheels, which showed above the top of the bank, entirely cut away by Minie-bullets, so that when she jumped in the recoil her wheels smashed and let her down. This covered all old scores. The other guns had been cut down by shells or solid shot; but never before had one been gnawed down by musket-balls. From this time all through the campaign the Cat held her own beside her brazen and bloody sisters, and in the cold trenches before Petersburg that winter, when the new general—Starvation—had joined the one already there, she made her bloody mark as often as any gun on the long lines.

Thus the old battery had come to be known, as its old commander, now Colonel of a battalion, had come to be known by those in yet higher command. And when in the opening spring of 1865 it became apparent to the leaders of both armies that the long line could not longer be held if a force should enter behind it, and, sweeping the one partially unswept portion of Virginia, cut the railways in the southwest, and a man was wanted to command the artillery in the expedition sent to meet this force, it was not remarkable that the old Colonel and his battalion should be selected for the work. The force sent out was but small; for the long line was worn to a thin one in those days, and great changes were taking place, the consequences of which were known only to the commanders. In a few days the commander of the expedition found that he must divide his small force for a time, at least, to accomplish his purpose, and sending the old Colonel with one battery of artillery to guard one pass, must push on over the mountain by another way to meet the expected force, if possible, and repel it before it crossed the farther range. Thus the old battery, on an April evening of 1865, found itself toiling alone up the steep mountain road which leads above the river to the gap, which formed the chief pass in that part of the Blue Ridge. Both men and horses looked, in the dim and waning light of the gray April day, rather like shadows of the beings they represented than the actual beings themselves. And anyone seeing them as they toiled painfully up, the thin horses floundering in the mud, and the men, often up to their knees, tugging at the sinking wheels, now stopping to rest, and always moving so slowly that they seemed scarcely to advance at all, might have thought them the ghosts of some old battery lost from some long gone and forgotten war on that deep and desolate mountain road. Often, when they stopped, the blowing of the horses and the murmuring of the river in its bed below were the only sounds heard, and the tired voices of the men when they spoke among themselves seemed hardly more articulate sounds than they. Then the voice of the mounted figure on the roan horse half hidden in the mist would cut in, clear and inspiring, in a tone of encouragement more than of command, and everything would wake up: the drivers would shout and crack their whips; the horses would bend themselves on the collars and flounder in the mud; the men would spring once more to the mud-clogged wheels, and the slow ascent would begin again.

The orders to the Colonel, as has been said, were brief: To hold the pass until he received further instructions, and not to lose his guns. To be ordered, with him, was to obey. The last streak of twilight brought them to the top of the pass; his soldier's instinct and a brief recognizance made earlier in the day told him that this was his place, and before daybreak next morning the point was as well fortified as a night's work by weary and supperless men could make it. A prettier spot could not have been found for the purpose; a small plateau, something over an acre in extent, where a charcoal-burner's hut had once stood, lay right at the top of the pass. It was a little higher on either side than in the middle, where a small brook, along which the charcoal-burner's track was yet visible, came down from the wooded mountain above, thus giving a natural crest to aid the fortification on either side, with open space for the guns, while the edge of the wood coming down from the mountain afforded shelter for the camp.

As the battery was unsupported it had to rely on itself for everything, a condition which most soldiers by this time were accustomed to. A dozen or so of rifles were in the camp, and with these pickets were armed and posted. The pass had been seized none too soon; a scout brought in the information before nightfall that the invading force had crossed the farther range before that sent to meet it could get there, and taking the nearest road had avoided the main body opposing it, and been met only by a rapidly moving detachment, nothing more than a scouting party, and now were advancing rapidly on the road on which they were posted, evidently meaning to seize the pass and cross the mountain at this point. The day was Sunday; a beautiful Spring Sunday; but it was no Sabbath for the old battery. All day the men worked, making and strengthening their redoubt to guard the pass, and bv the next morning, with the old battery at the top, it was impregnable. They were just in time. Before noon their vedettes brought in word that the enemy were ascending the mountain, and the sun had hardly turned when the advance guard rode up, came within range of the picket, and were fired on.

It was apparent that they supposed the force there only a small one, for they retired and soon came up again reinforced in some numbers, and a sharp little skirmish ensued, hot enough to make them more prudent afterwards, though the picket retired up the mountain. This gave them encouragement and probably misled them, for they now advanced boldly. They saw the redoubt on the crest as they came on, and unlimbering a section or two, flung a few shells up at it, which either fell short or passed over without doing material damage. None of the guns was allowed to respond, as the distance was too great with the ammunition the battery had, and, indifferent as it was, it was too precious to be wasted in a duel at an ineffectual range. Doubtless deceived by this, the enemy came on in force, being obliged by the character of the ground to keep almost entirely to the road, which really made them advance in column. The battery waited. Under orders of the Colonel the guns standing in line were double-shotted with canister, and, loaded to the muzzle, were trained down to sweep the road at from four to five hundred yards' distance. And when the column reached this point the six guns, aimed by old and skilful gunners, at a given word swept road and mountain-side with a storm of leaden hail. It was a fire no mortal man could stand up against, and the practised gunners rammed their pieces full again, and before the smoke had cleared or the reverberation had died away among the mountains, had fired the guns again and yet again. The road was cleared of living things when the draught setting down the river drew the smoke away; but it was no discredit to the other force; for no army that was ever uniformed could stand against that battery in that pass. Again and again the attempt was made to get a body of men up under cover of the woods and rocks on the mountain-side, while the guns below utilized their better ammunition from longer range; but it was useless. Although one of the lieutenants and several men were killed in the skirmish, and a number more were wounded, though not severely, the old battery commanded the mountain-side, and its skilful gunners swept it at every point the foot of man could scale. The sun went down, flinging his last flame on a victorious battery still crowning the mountain pass. The dead were buried by night in a corner of the little plateau, borne to their last bivouac on the old gun-carriages which they had stood by so often—which the men said would "sort of ease their minds."

The next day the fight was renewed, and with the same result. The old battery in its position was unconquerable. Only one fear now faced them; their ammunition was getting as low as their rations; another such day or half-day would exhaust it. A sergeant was sent back down the mountain to try to get more, or, if not, to get tidings. The next day it was supposed the fight would be renewed; and the men waited, alert, eager, vigilant, their spirits high, their appetite for victory whetted by success. The men were at their breakfast, or what went for breakfast, scanty at all times, now doubly so, hardly deserving the title of a meal, so poor and small were the portions of cornmeal, cooked in their frying-pans, which went for their rations, when the sound of artillery below broke on the quiet air. They were on their feet in an instant and at the guns, crowding upon the breastwork to look or to listen; for the road, as far as could be seen down the mountain, was empty except for their own picket, and lay as quiet as if sleeping in the balmy air. And yet volley after volley of artillery came rolling up the mountain. What could it mean? That the rest of their force had come up and was engaged with that at the foot of the mountain? The Colonel decided to be ready to go and help them; to fall on the enemy in the rear; perhaps they might capture the entire force. It seemed the natural thing to do, and the guns were limbered up in an incredibly short time, and a roadway made through the intrenchment, the men working like beavers under the excitement. Before they had left the redoubt, however, the vedettes sent out returned and reported that there was no engagement going on, and the firing below seemed to be only practising. There was quite a stir in the camp below; but they had not even broken camp. This was mysterious. Perhaps it meant that they had received reinforcements, but it was a queer way of showing it. The old Colonel sighed as he thought of the good ammunition they could throw away down there, and of his empty limber-chests. It was necessary to be on the alert, however; the guns were run back into their old places, and the horses picketed once more back among the trees. Meantime he sent another messenger back, this time a courier, for he had but one commissioned officer left, and the picket below was strengthened.

The morning passed and no one came; the day wore on and still no advance was made by the force below. It was suggested that the enemy had left; he had, at least, gotten enough of that battery. A reconnoissance, however, showed that he was still encamped at the foot of the mountain. It was conjectured that he was trying to find a way around to take them in the rear, or to cross the ridge by the foot-path. Preparation was made to guard more closely the mountain-path across the spur, and a detachment was sent up to strengthen the picket there. The waiting told on the men and they grew bored and restless. They gathered about the guns in groups and talked; talked of each piece some, but not with the old spirit and vim; the loneliness of the mountain seemed to oppress them; the mountains stretching up so brown and gray on one side of them, and so brown and gray on the other, with their bare, dark forests soughing from time to time as the wind swept up the pass. The minds of the men seemed to go back to the time when they were not so alone, but were part of a great and busy army, and some of them fell to talking of the past, and the battles they had figured in, and of the comrades they had lost. They told them off in a slow and colorless way, as if it were all part of the past as much as the dead they named. One hundred and nineteen times they had been in action. Only seventeen men were left of the eighty odd who had first enlisted in the battery, and of these four were at home crippled for life. Two of the oldest men had been among the half-dozen who had fallen in the skirmish just the day before. It looked tolerably hard to be killed that way after passing for four years through such battles as they had been in; and both had wives and children at home, too, and not a cent to leave them to their names. They agreed calmly that they'd have to "sort of look after them a little" if they ever got home. These were some of the things they talked about as they pulled their old worn coats about them, stuffed their thin, weather-stained hands in their ragged pockets to warm them, and squatted down under the breastwork to keep a little out of the wind. One thing they talked about a good deal was something to eat. They described meals they had had at one time or another as personal adventures, and discussed the chances of securing others in the future as if they were prizes of fortune. One listening and seeing their thin, worn faces and their wasted frames might have supposed they were starving, and they were, but they did not say so.

Towards the middle of the afternoon there was a sudden excitement in the camp. A dozen men saw them at the same time: a squad of three men down the road at the farthest turn, past their picket; but an advancing column could not have created as much excitement, for the middle man carried a white flag. In a minute every man in the battery was on the breastwork. What could it mean! It was a long way off, nearly half a mile, and the flag was small: possibly only a pocket-handkerchief or a napkin; but it was held aloft as a flag unmistakably. A hundred conjectures were indulged in. Was it a summons to surrender? A request for an armistice for some purpose? Or was it a trick to ascertain their number and position? Some held one view, some another. Some extreme ones thought a shot ought to be fired over them to warn them not to come on; no flags of truce were wanted. The old Colonel, who had walked to the edge of the plateau outside the redoubt and taken his position where he could study the advancing figures with his field-glass, had not spoken. The lieutenant who was next in command to him had walked out after him, and stood near him, from time to time dropping a word or two of conjecture in a half-audible tone; but the Colonel had not answered a word; perhaps none was expected. Suddenly he took his glass down, and gave an order to the lieutenant: "Take two men and meet them at the turn yonder; learn their business; and act as your best judgment advises. If necessary to bring the messenger farther, bring only the officer who has the flag, and halt him at that rock yonder, where I will join him." The tone was as placid as if such an occurrence came every day. Two minutes later the lieutenant was on his way down the mountain and the Colonel had the men in ranks. His face was as grave and his manner as quiet as usual, neither more nor less so. The men were in a state of suppressed excitement. Having put them in charge of the second sergeant the Colonel returned to the breastwork. The two officers were slowly ascending the hill, side by side, the bearer of the flag, now easily distinguishable in his jaunty uniform as a captain of cavalry, talking, and the lieutenant in faded gray, faced with yet more faded red, walking beside him with a face white even at that distance, and lips shut as though they would never open again. They halted at the big bowlder which the Colonel had indicated, and the lieutenant, having saluted ceremoniously, turned to come up to the camp; the Colonel, however, went down to meet him. The two men met, but there was no spoken question; if the Colonel inquired it was only with the eyes. The lieutenant spoke, however. "He says," he began and stopped, then began again—"he says, General Lee—" again he choked, then blurted out, "I believe it is all a lie—a damned lie."

"Not dead? Not killed?" said the Colonel, quickly.

"No, not so bad as that; surrendered: surrendered his entire army at Appomattox day before yesterday. I believe it is all a damned lie," he broke out again, as if the hot denial relieved him. The Colonel simply turned away his face and stepped a pace or two off, and the two men stood motionless back to back for more than a minute. Then the Colonel stirred.

"Shall I go back with you?" the lieutenant asked, huskily.

The Colonel did not answer immediately. Then he said: "No, go back to camp and await my return." He said nothing about not speaking of the report. He knew it was not needed. Then he went down the hill slowly alone, while the lieutenant went up to the camp.

The interview between the two officers beside the bowlder was not a long one. It consisted of a brief statement by the Federal envoy of the fact of Lee's surrender two days before near Appomattox Court-House, with the sources of his information, coupled with a formal demand on the Colonel for his surrender. To this the Colonel replied that he had been detached and put under command of another officer for a specific purpose, and that his orders were to hold that pass, which he should do until he was instructed otherwise by his superior in command. With that they parted, ceremoniously, the Federal captain returning to where he had left his horse in charge of his companions a little below, and the old Colonel coming slowly up the hill to camp. The men were at once set to work to meet any attack which might be made. They knew that the message was of grave import, but not of how grave. They thought it meant that another attack would be made immediately, and they sprang to their work with renewed vigor, and a zeal as fresh as if it were but the beginning and not the end.

The time wore on, however, and there was no demonstration below, though hour after hour it was expected and even hoped for. Just as the sun sank into a bed of blue cloud a horseman was seen coming up the darkened mountain from the eastward side, and in a little while practised eyes reported him one of their own men—the sergeant who had been sent back the day before for ammunition. He was alone, and had something white before him on his horse—it could not be the ammunition; but perhaps that might be coming on behind. Every step of his jaded horse was anxiously watched. As he drew near, the lieutenant, after a word with the Colonel, walked down to meet him, and there was a short colloquy in the muddy road; then they came back together and slowly entered the camp, the sergeant handing down a bag of corn which he had got somewhere below, with the grim remark to his comrades, "There's your rations," and going at once to the Colonel's camp-fire, a little to one side among the trees, where the Colonel awaited him. A long conference was held, and then the sergeant left to take his luck with his mess, who were already parching the corn he had brought for their supper, while the lieutenant made the round of the camp; leaving the Colonel seated alone on a log by his camp-fire. He sat without moving, hardly stirring until the lieutenant returned from his round. A minute later the men were called from the guns and made to fall into line. They were silent, tremulous with suppressed excitement; the most sunburned and weather-stained of them a little pale; the meanest, raggedest, and most insignificant not unimpressive in the deep and solemn silence with which they stood, their eyes fastened on the Colonel, waiting for him to speak. He stepped out in front of them, slowly ran his eye along the irregular line, up and down, taking in every man in his glance, resting on some longer than on others, the older men, then dropped them to the ground, and then suddenly, as if with an effort, began to speak. His voice had a somewhat metallic sound, as if it were restrained; but it was otherwise the ordinary tone of command. It was not much that he said: simply that it had become his duty to acquaint them with the information which he had received: that General Lee had surrendered two days before at Appomattox Court-House, yielding to overwhelming numbers; that this afternoon when he had first heard the report he had questioned its truth, but that it had been confirmed by one of their own men, and no longer admitted of doubt; that the rest of their own force, it was learned, had been captured, or had disbanded, and the enemy was now on both sides of the mountain; that a demand had been made on him that morning to surrender too; but that he had orders which he felt held good until they were countermanded, and he had declined. Later intelligence satisfied him that to attempt to hold out further would be useless, and would involve needless waste of life; he had determined, therefore, not to attempt to hold their position longer; but to lead them out, if possible, so as to avoid being made prisoners and enable them to reach home sooner and aid their families. His orders were not to let his guns fall into the enemy's hands, and he should take the only step possible to prevent it. In fifty minutes he should call the battery into line once more, and roll the guns over the cliff into the river, and immediately afterwards, leaving the wagons there, he would try to lead them across the mountain, and as far as they could go in a body without being liable to capture, and then he should disband them, and his responsibility for them would end. As it was necessary to make some preparations he would now dismiss them to prepare any rations they might have and get ready to march.

All this was in the formal manner of a common order of the day; and the old Colonel had spoken in measured sentences, with little feeling in his voice. Not a man in the line had uttered a word after the first sound, half exclamation, half groan, which had burst from them at the announcement of Lee's surrender. After that they had stood in their tracks like rooted trees, as motionless as those on the mountain behind them, their eyes fixed on their commander, and only the quick heaving up and down the dark line, as of horses overlaboring, told of the emotion which was shaking them. The Colonel, as he ended, half-turned to his subordinate officer at the end of the dim line, as though he were about to turn the company over to him to be dismissed; then faced the line again, and taking a step nearer, with a sudden movement of his hands towards the men as though he would have stretched them out to them, began again:

"Men," he said, and his voiced changed at the word, and sounded like a father's or a brother's, "My men, I cannot let you go so. We were neighbors when the war began—many of us, and some not here to-night; we have been more since then—comrades, brothers in arms; we have all stood for one thing—for Virginia and the South; we have all done our duty—tried to do our duty; we have fought a good fight, and now it seems to be over, and we have been overwhelmed by numbers, not whipped—and we are going home. We have the future before us—we don't know just what it will bring, but we can stand a good deal. We have proved it. Upon us depends the South in the future as in the past. You have done your duty in the past, you will not fail in the future. Go home and be honest, brave, self-sacrificing, God-fearing citizens, as you have been soldiers, and you need not fear for Virginia and the South. The war may be over; but you will ever be ready to serve your country. The end may not be as we wanted it, prayed for it, fought for it; but we can trust God; the end in the end will be the best that could be; even if the South is not free she will be better and stronger that she fought as she did. Go home and bring up your children to love her, and though you may have nothing else to leave them, you can leave them the heritage that they are sons of men who were in Lee's army."

He stopped, looked up and down the ranks again, which had instinctively crowded together and drawn around him in a half-circle; made a sign to the lieutenant to take charge, and turned abruptly on his heel to walk away. But as he did so, the long pent-up emotion burst forth. With a wild cheer the men seized him, crowding around and hugging him, as with protestations, prayers, sobs, oaths—broken, incoherent, inarticulate—they swore to be faithful, to live loyal forever to the South, to him, to Lee. Many of them cried like children; others offered to go down and have one more battle on the plain. The old Colonel soothed them, and quieted their excitement, and then gave a command about the preparations to be made. This called them to order at once; and in a few minutes the camp was as orderly and quiet as usual: the fires were replenished; the scanty stores were being overhauled; the place was selected, and being got ready to roll the guns over the cliff; the camp was being ransacked for such articles as could be carried, and all preparations were being hastily made for their march.

The old Colonel having completed his arrangements sat down by his camp-fire with paper and pencil, and began to write; and as the men finished their work they gathered about in groups, at first around their camp-fires, but shortly strolled over to where the guns still stood at the breastwork, black and vague in the darkness. Soon they were all assembled about the guns. One after another they visited, closing around it and handling it from muzzle to trail as a man might a horse to try its sinew and bone, or a child to feel its fineness and warmth. They were for the most part silent, and when any sound came through the dusk from them to the officers at their fire, it was murmurous and fitful as of men speaking low and brokenly. There was no sound of the noisy controversy which was generally heard, the give-and-take of the camp-fire, the firing backwards and forwards that went on on the march; if a compliment was paid a gun by one of its special detachment, it was accepted by the others; in fact, those who had generally run it down now seemed most anxious to accord the piece praise. Presently a small number of the men returned to a camp-fire, and, building it up, seated themselves about it, gathering closer and closer together until they were in a little knot. One of them appeared to be writing, while two or three took up flaming chunks from the fire and held them as torches for him to see by. In time the entire company assembled about them, standing in respectful silence, broken only occasionally by a reply from one or another to some question from the scribe. After a little there was a sound of a roll-call, and reading and a short colloquy followed, and then two men, one with a paper in his hand, approached the fire beside which the officers sat still engaged.

"What is it, Harris?" said the Colonel to the man with the paper, who bore remnants of the chevrons of a sergeant on his stained and faded jacket.

"If you please, sir," he said, with a salute, "we have been talking it over, and we'd like this paper to go in along with that you're writing." He held it out to the lieutenant, who was the nearer and had reached forward to take it. "We s'pose you're agoin' to bury it with the guns," he said, hesitatingly, as he handed it over.

"What is it?" asked the Colonel, shading his eyes with his hands.

"It's just a little list we made out in and among us," he said, "with a few things we'd like to put in, so's if anyone ever hauls 'em out they'll find it there to tell what the old battery was, and if they don't, it'll be in one of 'em down thar 'til judgment, and it'll sort of ease our minds a bit." He stopped and waited as a man who had delivered his message. The old Colonel had risen and taken the paper, and now held it with a firm grasp, as if it might blow away with the rising wind. He did not say a word, but his hand shook a little as he proceeded to fold it carefully, and there was a burning gleam in his deep-set eyes, back under his bushy, gray brows.

"Will you sort of look over it, sir, if you think it's worth while? We was in a sort of hurry and we had to put it down just as we come to it; we didn't have time to pick our ammunition; and it ain't written the best in the world, nohow." He waited again, and the Colonel opened the paper and glanced down at it mechanically. It contained first a roster, headed by the list of six guns, named by name: "Matthew," "Mark," "Luke," and "John," "The Eagle," and "The Cat"; then of the men, beginning with the heading:

"Those killed."

Then had followed "Those wounded," but this was marked out. Then came a roster of the company when it first entered service; then of those who had joined afterward; then of those who were present now. At the end of all there was this statement, not very well written, nor wholly accurately spelt:

"To Whom it may Concern: We, the above members of the old battery known, etc., of six guns, named, etc., commanded by the said Col. etc., left on the 11th day of April, 1865, have made out this roll of the battery, them as is gone and them as is left, to bury with the guns which the same we bury this night. We're all volunteers, every man; we joined the army at the beginning of the war, and we've stuck through to the end; sometimes we aint had much to eat, and sometimes we aint had nothin', but we've fought the best we could 119 battles and skirmishes as near as we can make out in four years, and never lost a gun. Now we're agoin' home. We aint surrendered; just disbanded, and we pledges ourselves to teach our children to love the South and General Lee; and to come when we're called anywheres an' anytime, so help us God."

There was a dead silence whilst the Colonel read.

" 'Taint entirely accurite, sir, in one particular," said the sergeant, apologetically; "but we thought it would be playin' it sort o' low down on the Cat if we was to say we lost her unless we could tell about gittin' of her back, and the way she done since, and we didn't have time to do all that." He looked around as if to receive the corroboration of the other men, which they signified by nods and shuffling.

The Colonel said it was all right, and the paper should go into the guns.

"If you please, sir, the guns are all loaded," said the sergeant; "in and about our last charge, too; and we'd like to fire 'em off once more, jist for old times' sake to remember 'em by, if you don't think no harm could come of it?"

The Colonel reflected a moment and said it might be done; they might fire each gun separately as they rolled it over, or might get all ready and fire together, and then roll them over, whichever they wished. This was satisfactory.

The men were then ordered to prepare to march immediately, and withdrew for the purpose. The pickets were called in. In a short time they were ready, horses and all, just as they would have been to march ordinarily, except that the wagons and caissons were packed over in one corner by the camp with the harness hung on poles beside them, and the guns stood in their old places at the breastwork ready to defend the pass. The embers of the sinking camp-fires threw a faint light on them standing so still and silent. The old Colonel took his place, and at a command from him in a somewhat low voice, the men, except a detail left to hold the horses, moved into company-front facing the guns. Not a word was spoken, except the words of command. At the order each detachment went to its gun; the guns were run back and the men with their own hands ran them up on the edge of the perpendicular bluff above the river, where, sheer below, its waters washed the base, as if to face an enemy on the black mountain on the other side. The pieces stood ranged in the order in which they had so often stood in battle, and the gray, thin fog rising slowly and silently from the river deep down between the cliffs, and wreathing the mountain-side above, might have been the smoke from some unearthly battle fought in the dim pass by ghostly guns, yet posted there in the darkness, manned by phantom gunners, while plantom horses stood behind, lit vaguely up by phantom camp-fires. At the given word the laniards were pulled together, and together as one the six black guns, belching flame and lead, roared their last challenge on the misty night, sending a deadly hail of shot and shell, tearing the trees and splintering the rocks of the farther side, and sending the thunder reverberating through the pass and down the mountain, startling from its slumber the sleeping camp on the hills below, and driving the browsing deer and the prowling mountain-fox in terror up the mountain.

There was silence among the men about the guns for one brief instant and then such a cheer burst forth as had never broken from them even in battle: cheer on cheer, the long, wild, old familiar rebel yell for the guns they had fought with and loved.

The noise had not died away and the men behind were still trying to quiet the frightened horses when the sergeant, the same who had written, received from the hand of the Colonel a long package or roll which contained the records of the battery furnished by the men and by the Colonel himself, securely wrapped to make them water-tight, and it was rammed down the yet warm throat of the nearest gun, the Cat: and then the gun was tamped to the muzzle to make her water-tight, and, like her sisters, was spiked, and her vent tamped tight. All this took but a minute, and the next instant the guns were run up once more to the edge of the cliff; and the men stood by them with their hands still on them. A deadly silence fell on the men, and even the horses behind seemed to feel the spell. There was a long pause, in which not a breath was heard from any man, and the soughing of the tree-tops above and the rushing of the rapids below were the only sounds. They seemed to come from far, very far away. Then the Colonel said, quietly, "Let them go, and God be our helper, Amen." There was the noise in the darkness of trampling and scraping on the cliff-top for a second; the sound as of men straining hard together, and then with a pant it ceased all at once, and the men held their breath to hear. One second of utter silence; then one prolonged, deep, resounding splash sending up a great mass of white foam as the brass-pieces together plunged into the dark water below, and then the soughing of the trees and the murmur of the river came again with painful distinctness. It was full ten minutes before the Colonel spoke, though there were other sounds enough in the darkness, and some of the men, as the dark, outstretched bodies showed, were lying on the ground flat on their faces. Then the Colonel gave the command to "fall in" in the same quiet, grave tone he had used all night. The line fell in, the men getting to their horses and mounting in silence; the Colonel put himself at their head and gave the order of march, and the dark line turned in the darkness, crossed the little plateau between the smouldering camp-fires and the spectral caissons with the harness hanging beside them, and slowly entered the dim charcoal-burner's track. Not a word was spoken as they moved off. They might all have been phantoms. Only, the sergeant in the rear, as he crossed the little breastwork which ran along the upper side and marked the boundary of the little camp, half turned and glanced at the dying fires, the low, newly made mounds in the corner, the abandoned caissons, and the empty redoubt, and said, slowly, in a low voice to himself,

"Well, by God!"

HENRY VAN DYKE

The First Christmas Tree

HENRY VAN DYKE (1852–1933)

IT IS TOO BAD *that the tides of literary fashion have left Henry Van Dyke's delicate craft stranded among the many undoubted wrecks of the genteel tradition. He was much more than a literary echo, more than a worthy contemporary of Mabie and Crothers and the rest. In mere bulk of output he is impressive—some seventy books, and a host of contributions to books by others, to say nothing of pamphlets! His range of interests was extremely wide; from concern with municipal reform and theological scholarship to a deep love of nature which informs his* Little Rivers *and* Fisherman's Luck *and gives them place with the work of Muir and Burroughs, if not of Thoreau and Gilbert White.*

He was a child of the manse, born in Germantown, Pennsylvania, but reared in old Brooklyn—not the raucous caricature of today's legend, but Beecher's Brooklyn, the City of Churches, whose shady streets and brick houses harbored a race more closely akin to New England than New York. The genial qualities of his Dutch ancestors showed in his humor and his love of field sport, but there was a stern Puritan idealist in him, too; it was this side of his nature which drove him always to active duty—as a student at Princeton, as a crusading minister at Fifth Avenue's Brick Presbyterian church, as an agitator for reform of the Westminster Confession as well as for reform of the copyright law, and of municipal corruption. In later years, he served as professor of English literature at Princeton University, and his active career was crowned by Woodrow Wilson's appointment of him to represent the United States at The Hague.

Van Dyke wrote like a poet. He saw the greatness in little things, and had a genuine mysticism. His writing was release for the tensions certain to disturb a man who felt his vocation divided between that of the artist and that of the moralist. The poet in him bowed to the preacher's urgencies, and so, too seldom did he attempt a purely literary flight. All this is clear in The First Christmas Tree, *a small volume, but one which well expresses van Dyke's highmindedness, vision and breadth of sympathy.*

THE FIRST CHRISTMAS TREE

I

THE CALL OF THE WOODSMAN

THE day before Christmas, in the year of our Lord 722.

Broad snow-meadows glistening white along the banks of the river Moselle; pallid hill-sides blooming with mystic roses where the glow of the setting sun still lingered upon them; an arch of clearest, faintest azure bending overhead; in the centre of the aerial landscape the massive walls of the cloister of Pfalzel, gray to the east, purple to the west; silence over all,—a gentle, eager, conscious stillness, diffused through the air like perfume, as if earth and sky were hushing themselves to hear the voice of the river faintly murmuring down the valley.

In the cloister, too, there was silence at the sunset hour. All day long there had been a strange and joyful stir among the nuns. A breeze of curiosity and excitement had swept along the corridors and through every quiet cell.

The elder sisters,—the provost, the deaconess, the stewardess, the portress with her huge bunch of keys jingling at her girdle,—had been hurrying to and fro, busied with household cares. In the huge kitchen there was a bustle of hospitable preparation. The little bandy-legged dogs that kept the spits turning before the fires had been trotting steadily for many an hour, until their tongues hung out for want of breath. The big black pots swinging from the cranes had bubbled and gurgled and shaken and sent out puffs of appetizing steam.

St. Martha was in her element. It was a field-day for her virtues.

The younger sisters, the pupils of the convent, had forsaken their Latin books and their embroidery-frames, their manuscripts and their miniatures, and fluttered through the halls in little flocks like merry snow-birds, all in black and white, chattering and whispering together. This was no day for tedious task-work, no day for grammar or arithmetic, no day for picking out illuminated letters in red and gold on stiff parchment, or patiently chasing intricate patterns over thick cloth with the slow needle. It was a holiday. A famous visitor had come to the convent.

It was Winfried of England, whose name in the Roman tongue was Boniface, and whom men called the Apostle of Germany. A great preacher; a wonderful scholar; he had written a Latin grammar himself,—think of it,—and he could hardly sleep without a book under his pillow; but, more than all, a great and daring traveller, a venturesome pilgrim, a high-priest of romance.

He had left his home and his fair estate in Wessex; he would not stay in the rich monastery of Nutescelle, even though they had chosen him as the abbot; he had refused a bishopric at the court of King Karl. Nothing would content him but to go out into the wild woods and preach to the heathen.

Up and down through the forests of Hesse and Thuringia, and along the borders of Saxony, he had wandered for years, with a handful of companions, sleeping under the trees, crossing mountains and marshes, now here, now there, never satisfied with ease and comfort, always in love with hardship and danger.

What a man he was! Fair and slight, but straight as a spear and strong as an oaken staff. His face was still young; the smooth skin was bronzed by wind and sun. His gray eyes, clear and kind, flashed like fire when he spoke of his adventures, and of the evil deeds of the false priests with whom he contended.

What tales he had told that day! Not of miracles wrought by sacred relics; not of courts and councils and splendid cathedrals; though he knew much of these things, and had been at Rome and received the Pope's blessing. But today he had spoken of long journeyings by sea and land; of perils by fire and flood; of wolves and bears and fierce snowstorms and black nights in the lonely forest; of dark altars of heathen gods, and weird, bloody sacrifices, and narrow escapes from murderous bands of wandering savages.

The little novices had gathered around him, and their faces had grown pale and their eyes bright as they listened with parted lips, entranced in admiration, twining their arms about one another's shoulders and holding closely together, half in fear, half in delight. The older nuns had turned from their tasks and paused, in passing by, to hear the pilgrim's story. Too well they knew the truth of what he spoke. Many a one among them had seen the smoke rising from the ruins of her father's roof. Many a one had a brother far away in the wild country to whom her heart went out night and day, wondering if he were still among the living.

But now the excitements of that wonderful day were over; the hour of the evening meal had come; the inmates of the cloister were assembled in the refectory.

On the daïs sat the stately Abbess Addula, daughter of King Dagobert, looking a princess indeed, in her violet tunic, with the hood and cuffs of her long white robe trimmed with fur, and a snowy veil resting like a crown on her snowy hair. At her right hand was the honoured guest, and at her left hand her grandson, the young Prince Gregor, a big, manly boy, just returned from the high school.

The long, shadowy hall, with its dark-brown rafters and beams; the double rows of nuns, with their pure veils and fair faces; the ruddy glow of the slanting sunbeams striking upwards through the tops of the windows and painting a pink glow high up on the walls,—it was all as beautiful as a picture, and as silent. For this was the rule of the cloister, that at the table all should sit in stillness for a little while, and then one should read aloud, while the rest listened.

"It is the turn of my grandson to read to-day," said the abbess to Winfried; "we shall see how much he has learned in the school. Read, Gregor; the place in the book is marked."

The tall lad rose from his seat and turned the pages of the manuscript. It was a copy of Jerome's version of the Scriptures in Latin, and the marked place was in the letter of St. Paul to the Ephesians,—the passage where he describes the preparation of the Christian as the arming of a warrior for glorious battle. The young voice rang out clearly, rolling the sonorous words, without slip or stumbling, to the end of the chapter.

Winfried listened smiling. "My son," said he, as the reader paused, "that was bravely read. Understandest thou what thou readest?"

"Surely, father," answered the boy; "it was taught me by the masters at Treves; and we have read this epistle clear through, from beginning to end, so that I almost know it by heart."

Then he began again to repeat the passage, turning away from the page as if to show his skill.

But Winfried stopped him with a friendly lifting of the hand.

"Not so, my son; that was not my meaning. When we pray, we speak to God; when we read, it is God who speaks to us. I ask whether thou hast heard what He has said to thee, in thine own words, in the common speech. Come, give us again the message of the warrior and his armour and his battle, in the mother-tongue, so that all can understand it."

The boy hesitated, blushed, stammered; then he came around to Winfried's seat, bringing the book. "Take the book, my father," he cried, "and read it for me. I cannot see the meaning plain, though I love the sound of the words. Religion I know, and the doctrines of our faith, and the life of priests and nuns in the cloister, for which my grandmother designs me, though it likes me little. And fighting I know, and the life of warriors and heroes, for I have read of it in Virgil and the ancients, and heard a bit from the soldiers at Treves; and I would fain taste more of it, for it likes me much. But how the two lives fit together, or what need there is of armour for a clerk in holy orders, I can never see. Tell me the meaning, for if there is a man in all the world that knows it, I am sure it is none other than thou."

So Winfried took the book and closed it, clasping the boy's hand with his own.

"Let us first dismiss the others to their vespers," said he, "lest they should be weary."

A sign from the abbess; a chanted benediction; a murmuring of sweet voices and a soft rustling of many feet over the rushes on the floor; the gentle tide of noise flowed out through the doors and ebbed away down the corridors; the three at the head of the table were left alone in the darkening room.

Then Winfried began to translate the parable of the soldier into the realities of life.

At every turn he knew how to flash a new light into the picture out of his own experience. He spoke of the combat with self, and of the wrestling with dark spirits in solitude. He spoke of the demons that men had worshipped for centuries in the wilderness, and whose malice they invoked against the stranger who ventured into the gloomy forest. Gods, they called them, and told strange tales of their dwelling among the impenetrable branches of the oldest trees and in the caverns of the shaggy hills; of their riding on the wind-horses and hurling spears of lightning against their foes. Gods they were not, but foul spirits of the air, rulers of the darkness. Was there not glory and honour in fighting with them, in daring their anger under the shield of faith, in putting them to flight with the sword of truth? What better adventure could a brave man ask than to go forth against them, and wrestle with them, and conquer them?

"Look you, my friends," said Winfried, "how sweet and peaceful is this convent to-night, on the eve of the nativity of the Prince of Peace! It is a garden full of flowers in the heart of winter; a nest among the branches of a great tree shaken by the winds; a still haven on the edge of a tempestuous sea. And this is what religion means for those who are chosen and called to quietude and prayer and meditation.

"But out yonder in the wide forest, who knows what storms are raving to-night in the hearts of men, though all the woods are still? Who knows what haunts of wrath and cruelty and fear are closed to-night against the advent of the Prince of Peace? And shall I tell you what religion means to those who are called and chosen to dare and to fight, and to conquer the world for Christ? It means to launch out into the deep. It means to go against the strongholds of the adversary. It means to struggle to win an entrance for their Master everywhere. What helmet is strong enough for this strife save the helmet of salvation? What breastplate can guard a man against these fiery darts but the breastplate of righteousness? What shoes can stand the wear of these journeys but the preparation of the gospel of peace?"

"Shoes?" he cried again, and laughed as if a sudden thought had struck him. He thrust out his foot, covered with a heavy cowhide boot, laced high about his leg with thongs of skin.

"See here,—how a fighting man of the cross is shod! I have seen the boots of the Bishop of Tours,—white kid, broidered with silk; a day in the bogs would tear them to shreds. I have seen the sandals that the monks use on the highroads,—yes, and worn them; ten pair of them have I worn out and thrown away in a single journey. Now I shoe my feet with the toughest hides, hard as iron; no rock can cut them, no branches can tear them. Yet more than one pair of these have I outworn, and many more shall I outwear ere my journeys are ended. And I think, if God is gracious to me, that I shall die wearing them. Better so than in a soft bed with silken coverings. The boots of a warrior, a hunter, a woodsman,—these are my preparation of the gospel of peace."

"Come, Gregor," he said, laying his brown hand on the youth's shoulder, "come, wear the forester's boots with me. This is the life to which we are called. Be strong in the Lord, a hunter of the demons, a subduer of the wilderness, a woodsman of the faith. Come!"

The boy's eyes sparkled. He turned to his grandmother. She shook her head vigorously.

"Nay, father," she said, "draw not the lad away from my side with these wild words. I need him to help me with my labours, to cheer my old age."

"Do you need him more than the Master does?" asked Winfried; "and will you take the wood that is fit for a bow to make a distaff?"

"But I fear for the child. Thy life is too hard for him. He will perish with hunger in the woods."

"Once," said Winfried, smiling, "we were camped by the bank of the river Ohru. The table was spread for the morning meal, but my comrades cried that it was empty; the provisions were exhausted; we must go without breakfast, and perhaps starve before we could escape from the wilderness. While they complained, a fish-hawk flew up from the river with flapping wings, and let fall a great pike in the midst of the camp. There was food enough and to spare. Never have I seen the righteous forsaken, nor his seed begging bread."

"But the fierce pagans of the forest," cried the abbess,—"they may pierce the boy with their arrows, or dash out his brains with their axes. He is but a child, too young for the dangers of strife."

"A child in years," replied Winfried, "but a man in spirit. And if the hero must fall early in the battle, he wears the brighter crown, not a leaf withered, not a flower fallen."

The aged princess trembled a little. She drew Gregor close to her side, and laid her hand gently on his brown hair.

"I am not sure that he wants to leave me yet. Besides, there is no horse in the stable to give him, now, and he cannot go as befits the grandson of a king."

Gregor looked straight into her eyes.

"Grandmother," said he, "dear grandmother, if thou wilt not give me a horse to ride with this man of God, I will go with him afoot."

II

THE TRAIL THROUGH THE FOREST

Two years had passed, to a day, almost to an hour, since that Christmas eve in the cloister of Pfalzel. A little company of pilgrims, less than a score of men, were creeping slowly northward through the wide forest that rolled over the hills of central Germany.

At the head of the band marched Winfried, clad in a tunic of fur, with his long black robe girt high about his waist, so that it might not hinder his stride. His hunter's boots were crusted with snow. Drops of ice sparkled like jewels along the thongs that bound his legs. There was no other ornament to his dress except the bishop's cross hanging on his breast, and the broad silver clasp that fastened his cloak about his neck. He carried a strong, tall staff in his hand, fashioned at the top into the form of a cross.

Close beside him, keeping step like a familiar comrade, was the young Prince Gregor. Long marches through the wilderness had stretched his limbs and broadened his back, and made a man of him in stature as well as in spirit. His jacket and cap were of wolfskin, and on his shoulder he carried an axe, with broad, shining blade. He was a mighty woodsman now, and could make a spray of chips fly around him as he hewed his way through the trunk of a spruce-tree.

Behind these leaders followed a pair of teamsters, guiding a rude sledge, loaded with food and the equipage of the camp, and drawn by two big, shaggy horses, blowing thick clouds of steam from their frosty nostrils. Tiny icicles hung from the hairs on their lips. Their flanks were smoking. They sank above the fetlocks at every step in the soft snow.

Last of all came the rear guard, armed with bows and javelins. It was no child's play, in those days, to cross Europe afoot.

The weird woodland, sombre and illimitable, covered hill and vale, tableland and mountain-peak. There were wide moors where the wolves hunted in packs as if the devil drove them, and tangled thickets where the lynx and the boar made their lairs. Fierce bears lurked among the rocky passes, and had not yet learned to fear the face of man. The gloomy recesses of the forest gave shelter to inhabitants who were still more cruel and dangerous than beasts of prey,—outlaws and sturdy robbers and mad were-wolves and bands of wandering pillagers.

The pilgrim who would pass from the mouth of the Tiber to the mouth of the Rhine must travel with a little army of retainers, or else trust in God and keep his arrows loose in the quiver.

The travellers were surrounded by an ocean of trees, so vast, so full of endless billows, that it seemed to be pressing on every side to overwhelm them. Gnarled oaks, with branches twisted and knotted as if in rage, rose in groves like tidal waves. Smooth forests of beech-trees, round and gray, swept over the knolls and slopes of land in a mighty ground-swell. But most of all, the multitude of pines and firs, innumerable and monotonous, with straight, stark trunks, and branches woven together in an unbroken flood of darkest green, crowded through the valleys and over the hills, rising on the highest ridges into ragged crests, like the foaming edge of breakers.

Through this sea of shadows ran a narrow stream of shining whiteness,—an ancient Roman road, covered with snow. It was as if some great ship had ploughed through the green ocean long ago, and left behind it a thick, smooth wake of foam. Along this open track the travellers held their way,—heavily, for the drifts were deep; warily, for the hard winter had driven many packs of wolves down from the moors.

The steps of the pilgrims were noiseless; but the sledges creaked over the dry snow, and the panting of the horses throbbed through the still, cold air. The pale-blue shadows on the western side of the road grew longer. The sun, declining through its shallow arch, dropped behind the tree-tops. Darkness followed swiftly, as if it had been a bird of prey waiting for this sign to swoop down upon the world.

"Father," said Gregor to the leader, "surely this day's march is done. It is time to rest, and eat, and sleep. If we press onward now, we cannot see our steps; and will not that be against the word of the psalmist David, who bids us not to put confidence in the legs of a man?"

Winfried laughed. "Nay, my son Gregor," said he, "thou hast tripped, even now, upon thy text. For David said only, 'I take no pleasure in the legs of a man.' And so say I, for I am not minded to spare thy legs or mine, until we come farther on our way, and do what must be done this night. Draw the belt tighter, my son, and hew me out this tree that is fallen across the road, for our camp-ground is not here."

The youth obeyed; two of the foresters sprang to help him; and while the soft fir-wood yielded to the stroke of the axes, and the snow flew from the bending branches, Winfried turned and spoke to his followers in a cheerful voice, that refreshed them like wine.

"Courage, brothers, and forward yet a little! The moon will light us presently, and the path is plain. Well know I that the journey is weary; and my own heart wearies also for the home in England, where those I love are keeping feast this Christmas eve. But we have work to do before we feast to-night. For this is the Yuletide, and the heathen people of the forest have gathered at the thunder-oak of Geismar to worship their god, Thor. Strange things will be seen there, and deeds which make the soul black. But we are sent to lighten their darkness; and we will teach our kinsmen to keep a Christmas with us such as the woodland has never known. Forward, then, and let us stiffen up our feeble knees!"

A murmur of assent came from the men. Even the horses seemed to take fresh heart. They flattened their backs to draw the heavy loads, and blew the frost from their nostrils as they pushed ahead.

The night grew broader and less oppressive. A gate of brightness was opened secretly somewhere in the sky; higher and higher swelled the clear moon-flood, until it poured over the eastern wall of forest into the road. A drove of wolves howled faintly in the distance, but they were receding, and the sound soon died away. The stars sparkled merrily through the stringent air; the small, round moon shone like silver; little breaths of the dreaming wind wandered whispering across the pointed fir-tops, as the pilgrims toiled bravely onward, following their clue of light through a labyrinth of darkness.

After a while the road began to open out a little. There were spaces of meadow-land, fringed with alders, behind which a boisterous river ran, clashing through spears of ice.

Rude houses of hewn logs appeared in the openings, each one casting a patch of inky blackness upon the snow. Then the travellers passed a larger group of dwellings, all silent and unlighted; and beyond, they saw a great house, with many outbuildings and enclosed courtyards, from which the hounds bayed furiously, and a noise of stamping horses came from the stalls. But there was no other sound of life. The fields around lay bare to the moon. They saw no man, except that once, on a path that skirted the farther edge of a meadow, three dark figures passed by, running very swiftly.

Then the road plunged again into a dense thicket, traversed it, and climbing to the left, emerged suddenly upon a glade, round and level except at the northern side, where a swelling hillock was crowned with a huge oak-tree. It towered above the heath, a giant with contorted arms, beckoning to the host of lesser trees. "Here," cried Winfried, as his eyes flashed and his hand lifted his heavy staff, "here is the Thunder-oak; and here the cross of Christ shall break the hammer of the false god Thor."

III
THE SHADOW OF THE THUNDER-OAK

Withered leaves still clung to the branches of the oak: torn and faded banners of the departed summer. The bright crimson of autumn had long since disappeared, bleached away by the storms and the cold. But to-night these tattered remnants of glory were red again: ancient bloodstains against the dark-blue sky. For an immense fire had been kindled in front of the tree. Tongues of ruddy flame, fountains of ruby sparks, ascended through the spreading limbs and flung a fierce illumination upward and around. The pale, pure moonlight that bathed the surrounding forests was quenched and eclipsed here. Not a beam of it sifted downward through the branches of the oak. It stood like a pillar of cloud between the still light of heaven and the crackling, flashing fire of earth.

But the fire itself was invisible to Winfried and his companions. A great throng of people were gathered around it in a half-circle, their backs to the open glade, their faces towards the oak. Seen against that glowing background, it was but the silhouette of a crowd, vague, black, formless, mysterious.

The travellers paused for a moment at the edge of the thicket, and took counsel together.

"It is the assembly of the tribe," said one of the foresters, "the great night of the council. I heard of it three days ago, as we passed through one of the villages. All who swear by the old gods have been summoned. They will sacrifice a steed to the god of war, and drink blood, and eat horse-flesh to make them strong. It will be at the peril of our lives if we approach them. At least we must hide the cross, if we would escape death."

"Hide me no cross," cried Winfried, lifting his staff, "for I have come to show it, and to make these blind folk see its power. There is more to be done here to-night than the slaying of a steed, and a greater evil to be stayed than the shameful eating of meat sacrificed to idols. I have seen it in a dream. Here the cross must stand and be our rede."

At his command the sledge was left in the border of the wood, with two of the men to guard it, and the rest of the company moved forward across the open ground. They approached unnoticed, for all the multitude were looking intently towards the fire at the foot of the oak.

Then Winfried's voice rang out, "Hail, ye sons of the forest! A stranger claims the warmth of your fire in the winter night."

Swiftly, and as with a single motion, a thousand eyes were bent upon the speaker. The semicircle opened silently in the middle; Winfried entered with his followers; it closed again behind them.

Then, as they looked round the curving ranks, they saw that the hue of the assemblage was not black, but white,—dazzling, radiant, solemn. White, the robes of the women clustered together at the points of the wide crescent; white, the glittering byrnies of the warriors standing in close ranks; white, the fur mantles of the aged men who held the central place in the circle; white, with the shimmer of silver ornaments and the purity of lamb's-wool, the raiment of a little group of children who stood close by the fire; white, with awe and fear, the faces of all who looked at them; and over all the flickering, dancing radiance of the flames played and glimmered like a faint, vanishing tinge of blood on snow.

The only figure untouched by the glow was the old priest, Hunrad, with his long, spectral robe, flowing hair and beard, and dead-pale face, who stood with his back to the fire and advanced slowly to meet the strangers.

"Who are you? Whence come you, and what seek you here?" His voice was heavy and toneless as a muffled bell.

"Your kinsman am I, of the German brotherhood," answered Winfried, "and from England, beyond the sea, have I come to bring you a greeting from that land, and a message from the All-Father, whose servant I am."

"Welcome, then," said Hunrad, "welcome, kinsman, and be silent; for what passes here is too high to wait, and must be done before the moon crosses the middle heaven, unless, indeed, thou hast some sign or token from the gods. Canst thou work miracles?"

The question came sharply, as if a sudden gleam of hope had flashed through the tangle of the old priest's mind. But Winfried's voice sank lower and a cloud of disappointment passed over his face as he replied: "Nay, miracles have I never wrought, though I have heard of many; but the All-Father has given no power to my hands save such as belongs to common man."

"Stand still, then, thou common man," said Hunrad, scornfully, "and behold what the gods have called us hither to do. This night is the death-night of the sun-god, Baldur the Beautiful, beloved of gods and men. This night is the hour of darkness and the power of winter, of sacrifice and mighty fear. This night the great Thor, the god of thunder and war, to whom this oak is sacred, is grieved for the death of Baldur, and angry with this people because they have forsaken his worship. Long is it since an offering has been laid upon his altar, long since the roots of his holy tree have been fed with blood. Therefore its leaves have withered before the time, and its boughs are heavy with death. Therefore the Slavs and the Wends have beaten us in battle. Therefore the harvests have failed, and the wolf-hordes have ravaged the folds, and the strength has departed from the bow, and the wood of the spear has broken, and the wild boar has slain the huntsman. Therefore the plague has fallen on our dwellings, and the dead are more than the living in all our villages. Answer me, ye people, are not these things true?"

A hoarse sound of approval ran through the circle. A chant, in which the voices of the men and women blended, like the shrill wind in the pine-trees above the rumbling thunder of a waterfall, rose and fell in rude cadences.

O Thor, the Thunderer,
Mighty and merciless,
Spare us from smiting!
Heave not thy hammer,
Angry, against us;
Plague not thy people.
Take from our treasure
Richest of ransom.
Silver we send thee,
Jewels and javelins,
Goodliest garments,
All our possessions,
Priceless, we proffer.
Sheep will we slaughter,
Steeds will we sacrifice;
Bright blood shall bathe thee,
O tree of Thunder,
Life-bloods shall lave thee,
Strong wood of wonder.
Mighty, have mercy,
Smite us no more,
Spare us and save us,
Spare us, Thor! Thor!

With two great shouts the song ended, and a stillness followed so intense that the crackling of the fire was heard distinctly. The old priest stood silent for a moment. His shaggy brows swept down over his eyes like ashes quenching flame. Then he lifted his face and spoke.

"None of these things will please the god. More costly is the offering that shall cleanse your sin, more precious the crimson dew that shall send new life into this holy tree of blood. Thor claims your dearest and your noblest gift."

Hunrad moved nearer to the handful of children who stood watching the red mines in the fire and the swarms of spark-serpents darting upward. They had heeded none of the priest's words, and did not notice now that he approached them, so eager were they to see which fiery snake would go highest among the oak branches. Foremost among them, and most intent on the pretty game, was a boy like a sunbeam, slender and quick, with blithe brown eyes and laughing lips. The priest's hand was laid upon his shoulder. The boy turned and looked up in his face.

"Here," said the old man, with his voice vibrating as when a thick rope is strained by a ship swinging from her moorings, "here is the chosen one, the eldest son of the Chief, the darling of the people. Hearken, Bernhard, wilt thou go to Valhalla, where the heroes dwell with the gods, to bear a message to Thor?"

The boy answered, swift and clear:

"Yes, priest, I will go if my father bids me. Is it far away? Shall I run quickly? Must I take my bow and arrows for the wolves?"

The boy's father, the Chieftain Gundhar, standing among his bearded warriors, drew his breath deep, and leaned so heavily on the handle of his spear that the wood cracked. And his wife, Irma, bending forward from the ranks of women, pushed the golden hair from her forehead with one hand. The other dragged at the silver chain about her neck until the rough links pierced her flesh, and the red drops fell unheeded on the snow of her breast.

A sigh passed through the crowd, like the murmur of the forest before the storm breaks. Yet no one spoke save Hunrad:

"Yes, my Prince, both bow and spear shalt thou have, for the way is long, and thou art a brave huntsman. But in darkness thou must journey for a little space, and with eyes blindfolded. Fearest thou?"

"Naught fear I," said the boy, "neither darkness, nor the great bear, nor the were-wolf. For I am Gundhar's son, and the defender of my folk."

Then the priest led the child in his raiment of lamb's-wool to a broad stone in front of the fire. He gave him his little bow tipped with silver, and his spear with shining head of steel. He bound the child's eyes with a white cloth, and bade him kneel beside the stone with his face to the east. Unconsciously the wide arc of spectators drew inward toward the centre, as the ends of the bow draw together when the cord is stretched. Winfried moved noiselessly until he stood close behind the priest.

The old man stooped to lift a black hammer of stone from the ground,—the sacred hammer of the god Thor. Summoning all the strength of his withered arms, he swung it high in the air. It poised for an instant above the child's fair head—then turned to fall.

One keen cry shrilled out from where the women stood: "Me! take me! not Bernhard!"

The flight of the mother towards her child was swift as the falcon's swoop. But swifter still was the hand of the deliverer.

Winfried's heavy staff thrust mightily against the hammer's handle as it fell. Sideways it glanced from the old man's grasp, and the black stone, striking on the altar's edge, split in twain. A shout of awe and joy rolled along the living circle. The branches of the oak shivered. The flames leaped higher. As the shout died away the people saw the lady Irma, with her arms clasped round her child, and above them, on the altar-stone, Winfried, his face shining like the face of an angel.

IV

THE FELLING OF THE TREE

A swift mountain-flood rolling down its channel; a huge rock tumbling from the hill-side and falling in mid-stream; the baffled waters broken and confused, pausing in their flow, dash high against the rock, foaming and murmuring, with divided impulse, uncertain whether to turn to the right or the left.

Even so Winfried's bold deed fell into the midst of the thoughts and passions of the council. They were at a standstill. Anger and wonder, reverence and joy and confusion surged through the crowd. They knew not which way to move: to resent the intrusion of the stranger as an insult to their gods, or to welcome him as the rescuer of their darling prince.

The old priest crouched by the altar, silent. Conflicting counsels troubled the air. Let the sacrifice go forward; the gods must be appeased. Nay, the boy must not die; bring the chieftain's best horse and slay it in his stead; it will be enough; the holy tree loves the blood of horses. Not so, there is a better counsel yet; seize the stranger whom the gods have led hither as a victim and make his life pay the forfeit of his daring.

The withered leaves on the oak rustled and whispered overhead. The fire flared and sank again. The angry voices clashed against each other and fell like opposing waves. Then the chieftain Gundhar struck the earth with his spear and gave his decision.

"All have spoken, but none are agreed. There is no voice of the council. Keep silence now, and let the stranger speak. His words shall give us judgment, whether he is to live or to die."

Winfried lifted himself high upon the altar, drew a roll of parchment from his bosom, and began to read.

"A letter from the great Bishop of Rome, who sits on a golden throne, to the people of the forest, Hessians and Thuringians, Franks and Saxons. *In nomine Domini, sanctae et individuae Trinitatis, amen!*"

A murmur of awe ran through the crowd. "It is the sacred tongue of the Romans: the tongue that is heard and understood by the wise men of every land. There is magic in it. Listen!"

Winfried went on to read the letter, translating it into the speech of the people.

" 'We have sent unto you our Brother Boniface, and appointed him your bishop, that he may teach you the only true faith, and baptize you, and lead you back from the ways of error to the path of salvation. Hearken to him in all things like a father. Bow your hearts to his teaching. He comes not for earthly gain, but for the gain of your souls. Depart from evil works. Worship not the false gods, for they are devils. Offer no more bloody sacrifices, nor eat the flesh of horses, but do as our Brother Boniface commands you. Build a house for him that he may dwell among you, and a church where you may offer your prayers to the only living God, the Almighty King of Heaven.' "

It was a splendid message: proud, strong, peaceful, loving. The dignity of the words imposed mightily upon the hearts of the people. They were quieted as men who have listened to a lofty strain of music.

"Tell us, then," said Gundhar, "what is the word that thou bringest to us from the Almighty. What is thy counsel for the tribes of the woodland on this night of sacrifice?"

"This is the word, and this is the counsel," answered Winfried. "Not a drop of blood shall fall to-night, save that which pity has drawn from the breast of your princess, in love for her child. Not a life shall be blotted out in the darkness to-night; but the great shadow of the tree which hides you from the light of heaven shall be swept away. For this is the birth-night of the white Christ, son of the All-Father, and Saviour of mankind. Fairer is He than Baldur the Beautiful, greater than Odin the Wise, kinder than Freya the Good. Since He has come to earth, the bloody sacrifices must cease. The dark Thor, on whom you vainly call, is dead. Deep in the shades of Niffelheim he is lost forever. His power in the world is broken. Will you serve a helpless god? See, my brothers, you call this tree his oak. Does he dwell here? Does he protect it?"

A troubled voice of assent rose from the throng. The people stirred uneasily. Women covered their eyes. Hunrad lifted his head and muttered hoarsely, "Thor! take vengeance! Thor!"

Winfried beckoned to Gregor. "Bring the axes, thine and one for me. Now, young woodsman, show thy craft! The king-tree of the forest must fall, and swiftly, or all is lost!"

The two men took their places facing each other, one on each side of the oak. Their cloaks were flung aside, their heads bare.

Carefully they felt the ground with their feet, seeking a firm grip of the earth. Firmly they grasped the axe-helves and swung the shining blades.

"Tree-god!" cried Winfried, "art thou angry? Thus we smite thee!"

"Tree-god!" answered Gregor, "art thou mighty? Thus we fight thee!"

Clang! clang! the alternate strokes beat time upon the hard, ringing wood. The axe-heads glittered in their rhythmic flight, like fierce eagles circling about their quarry.

The broad flakes of wood flew from the deepening gashes in the sides of the oak. The huge trunk quivered. There was a shuddering in the branches. Then the great wonder of Winfried's life came to pass.

Out of the stillness of the winter night, a mighty rushing noise sounded overhead.

Was it the ancient gods on their white battle-steeds, with their black hounds of wrath and their arrows of lightning, sweeping through the air to destroy their foes?

A strong, whirling wind passed over the tree-tops. It gripped the oak by its branches and tore it from its roots. Backward it fell, like a ruined tower, groaning and crashing as it split asunder in four great pieces.

Winfried let his axe drop, and bowed his head for a moment in the presence of almighty power.

Then he turned to the people, "Here is the timber," he cried, "already felled and split for your new building. On this spot shall rise a chapel to the true God and his servant St. Peter.

"And here," said he, as his eyes fell on a young fir-tree, standing straight and green, with its top pointing towards the stars, amid the divided ruins of the fallen oak, "here is the living tree, with no stain of blood upon it, that shall be the sign of your new worship. See how it points to the sky. Let us call it the tree of the Christ-child. Take it up and carry it to the chieftain's hall. You shall go no more into the shadows of the forest to keep your feasts with secret rites of shame. You shall keep them at home, with laughter and song and rites of love. The thunder-oak has fallen, and I think the day is coming when there shall not be a home in all Germany where the children are not gathered around the green fir-tree to rejoice in the birth-night of Christ."

So they took the little fir from its place, and carried it in joyous procession to the edge of the glade, and laid it on the sledge. The horses tossed their heads and drew their load bravely, as if the new burden had made it lighter.

When they came to the house of Gundhar, he bade them throw open the doors of the hall and set the tree in the midst of it. They kindled lights among the branches until it seemed to be tangled full of fire-flies. The children encircled it, wondering, and the sweet odour of the balsam filled the house.

Then Winfried stood beside the chair of Gundhar, on the daïs at the end of the hall, and told the story of Bethlehem; of the babe in the manger, of the shepherds on the hills, of the host of angels and their midnight song. All the people listened, charmed into stillness.

But the boy Bernhard, on Irma's knee, folded by her soft arm, grew restless as the story lengthened, and began to prattle softly at his mother's ear.

"Mother," whispered the child, "why did you cry out so loud, when the priest was going to send me to Valhalla?"

"Oh, hush, my child," answered the mother, and pressed him closer to her side.

"Mother," whispered the boy again, laying his finger on the stains upon her breast, "see, your dress is red! What are these stains? Did some one hurt you?"

The mother closed his mouth with a kiss. "Dear, be still, and listen!"

The boy obeyed. His eyes were heavy with sleep. But he heard the last words of Winfried as he spoke of the angelic messengers, flying over the hills of Judea and singing as they flew. The child wondered and dreamed and listened. Suddenly his face grew bright. He put his lips close to Irma's cheek again.

"Oh, mother!" he whispered very low, "do not speak. Do you hear them? Those angels have come back again. They are singing now behind the tree."

And some say that it was true; but others say that it was only Gregor and his companions at the lower end of the hall, chanting their Christmas hymn:

All glory be to God on high,
And to the earth be peace!
Good-will, henceforth, from heaven to men
Begin, and never cease.

ANNIE TRUMBULL SLOSSON

Fishin' Jimmy

Annie Trumbull Slosson (1838–1926)

A CRITIC OF AN EARLIER DAY called Mrs. Slosson "the defender of the eccentric mystic . . . of God's Fools," adding that the other-worldliness of her characters linked her in spirit with the greater writers who had dealt with the transcendental aspects of the New England mind. Indeed, he confessed that readers who had not encountered the type in person among the remoter hills of Vermont and New Hampshire might refuse belief in it as the central character of a story.

In her tiny output of fiction, Annie Trumbull Slosson portrayed people who were all shrewd, witty, of simple dignity and undoubtedly "off." Her story-telling technique is as unpretentious as china-painting, and as effective within its limits. She admired the people of whom she wrote, and trusted that her readers would understand and admire them. Hers are gentle stories, filled with New England bitter-sweet, and the wild flowers she knew and loved so well, and the song of birds. Fishin' Jimmy is truly representative of her slight but genuine talent.

FISHIN' JIMMY

I

IT WAS on the margin of Pond Brook, just back of Uncle Eben's, that I first saw Fishin' Jimmy. It was early June, and we were again at Franconia, that peaceful little village among the northern hills.

The boys, as usual, were tempting the trout with false fly or real worm, and I was roaming along the bank, seeking spring flowers, and hunting early butterflies and moths. Suddenly there was a little plash in the water at the spot where Ralph was fishing, the slender tip of his rod bent, I heard a voice cry out, "Strike him, sonny, strike him!" and an old man came quickly but noiselessly through the bushes, just as Ralph's line flew up into space, with, alas! no shining, spotted trout upon the hook. The new comer was a spare, wiry man of middle height, with a slight stoop in his shoulders, a thin brown face, and scanty gray hair. He carried a fishing-rod and had some small trout strung on a forked stick in one hand. A simple, homely figure, yet he stands out in memory just as I saw him then, no more to be forgotten than the granite hills, the rushing streams, the cascades of that north country I love so well.

We fell into talk at once, Ralph and Waldo rushing eagerly into questions about the fish, the bait, the best spots in the stream, advancing their own small theories, and asking advice from their new friend. For friend he seemed even in that first hour, as he began simply, but so wisely, to teach my boys the art he loved. They are older now, and are no mean anglers, I believe; but they look back gratefully to those brookside lessons, and acknowledge gladly their obligations to Fishin' Jimmy. But it is not of these practical teachings I would now speak; rather of the lessons of simple faith, of unwearied patience, of self-denial and cheerful endurance, which the old man himself seemed to have learned, strangely enough, from the very sport so often called cruel and murderous. Incomprehensible as it may seem, to his simple intellect the fisherman's art was a whole system of morality, a guide for every-day life, an education, a gospel. It was all any poor mortal man, woman, or child, needed in this world to make him or her happy, useful, good.

At first we scarcely realized this, and wondered greatly at certain things he said, and the tone in which he said them. I remember at that first meeting I asked him, rather carelessly, "Do you like fishing?" He did not reply at first; then he looked at me with those odd, limpid, green-gray eyes of his which always seemed to reflect the clear waters of mountain streams, and said very quietly: "You would n't ask me if I liked my mother—or my wife." And he always spoke of his pursuit as one speaks of something very dear, very sacred. Part of his story I learned from others, but most of it from himself, bit by bit, as we wandered together day by day in that lovely hill-country. As I tell it over again I seem to hear the rush of mountain streams, the "sound of a going in the tops of the trees," the sweet, pensive strain of white-throat sparrow, and the plash of leaping trout; to see the crystal-clear waters pouring over granite rock, the wonderful purple light upon the mountains, the flash and glint of darting fish, the tender green of early summer in the north country.

Fishin' Jimmy's real name was James Whitcher. He was born in the Franconia Valley of northern New Hampshire, and his whole life had been passed there. He had always fished; he could not remember when or how he learned the art. From the days when, a tiny, bare-legged urchin in ragged frock, he had dropped his piece of string with its bent pin at the end into the narrow, shallow brooklet behind his father's house, through early boyhood's season of roaming along Gale River, wading Black Brook, rowing a leaky boat on Streeter or Mink Pond, through youth, through manhood, on and on into old age, his life had apparently been one long day's fishing—an angler's holiday. Had it been only that? He had not cared for books, or school, and all efforts to tie him down to study were unavailing. But he knew well the books of running brooks. No dry botanical text-book or manual could have taught him all he now knew of plants and flowers and trees.

He did not call the yellow spatterdock *Nuphar advena,* but he knew its large leaves of rich green, where the black bass or pickerel sheltered themselves from the summer sun, and its yellow balls on stout stems, around which his line so often twined and twisted, or in which the hook caught, not to be jerked out till the long, green, juicy stalk itself, topped with globe of greenish gold, came up from its wet bed. He knew the sedges along the bank with their nodding tassels and stiff lance-like leaves, the feathery grasses, the velvet moss upon the wet stones, the sea-green lichen on boulder or tree-trunk. There, in that corner of Echo Lake, grew the thickest patch of pipe-wort, with its small, round, grayish-white, mushroom-shaped tops on long, slender stems. If he had styled it *Eriocaulon septangulare,* would it have shown a closer knowledge of its habits than did his careful avoidance of its vicinity, his keeping line and flies at a safe distance, as he muttered to himself, "Them pesky butt'ns agin!" He knew by sight the bur-reed of mountain ponds, with its round, prickly balls strung like big beads on the stiff, erect stalks; the little water-lobelia, with tiny purple blossoms, springing from the waters of lake and pond. He knew, too, all the strange, beautiful under-water growth: bladderwort in long, feathery garlands, pellucid water-weed, quillwort in stiff little bunches with sharp-pointed leaves of olive-green,—all so seldom seen save by the angler whose hooks draw up from time to time the wet, lovely tangle. I remember the amusement with which a certain well-known botanist, who had journeyed to the mountains in search of a little plant, found many years ago near Echo Lake, but not since seen, heard me propose to consult Fishin' Jimmy on the subject. But I was wiser than he knew. Jimmy looked at the specimen brought as an aid to identification. It was dry and flattened, and as unlike a living, growing plant as are generally the specimens from an herbarium. But it showed the awl-shaped leaves, and thread-like stalk with its tiny round seed-vessels, like those of our common shepherd's-purse, and Jimmy knew it at once. "There's a dreffle lot o' that peppergrass out in deep water there, jest where I ketched the big pick'ril," he said quietly. "I seen it nigh a foot high, an' it 's juicier and livin'er than them dead sticks in your book." At our request he accompanied the unbelieving botanist and myself to the spot; and there, looking down through the sunlit water, we saw great patches of that rare and long-lost plant of the Cruciferae known to science as *Subularia aquatica.* For forty years it had hidden itself away, growing and blossoming and casting abroad its tiny seeds in its watery home, unseen, or at least unnoticed, by living soul, save by the keen, soft, limpid eyes of Fishin' Jimmy. And he knew the trees and shrubs so well: the alder and birch from which as a boy he cut his simple, pliant pole; the shadblow and iron-wood (he called them, respectively, sugarplum and hard-hack) which he used for the more ambitious rods of maturer years; the mooseberry, wayfaring-tree, hobble-bush, or triptoe,—it has all these names, with stout, trailing branches, over which he stumbled as he hurried through the woods and underbrush in the darkening twilight.

He had never heard of entomology. Guénée, Hübner, and Fabricius were unknown names; but he could have told these worthies many new things. Did they know just at what hour the trout ceased leaping at dark fly or moth, and could see only in the dim light the ghostly white miller? Did they know the comparative merits, as a tempting bait, of grasshopper, cricket, spider, or wasp; and could they, with bits of wool, tinsel, and feather, copy the real dipterous, hymenopterous, or orthopterous insect? And the birds: he knew them as do few ornithologists, by sight, by sound, by little ways and tricks of their own, known only to themselves and him. The white-throat sparrow with its sweet, far-reaching chant; the hermit-thrush with its chime of bells in the calm summer twilight; the vesper-sparrow that ran before him as he crossed the meadow, or sang for hours, as he fished the stream, its unvarying, but scarcely monotonous little strain; the cedar-bird, with its smooth brown coat of Quaker simplicity, and speech as brief and simple as Quaker yea or nay; the winter-wren sending out his strange, lovely, liquid warble from the high, rocky side of Cannon Mountain; the bluebird of the early spring, so welcome to the winter-weary dwellers in that land of ice and snow, as he

"From the bluer deeps
Lets fall a quick, prophetic strain,"

of summer, of streams freed and flowing again, of waking, darting, eager fish; the veery, the phoebe, the jay, the vireo,—all these were friends, familiar, tried, and true to Fishin' Jimmy. The cluck and coo of the cuckoo, the bubbling song of bobolink in buff and black, the watery trill of the stream-loving swamp-sparrow, the whispered whistle of the stealthy, darkness-haunting whippoorwill, the gurgle and gargle of the cow-bunting,—he knew each and all, better than did Audubon, Nuttall, or Wilson. But he never dreamed that even the tiniest of his little favorites bore, in the scientific world, far away from that quiet mountain nest, such names as *Troglodytes hyemalis* or *Melospiza palutris*. He could tell you, too, of strange, shy creatures rarely seen except by the early-rising, late-fishing angler, in quiet, lonesome places: the otter, muskrat, and mink of ponds and lakes,—rival fishers, who bore off prey sometimes from under his very eyes,—field-mice in meadow and pasture, blind, burrowing moles, prickly hedgehogs, brown hares, and social, curious squirrels.

Sometimes he saw deer, in the early morning or in the dusk of the evening, as they came to drink at the lake shore, and looked at him with big, soft eyes not unlike his own. Sometimes a shaggy bear trotted across his path and hid himself in the forest, or a sharp-eared fox ran barking through the bushes. He loved to tell of these things to us who cared to listen, and I still seem to hear his voice saying in hushed tones, after a story of woodland sight or sound: "Nobody don't see 'em but fishermen. Nobody don't hear 'em but fishermen."

II

But it was of another kind of knowledge he oftenest spoke, and of which I shall try to tell you, in his own words as nearly as possible.

First let me say that if there should seem to be the faintest tinge of irreverence in aught I write, I tell my story badly. There was no irreverence in Fishin' Jimmy. He possessed a deep and profound veneration for all things spiritual and heavenly; but it was the veneration of a little child, mingled as is that child's with perfect confidence and utter frankness. And he used the dialect of the country in which he lived.

"As I was tellin' ye," he said, "I allers loved fishin' an' knowed 't was the best thing in the hull airth. I knowed it larnt ye more about creeters an' yarbs an' stuns an' water than books could tell ye. I knowed it made folks patienter an' commonsenser an' weather-wiser an' cuter gen'ally; gin 'em more fac'lty than all the school larnin' in creation. I knowed it was more fillin' than vittles, more rousin' than whisky, more soothin' than lodlum. I knowed it cooled ye off when ye was het, an' het ye when ye was cold. I knowed all that, o' course—any fool knows it. But—will ye b'l'eve it?—I was more 'n twenty-one year old, a man growed, 'fore I foun' out why 't was that away. Father an' mother was Christian folks, good out-an'-out Calv'nist Baptists from over East'n way. They fetched me up right, made me go to meetin' an' read a chapter every Sunday, an' say a hymn Sat'day night a'ter washin'; an' I useter say my prayers mos' nights. I wa'n't a bad boy as boys go. But nobody thought o' tellin' me the one thing, jest the one single thing, that'd ha' made all the diffunce. I knowed about God, an' how he made me an' made the airth, an' everythin', an' once I got thinkin' about that, an' I asked my father if God made the fishes. He said 'course he did, the sea an' all that in 'em is; but somehow that did n't seem to mean nothin' much to me, an' I lost my int'rist agin. An' I read the Scripter account o' Jonah an' the big fish, an' all that in Job about pullin' out levi'thing with a hook an' stickin' fish spears in his head, an' some parts in them queer books nigh the end o' the ole Test'ment about fish-ponds an' fish-gates an' fish-pools, an' how the fishers shall l'ment—everything I could pick out about fishin' an' sech; but it did n't come home to me; 't wa'n't my kind o' fishin' an' I did n't seem ter sense it.

"But one day—it 's more 'n forty year ago now, but I rec'lect it same 's 't was yest'day, an' I shall rec'lect it forty thousand year from now if I 'm 'round, an' I guess I shall be—I heerd—suthin'—diffunt. I was down in the village one Sunday; it wa'n't very good fishin'—the streams was too full; an' I thought I'd jest look into the meetin'-house 's I went by. 'T was the ole union meetin'-house, down to the corner, ye know, an' they had n't got no reg'lar s'pply, an' ye never knowed what sort ye 'd hear, so 't was kind o' excitin'.

"'T was late, 'most 'leven o'clock, an' the sarm'n had begun.

There was a strange man a-preachin', some one from over to the hotel. I never heerd his name, I never seed him from that day to this; but I knowed his face. Queer enough I 'd seed him a-fishin'. I never knowed he was a min'ster; he did n't look like one. He went about like a real fisherman, with ole clo'es an' an ole hat with hooks stuck in it, an' big rubber boots, an' he fished, reely fished, I mean—ketched 'em. I guess 't was that made me liss'n a leetle sharper 'n us'al, for I never seed a fishin' min'ster afore. Elder Jacks'n, he said 't was a sinf'l waste o' time, an' ole Parson Loomis, he 'd an idee it was cruel an' onmarciful; so I thought I 'd jest see what this man 'd preach about, an' I settled down to liss'n to the sarm'n.

"But there wa'n't no sarm'n; not what I 'd been raised to think was the on'y true kind. There wa'n't no heads, no fustlys nor sec'ndlys, nor fin'ly bruthrins, but the first thing I knowed I was hearin' a story, an' 't was a fishin' story. 'T was about Some One—I had n't the least idee then who 't was, an' how much it all meant—Some One that was dreffle fond o' fishin' an' fishermen, Some One that sot every-thin' by the water, an' useter go along by the lakes an' ponds, an' sail on 'em, an' talk with the men that was fishin'. An' how the fishermen all liked him, 'nd asked his 'dvice, an' done jest 's he telled 'em about the likeliest places to fish; an' how they allers ketched more for mindin' him; an' how when he was a-preachin' he would n't go into a big meetin'-house an' talk to rich folks all slicked up, but he 'd jest go out in a fishin' boat, an' ask the men to shove out a mite, an' he 'd talk to the folks on shore, the fishin' folks an' their wives an' the boys an' gals playin' on the shore. An' then, best o' everythin', he telled how when he was a-choosin' the men to go about with him an' help him an' larn his ways so 's to come a'ter him, he fust o' all picked out the men he'd seen every day fishin', an' mebbe fished with hisself; for he knowed 'em an' knowed he could trust 'em.

"An' then he telled us about the day when this preacher come along by the lake—a dreffle sightly place, this min'ster said; he 'd seed it hisself when he was trav'lin' in them countries—an' come acrost two men he knowed well; they was brothers, an' they was a-fishin'. An' he jest asked 'em in his pleasant-spoken, frien'ly way—there wa'n't never sech a drawin', takin', lovin' way with any one afore as this man had, the min'ster said—he jest asked 'em to come along with him; an' they lay down their poles an' their lines an' everythin', an' jined him. An' then he come along a spell further, an' he sees two boys out with their ole father, an' they was settin' in a boat an' fixin' up their tackle, an' he asked 'em if they'd jine him, too, an' they jest dropped all their things, an' left the ole man with the boat an' the fish an' the bait an' follered the preacher. I don't tell it very good. I 've read it an' read it sence that; but I want to make ye see how it sounded to me, how I took it, as the min'ster telled it that summer day in Francony meetin'. Ye see I'd no idee who the story was about, the man put it so plain, in common kind o' talk, without any come-to-passes an' whuffers an' thuffers, an' I never conceited 't was a Bible narr'tive.

"An' so fust thing I knowed I says to myself, 'That 's the kind o' teacher I want. If I could come acrost a man like that, I 'd jest foller him, too, through thick an' thin.' Well, I can't put the rest on it into talk very good; 't aint jest the kind o' thing to speak on 'fore folks, even sech good friends as you. I aint the sort to go back on my word,—fishermen aint, ye know,—an' what I'd said to myself 'fore I knowed who I was bindin' myself to, I stuck to a'terwards when I knowed all about him. For 't aint for me to tell ye, who've got so much more larnin' than me, that there was a dreffle lot more to that story than the fishin' part. That lovin', givin' up, suff'rin', dyin' part, ye know it all yerself, an' I can't kinder say much on it, 'cept when I 'm jest all by myself, or—'long o' him.

"That a'ternoon I took my ole Bible that I had n't read much sence I growed up, an' I went out into the woods 'long the river, an' 'stid o' fishin' I jest sot down an' read that hull story. Now ye know it yerself by heart, an' ye 've knowed it all yer born days, so ye can't begin to tell how new an' 'stonishin' 't was to me, an' how findin' so much fishin' in it kinder helped me unnerstan' an' b'l'eve it every mite, an' take it right hum to me to foller an' live up to 's long 's I live an' breathe. Did j'ever think on it, reely? I tell ye, his r'liging 's a fishin' r'liging all through. His friends was fishin' folks; his pulpit was a fishin' boat, or the shore o' the lake; he loved the ponds an' streams; an' when his d'sciples went out fishin', if he did n't go hisself with 'em, he'd go a'ter 'em, walkin' on the water, to cheer 'em up an' comfort 'em.

"An' he was allers 'round the water; for the story 'll say, 'he come to the seashore,' or 'he begun to teach by the seaside,' or again, 'he entered into a boat,' an' 'he was in the stern o' the boat, asleep.'

"An' he used fish in his mir'cles. He fed that crowd o' folks on fish when they was hungry, bought 'em from a little chap on the shore. I 've oft'n thought how dreffle tickled that boy must 'a' ben to have him take them fish. Mebbe they wa'n't nothin' but shiners, but the fust the little feller 'd ever ketched; an' boys set a heap on their fust ketch. He was dreffle good to child'en, ye know. An' who 'd he come to a'ter he 'd died, an' ris agin? Why, he come down to the shore 'fore daylight, an' looked off over the pond to where his ole frien's was a-fishin'. Ye see they 'd gone out jest to quiet their minds an' keep up their sperrits; ther 's nothin' like fishin' for that, ye know, an' they 'd ben in a heap o' trubble. When they was settin' up the night afore, worryin' an' wond'rin' an' s'misin' what was goin' ter become on 'em without their master, Peter 'd got kinder desprit, an' he up an' says in his quick way, says he, 'Anyway, *I* 'm goin' a-fishin'.' An' they all see the sense on it,—any fisherman would,—an' they says, says they, 'We 'll go 'long too.' But they did n't ketch anythin'. I suppose they could n't fix their minds on it, an' everythin' went wrong like. But when mornin' come creepin' up over the mountings, fust thin' they knowed they see him on the bank, an' he called out to 'em to know if they'd ketched anythin'. The water jest run down my cheeks when I heerd the min'ster tell that, an' it kinder makes my eyes wet every time I think on 't. For 't seems 's if it might 'a' ben me in that boat, who heern that v'ice I loved so dreffle well speak up agin so nat'ral from the bank there. An' he eat some o' their fish! O' course he done it to sot their minds easy, to show 'em he wa'n't quite a sperrit yit, but jest their own ole frien' who 'd ben out in the boat with 'em so many, many times. But seems to me, jest the fac' he done it kinder makes fish an' fishin' diffunt from any other thing in the hull airth. I tell ye them four books that gin his story is chock full o' things that go right to the heart o' fishermen,—nets, an' hooks, an' boats, an' the shores, an' the sea, an' the mountings, Peter's fishin'-coat, lilies, an' sparrers, an' grass o' the fields, an' all about the evenin' sky bein' red or lowerin', an' fair or foul weather.

"It 's an out-doors, woodsy, country story, 'sides bein' the heav'n-liest one that was ever telled. I read the hull Bible, as a duty ye know. I read the epis'les, but somehow they don't come home to me. Paul was a great man, a dreffle smart scholar, but he was raised in the city, I guess, an' when I go from the gospils into Paul's writin's it 's like goin' from the woods an' hills an' streams o' Francony into the streets of a big city like Concord or Manch'ster."

The old man did not say much of his after life and the fruits of this strange conversion, but his neighbors told us a great deal. They spoke of his unselfishness, his charity, his kindly deeds; told of his visiting the poor and unhappy, nursing the sick. They said the little children loved him, and every one in the village and for miles around trusted and leaned upon Fishin' Jimmy. He taught the boys to fish, sometimes the girls too; and while learning to cast and strike, to whip the stream, they drank in knowledge of higher things, and came to know and love Jimmy's "fishin' r'liging." I remember they told me of a little French Canadian girl, a poor, wretched waif, whose mother, an unknown tramp, had fallen dead in the road near the village. The child, an untamed little heathen, was found clinging to her mother's body in an agony of grief and rage, and fought like a tiger when they tried to take her away. A boy in the little group attracted to the spot, ran away, with a child's faith in his old friend, to summon Fishin' Jimmy. He came quickly, lifted the little savage tenderly, and carried her away.

No one witnessed the taming process, but in a few days the pair were seen together on the margin of Black Brook, each with a fish-pole. Her dark face was bright with interest and excitement as she took her first lesson in the art of angling. She jabbered and chattered in her odd patois, he answered in broadest New England dialect, but the two quite understood each other, and though Jimmy said afterward that it was "dreffle to hear her call the fish pois'n," they were soon great friends and comrades. For weeks he kept and cared for the child, and when she left him for a good home in Bethlehem, one would scarcely have recognized in the gentle, affectionate girl the wild creature of the past. Though often questioned as to the means used to effect this change, Jimmy's explanation seemed rather vague and unsatisfactory. " 'T was fishin' done it," he said; "on'y fishin'; it allers works. The Christian r'liging itself had to begin with fishin', ye know."

III

But one thing troubled Fishin' Jimmy. He wanted to be a "fisher of men." That was what the Great Teacher had promised he would make the fishermen who left their boats to follow him. What strange, literal meaning he attached to the terms, we could not tell. In vain we—especially the boys, whose young hearts had gone out in warm affection to the old man—tried to show him that he was, by his efforts to do good and make others better and happier, fulfilling the Lord's directions. He could not understand it so. "I allers try to think," he said, "that 't was me in that boat when he come along. I make b'l'eve that it was out on Streeter Pond, an' I was settin' in the boat, fixin' my lan'in' net, when I see him on the shore. I think mebbe I 'm that James—for that 's my given name, ye know, though they allers call me Jimmy—an' then I hear him callin' me 'James, James.' I can hear him jest 's plain sometimes, when the wind 's blowin' in the trees, an' I jest ache to up an' foller him. But says he, 'I 'll make ye a fisher o' men,' an' he aint done it. I 'm waitin'; mebbe he 'll larn me some day."

He was fond of all living creatures, merciful to all. But his love for our dog Dash became a passion, for Dash was an angler. Who that ever saw him sitting in the boat beside his master, watching with eager eye and whole body trembling with excitement the line as it was cast, the flies as they touched the surface—who can forget old Dash? His fierce excitement at rise of trout, the efforts at self-restraint, the disappointment if the prey escaped, the wild exultation if it was captured, how plainly—he who runs might read—were shown these emotions in eye, in ear, in tail, in whole quivering body! What wonder that it all went straight to the fisher's heart of Jimmy! "I never knowed afore they could be Christians," he said, looking, with tears in his soft, keen eyes, at the every-day scene, and with no faintest thought of irreverence. "I never knowed it, but I 'd give a stiffikit o' membership in the orthodoxest church goin' to that dog there."

It is almost needless to say that as years went on Jimmy came to know many "fishin' min'sters"; for there are many of that school who know our mountain country, and seek it yearly. All these knew and loved the old man. And there were others who had wandered by that sea of Galilee, and fished in the waters of the Holy Land, and with them Fishin' Jimmy dearly loved to talk. But his wonder was never-ending that, in the scheme of evangelizing the world, more use was not made of the "fishin' side" of the story. "Haint they ever tried it on them poor heathen?" he would ask earnestly of some clerical angler casting a fly upon the clear water of pond or brook. "I should think 't would 'a' ben the fust thing they 'd done. Fishin' fust, an' r'liging 's sure to foller. An' it 's so easy; fur heath'n mostly r'sides on islands, don't they? So ther 's plenty o' water, an' o' course ther 's fishin'; an' oncet gin 'em poles an' git 'em to work, an' they 're out o' mischief fur that day. They 'd like it better 'n cannib'ling, or cuttin' out idles, or scratchin' picters all over theirselves, an' bimeby—not too suddent, ye know, to scare 'em—ye could begin on that story, an' they could n't stan' that, not a heath'n on 'em. Won't ye speak to the 'Merican Board about it, an' sen' out a few fishin' mishneries, with poles an' lines an' tackle gen'ally? I 've tried it on dreffle bad folks, an' it allers done 'em good. But"—so almost all his simple talk ended—"I wish I could begin to be a fisher o' men. I 'm gettin' on now, I 'm nigh seventy, an' I aint got much time, ye see."

One afternoon in July there came over Franconia Notch one of those strangely sudden tempests which sometimes visit that mountain country. It had been warm that day, unusually warm for that refreshingly cool spot; but suddenly the sky grew dark and darker, almost to blackness, there was roll of thunder and flash of lightning, and then poured down the rain—rain at first, but soon hail in large frozen bullets, which fiercely pelted any who ventured outdoors, rattled against the windows of the Profile House with sharp cracks like sounds of musketry, and lay upon the piazza in heaps like snow. And in the midst of the wild storm it was remembered that two boys, guests at the hotel, had gone up Mount Lafayette alone that day. They were young boys, unused to mountain climbing, and their friends were anxious. It was found that Dash had followed them; and just as some one was to be sent in search of them, a boy from the stables brought the information that Fishin' Jimmy had started up the mountain after them as the storm broke. "Said if he could n't be a fisher o' men, mebbe he knowed nuff to ketch boys," went on our informant, seeing nothing more in the speech, full of pathetic meaning to us who knew him, than the idle talk of one whom many considered "lackin'." Jimmy was old now, and had of late grown very feeble, and we did not like to think of him out in that wild storm. And now suddenly the lost boys themselves appeared through the opening in the woods opposite the house, and ran in through the sleet, now falling more quietly. They were wet, but no worse apparently for their adventure, though full of contrition and distress at having lost sight of the dog. He had rushed off into the woods some hours before, after a rabbit or hedgehog, and had never returned. Nor had they seen Fishin' Jimmy.

As hours went by and the old man did not return, a search party was sent out, and guides familiar with the mountain paths went up Lafayette to seek for him. It was nearly night when they at last found him, and the grand old mountains had put on those robes of royal purple which they sometimes assume at eventide. At the foot of a mass of rock, which looked like amethyst or wine-red agate in that marvellous evening light, the old man was lying, and Dash was with him. From the few faint words Jimmy could then gasp out, the truth was gathered. He had missed the boys, leaving the path by which they had returned, and while stumbling along in search of them, feeble and weary, he had heard far below a sound of distress. Looking down over a steep, rocky ledge, he had seen his friend and fishing comrade, old Dash, in sore trouble. Poor Dash! He never dreamed of harming his old friend, for he had a kind heart. But he was a sad coward in some matters, and a very baby when frightened and away from master and friends. So I fear he may have assumed the rôle of wounded sufferer when in reality he was but scared and lonesome. He never owned this afterward, and you may be sure we never let him know, by word or look, the evil he had done. Jimmy saw him holding up one paw helplessly, and looking at him with wistful, imploring brown eyes, heard his pitiful whimpering cry for aid, and never doubted his great distress and peril. Was Dash not a fisherman? And fishermen, in Fishin' Jimmy's category, were always true and trusty. So the old man without a second's hesitation started down the steep, smooth decline to the rescue of his friend.

We do not know just how or where in that terrible descent he fell. To us who afterward saw the spot, and thought of the weak old man, chilled by the storm, exhausted by his exertions, and yet clambering down that precipitous cliff, made more slippery and treacherous by the sleet and hail still falling, it seemed impossible that he could have kept a foothold for an instant. Nor am I sure that he expected to save himself, and Dash too. But he tried. He was sadly hurt. I will not tell you of that.

Looking out from the hotel windows through the gathering darkness, we who loved him—it was not a small group—saw a sorrowful sight. Flickering lights thrown by the lanterns of the guides came through the woods. Across the road, slowly, carefully, came strong men, bearing on a rough, hastily made litter of boughs the dear old man. All that could have been done for the most distinguished guest, for the dearest, best-beloved friend, was done for the gentle fisherman. We, his friends, and proud to style ourselves thus, were of different, widely separated lands, greatly varying creeds. Some were nearly as old as the dying man, some in the prime of manhood. There were youths and maidens and little children. But through the night we watched together. The old Roman bishop, whose calm, benign face we all know and love; the Churchman, ascetic in faith, but with the kindest, most indulgent heart when one finds it; the gentle old Quakeress with placid, unwrinkled brow and silvery hair; Presbyterian, Methodist, and Baptist,—we were all one that night. The old angler did not suffer—we were so glad of that! But he did not appear to know us, and his talk seemed strange. It rambled on quietly, softly, like one of his own mountain brooks, babbling of green fields, of sunny summer days, of his favorite sport, and ah! of other things. But he was not speaking to us. A sudden, awed hush and thrill came over us as, bending to catch the low words, we all at once understood what only the bishop put into words as he said, half to himself, in a sudden, quick, broken whisper, "God bless the man, he 's talking to his Master!"

"Yes, sir, that 's so," went on the quiet voice; " 't was on'y a dog sure nuff; 'twa'n't even a boy, as ye say, an' ye ast me to be a fisher o' men. But I haint had no chance for that, somehow; mebbe I wa'n't fit for 't. I 'm on'y jest a poor old fisherman, Fishin' Jimmy, ye know, sir. Ye useter call me James—no one else ever done it. On'y a dog? But he wa'n't jest a common dog, sir; he was a fishin' dog. I never seed a man love fishin' mor 'n Dash." The dog was in the room, and heard his name. Stealing to the bedside, he put a cold nose into the cold hand of his old friend, and no one had the heart to take him away. The touch turned the current of the old man's talk for a moment, and he was fishing again with his dog friend. "See 'em break, Dashy! See 'em break! Lots on 'em to-day, aint they? Keep still, there 's a good dog, while I put on a diffunt fly. Don't ye see they 're jumpin' at them gnats? Aint the water jest 'live with 'em? Aint it shinin' an' clear an'—" The voice faltered an instant, then went on: "Yes, sir, I 'm comin'—I 'm glad, dreffle glad to come. Don't mind 'bout my leavin' my fishin'; do ye think I care 'bout that? I 'll jest lay down my pole ahin' the alders here, an' put my lan'in' net on the stuns, with my flies an' tackle—the boys 'll like 'em, ye know—an' I 'll be right along.

"I mos' knowed ye was on'y a-tryin' me when ye said that 'bout how I had n't been a fisher o' men, nor even boys, on'y a dog. 'T was a—fishin' dog—ye know—an' ye was allers dreffle good to fishermen, —dreffle good to—everybody; died—for 'em, did n't ye?—

"Please wait—on—the bank there, a minnit; I 'm comin' 'crost. Water 's pretty—cold this—spring—an' the stream 's risin'—but—I—can—do it;—don't ye mind—'bout me, sir. I 'll get acrost." Once more the voice ceased, and we thought we should not hear it again this side that stream.

But suddenly a strange light came over the thin face, the soft gray eyes opened wide, and he cried out, with the strong voice we had so often heard come ringing out to us across the mountain streams above the sound of their rushing: "Here I be, sir! It 's Fishin' Jimmy, ye know, from Francony way; him ye useter call James when ye come 'long the shore o' the pond an' I was a-fishin'. I heern ye agin, jest now—an' I—straightway—f'sook—my—nets—an'—follered—"

Had the voice ceased utterly? No, we could catch faint, low murmurs and the lips still moved. But the words were not for us; and we did not know when he reached the other bank.

ERNEST THOMPSON SETON

The Trail of the Sandhill Stag

Ernest Thompson Seton (1860–1946)

SETON'S FAME *as illustrator and prose-poet of the outdoors and its creatures was the reward of a hard apprenticeship. His family emigrated to the Canadian backwoods from their native South Shields in England when he was about six years of age, and his childhood was passed near Lindsay, Ontario, amid the screech of sawmills and a great bustle of frontier activity. His chief memory of the place was "the pervading, sweet, sanctifying smell of new-cut boards of pine."*

Soon he was acquiring a unique education in his "college of handicraft" as he called it; for all the family turned to, and were axemen, hunters, carpenters and woodsmen as occasion demanded. He learned to fight his own battles, to observe the smallest details of plant and animal life, and to love every wild thing that ran or crawled or flew—indeed, to become the apologist for even the least beautiful of them.

In April, 1870, the family said goodbye to the woods and moved to Toronto, but Ernest had found his vocation in those early years. Along with his passion for natural history, he showed a talent for drawing and made formal art studies in Canada and at the Royal Academy in London. His evenings were spent in libraries, wherever he might be; in close study of the classic books on nature and the animal kingdom. In his London days, and later when he attended Julian's atelier in Paris, he was to be found sketching as often in the zoo as in the studio, and his skill as an animal painter developed rapidly and surely.

Overwork reduced his health, and in a kind of despair he returned to Canada, to Manitoba, where, in the wild country, he soon regained his tone and broadened enormously his practical knowledge of wood and stream. More than this, he learned that only in the closest communion with nature did he thrive, and in a symbolic gesture he destroyed whatever souvenirs he had kept of his European adventures.

Thereafter, he was to work as a naturalist for the government of Manitoba, to write more than thirty books on wild life and woodcraft and illustrate them as only he could, to travel widely, to know all sorts and conditions of men. Kipling was to pay him graceful tribute and credit several of his early stories as the inspiration for his own Jungle Books. *But his philosophy was to remain simple, indeed primitive—a mysticism of the inter-relation of man and the wild more akin to the Indian's pattern of life than the white man's. This attitude of mind is dominant in* The Trail of the Sandhill Stag*—a splendid tale, filled with Seton's memories of his Canadian youth.*

THE TRAIL OF THE SANDHILL STAG

I

IT WAS a burning hot day. Yan was wandering in pursuit of birds among the endless groves and glades of the Sandhill wilderness about Carberry. The water in the numerous marshy ponds was warm with the sun heat, so Yan cut across to the trail spring, the only place in the country where he might find a cooling drink. As he stooped beside it his eye fell on a small hoof-mark in the mud, a sharp and elegant track. He had never seen one like it before, but it gave him a thrill, for he knew at once it was the track of a wild deer.

"There are no deer in those hills now," the settlers told Yan. Yet when the first snow came that autumn he, remembering the hoof-mark in the mud, quietly took down his rifle and said to himself, "I am going into the hills every day till I bring out a deer." Yan was a tall, raw lad in the last of his teens. He was no hunter yet, but he was a tireless runner, and filled with unflagging zeal. Away to the hills he went on his quest day after day, and many a score of long white miles he coursed, and night after night he returned to the shanty without seeing even a track. But the longest chase will end. On a far, hard trip in the southern hills he came at last on the trail of a deer—dim and stale, but still a deer-trail—and again he felt a thrill as the thought came, "At the other end of that line of dimples in the snow is the creature that made them; each one is fresher than the last, and it is only a question of time for me to come up with their maker."

At first Yan could not tell by the dim track which way the animal had gone. But he soon found that the mark was a little sharper at one end, and rightly guessed that that was the toe; also he noticed that the spaces shortened in going up hill, and at last a clear imprint in a sandy place ended all doubt. Away he went with a new fire in his blood, and an odd prickling in his hair; away on a long, hard follow through interminable woods and hills, with the trail growing fresher as he flew. All day he followed, and toward night it turned and led him homeward. On it went, soon over familiar ground, back to the sawmill, then over Mitchell's Plain, and at last into the thick poplar woods near by, where Yan left it when it was too dark to follow. He was only seven miles from home, and this he easily trotted in an hour.

In the morning he was back to take it up, but instead of an old track, there were now so many fresh ones, crossing and winding, that he could not follow at all. So he prowled along haphazard, until he found two tracks so new that he could easily trail them as before, and he eagerly gave chase. As he sneaked along watching the tracks at his feet instead of the woods ahead, he was startled by two big-eared grayish animals springing from a little glade into which he had stumbled. They trotted to a bank fifty yards away and then turned to gaze at him.

How they did seem to *look* with their great ears! How they spell-bound him by the soft gaze that he felt rather than saw! He knew what they were. Had he not for weeks been holding ready, preparing and hungering for this very sight! And yet how useless were his preparations; how wholly all his preconcepts were swept away, and a wonder-stricken "Oh-h-h!" went softly from his throat.

As he stood and gazed, they turned their heads away, though they still seemed to look at him with their great ears, and trotting a few steps to a smoother place, began to bound up and down in a sort of play. They seemed to have forgotten him, and it was bewildering to see the wonderful effortless way in which, by a tiny toe-touch, they would rise six or eight feet in air. Yan stood fascinated by the strange play of the light-limbed, gray-furred creatures. There was no haste or alarm in their movements; he would watch them until they began to run away—till they should take fright and begin the labored straining, the vast athletic bounds, he had heard of. And it was only on noting that they were rapidly fading into the distance that he realized that *now* they were running away, *already* were flying for safety.

Higher and higher they rose each time; gracefully their bodies swayed inward as they curved along some bold ridge, or for a long space the buff-white scutcheons that they bore behind them seemed hanging in the air while these wingless birds were really sailing over some deep gully.

Yan stood intensely gazing until they were out of sight, and it never once occurred to him to shoot.

When they were gone he went to the place where they had begun their play. Here was one track; where was the next? He looked all around and was surprised to see a blank for fifteen feet; and then another blank, and on farther, another: then the blanks increased to eighteen feet, then to twenty, then to twenty-five and sometimes thirty feet. Each of these playful, effortless bounds covered a space of eighteen to thirty feet.

Gods above! They do not run at all, they fly; and once in a while come down again to tap the hill-tops with their dainty hoofs.

"I'm glad they got away," said Yan. "They've shown me something to-day that never man saw before. I know that no one else has ever seen it, or he would have told of it."

II

Yet when the morning came the old wolfish instinct was back in his heart. "I must away to the hills," he said, "take up the trail, and be a beast of the chase once more; my wits against their wits; my strength against their strength; and against their speed, my gun."

Oh! those glorious hills—an endless rolling stretch of sandy dunes, with lakes and woods and grassy lawns between. Life—life on every side, and life within, for Yan was young and strong and joyed in powers complete. "These are the best days of my life," he said, "these are my golden days." He thought it then, and oh, how well he came to know it in the after years!

All day at a long wolf-lope he would go and send the white hare and the partridge flying from his path, and swing along and scan the ground for sign and the telltale inscript in the snow, the oldest of all writing, more thrillful of interest by far than the finest glyph or scarab that ever Egypt gave to modern day.

But the driving snow was the wild deer's friend, as the driven snow was his foe, and down it came that day and wiped out every trace.

The next day and the next still found Yan careering in the hills, but never a track or sign did he see. And the weeks went by, and many a rolling mile he ran, and many a bitter day and freezing night he passed in the snow-clad hills, sometimes on a deer-trail but more often without; sometimes in the barren hills, and sometimes led by woodmen's talk to far-off sheltering woods, and once or twice he saw indeed the buff-white bannerets go floating up the hills. Sometimes reports came of a great buck that frequented the timber-lands near the sawmill, and more than once Yan found his trail, but never got a glimpse of him; and the few deer there were now grew so wild with long pursuit that he had no further chances to shoot, and the hunting season passed in one long train of failures.

Bright, unsad failures they. He seemed indeed to come back empty-handed, but he really came home laden with the best spoils of the chase, and he knew it more and more, as time went on, till every day, at last, on the clear unending trail, was a glad triumphant march.

III

The year went by. Another season came, and Yan felt in his heart the hunter fret once more. Even had he not, the talk he heard would have set him all afire.

It told of a mighty buck that now lived in the hills—the Sandhill Stag they called him. It told of his size, his speed, and the crowning glory that he bore on his brow, a marvellous growth like sculptured bronze with gleaming ivory points.

So when the first tracking snow came, Yan set out with some comrades who had caught a faint reflected glow of his ardor. They drove in a sleigh to the Spruce Hill, then scattered to meet again at sunset. The woods about abounded in hares and grouse, and the powder burned all around. But no deer-track was to be found, so Yan quietly left the woods and set off alone for Kennedy's Plain, where last this wonderful buck had been seen.

After a few miles he came on a great deer-track, so large and sharp and broken by such mighty bounds that he knew it at once for the trail of the Sandhill Stag.

With a sudden rush of strength to his limbs he led away like a wolf on the trail. And down his spine and in his hair he felt as before, and yet as never before, the strange prickling that he knew was the same as makes the wolf's mane bristle when he hunts. He followed till night was near and he must needs turn, for the Spruce Hill was many miles away.

He knew that it would be long after sunset before he could get there, and he scarcely expected that his comrades would wait for him, but he did not care; he gloried in the independence of his strength, for his legs were like iron and his wind was like a hound's. Ten miles were no more to him than a mile to another man, for he could run all day and come home fresh, and always when alone in the lone hills he felt within so glad a gush of wild exhilaration that his joy was full.

So when when his friends, feeling sure that he could take care of himself, drove home and left him, he was glad to be left. They seemed rather to pity him for imposing on himself such long, toilsome tramps. They had no realization of what he found in those wind-swept hills. They never once thought what they and all their friends and every man that ever lived has striven for and offered his body, his brain, his freedom, and his life to buy; what they were vainly wearing out their lives in fearful, hopeless drudgery to gain, that boy was daily finding in those hills. The bitter, biting, blizzard wind was without, but the fire of health and youth was within; and at every stride in his daily march, it was *happiness* he found, and he knew it. And he smiled such a gentle smile when he thought of those driven home in the sleigh shivering and miserable, *yet pitying him.*

Oh, what a glorious sunset he saw that day on Kennedy's Plain, with the snow dyed red and the poplar woods aglow in pink and gold! What a glorious tramp through the darkening woods as the shadows fell and the yellow moon came up!

"These are the best days of my life," he sang. "These are my golden days!"

And as he neared the great Spruce Hill, Yan yelled a long hurrah! "In case they are still there," he told himself, but really for very joy of feeling all alive.

As he listened for the improbable response, he heard a faint howling of wolves away over Kennedy's Plain. He mimicked their cry and quickly got response, and noticed that they were gathering together, doubtless hunting something, for now it was their hunting-cry. Nearer and nearer it came, and his howls brought ready answers from the gloomy echoing woods, when suddenly it flashed upon him: "It's *my* trail you are on. *You are hunting me.*"

The road now led across a little open plain. It would have been madness to climb a tree in such a fearful frost, so he went out to the middle of the open place and sat down in the moonlit snow—a glittering rifle in his hands, a row of shining brass pegs in his belt, and a strange, new feeling in his heart. On came the chorus, a deep, melodious howling, on to the very edge of the woods, and there the note changed. Then there was silence. They must have seen him sitting there, for the light was like day, but they went around in the edge of the woods. A stick snapped to the right and a low '*Woof*' came from the left. Then all was still. Yan felt them sneaking around, felt them watching him from the cover, and strained his eyes in vain to see some form that he might shoot. But they were wise, and he was wise, for had he run he would soon have seen them closing in on him. They must have been but few, for after their council of war they decided he was better let alone, and he never saw them at all. For twenty minutes he waited, but hearing no more of them, arose and went homeward. And as he tramped he thought, "Now I know how a deer feels when the grind of a moccasined foot or the click of a lock is heard in the trail behind him."

In the days that followed he learned those Sandhills well, for many a frosty day and bitter night he spent in them. He learned to follow fast the faintest trail of deer. He learned just why that trail went never past a tamarack-tree, and why it pawed the snow at every oak, and why the buck's is plainest and the fawn's down wind. He learned just what the club-rush has to say, when its tussocks break the snow. He came to know how the musk-rat lives beneath the ice, and why the mink slides down a hill, and what the ice says when it screams at night. The squirrels taught him how best a fir-cone can be stripped and which of toadstools one might eat. The partridge, why it dives beneath the snow, and the fox, just why he sets his feet so straight, and why he wears so huge a tail.

He learned the ponds, the woods, the hills, and a hundred secrets of the trail, but—*he got no deer*.

And though many a score of crooked frosty miles he coursed, and sometimes had a track to lead and sometimes none, he still went on, like Galahad when the Grail was just before him. For more than once, the guide that led was the trail of the Sandhill Stag.

IV

The hunt was nearly over, for the season's end was nigh. The moose-birds had picked the last of the saskatoons, all the spruce-cones were scaled, and the hunger-moon was at hand. But a hopeful chickadee sang '*See soon*' as Yan set off one frosty day for the great Spruce Woods. On the road he overtook a wood-cutter, who told him that at such a place he had seen two deer last night, a doe and a monstrous stag with "a rocking-chair on his head."

Straight to the very place went Yan, and found the tracks—one like those he had seen in the mud long ago, another a large unmistakable print, the mark of the Sandhill Stag.

How the wild beast in his heart did ramp—he wanted to howl like a wolf on a hot scent; and away they went through woods and hills, the trail and Yan and the inner wolf.

All day he followed and, grown crafty himself, remarked each sign, and rejoiced to find that nowhere had the deer been bounding. And when the sun was low the sign was warm, so laying aside unneeded things, Yan crawled along like a snake on the track of a hare. All day the animals had zigzagged as they fed; their drink was snow, and now at length away across a lawn in a bank of brush Yan spied a *something* flash. A bird perhaps; he lay still and watched. Then gray among the gray brush, he made out a great log, and from one end of it rose two gnarled oaken boughs. Again the flash—the move of a restless ear, then the oak boughs moved and Yan trembled, for he knew that the log in the brush was the form of the Sandhill Stag. So grand, so charged with *life*. He seemed a precious, sacred thing—a king, fur-robed and duly crowned. To think of shooting now as he lay unconscious, resting, seemed an awful crime. But Yan for weeks and months had pined for this. His chance had come, and shoot he must. The long, long strain grew tighter yet—grew taut—broke down, as up the rifle went. But the wretched thing kept wabbling and pointing all about the little glade. His breath came hot and fast and choking—so much, so very much, so clearly all, hung on a single touch. He laid the rifle down, revulsed—and trembled in the snow. But he soon regained the mastery, his hand was steady now, the sights in line—'twas but a deer out yonder. But at that moment the Stag turned full Yan's way, with those regardful eyes and ears, and nostrils too, and gazed.

"Darest thou slay me?" said an uncrowned, unarmed king once, as his eyes fell on the assassin's knife, and in that clear, calm gaze the murderer quailed and cowed.

So trembled Yan; but he knew it was only stag-fever, and he despised it then as he came in time to honor it; and the beast that dwelt within him fired the gun.

The ball splashed short. The buck sprang up and the doe appeared. Another shot; then, as they fled, another and another. But away the deer went, lightly drifting across the low round hills.

V

He followed their trail for some time, but gnashed his teeth to find no sign of blood, and he burned with a raging animal sense that was neither love nor hate. Within a mile there was a new sign that joined on and filled him with another rage and shed light on many a bloody page of frontier history—a moccasin-track, a straight-set, broad-toed, moosehide track, the track of a Cree brave. He followed in savage humor, and as he careered up a slope a tall form rose from a log, raising one hand in peaceable gesture. Although Yan was behind, the Indian had seen him first.

"Who are you?" said Yan, roughly.

"Chaska."

"What are you doing in my country?"

"It was my country first," he replied gravely.

"Those are my deer," Yan said, and thought.

"No man owns wild deer till he kills them," said Chaska. "You better keep off any trail I'm following."

"Not afraid," said he, and made a gesture to include the whole settlement, then added gently, "No good to fight; the best man will get the most deer anyhow."

And the end of it was that Yan stayed for several days with Chaska, and got, not an antlered buck indeed, but, better far, an insight into the ways of a man who could hunt. The Indian taught him *not* to follow the trail over the hills, for deer watch their back track, and cross the hills to make this more easy. He taught him to tell by touch and smell of sign just how far ahead they are, as well as the size and condition of the deer, and not to trail closely when the game is near. He taught him to study the wind by raising his moistened finger in the air, and Yan thought, "Now I know why a deer's nose is always moist, for he must always watch the wind." He showed Yan how much may be gained at times by patient waiting, and that it is better to tread like an Indian with foot set straight, for thereby one gains an inch or two at each stride and can come back in one's own track through deep snow. And he also unwittingly taught him that an Indian *cannot* shoot with a rifle, and Natty Bumpo's adage came to mind, "A white man can shoot with a gun, but it ain't accordin' to an Injun's gifts."

Sometimes they went out together and sometimes singly. One day, while out alone, Yan had followed a deer-track into a thicket by what is now called Chaska Lake. The sign was fresh, and as he sneaked around there was a rustle in the brush. Then he saw the kinni-kinnick boughs shaking. His gun flew up and covered the spot. As soon as he was sure of the place he meant to fire. But when he saw the creature as a dusky moving form through the twigs, he awaited a better view, which came, and he had almost pulled the trigger when his hand was stayed by a glimpse of red, and a moment later out stepped—Chaska.

"Chaska," Yan gasped, "I nearly did for you."

For reply the Indian drew his finger across the red handkerchief on his brow. Yan knew then one reason why a hunting Indian always wears it; after that he wore one himself.

One day a flock of prairie-chickens flew high overhead toward the thick Spruce Woods. Others followed, and it seemed to be a general move. Chaska looked toward them and said, "Chickens go hide in bush. Blizzard to-night."

It surely came, and the hunters stayed all day by the fire. Next day it was as fierce as ever. On the third day it ceased somewhat, and they hunted again. But Chaska returned with his gun broken by a fall, and after a long silent smoke he said:

"Yan hunt in Moose Mountain?"

"No!"

"Good hunting. Go?"

Yan shook his head.

Presently the Indian, glancing to the eastward, said, "Sioux tracks there to-day. All bad medicine here." And Yan knew that his mind was made up. He went away and they never met again, and all that is left of him now is his name, borne by the lonely lake that lies in the Carberry Hills.

VI

"There are more deer round Carberry now than ever before, and the Big Stag has been seen between Kennedy's Plain and the mill." So said a note that reached Yan away in the East, where he had been chafing in a new and distasteful life. It was the beginning of the hunting season, the fret was already in his blood, and that letter decided him. For a while the iron horse, for a while the gentle horse, then he donned his moosehide wings and flew as of old on many a long, hard flight, to return as so often before.

Then he heard that at a certain lake far to the eastward seven deer had been seen; their leader a wonderful buck.

With three others he set out in a sleigh to the eastward lake, and soon found the tracks—six of various sizes and one large one, undoubtedly that of the famous Stag.

How utterly the veneer was torn to tatters by those seven chains of tracks! How completely the wild paleolithic beast stood revealed in each of the men, in spite of semi-modern garb, as they drove away on the trail with a wild, excited gleam in every eye!

It was nearly night before the trail warmed up, but even then, in spite of Yan's earnest protest, they drove on in the sleigh. And soon they came to where the trail told of seven keen observers looking backward from a hill, then an even sevenfold chain of twenty-five-foot bounds. The hunters got no glimpse at all, but followed till the night came down, then hastily camped in the snow.

In the morning they followed as before, and soon came to where seven spots of black, bare ground showed where the deer had slept.

Now when the trail grew warm Yan insisted on hunting on foot. He trailed the deer into a great thicket, and knew just where they were by a grouse that flew cackling from its farther side.

He arranged a plan, but his friends would not await the blue-jay's 'all-right' note, and the deer escaped. But finding themselves hard pressed, they split their band, two going one way and five another. Yan kept with him one, Duff, and leaving the others to follow the five deer, he took up the twofold trail. Why? Because in it was the great broad track he had followed for two years back.

On they went, overtaking the deer and causing them again to split. Yan sent Duff after the doe, while he stuck relentlessly to the track of the famous Stag. As the sun got low, the chase led to a great half-wooded stretch, in a country new to him; for he had driven the Stag far from his ancient range. The trail again grew hot, but just as Yan felt sure he soon would close, two distant shots were heard, and the track of the Stag as he found it then went off in a fear-winged flight that might keep on for miles.

Yan went at a run, and soon found Duff. He had had two long shots at the doe. The second he thought had hit her. Within half a mile they found blood on the trail; within another half-mile the blood was no more seen and the track seemed to have grown very large and strong. The snow was drifting and the marks not easily read, yet Yan knew very soon that the track they were on was not that of the wounded doe, but was surely that of her antlered mate. Back on the trail they ran till they solved the doubt, for there they learned that the Stag, after making his own escape, had come back to change off: an old, old trick of the hunted whereby one deer will cleverly join on and carry on the line of tracks to save another that is too hard pressed, while it leaps aside to hide or fly in a different direction. Thus the Stag had sought to save his wounded mate, but the hunters remorselessly took up her trail and gloated like wolves over the slight drip of blood. Within another short run they found that the Stag, having failed to divert the chase to himself, had returned to her, and at sundown they sighted them a quarter of a mile ahead mounting a long snow-slope. The doe was walking slowly, with hanging head and ears. The buck was running about as though in trouble that he did not understand, and coming back to caress the doe and wonder why she walked so slowly. In another half-mile the hunters came up with them. She was down in the snow. When he saw them coming, the great Stag shook the oak-tree on his brow and circled about in doubt, then fled from a foe he was powerless to resist.

As the men came near, the doe made a convulsive effort to rise, but could not. Duff drew his knife. It never before occurred to Yan why he and each of them carried a long knife. The poor doe turned on her foes her great lustrous eyes; they were brimming with tears, but she made no moan. Yan turned his back on the scene and covered his face with his hands, but Duff went forward with the knife and did some dreadful, unspeakable thing, Yan scarcely knew what, and when Duff called him he slowly turned, and the big Stag's mate was lying quiet in the snow, and the only living thing that they saw as they quit the scene was the great round form bearing aloft the oak-tree on its brow as it haunted the nearer hills.

And when, an hour later, the men came with the sleigh to lift the doe's body from the crimsoned snow, there were large fresh tracks about it, and a dark shadow passed over the whitened hill into the silent night.

What morbid thoughts came from the fire that night! How the man in Yan did taunt the glutted brute! Was this the end? Was this the real chase? After long weeks, with the ideal alone in mind, after countless blessed failures, was this the vile success—a beautiful, glorious, living creature tortured into a loathsome mass of carrion?

VII

But when the morning came the impress of the night was dim. A long howl came over the hill, and the thought that a wolf was on the trail that he was quitting smote sadly on Yan's heart. They all set out for the settlement, but within an hour Yan only wanted an excuse to stay. And when at length they ran onto the fresh track of the Sandhill Stag himself, the lad was all ablaze once more.

"I cannot go back—something tells me that I must stay—I must see him face to face again."

The rest had had enough of the bitter frost, so Yan took from the sleigh a small pot, a blanket, and some food, and left them, to follow alone the great sharp imprint in the snow.

"Good-by—good luck!"

He watched the sleigh out of sight, in the low hills, and then felt as he never had before. Though he had been so many months alone in the wilds, he had never known loneliness, but as soon as his friends were gone he was overwhelmed by a sense of the utter heart-sickening dreariness of the endless, snowy waste. Where were the charms that he had never failed to find until now? He wanted to recall the sleigh, but pride kept him silent.

In a little while it was too late, and soon he was once more in the power of that fascinating, endless chain of tracks,—a chain begun years ago, when in a June the track of a mother Blacktail was suddenly joined by two little ones' tracks. Since then the three had gone on winding over the land the trail-chains they were forging,—knotted and kinked, and twisted with every move and thought of the makers, imprinted with every hap of their lives, but interrupted never wholly. At times the tracks were joined by that of some fierce foe and the kind of mark was changed, but the chains went on for months and years, now fast, now slow, but endless, until some foe more strong joined on and there one trail was ended. But this great Stag was forging still that mystic chain. A million roods of hills had he overlaid with its links, had scribbled over in this oldest script with the story of his life. If only our eyes were bright enough to follow up that twenty thousand miles of trail, what light unguessed we might obtain where the wisest now are groping!

But skin deep, man is brute. Just a little while ago we were mere hunting brutes—our bellies were our only thought, that telltale line of dots was the road to food. No man can follow it far without feeling a wild beast prickling in his hair and down his spine.

Away Yan went, a hunter-brute once more, all other feelings swamped.

Late that day the trail, after many a kink and seeming break, led into a great dense thicket of brittle, quaking asp. Yan knew that the Stag was there to lie at rest. The deer went in up-wind, of course. His eyes and ears would watch his trail, and his nose would guard in front, so Yan went in at one side, trusting to get a shot. With a very agony of care he made his way, step by step, and, after many minutes, surely found the track, still leading on. Another lengthy crawl, with nerves at tense, and then the lad thought he heard a twig snapped behind him, though the track was still ahead. And after long he found it true. Before lying down the Stag had doubled back, and while Yan had thought him still ahead, he was lying far behind, so had gotten wind of the man and now was miles away.

Once more into the unknown north away, till cold, black night came down; then Yan sought out a sheltered spot and made a tiny, redman's fire. As Chaska had taught him long ago—'Big fire for fool.'

When the lad curled up to sleep he felt a vague wish to turn three times like a dog, and a well-defined wish that he had fur on his face and a bushy tail to lay around his freezing hands and feet, for it was a night of northern frost. Old Peboan was stalking on the snow. The stars seemed to crackle, so one could almost hear. The trees and earth were bursting with the awful frost. The ice on a near lake was rent all night by cracks that went whooping from shore to shore; and down between the hills there poured the cold that burns.

A prairie-wolf came by in the night, but he did not howl or treat Yan like an outsider now. He gave a gentle, doglike '*Woof, woof,*' a sort of 'Oho! so you have come to it at last,' and passed away. Toward morning the weather grew milder, but with the change there came a driving snow. The track was blotted out. Yan had heeded nothing else, and did not know where he was. After travelling an aimless mile or two he decided to make for Pine Creek, which ought to lie southeastward. But which way was southeast? The powdery snow was driven along through the air, blinding, stinging, burning. On all things near it was like smoke, and on farther things, a driving fog.

But he made for a quaking asp grove, and there, sticking through the snow, he found a crosier golden-rod, dead and dry, but still faithfully delivering its message, 'Yon is the north.' With course corrected, on he went, and, whenever in doubt, dug out this compass-flower, till the country dipped and Pine Creek lay below.

There was good camping here, the very spot indeed where, fifteen years before, Butler had camped on his Loneland Journey; but now the blizzard had ceased, so Yan spent the day hunting without seeing a track, and he spent the night as before, wishing that nature had been kinder to him in the matter of fur. During that first lone night his face and toes had been frozen and now bore burning sores. But still he kept on the chase, for something within had told him that the Grail was surely near. Next day a strange, unreasoning guess sent him east across the creek in a deerless-looking barren land. Within half a mile he came on dim tracks made lately in the storm. He followed, and soon found where six deer had lain at rest, and among them a great, broad bed and a giant track that only one could have made. The track was almost fresh, the sign unfrozen still. "Within a mile," he thought. But within a hundred yards there loomed up on a fog-wrapped hillside five heads with ears regardant, and at that moment, too, there rose up from the snowy top a great form like a blasted trunk with two dead boughs still on. But they had seen him first, and before the deadly gun could play, six beacons waved and a friendly hill had screened them from its power.

The Sandhill Stag had gathered his brood again, yet now that the murderer was on the track once more, he scattered them as before. But there was only one track for Yan.

At last the chase led away to the great dip of Pine Creek—a mile-wide flat, with a long, dense thicket down the middle.

"There is where he is hiding and watching now, but there he will not rest," said the something within, and Yan kept out of sight and watched; after half an hour a dark spot left the willow belt and wandered up the farther hill. When he was well out of sight over the hill Yan ran across the valley and stalked around to get the trail on the down-wind side. He found it, and there learned that the Stag was as wise as he—he had climbed a good lookout and watched his back trail, then seeing Yan crossing the flat, his track went swiftly bounding, bounding—.

The Stag knew just how things stood; a single match to a finish now, and he led away for a new region. But Yan was learning something he had often heard—that the swiftest deer can be run down by a hardy man; for he was as fresh as ever, but the great Stag's bounds were shortening, he was surely tiring out, he must throw off the hunter now, or he is lost.

He often mounted a high hill to scan the white world for his foe, and the after-trail was a record of what he learned or feared. At last his trail came to a sudden end. This was a mystery until long study showed how he had returned backward on his own track for a hundred yards, then bounded aside to fly in another direction. Three times he did this, and then passed through an aspen thicket and, returning, lay down in this thicket near his own track, so that in following, Yan must pass where the Stag could smell and hear him long before the trail brought the hunter over-close.

All these doublings and many more like them were patiently unravelled and the shortening bounds were straightened out once more till, as daylight waned, the tracks seemed to grow stale and the bounds again grow long. After a little, Yan became wholly puzzled, so he stopped right there and spent another wretched night. Next day at dawn he worked it out.

He found he had been running the trail he had already run. With a long hark-back, the doubt was cleared. The desperate Stag had joined onto his old track and bounded aside at length to let the hunter follow the cold scent. But the join-on was found and the real trail read, and the tale that it told was of a great Stag wearing out, too tired to eat, too scared to sleep, with a tireless hunter after.

VIII

A last long follow brought the hunt back to familiar ground—a marsh-encompassed tract of woods with three ways in. There was the deer's trail entering. Yan felt he would not come out there, for he knew his foe was following. So swiftly and silently the hunter made for the second road on the down-wind side, and having hung his coat and sash there on a swaying sapling, he hastened to the third way out, and hid. After a while, seeing nothing, Yan gave the low call that the jaybird gives when there's danger abroad in the woods.

All deer take guidance from the jay, and away off in the encompassed woods Yan saw the great Stag with wavering ears go up a high lookout. A low whistle turned him to a statue, but he was far away with many a twig between. For some seconds he stood sniffing the wind and gazing with his back to his foe, watching the back trail, where so long his enemy had been, but never dreaming of that enemy in ambush ahead. Then the breeze set the coat on the sapling a-fluttering. The Stag quickly quit the hillock, not leaping or crashing through the brush,—he had years ago got past that,—but silent and weasel-like threading the maze, he disappeared. Yan crouched in the willow thicket and strained his every sense and tried to train his ears for keener watching. A twig ticked in the copse that he was in. Yan slowly rose with nerve and sense at tightest tense, the gun in line—and as he rose, there also rose, but fifteen feet away, a wondrous pair of bronze and ivory horns, a royal head, a noble form behind it, and face to face they stood, Yan and the Sandhill Stag. At last—at last, his life was in Yan's hands. The Stag flinched not, but stood and gazed with those great ears and mournful, truthful eyes, and the rifle leaped but sank again, for the Stag stood still and calmly looked him in the eyes, and Yan felt the prickling fading from his scalp, his clenched teeth eased, his limbs, bent as to spring, relaxed and man-like stood erect.

'*Shoot, shoot, shoot now! This is what you have toiled for,*' said a faint and fading voice, and spoke no more.

But Yan remembered the night when he, himself run down, had turned to face the hunting wolves; he remembered too that night when the snow was red with crime, and now between him and the other there he dimly saw a vision of an agonizing, dying doe, with great, sad eyes, that only asked, 'What harm have I done you?' A change came over him, and every thought of murder went from Yan as they gazed into each other's eyes—and hearts. Yan could not look him in the eyes and take his life, and different thoughts and a wholly different concept of the Stag, coming—coming—long coming—had come.

"Oh, beautiful creature! One of our wise men has said, the body is the soul made visible; is your spirit then so beautiful—as beautiful as wise? We have long stood as foes, hunter and hunted, but now that is changed and we stand face to face, fellow-creatures looking in each other's eyes, not knowing each other's speech—but knowing motives and feelings. Now I understand you as I never did before; surely you at least in part understand me. For your life is at last in my power, yet you have no fear. I knew of a deer once, that, run down by the hounds, sought safety with the hunter, and he saved it—and you also I have run down and you boldly seek safety with me. Yes! you are as wise as you are beautiful, for I will never harm a hair of you. We are brothers, oh, bounding Blacktail! only I am the elder and stronger, and if only my strength could always be at hand to save you, you would never come to harm. Go now, without fear, to range the piney hills; never more shall I follow your trail with the wild wolf rampant in my heart. Less and less as I grow do I see in your race mere flying marks, or butcher-meat. We have grown, Little Brother, and learned many things that you know not, but you have many a precious sense that is wholly hidden from us. Go now without fear of me.

"I may never see you again. But if only you would come sometimes and look me in the eyes and make me feel as you have done to-day, you would drive the wild beast wholly from my heart, and then the veil would be a little drawn and I should know more of the things that wise men have prayed for knowledge of. And yet I feel it never will be—I have found the Grail. I have learned what Buddha learned. I shall never see you again. Farewell."

RICHARD HARDING DAVIS

The Bar Sinister

Richard Harding Davis (1864–1916)

THE ACADEMIC CRITIC, *when he condescends to discuss Davis's work, contrasts it as a rule with his mother's, and much to the lady's advantage. Rebecca Davis's slow, grim sketches of life in mill and mine are as different as can be from her son's fast-paced, high-climaxed stories but not necessarily better for their earnestness. If good fiction be among other things the creation of characters, and the doing to perfection precisely what one sets out to do, Richard Harding Davis wins on both these counts, and scores high in ability to entertain.*

Davis's reputation has suffered in our day from some of the very characteristics of the man which won him success in his own. We find it intolerable that an intelligent creature should concern himself with the feelings and experiences of Upper-Tendom; incredible that the young girls of his time should sigh over his portrait as the original of the "Gibson Man." We refuse to judge him by his skill in portraying what he saw during the last days of the hansom-cab and the first days of the motor, and write him off as the first of the superficial slick-paper magazine fictioneers. The high sense of honor which animated him and which fills his stories, we appear to resent as if our own reversion to tooth and claw in fiction were somehow more admirable an aberration. Yet today's hero of popular fiction—advertising-man, professor, banker—is as apt as not to be only Van Bibber *without morals or manners.*

It must be confessed that the durable virtues in Davis's work are not shown to advantage in his love stories; it may be conceded that each generation's romantic flights are absurd to its successors. And his taste for the sharply dramatic scene is no less an affectation than the contemporary taste for underplaying. Yet when Davis deals with any perennial subject—one in which the conventions of his day are not vitally involved—he writes with the superb assurance of a great reporter and a true teller of tales. The three stories we have chosen for The Scribner Treasury, *of which the first is* The Bar Sinister (The Deserter *and* The Consul *will appear later on in their proper chronological position), seem typical of Davis at his best. In this personal view, we are supported by the public demand for these stories ever since their first publication.*

THE BAR SINISTER

PART I

THE Master was walking most unsteady, his legs tripping each other. After the fifth or sixth round, my legs often go the same way.

But even when the Master's legs bend and twist a bit, you mustn't think he can't reach you. Indeed, that is the time he kicks most frequent. So I kept behind him in the shadow, or ran in the middle of the street. He stopped at many public-houses with swinging doors, those doors that are cut so high from the sidewalk that you can look under them, and see if the Master is inside. At night when I peep beneath them the man at the counter will see me first and say, "Here's the Kid, Jerry, come to take you home. Get a move on you," and the Master will stumble out and follow me. It's lucky for us I'm so white, for no matter how dark the night, he can always see me ahead, just out of reach of his boot. At night the Master certainly does see most amazing. Sometimes he sees two or four of me, and walks in a circle, so that I have to take him by the leg of his trousers and lead him into the right road. One night, when he was very nasty-tempered and I was coaxing him along, two men passed us and one of them says, "Look at that brute!" and the other asks "Which?" and they both laugh. The Master, he cursed them good and proper.

This night, whenever we stopped at a public-house, the Master's pals left it and went on with us to the next. They spoke quite civil to me, and when the Master tried a flying kick, they gives him a shove. "Do you want we should lose our money?" says the pals.

I had had nothing to eat for a day and a night, and just before we set out the Master gives me a wash under the hydrant. Whenever I am locked up until all the slop-pans in our alley are empty, and made to take a bath, and the Master's pals speak civil, and feel my ribs, I know something is going to happen. And that night, when every time they see a policeman under a lamp-post, they dodged across the street, and when at the last one of them picked me up and hid me under his jacket, I began to tremble; for I knew what it meant. It meant that I was to fight again for the Master.

I don't fight because I like it. I fight because if I didn't the other dog would find my throat, and the Master would lose his stakes, and I would be very sorry for him and ashamed. Dogs can pass me and I can pass dogs, and I'd never pick a fight with none of them. When I see two dogs standing on their hind-legs in the streets, clawing each other's ears, and snapping for each other's windpipes, or howling and swearing and rolling in the mud, I feel sorry they should act so, and pretend not to notice. If he'd let me, I'd like to pass the time of day with every dog I meet. But there's something about me that no nice dog can abide. When I trot up to nice dogs, nodding and grinning, to make friends, they always tell me to be off. "Go to the devil!" they bark at me; "Get out!" and when I walk away they shout "mongrel," and "gutter-dog," and sometimes, after my back is turned, they rush me. I could kill most of them with three shakes, breaking the backbone of the little ones, and squeezing the throat of the big ones. But what's the good? They *are* nice dogs; that's why I try to make up to them, and though it's not for them to say it, I *am* a street-dog, and if I try to push into the company of my betters, I suppose it's their right to teach me my place.

Of course, they don't know I'm the best fighting bull-terrier of my weight in Montreal. That's why it wouldn't be right for me to take no notice of what they shout. They don't know that if I once locked my jaws on them I'd carry away whatever I touched. The night I fought Kelley's White Rat, I wouldn't loosen up until the Master made a noose in my leash and strangled me, and if the handlers hadn't thrown red pepper down my nose, I *never* would have let go of that Ottawa dog. I don't think the handlers treated me quite right that time, but maybe they didn't know the Ottawa dog was dead. I did.

I learned my fighting from my mother when I was very young. We slept in a lumber-yard on the river-front, and by day hunted for food along the wharfs. When we got it, the other tramp-dogs would try to take it off us, and then it was wonderful to see mother fly at them, and drive them away. All I know of fighting I learned from mother, watching her picking the ash-heaps for me when I was too little to fight for myself. No one ever was so good to me as mother. When it snowed and the ice was in the St. Lawrence she used to hunt alone, and bring me back new bones, and she'd sit and laugh to see me trying to swallow 'em whole. I was just a puppy then, my teeth was falling out. When I was able to fight we kept the whole river-range to ourselves. I had the genuine long, "punishing" jaw, so mother said, and there wasn't a man or a dog that dared worry us. Those were happy days, those were; and we lived well, share and share alike, and when we wanted a bit of fun, we chased the fat old wharf-rats. My! how they would squeal!

Then the trouble came. It was no trouble to me. I was too young to care then. But mother took it so to heart that she grew ailing, and wouldn't go abroad with me by day. It was the same old scandal that they're always bringing up against me. I was so young then that I didn't know. I couldn't see any difference between mother—and other mothers.

But one day a pack of curs we drove off snarled back some new names at her, and mother dropped her head and ran, just as though they had whipped us. After that she wouldn't go out with me except in the dark, and one day she went away and never came back, and though I hunted for her in every court and alley and back street of Montreal, I never found her.

One night, a month after mother ran away, I asked Guardian, the old blind mastiff, whose Master is the night-watchman on our slip, what it all meant. And he told me.

"Every dog in Montreal knows," he says, "except you, and every Master knows. So I think it's time you knew."

Then he tells me that my father, who had treated mother so bad, was a great and noble gentleman from London. "Your father had twenty-two registered ancestors, had your father," old Guardian says, "and in him was the best bull-terrier blood of England, the most ancientest, the most royal; the winning 'blue-ribbon' blood, that breeds champions. He had sleepy pink eyes, and thin pink lips, and he was as white all over as his own white teeth, and under his white skin you could see his muscles, hard and smooth, like the links of a steel chain. When your father stood still, and tipped his nose in the air, it was just as though he was saying, 'Oh, yes, you common dogs and men, you may well stare. It must be a rare treat for you Colonials to see a real English royalty.' He certainly was pleased with hisself, was your father. He looked just as proud and haughty as one of them stone dogs in Victoria Park—them as is cut out of white marble. And you're like him," says the old mastiff—"by that, of course, meaning you're white, same as him. That's the only likeness. But, you see, the trouble is, Kid—well, you see, Kid, the trouble is—your mother——"

"That will do," I said, for I understood then without his telling me, and I got up and walked away, holding my head and tail high in the air.

But I was, oh, so miserable, and I wanted to see mother that very minute, and tell her that I didn't care.

Mother is what I am, a street-dog; there's no royal blood in mother's veins, nor is she like that father of mine, nor—and that's the worst—she's not even like me. For while I, when I'm washed for a fight, am as white as clean snow, she—and this is our trouble, she—my mother, is a black-and-tan.

When mother hid herself from me, I was twelve months old and able to take care of myself, and, as after mother left me, the wharfs were never the same, I moved up-town and met the Master. Before he came, lots of other men-folks had tried to make up to me, and to whistle me home. But they either tried patting me or coaxing me with a piece of meat; so I didn't take to 'em. But one day the Master pulled me out of a street-fight by the hind-legs, and kicked me good.

"You want to fight, do you?" says he. "I'll give you all the *fighting* you want!" he says, and he kicks me again. So I knew he was my Master, and I followed him home. Since that day I've pulled off many fights for him, and they've brought dogs from all over the province to have a go at me, but up to that night none under thirty pounds had never downed me.

But that night, as soon as they carried me into the ring, I saw the dog was over-weight, and that I was no match for him. It was asking too much of a puppy. The Master should have known I couldn't do it. Not that I mean to blame the Master, for when sober, which he sometimes was, though not, as you might say, his habit, he was most kind to me, and let me out to find food, if I could get it, and only kicked me when I didn't pick him up at night and lead him home.

But kicks will stiffen the muscles, and starving a dog so as to get him ugly-tempered for a fight may make him nasty, but it's weakening to his insides, and it causes the legs to wabble.

The ring was in a hall, back of a public-house. There was a red-hot whitewashed stove in one corner, and the ring in the other. I lay in the Master's lap, wrapped in my blanket, and, spite of the stove, shivering awful; but I always shiver before a fight; I can't help gettin' excited. While the men-folks were a-flashing their money and taking their last drink at the bar, a little Irish groom in gaiters came up to me and give me the back of his hand to smell, and scratched me behind the ears.

"You poor little pup," says he. "You haven't no show," he says. "That brute in the tap-room, he'll eat your heart out."

"That's what you think," says the Master, snarling. "I'll lay you a quid the Kid chews him up."

The groom, he shook his head, but kept looking at me so sorry-like, that I begun to get a bit sad myself. He seemed like he couldn't bear to leave off a-patting of me, and he says, speaking low just like he would to a man-folk, "Well, good-luck to you, little pup," which I thought so civil of him, that I reached up and licked his hand. I don't do that to many men. And the Master, he knew I didn't, and took on dreadful.

"What 'ave you got on the back of your hand?" says he, jumping up.

"Soap!" says the groom, quick as a rat. "That's more than you've got on yours. Do you want to smell of it?" and he sticks his fist under the Master's nose. But the pals pushed in between 'em.

"He tried to poison the Kid!" shouts the Master.

"Oh, one fight at a time," says the referee. "Get into the ring, Jerry. We're waiting." So we went into the ring.

I never could just remember what did happen in that ring. He give me no time to spring. He fell on me like a horse. I couldn't keep my feet against him, and though, as I saw, he could get his hold when he liked, he wanted to chew me over a bit first. I was wondering if they'd be able to pry him off me, when, in the third round, he took his hold; and I began to drown, just as I did when I fell into the river off the Red C slip. He closed deeper and deeper, on my throat, and everything went black and red and bursting; and then, when I were sure I were dead, the handlers pulled him off, and the Master give me a kick that brought me to. But I couldn't move none, or even wink, both eyes being shut with lumps.

"He's a cur!" yells the Master, "a sneaking, cowardly cur. He lost the fight for me," says he, "because he's a —— —— —— cowardly cur." And he kicks me again in the lower ribs, so that I go sliding across the sawdust. "There's gratitude fer yer," yells the Master. "I've fed that dog, and nussed that dog, and housed him like a prince; and now he puts his tail between his legs, and sells me out, he does. He's a coward; I've done with him, I am. I'd sell him for a pipeful of tobacco." He picked me up by the tail, and swung me for the men-folks to see. "Does any gentleman here want to buy a dog," he says, "to make into sausage meat?" he says. "That's all he's good for."

Then I heard the little Irish groom say, "I'll give you ten bob for the dog."

And another voice says, "Ah, don't you do it; the dog's same as dead—mebby he is dead."

"Ten shillings!" says the Master, and his voice sobers a bit; "make it two pounds, and he's yours."

But the pals rushed in again.

"Don't you be a fool, Jerry," they say. "You'll be sorry for this when you're sober. The Kid's worth a fiver."

One of my eyes was not so swelled up as the other, and as I hung by my tail, I opened it, and saw one of the pals take the groom by the shoulder.

"You ought to give 'im five pounds for that dog, mate," he says; "that's no ordinary dog. That dog's got good blood in him, that dog has. Why, his father—that very dog's father——"

I thought he never would go on. He waited like he wanted to be sure the groom was listening.

"That very dog's father," says the pal, "is Regent Royal, son of Champion Regent Monarch, champion bull-terrier of England for four years."

I was sore, and torn, and chewed most awful, but what the pal said sounded so fine that I wanted to wag my tail, only couldn't, owing to my hanging from it.

But the Master calls out, "Yes, his father was Regent Royal; who's saying he wasn't? but the pup's a cowardly cur, that's what his pup is, and why—I'll tell you why—because his mother was a black-and-tan street-dog, that's why!"

I don't see how I got the strength, but some way I threw myself out of the Master's grip and fell at his feet, and turned over and fastened all my teeth in his ankle, just across the bone.

When I woke, after the pals had kicked me off him, I was in the smoking-car of a railroad-train, lying in the lap of the little groom, and he was rubbing my open wounds with a greasy, yellow stuff, exquisite to the smell, and most agreeable to lick off.

PART II

"Well—what's your name—Nolan? Well, Nolan, these references are satisfactory," said the young gentleman my new Master called "Mr. Wyndham, sir." "I'll take you on as second man. You can begin to-day."

My new Master shuffled his feet, and put his finger to his forehead. "Thank you, sir," says he. Then he choked like he had swallowed a fish-bone. "I have a little dawg, sir," says he.

"You can't keep him," says "Mr. Wyndham, sir," very short.

" 'Es only a puppy, sir," says my new Master; " 'e wouldn't go outside the stables, sir."

"It's not that," says "Mr. Wyndham, sir"; "I have a large kennel of very fine dogs; they're the best of their breed in America. I don't allow strange dogs on the premises."

The Master shakes his head, and motions me with his cap, and I crept out from behind the door. "I'm sorry, sir," says the Master.

"Then I can't take the place. I can't get along without the dog, sir."

"Mr. Wyndham, sir," looked at me that fierce that I guessed he was going to whip me, so I turned over on my back and begged with my legs and tail.

"Why, you beat him!" says "Mr. Wyndham, sir," very stern.

"No fear!" the Master says, getting very red. "The party I bought him off taught him that. He never learnt that from me!" He picked me up in his arms, and to show "Mr. Wyndham, sir," how well I loved the Master, I bit his chin and hands.

"Mr. Wyndham, sir," turned over the letters the Master had given him. "Well, these references certainly are very strong," he says. "I guess I'll let the dog stay this time. Only see you keep him away from the kennels—or you'll both go."

"Thank you, sir," says the Master, grinning like a cat when she's safe behind the area-railing.

"He's not a bad bull-terrier," says "Mr. Wyndham, sir," feeling my head. "Not that I know much about the smooth-coated breeds. My dogs are St. Bernards." He stopped patting me and held up my nose. "What's the matter with his ears?" he says. "They're chewed to pieces. Is this a fighting dog?" he asks, quick and rough-like.

I could have laughed. If he hadn't been holding my nose, I certainly would have had a good grin at him. Me, the best under thirty pounds in the Province of Quebec, and him asking if I was a fighting dog! I ran to the Master and hung down my head modest-like, waiting for him to tell of my list of battles, but the Master he coughs in his cap most painful. "Fightin' dog, sir," he cries. "Lor' bless you, sir, the Kid don't know the word. 'Es just a puppy, sir, same as you see; a pet dog, so to speak. 'Es a regular old lady's lap-dog, the Kid is."

"Well, you keep him away from my St. Bernards," says "Mr. Wyndham, sir," "or they might make a mouthful of him."

"Yes, sir, that they might," says the Master. But when we gets outside he slaps his knee and laughs inside hisself, and winks at me most sociable.

The Master's new home was in the country, in a province they called Long Island. There was a high stone wall about his home with big iron gates to it, same as Godfrey's brewery; and there was a house with five red roofs, and the stables, where I lived, was cleaner than the aerated bakery-shop, and then there was the kennels, but they was like nothing else in this world that ever I see. For the first days I couldn't sleep of nights for fear some one would catch me lying in such a cleaned-up place, and would chase me out of it, and when I did fall to sleep I'd dream I was back in the old Master's attic, shivering under the rusty stove, which never had no coals in it, with the Master flat on his back on the cold floor with his clothes on. And I'd wake up, scared and whimpering, and find myself on the new Master's cot with his hand on the quilt beside me; and I'd see the glow of the big stove, and hear the high-quality horses below-stairs stamping in their straw-lined boxes, and I'd snoop the sweet smell of hay and harness-soap, and go to sleep again.

The stables was my jail, so the Master said, but I don't ask no better home than that jail.

"Now, Kid," says he, sitting on the top of a bucket upside down, "you've got to understand this. When I whistle it means you're not to go out of this 'ere yard. These stables is your jail. And if you leave 'em I'll have to leave 'em, too, and over the seas, in the County Mayo, an old mother will 'ave to leave her bit of a cottage. For two pounds I must be sending her every month, or she'll have naught to eat, nor no thatch over 'er head; so, I can't lose my place, Kid, an' see you don't lose it for me. You must keep away from the kennels," says he; "they're not for the likes of you. The kennels are for the quality. I wouldn't take a litter of them woolly dogs for one wag of your tail, Kid, but for all that they are your betters, same as the gentry up in the big house are my betters. I know my place and keep away from the gentry, and you keep away from the champions."

So I never goes out of the stables. All day I just lay in the sun on the stone flags, licking my jaws, and watching the grooms wash down the carriages, and the only care I had was to see they didn't get gay and turn the hose on me. There wasn't even a single rat to plague me. Such stables I never did see.

"Nolan," says the head-groom, "some day that dog of yours will give you the slip. You can't keep a street-dog tied up all his life. It's against his natur'." The head-groom is a nice old gentleman, but he doesn't know everything. Just as though I'd been a street-dog because

I liked it. As if I'd rather poke for my vittles in ash-heaps than have 'em handed me in a wash-basin and would sooner bite and fight than be polite and sociable. If I'd had mother there I couldn't have asked for nothing more. But I'd think of her snooping in the gutters, or freezing of nights under the bridges, or, what's worse of all, running through the hot streets with her tongue down, so wild and crazy for a drink, that the people would shout "mad dog" at her, and stone her. Water's so good, that I don't blame the men-folks for locking it up inside their houses, but when the hot days come, I think they might remember that those are the dog-days and leave a little water outside in a trough, like they do for the horses. Then we wouldn't go mad, and the policemen wouldn't shoot us. I had so much of everything I wanted that it made me think a lot of the days when I hadn't nothing, and if I could have given what I had to mother, as she used to share with me, I'd have been the happiest dog in the land. Not that I wasn't happy then, and most grateful to the Master, too, and if I'd only minded him, the trouble wouldn't have come again.

But one day the coachman says that the little lady they called Miss Dorothy had come back from school, and that same morning she runs over to the stables to pat her ponies, and she sees me.

"Oh, what a nice little, white little dog," said she; "whose little dog are you?" says she.

"That's my dog, miss," says the Master. " 'Is name is Kid," and I ran up to her most polite, and licks her fingers, for I never see so pretty and kind a lady.

"You must come with me and call on my new puppies," says she, picking me up in her arms and starting off with me.

"Oh, but please, miss," cries Nolan, "Mr. Wyndham give orders that the Kid's not to go to the kennels."

"That'll be all right," says the little lady; "they're my kennels too. And the puppies will like to play with him."

You wouldn't believe me if I was to tell you of the style of them quality-dogs. If I hadn't seen it myself I wouldn't have believed it neither. The Viceroy of Canada don't live no better. There was forty of them, but each one had his own house and a yard—most exclusive —and a cot and a drinking-basin all to hisself. They had servants standing 'round waiting to feed 'em when they was hungry, and valets to wash 'em; and they had their hair combed and brushed like the grooms must when they go out on the box. Even the puppies had overcoats with their names on 'em in blue letters, and the name of each of those they called champions was painted up fine over his front door just like it was a public-house or a veterinary's. They were the biggest St. Bernards I ever did see. I could have walked under them if they'd have let me. But they were very proud and haughty dogs, and looked only once at me, and then sniffed in the air. The little lady's own dog was an old gentleman bull-dog. He'd come along with us, and when he notices how taken aback I was with all I see, he turned quite kind and affable and showed me about.

"Jimmy Jocks," Miss Dorothy called him, but, owing to his weight, he walked most dignified and slow, waddling like a duck as you might say, and looked much too proud and handsome for such a silly name.

"That's the runway, and that's the Trophy House," says he to me, "and that over there is the hospital, where you have to go if you get distemper, and the vet. gives you beastly medicine."

"And which of these is your 'ouse, sir?" asks I, wishing to be respectful. But he looked that hurt and haughty. "I don't live in the kennels," says he, most contemptuous. "I am a house-dog. I sleep in Miss Dorothy's room. And at lunch I'm let in with the family, if the visitors don't mind. They most always do, but they're too polite to say so. Besides," says he, smiling most condescending, "visitors are always afraid of me. It's because I'm so ugly," says he. "I suppose," says he, screwing up his wrinkles and speaking very slow and impressive, "I suppose I'm the ugliest bull-dog in America," and as he seemed to be so pleased to think hisself so, I said, "Yes, sir, you certainly are the ugliest ever I see," at which he nodded his head most approving.

"But I couldn't hurt 'em, as you say," he goes on, though I hadn't said nothing like that, being too polite. "I'm too old," he says; "I haven't any teeth. The last time one of those grizzly bears," said he, glaring at the big St. Bernards, "took a hold of me, he nearly was my death," says he. I thought his eyes would pop out of his head, he seemed so wrought up about it. "He rolled me around in the dirt, he did," says Jimmy Jocks, "an' I couldn't get up. It was low," says Jimmy Jocks, making a face like he had a bad taste in his mouth. "Low, that's what I call it, bad form, you understand, young man, not done in our circles—and—and low." He growled, way down in his stomach, and puffed hisself out, panting and blowing like he had been on a run.

"I'm not a street-fighter," he says, scowling at a St. Bernard marked "Champion." "And when my rheumatism is not troubling me," he says, "I endeavor to be civil to all dogs, so long as they are gentlemen."

"Yes, sir," said I, for even to me he had been most affable.

At this we had come to a little house off by itself and Jimmy Jocks invites me in. "This is their trophy-room," he says, "where they keep their prizes. Mine," he says, rather grand-like, "are on the sideboard." Not knowing what a sideboard might be, I said, "Indeed, sir, that must be very gratifying." But he only wrinkled up his chops as much as to say, "It is my right."

The trophy-room was as wonderful as any public-house I ever see. On the walls was pictures of nothing but beautiful St. Bernard dogs, and rows and rows of blue and red and yellow ribbons; and when I asked Jimmy Jocks why they was so many more of blue than of the others, he laughs and says, "Because these kennels always win." And there was many shining cups on the shelves which Jimmy Jocks told me were prizes won by the champions.

"Now, sir, might I ask you sir," says I, "wot is a champion?"

At that he panted and breathed so hard I thought he would bust hisself. "My dear young friend!" says he. "Wherever have you been educated? A champion is a—a champion," he says. "He must win nine blue ribbons in the 'open' class. You follow me—that is—against all comers. Then he has the title before his name, and they put his photograph in the sporting papers. You know, of course, that I am a champion," says he. "I am Champion Woodstock Wizard III, and the two other Woodstock Wizards, my father and uncle, were both champions."

"But I thought your name was Jimmy Jocks," I said.

He laughs right out at that.

"That's my kennel name, not my registered name," he says. "Why you certainly know that every dog has two names. Now, what's your registered name and number, for instance?" says he.

"I've only got one name," I says. "Just Kid."

Woodstock Wizard puffs at that and wrinkles up his forehead and pops out his eyes.

"Who are your people?" says he. "Where is your home?"

"At the stable, sir," I said. "My Master is the second groom."

At that Woodstock Wizard III looks at me for quite a bit without winking, and stares all around the room over my head.

"Oh, well," says he at last, "you're a very civil young dog," says he, "and I blame no one for what he can't help," which I thought most fair and liberal. "And I have known many bull-terriers that were champions," says he, "though as a rule they mostly run with fire-engines, and to fighting. For me, I wouldn't care to run through the streets after a hose-cart, nor to fight," says he; "but each to his taste."

I could not help thinking that if Woodstock Wizard III tried to follow a fire-engine he would die of apoplexy, and that, seeing he'd lost his teeth, it was lucky he had no taste for fighting, but, after his being so condescending, I didn't say nothing.

"Anyway," says he, "every smooth-coated dog is better than any hairy old camel like those St. Bernards, and if ever you're hungry down at the stables, young man, come up to the house and I'll give you a bone. I can't eat them myself, but I bury them around the garden from force of habit, and in case a friend should drop in. Ah, I see my Mistress coming," he says, "and I bid you good-day. I regret," he says, "that our different social position prevents our meeting frequent, for you're a worthy young dog with a proper respect for your betters, and in this country there's precious few of them have that." Then he waddles off, leaving me alone and very sad, for he was the first dog in many days that had spoken to me. But since he showed, seeing that I was a stable-dog, he didn't want my company, I waited for him to get well away. It was not a cheerful place to wait, the Trophy House. The pictures of the champions seemed to scowl at me, and ask what right had such as I even to admire them, and the blue and gold ribbons and the silver cups made me very miserable. I had never won no blue ribbons or silver cups; only stakes for the old

Master to spend in the publics, and I hadn't won them for being a beautiful, high-quality dog, but just for fighting—which, of course, as Woodstock Wizard III says, is low. So I started for the stables, with my head down and my tail between my legs, feeling sorry I had ever left the Master. But I had more reason to be sorry before I got back to him.

The Trophy House was quite a bit from the kennels, and as I left it I see Miss Dorothy and Woodstock Wizard III walking back toward them, and that a fine, big St. Bernard, his name was Champion Red Elfberg, had broke his chain, and was running their way. When he reaches old Jimmy Jocks he lets out a roar like a grain-steamer in a fog, and he makes three leaps for him. Old Jimmy Jocks was about a fourth his size; but he plants his feet and curves his back, and his hair goes up around his neck like a collar. But he never had no show at no time, for the grizzly bear, as Jimmy Jocks had called him, lights on old Jimmy's back and tries to break it, and old Jimmy Jocks snaps his gums and claws the grass, panting and groaning awful. But he can't do nothing, and the grizzly bear just rolls him under him, biting and tearing cruel. The odds was all that Woodstock Wizard III was going to be killed. I had fought enough to see that, but not knowing the rules of the game among champions, I didn't like to interfere between two gentlemen who might be settling a private affair, and, as it were, take it as presuming of me. So I stood by, though I was shaking terrible, and holding myself in like I was on a leash. But at that Woodstock Wizard III, who was underneath, sees me through the dust, and calls very faint, "Help, you!" he says. "Take him in the hind-leg," he says. "He's murdering me," he says. And then the little Miss Dorothy, who was crying, and calling to the kennel-men, catches at the Red Elfberg's hind-legs to pull him off, and the brute, keeping his front pats well in Jimmy's stomach, turns his big head and snaps at her. So that was all I asked for, thank you. I went up under him. It was really nothing. He stood so high that I had only to take off about three feet from him and come in from the side, and my long, "punishing jaw" as mother was always talking about, locked on his woolly throat, and my back teeth met. I couldn't shake him, but I shook myself, and every time I shook myself there was thirty pounds of weight tore at his windpipes. I couldn't see nothing for his long hair, but I heard Jimmy Jocks puffing and blowing on one side, and munching the brute's leg with his old gums. Jimmy was an old sport that day, was Jimmy, or, Woodstock Wizard III., as I should say. When the Red Elfberg was out and down I had to run, or those kennel-men would have had my life. They chased me right into the stables; and from under the hay I watched the head-groom take down a carriage-whip and order them to the right about. Luckily Master and the young grooms were out, or that day there'd have been fighting for everybody.

Well, it nearly did for me and the Master. "Mr. Wyndham, sir, comes raging to the stables and said I'd half-killed his best prize-winner, and had oughter be shot, and he gives the Master his notice. But Miss Dorothy she follows him, and says it was his Red Elfberg what began the fight, and that I'd saved Jimmy's life, and that old Jimmy Jocks was worth more to her than all the St. Bernards in the Swiss mountains—wherever they be. And that I was her champion, anyway. Then she cried over me most beautiful, and over Jimmy Jocks, too, who was that tied up in bandages he couldn't even waddle. So when he heard that side of it, "Mr. Wyndham, sir," told us that if Nolan put me on a chain, we could stay. So it came out all right for everybody but me. I was glad the Master kept his place, but I'd never worn a chain before, and it disheartened me—but that was the least of it. For the quality-dogs couldn't forgive my whipping their champion, and they came to the fence between the kennels and the stables, and laughed through the bars, barking most cruel words at me. I couldn't understand how they found it out, but they knew. After the fight Jimmy Jocks was most condescending to me, and he said the grooms had boasted to the kennel-men that I was a son of Regent Royal, and that when the kennel-men asked who was my mother they had had to tell them that too. Perhaps that was the way of it, but, however, the scandal was out, and every one of the quality-dogs knew that I was a street-dog and the son of a black-and-tan.

"These misalliances will occur," said Jimmy Jocks, in his old-fashioned way, "but no well-bred dog," says he, looking most scornful at the St. Bernards, who were howling behind the palings, "would refer to your misfortune before you, certainly not cast it in your face. I, myself, remember your father's father, when he made his début at the Crystal Palace. He took four blue ribbons and three specials."

But no sooner than Jimmy would leave me, the St. Bernards would take to howling again, insulting mother and insulting me. And when I tore at my chain, they, seeing they were safe, would howl the more. It was never the same after that; the laughs and the jeers cut into my heart, and the chain bore heavy on my spirit. I was so sad that sometimes I wished I was back in the gutter again, where no one was better than me, and some nights I wished I was dead. If it hadn't been for the Master being so kind, and that it would have looked like I was blaming mother, I would have twisted my leash and hanged myself.

About a month after my fight, the word was passed through the kennels that the New York Show was coming, and such goings on as followed I never did see. If each of them had been matched to fight for a thousand pounds and the gate, they couldn't have trained more conscientious. But, perhaps, that's just my envy. The kennel-men rubbed 'em and scrubbed 'em and trims their hair and curls and combs it, and some dogs they fatted, and some they starved. No one talked of nothing but the Show, and the chances "our kennels" had against the other kennels, and if this one of our champions would win over that one, and whether them as hoped to be champions had better show in the "open" or the "limit" class, and whether this dog would beat his own dad, or whether his little puppy sister couldn't beat the two of them. Even the grooms had their money up, and day or night you heard nothing but praises of "our" dogs, until I, being so far out of it, couldn't have felt meaner if I had been running the streets with a can to my tail. I knew shows were not for such as me, and so I lay all day stretched at the end of my chain, pretending I was asleep, and only too glad that they had something so important to think of, that they could leave me alone.

But one day before the Show opened, Miss Dorothy came to the stables with "Mr. Wyndham, sir," and seeing me chained up and so miserable, she takes me in her arms.

"You poor little tyke," says she. "It's cruel to tie him up so; he's eating his heart out, Nolan," she says. "I don't know nothing about bull-terriers," says she, "but I think Kid's got good points," says she, "and you ought to show him. Jimmy Jocks has three legs on the Rensselaer Cup now, and I'm going to show him this time so that he can get the fourth, and if you wish, I'll enter your dog too. How would you like that, Kid?" says she. "How would you like to see the most beautiful dogs in the world? Maybe, you'd meet a pal or two," says she. "It would cheer you up, wouldn't it, Kid?" says she. But I was so upset, I could only wag my tail most violent. "He says it would!" says she, though, being that excited, I hadn't said nothing.

So, "Mr. Wyndham, sir," laughs and takes out a piece of blue paper, and sits down at the head-groom's table.

"What's the name of the father of your dog, Nolan?" says he. And Nolan says, "The man I got him off told me he was a son of Champion Regent Royal, sir. But it don't seem likely, does it?" says Nolan.

"It does not!" says "Mr. Wyndham, sir," short-like.

"Aren't you sure, Nolan?" says Miss Dorothy.

"No, miss," says the Master.

"Sire unknown," says "Mr. Wyndham, sir," and writes it down.

"Date of birth?" asks "Mr. Wyndham, sir."

"I—I—unknown, sir," says Nolan. And "Mr. Wyndham, sir," writes it down.

"Breeder?" says "Mr. Wyndham, sir."

"Unknown," says Nolan, getting very red around the jaws, and I drops my head and tail. And "Mr. Wyndham, sir," writes that down.

"Mother's name?" says "Mr. Wyndham, sir."

"She was a—unknown," says the Master. And I licks his hand.

"Dam unknown," says "Mr. Wyndham, sir," and writes it down. Then he takes the paper and reads out loud: "Sire unknown, dam unknown, breeder unknown, date of birth unknown. You'd better call him the 'Great Unknown,' " says he. "Who's paying his entrance-fee?"

"I am," says Miss Dorothy.

Two weeks after we all got on a train for New York; Jimmy Jocks and me following Nolan in the smoking-car, and twenty-two of the

St. Bernards, in boxes and crates, and on chains and leashes. Such a barking and howling I never did hear, and when they sees me going, too, they laughs fit to kill.

"Wot is this; a circus?" says the railroad-man.

But I had no heart in it. I hated to go. I knew I was no "show" dog, even though Miss Dorothy and the Master did their best to keep me from shaming them. For before we set out Miss Dorothy brings a man from town who scrubbed and rubbed me, and sand-papered my tail, which hurt most awful, and shaved my ears with the Master's razor, so that you could most see clear through 'em, and sprinkles me over with pipe-clay, till I shines like a Tommy's cross-belts.

"Upon my word!" says Jimmy Jocks when he first sees me. "What a swell you are! You're the image of your grand-dad when he made his début at the Crystal Palace. He took four firsts and three specials." But I knew he was only trying to throw heart into me. They might scrub, and they might rub, and they might pipe-clay, but they couldn't pipe-clay the insides of me, and they was black-and-tan.

Then we came to a Garden, which it was not, but the biggest hall in the world. Inside there was lines of benches, a few miles long, and on them sat every dog in the world. If all the dog-snatchers in Montreal had worked night and day for a year, they couldn't have caught so many dogs. And they was all shouting and barking and howling so vicious, that my heart stopped beating. For at first I thought they was all enraged at my presuming to intrude, but after I got in my place, they kept at it just the same, barking at every dog as he come in; daring him to fight, and ordering him out, and asking him what breed of dog he thought he was, anyway. Jimmy Jocks was chained just behind me, and he said he never see so fine a show. "That's a hot class you're in, my lad," he says, looking over into my street, where there were thirty bull-terriers. They was all as white as cream, and each so beautiful that if I could have broke my chain, I would have run all the way home and hid myself under the horse-trough.

All night long they talked and sang, and passed greetings with old pals, and the home-sick puppies howled dismal. Them that couldn't sleep wouldn't let no others sleep, and all the electric lights burned in the roof, and in my eyes. I could hear Jimmy Jocks snoring peaceful, but I could only doze by jerks, and when I dozed I dreamed horrible. All the dogs in the hall seemed coming at me for daring to intrude, with their jaws red and open, and their eyes blazing like the lights in the roof. "You're a street-dog! Get out, you street-dog!" they yells. And as they drives me out, the pipe-clay drops off me, and they laugh and shriek; and when I looks down I see that I have turned into a black-and-tan.

They was most awful dreams, and next morning, when Miss Dorothy comes and gives me water in a pan, I begs and begs her to take me home, but she can't understand. "How well Kid is!" she says. And when I jumps into the Master's arms, and pulls to break my chain, he says, "If he knew all as he had against him, miss, he wouldn't be so gay." And from a book they reads out the names of the beautiful high-bred terriers which I have got to meet. And I can't make 'em understand that I only want to run away, and hide myself where no one will see me.

Then suddenly men comes hurrying down our street and begins to brush the beautiful bull-terriers, and Nolan rubs me with a towel so excited that his hands trembles awful, and Miss Dorothy tweaks my ears between her gloves, so that the blood runs to 'em, and they turn pink and stand straight and sharp.

"Now, then, Nolan," says she, her voice shaking just like his fingers, "Keep his head up—and never let the Judge lose sight of him." When I hears that my legs breaks under me, for I knows all about judges. Twice, the old Master goes up before the Judge for fighting me with other dogs, and the Judge promises him if he ever does it again, he'll chain him up in jail. I knew he'd find me out. A judge can't be fooled by no pipe-clay. He can see right through you, and he reads your insides.

The judging-ring, which is where the Judge holds out, was so like a fighting-pit, that when I came in it, and find six other dogs there, I springs into position, so that when they lets us go I can defend myself. But the Master smoothes down my hair and whispers, "Hold 'ard, Kid, hold 'ard. This ain't a fight," says he. "Look your prettiest," he whispers. "Please, Kid, look your prettiest," and he pulls my leash so tight that I can't touch my pats to the sawdust, and my nose goes up in the air. There was millions of people a-watching us from the railings, and three of our kennel-men, too, making fun of Nolan and me, and Miss Dorothy with her chin just reaching to the rail, and her eyes so big that I thought she was a-going to cry. It was awful to think that when the Judge stood up and exposed me, all those people, and Miss Dorothy, would be there to see me driven from the show.

The Judge, he was a fierce-looking man with specs on his nose, and a red beard. When I first come in he didn't see me owing to my being too quick for him and dodging behind the Master. But when the Master drags me round and I pulls at the sawdust to keep back, the Judge looks at us careless-like, and then stops and glares through his specs, and I knew it was all up with me.

"Are there any more?" asks the Judge, to the gentleman at the gate, but never taking his specs from me.

The man at the gate looks in his book. "Seven in the novice-class," says he. "They're all here. You can go ahead," and he shuts the gate.

The Judge, he doesn't hesitate a moment. He just waves his hand toward the corner of the ring. "Take him away." he says to the Master. "Over there and keep him away," and he turns and looks most solemn at the six beautiful bull-terriers. I don't know how I crawled to that corner. I wanted to scratch under the sawdust and dig myself a grave. The kennel-men they slapped the rail with their hands and laughed at the Master like they would fall over. They pointed at me in the corner, and their sides just shaked. But little Miss Dorothy she presses her lips tight against the rail, and I see tears rolling from her eyes. The Master, he hangs his head like he had been whipped. I felt most sorry for him, than all. He was so red, and he was letting on not to see the kennel-men, and blinking his eyes. If the Judge had ordered me right out, it wouldn't have disgraced us so, but it was keeping me there while he was judging the high-bred dogs that hurt so hard. With all those people staring too. And his doing it so quick, without no doubt nor questions. You can't fool the judges. They see insides you.

But he couldn't make up his mind about them high-bred dogs. He scowls at 'em, and he glares at 'em, first with his head on the one side and then on the other. And he feels of 'em, and orders 'em to run about. And Nolan leans against the rails, with his head hung down, and pats me. And Miss Dorothy comes over beside him, but don't say nothing, only wipes her eye with her finger. A man on the other side of the rail he says to the Master, "The Judge don't like your dog?"

"No," says the Master.

"Have you ever shown him before?" says the man.

"No," says the Master, "and I'll never show him again. He's my dog," says the Master, "an' he suits me! And I don't care what no judges think." And when he says them kind words, I licks his hand most grateful.

The Judge had two of the six dogs on a little platform in the middle of the ring, and he had chased the four other dogs into the corners, where they was licking their chops, and letting on they didn't care, same as Nolan was.

The two dogs on the platform was so beautiful that the Judge hisself couldn't tell which was the best of 'em, even when he stoops down and holds their heads together. But at last he gives a sigh, and brushes the sawdust off his knees and goes to the table in the ring, where there was a man keeping score, and heaps and heaps of blue and gold and red and yellow ribbons. And the Judge picks up a bunch of 'em and walks to the two gentlemen who was holding the beautiful dogs, and he says to each "What's his number?" and he hands each gentleman a ribbon. And then he turned sharp, and comes straight at the Master.

"What's his number?" says the Judge. And Master was so scared that he couldn't make no answer.

But Miss Dorothy claps her hands and cries out like she was laughing, "Three twenty-six," and the Judge writes it down, and shoves Master the blue ribbon.

I bit the Master, and I jumps and bit Miss Dorothy, and I waggled so hard that the Master couldn't hold me. When I get to the gate Miss Dorothy snatches me up and kisses me between the ears, right before millions of people, and they both hold me so tight that I didn't know which of them was carrying of me. But one thing I knew, for I listened hard, as it was the Judge hisself as said it.

"Did you see that puppy I gave 'first' to?" says the Judge to the gentleman at the gate.

"I did. He was a bit out of his class," says the gate-gentleman.

"He certainly was!" says the Judge, and they both laughed.

But I didn't care. They couldn't hurt me then, not with Nolan holding the blue ribbon and Miss Dorothy hugging my ears, and the kennel-men sneaking away, each looking like he'd been caught with his nose under the lid of the slop-can.

We sat down together, and we all three just talked as fast as we could. They was so pleased that I couldn't help feeling proud myself, and I barked and jumped and leaped about so gay, that all the bull-terriers in our street stretched on their chains, and howled at me.

"Just look at him!" says one of those I had beat. "What's he giving hisself airs about?"

"Because he's got one blue ribbon!" says another of 'em. "Why, when I was a puppy I used to eat em, and if that Judge could ever learn to know a toy from a mastiff, I'd have had this one."

But Jimmy Jocks he leaned over from his bench, and says, "Well done, Kid. Didn't I tell you so!" What he 'ad told me was that I might get a "commended," but I didn't remind him.

"Didn't I tell you," says Jimmy Jocks, "that I saw your grandfather make his début at the Crystal——"

"Yes, sir, you did, sir," says I, for I have no love for the men of my family.

A gentleman with a showing leash around his neck comes up just then and looks at me very critical. "Nice dog you've got, Miss Wyndham," says he; "would you care to sell him?"

"He's not my dog," says Miss Dorothy, holding me tight. "I wish he were."

"He's not for sale, sir," says the Master, and I was *that* glad.

"Oh, he's yours, is he?" says the gentleman, looking hard at Nolan. "Well, I'll give you a hundred dollars for him," says he, careless-like.

"Thank you, sir, he's not for sale," says Nolan, but his eyes get very big. The gentleman, he walked away, but I watches him, and he talks to a man in a golf-cap, and by and by the man comes along our street, looking at all the dogs, and stops in front of me.

"This your dog?" says he to Nolan. "Pity he's so leggy," says he. "If he had a good tail, and a longer stop, and his ears were set higher, he'd be a good dog. As he is, I'll give you fifty dollars for him."

But, before the Master could speak, Miss Dorothy laughs, and says, "You're Mr. Polk's kennel-man, I believe. Well, you tell Mr. Polk from me that the dog's not for sale now any more than he was five minutes ago, and that when he is, he'll have to bid against me for him." The man looks foolish at that, but he turns to Nolan quick-like. "I'll give you three hundred for him," he says.

"Oh, indeed!" whispers Miss Dorothy, like she was talking to herself. "That's it, is it," and she turns and looks at me as though she had never seen me before. Nolan, he was gaping, too, with his mouth open. But he holds me tight.

"He's not for sale," he growls, like he was frightened, and the man looks black and walks away.

"Why, Nolan!" cries Miss Dorothy, "Mr. Polk knows more about bull-terriers than any amateur in America. What can he mean? Why, Kid is no more than a puppy! Three hundred dollars for a puppy!"

"And he ain't no thoroughbred neither!" cries the Master. "He's 'Unknown,' ain't he? Kid can't help it, of course, but his mother, Miss——"

I dropped my head. I couldn't bear he should tell Miss Dorothy. I couldn't bear she should know I had stolen my blue ribbon.

But the Master never told, for at that, a gentleman runs up, calling, "Three Twenty-Six, Three Twenty-Six," and Miss Dorothy says, "Here he is, what is it?"

"The Winner's Class," says the gentleman. "Hurry, please. The Judge is waiting for him."

Nolan tries to get me off the chain onto a showing leash, but he shakes so, he only chokes me. "What is it, Miss?" he says. "What is it?"

"The Winner's Class," says Miss Dorothy. "The Judge wants him with the winners of the other classes—to decide which is the best. It's only a form," says she. "He has the champions against him now."

"Yes," says the gentleman, as he hurries us to the ring. "I'm afraid it's only a form for your dog, but the Judge wants all the winners, puppy class even."

We had got to the gate, and the gentleman there was writing down my number.

"Who won the open?" asks Miss Dorothy.

"Oh, who would?" laughs the gentleman. "The old champion, of course. He's won for three years now. There he is. Isn't he wonderful?" says he, and he points to a dog that's standing proud and haughty on the platform in the middle of the ring.

I never see so beautiful a dog, so fine and clean and noble, so white like he had rolled hisself in flour, holding his nose up and his eyes shut, same as though no one was worth looking at. Aside of him, we other dogs, even though we had a blue ribbon apiece, seemed like lumps of mud. He was a royal gentleman, a king, he was. His Master didn't have to hold his head with no leash. He held it hisself, standing as still as an iron dog on a lawn, like he knew all the people was looking at him. And so they was, and no one around the ring pointed at no other dog but him.

"Oh, what a picture," cried Miss Dorothy; "he's like a marble figure by a great artist—one who loved dogs. Who is he?" says she, looking in her book. "I don't keep up with terriers."

"Oh, you know him," says the gentleman. "He is the Champion of champions, Regent Royal."

The Master's face went red.

"And this is Regent Royal's son," cries he, and he pulls me quick into the ring, and plants me on the platform next my father.

I trembled so that I near fell. My legs twisted like a leash. But my father he never looked at me. He only smiled, the same sleepy smile, and he still keep his eyes half-shut, like as no one, no, not even his son, was worth his lookin' at.

The Judge, he didn't let me stay beside my father, but, one by one, he placed the other dogs next to him and measured and felt and pulled at them. And each one he put down, but he never put my father down. And then he comes over and picks up me and sets me back on the platform, shoulder to shoulder with the Champion Regent Royal, and goes down on his knees, and looks into our eyes.

The gentleman with my father, he laughs, and says to the Judge, "Thinking of keeping us here all day, John?" but the Judge, he doesn't hear him, and goes behind us and runs his hand down my side, and holds back my ears, and takes my jaw between his fingers. The crowd around the ring is very deep now, and nobody says nothing. The gentleman at the score-table, he is leaning forward, with his elbows on his knees, and his eyes very wide, and the gentleman at the gate is whispering quick to Miss Dorothy, who has turned white. I stood as stiff as stone. I didn't even breathe. But out of the corner of my eye I could see my father licking his pink chops, and yawning just a little, like he was bored.

The Judge, he had stopped looking fierce, and was looking solemn. Something inside him seemed a-troubling him awful. The more he stares at us now, the more solemn he gets, and when he touches us he does it gentle, like he was patting us. For a long time he kneels in the sawdust, looking at my father and at me, and no one around the ring says nothing to nobody.

Then the Judge takes a breath and touches me sudden. "It's his," he says, but he lays his hand just as quick on my father. "I'm sorry," says he.

The gentleman holding my father cries:

"Do you mean to tell me——"

And the Judge, he answers, "I mean the other is the better dog." He takes my father's head between his hands and looks down at him, most sorrowful. "The King is dead," says he, "long live the King. Good-by, Regent," he says.

The crowd around the railings clapped their hands, and some laughed scornful, and every one talks fast, and I start for the gate so dizzy that I can't see my way. But my father pushes in front of me, walking very daintily, and smiling sleepy, same as he had just been waked, with his head high, and his eyes shut, looking at nobody.

So that is how I "came by my inheritance," as Miss Dorothy calls it, and just for that, though I couldn't feel where I was any different, the crowd follows me to my bench, and pats me, and coos at me, like I was a baby in a baby-carriage. And the handlers have to hold 'em back so that the gentlemen from the papers can make pictures of me, and Nolan walks me up and down so proud, and the men shakes their heads and says, "He certainly is the true type, he is!" And the pretty ladies asks Miss Dorothy, who sits beside me letting me lick her gloves to show the crowd what friends we is, "Aren't you afraid he'll bite you?" and Jimmy Jocks calls to me, "Didn't I tell you so! I always knew you were one of us. Blood will out, Kid, blood will out. I saw your grandfather," says he, "make his début at the Crystal Palace. But he was never the dog you are!"

After that, if I could have asked for it, there was nothing I couldn't get. You might have thought I was a snow-dog, and they was afeerd I'd melt. If I wet my pats, Nolan gave me a hot bath and chained me to the stove; if I couldn't eat my food, being stuffed full by the cook, for I am a house-dog now, and let in to lunch whether there is visitors or not, Nolan would run to bring the vet. It was all tommy-rot, as Jimmy says, but meant most kind. I couldn't scratch myself comfortable, without Nolan giving me nasty drinks, and rubbing me outside till it burnt awful, and I wasn't let to eat bones for fear of spoiling my "beautiful" mouth, what mother used to call my "punishing jaw," and my food was cooked special on a gas-stove, and Miss Dorothy gives me an overcoat, cut very stylish like the champions', to wear when we goes out carriage-driving.

After the next show, where I takes three blue ribbons, four silver cups, two medals, and brings home forty-five dollars for Nolan, they gives me a "Registered" name, same as Jimmy's. Miss Dorothy wanted to call me "Regent Heir Apparent," but I was THAT glad when Nolan says, "No. Kid don't owe nothing to his father, only to you and hisself. So, if you please, Miss, we'll call him Wyndham Kid." And so they did, and you can see it on my overcoat in blue letters, and painted top of my kennel. It was all too hard to understand. For days I just sat and wondered if I was really me, and how it all come about, and why everybody was so kind. But, oh, it was so good they was, for if they hadn't been, I'd never have got the thing I most wished after.

But, because they was kind, and not liking to deny me nothing, they gave it me, and it was more to me than anything in the world.

It came about one day when we was out driving. We was in the cart they calls the dog-cart, because it's the one Miss Dorothy keeps to take Jimmy and me for an airing. Nolan was up behind, and me in my new overcoat was sitting beside Miss Dorothy. I was admiring the view, and thinking how good it was to have a horse pull you about so that you needn't get yourself splashed and have to be washed, when I hears a dog calling loud for help, and I pricks up my ears and looks over the horse's head. And I sees something that makes me tremble down to my toes. In the road before us three big dogs was chasing a little, old lady-dog. She had a string to her tail, where some boys had tied a can, and she was dirty with mud and ashes, and torn most awful. She was too far done up to get away, and too old to help herself, but she was making a fight for her life, snapping her old gums savage, and dying game. All this I see in a wink, and then the three dogs pinned her down, and I can't stand it no longer and clears the wheel and lands in the road on my head. It was my stylish overcoat done that, and I curse it proper, but I gets my pats again quick, and makes a rush for the fighting. Behind me I hear Miss Dorothy cry, "They'll kill that old dog. Wait, take my whip. Beat them off her! The Kid can take care of himself," and I hear Nolan fall into the road, and the horse come to a stop. The old lady-dog was down, and the three was eating her vicious, but as I come up, scattering the pebbles, she hears, and thinking it's one more of them, she lifts her head and my heart breaks open like some one had sunk his teeth in it. For, under the ashes and the dirt and the blood, I can see who it is, and I know that my mother has come back to me.

I gives a yell that throws them three dogs off their legs.

"Mother!" I cries. "I'm the Kid," I cries. "I'm coming to you, mother, I'm coming."

And I shoots over her, at the throat of the big dog, and the other two, they sinks their teeth into that stylish overcoat, and tears it off me, and that sets me free, and I lets them have it. I never had so fine a fight as that! What with mother being there to see, and not having been let to mix up in no fights since I become a prize-winner, it just naturally did me good, and it wasn't three shakes before I had 'em yelping. Quick as a wink, mother, she jumps in to help me, and I just laughed to see her. It was so like old times. And Nolan, he made me laugh too. He was like a hen on a bank, shaking the butt of his whip, but not daring to cut in for fear of hitting me.

"Stop it, Kid," he says, "stop it. Do you want to be all torn up?" says he. "Think of the Boston show next week," says he. "Think of Chicago. Think of Danbury. Don't you never want to be a champion?" How was I to think of all them places when I had three dogs to cut up at the same time. But in a minute two of 'em begs for mercy, and mother and me lets 'em run away. The big one, he ain't able to run away. Then mother and me, we dances and jumps, and barks and laughs, and bites each other and rolls each other in the road. There never was two dogs so happy as we, and Nolan, he whistles and calls and begs me to come to him, but I just laugh and play larks with mother.

"Now, you come with me," says I, "to my new home, and never try to run away again." And I shows her our house with the five red roofs, set on the top of the hill. But mother trembles awful, and says: "They'd never let the likes of me in such a place. Does the Viceroy live there, Kid?" says she. And I laugh at her. "No, I do," I says; "and if they won't let you live there, too, you and me will go back to the streets together, for we must never be parted no more." So we trots up the hill, side by side, with Nolan trying to catch me, and Miss Dorothy laughing at him from the cart.

"The Kid's made friends with the poor old dog," says she. "Maybe he knew her long ago when he ran the streets himself. Put her in here beside me, and see if he doesn't follow."

So when I hears that, I tells mother to go with Nolan and sit in the cart, but she says no, that she'd soil the pretty lady's frock; but I tells her to do as I say, and so Nolan lifts her, trembling still, into the cart, and I runs alongside, barking joyful.

When we drives into the stables I takes mother to my kennel, and tells her to go inside it and make herself at home. "Oh, but he won't let me!" says she.

"Who won't let you?" says I, keeping my eye on Nolan, and growling a bit nasty, just to show I was meaning to have my way.

"Why, Wyndham Kid," says she, looking up at the name on my kennel.

"But I'm Wyndham Kid!" says I.

"You!" cries mother. "You! Is my little Kid the great Wyndham Kid the dogs all talk about?" And at that, she, being very old, and sick, and hungry, and nervous, as mothers are, just drops down in the straw and weeps bitter.

Well, there ain't much more than that to tell. Miss Dorothy, she settled it.

"If the Kid wants the poor old thing in the stables," says she, "let her stay."

"You see," says she, "she's a black-and-tan, and his mother was a black-and-tan, and maybe that's what makes Kid feel so friendly toward her," says she.

"Indeed, for me," says Nolan, "she can have the best there is. I'd never drive out no dog that asks for a crust nor a shelter," he says. "But what will Mr. Wyndham do?"

"He'll do what I say," says Miss Dorothy, "and if I say she's to stay, she will stay, and I say—she's to stay!"

And so mother and Nolan, and me, found a home. Mother was scared at first—not being used to kind people—but she was so gentle and loving, that the grooms got fonder of her than of me, and tried to make me jealous by patting of her, and giving her the pick of the vittles. But that was the wrong way to hurt my feelings. That's all, I think. Mother is so happy here that I tell her we ought to call it the Happy Hunting Grounds, because no one hunts you, and there is nothing to hunt; it just all comes to you. And so we live in peace, mother sleeping all day in the sun, or behind the stove in the head-groom's office, being fed twice a day regular by Nolan, and all the day by the other grooms most irregular. And, as for me, I go hurrying around the country to the bench-shows; winning money and cups for Nolan, and taking the blue ribbons away from father.

[illegible]

[illegible] and [illegible] way I [illegible] cause [illegible] and [illegible] a [illegible] now [illegible] to [illegible]

"[illegible] were [illegible] to [illegible] the [illegible] Some."

"[illegible]" said I.

"[illegible] are little and the great [illegible] will [illegible] And at [illegible] are [illegible] ... is [illegible] are, [illegible] always better."

"[illegible] go [illegible] much [illegible] that [illegible] Miss [illegible]."

"If the [illegible] is the great old thing [illegible]," says the [illegible] horse.

"Now [illegible] there is one [illegible] and [illegible] [illegible] and [illegible] what [illegible] [illegible] and [illegible] says [illegible]."

"[illegible] Yolan [illegible] have [illegible] best [illegible] [illegible] and [illegible] that [illegible] [illegible] and [illegible] with [illegible] a [illegible] [illegible]?"

[illegible] and I [illegible] [illegible] [illegible]

And [illegible] and Yolan [illegible] me [illegible] a [illegible] [illegible] of [illegible] being used to [illegible] people—[illegible] that [illegible] that the [illegible] is [illegible] of [illegible] than [illegible] [illegible] kind of [illegible] that [illegible] [illegible] as the [illegible] [illegible] [illegible] that [illegible] [illegible] [illegible] and [illegible] and [illegible] [illegible] the [illegible] being [illegible] and [illegible] [illegible] [illegible] and [illegible] of [illegible] [illegible] [illegible] and [illegible] from [illegible]

CARL EWALD

My Little Boy

Carl Ewald (1856–1908)

CARL EWALD'S BIRTHPLACE was in Danish Schleswig; after the seizure of that province by Prussia, however, his parents moved to Copenhagen and he was brought up in that pleasant capital. He was first a forester, and then a schoolmaster. Even after he gave himself up wholly to literature, his interest in the proper training of children continued as My Little Boy *will testify.*

Ewald's work in literature followed an odd course. He began as a compiler of school textbooks, turned then to write a series of novels analyzing morbid psychological states, was for a while a satirist of society, and finally won fame as author of books for children in which fantasy and instruction were admirably blended.

My Little Boy*—wise, kindly and unpretentious—offers an ideal system of education in story form. It was one of the small number of his books to be published in English. The late Alexander Woollcott, with whom it was a favorite book, once described it as "as simple and as modest and as perfect as a Vermeer," and gave high praise to the translation by Alexander Teixeira de Mattos.*

MY LITTLE BOY

I

MY little boy is beginning to live.

Carefully, stumbling now and then on his little knock-kneed legs, he makes his way over the paving-stones, looks at everything that there is to look at and bites at every apple, both those which are his due and those which are forbidden him.

He is not a pretty child and is the more likely to grow into a fine lad. But he is charming.

His face can light up suddenly and become radiant; he can look at you with quite cold eyes. He has a strong intuition and he is incorruptible. He has never yet bartered a kiss for barley-sugar. There are people whom he likes and people whom he dislikes. There is one who has long courted his favour indefatigably and in vain; and, the other day, he formed a close friendship with another who had not so much as said "Good day" to him before he had crept into her lap and nestled there with glowing resolution.

He has a habit which I love.

When we are walking together and there is anything that impresses him, he lets go my hand for a moment. Then, when he has investigated the phenomenon and arrived at a result, I feel his little fist in mine again.

He has bad habits too.

He is apt, for instance, suddenly and without the slightest reason, to go up to people whom he meets in the street and hit them with his little stick. What is in his mind, when he does so, I do not know; and, so long as he does not hit me, it remains a matter between himself and the people concerned.

He has an odd trick of seizing big words in a grown-up conversation, storing them up for a while and then asking me for an explanation:

"Father," he says, "what is life?"

I give him a tap in his little stomach, roll him over on the carpet and conceal my emotion under a mighty romp. Then, when we sit breathless and tired, I answer, gravely:

"Life is delightful, my little boy. Don't you be afraid of it!"

II

Today my little boy gave me my first lesson.

It was in the garden.

I was writing in the shade of the big chestnut-tree, close to where the brook flows past. He was sitting a little way off, on the grass, in the sun, with Hans Christian Andersen in his lap.

Of course, he does not know how to read, but he lets you read to him, likes to hear the same tales over and over again. The better he knows them, the better he is pleased. He follows the story page by page, knows exactly where everything comes and catches you up immediately should you skip a line.

There are two tales which he loves more than anything in the world.

These are Grimm's *Faithful John* and Andersen's *The Little Mermaid*. When anyone comes whom he likes, he fetches the big Grimm, with those heaps of pictures, and asks for *Faithful John*. Then, if the reader stops, because it is so terribly sad, with all those little dead children, a bright smile lights up his small, long face and he says, reassuringly and pleased at "knowing better":

"Yes, but they come to life again."

Today, however, it is *The Little Mermaid*.

"Is that the sort of stories you write?" he asks.

"Yes," I say, "but I am afraid mine will not be so pretty."

"You must take pains," he says.

And I promise.

For a time he makes no sound. I go on writing and forget about him.

"Is there a little mermaid down there, in the water?" he asks.

"Yes, she swims up to the top in the summer."

He nods and looks out across the brook, which ripples so softly and smoothly that one can hardly see the water flow. On the opposite side, the rushes grow green and thick and there is also a bird, hidden in the rushes, which sings. The dragon-flies are whirling and humming. I am sitting with my head in my hand, absorbed in my work.

Suddenly, I hear a splash.

I jump from my chair, upset the table, dart forward and see that my little boy is gone. The brook is billowing and foaming; there are wide circles on the surface.

In a moment, I am in the water and find him and catch hold of him.

He stands on the grass, dripping with wet, spluttering and coughing. His thin clothes are clinging to his thin body, his face is black with mud. But out of the mud gleams a pair of angry eyes:

"There was no mermaid," he says.

I do not at once know what to reply and I have no time to think.

"Do you write that sort of stories?" he asks.

"Yes," I say, shamefaced.

"I don't like any of you," he says. "You make fun of a little boy."

He turns his back on me and, proud and wet, goes indoors without once looking round.

This evening, Grimm and Hans Christian Andersen disappear in a mysterious manner, which is never explained. He will miss them greatly, at first; but he will never be fooled again, not if I were to give him the sun and moon in his hand.

III

My little boy and I have had an exceedingly interesting walk in the Frederiksberg Park.

There was a mouse, which was irresistible. There were two chaffinches, husband and wife, which built their nest right before our eyes, and a snail, which had no secrets for us. And there were flowers, yellow and white, and there were green leaves, which told us the oddest adventures: in fact, as much as we can find room for in our little head.

Now we are sitting on a bench and digesting our impressions.

Suddenly the air is shaken by a tremendous roar:

"What was that?" asks my little boy.

"That was the lion in the Zoological Gardens," I reply.

No sooner have I said this than I curse my own stupidity.

I might have said that it was a gunshot announcing the birth of a prince; or an earthquake; or a china dish falling from the sky and breaking into pieces: anything whatever, rather than the truth.

For now my little boy wants to know what sort of thing the Zoological Gardens is.

I tell him.

The Zoological Gardens is a horrid place, where they lock up wild beasts who have done no wrong and who are accustomed to walk about freely in the distant foreign countries where they come from. The lion is there, whom we have just heard roaring. He is so strong that he can kill a policeman with one blow of his paw; he has great, haughty eyes and awfully sharp teeth. He lives in Africa and, at night, when he roars, all the other beasts tremble in their holes for fear. He is called the king of beasts. They caught him one day in a cunning trap and bound him and dragged him here and locked him up in a cage with iron bars to it. The cage is no more than half as big as Petrine's room. And there the king walks up and down, up and down, and gnashes his teeth with sorrow and rage and roars so that you can hear him ever so far away. Outside his cage stand cowardly people and laugh at him, because he can't get out and eat them up, and poke their sticks through the rails and tease him.

My little boy stands in front of me and looks at me with wide-open eyes:

"Would he eat them up, if he got out?" he asks.

"In a moment."

"But he can't get out, can he?"

"No. That's awfully sad. He can't get out."

"Father, let us go and look at the lion."

I pretend not to hear and go on to tell him of the strange birds there: great eagles, which used to fly over every church-steeple and over the highest trees and mountains and swoop down upon lambs and hares and carry them up to their young in the nest. Now they are sitting in cages, on a perch, like canaries, with clipped wings and blind eyes. I tell him of gulls, which used to fly all day long over the stormy sea: now they splash about in a puddle of water, screaming pitifully. I tell him of wonderful blue and red birds, which, in their youth, used to live among wonderful blue and red flowers, in balmy forests a thousand times bigger than the Frederiksberg Park, where it was as dark as night under the trees with the brightest sun shining down upon the tree-tops: now they sit there in very small cages and hang their beaks while they stare at tiresome boys in dark-blue suits and black stockings and waterproof boots and sailor-hats.

"Are those birds really blue?" asks my little boy.

"Sky-blue," I answer. "And utterly broken-hearted."

"Father, can't we go and look at the birds?"

I take my little boy's hands in mine:

"I don't think we will," I say. "Why should still more silly boys do so? You can't imagine how it goes to one's heart to look at those poor captive beasts."

"Father, I should so much like to go."

"Take my advice and don't. The animals there are not the real animals, you see. They are ill and ugly and angry because of their captivity and their longing and their pain."

"I should so much like to see them."

"Now let me tell you something. To go to the Zoological Gardens costs five cents for you and ten cents for me. That makes fifteen cents altogether, which is an awful lot of money. We won't go there now, but we'll buy the biggest money-box we can find: one of those money-boxes shaped like a pig. Then we'll put fifteen cents in it. And every Thursday we'll put fifteen cents in the pig. By-and-by, that will grow into quite a fortune: it will make such a lot of money that, when you are grown up, you can take a trip to Africa and go to the desert and hear the wild, the real lion roaring and tremble just like the people tremble down there. And you can go to the great, dark forests and see the real blue birds flying proud and free among the flowers. You can't think how glad you will be, how beautiful they will look and how they will sing to you. . . ."

"Father, I would rather go to the Zoological Gardens now."

My little boy does not understand a word of what I say. And I am at my wits' end.

"Shall we go and have some cakes at Josty's?" I ask.

"I would rather go to the Zoological Gardens."

I can read in his eyes that he is thinking of the captive lion. Ugly human instincts are waking up in his soul. The mouse is forgotten and the snail; and the chaffinches have built their nest to no purpose.

At last I get up and say, bluntly, without any further explanation:

"You are *not* going to the Zoological Gardens. Now we'll go home."

And home we go. But we are not in a good temper.

Of course, I get over it and I buy an enormous money-box pig. Also we put the money into it and he thinks that most interesting.

But, later in the afternoon, I find him in the bed-room engaged in a piteous game.

He has built a cage, in which he has imprisoned the pig. He is teasing it and hitting it with his whip, while he keeps shouting to it:

"You can't get out and bite me, you stupid pig! You can't get out!"

IV

We have beer-soup and Aunt Anna to dinner. Now beer-soup is a nasty dish and Aunt Anna is not very nice either.

She has yellow teeth and a little hump and very severe eyes, which are not even both equally severe. She is nearly always scolding us and, when she sees a chance, she pinches us.

The worst of all, however, is that she is constantly setting us a good example, which can easily end by gradually and inevitably driving us to embrace wickedness.

Aunt Anna does not like beer-soup any more than we do. But of course she eats it with a voluptuous expression on her face and looks angrily at my little boy, who does not even make an attempt to behave nicely:

"Why doesn't the little boy eat his delicious beer-soup?" she asks.

A scornful silence.

"Such delicious beer-soup! I know a poor, wretched boy who would be awfully glad to have such delicious beer-soup."

My little boy looks with great interest at Auntie, who is swallowing her soup with eyes full of ecstatic bliss:

"Where is he?" he asks.

Aunt Anna pretends not to hear.

"Where is the poor boy?" he asks again.

"Yes, where is he?" I ask. "What's his name?"

Aunt Anna gives me a furious glance.

"What's his name, Aunt Anna?" asks my little boy. "Where does he live? He can have my beer-soup with pleasure."

"Mine too," I say, resolutely, and I push my plate from me.

My little boy never takes his great eyes off Aunt Anna's face. Meanwhile, she has recovered herself:

"There are many poor boys who would thank God if they could get such delicious beer-soup," she says. "Very many. Everywhere."

"Yes, but tell us of one, Auntie," I say.

My little boy has slipped down from his chair. He stands with his chin just above the table and both his hands round his plate, ready to march off with the beer-soup to the poor boy, if only he can get his address.

But Aunt Anna does not allow herself to be played with:

"Heaps of poor boys," she says again. "Hun-dreds! And therefore another little boy, whom I will not name, but who is in this room, ought to be ashamed that he is not thankful for his beer-soup."

My little boy stares at Aunt Anna like the bird fascinated by the snake.

"Such delicious beer-soup!" she says. "I must really ask for another little helping."

Aunt Anna revels in her martyrdom. My little boy stands speechless, with open mouth and round eyes.

I push my chair back and say, with genuine exasperation:

"Now, look here, Aunt Anna, this is really too bad! Here we are, with a whole lot of beer-soup which we don't care about in the least and which we would be very glad to get rid of, if we only knew someone who would have it. You are the only one that knows of anybody. You know a poor boy who would dance for joy if he got some beer-soup. You know hundreds. But you won't tell us their names or where they live."

"Why, what do you mean?"

"And you yourself sit quite calmly eating two whole helpings, though you know quite well that you're going to have an omelette to follow. That's really very naughty of you, Aunt Anna."

Aunt Anna chokes with annoyance. My little boy locks his teeth with a snap and looks with every mark of disgust at that wicked old woman.

And I turn with calm earnestness to his mother and say:

"After this, it would be most improper for us ever to have beer-soup here again. We don't care for it and there are hundreds of little boys who love it. If it must be made, then Aunt Anna must come every Saturday and fetch it. She knows where the boys live."

The omelette is eaten in silence, after which Aunt Anna shakes the dust from her shoes. She won't have any coffee today.

While she is standing in the hall and putting on her endless wraps, a last doubt arises in my little boy's soul. He opens his green eyes wide before her face and whispers:

"Aunt Anna, where do the boys live?"

Aunt Anna pinches him and is shocked and goes off, having suffered a greater defeat than she can ever repair.

V

My little boy comes into my room and tells me, with a very long face, that Jean is dead. And we put all nonsense on one side and hurry away to the Klampenborg train, to go where Jean is.

For Jean is the biggest dog that has lived for some time.

He once bit a boy so hard that the boy still walks lame. He once bit his own master. He could give such a look out of his eyes and open such a mouth that there was no more horrible sight in the world. And then he would be the mildest of the mild: my little boy could put his hand in his mouth and ride on his back and pull his tail.

When we get there, we hear that Jean is already buried.

We look at each other in dismay, to think how quickly that happens! And we go to the grave, which is in the grounds of the factory, where the tall chimneys stand.

We sit down and can't understand it.

We tell each other all the stories that we know of Jean's wonderful size and strength. The one remembers this, the other that. And, as each story is told, the whole thing becomes only more awful and obscure.

At last we go home by train.

Besides ourselves, there is a kind old gentleman in the compartment, who would like to make friends with my little boy. But the boy has nothing to talk about to the kind old gentleman. He stands at the window, which comes just under his chin, and stares out.

His eyes light upon some tall chimneys:

"That's where Jean is buried," he says.

"Yes."

The landscape flies past. He can think only of *that* and see only *that* and, when some more chimneys appear, he says again:

"That's where Jean is buried."

"No, my little friend," says the kind old gentleman. "That was over there."

The boy looks at him with surprise. I hasten to reassure him:

"Those *are* Jean's chimneys," I say.

And, while he is looking out again, I take the old gentleman to the further corner of the compartment and tell him the state of the case.

I tell him that, if I live, I hope, in years to come, to explain to the boy the difference between Petersen's and Hansen's factories and, should I die, I will confidently leave that part of his education to others. Yes, even if he should never learn this difference, I would still be resigned. Today it is a question of other and more important matters. The strongest, the most living thing he knew is dead. . . .

"Really?" says the old gentleman, sympathetically. "A relation, perhaps?"

"Yes," I say. "Jean is dead, a dog. . . ."

"A dog?"

"It is not because of the *dog*—don't you understand?—but of *death*, which he sees for the first time: death, with all its might, its mystery. . . ."

"Father," says my little boy and turns his head towards us. "When do we die?"

"When we grow old," says the kind old gentleman.

"No," says the boy. "Einar has a brother, at home, in the courtyard, and he is dead. And he was only a little boy."

"Then Einar's brother was so good and learnt such a lot that he was already fit to go to Heaven," says the old gentleman.

"Mind you don't become too good," I say and laugh and tap my little boy in the stomach.

And my little boy laughs too and goes back to his window, where new chimneys rise over Jean's grave.

But I take the old gentleman by the shoulders and forbid him most strictly to talk to my little boy again. I give up trying to make him understand me. I just shake him. He eyes the communication-cord and, when we reach the station, hurries away.

I go with my little boy, holding his hand, through the streets full of live people. In the evening, I sit on the edge of his bed and talk with him about that incomprehensible thing: Jean, who is dead; Jean, who was so much alive, so strong, so big. . . .

VI

Our courtyard is full of children and my little boy has picked a bosom-friend out of the band: his name is Einar and he can be as good as another.

My little boy admires him and Einar allows himself to be

admired, so that the friendship is established on the only proper basis.

"Einar says . . . Einar thinks . . . Einar does," is the daily refrain; and we arrange our little life accordingly.

"I can't see anything out of the way in Einar," says the mother of my little boy.

"Nor can I," say I. "But our little boy can and that is enough. I once had a friend who could see nothing at all charming in you. And you yourself, if I remember right, had three friends who thought *your* taste inexcusable. Luckily for our little boy. . . ."

"Luckily!"

"It is the feeling that counts," I go on lecturing, "and not the object."

"Thanks!" she says.

Now something big and unusual takes place in our courtyard and makes an extraordinary impression on the children and gives their small brains heaps to struggle with for many a long day.

The scarlatina comes.

And scarlatina is not like a pain in your stomach, when you have eaten too many pears, or like a cold, when you have forgotten to put on your jacket. Scarlatina is something quite different, something powerful and terrible. It comes at night and takes a little boy who was playing quite happily that same evening. And then the little boy is gone.

Perhaps a funny carriage comes driving in through the gate, with two horses and a coachman and two men with bright brass buttons on their coats. The two men take out of the carriage a basket, with a red blanket and white sheets, and carry it up to where the boy lives. Presently, they carry the basket down again and then the boy is inside. But nobody can see him, because the sheet is over his face. The basket is shoved into the carriage, which is shut with a bang, and away goes the carriage with the boy, while his mother dries her eyes and goes up to the others.

Perhaps no carriage comes. But then the sick boy is shut up in his room and no one may go to him for a long time, because he is infectious. And anyone can understand that this must be terribly sad.

The children in the courtyard talk of nothing else.

They talk with soft voices and faces full of mystery, because they know nothing for certain. They hear that one of them, who rode away in the carriage, is dead; but that makes no more impression on them than when one of them falls ill and disappears.

Day by day, the little band is being thinned out and not one of them has yet come back.

I stand at my open window and look at my little boy, who is sitting on the steps below with his friend. They have their arms around each other's necks and see no one except each other; that is to say, Einar sees himself and my little boy sees Einar.

"If you fall ill, I will come and see you," says my little boy.

"No, you won't!"

"I will come and see you."

His eyes beam at this important promise. Einar cries as though he were already ill.

And the next day he is ill.

He lies in a little room all by himself. No one is allowed to go to him. A red curtain hangs before the window.

My little boy sits alone on the steps outside and stares up at the curtain. His hands are thrust deep into his pockets. He does not care to play and he speaks to nobody.

And I walk up and down the room, uneasy as to what will come next.

"You are anxious about our little boy," says his mother. "And it will be a miracle if he escapes."

"It's not that. We've all had a touch of scarlatina."

But just as I want to talk to her about it, I hear a fumbling with the door-handle which there is no mistaking and then he stands before us in the room.

I know you so well, my little boy, when you come in sideways like that, with a long face, and go and sit in a corner and look at the two people who owe so much happiness to you—look from one to the other. Your eyes are greener than usual. You can't find your words and you sit huddled up and you are ever so good.

"Mother, is Einar ill?"

"Yes. But he will soon be better again. The doctor says that he is not so bad."

"Is he infectious, Mother?"

"Yes, he is. His little sister has been sent to the country, so that she may not fall ill too. No one is allowed to go to him except his mother, who gives him his milk and his medicine and makes his bed."

A silence.

The mother of my little boy looks down at her book and suspects nothing. The father of my little boy looks in great suspense from the window.

"Mother, I want to go to Einar."

"You can't go there, my little man. You hear, he's infectious. Just think, if you should fall ill yourself! Einar isn't bothering at all about chatting with you. He sleeps the whole day long."

"But when he wakes, Mother?"

"You can't go up there."

This tells upon him and he is nearly crying. I see that the time has come for me to come to his rescue:

"Have you promised Einar to go and see him?" I ask.

"Yes, Father. . . ."

He is over his trouble. His eyes beam. He stands erect and glad beside me and puts his little hand in mine.

"Then of course you must do so," I say, calmly. "So soon as he wakes."

Our mother closes her book with a bang:

"Go down to the courtyard and play, while Father and I have a talk."

The boy runs away.

And she comes up to me and lays her hand on my shoulder and says, earnestly:

"I *daren't* do that, do you hear?"

And I take her hand and kiss it and say, quite as earnestly:

"And I *daren't refuse!*"

We look at each other, we two, who share the empire, the power and the glory.

"I heard our little boy make his promise," I say, "I saw him. Sir

Galahad himself was not more in earnest when swearing his knightly oath. You see, we have no choice here. He can catch the scarlatina in any case and it is not even certain that he will catch it. . . ."

"If it was diphtheria, you wouldn't talk like that!"

"You may be right. But am I to become a thief for the sake of a nickel, because I am not sure that I could resist the temptation to steal a kingdom?"

"You would not find a living being to agree with you."

"Except yourself. And that is all I want. The infection is really only a side matter. It can come this way or that way. We can't safeguard him, come what may. . . ."

"But are we to send him straight to where it is?"

"We're not doing that; it's not we who are doing that."

She is very much excited. I put my arm round her waist and we walk up and down the room together:

"Darling, today our little boy may meet with a great misfortune. He may receive a shock from which he will never recover. . . ."

"That is true," she says.

"If he doesn't keep his promise, the misfortune has occurred. It would already be a misfortune if he could ever think that it was possible for him to break it, if it appeared to him that there was anything great or remarkable about keeping it."

"Yes, but . . ."

"Darling, the world is full of careful persons. One step more and they become mere paltry people. Shall we turn that into a likely thing, into a virtue, for our little boy? His promise was stupid: let that pass. . . ."

"He is so little."

"Yes, that he is; and God be praised for it! Think what good luck it is that he did not know the danger, when he made his promise, that he does not understand it now, when he is keeping it. What a lucky beggar! He is learning to keep his word, just as he has learnt to be clean. By the time that he is big enough to know his danger, it will be an indispensable habit with him. And he gains all that at the risk of a little scarlatina."

She lays her head on my shoulder and says nothing more.

That afternoon, she takes our little boy by the hand and goes up with him to Einar. They stand on the threshold of his room, bid him good-day and ask him how he is.

Einar is not at all well and does not look up and does not answer. But that does not matter in the least.

VII

My little boy is given a cent by Petrine with instructions to go to the baker's and buy some biscuits.

By that which fools call an accident, but which is really a divine miracle, if miracles there be, I overhear this instruction. Then I stand at my window and see him cross the street in his slow way and with bent head; only, he goes slower than usual and with his head bent more deeply between his small shoulders.

He stands long outside the baker's window, where there is a confused heap of lollipops and chocolates and sugar-sticks and other things created for a small boy's delight. Then he lifts his young hand, opens the door, disappears and presently returns with a great paper bag, eating with all his might.

And I, who, Heaven be praised, have myself been a thief in my time, run all over the house and give my orders.

My little boy enters the kitchen.

"Put the biscuits on the table," says Petrine.

He stands still for a moment and looks at her and at the table and at the floor. Then he goes silently to his mother.

"You're quite a big boy now, that you can buy biscuits for Petrine," says she, without looking up from her work.

His face is very long, but he says nothing. He comes quietly in to me and sits down on the edge of a chair.

"You have been over the way, at the baker's."

He comes up to me, where I am sitting and reading, and presses himself against me. I do not look at him, but I can perceive what is going on inside him.

"What did you buy at the baker's?"

"Lollipops."

"Well, I never! What fun! Why, you had some lollipops this morning. Who gave you the money this time?"

"Petrine."

"Really! Well, Petrine is certainly very fond of you. Do you remember the lovely ball she gave you on your birthday?"

"Father, Petrine told me to buy a cent's worth of biscuits."

"Oh, dear!"

It is very quiet in the room. My little boy cries bitterly and I look anxiously before me, stroking his hair the while.

"Now you have fooled Petrine badly. She wants those biscuits, of course, for her cooking. She thinks they're on the kitchen-table and, when she goes to look, she won't find any. Mother gave her a cent for biscuits. Petrine gave you a cent for biscuits and you go and spend it on lollipops. What are we to do?"

He looks at me in despair, holds me tight, says a thousand things without speaking a word.

"If only we had a cent," I say. "Then you could rush over the way and fetch the biscuits."

"Father. . . ." His eyes open very wide and he speaks so softly that I can hardly hear him. "There is a cent on mother's writing-table."

"Is there?" I cry with delight. But, at the same moment, I shake my head and my face is overcast again. "That is no use to us, my little boy. That cent belongs to mother. The other was Petrine's. People are so terribly fond of their money and get so angry when you take it from them. I can understand that, for you can buy such an awful lot of things with money. You can get biscuits and lollipops and clothes and toys and half the things in the world. And it is not so easy either to make money. Most people have to drudge all day long to earn as much as they want. So it is no wonder that they get angry when you take it. Especially when it is only for lollipops. Now Petrine . . . she has to spend the whole day cleaning rooms and cooking dinner and washing up before she gets her wages. And out of that she has to buy clothes and shoes . . . and you know that she has a little girl whom she has to pay for at Madam Olsen's. She must certainly have saved very cleverly before she managed to buy you that ball."

We walk up and down the room, hand in hand. He keeps on falling over his legs, for he can't take his eyes from my face.

"Father . . . haven't you got a cent?"

I shake my head and give him my purse:

"Look for yourself," I say. "There's not a cent in it. I spent the last this morning."

We walk up and down. We sit down and get up and walk about again. We are very gloomy. We are bowed down with sorrow and look at each other in great perplexity.

"There might be one hidden away in a drawer somewhere," I say. We fly to the drawers.

We pull out thirty drawers and rummage through them. We fling papers in disorder, higgledy-piggledy, on the floor: what do we care? If only, if only we find a cent. . . .

Hurrah!

We both, at last, grasp at a cent, as though we would fight for it . . . we have found a beautiful, large cent. Our eyes gleam and we laugh through our tears.

"Hurry now," I whisper. "You can go this way . . . through my door. Then run back quickly up the kitchen stairs, with the biscuits, and put them on the table. I shall call Petrine, so that she doesn't see. And we won't tell anybody."

He is down the stairs before I have done speaking. I run after him and call to him:

"Wasn't it a splendid thing that we found that cent?" I say.

"Yes," he answers, earnestly.

And he laughs for happiness and I laugh too and his legs go like drumsticks across to the baker's.

From my window, I see him come back, at the same pace, with red cheeks and glad eyes. He has committed his first crime. He has understood it. And he has not the sting of remorse in his soul nor the black cockade of forgiveness in his cap.

The mother of my little boy and I sit until late at night talking about money, which seems to us the most difficult matter of all.

For our little boy must learn to know the power of money and the glamour of money and the joy of money. He must earn much money and spend much money. . . .

Yet there were two people, yesterday, who killed a man to rob him of four dollars and thirty-seven cents. . . .

VIII

It has been decreed in the privy council that my little boy shall have a weekly income of one cent. Every Sunday morning, that sum shall be paid to him, free of income-tax, out of the treasury and he has leave to dispose of it entirely at his own pleasure.

He receives this announcement with composure and sits apart for a while and ponders on it.

"Every Sunday?" he asks.

"Every Sunday."

"All the time till the summer holidays?"

"All the time till the summer holidays."

In the summer holidays, he is to go to the country, to stay with his godmother, in whose house he was pleased to allow himself to be born. The summer holidays are, consequently, the limits of his calculation of time: beyond them lies, for the moment, his Nirvana.

And we employ this restricted horizon of ours to further our true happiness.

That is to say, we calculate, with the aid of the almanac, that, if everything goes as heretofore, there will be fifteen Sundays before the summer holidays. We arrange a drawer with fifteen compartments and in each compartment we put one cent. Thus we know exactly what we have and are able at any time to survey our financial status.

And, when he sees that great lot of cents lying there, my little boy's breast is filled with mad delight. He feels endlessly rich, safe for a long time. The courtyard rings with his bragging, with all that he is going to do with his money. His special favourites are invited to come up and view his treasure.

The first Sunday passes in a normal fashion, as was to be expected.

He takes his cent and turns it straightway into a stick of chocolate of the best sort, with almonds on it and sugar, in short, an ideal stick in every way. The whole performance is over in five minutes: by that time, the stick of chocolate is gone, with the sole exception of a remnant in the corners of our mouth, which our ruthless mother wipes away, and a stain on our collar, which annoys us.

He sits by me, with a vacant little face, and swings his legs. I open the drawer and look at the empty space and at the fourteen others:

"So *that's* gone," I say.

My accent betrays a certain melancholy, which finds an echo in his breast. But he does not deliver himself of it at once.

"Father . . . is it long till next Sunday?"

"Very long, my boy; ever so many days."

We sit a little, steeped in our own thoughts. Then I say, pensively:

"Now, if you had bought a top, you would perhaps have had more pleasure out of it. I know a place where there is a lovely top: red, with a green ring round it. It is just over the way, in the toy-shop. I saw it yesterday. I should be greatly mistaken if the toy-man was not willing to sell it for a cent. And you've got a whip, you know."

We go over the way and look at the top in the shop-window. It is really a splendid top.

"The shop's shut," says my little boy, despondently.

I look at him with surprise:

"Yes, but what does that matter to us? Anyway, we can't buy the top before next Sunday. You see, you've spent your cent on chocolate. Give me your handkerchief: there's still a bit on your cheek."

There is no more to be said. Crestfallen and pensively, we go home. We sit a long time at the dining-room window, from which we can see the window of the shop.

During the course of the week, we look at the top daily, for it does not do to let one's love grow cold. One might so easily forget it. And the top shines always more seductively. We go in and make sure that the price is really in keeping with our means. We make the shopkeeper take a solemn oath to keep the top for us till Sunday morning, even if boys should come and bid him much higher sums for it.

On Sunday morning, we are on the spot before nine o'clock and acquire our treasure with trembling hands. And we play with it all day and sleep with it at night, until, on Wednesday morning, it disappears without a trace, after the nasty manner which tops have.

When the turn comes of the next cent, something remarkable happens.

There is a boy in the courtyard who has a skipping-rope and my little boy, therefore, wants to have a skipping-rope too. But this is a difficult matter. Careful enquiries establish the fact that a skipping rope of the sort used by the upper classes is nowhere to be obtained for less than five cents.

The business is discussed as early as Saturday:

"It's the simplest thing in the world," I say. "You must not spend your cent tomorrow. Next Sunday you must do the same and the next and the next. On the Sunday after that, you will have saved your five cents and can buy your skipping-rope at once."

"When shall I get my skipping-rope then?"

"In five Sundays from now."

He says nothing, but I can see that he does not think my idea very brilliant. In the course of the day, he derives, from sources unknown to me, an acquaintance with financial circumstances which he serves up to me on Sunday morning in the following words:

"Father, you must lend me five cents for the skipping-rope. If you will lend me five cents for the skipping-rope, I'll give you *forty* cents back. . . ."

He stands close to me, very red in the face and quite confused. I perceive that he is ripe for falling into the claws of the usurers:

"I don't do that sort of business, my boy," I say. "It wouldn't do you any good either. And you're not even in a position to do it, for you have only thirteen cents, as you know."

He collapses like one whose last hope is gone.

"Let us just see," I say.

And we go to our drawer and stare at it long and deeply.

"We might perhaps manage it this way, that I give you five cents now. And then I should have your cent and the next four cents. . . ."

He interrupts me with a loud shout. I take out my purse, give him five cents and take one cent out of the drawer:

"That won't be pleasant next Sunday," I say, "and the next and the next and the next. . . ."

But the thoughtless youth is gone.

Of course, the instalments of his debt are paid off with great ceremony. He is always on the spot himself when the drawer is opened and sees how the requisite cent is removed and finds its way into my pocket instead of his.

The first time, all goes well. It is simply an amusing thing that I should have the cent; and the skipping-rope is still fresh in his memory, because of the pangs which he underwent before its purchase. Next Sunday, already the thing is not *quite* so pleasant and, when the fourth instalment falls due, my little boy's face looks very gloomy:

"Is anything the matter?" I ask.

"I should so much like a stick of chocolate," he says, without looking at me.

"Is that all? You can get one in a fortnight. By that time, you will have paid for the skipping-rope and the cent will be your own again."

"I should so much like to have the stick of chocolate now."

Of course, I am full of the sincerest compassion, but I can't help it. What's gone is gone. We saw it with our own eyes and we know exactly where it has gone to. And, that Sunday morning, we part in a dejected mood.

Later in the day, however, I find him standing over the drawer with raised eyebrows and a pursed-up mouth. I sit down quietly and wait. And I do not have to wait long before I learn that his development as an economist is taking quite its normal course.

"Father, suppose we moved the cent now from here into this Sunday's place and I took it and bought the chocolate-stick. . . ."

"Why, then you won't have your cent for the other Sunday."

"I don't mind that, Father. . . ."

We talk about it, and then we do it. And, with that, as a matter of course, we enter upon the most reckless peculations.

The very next Sunday, he is clever enough to take the furthest cent, which lies just before the summer holidays. He pursues the path of vice without a scruple, until, at last, the blow falls and five long Sundays come in a row without the least chance of a cent.

Where should they come from? They were there. We know that. They are gone. We have spent them ourselves.

But, during those drab days of poverty, we sit every morning over the empty drawer and talk long and profoundly about that painful phenomenon, which is so simple and so easy to understand and which one must needs make the best of.

And we hope and trust that our experience will do us good, when, after our trip, we start a new set of cents.

IX

My little boy is engaged to be married.

She is a big, large-limbed young woman, three years his senior, and no doubt belongs to the minor aristocracy. Her name is Gertie. By a misunderstanding, however, which is pardonable at his age and moreover quite explained by Gertie's appearance, he calls her Dirty—little Dirty—and by this name she will be handed down to history.

He met her on the boulevard, where he was playing, in the fine spring weather, with other children. His reason for the engagement is good enough:

"I wanted a girl for myself," he says.

Either I know very little of mankind or he has made a fortunate choice. No one is likely to take Dirty from him.

Like the gentleman that he is, he at once brings the girl home to us and introduces her. In consequence of the formality of the occasion, he does not go in by the kitchen way, as usual, but rings the front-door bell. I open the door myself. There he stands on the mat, hand in hand with Dirty, his bride, and, with radiant eyes:

"Father," he says, "this is little Dirty. She is my sweetheart. We are going to be married."

"That is what people usually do with their sweethearts," I answer, philosophically. "Pray, Dirty, come in and be welcomed by the family."

"Wipe your feet, Dirty," says my little boy.

The mother of my little boy does not think much of the match. She has even spoken of forbidding Dirty the house.

"We can't do that," I say. "I am not in ecstasies over it either, but it is not at all certain that it will last."

"Yes, but . . ."

"Do you remember what little use it was when your mother forbade me the house? We used to meet in the most incredible places and kiss each other terribly. I can quite understand that you have forgotten, but you ought to bear it in mind now that your son's beginning. And you ought to value the loyalty of his behaviour towards his aged parents."

"My dear! . . ."

"And then I must remind you that it is spring. The trees are budding. You can't see it, perhaps, from the kitchen-window or from your work-table, but I, who go about all day, have noticed it. You know what Byron says:

March has its hares, and May must have its heroine."

And so Dirty is accepted.

But, when she calls, she has first to undergo a short quarantine, while the mother of my little boy washes her and combs her hair thoroughly.

Dirty does not like this, but the boy does. He looks on with extraordinary interest and at once complains if there is a place that has escaped the sponge. I can't make out what goes on within him on these occasions. There is a good deal of cruelty in love; and he himself hates to be washed. Perhaps he is rapt in fancies and wants to see his sweetheart rise daily from the waves, like Venus Anadyomene. Perhaps it is merely his sense of duty: last Friday, in cold blood, he allowed Dirty to wait outside, on the step, for half an hour, until his mother came home.

Another of his joys is to see Dirty eat.

I can quite understand that. Here, as at her toilet, there is something worth looking at. The mother of my little boy and I would be glad too to watch her, if there were any chance of giving Dirty her fill. But there is none. At least, not with my income.

When I see all that food disappear, without as much as a shade of satisfaction coming into her eyes, I tremble for the young couple's future. But he is cheerful and unconcerned.

Of course, there are also clouds in their sky.

A few days ago, they were sitting quietly together in the dining-room and talking of their wedding. My little boy described what the house would be like and the garden and the horses. Dirty made no remarks and she had no grounds for doing so, for everything was particularly nice. But, after that, things went wrong:

"We shall have fourteen children," said the boy.

"No," said Dirty. "We shall only have two: a boy and a girl."

"I want to have fourteen."

"I won't have more than two."

"Fourteen."

"Two."

There was no coming to an agreement. My little boy was speechless at Dirty's meanness. And Dirty pinched her lips together and nodded her head defiantly. Then he burst into tears.

I could have explained to him that Dirty, who sits down every day as the seventh at the children's table at home, cannot look upon children with his eyes, as things forming an essential part of every well-regulated family, but must regard them rather as bandits who eat up other people's food. But I did not feel entitled to discuss the young lady's domestic circumstances unasked.

One good thing about Dirty is that she is not dependent upon her family nor they upon her. It has not yet happened that any inquiries have been made after her, however long she remained with us. We know just where she lives and what her father's name is. Nothing more.

However, we notice in another way that our daughter-in-law is not without relations.

Whenever, for instance, we give her a pair of stockings or some other article of clothing, it is always gone the next day; and so on until all the six brothers and sisters have been supplied. Not till then do we have the pleasure of seeing Dirty look neat. She has been so long accustomed to going shares that she does so in every conceivable circumstance.

And I console the mother of my little boy by saying that, should he fall out with Dirty, he can take one of the sisters and that, in this way, nothing would be lost.

X

My little boy confides to me that he would like a pear.

Now pears fall within his mother's province and I am sure that he has had as many as he is entitled to. And so we are at once agreed that what he wants is a wholly irrelevant, uncalled-for, delightful extra pear.

Unfortunately, it also appears that the request has already been laid before Mamma and met with a positive refusal.

The situation is serious, but not hopeless. For I am a man who knows how mean is the supply of pears to us poor wretched children of men and how wonderful an extra pear tastes.

And I am glad that my little boy did not give up all hope of the pear at the first obstacle. I can see by the longing in his green eyes how big the pear is and I reflect with lawful paternal pride that he will win his girl and his position in life when their time comes.

We now discuss the matter carefully.

First comes the prospect of stomach-ache:

"Never mind about that," says he.

I quite agree with his view.

Then perhaps Mother will be angry.

No, Mother is never angry. She is sorry; and that is not nice. But then we must see and make it up to her in another way.

So we slink in and steal the pear.

I put it to him whether, perhaps—when we have eaten the pear—we ought to tell Mother. But that does not appeal to him:

"Then I shan't get one this evening," he says.

And when I suggest that, possibly, Mother might be impressed with such audacious candour, he shakes his head decisively:

"You don't know Mother," he says.

So I, of course, have nothing to say.

Shortly after this, the mother of my little boy and I are standing at the window laughing at the story.

We catch sight of him below, in the courtyard.

He is sitting on the steps with his arm round little Dirty's neck. They have shared the pear. Now they are both singing, marvellously out of tune and with a disgustingly sentimental expression on their faces, a song which Dirty knows:

For riches are only a lo-oan from Heaven
And poverty is a reward.

And we are overcome with a great sense of desolation.

We want to make life green and pleasant for our little boy, to make his eyes open wide to see it, his hands strong to grasp it. But we feel powerless in the face of all the contentment and patience and resignation that are preached from cellar to garret, in church and in school: all those second-rate virtues, which may lighten an old man's last few steps as he stumbles on towards the grave, but which are only so many shabby lies for the young.

XI

Dirty is paying us a visit and my little boy is sitting at her feet.

She has buried her fingers in her hair and is reading, reading, reading. . . .

She is learning the Ten Commandments by heart. She stammers and repeats herself, with eyes fixed in her head and a despairing mouth:

"Thou shalt . . . Thou shalt not . . . Thou shalt . . ."

The boy watches her with tender compassion.

He has already learnt a couple of the commandments by listening to her and helps her, now and then, with a word. Then he comes to me and asks, anxiously:

"Father, must Dirty do all that the Ten Commandments say?"

"Yes."

He sits down by her again. His heart is overflowing with pity, his eyes are moist. She does not look at him, but plods on bravely:

"Thou shalt . . . Thou shalt not . . ."

"Father, when I grow big, must I also do all that the Ten Commandments say?"

"Ye-es."

He looks at me in utter despair. Then he goes back to Dirty and listens, but now he keeps his thoughts to himself.

Suddenly, something seems to flash across his mind.

He comes to me again, puts his arms on my knee and looks with his green eyes firmly into mine:

"Father, do you do all that the Ten Commandments say?"

"Ye-e-es."

He looks like a person whose last hope has escaped him. I would so much like to help him; but what, in Heaven's name, can I do?

Then he collects himself, shakes his head a little and says, with great tears in his eyes:

"Father, I don't believe that I can do all those things that the Ten Commandments say."

And I draw him to me and we cry together because life is so difficult, while Dirty plods away like a good girl.

XII

This we all know, that sin came into the world by the law.

Dirty's Ten Commandments have brought it to us.

When she comes, she now always has Luther's terrible Little Catechism [1] and Balslev's equally objectionable work with her. Her parents evidently look upon it as most natural that she should also cultivate her soul at our house.

Her copies of these two classics were not published yesterday. They are probably heirlooms in Dirty's family. They are covered in thick brown paper, which again is protected by a heavy layer of dirt against any touch of clean fingers. They can be smelt at a distance.

But my little boy is no snob.

When Dirty has finished her studies—she always reads out aloud—he asks her permission to turn over the pages of the works in which she finds those strange words. He stares respectfully at the letters which he cannot read. And then he asks questions.

He asks Dirty, he asks the servant, he asks us. Before anyone suspects it, he is at home in the whole field of theology.

[1] *Luther's Lille Katekismus,* the Lutheran catechism in general use in Denmark.—A. T. de M.

He knows that God is in Heaven, where all good people go to Him, while the wicked are put down below in Hell. That God created the world in six days and said that we must not do anything on Sundays. That God can do everything and knows everything and sees everything.

He often prays, creeps upstairs as high as he can go, so as to be nearer Heaven, and shouts as loud as he can. The other day I found him at the top of the folding-steps:

"Dear God! You must please give us fine weather tomorrow, for we are going to the wood."

He says *Du* to everybody except God and the grocer.

He never compromises.

The servant is laying the table; we have guests coming and we call her attention to a little hole in the cloth:

"I must lay it so that no one can see it," she says.

"God will see it."

"He is not coming this evening," says the blasphemous hussy.

"Yes, He is everywhere," answers my little boy, severely.

He looks after me in particular:

"You mustn't say 'gad,' Father. Dirty's teacher says that people who say 'gad' go to Hell."

"I shan't say it again," I reply, humbly.

One Sunday morning, he finds me writing and upbraids me seriously.

"My little boy," I say, distressfully, "I must work every day. If I do nothing on Sunday, I do nothing on Monday either. If I do nothing on Monday, I am idle on Tuesday too. And so on."

He ponders; and I continue, with the courage of despair.

"You must have noticed that Dirty wants a new catechism? The one she has is dirty and old."

He agrees to this.

"She will never have one, you see," I say, emphatically. "Her father rests so tremendously on Sunday that he is hardly able to do anything on the other days. He never earns enough to buy a new catechism."

I have won—this engagement. But the war is continued without cessation of hostilities.

The mother of my little boy and I are sitting in the twilight by his bedside and softly talking about this.

"What are we to do?" she asks.

"We can do nothing?" I reply. "Dirty is right: God is everywhere. We can't keep Him out. And if we could, for a time: what then? A day would come perhaps when our little boy was ill or sad and the priests would come to him with their God as a new and untried miraculous remedy and bewilder his mind and his senses. Our little boy too will have to go through Luther and Balslev and Assens and confirmation and all the rest of it. Then this will become a commonplace to him; and one day he will form his own views, as we have done."

But, when he comes and asks how big God is, whether He is bigger than the Round Tower, how far it is to Heaven, why the weather was not fine on the day when he prayed so hard for it: then we fly from the face of the Lord and hide like Adam and Eve in the Garden of Eden.

And we leave Dirty to explain.

XIII

My little boy has got a rival, whose name is Henrik, a popinjay who not only is six years old, but has an unlimited supply of liquorice at his disposal. And, to fill the measure of my little boy's bitterness, Henrik is to go to the dancing-school; and I am, therefore, not surprised when my little boy asks to be taught to dance, so that he may not be left quite behind in the contest.

"I don't advise you to do that," I say. "The dancing which you learn at school is not pretty and does not play so great a part in love as you imagine. I don't know how to dance; and many charming ladies used to prefer me to the most accomplished ornaments of the ballroom. Besides, you know, you are knock-kneed."

And, to cheer him up, I sing a little song which we composed when we were small and had a dog and did not think about women:

See, my son, that little basset,
Running with his knock-kneed legs!
His own puppy, he can't catch it:
He'll fall down as sure as eggs!
Knock-kneed Billy!
Isn't he silly?
Silly Billy!

But poetry fails to comfort him. Dark is his face and desperate his glance. And, when I see that the case is serious, I resolve to resort to serious measures.

I take him with me to a ball, a real ball, where people who have learnt to dance go to enjoy themselves. It is difficult to keep him in a more or less waking condition, but I succeed.

We sit quietly in a corner and watch the merry throng. I say not a word, but look at his wide-open eyes.

"Father, why does that man jump like that, when he is so awfully hot?"

"Yes; can you understand it?"

"Why does that lady with her head on one side look so tired? . . . Why does that fat woman hop about so funnily, Father? . . . Father, what queer legs that man there has!"

It rains questions and observations. We make jokes and laugh till the tears come to our eyes. We whisper naughty things to each other and go into a side-room and mimic a pair of crooked legs till we can't hold ourselves for laughter. We sit and wait till a steam thrashing-machine on its round comes past us; and we are fit to die when we hear it puff and blow.

We enjoy ourselves beyond measure.

And we make a hit.

The steam thrashing-machine and the crooked legs and the fat woman and the hot gentleman and others crowd round us and admire the dear little boy. We accept their praises, for we have agreed not to say what we think to anybody, except to Mother, when we come home, and then, of course, to Dirty.

And we wink our eyes and enjoy our delightful fun until we fall asleep and are driven home and put to bed.

And then we have done with the dancing-school.

My little boy paints in strong colours, for his Dirty's benefit, what Henrik will look like when he dances. It is no use for that young man to deny all that my little boy says and to execute different elegant steps. I was prepared for this; and my little boy tells exultantly that this is only something with which they lure stupid people at the start and that it will certainly end with Henrik's getting very hot and hopping round on crooked legs with a fat woman and a face of despair.

In the meantime, of course, I do not forget that, if we pull down without building up we shall end by landing ourselves in an unwholesome scepticism.

We therefore invent various dances, which my little boy executes in the courtyard to Dirty's joy and to Henrik's most jealous envy. We point emphatically to the fact that the dances are our own, that they are composed only for the woman we love and performed only for her.

There is, for instance, a dance with a stick, which my little boy wields, while Henrik draws back. Another with a pair of new mittens for Dirty. And, lastly, the liquorice dance, which expresses an extraordinary contempt for that foodstuff.

That Dirty should suck a stick of liquorice, which she has received from Henrik, while enjoying her other admirer's satire, naturally staggers my little boy. But I explain to him that that is because she is a woman and that *that* is a thing which can't be helped.

What Bournonville[1] would say, if he could look down upon us from his place in Heaven, I do not know.

But I don't believe that he can.

If he, up there, could see how people dance down here, he really would not stay there.

XIV

There is a battle royal and a great hullabaloo among the children in the courtyard.

I hear them shouting "Jew!" and I go to the window and see my

[1] A famous French ballet-master who figured at the Copenhagen Opera House in the eighteenth century.—A. T. de M.

little boy in the front rank of the bandits, screaming, fighting with clenched fists and without his cap.

I sit down quietly to my work again, certain that he will appear before long and ease his heart.

And he comes directly after.

He stands still, as is his way, by my side and says nothing. I steal a glance at him: he is greatly excited and proud and glad, like one who has fearlessly done his duty.

"What fun you've been having down there!"

"Oh," he says, modestly, "it was only a Jew boy whom we were licking."

I jump up so quickly that I upset my chair:

"A Jew boy? Were you licking him? What had he done?"

"Nothing. . . ."

His voice is not very certain, for I look so queer.

And that is only the beginning. For now I snatch my hat and run out of the door as fast as I can and shout:

"Come . . . come . . . we must find him and beg his pardon!"

My little boy hurries after me. He does not understand a word of it, but he is terribly in earnest. We look in the courtyard, we shout and call. We rush into the street and round the corner, so eager are we to come up with him. Breathlessly, we ask three passers-by if they have not seen a poor, ill-used Jew boy.

All in vain: the Jew boy and all his persecutors are blown away into space.

So we go and sit up in my room again, the laboratory where our soul is crystallized out of the big events of our little life. My forehead is wrinkled and I drum disconsolately with my fingers on the table. The boy has both his hands in his pockets and does not take his eyes from my face.

"Well," I say, decidedly, "there is nothing more to be done. I hope you will meet that Jew boy one day, so that you can give him your hand and ask him to forgive you. You must tell him that you did that only because you were stupid. But if, another time, anyone does him any harm, I hope you will help him and lick the other one as long as you can stir a limb."

I can see by my little boy's face that he is ready to do what I wish. For he is still a mercenary, who does not ask under which flag, so long as there is a battle and booty to follow. It is my duty to train him to be a brave recruit, who will defend his fair mother-land, and so I continue:

"Let me tell you, the Jews are by way of being quite wonderful people. You remember David, about whom Dirty reads at school: he was a Jew boy. And the Child Jesus, Whom everybody worships and loves, although He died two thousand years ago: He was a little Jew also."

My little boy stands with his arms on my knee and I go on with my story.

The old Hebrews rise before our eyes in all their splendour and power, quite different from Dirty's Balslev. They ride on their camels in coats of many colours and with long beards: Moses and Joseph and his brethren and Samson and David and Saul. We hear wonderful stories. The walls of Jericho fall at the sound of the trumpet.

"And what next?" says my little boy, using the expression which he employed when he was much smaller and which still comes to his lips whenever he is carried away.

We hear of the destruction of Jerusalem and how the Jews took their little boys by the hand and wandered from place to place, scoffed at, despised and ill-treated. How they were allowed to own neither house nor land, but could only be merchants, and how the Christian robbers took all the money which they had got together. How, nevertheless, they remained true to their God and kept up their old sacred customs in the midst of the strangers who hated and persecuted them.

The whole day is devoted to the Jews.

We look at old books on the shelves which I love best to read and which are written by a Jew with a wonderful name, which a little boy can't remember at all. We learn that the most famous man now living in Denmark is a Jew.

And, when evening comes and Mother sits down at the piano and sings the song which Father loves above all other songs, it appears that the words were written by one Jew and the melody composed by another.

My little boy is hot and red when he falls to sleep that night. He turns restlessly in bed and talks in his sleep.

"He is a little feverish," says his mother.

And I bend down and kiss his forehead and answer, calmly:

"That is not surprising. Today I have vaccinated him against the meanest of all mean and vulgar diseases."

XV

We are staying in the country, a long way out, where the real country is.

Cows and horses, pigs and sheep, a beautiful dog and hens and ducks form our circle of acquaintances. In addition to these, there are of course the two-legged beings who own and look after the four-legged ones and who, in my little boy's eyes, belong to quite the same kind.

The great sea lies at the foot of the slope. Ships float in the distance and have nothing to say to us. The sun burns us and bronzes us. We eat like thrashers, sleep like guinea-pigs and wake like larks. The only real sorrow that we have suffered is that we were not allowed to have our breeches made with a flap at the side, like the old woodcutter's.

Presently, it happens that, for better or worse, we get neighbours.

They are regular Copenhageners. They were prepared not to find electric light in the farm-house; but, if they had known that there was no water in the kitchen, God knows they would not have come. They trudge through the clover as though it were mire and are sorry to find so few cornflowers in the rye. A cow going loose along the roads fills them with a terror which might easily have satisfied a royal tiger.

The pearl of the family is Erna.

Erna is five years old; her very small face is pale green, with watery blue eyes and yellow curls. She is richly and gaily dressed in a broad and slovenly sash, daintily-embroidered pantalets, short open-work socks and patent-leather shoes. She falls if she but moves a foot, for she is used only to gliding over polished floors or asphalt.

I at once perceive that my little boy's eyes have seen a woman.

He has seen the woman that comes to us all at one time or another and turns our heads with her rustling silks and her glossy hair and wears her soul in her skirts and our poor hearts under her heel.

"Now comes the perilous moment for Dirty," I say to the mother of my little boy.

This time it is my little boy's turn to be superior.

He knows the business thoroughly and explains it all to Erna. When he worries the horse, she trembles, impressed with his courage and manliness. When she has a fit of terror at the sight of a hen, he is charmed with her delicacy. He knows the way to the smith's, he dares to roll down the high slope, he chivalrously carries her ridiculous little cape.

Altogether, there is no doubt as to the condition of his heart. And, while Erna's family apparently favour the position—for which may the devil take them!—I must needs wait with resignation like one who knows that love is every man's master.

One morning he proposes.

He is sitting with his beloved on the lawn. Close to them, her aunt is nursing her chlorosis under a red parasol and with a novel in her bony lap. Up in the balcony above sit I, as Providence, and see everything, myself unseen.

"You shall be my sweetheart," says my little boy.

"Yes," says Erna.

"I have a sweetheart already in Copenhagen," he says, proudly.

This communication naturally by no means lowers Erna's suitor in her eyes. But it immediately arouses all Auntie's moral instincts:

"If you have a sweetheart, you must be true to her."

"Erna shall be my sweetheart."

Auntie turns her eyes up to Heaven:

"Listen, child," she says. "You're a very naughty boy. If you have given Dir—Dir——"

"Dirty," says the boy.

"Well, that's an extraordinary name! But, if you have given her your word, you must keep it till you die. Else you'll never, never be happy."

My little boy understands not a word and answers not a word.

Erna begins to cry at the prospect that this good match may not come off. But I bend down over the baluster and raise my hat:

"I beg your pardon, Fröken. Was it not you who jilted Hr. Petersen? . . ."

"Good heavens! . . ."

She packs up her chlorosis and disappears with Erna, mumbling something about like father, like son, and goodness knows what.

Presently, my little boy comes up to me and stands and hangs about.

"Where has Erna gone to?" I ask my little boy.

"She mustn't go out," he says, dejectedly.

He puts his hands in his pockets and looks straight before him.

"Father," he says, "can't you have two sweethearts?"

The question comes quite unexpectedly and, at the moment, I don't know what to answer.

"Well?" says the mother of my little boy, amiably, and looks up from her newspaper.

And I pull my waistcoat down and my collar up:

"Yes," I say, firmly. "You can. But it is wrong. It leads to more fuss and unpleasantness than you can possibly conceive."

A silence.

"Are you so fond of Erna?" asks our mother.

"Yes."

"Do you want to marry her?"

"Yes."

I get up and rub my hands:

"Then the thing is settled," I say. "We'll write to Dirty and give her notice. There's nothing else to be done. I will write now and you can give the letter yourself to the postman, when he comes this afternoon. If you take my advice, you will make her a present of your ball. Then she will not be so much upset."

"She can have my gold-fish too, if she likes," says the boy.

"Excellent, excellent. We will give her the gold-fish. Then she will really have nothing in the world to complain of."

My little boy goes away. But, presently, he returns:

"Father, have you written the letter to Dirty?"

"Not yet, my boy. There is time enough. I sha'n't forget it."

"Father, I am so fond of Dirty."

"She was certainly a dear little girl."

A silence.

"Father, I am also so fond of Erna."

We look at each other. This is no joke:

"Perhaps we had better wait with the letter till tomorrow," I say. "Or perhaps it would be best if we talked to Dirty ourselves, when we get back to town."

We both ponder over the matter and really don't know what to do.

Then my eyes surprise an indescribable smile on our mother's face. All a woman's incapacity to understand man's honesty is contained within that smile and I resent it greatly:

"Come," I say and give my hand to my little boy. "Let us go."

And we go to a place we know of, far away behind the hedge, where we lie on our backs and look up at the blue sky and talk together sensibly, as two gentlemen should.

XVI

My little boy is to go to school.

We can't keep him at home any longer, says his mother. He himself is glad to go, of course, because he does not know what school is.

I know what it is and I know also that there is no escape for him, that he must go. But I am sick at heart. All that is good within me revolts against the inevitable.

So we go for our last morning walk, along the road where something wonderful has always happened to us. It looks to me as if the trees have crape wound round their tops and the birds sing in a minor key and the people stare at me with earnest and sympathetic eyes.

But my little boy sees nothing. He is only excited at the prospect. He talks and asks questions without stopping.

We sit down by the edge of our usual ditch—alas, that ditch!

And suddenly my heart triumphs over my understanding. The

voice of my clear conscience penetrates through the whole well-trained and harmonious choir which is to give the concert; and it sings its solo in the ears of my little boy:

"I just want to tell you that school is a horrid place," I say. "You can have no conception of what you will have to put up with there. They will tell you that two and two are four. . . ."

"Mother has taught me that already," says he, blithely.

"Yes, but that is wrong, you poor wretch!" I cry. "Two and two are never four, or only very seldom. And that's not all. They will try to make you believe that Teheran is the capital of Persia and that Mont Blanc is 15,781 feet high and you will take them at their word. But I tell you that both Teheran and Persia are nothing at all, an empty sound, a stupid joke. And Mont Blanc is not half as big as the mound in the tallow-chandler's back-garden. And listen: you will never have any more time to play in the courtyard with Einar. When he shouts to you to come out, you'll have to sit and read about a lot of horrible old kings who have been dead for hundreds and hundreds of years, if they ever existed at all, which I, for my part, simply don't believe."

My little boy does not understand me. But he sees that I am sad and puts his hand in mine:

"Mother says that you must go to school to become a clever boy," he says. "Mother says that Einar is ever so much too small and stupid to go to school."

I bow my head and nod and say nothing.

That is past.

And I take him to school and see how he storms up the steps without so much as turning his head to look back at me.

XVII

Here ends this book about my little boy.

What more can there be to tell?

He is no longer mine. I have handed him over to society. Hr. Petersen, candidate in letters, Hr. Nielsen, student of theology, and

Fröken Hansen, certificated teacher, will now set their distinguished example before him for five hours daily. He will form himself in their likeness. Their spirit hovers over him at school: he brings it home with him, it overshadows him when he is learning the lessons which they zealously mete out to him.

I don't know these people. But I pay them.

I, who have had a hard fight to keep my thoughts free and my limbs unrestrained and who have not retired from the fight without deep wounds of which I am reminded when the weather changes, I have, of my own free will, brought him to the institution for maiming human beings. I, who at times have soared to peaks that were my own, because the other birds dared not follow me, have myself brought him to the place where wings are clipped for flying respectably, with the flock.

"There was nothing else to be done," says the mother of my little boy.

"Really?" I reply, bitterly. "Was there nothing else to be done? But suppose that I had put by some money, so that I could have saved Messrs. Petersen and Nielsen and Fröken Hansen their trouble and employed my day in myself opening out lands for that little traveller whom I myself have brought into the land? Suppose that I had looked round the world for people with small boys who think as I do and that we had taken upon us to bring up these young animals so that they kept sight of horns and tails and fairy-tales?"

"Yes," she says.

"Small boys have a bad time of it, you know."

"They had a worse time of it in the old days."

"That is a poor comfort. And it can become worse again. The world is full of parents and teachers who shake their foolish heads and turn up their old eyes and cross their flat chests with horror at the depravity of youth: children are so disobedient, so naughty, so self-willed and talk so disrespectfully to their elders! . . . And what do we do, we who know better?"

"We do what we can."

But I walk about the room, more and more indignant and ashamed of the pitiful part which I am playing:

"Do you remember, a litle while ago, he came to me and said that he longed so for the country and asked if we couldn't go there for a little? There were horses and cows and green fields to be read in his eyes. Well, I couldn't leave my work. And I couldn't afford it. So I treated him to a shabby and high-class sermon about the tailor to whom I owed money. Don't you understand that I let my little boy do *my* work, that I let him pay *my* debt? . . ." I bend down over her and say earnestly, "You must know; do please tell me—God help me, I do not know—if I ought not rather to have paid my debt to the boy and cheated the other?"

"You know quite well," she says.

She says it in such a way and looks at me with two such sensible eyes and is so strong and so true that I suddenly think things look quite well for our little boy; and I become restful and cheerful like herself:

"Let Petersen and Nielsen and Hansen look out!" I say. "My little boy, for what I care, may take from them all the English and geography and history that he can. But they shall throw no dust in his eyes. I shall keep him awake and we shall have great fun and find them out."

"And I shall help him with his English and geography and history," says she.

MARY RAYMOND SHIPMAN ANDREWS

The Perfect Tribute

Mary Raymond Shipman Andrews
(186?–1936)

THE IDEA OF The Perfect Tribute *grew from an anecdote of what took place on the way to the dedication services at Gettysburg Cemetery, told to the author on the ultimate authority of Edward Everett but only after it had passed through the memories of three intermediate witnesses. Recent scholarship has played ducks and drakes with the story's basis in fact, but its popularity as a contribution to the myth of Abraham Lincoln is unharmed. The historians, those chilly guardians of truth, may gnash their teeth; the men of letters may say (as one did) that Mrs. Andrews's fiction possessed only "saccharine and mystic tendencies relieved by a mild and harmless humor"; yet the public has taken her work to its heart. Almost three-quarters of a million copies of* The Perfect Tribute *have been sold.*

Mrs. Andrews did not court publicity during her long, useful life, nor was she ever aggressively "literary." She was born in Mobile, Alabama, schooled in Lexington, Kentucky, and after her marriage to Justice W. S. Andrews of the New York Court of Appeals became a New Yorker by adoption. She contributed extensively to the magazines and added a second piece of apocrypha to the Lincoln canon in The Counsel Assigned *(1912), which will be found in its proper chronological position in* The Scribner Treasury.

THE PERFECT TRIBUTE

ON the morning of November 18, 1863, a special train drew out from Washington, carrying a distinguished company. The presence with them of the Marine Band from the Navy Yard spoke a public occasion to come, and among the travellers there were those who might be gathered only for an occasion of importance. There were judges of the Supreme Court of the United States; there were heads of departments; the general-in-chief of the army and his staff; members of the cabinet. In their midst, as they stood about the car before settling for the journey, towered a man sad, preoccupied, unassuming; a man awkward and ill-dressed; a man, as he leaned slouchingly against the wall, of no grace of look or manner, in whose haggard face seemed to be the suffering of the sins of the world. Abraham Lincoln, President of the United States, journeyed with his party to assist at the consecration, the next day, of the national cemetery at Gettysburg. The quiet November landscape slipped past the rattling train, and the President's deep-set eyes stared out at it gravely, a bit listlessly. From time to time he talked with those who were about him; from time to time there were flashes of that quaint wit which is linked, as his greatness, with his name, but his mind was to-day dispirited, unhopeful. The weight on his shoulders seemed pressing more heavily than he had courage to press back against it, the responsibility of one almost a dictator in a wide, war-torn country came near to crushing, at times, the mere human soul and body. There was, moreover, a speech to be made to-morrow to thousands who would expect their President to say something to them worth the listening of a people who were making history; something brilliant, eloquent, strong. The melancholy gaze glittered with a grim smile. He—Abraham Lincoln—the lad bred in a cabin, tutored in rough schools here and there, fighting for, snatching at crumbs of learning that fell from rich tables, struggling to a hard knowledge which well knew its own limitations—it was he of whom this was expected. He glanced across the car. Edward Everett sat there, the orator of the following day, the finished gentleman, the careful student, the heir of traditions of learning and breeding, of scholarly instincts and resources. The self-made President gazed at him wistfully. From him the people might expect and would get a balanced and polished oration. For that end he had been born, and inheritance and opportunity and inclination had worked together for that end's perfection. While Lincoln had wrested from a scanty schooling a command of English clear and forcible always, but, he feared, rough-hewn, lacking, he feared, in finish and in breadth—of what use was it for such a one to try to fashion a speech fit to take a place by the side of Everett's silver sentences? He sighed. Yet the people had a right to the best he could give, and he would give them his best; at least he could see to it that the words were real and were short; at least he would not, so, exhaust their patience. And the work might as well be done now in the leisure of the journey. He put a hand, big, powerful, labor-knotted, into first one sagging pocket and then another, in search of a pencil, and drew out one broken across the end. He glanced about inquiringly—there was nothing to write upon. Across the car the Secretary of State had just opened a package of books and their wrapping of brown paper lay on the floor, torn carelessly in a zig-zag. The President stretched a long arm.

"Mr. Seward, may I have this to do a little writing?" he asked, and the Secretary protested, insisting on finding better material.

But Lincoln, with few words, had his way, and soon the untidy stump of a pencil was at work and the great head, the deep-lined face, bent over Seward's bit of brown paper, the whole man absorbed in his task.

Earnestly, with that "capacity for taking infinite pains" which has been defined as genius, he labored as the hours flew, building together close-fitted word on word, sentence on sentence. As the sculptor must dream the statue prisoned in the marble, as the artist must dream the picture to come from the brilliant unmeaning of his palette, as the musician dreams a song, so he who writes must have a vision of his finished work before he touches, to begin it, a medium more elastic, more vivid, more powerful than any other—words—prismatic bits of humanity, old as the Pharaohs, new as the Arabs of the street, broken, sparkling, alive, from the age-long life of the race. Abraham Lincoln, with the clear thought in his mind of what he would say, found the sentences that came to him colorless, wooden. A wonder flashed over him once or twice of Everett's skill with these symbols which, it seemed to him, were to the Bostonian a key-board facile to make music, to Lincoln tools to do his labor. He put the idea aside, for it hindered him. As he found the sword fitted to his hand he must fight with it; it might be that he, as well as Everett, could say that which should go straight from him to his people, to the nation who struggled at his back towards a goal. At least each syllable he said should be chiselled from the rock of his sincerity. So he cut here and there an adjective, here and there a phrase, baring the heart of his thought, leaving no ribbon or flower of rhetoric to flutter in the eyes of those with whom he would be utterly honest. And when he had done he read the speech and dropped it from his hand to the floor and stared again from the window. It was the best he could do, and it was a failure. So, with the pang of the workman who believes his work done wrong, he lifted and folded the torn bit of paper and put it in his pocket, and put aside the thought of it, as of a bad thing which he might not better, and turned and talked cheerfully with his friends.

At eleven o'clock on the morning of the day following, on November 19, 1863, a vast, silent multitude billowed, like waves of the sea, over what had been not long before the battle-field of Gettysburg. There were wounded soldiers there who had beaten their way four months before through a singing fire across these quiet fields, who had seen the men die who were buried here; there were troops, grave and responsible, who must soon go again into battle; there were the rank and file of an everyday American gathering in surging thousands; and above them all, on the open-air platform, there were the leaders of the land, the pilots who today lifted a hand from the wheel of the ship of state to salute the memory of those gone down in the storm. Most of the men in that group of honor are now passed over to the majority, but their names are not dead in American history—great ghosts who walk still in the annals of their country, their flesh-and-blood faces were turned attentively that bright, still November afternoon towards the orator of the day, whose voice held the audience.

For two hours Everett spoke and the throng listened untired, fascinated by the dignity of his high-bred look and manner almost as much, perhaps, as by the speech which has taken a place in literature. As he had been expected to speak he spoke, of the great battle, of the causes of the war, of the results to come after. It was an oration which missed no shade of expression, no reach of grasp. Yet there were those in the multitude, sympathetic to a unit as it was with the Northern cause, who grew restless when this man who had been crowned with so thick a laurel wreath by Americans spoke of Americans as rebels, of a cause for which honest Americans were giving their lives as a crime. The days were war days, and men's passions were inflamed, yet there were men who listened to Edward Everett who believed that his great speech would have been greater unenforced with bitterness.

As the clear, cultivated voice fell into silence, the mass of people burst into a long storm of applause, for they knew that they had heard an oration which was an event. They clapped and cheered him again and again and again, as good citizens acclaim a man worthy of honor whom they have delighted to honor. At last, as the ex-Governor of Massachusetts, the ex-ambassador to England, the ex-Secretary of State, the ex-Senator of the United States—handsome, distinguished, graceful, sure of voice and of movement—took his seat, a tall, gaunt figure detached itself from the group on the platform and slouched slowly across the open space and stood facing the audience. A stir and a whisper brushed over the field of humanity, as if a breeze had rippled a monstrous bed of poppies. This was the President. A quivering silence settled down and every eye was wide to watch this strange, disappointing appearance, every ear alert to catch the first sound of his voice. Suddenly the voice came, in a queer, squeaking falsetto. The effect on the audience was irrepressible, ghastly. After Everett's deep tones, after the strain of expectancy, this extraordinary, gaunt apparition, this high, thin sound from the huge body, were too much for the American crowd's sense of humor, always stronger than its sense of reverence. A suppressed yet unmistakable titter caught the throng, ran through it, and was gone. Yet no one who knew the President's face could doubt that he had heard it and had understood. Calmly enough, after a pause almost too slight to be recognized, he went on, and in a dozen words his tones had gathered volume, he had come to his power and dignity. There was no smile now on any face of those who listened. People stopped breathing rather, as if they feared to miss an inflection. A loose-hung figure, six feet four inches high, he towered above them, conscious of and quietly ignoring the bad first impression, unconscious of a charm of personality which reversed that impression within a sentence. That these were his people was his only thought. He had something to say to them; what did it matter about him or his voice?

"Fourscore and seven years ago," spoke the President, "our fathers brought forth on this continent a new nation, conceived in liberty and dedicated to the proposition that all men are created equal. Now we are engaged in a great civil war, testing whether that nation, or any nation, so conceived and so dedicated can long endure. We are met on a great battlefield of that war. We have come to dedicate a portion of it as a final resting-place for those who here gave their lives that that nation might live. It is altogether fitting and proper that we should do this.

"But in a larger sense we cannot dedicate, we cannot consecrate, we cannot hallow, this ground. The brave men, living and dead, who struggled here, have consecrated it far above our poor power to add or to detract. The world will little note nor long remember what we say here, but it can never forget what they did here. It is for us, the living, rather, to be dedicated here to the unfinished work which they who fought here have thus far so nobly advanced. It is rather for us to be here dedicated to the great task remaining before us—that from these honored dead we take increased devotion to that cause for which they here gave the last full measure of devotion—that we here highly resolve that these dead shall not have died in vain, that this nation, under God, shall have a new birth of freedom, and that government of the people, by the people, for the people shall not perish from the earth."

There was no sound from the silent, vast assembly. The President's large figure stood before them, at first inspired, glorified with the thrill and swing of his words, lapsing slowly in the stillness into lax, ungraceful lines. He stared at them a moment with sad eyes full of gentleness, of resignation, and in the deep quiet they stared at him. Not a hand was lifted in applause. Slowly the big, awkward man slouched back across the platform and sank into his seat, and yet there was no sound of approval, of recognition from the audience; only a long sigh ran like a ripple on an ocean through rank after rank. In Lincoln's heart a throb of pain answered it. His speech had been, as he feared it would be, a failure. As he gazed steadily at these his countrymen who would not give him even a little perfunctory applause for his best effort, he knew that the disappointment of it cut into his soul. And then he was aware that there was music, the choir was singing a dirge; his part was done, and his part had failed.

When the ceremonies were over Everett at once found the President. "Mr. President," he began, "your speech—" but Lincoln had interrupted, flashing a kindly smile down at him, laying a hand on his shoulder.

"We'll manage not to talk about my speech, Mr. Everett," he said. "This isn't the first time I've felt that my dignity ought not to permit me to be a public speaker."

He went on in a few cordial sentences to pay tribute to the orator of the occasion. Everett listened thoughtfully and when the chief had done, "Mr. President," he said simply, "I should be glad if I could flatter myself that I came as near the central idea of the occasion in two hours as you did in two minutes."

But Lincoln shook his head and laughed and turned to speak to a newcomer with no change of opinion—he was apt to trust his own judgments.

The special train which left Gettysburg immediately after the solemnities on the battle-field cemetery brought the President's party into Washington during the night. There was no rest for the man at the wheel of the nation next day, but rather added work until, at about four in the afternoon, he felt sorely the need of air and went out from the White House alone, for a walk. His mind still ran on the events of the day before—the impressive, quiet multitude, the serene sky of November arched, in the hushed interregnum of the year, between the joy of summer and the war of winter, over those who had gone from earthly war to heavenly joy. The picture was deeply engraved in his memory; it haunted him. And with it came a soreness, a discomfort of mind which had haunted him as well in the hours between—the chagrin of the failure of his speech. During the day he had gently but decisively put aside all reference to it from those about him; he had glanced at the head-lines in the newspapers with a sarcastic smile; the Chief Executive must be flattered, of course; newspaper notices meant nothing. He knew well that he had made many successful speeches; no man of his shrewdness could be ignorant that again and again he had carried an audience by storm; yet he had no high idea of his own speech-making, and yesterday's affair had shaken his confidence more. He remembered sadly that, even for the President, no hand, no voice had been lifted in applause.

"It must have been pretty poor stuff," he said half aloud; "yet I thought it was a fair little composition. I meant to do well by them."

His long strides had carried him into the outskirts of the city, and suddenly, at a corner, from behind a hedge, a young boy of fifteen years or so came rushing toward him and tripped and stumbled against him, and Lincoln kept him from falling with a quick, vigorous arm. The lad righted himself and tossed back his thick, light hair and stared haughtily, and the President, regarding him, saw that his blue eyes were blind with tears.

"Do you want all of the public highway? Can't a gentleman from the South even walk in the streets without—without—" and the broken sentence ended in a sob.

The anger and the insolence of the lad were nothing to the man who towered above him—to that broad mind this was but a child in trouble. "My boy, the fellow that's interfering with your walking is down inside of you," he said gently, and with that the astonished youngster opened his wet eyes wide and laughed—a choking childish laugh that pulled at the older man's heart-strings. "That's better, sonny," he said, and patted the slim shoulder. "Now tell me what's wrong with the world. Maybe I might help straighten it."

"Wrong, wrong!" the child raved; "everything's wrong," and launched into a mad tirade against the government from the President down.

Lincoln listened patiently, and when the lad paused for breath, "Go ahead," he said good-naturedly. "Every little helps."

With that the youngster was silent and drew himself up with stiff dignity, offended yet fascinated; unable to tear himself away from this strange giant who was so insultingly kind under his abuse, who yet inspired him with such a sense of trust and of hope.

"I want a lawyer," he said impulsively, looking up anxiously into the deep-lined face inches above him. "I don't know where to find a lawyer in this horrible city, and I must have one—I can't wait—it may be too late—I want a lawyer *now*," and once more he was in a fever of excitement.

"What do you want with a lawyer?" Again the calm, friendly tone quieted him.

"I want him to draw a will. My brother is—" he caught his breath with a gasp in a desperate effort for self-control. "They say he's—dying." He finished the sentence with a quiver in his voice, and the brave front and the trembling, childish tone went to the man's heart. "I don't believe it—he can't be dying," the boy talked on, gathering courage. "But anyway, he wants to make a will, and—and I reckon—it may be that he—he must."

"I see," the other answered gravely, and the young, torn soul felt an unreasoning confidence that he had found a friend. "Where is your brother?"

"He's in the prison hospital there—in that big building," he pointed down the street. "He's captain in our army—in the Confederate army. He was wounded at Gettysburg."

"Oh!" The deep-set eyes gazed down at the fresh face, its muscles straining under grief and responsibility, with the gentlest, most fatherly pity. "I think I can manage your job, my boy," he said. "I used to practise law in a small way myself, and I'll be glad to draw the will for you."

The young fellow had whirled him around before he had finished the sentence. "Come," he said. "Don't waste time talking—why didn't you tell me before?" and then he glanced up. He saw the ill-fitting clothes, the craglike, rough-modelled head, the awkward carriage of the man; he was too young to know that what he felt beyond these was greatness. There was a tone of patronage in his voice and in the cock of his aristocratic young head as he spoke. "We can pay you, you know—we're not paupers." He fixed his eyes on Lincoln's face to watch the impression as he added, "My brother is Carter Hampton Blair, of Georgia. I'm Warrington Blair. The Hampton Court Blairs, you know."

"Oh!" said the President.

The lad went on:

"It would have been all right if Nellie hadn't left Washington to-day—my sister, Miss Eleanor Hampton Blair. Carter was better this morning, and so she went with the Senator. She's secretary to Senator Warrington, you know. He's on the Yankee side"—the tone was full of contempt—"but yet he's our cousin, and when he offered Nellie the position she would take it in spite of Carter and me. We were so poor"—the lad's pride was off its guard for the moment, melted in the soothing trust with which this stranger thrilled his soul. It was a relief to him to talk, and the large hand which rested on his shoulder as they walked seemed an assurance that his words were accorded respect and understanding. "Of course, if Nellie had been here she would have known how to get a lawyer, but Carter had a bad turn half an hour ago, and the doctor said he might get better or he might die any minute, and Carter remembered about the money, and got so excited that they said it was hurting him, so I said I'd get a lawyer, and I rushed out, and the first thing I ran against you. I'm afraid I wasn't very polite." The smile on the gaunt face above him was all the answer he needed. "I'm sorry. I apologize. It certainly was good of you to come right back with me." The child's manner was full of the assured graciousness of a high-born gentleman; there was a lovable quality in his very patronage, and the suffering and the sweetness and the pride combined held Lincoln by his sense of humor as well as by his soft heart. "You sha'n't lose anything by it," the youngster went on. "We may be poor, but we have more than plenty to pay you, I'm sure. Nellie has some jewels, you see—oh, I think several things yet. Is it very expensive to draw a will?" he asked wistfully.

"No, sonny; it's one of the cheapest things a man can do," was the hurried answer, and the child's tone showed a lighter heart.

"I'm glad of that, for, of course, Carter wants to leave—to leave as much as he can. You see, that's what the will is about—Carter is engaged to marry Miss Sally Maxfield, and they would have been married now if he hadn't been wounded and taken prisoner. So, of course, like any gentleman that's engaged, he wants to give her everything that he has. Hampton Court has to come to me after Carter, but there's some money—quite a lot—only we can't get it now. And that ought to go to Carter's wife, which is what she is—just about—and if he doesn't make a will it won't. It will come to Nellie and me if—if anything should happen to Carter."

"So you're worrying for fear you'll inherit some money?" Lincoln asked meditatively.

"Of course," the boy threw back impatiently. "Of course, it would be a shame if it came to Nellie and me, for we couldn't ever make her take it. We don't need it—I can look after Nellie and myself," he said proudly, with a quick, tossing motion of his fair head that was like the motion of a spirited, thoroughbred horse. They had arrived at the prison. "I can get you through all right. They all know me here," he spoke over his shoulder reassuringly to the President with a friendly glance. Dashing down the corridors in front, he did not see the guards salute the tall figure which followed him; too preoccupied to wonder at the ease of their entrance, he flew along through the big building, and behind him in large strides came his friend.

A young man—almost a boy, too—of twenty-three or twenty-four, his handsome face a white shadow, lay propped against the pillows, watching the door eagerly as they entered.

"Good boy, Warry," he greeted the little fellow; "you've got me a lawyer," and the pale features lighted with a smile of such radiance as seemed incongruous in the gruesome place. He held out his hand to the man who swung toward him, looming mountainous behind his brother's slight figure. "Thank you for coming," he said cordially, and in his tone was the same air of a *grand seigneur* as in the lad's. Suddenly a spasm of pain caught him, his head fell into the pillows, his muscles twisted, his arm about the neck of the kneeling boy tightened convulsively. Yet while the agony still held him he was smiling again with gay courage. "It nearly blew me away," he whispered, his voice shaking, but his eyes bright with amusement. "We'd better get to work before one of those little breezes carries me too far. There's pen and ink on the table, Mr.—my brother did not tell me your name."

"Your brother and I met informally," the other answered, setting the materials in order for writing. "He charged into me like a young steer," and the boy, out of his deep trouble, laughed delightedly. "My name is Lincoln."

The young officer regarded him. "That's a good name from your standpoint—you are, I take it, a Northerner?"

The deep eyes smiled whimsically. "I'm on that side of the fence. You may call me a Yankee if you'd like."

"There's something about you, Mr. Lincoln," the young Georgian answered gravely, with a kindly and unconscious condescension, "which makes me wish to call you, if I may, a friend."

He had that happy instinct which shapes a sentence to fall on its smoothest surface, and the President, in whom the same instinct was strong, felt a quick comradeship with this enemy who, about to die, saluted him. He put out his great fist swiftly.

"Shake hands," he said. "Friends it is."

" 'Till death us do part,' " said the officer slowly, and smiled, and then threw back his head with a gesture like the boy's. "We must do the will," he said peremptorily.

"Yes, now we'll fix this will business, Captain Blair," the big man answered cheerfully. "When your mind's relieved about your plunder you can rest easier and get well faster."

The sweet, brilliant smile of the Southerner shone out, his arm drew the boy's shoulder closer, and the President, with a pang, knew that his friend knew that he must die.

With direct, condensed question and clear answer the simple will was shortly drawn and the impromptu lawyer rose to take his leave. But the wounded man put out his hand.

"Don't go yet," he pleaded, with the imperious, winning accent which was characteristic of both brothers. The sudden, radiant smile broke again over the face, young, drawn with suffering, prophetic of close death. "I like you," he brought out frankly. "I've never liked a stranger as much in such short order before."

His head, fair as the boy's, lay back on the pillows, locks of hair damp against the whiteness, the blue eyes shone like jewels from the colorless face, a weak arm stretched protectingly about the young brother who pressed against him. There was so much courage, so much helplessness, so much pathos in the picture that the President's great heart throbbed with a desire to comfort them.

"I want to talk to you about that man Lincoln, your namesake," the prisoner's deep, uncertain voice went on, trying pathetically to make conversation which might interest, might hold his guest. The man who stood hesitating controlled a startled movement. "I'm Southern to the core of me, and I believe with my soul in the cause I've fought for, the cause I'm—" he stopped, and his hand caressed the boy's shoulder. "But that President of yours is a remarkable man. He's regarded as a red devil by most of us down home, you know," and he laughed, "but I've admired him all along. He's inspired by principle, not by animosity, in this fight; he's real and he's powerful and"—he lifted his head impetuously and his eyes flashed—"and, by Jove, have you read his speech of yesterday in the papers?"

Lincoln gave him an odd look. "No," he said, "I haven't."

"Sit down," Blair commanded. "Don't grudge a few minutes to a man in hard luck. I want to tell you about that speech. You're not so busy but that you ought to know."

"Well, yes," said Lincoln, "perhaps I ought." He took out his watch and made a quick mental calculation. "It's only a question of going without my dinner, and the boy is dying," he thought. "If I can give him a little pleasure the dinner is a small matter." He spoke again. "It's the soldiers who are the busy men, not the lawyers, nowadays," he said. "I'll be delighted to spend a half hour with you, Captain Blair, if I won't tire you."

"That's good of you," the young officer said, and a king on his throne could not have been gracious in a more lordly yet unconscious way. "By the way, this great man isn't any relation of yours, is he, Mr. Lincoln?"

"He's a kind of connection—through my grandfather," Lincoln acknowledged. "But I know just the sort of fellow he is—you can say what you want."

"What I want to say first is this: that he yesterday made one of the great speeches of history."

"What?" demanded Lincoln, staring.

"I know what I'm talking about." The young fellow brought his thin fist down on the bedclothes. "My father was a speaker—all my uncles and my grandfather were speakers. I've been brought up on oratory. I've studied and read the best models since I was a lad in knee-breeches. And I know a great speech when I see it. And when Nellie—my sister—brought in the paper this morning and read that to me I told her at once that not six times since history began has a speech been made which was its equal. That was before she told me what the Senator said."

"What did the Senator say?" asked the quiet man who listened.

"It was Senator Warrington, to whom my sister is—is acting as secretary." The explanation was distasteful, but he went on, carried past the jog by the interest of his story. "He was at Gettysburg yesterday, with the President's party. He told my sister that the speech so went home to the hearts of all those thousands of people that when it was ended it was as if the whole audience held its breath—there was not a hand lifted to applaud. One might as well applaud the Lord's Prayer—it would have been sacrilege. And they all felt it—down to the lowest. There was a long minute of reverent silence, no sound from all that great throng—it seems to me, an enemy, that it was the most perfect tribute that has ever been paid by any people to any orator."

The boy, lifting his hand from his brother's shoulder to mark the effect of his brother's words, saw with surprise that in the strange lawyer's eyes were tears. But the wounded man did not notice.

"It will live, that speech. Fifty years from now American schoolboys will be learning it as part of their education. It is not merely my opinion," he went on. "Warrington says the whole country is ringing with it. And you haven't read it? And your name's Lincoln? Warry, boy, where's the paper Nellie left? I'll read the speech to Mr. Lincoln myself."

The boy had sprung to his feet and across the room, and had lifted a folded newspaper from the table. "Let me read it, Carter—it might tire you."

The giant figure which had crouched, elbows on knees, in the shadows by the narrow hospital cot, heaved itself slowly upward till it loomed at its full height in air. Lincoln turned his face toward the boy standing under the flickering gas-jet and reading with soft, sliding inflections the words which had for twenty-four hours been gall and wormwood to his memory. And as the sentences slipped from the lad's mouth, behold, a miracle happened, for the man who had written them knew that they were great. He knew then, as many a lesser one has known, that out of a little loving-kindness had come great joy; that he had wrested with gentleness a blessing from his enemy.

" 'Fourscore and seven years ago,' " the fresh voice began, and the face of the dying man stood out white in the white pillows, sharp with eagerness, and the face of the President shone as he listened as if to new words. The field of yesterday, the speech, the deep silence which followed it, all were illuminated, as his mind went back, with new meaning. With the realization that the stillness had meant, not indifference, but perhaps, as this generous enemy had said, "The most perfect tribute ever paid by any people to any orator," there came to him a rush of glad strength to bear the burdens of the nation. The boy's tones ended clearly, deliberately:

" 'We here highly resolve that these dead shall not have died in vain, that this nation, under God, shall have a new birth of freedom, and that government of the people, by the people, for the people shall not perish from the earth.' "

There was deep stillness in the hospital ward as there had been stillness on the field of Gettysburg. The soldier's voice broke it. "It's a wonderful speech," he said. "There's nothing finer. Other men have spoken stirring words, for the North and for the South, but never before, I think, with the love of both breathing through them. It is only the greatest who can be a partisan without bitterness, and only such to-day may call himself not Northern or Southern, but American. To feel that your enemy can fight you to death without malice, with charity—it lifts country, it lifts humanity to something worth dying for. They are beautiful, broad words and the sting of war would be drawn if the soul of Lincoln could be breathed into the armies. Do you agree with me?" he demanded abruptly, and Lincoln answered slowly from a happy heart.

"I believe it is a good speech," he said.

The impetuous Southerner went on: "Of course, it's all wrong from my point of view," and the gentleness of his look made the words charming. "The thought which underlies it is warped, inverted, as I look at it, yet that doesn't alter my admiration of the man and of his words. I'd like to put my hand in his before I die," he said, and the sudden, brilliant, sweet smile lit the transparency of his face like a lamp; "and I'd like to tell him that I know that what we're all fighting for, the best of us, is the right of our country as it is given us to see it." He was laboring a bit with the words now as if he were tired, but he hushed the boy imperiously. "When a man gets so close to death's door that he feels the wind through it from a larger atmosphere, then the small things are blown away. The bitterness of the fight has faded for me. I only feel the love of country, the satisfaction of giving my life for it. The speech—that speech—has made it look higher and simpler—your side as well as ours. I would like to put my hand in Abraham Lincoln's——"

The clear, deep voice, with its hesitations, its catch of weakness, stopped short. Convulsively the hand shot out and caught at the great fingers that hung near him, pulling the President, with the strength of agony, to his knees by the cot. The prisoner was writhing in an attack of mortal pain, while he held, unknowing that he held it, the hand of his new friend in a torturing grip. The door of death had opened wide and a stormy wind was carrying the bright, conquered spirit into that larger atmosphere of which he had spoken. Suddenly the struggle ceased, the unconscious head rested in the boy's arms, and the hand of the Southern soldier lay quiet, where he had wished to place it, in the hand of Abraham Lincoln.

JOHN FOX, JR.

A Knight of the Cumberland

John Fox, Jr. (1863–1919)

THE CUMBERLAND MOUNTAINS were Fox's special territory. His chief theme was the conflict between the cultures of the hill-people—proud, Elizabethan, deprived—and the law-abiding children of the lowlands. He had first-hand knowledge to work with, for he was himself a Kentuckian who, after some early newspaper work in cities, had returned to live in the mountains. His business took him among the people and obliged him to win their confidence and have the subtleties of their dialect at his tongue's end.

The public acclaimed this able writer in his own time, and he ranked among the first writers of his era in point of sales, yet his fame has been transitory. As our century moves along its course, his surfaces though brilliant seem to us hard; his depths untried, if existent. Today's critics are harsh in judgment of Fox; they find his work oversentimental and filled with bustle rather than life.

An unbiassed reading of the story we have included in The Scribner Treasury will show sufficient reasons for his popularity, however. Like his other great successes, The Little Shepherd of Kingdom Come (1903) and The Trail of the Lonesome Pine (1908), A Knight of the Cumberland was worked from a new American vein with shrewd observation and great skill in pacing a narrative.

A KNIGHT OF THE CUMBERLAND

I

THE BLIGHT IN THE HILLS

HIGH noon of a crisp October day, sunshine flooding the earth with the warmth and light of old wine and, going single-file up through the jagged gap that the dripping of water has worn down through the Cumberland Mountains from crest to valley-level, a gray horse and two big mules, a man and two young girls. On the gray horse, I led the tortuous way. After me came my small sister—and after her and like her, muleback, rode the Blight—dressed as she would be for a gallop in Central Park or to ride a hunter in a horse show.

I was taking them, according to promise, where the feet of other women than mountaineers had never trod—beyond the crest of the Big Black—to the waters of the Cumberland—the lair of moonshiner and feudsman, where is yet pocketed a civilization that, elsewhere, is long ago gone. This had been a pet dream of the Blight's for a long time, and now the dream was coming true. The Blight was in the hills.

Nobody ever went to her mother's house without asking to see her even when she was a little thing with black hair, merry face and black eyes. Both men and women, with children of their own, have told me that she was, perhaps, the most fascinating child that ever lived. There be some who claim that she has never changed—and I am among them. She began early, regardless of age, sex or previous condition of servitude—she continues recklessly as she began—and none makes complaint. Thus was it in her own world—thus it was when she came to mine. On the way down from the North, the conductor's voice changed from a command to a request when he asked for her ticket. The jacketed lord of the dining-car saw her from afar and advanced to show her to a seat—that she might ride forward, sit next to a shaded window and be free from the glare of the sun on the other side. Two porters made a rush for her bag when she got off the car, and the proprietor of the little hotel in the little town where we had to wait several hours for the train into the mountains gave her the bridal chamber for an afternoon nap. From this little town to "The Gap" is the worst sixty-mile ride, perhaps, in the world. She sat in a dirty day-coach; the smoke rolled in at the windows and doors; the cars shook and swayed and lumbered around curves and down and up gorges; there were about her rough men, crying children, slatternly women, tobacco juice, peanuts, popcorn and apple cores, but dainty, serene and as merry as ever, she sat through that ride with a radiant smile, her keen black eyes noting everything unlovely within and the glory of hill, tree and chasm without. Next morning at home, where we rise early, no one was allowed to waken her and she had breakfast in bed—for the Blight's gentle tyranny was established on sight and varied not at the Gap.

When she went down the street that day everybody stared surreptitiously and with perfect respect, as her dainty black-plumed figure passed; the post-office clerk could barely bring himself to say that there was no letter for her. The soda-fountain boy nearly filled her glass with syrup before he saw that he was not strictly minding his own business; the clerk, when I bought chocolate for her, unblushingly added extra weight and, as we went back, she met them both—Marston, the young engineer from the North, crossing the street and, at the same moment, a drunken young tough with an infuriated face reeling in a run around the corner ahead of us as though he were being pursued. Now we have a volunteer police guard some forty strong at the Gap—and from habit, I started for him, but the Blight caught my arm tight. The young engineer in three strides had reached the curb-stone and all he sternly said was:

"Here! Here!"

The drunken youth wheeled and his right hand shot toward his hip pocket. The engineer was belted with a pistol, but with one lightning movement and an incredibly long reach, his right fist caught the fellow's jaw so that he pitched backward and collapsed like an empty bag. Then the engineer caught sight of the Blight's bewildered face, flushed, gripped his hands in front of him and simply stared. At last he saw me:

"Oh," he said, "how do you do?" and he turned to his prisoner, but the panting sergeant and another policeman—also a volunteer—were already lifting him to his feet. I introduced the boy and the Blight then, and for the first time in my life I saw the Blight—shaken. Round-eyed, she merely gazed at him.

"That was pretty well done," I said.

"Oh, he was drunk and I knew he would be slow." Now something curious happened. The dazed prisoner was on his feet, and his captors were starting with him to the calaboose when he seemed suddenly to come to his senses.

"Jes wait a minute, will ye?" he said quietly, and his captors, thinking perhaps that he wanted to say something to me, stopped. The mountain youth turned a strangely sobered face and fixed his blue eyes on the engineer as though he were searing every feature of that imperturbable young man in his brain forever. It was not a bad face, but the avenging hatred in it was fearful. Then he, too, saw the Blight, his face calmed magically and he, too, stared at her, and turned away with an oath checked at his lips. We went on—the Blight thrilled, for she had heard much of our volunteer force at the Gap and had seen something already. Presently I looked back. Prisoner and captors were climbing the little hill toward the calaboose and the mountain boy just then turned his head and I could swear that his eyes sought not the engineer, whom we left at the corner, but, like the engineer, he was looking at the Blight. Whereat I did not wonder—particularly as to the engineer. He had been in the mountains for a long time and I knew what this vision from home meant to him. He turned up at the house quite early that night.

"I'm not on duty until eleven," he said hesitantly, "and I thought I'd——"

"Come right in."

I asked him a few questions about business and then I left him and the Blight alone. When I came back she had a Gatling gun of eager questions ranged on him and—happy withal—he was squirming no little. I followed him to the gate.

"Are you really going over into those God-forsaken mountains?" he asked.

"I thought I would."

"And you are going to take *her*?"

"And my sister."

"Oh, I beg your pardon." He strode away.

"Coming up by the mines?" he called back.

"Perhaps—will you show us around?"

"I guess I will," he said emphatically, and he went on to risk his neck on a ten-mile ride along a mountain road in the dark.

"I *like* a man," said the Blight. "I like a *man*."

Of course the Blight must see everything, so she insisted on going to the police court next morning for the trial of the mountain boy. The boy was in the witness chair when we got there, and the Hon. Samuel Budd was his counsel. He had volunteered to defend the prisoner, I was soon told, and then I understood. The November election was not far off and the Hon. Samuel Budd was candidate for legislature. More even, the boy's father was a warm supporter of Mr. Budd and the boy himself might perhaps render good service in the cause when the time came—as indeed he did. On one of the front chairs sat the young engineer and it was a question whether he or the prisoner saw the Blight's black plumes first. The eyes of both flashed toward her simultaneously, the engineer colored perceptibly and the mountain boy stopped short in speech and his pallid face flushed with unmistakable shame. Then he went on: "He had liquered up," he said, "and had got tight afore he knowed it and he didn't mean no harm and had never been arrested afore in his whole life."

"Have you ever been drunk before?" asked the prosecuting attorney severely. The lad looked surprised.

"Co'se I have, but I ain't goin' to agin—leastwise not in this here town." There was a general laugh at this and the aged mayor rapped loudly.

"That will do," said the attorney.

The lad stepped down, hitched his chair slightly so that his back was to the Blight, sank down in it until his head rested on the back of the chair and crossed his legs. The Hon. Samuel Budd arose and the Blight looked at him with wonder. His long yellow hair was parted in the middle and brushed with plaster-like precision behind two enormous ears, he wore spectacles, gold-rimmed and with great staring lenses, and his face was smooth and ageless. He caressed his chin ruminatingly and rolled his lips until they settled into a fine resultant of wisdom, patience, toleration and firmness. His manner was profound and his voice oily and soothing.

"May it please your Honor—my young friend frankly pleads guilty." He paused as though the majesty of the law could ask no more. "He is a young man of naturally high and somewhat—naturally, too, no doubt—bibulous spirits. Homeopathically—if inversely—the result was logical. In the untrammelled life of the liberty-breathing mountains, where the stern spirit of law and order, of which your Honor is the august symbol, does not prevail as it does here—thanks to your Honor's wise and just dispensations—the lad has, I may say, naturally acquired a certain recklessness of mood—indulgence which, however easily condoned there, must here be sternly rebuked. At the same time, he knew not the conditions here, he became exhilarated without malice, prepensey or even, I may say, consciousness. He would not have done as he has, if he had known what he knows now, and, knowing, he will not repeat the offence. I need say no more. I plead simply that your Honor will temper the justice that is only yours with the mercy that is yours—only."

His Honor was visibly affected and to cover it—his methods being informal—he said with sharp irrelevancy:

"Who bailed this young feller out last night?" The sergeant spoke:

"Why, Mr. Marston thar"—with outstretched finger toward the young engineer. The Blight's black eyes leaped with exultant appreciation and the engineer turned crimson. His Honor rolled his quid around in his mouth once, and peered over his glasses:

"I fine this young feller two dollars and costs." The young fellow had turned slowly in his chair and his blue eyes blazed at the engineer with unappeasable hatred. I doubt if he had heard his Honor's voice.

"I want ye to know that I'm obleeged to ye an' I ain't a-goin' to fergit it; but if I'd a known hit was you I'd a stayed in jail an' seen you in hell afore I'd a been bounden to ye."

"Ten dollars fer contempt of couht." The boy was hot now.

"Oh, fine and be—" The Hon. Samuel Budd had him by the shoulder, the boy swallowed his voice and his starting tears of rage, and after a whisper to his Honor, the Hon. Samuel led him out. Outside, the engineer laughed to the Blight:

"Pretty peppery, isn't he?" but the Blight said nothing, and later we saw the youth on a gray horse crossing the bridge and conducted by the Hon. Samuel Budd, who stopped and waved him toward the mountains. The boy went on and across the plateau, the gray Gap swallowed him.

That night, at the post-office, the Hon. Sam plucked me aside by the sleeve.

"I know Marston is agin me in this race—but I'll do him a good turn just the same. You tell him to watch out for that young fellow. He's all right when he's sober, but when he's drunk—well, over in Kentucky, they call him the Wild Dog."

Several days later we started out through that same Gap. The glum stableman looked at the Blight's girths three times, and with my own eyes starting and my heart in my mouth, I saw her pass behind her sixteen-hand-high mule and give him a friendly tap on the rump as she went by. The beast gave an appreciative flop of one ear and that was all. Had I done that, any further benefit to me or mine would be incorporated in the terms of an insurance policy. So, stating this, I believe I state the limit and can now go on to say at last that it was because she seemed to be loved by man and brute alike that a big man of her own town, whose body, big as it was, was yet too small for his heart and from whose brain things went off at queer angles, always christened her perversely as—"The Blight."

II

ON THE WILD DOG'S TRAIL

So up we went past Bee Rock, Preacher's Creek and Little Looney, past the mines where high on a "tipple" stood the young engineer looking down at us, and looking after the Blight as we passed on into a dim rocky avenue walled on each side with rhododendrons. I waved at him and shook my head—we would see him coming back. Beyond a deserted log-cabin we turned up a spur of the mountain. Around a clump of bushes we came on a gray-bearded mountaineer holding his horse by the bridle and from a covert high above two more men appeared with Winchesters. The Blight breathed forth an awed whisper:

"Are they moonshiners?"

I nodded sagely, "Most likely," and the Blight was thrilled. They might have been squirrel-hunters most innocent, but the Blight had heard much talk of moonshine stills and mountain feuds and the men who run them and I took the risk of denying her nothing. Up and up we went, those two mules swaying from side to side with a motion little short of elephantine and, by and by, the Blight called out:

"You ride ahead and don't you *dare* look back."

Accustomed to obeying the Blight's orders, I rode ahead with eyes to the front. Presently, a shriek made me turn suddenly. It was nothing—my little sister's mule had gone near a steep cliff—perilously near, as its rider thought, but I saw why I must not look back; those two little girls were riding astride on side-saddles, the booted little right foot of each dangling stirrupless—a posture quite decorous but ludicrous.

"Let us know if anybody comes," they cried. A mountaineer descended into sight around a loop of the path above.

"Change cars," I shouted.

They changed and, passing, were grave, demure—then they changed again, and thus we climbed.

Such a glory as was below, around and above us; the air like champagne; the sunlight rich and pouring like a flood on the gold that the beeches had strewn in the path, on the gold that the poplars still shook high above, and shimmering on the royal scarlet of the maple and the sombre russet of the oak. From far below us to far above us a deep curving ravine was slashed into the mountain side as by one stroke of a gigantic scimitar. The darkness deep down was lighted up with cool green, interfused with liquid gold. Russet and yellow splashed the mountain sides beyond and high up the maples were in a shaking blaze. The Blight's swift eyes took all in and with indrawn breath she drank it all deep down.

An hour by sun we were near the top, which was bared of trees and turned into rich farm-land covered with blue-grass. Along these upland pastures, dotted with grazing cattle, and across them we rode toward the mountain wildernesses on the other side, down into which a zigzag path wriggles along the steep front of Benham's spur. At the edge of the steep was a cabin and a bushy-bearded mountaineer, who looked like a brigand, answered my hail. He "mought" keep us all night, but he'd "ruther not, as we could git a place to stay down the spur." Could we get down before dark? The mountaineer lifted his eyes to where the sun was breaking the horizon of the west into streaks and splashes of yellow and crimson.

"Oh, yes, you can git thar afore dark."

Now I knew that the mountaineer's idea of distance is vague—but he knows how long it takes to get from one place to another. So we started down—dropping at once into thick dark woods, and as we went looping down, the deeper was the gloom. That sun had suddenly severed all connection with the laws of gravity and sunk, and it was all the darker because the stars were not out. The path was steep and coiled downward like a wounded snake. In one place a tree had fallen across it, and to reach the next coil of the path below was dangerous. So I had the girls dismount and I led the gray horse down on his haunches. The mules refused to follow, which was rather unusual. I went back and from a safe distance in the rear I belabored them down. They cared neither for gray horse nor crooked path, but turned of their own devilish wills along the bushy mountain side. As

I ran after them the gray horse started calmly on down and those two girls shrieked with laughter—they knew no better. First one way and then the other down the mountain went those mules, with me after them, through thick bushes, over logs, stumps and bowlders and holes—crossing the path a dozen times. What that path was there for never occurred to those long-eared half asses, whole fools, and by and by, when the girls tried to shoo them down they clambered around and above them and struck the path back up the mountain. The horse had gone down one way, the mules up the other, and there was no health in anything. The girls could not go up—so there was nothing to do but go down, which, hard as it was, was easier than going up. The path was not visible now. Once in a while I would stumble from it and crash through the bushes to the next coil below. Finally I went down, sliding one foot ahead all the time—knowing that when leaves rustled under that foot I was on the point of going astray. Sometimes I had to light a match to make sure of the way, and thus the ridiculous descent was made with those girls in high spirits behind. Indeed, the darker, rockier, steeper it got, the more they shrieked from pure joy—but I was anything than happy. It was dangerous. I didn't know the cliffs and high rocks we might skirt and an unlucky guidance might land us in the creek-bed far down. But the blessed stars came out, the moon peered over a farther mountain and on the last spur there was the gray horse browsing in the path—and the sound of running water not far below. Fortunately on the gray horse were the saddle-bags of the chattering infants who thought the whole thing a mighty lark. We reached the running water, struck a flock of geese and knew, in consequence, that humanity was somewhere near. A few turns of the creek and a beacon light shone below. The pales of a picket fence, the cheering outlines of a log-cabin came in view and at a peaked gate I shouted:

"Hello!"

You enter no mountaineer's yard without that announcing cry. It was mediaeval, the Blight said, positively—two lorn damsels, a benighted knight partially stripped of his armor by bush and sharp-edged rock, a gray palfrey (she didn't mention the impatient asses that had turned homeward) and she wished I had a horn to wind.

I wanted a "horn" badly enough—but it was not the kind men wind. By and by we got a response:

"Hello!" was the answer, as an opened door let out into the yard a broad band of light. Could we stay all night? The voice replied that the owner would see "Pap." "Pap" seemed willing, and the boy opened the gate and into the house went the Blight and the little sister. Shortly, I followed.

There, all in one room, lighted by a huge wood-fire, rafters above, puncheon floor beneath—cane-bottomed chairs and two beds the only furniture—"pap," barefooted, the old mother in the chimney-corner with a pipe, strings of red pepperpods, beans and herbs, hanging around and above, a married daughter with a child at her breast, two or three children with yellow hair and bare feet—all looking with all their eyes at the two visitors who had dropped upon them from another world. The Blight's eyes were brighter than usual—that was the only sign she gave that she was not in her own drawing-room. Apparently she saw nothing strange or unusual even, but there was really nothing that she did not see or hear and absorb, as few others than the Blight can.

Straightway, the old woman knocked the ashes out of her pipe.

"I reckon you hain't had nothin' to eat," she said and disappeared. The old man asked questions, the young mother rocked her baby on her knees, the children got less shy and drew near the fireplace, the Blight and the little sister exchanged a furtive smile and the contrast of the extremes in American civilization, as shown in that little cabin, interested me mightily.

"Yer snack's ready," said the old woman. The old man carried the chairs into the kitchen, and when I followed the girls were seated. The chairs were so low that their chins came barely over their plates, and demure and serious as they were they surely looked most comical. There was the usual bacon and corn-bread and potatoes and sour milk, and the two girls struggled with the rude fare nobly.

After supper I joined the old man and the old woman with a pipe —exchanging my tobacco for their long green with more satisfaction probably to me than to them, for the long green was good, and strong and fragrant.

The old woman asked the Blight and the little sister many questions and they, in turn, showed great interest in the baby in arms, whereat the eighteen-year-old mother blushed and looked greatly pleased.

"You got mighty purty black eyes," said the old woman to the Blight, and not to slight the little sister she added, "An' you got mighty purty teeth."

The Blight showed hers in a radiant smile and the old woman turned back to her.

"Oh, you've got both," she said and she shook her head, as though she were thinking of the damage they had done. It was my time now—to ask questions.

They didn't have many amusements on that creek, I discovered—and no dances. Sometimes the boys went coon-hunting and there were corn-shuckings, house-raisings and quilting-parties.

"Does anybody round here play the banjo?"

"None o' my boys," said the old woman, "but Tom Green's son down the creek—he follers pickin' the banjo a leetle." "Follows pickin' "—the Blight did not miss that phrase.

"What do you foller fer a livin'?" the old man asked me suddenly.

"I write for a living." He thought a while.

"Well, it must be purty fine to have a good handwrite." This nearly dissolved the Blight and the little sister, but they held on heroically.

"Is there much fighting around here?" I asked presently.

"Not much 'cept when one young feller up the river gets to tearin' up things. I heerd as how he was over to the Gap last week—raisin' hell. He comes by here on his way home." The Blight's eyes opened wide—apparently we were on his trail. It is not wise for a member of the police guard at the Gap to show too much curiosity about the lawless ones of the hills, and I asked no questions.

"They calls him the Wild Dog over here," he added, and then he yawned cavernously.

I looked around with divining eye for the sleeping arrangements soon to come, which sometimes are embarrassing to "furriners" who are unable to grasp at once the primitive unconsciousness of the mountaineers and, in consequence, accept a point of view natural to them because enforced by architectural limitations and a hospitality that turns no one seeking shelter from any door. They were, however, better prepared than I had hoped for. They had a spare room on the porch and just outside the door, and when the old woman led the two girls to it, I followed with their saddle-bags. The room was about seven feet by six and was windowless.

"You'd better leave your door open a little," I said, "or you'll smother in there."

"Well," said the old woman, "hit's all right to leave the door open. Nothin's goin' ter bother ye, but one o' my sons is out a coon-huntin' and he mought come in, not knowin' you're thar. But you jes' holler an' he'll move on." She meant precisely what she said and saw no humor at all in such a possibility—but when the door closed, I could hear those girls stifling shrieks of laughter.

Literally, that night, I was a member of the family. I had a bed to myself (the following night I was not so fortunate)—in one corner; behind the head of mine the old woman, the daughter-in-law and the baby had another in the other corner, and the old man with the two boys spread a pallet on the floor. That is the invariable rule of courtesy with the mountaineer, to give his bed to the stranger and take to the floor himself, and, in passing, let me say that never, in a long experience, have I seen the slightest consciousness—much less immodesty—in a mountain cabin in my life. The same attitude on the part of the visitors is taken for granted—any other indeed holds mortal possibilities of offence—so that if the visitor has common sense, all embarrassment passes at once. The door was closed, the fire blazed on uncovered, the smothered talk and laughter of the two girls ceased, the coon-hunter came not and the night passed in peace.

It must have been near daybreak that I was aroused by the old man leaving the cabin and I heard voices and the sound of horses' feet outside. When he came back he was grinning.

"Hit's your mules."

"Who found them?"

"The Wild Dog had 'em," he said.

III

THE AURICULAR TALENT OF THE HON. SAMUEL BUDD

Behind us came the Hon. Samuel Budd. Just when the sun was slitting the east with a long streak of fire, the Hon. Samuel was, with the jocund day, standing tiptoe in his stirrups on the misty mountain top and peering into the ravine down which we had slid the night before, and he grumbled no little when he saw that he, too, must get off his horse and slide down. The Hon. Samuel was ambitious, Southern, and a lawyer. Without saying, it goes that he was also a politician. He was not a native of the mountains, but he had cast his fortunes in the highlands, and he was taking the first step that he hoped would, before many years, land him in the National Capitol. He really knew little about the mountaineers, even now, and he had never been among his constituents on Devil's Fork, where he was bound now. The campaign had so far been full of humor and full of trials—not the least of which sprang from the fact that it was sorghum time. Everybody through the mountains was making sorghum, and every mountain child was eating molasses.

Now, as the world knows, the straightest way to the heart of the honest voter is through the women of the land, and the straightest way to the heart of the women is through the children of the land; and one method of winning both, with rural politicians, is to kiss the babies wide and far. So as each infant, at sorghum time, has a circle of green-brown stickiness about his chubby lips, and as the Hon. Sam was averse to "long sweetenin'" even in his coffee, this particular political device just now was no small trial to the Hon. Samuel Budd. But in the language of one of his firmest supporters—Uncle Tommie Hendricks:

"The Hon. Sam done his duty, and he done it damn well."

The issue at stake was the site of the new Court-House—two localities claiming the right undisputed, because they were the only two places in the county where there was enough level land for the Court-House to stand on. Let no man think this a trivial issue. There had been a similar one over on the Virginia side once, and the opposing factions agreed to decide the question by the ancient wager of battle, fist and skull—two hundred men on each side—and the women of the county with difficulty prevented the fight. Just now, Mr. Budd was on his way to "The Pocket"—the voting place of one faction—where he had never been, where the hostility against him was most bitter, and, that day, he knew he was "up against" Waterloo, the crossing of the Rubicon, holding the pass at Thermopylae, or any other historical crisis in the history of man. I was saddling the mules when the cackling of geese in the creek announced the coming of the Hon. Samuel Budd, coming with his chin on his breast—deep in thought. Still his eyes beamed cheerily, he lifted his slouched hat gallantly to the Blight and the little sister, and he would wait for us to jog along with him. I told him of our troubles, meanwhile. The Wild Dog had restored our mules—and the Hon. Sam beamed:

"He's a wonder—where is he?"

"He never waited—even for thanks."

Again the Hon. Sam beamed:

"Ah! just like him. He's gone ahead to help me."

"Well, how did he happen to be here?" I asked.

"He's everywhere," said the Hon. Sam.

"How did he know the mules were ours?"

"Easy. That boy knows everything."

"Well, why did he bring them back and then leave so mysteriously?"

The Hon. Sam silently pointed a finger at the laughing Blight ahead, and I looked incredulous.

"Just the same, that's another reason I told you to warn Marston. He's already got it in his head that Marston is his rival."

"Pshaw!" I said—for it was too ridiculous.

"All right," said the Hon. Sam placidly.

"Then why doesn't he want to see her?"

"How do you know he ain't watchin' her now, for all we know? Mark me," he added, "you won't see him at the speakin', but I'll bet fruit cake agin gingerbread he'll be somewhere around."

So we went on, the two girls leading the way and the Hon. Sam now telling his political troubles to me. Half a mile down the road, a solitary horseman stood waiting, and Mr. Budd gave a low whistle.

"One o' my rivals," he said, from the corner of his mouth.

"Mornin'," said the horseman; "lemme see you a minute."

He made a movement to draw aside, but the Hon. Samuel made a counter-gesture of dissent.

"This gentleman is a friend of mine," he said firmly, but with great courtesy, "and he can hear what you have to say to me."

The mountaineer rubbed one huge hand over his stubbly chin, threw one of his long legs over the pommel of his saddle, and dangled a heavy cowhide shoe to and fro.

"Would you mind tellin' me whut pay a member of the House of Legislatur' gits a day?"

The Hon. Sam looked surprised.

"I think about two dollars and a half."

"An' his meals?"

"No!" laughed Mr. Budd.

"Well, look-ee here, stranger. I'm a pore man an' I've got a mortgage on my farm. That money don't mean nothin' to you—but if you'll draw out now an' I win, I'll tell ye whut I'll do." He paused as though to make sure that the sacrifice was possible. "I'll just give ye half of that two dollars and a half a day, as shore as you're a-settin' on that hoss, and you won't hav' to hit a durn lick to earn it."

I had not the heart to smile—nor did the Hon. Samuel—so artless and simple was the man and so pathetic his appeal.

"You see—you'll divide my vote, an' ef we both run, ole Josh Barton'll git it shore. Ef you git out o' the way, I can lick him easy."

Mr. Budd's answer was kind, instructive, and uplifted.

"My friend," said he, "I'm sorry, but I cannot possibly accede to your request for the following reasons: First, it would not be fair to my constituents; secondly, it would hardly be seeming to barter the noble gift of the people to which we both aspire; thirdly, you might lose with me out of the way; and fourthly, I'm going to win whether you are in the way or not."

The horseman slowly collapsed while the Hon. Samuel was talking, and now he threw the leg back, kicked for his stirrup twice, spat once, and turned his horse's head.

"I reckon you will, stranger," he said sadly, "with that gift o' gab o' yourn." He turned without another word or nod of good-by and started back up the creek whence he had come.

"One gone," said the Hon. Samuel Budd grimly, "and I swear I'm right sorry for him." And so was I.

An hour later we struck the river, and another hour upstream brought us to where the contest of tongues was to come about. No sylvan dell in Arcady could have been lovelier than the spot. Above the road, a big spring poured a clear little stream over shining pebbles into the river; above it the bushes hung thick with autumn leaves, and above them stood yellow beeches like pillars of pale fire. On both sides of the road sat and squatted the honest voters, sour-looking, disgruntled—a distinctly hostile crowd. The Blight and my little sister drew great and curious attention as they sat on a bowlder above the spring while I went with the Hon. Samuel Budd under the guidance of Uncle Tommie Hendricks, who introduced him right and left. The Hon. Samuel was cheery, but he was plainly nervous. There were two lanky youths whose names, oddly enough, were Budd. As they gave him their huge paws in lifeless fashion, the Hon. Samuel slapped one on the shoulder, with the true democracy of the politician, and said jocosely:

"Well, we Budds may not be what you call great people, but, thank God, none of us have ever been in the penitentiary," and he laughed loudly, thinking that he had scored a great and jolly point. The two young men looked exceedingly grave and Uncle Tommie panic-stricken. He plucked the Hon. Sam by the sleeve and led him aside:

"I reckon you made a leetle mistake thar. Them two fellers' daddy died in the penitentiary last spring." The Hon. Sam whistled mournfully, but he looked game enough when his opponent rose to speak—Uncle Josh Barton, who had short, thick, upright hair, little sharp eyes, and a rasping voice. Uncle Josh wasted no time:

"Feller-citizens," he shouted, "this man is a lawyer—he's a corporation lawyer"; the fearful name—pronounced "lie-yer"—rang through the crowd like a trumpet, and like lightning the Hon. Sam was on his feet.

"The man who says that is a liar," he said calmly, "and I demand your authority for the statement. If you won't give it—I shall hold you personally responsible, sir."

It was a strike home, and under the flashing eyes that stared unwaveringly through the big goggles, Uncle Josh halted and stammered and admitted that he might have been misinformed.

"Then I advise you to be more careful," cautioned the Hon. Samuel sharply.

"Feller-citizens," said Uncle Josh, "if he ain't a corporation lawyer —who is this man? Where did he come from? I have been born and raised among you. You all know me—do you know him? Whut's he a'doin' now? He's a fine-haired furriner, an' he's come down hyeh from the settlemints to tell ye that you hain't got no man in yo' own deestrict that's fittin' to represent ye in the legislatur'. Look at him—look at him! He's got *four* eyes! Look at his hair—hit's *parted in the middle*!" There was a storm of laughter—Uncle Josh had made good—and if the Hon. Samuel could straightway have turned bald-headed and sightless, he would have been a happy man. He looked sick with hopelessness, but Uncle Tommie Hendricks, his mentor, was vigorously whispering something in his ear, and gradually his face cleared. Indeed, the Hon. Samuel was smilingly confident when he rose.

Like his rival, he stood in the open road, and the sun beat down on his parted yellow hair, so that the eyes of all could see, and the laughter was still running round.

"Who is your Uncle Josh?" he asked with threatening mildness. "I know I was not born here, but, my friends, I couldn't help that. And just as soon as I could get away from where I was born, I came here and," he paused with lips parted and long finger outstretched, "and—I—came—because—I *wanted*—to come—and *not* because *I had to*."

Now it seems that Uncle Josh, too, was not a native and that he had left home early in life for his State's good and for his own. Uncle

Tommie had whispered this, and the Hon. Samuel raised himself high on both toes while the expectant crowd, on the verge of a roar, waited—as did Uncle Joshua, with a sickly smile.

"Why did your Uncle Josh come among you? Because he was hoop-poled away from home." Then came the roar—and the Hon. Samuel had to quell it with uplifted hand.

"And did your Uncle Joshua marry a mountain wife? No! He didn't think any of your mountain women were good enough for him, so he slips down into the settlemints and *steals* one. And now, fellow-citizens, that is just what I'm here for—I'm looking for a nice mountain girl, and I'm going to have her." Again the Hon. Samuel had to still the roar, and then he went on quietly to show how they must lose the Court-House site if they did not send him to the legislature, and how, while they might not get it if they did send him, it was their only hope to send only him. The crowd had grown somewhat hostile again, and it was after one telling period, when the Hon. Samuel stopped to mop his brow, that a gigantic mountaineer rose in the rear of the crowd:

"Talk on, stranger; you're talking sense. I'll trust ye. You've got big ears!"

Now the Hon. Samuel possessed a primordial talent that is rather rare in these physically degenerate days. He said nothing, but stood quietly in the middle of the road. The eyes of the crowd on either side of the road began to bulge, the lips of all opened with wonder, and a simultaneous burst of laughter rose around the Hon. Samuel Budd. A dozen men sprang to their feet and rushed up to him—looking at those remarkable ears, as they gravely wagged to and fro. That settled things, and as we left, the Hon. Sam was having things his own way, and on the edge of the crowd Uncle Tommie Hendricks was shaking his head:

"I tell ye, boys, he ain't no jackass—even if he can flop his ears."

At the river we started upstream, and some impulse made me turn in my saddle and look back. All the time I had had an eye open for the young mountaineer whose interest in us seemed to be so keen. And now I saw, standing at the head of a gray horse, on the edge of the crowd, a tall figure with his hands on his hips and looking after us. I couldn't be sure, but it looked like the Wild Dog.

IV

CLOSE QUARTERS

Two hours up the river we struck Buck. Buck was sitting on the fence by the roadside, barefooted and hatless.

"How-dye-do?" I said.

"Purty well," said Buck.

"Any fish in this river?"

"Several," said Buck. Now in mountain speech, "several" means simply "a good many."

"Any minnows in these branches?"

"I seed several in the branch back o' our house."

"How far away do you live?"

"Oh, 'bout one whoop an' a holler." If he had spoken Greek the Blight could not have been more puzzled. He meant he lived as far as a man's voice would carry with one yell and a holla.

"Will you help me catch some?" Buck nodded.

"All right," I said, turning my horse up to the fence. "Get on behind." The horse shied his hind quarters away, and I pulled him back.

"Now, you can get on, if you'll be quick." Buck sat still.

"Yes," he said imperturbably; "but I ain't quick." The two girls laughed aloud, and Buck looked surprised.

Around a curving cornfield we went, and through a meadow which Buck said was a "nigh cut." From the limb of a tree that we passed hung a piece of wire with an iron ring swinging at its upturned end. A little farther was another tree and another ring, and farther on another and another.

"For heaven's sake, Buck, what are these things?"

"Mart's a-gittin' ready fer a tourneyment."

"A what?"

"That's whut Mart calls hit. He was over to the Gap last Fourth o' July, an' he says fellers over thar fix up like Kuklux and go a-chargin' on hosses and takin' off them rings with a ash-stick—'spear,' Mart calls hit. He come back an' he says he's a-goin' to win that ar tourney-ment next Fourth o' July. He's got the best hoss up this river, and on Sundays him an' Dave Branham goes a-chargin' along here a-picking off these rings jus' a-flyin'; an' Mart can do hit, I'm tellin' ye. Dave's mighty good hisself, but he ain't nowhar 'longside o' Mart."

This was strange. I had told the Blight about our Fourth of July, and how on the Virginia side the ancient custom of the tournament still survived. It was on the last Fourth of July that she had meant to come to the Gap. Truly civilization was spreading throughout the hills.

"Who's Mart?"

"Mart's my brother," said little Buck. "He was over to the Gap not long ago, an' he come back mad as hops—" He stopped suddenly, and in such a way that I turned my head, knowing that caution had caught Buck.

"What about?"

"Oh, nothin'," said Buck carelessly; "only he's been quar ever since. My sisters says he's got a gal over thar, an' he's a-pickin' off these rings more'n ever now. He's going to win or bust a bellyband."

"Well, who's Dave Branham?"

Buck grinned. "You jes axe my sister Mollie. Thar she is."

Before us was a white-framed house of logs in the porch of which stood two stalwart, good-looking girls. Could we stay all night? We could—there was no hesitation—and straight in we rode.

"Where's your father?" Both girls giggled, and one said, with frank unembarrassment:

"Pap's tight!" That did not look promising, but we had to stay just the same. Buck helped me to unhitch the mules, helped me also to catch minnows, and in half an hour we started down the river to try fishing before dark came. Buck trotted along.

"Have you got a wagon, Buck?"

"What fer?"

"To bring the fish back." Buck was not to be caught napping.

"We got that sled thar, but hit won't be big enough," he said gravely. "An' our two-hoss wagon's out in the cornfield. We'll have to string the fish, leave 'em in the river and go fer 'em in the mornin'."

"All right, Buck." The Blight was greatly amused at Buck.

Two hundred yards down the road stood his sisters over the figure of a man outstretched in the road. Unashamed, they smiled at us. The man in the road was "pap"—tight—and they were trying to get him home.

We cast into a dark pool farther down and fished most patiently; not a bite—not a nibble.

"Are there any fish in here, Buck?"

"Dunno—used ter be." The shadows deepened; we must go back to the house.

"Is there a dam below here, Buck?"

"Yes, thar's a dam about a half-mile down the river."

I was disgusted. No wonder there were no bass in that pool.

"Why didn't you tell me that before?"

"You never axed me," said Buck placidly.

I began winding in my line.

"Ain't no bottom to that pool," said Buck.

Now I never saw any rural community where there was not a bottomless pool, and I suddenly determined to shake one tradition in at least one community. So I took an extra fish-line, tied a stone to it, and climbed into a canoe, Buck watching me, but not asking a word.

"Get in, Buck."

Silently he got in and I pushed off—to the centre.

"This the deepest part, Buck?"

"I reckon so."

I dropped in the stone and the line reeled out some fifty feet and began to coil on the surface of the water.

"I guess that's on the bottom, isn't it, Buck?"

Buck looked genuinely distressed; but presently he brightened.

"Yes," he said, "ef hit ain't on a turtle's back."

Literally I threw up both hands and back we trailed—fishless.

"Reckon you won't need that two-hoss wagon," said Buck.

"No, Buck, I think not." Buck looked at the Blight and gave himself the pleasure of his first chuckle. A big crackling, cheerful fire awaited us. Through the door I could see, outstretched on a bed in the next room, the limp figure of "pap" in alcoholic sleep. The old mother, big, kind-faced, explained—and there was a heaven of kindness and charity in her drawling voice.

"Dad didn' often git that a-way," she said; "but he'd been out a-huntin' hawgs that mornin' and had met up with some teamsters and gone to a political speakin' and had tuk a dram or two of their mean whiskey, and not havin' nothin' on his stummick, hit had all gone to his head. No, 'pap' didn't git that a-way often, and he'd be all right jes' as soon as he slept it off a while." The old woman moved about with a cane and the sympathetic Blight merely looked a question at her.

"Yes, she'd fell down a year ago—and had sort o' hurt herself—didn't do nothin', though, 'cept break one hip," she added, in her kind, patient old voice. Did many people stop there? Oh, yes, sometimes fifteen at a time—they "never turned nobody away." And she had a big family, little Cindy and the two big girls and Buck and Mart—who was out somewhere—and the hired man, and yes—"Thar was another boy, but he was fitified," and one of the big sisters.

"I beg your pardon," said the wondering Blight, but she knew that phrase wouldn't do, so she added politely:

"What did you say?"

"Fitified—Tom has fits. He's in a asylum in the settlements."

"Tom come back once an' he was all right," said the old mother; "but he worried so much over them gals workin' so hard that it plum' throwed him off ag'in, and we had to send him back."

"Do you work pretty hard?" I asked presently. Then a story came that was full of unconscious pathos, because there was no hint of complaint—simply a plain statement of daily life. They got up before the men, in order to get breakfast ready; then they went with the men into the fields—those two girls—and worked like men. At dark they got supper ready, and after the men went to bed they worked on—washing dishes and clearing up the kitchen. They took it turn about getting supper, and sometimes, one said, she was "so plumb tuckered out that she'd drap on the bed and go to sleep ruther than eat her own supper." No wonder poor Tom had to go back to the asylum. All the while the two girls stood by the fire looking, politely but minutely, at the two strange girls and their curious clothes and their boots, and the way they dressed their hair. Their hard life seemed to have hurt them none—for both were the pictures of health—whatever that phrase means.

After supper "pap" came in, perfectly sober, with a big ruddy face, giant frame and twinkling gray eyes. He was the man who had risen to speak his faith in the Hon. Samuel Budd that day on the size of the Hon. Samuel's ears. He, too, was unashamed and, as he explained his plight again, he did it with little apology.

"I seed ye at the speakin' to-day. That man Budd is a good man. He done somethin' fer a boy o' mine over at the Gap." Like little Buck, he, too, stopped short. "He's a good man an' I'm a-goin' to help him."

Yes, he repeated, quite irrelevantly, it was hunting hogs all day with nothing to eat and only mean whiskey to drink. Mart had not come in yet—he was "workin' out" now.

"He's the best worker in these mountains," said the old woman; "Mart works too hard."

The hired man appeared and joined us at the fire. Bedtime came, and I whispered jokingly to the Blight:

"I believe I'll ask that good-looking one to 'set up' with me." "Settin' up" is what courting is called in the hills. The couple sit up in front of the fire after everybody else has gone to bed. The man puts his arm around the girl's neck and whispers; then she puts her arm around his neck and whispers—so that the rest may not hear. This I had related to the Blight, and now she withered me.

"You just do, now!"

I turned to the girl in question, whose name was Mollie. "Buck told me to ask you who Dave Branham was." Mollie wheeled, blushing and angry, but Buck had darted cackling out the door. "Oh," I said, and I changed the subject. "What time do you get up?"

"Oh, 'bout crack o' day." I was tired, and that was discouraging. "Do you get up that early every morning?"

"No," was the quick answer; "a mornin' later."

A morning later, Mollie got up, each morning. The Blight laughed.

Pretty soon the two girls were taken into the next room, which was a long one, with one bed in one dark corner, one in the other, and a third bed in the middle. The feminine members of the family all followed them out on the porch and watched them brush their teeth, for they had never seen tooth-brushes before. They watched them prepare for bed—and I could hear much giggling and comment and many questions, all of which culminated, by and by, in a chorus of shrieking laughter. That climax, as I learned next morning, was over the Blight's hot-water bag. Never had their eyes rested on an article of more wonder and humor than that water bag.

By and by, the feminine members came back and we sat around the fire. Still Mart did not appear, though somebody stepped into the kitchen, and from the warning glance that Mollie gave Buck when she left the room I guessed that the newcomer was her lover Dave. Pretty soon the old man yawned.

"Well, mammy, I reckon this stranger's about ready to lay down, if you've got a place fer him."

"Git a light, Buck," said the old woman. Buck got a light—a chimneyless, smoking oil-lamp—and led me into the same room where the Blight and my little sister were. Their heads were covered up, but the bed in the gloom of one corner was shaking with their smothered laughter. Buck pointed to the middle bed.

"I can get along without that light, Buck," I said, and I must have been rather haughty and abrupt, for a stifled shriek came from under the bedclothes in the corner and Buck disappeared swiftly. Preparations for bed are simple in the mountains—they were primitively simple for me that night. Being in knickerbockers, I merely took off my coat and shoes. Presently somebody else stepped into the room and the bed in the other corner creaked. Silence for a while. Then the door opened, and the head of the old woman was thrust in.

"Mart!" she said coaxingly; "git up thar now an' climb over inter bed with that ar stranger."

That was Mart at last, over in the corner. Mart turned, grumbled, and, to my great pleasure, swore that he wouldn't. The old woman waited a moment.

"Mart," she said again with gentle imperiousness, "git up thar now, I tell ye—you've got to sleep with that thar stranger."

She closed the door and with a snort Mart piled into bed with me. I gave him plenty of room and did not introduce myself. A little more dark silence—the shaking of the bed under the hilarity of those astonished, bethrilled, but thoroughly unfrightened young women in the dark corner on my left ceased, and again the door opened. This time it was the hired man, and I saw that the trouble was either that neither Mart nor Buck wanted to sleep with the hired man or that neither wanted to sleep with me. A long silence and then the boy Buck slipped in. The hired man delivered himself with the intonation somewhat of a circuit rider.

"I've been a-watchin' that star thar, through the winder. Sometimes hit moves, then hit stands plum' still, an' ag'in hit gits to pitchin'." The hired man must have been touching up mean whiskey himself. Meanwhile, Mart seemed to be having spells of troubled slumber. He would snore gently, accentuate said snore with a sudden quiver of his body and then wake up with a climacteric snort and start that would shake the bed. This was repeated several times, and I began to think of the unfortunate Tom who was "fitified." Mart seemed on the verge of a fit himself, and I waited apprehensively for each snorting climax to see if fits were a family failing. They were not. Peace overcame Mart and he slept deeply, but not I. The hired man began to show symptoms. He would roll and groan, dreaming of feuds, *quorum pars magna fuit*, it seemed, and of religious conversion, in which he feared he was not so great. Twice he said aloud:

"An' I tell you thar wouldn't a one of 'em have said a word if I'd been killed stone-dead." Twice he said it almost weepingly, and now and then he would groan appealingly:

"O Lawd, have mercy on my pore soul!"

Fortunately those two tired girls slept—I could hear their breathing—but sleep there was little for me. Once the troubled soul with the hoe got up and stumbled out to the water-bucket on the porch to soothe the fever or whatever it was that was burning him, and after that he was quiet. I awoke before day. The dim light at the window showed an empty bed—Buck and the hired man were gone. Mart was slipping out of the side of my bed, but the girls still slept on. I watched Mart, for I guessed I might now see what, perhaps, is the distinguishing trait of American civilization down to its bed-rock, as you find it through the West and in the Southern hills—a chivalrous respect for women. Mart thought I was asleep. Over in the corner were two creatures the like of which I supposed he had never seen and would not see, since he came in too late the night before, and was going away too early now—and two angels straight from heaven could not have stirred my curiosity any more than they already must have stirred his. But not once did Mart turn his eyes, much less his face, toward the corner where they were—not once, for I watched him closely. And when he went out he sent his little sister back for his shoes, which the night-walking hired man had accidentally kicked toward the foot of the strangers' bed. In a minute I was out after him, but he was gone. Behind me the two girls opened their eyes on a room that was empty save for them. Then the Blight spoke (this I was told later).

"Dear," she said, "have our roommates gone?"

Breakfast at dawn. The mountain girls were ready to go to work. All looked sorry to have us leave. They asked us to come back again, and they meant it. We said we would like to come back—and we meant it—to see them—the kind old mother, the pioneer-like old man, sturdy little Buck, shy little Cindy, the elusive, hard-working, unconsciously shivery Mart, and the two big sisters. As we started back up the river the sisters started for the fields, and I thought of their stricken brother in the settlements, who must have been much like Mart.

Back up the Big Black Mountain we toiled, and late in the afternoon we were on the State line that runs the crest of the Big Black. Right on top and bisected by that State line sat a dingy little shack, and there, with one leg thrown over the pommel of his saddle, sat Marston, drinking water from a gourd.

"I was coming over to meet you," he said, smiling at the Blight, who, greatly pleased, smiled back at him. The shack was a "blind Tiger" where whiskey could be sold to Kentuckians on the Virginia side and to Virginians on the Kentucky side. Hanging around were the slouching figures of several moonshiners and the villainous fellow who ran it.

"They are real ones all right," said Marston. "One of them killed a revenue officer at that front door last week, and was killed by the posse as he was trying to escape out of the back window. That house will be in ashes soon," he added. And it was.

As we rode down the mountain we told him about our trip and the people with whom we had spent the night—and all the time he was smiling curiously.

"Buck," he said. "Oh, yes, I know that little chap. Mart had him posted down there on the river to toll you to his house—to toll *you,*" he added to the Blight. He pulled in his horse suddenly, turned and looked up toward the top of the mountain.

"Ah, I thought so." We all looked back. On the edge of the cliff, far upward, on which the "blind Tiger" sat was a gray horse, and on it was a man who, motionless, was looking down at us. "He's been following you all the way," said the engineer.

"Who's been following us?" I asked.

"That's Mart up there—my friend and yours," said Marston to the Blight. "I'm rather glad I didn't meet you on the other side of the mountain—that's 'the Wild Dog.' " The Blight looked incredulous, but Marston knew the man and knew the horse.

So Mart—hard-working Mart—was the Wild Dog, and he was content to do the Blight all service without thanks, merely for the privilege of secretly seeing her face now and then; and yet he would not look upon that face when she was a guest under his roof and asleep.

Still, when we dropped behind the two girls I gave Marston the Hon. Sam's warning, and for a moment he looked rather grave.

"Well," he said, smiling, "if I'm found in the road some day, you'll know who did it."

I shook my head. "Oh, no; he isn't that bad."

"I don't know," said Marston.

The smoke of the young engineer's coke ovens lay far below us and the Blight had never seen a coke-plant before. It looked like

Hades even in the early dusk—the snake-like coil of fiery ovens stretching up the long, deep ravine, and the smoke-streaked clouds of fire, trailing like a yellow mist over them, with a fierce white blast shooting up here and there when the lid of an oven was raised, as though to add fresh temperature to some particular malefactor in some particular chamber of torment. Humanity about was joyous, however. Laughter and banter and song came from the cabins that lined the big ravine and the little ravines opening into it. A banjo tinkled at the entrance of "Possum Trot," sacred to the darkies. We moved toward it. On the stoop sat an ecstatic picker and in the dust shuffled three pickaninnies—one boy and two girls—the youngest not five years old. The crowd that was gathered about them gave way respectfully as we drew near; the little darkies showed their white teeth in jolly grins, and their feet shook the dust in happy competition. I showered a few coins for the Blight and on we went—into the mouth of the many-peaked Gap. The night train was coming in and everybody had a smile of welcome for the Blight—post-office assistant, drug clerk, soda-water boy, telegraph operator, hostler, who came for the mules—and when tired, but happy, she slipped from her saddle to the ground, she then and there gave me what she usually reserves for Christmas morning, and that, too, while Marston was looking on. Over her shoulder I smiled at him.

That night Marston and the Blight sat under the vines on the porch until the late moon rose over Wallens Ridge, and, when bedtime came, the Blight said impatiently that she did not want to go home. She had to go, however, next day, but on the next Fourth of July she would surely come again; and, as the young engineer mounted his horse and set his face toward Black Mountain, I knew that until that day, for him, a blight would still be in the hills.

V

BACK TO THE HILLS

Winter drew a gray veil over the mountains, wove into it tiny jewels of frost and turned it many times into a mask of snow, before spring broke again among them and in Marston's impatient heart. No spring had ever been like that to him. The coming of young leaves and flowers and bird-song meant but one joy for the hills to him—the Blight was coming back to them. All those weary waiting months he had clung grimly to his work. He must have heard from her sometimes, else I think he would have gone to her; but I knew the Blight's pen was reluctant and casual for anybody, and, moreover, she was having a strenuous winter at home. That he knew as well, for he took one paper, at least, that he might simply read her name. He saw accounts of her many social doings as well, and ate his heart out as lovers have done for all time gone and will do for all time to come.

I, too, was away all winter, but I got back a month before the Blight, to learn much of interest that had come about. The Hon. Samuel Budd had ear-wagged himself into the legislature, had moved that Court-House, and was going to be State Senator. The Wild Dog had confined his reckless career to his own hills through the winter, but when spring came, migratory-like, he began to take frequent wing to the Gap. So far, he and Marston had never come into personal conflict, though Marston kept ever ready for him, and several times they had met in the road, eyed each other in passing and made no hipward gesture at all. But then Marston had never met him when the Wild Dog was drunk—and when sober, I took it that the one act of kindness from the engineer always stayed his hand. But the Police Guard at the Gap saw him quite often—and to it he was a fearful and elusive nuisance. He seemed to be staying somewhere within a radius of ten miles, for every night or two he would circle about the town, yelling and firing his pistol, and when we chased him, escaping through the Gap or up the valley or down in Lee. Many plans were laid to catch him, but all failed, and finally he came in one day and gave himself up and paid his fines. Afterward I recalled that the time of this gracious surrender to law and order was but little subsequent to one morning when a woman who brought butter and eggs to my little sister casually asked when that "purty slim little gal with the snappin' black eyes was a-comin' back." And the little sister, pleased with the remembrance, had said cordially that she was coming soon.

Thereafter the Wild Dog was in town every day, and he behaved well until one Saturday he got drunk again, and this time, by a peculiar chance, it was Marston again who leaped on him, wrenched his pistol away, and put him in the calaboose. Again he paid his fine, promptly visited a "blind Tiger," came back to town, emptied another pistol at Marston on sight and fled for the hills.

The enraged guard chased him for two days and from that day the Wild Dog was a marked man. The Guard wanted many men, but if they could have had their choice they would have picked out of the world of malefactors that same Wild Dog.

Why all this should have thrown the Hon. Samuel Budd into such gloom I could not understand—except that the Wild Dog had been so loyal a henchman to him in politics, but later I learned a better reason, that threatened to cost the Hon. Sam much more than the fines that, as I later learned, he had been paying for his mountain friend.

Meanwhile, the Blight was coming from her Northern home through the green lowlands of Jersey, the fat pastures of Maryland, and, as the white dresses of schoolgirls and the shining faces of darkies thickened at the stations, she knew that she was getting southward. All the way she was known and welcomed, and next morning she awoke with the keen air of the distant mountains in her nostrils and an expectant light in her happy eyes. At least the light was there when she stepped daintily from the dusty train and it leaped a little, I fancied, when Marston, bronzed and flushed, held out his sunburnt hand. Like a convent girl she babbled questions to the little sister as the dummy puffed along and she bubbled like wine over the midsummer glory of the hills. And well she might, for the glory of the mountains, full-leafed, shrouded in evening shadows, blue-veiled in the distance, was unspeakable, and through the Gap the sun was sending his last rays as though he, too, meant to take a peep at her before he started around the world to welcome her next day. And she must know everything at once. The anniversary of the Great Day on which all men were pronounced free and equal was only ten days distant and preparations were going on. There would be a big crowd of mountaineers and there would be sports of all kinds, and games, but the tournament was to be the feature of the day. "A tournament?" "Yes, a tournament," repeated the little sister, and Marston was going to ride and the mean thing would not tell what mediaeval name he meant to take. And the Hon. Sam Budd—did the Blight remember him? (Indeed, she did)—had a "dark horse," and he had bet heavily that his dark horse would win the tournament—whereat the little sister looked at Marston and at the Blight and smiled disdainfully. And the Wild Dog—*did* she remember him? I checked the sister here with a glance, for Marston looked uncomfortable and the Blight saw me do it, and on the point of saying something she checked herself, and her face, I thought, paled a little.

That night I learned why—when she came in from the porch after Marston was gone. I saw she had wormed enough of the story out of him to worry her, for her face this time was distinctly pale. I would tell her no more than she knew, however, and then she said she was sure she had seen the Wild Dog herself that afternoon, sitting on his horse in the bushes near a station in Wildcat Valley. She was sure that he saw her, and his face had frightened her. I knew her fright was for Marston and not for herself, so I laughed at her fears. She was mistaken—Wild Dog was an outlaw now and he would not dare appear at the Gap, and there was no chance that he could harm her or Marston. And yet I was uneasy.

It must have been a happy ten days for those two young people. Every afternoon Marston would come in from the mines and they would go off horseback together, over ground that I well knew—for I had been all over it myself—up through the gray-peaked rhododendron-bordered Gap with the swirling water below them and the gray rock high above where another such foolish lover lost his life, climbing to get a flower for his sweetheart, or down the winding dirt road into Lee, or up through the beech woods behind Imboden Hill, or climbing the spur of Morris's Farm to watch the sunset over the majestic Big Black Mountains, where the Wild Dog lived, and back through the fragrant, cool, moonlit woods. He was doing his best, Marston was, and he was having trouble—as every man should. And that trouble I knew even better than he, for I had once known a

Southern girl who was so tender of heart that she could refuse no man who really loved her—she accepted him and sent him to her father, who did all of her refusing for her. And I knew no man would know that he had won the Blight until he had her at the altar and the priestly hand of benediction was above her head.

Of such kind was the Blight. Every night when they came in I could read the story of the day, always in his face and sometimes in hers; and it was a series of ups and downs that must have wrung the boy's heart bloodless. Still I was in good hope for him, until the crisis came on the night before the Fourth. The quarrel was as plain as though typewritten on the face of each. Marston would not come in that night and the Blight went dinnerless to bed and cried herself to sleep. She told the little sister that she had seen the Wild Dog again peering through the bushes, and that she was frightened. That was her explanation—but I guessed a better one.

VI

THE GREAT DAY

It was a day to make glad the heart of slave or freeman. The earth was cool from a night-long rain, and a gentle breeze fanned coolness from the north all day long. The clouds were snow-white, tumbling, ever-moving, and between them the sky showed blue and deep. Grass, leaf, weed and flower were in the richness that comes to the green things of the earth just before that full tide of summer whose foam is drifting thistle-down. The air was clear and the mountains seemed to have brushed the haze from their faces and drawn nearer that they, too, might better see the doings of that day.

From the four winds of heaven, that morning, came the brave and the free. Up from Lee, down from Little Stone Gap, and from over in Scott, came the valley-farmers—horseback, in buggies, hacks, two-horse wagons, with wives, mothers, sisters, sweethearts, in white dresses, beflowered hats, and many ribbons, and with dinner-baskets stuffed with good things to eat—old ham, young chicken, angel-cake and blackberry wine—to be spread in the sunless shade of great poplar and oak. From Bum Hollow and Wildcat Valley and from up the slopes that lead to Cracker's Neck came smaller tillers of the soil—as yet but faintly marked by the gewgaw trappings of the outer world; while from beyond High Knob, whose crown is in cloud-land, and through the Gap, came the mountaineer in the primitive simplicity of homespun and cowhide, wide-brimmed hat and poke-bonnet, quaint speech, and slouching gait. Through the Gap he came in two streams—the Virginians from Crab Orchard and Wise and Dickinson, the Kentuckians from Letcher and feudal Harlan, beyond the Big Black—and not a man carried a weapon in sight, for the stern spirit of that Police Guard at the Gap was respected wide and far. Into the town, which sits on a plateau some twenty feet above the level of the two rivers that all but encircle it, they poured, hitching their horses in the strip of woods that runs through the heart of the place, and broadens into a primeval park that, fan-like, opens on the oval level field where all things happen on the Fourth of July. About the street they loitered—lovers hand in hand—eating fruit and candy and drinking soda-water, or sat on the curb-stone, mothers with babies at their breasts and toddling children clinging close—all waiting for the celebration to begin.

It was a great day for the Hon. Samuel Budd. With a cheery smile and beaming goggles, he moved among his constituents, joking with yokels, saying nice things to mothers, paying gallantries to girls, and chucking babies under the chin. He felt popular and he was—so popular that he had begun to see himself with prophetic eye in a congressional seat at no distant day; and yet, withal, he was not wholly happy.

"Do you know," he said, "them fellers I made bets with in the tournament got together this morning and decided, all of 'em, that they wouldn't let me off? Jerusalem, it's most five hundred dollars!" And, looking the picture of dismay, he told me his dilemma.

It seems that his "dark horse" was none other than the Wild Dog, who had been practising at home for this tournament for nearly a year; and now that the Wild Dog was an outlaw, he, of course, wouldn't and couldn't come to the Gap. And said the Hon. Sam Budd:

"Them fellers says I bet I'd *bring in* a dark horse who would *win* this tournament, and if I don't *bring* him in, I lose just the same as though I had brought him in and he hadn't won. An' I reckon they've got me."

"I guess they have."

"It would have been like pickin' money off a blackberry-bush, for I was goin' to let the Wild Dog have that black horse o' mine—the steadiest and fastest runner in this country—and my, how that fellow can pick off the rings! He's been a-practising for a year, and I believe he could run the point o' that spear of his through a lady's finger-ring."

"You'd better get somebody else."

"Ah—that's it. The Wild Dog sent word he'd send over another feller, named Dave Branham, who has been practising with him, who's just as good, he says, as he is. I'm looking for him at twelve o'clock, an' I'm goin' to take him down an' see what he can do on that black horse o' mine. But if he's no good, I lose five hundred, all right," and he sloped away to his duties. For it was the Hon. Sam who was master of ceremonies that day. He was due now to read the Declaration of Independence in a poplar grove to all who would listen; he was to act as umpire at the championship base-ball game in the afternoon, and he was to give the "Charge" to the assembled knights before the tournament.

At ten o'clock the games began—and I took the Blight and the little sister down to the "grandstand"—several tiers of backless benches with leaves for a canopy and the river singing through rhododendrons behind. There was jumping broad and high, and a 100-yard dash and hurdling and throwing the hammer, which the Blight said were not interesting—they were too much like college sports—and she wanted to see the base-ball game and the tournament. And yet Marston was in them all—dogged and resistless—his teeth set and his eyes anywhere but lifted toward the Blight, who secretly proud, as I believed, but openly defiant, mentioned not his name even when he lost, which was twice only.

"Pretty good, isn't he?" I said.

"Who?" she said indifferently.

"Oh, nobody," I said, turning to smile, but not turning quickly enough.

"What's the matter with you?" asked the Blight sharply.

"Nothing, nothing at all," I said, and straightway the Blight thought she wanted to go home. The thunder of the Declaration was still rumbling in the poplar grove.

"That's the Hon. Sam Budd," I said. "Don't you want to hear him?"

"I don't care who it is—and I don't want to hear him and I think you are hateful."

Ah, dear me, it was more serious than I thought. There were tears in her eyes, and I led the Blight and the little sister home—conscience-stricken and humbled. Still I would find that young jackanapes of an engineer and let him know that anybody who made the Blight unhappy must deal with me. I would take him by the neck and pound some sense into him. I found him lofty, uncommunicative, perfectly alien to any consciousness that I could have any knowledge of what was going or any right to poke my nose into anybody's business—and I did nothing except go back to lunch—to find the Blight upstairs and the little sister indignant with me.

"You just let them alone," she said severely.

"Let who alone?" I said, lapsing into the speech of childhood.

"You—just—let—them—alone," she repeated.

"I've already made up my mind to that."

"Well, then!" she said, with an air of satisfaction, but why I don't know.

I went back to the poplar grove. The Declaration was over and the crowd was gone, but there was the Hon. Samuel Budd, mopping his brow with one hand, slapping his thigh with the other, and all but executing a pigeon-wing on the turf. He turned goggles on me that literally shone triumph.

"He's come—Dave Branham's come!" he said. "He's better than the Wild Dog. I've been trying him on the black horse and, Lord, how he can take them rings off! Ha, won't I get into them fellows who wouldn't let me off this morning! Oh, yes, I agreed to bring in a dark horse, and I'll bring him in all right. That five hundred is in my clothes now. You see that point yonder? Well, there's a hollow there and bushes all around. That's where I'm going to dress him. I've got his clothes all right and a name for him. This thing is a-goin' to come off accordin' to Hoyle, Ivanhoe, Four-Quarters-of-Beef, and all them mediaeval fellows. Just watch me!"

I began to get newly interested, for that knight's name I suddenly recalled. Little Buck, the Wild Dog's brother, had mentioned him, when we were over in the Kentucky hills, as practising with the Wild Dog—as being "mighty good, but nowhar 'longside o' Mart." So the Hon. Sam might have a good substitute, after all, and being a devoted disciple of Sir Walter, I knew his knight would rival, in splendor, at least, any that rode with King Arthur in days of old.

The Blight was very quiet at lunch, as was the little sister, and my effort to be jocose was a lamentable failure. So I gave news.

"The Hon. Sam has a substitute." No curiosity and no question.

"Who—did you say? Why, Dave Branham, a friend of the Wild Dog. Don't you remember Buck telling us about him?" No answer. "Well, I do—and, by the way, I saw Buck and one of the big sisters just a while ago. Her name is Mollie. Dave Branham, you will recall, is her sweetheart. The other big sister had to stay at home with her mother and little Cindy, who's sick. Of course, I didn't ask them about Mart—the Wild Dog. They knew I knew and they wouldn't have liked it. The Wild Dog's around, I understand, but he won't dare show his face. Every policeman in town is on the lookout for him." I thought the Blight's face showed a signal of relief.

"I'm going to play short-stop," I added.

"Oh!" said the Blight, with a smile, but the little sister said with some scorn:

"You!"

"I'll show you," I said, and I told the Blight about base-ball at the Gap. We had introduced base-ball into the region and the valley boys and mountain boys, being swift runners, throwing like a rifle-shot from constant practice with stones, and being hard as nails, caught the game quickly and with great ease. We beat them all the time at first, but now they were beginning to beat us. We had a league now, and this was the championship game for the pennant.

"It was right funny the first time we beat a native team. Of course, we got together and cheered 'em. They thought we were cheering ourselves, so they got red in the face, rushed together and whooped it up for themselves for about half an hour."

The Blight almost laughed.

"We used to have to carry our guns around with us at first when we went to other places, and we came near having several fights."

"Oh!" said the Blight excitedly. "Do you think there might be a fight this afternoon?"

"Don't know," I said, shaking my head. "It's pretty hard for eighteen people to fight when nine of them are policemen and there are forty more around. Still the crowd might take a hand."

This, I saw, quite thrilled the Blight and she was in good spirits when we started out.

"Marston doesn't pitch this afternoon," I said to the little sister. "He plays first base. He's saving himself for the tournament. He's done too much already." The Blight merely turned her head while I was speaking. "And the Hon. Sam will not act as umpire. He wants to save his voice—and his head."

The seats in the "grandstand" were in the sun now, so I left the girls in a deserted band-stand that stood on stilts under the trees on the southern side of the field, and on a line midway between third base and the position of short-stop. Now there is no enthusiasm in any sport that equals the excitement aroused by a rural base-ball game and I never saw the enthusiasm of that game outdone except by the excitement of the tournament that followed that afternoon. The game was close and Marston and I assuredly were stars—Marston one of the first magnitude. "Goose-egg" on one side matched "goose-egg" on the other until the end of the fifth inning, when the engineer knocked a home-run. Spectators threw their hats into the trees, yelled themselves hoarse, and I saw several old mountaineers who understood no more of base-ball than of the lost *digamma* in Greek going wild with the general contagion. During these innings I had "assisted" in two doubles and had fired in three "daisy-cutters" to first myself in spite of the guying I got from the opposing rooters. "Four-eyes" they called me on account of my spectacles until a new nickname came at the last half of the ninth inning, when we were in the field with the score four to three in our favor. It was then that a small, fat boy with a paper megaphone longer than he was waddled out almost to first base and levelling his trumpet at me, thundered out in a sudden silence:

"Hello, Foxy Grandpa!" That was too much. I got rattled, and when there were three men on bases and two out, a swift grounder came to me, I fell—catching it—and threw wildly to first from my knees. I heard shouts of horror, anger, and distress from everywhere and my own heart stopped beating—I had lost the game—and then Marston leaped in the air—surely it must have been four feet—caught the ball with his left hand and dropped back on the bag. The sound of his foot on it and the runner's was almost simultaneous, but the umpire said Marston's was there first. Then bedlam! One of my brothers was umpire and the captain of the other team walked threateningly out toward him, followed by two of his men with base-ball bats. As I started off myself towards them I saw, with the corner of my eye, another brother of mine start in a run from the left field, and I wondered why a third, who was scoring, sat perfectly still in his chair, particularly as a well-known, red-headed tough from one of the mines who had been officiously antagonistic ran toward the pitcher's box directly in front of him. Instantly a dozen of the guard sprang toward it, some man pulled his pistol, a billy cracked straightway on his head, and in a few minutes order was restored. And still the brother scoring hadn't moved from his chair, and I spoke to him hotly.

"Keep your shirt on," he said easily, lifting his score-card with his left hand and showing his right clinched about his pistol under it.

"I was just waiting for that red-head to make a move. I guess I'd have got him first."

I walked back to the Blight and the little sister and both of them looked very serious and frightened.

"I don't think I want to see a real fight, after all," said the Blight. "Not this afternoon."

It was a little singular and prophetic, but just as the words left her lips one of the Police Guard handed me a piece of paper.

"Somebody in the crowd must have dropped it in my pocket," he said. On the paper were scrawled these words:

"Look out for the Wild Dog!"

I sent the paper to Marston.

VII

AT LAST—THE TOURNAMENT

At last—the tournament!

Ever afterward the Hon. Samuel Budd called it "The Gentle and Joyous Passage of Arms—not of Ashby—but of the Gap, by-suh!" The Hon. Samuel had arranged it as nearly after Sir Walter as possible. And a sudden leap it was from the most modern of games to a game most ancient.

No knights of old ever jousted on a lovelier field than the green little valley toward which the Hon. Sam waved one big hand. It was level, shorn of weeds, elliptical in shape, and bound in by trees that ran in a semicircle around the bank of the river, shut in the southern border, and ran back to the northern extremity in a primeval little forest that wood-thrushes, even then, were making musical—all of it shut in by a wall of living green, save for one narrow space through which the knights were to enter. In front waved Wallens' leafy ridge and behind rose the Cumberland Range shouldering itself spur by spur, into the coming sunset and crashing eastward into the mighty bulk of Powell's Mountain, which loomed southward from the head of the valley—all nodding sunny plumes of chestnut.

The Hon. Sam had seen us coming from afar apparently, had come forward to meet us, and he was in high spirits.

"I am Prince John and Waldemar and all the rest of 'em this day," he said, "and 'it is thus,' " quoting Sir Walter, "that we set the dutiful example of loyalty to the Queen of Love and Beauty, and are ourselves her guide to the throne which she must this day occupy." And so saying, the Hon. Sam marshalled the Blight to a seat of honor next his own.

"And how do you know she is going to be the Queen of

Love and Beauty?" asked the little sister. The Hon. Sam winked at me.

"Well, this tournament lies between two gallant knights. One will make her the Queen of his own accord, if he wins, and if the other wins, he's got to, or I'll break his head. I've given orders." And the Hon. Sam looked about right and left on the people who were his that day.

"Observe the nobles and ladies," he said, still following Sir Walter, and waving at the towns-people and visitors in the rude grandstand. "Observe the yeomanry and spectators of a better degree than the mere vulgar"—waving at the crowd on either side of the stand—"and the promiscuous multitude down the river banks and over the woods and clinging to the tree-tops and to yon telegraph-pole. And there is my herald"—pointing to the cornetist of the local band—"and wait—by my halidom—please just wait until you see my knight on that black charger o' mine."

The Blight and the little sister were convulsed and the Hon. Sam went on:

"Look at my men-at-arms"—the volunteer policemen with bulging hip-pockets, dangling billies and gleaming shields of office—"and at my refreshment tents behind"—where peanuts and pink lemonade were keeping the multitude busy—"and my attendants"—colored gentlemen with sponges and water-buckets—"the armorers and farriers haven't come yet. But my knight—I got his clothes in New York—just wait—Love of Ladies and Glory to the Brave!" Just then there was a commotion in the free seats on one side of the grandstand. A darky starting, in all ignorance, to mount them was stopped and jostled none too good-naturedly back to the ground.

"And see," mused the Hon. Sam, "in lieu of the dog of an unbeliever we have a dark analogy in that son of Ham."

The little sister plucked me by the sleeve and pointed toward the entrance. Outside and leaning on the fence were Mollie, the big sister, and little Buck. Straightway I got up and started for them. They hung back, but I persuaded them to come, and I led them to seats two tiers below the Blight—who, with my little sister, rose smiling to greet them and shake hands—much to the wonder of the nobles and ladies close about, for Mollie was in brave and dazzling array, blushing fiercely, and little Buck looked as though he would die of such conspicuousness. No embarrassing questions were asked about Mart or Dave Branham, but I noticed that Mollie had purple and crimson ribbons clinched in one brown hand. The purpose of them was plain, and I whispered to the Blight:

"She's going to pin them on Dave's lance." The Hon. Sam heard me.

"Not on your life," he said emphatically. "I ain't takin' chances," and he nodded toward the Blight. "She's got to win, no matter who loses." He rose to his feet suddenly.

"Glory to the Brave—they're comin'! Toot that horn, son," he said; "they're comin'," and the band burst into discordant sounds that would have made the "wild barbaric music" on the field of Ashby sound like a lullaby. The Blight stifled her laughter over that amazing music with her handkerchief, and even the Hon. Sam scowled.

"Gee!" he said; "it is pretty bad, isn't it?"

"Here they come!"

The nobles and ladies on the grandstand, the yeomanry and spectators of better degree, and the promiscuous multitude began to sway expectantly and over the hill came the knights, single file, gorgeous in velvets and in caps, with waving plumes and with polished spears, vertical, resting on the right stirrup foot and gleaming in the sun.

"A goodly array!" murmured the Hon. Sam.

A crowd of small boys gathered at the fence below, and I observed the Hon. Sam's pockets bulging with peanuts.

"Largesse!" I suggested.

"Good!" he said, and rising he shouted:

"Largessy! largessy!" scattering peanuts by the handful among the scrambling urchins.

Down wound the knights behind the back stand of the base-ball field, and then, single file, in front of the nobles and ladies, before whom they drew up and faced, saluting with inverted spears.

The Hon. Sam arose—his truncheon a hickory stick—and in a

stentorian voice asked the names of the doughty knights who were there to win glory for themselves and the favor of fair women.

Not all will be mentioned, but among them was the Knight of the Holston—Athelstanic in build—in black stockings, white negligee shirt, with Byronic collar, and a broad crimson sash tied with a bow at his right side. There was the Knight of the Green Valley, in green and gold, a green hat with a long white plume, lace ruffles at his sleeves, and buckles on dancing-pumps; a bonny fat knight of Maxwelton Braes, in Highland kilts and a plaid; and the Knight at Large.

"He ought to be caged," murmured the Hon. Sam; for the Knight at Large wore plum-colored velvet, red base-ball stockings, held in place with safety-pins, white tennis shoes, and a very small hat with a very long plume, and the dye was already streaking his face. Marston was the last—sitting easily on his iron gray.

"And your name, Sir Knight?"

"The Discarded," said Marston, with steady eyes. I felt the Blight start at my side and sidewise I saw that her face was crimson.

The Hon. Sam sat down, muttering, for he did not like Marston.

Just then my attention was riveted on Mollie and little Buck. Both had been staring silently at the knights as though they were apparitions, but when Marston faced them I saw Buck clutch his sister's arm suddenly and say something excitedly in her ear. Then the mouths of both tightened fiercely and their eyes seemed to be darting lightning at the unconscious knight, who suddenly saw them, recognized them, and smiled past them at me. Again Buck whispered, and from his lips I could make out what he said:

"I wonder whar's Dave?" but Mollie did not answer.

"Which is yours, Mr. Budd?" asked the little sister. The Hon. Sam had leaned back with his thumbs in the armholes of his white waistcoat.

"He ain't come yet. I told him to come last."

The crowd waited and the knights waited—so long that the Mayor rose in his seat some twenty feet away and called out:

"Go ahead, Budd."

"You jus' wait a minute—my man ain't come yet," he said easily, but from various places in the crowd came jeering shouts from the men with whom he had wagered and the Hon. Sam began to look anxious.

"I wonder what is the matter?" he added in a lower tone. "I dressed him myself more than an hour ago and I told him to come last, but I didn't mean for him to wait till Christmas—ah!"

The Hon. Sam sank back in his seat again. From somewhere had come suddenly the blare of a solitary trumpet that rang in echoes around the amphitheatre of the hills, and, a moment later, a dazzling something shot into sight above the mound that looked like a ball of fire, coming in mid-air. The new knight wore a shining helmet and the Hon. Sam chuckled at the murmur that rose and then he sat up suddenly. There was no face under that helmet—the Hon. Sam's knight was *masked* and the Hon. Sam slapped his thigh with delight.

"Bully—bully! I never thought of it—I never thought of it—bully!"

This was thrilling, indeed—but there was more; the strange knight's body was cased in a flexible suit of glistening mail, his spear point, when he raised it on high, shone like silver, and he came on like a radiant star—on the Hon. Sam's charger, white-bridled, with long mane and tail and black from tip of nose to tip of that tail as midnight. The Hon. Sam was certainly doing it well. At a slow walk the stranger drew alongside of Marston and turned his spear point downward.

"Gawd!" said an old darky. "Ku-klux done come again." And, indeed, it looked like a Ku-klux mask, white, dropping below the chin, and with eye-holes through which gleamed two bright fires.

The eyes of Buck and Molllie were turned from Marston at last, and open-mouthed they stared.

"Hit's the same hoss—hit's Dave!" said Buck aloud.

"Well, my Lord!" said Mollie simply.

The Hon. Sam rose again.

"And who is Sir Tardy Knight that hither comes with maskèd face?" he asked courteously. He got no answer.

"What's your name, son?"

The white mask puffed at the wearer's lips.

"The Knight of the Cumberland," was the low, muffled reply.

"Make him take that thing off!" shouted some one.

"What's he got it on fer?" shouted another.

"I don't know, friend," said the Hon. Sam; "but it is not my business nor prithee thine; since by the laws of the tournament a knight may ride masked for a specified time or until a particular purpose is achieved, that purpose being, I wot, victory for himself and for me a handful of byzants from thee."

"Now, go ahead, Budd," called the Mayor again. "Are you going crazy?"

The Hon. Sam stretched out his arms once to loosen them for gesture, thrust his chest out, and uplifted his chin: "Fair ladies, nobles of the realm, and good knights," he said sonorously, and he raised one hand to his mouth and behind it spoke aside to me: "How's my voice—how's my voice?"

"Great!"

His question was genuine, for the mask of humor had dropped and the man was transformed. I knew his inner seriousness, his oratorical command of good English, and I knew the habit, not uncommon among stump-speakers in the South, of falling, through humor, carelessness, or for the effect of flattering comradeship, into all the lingual sins of rural speech; but I was hardly prepared for the soaring flight the Hon. Sam took now. He started with one finger pointed heavenward:

"The knights are dust
And their good swords are rust;
Their souls are with the saints, we trust.

"Scepticism is but a harmless phantom in these mighty hills. We *believe* that with the saints is the *good* knight's soul, and if, in the radiant unknown, the eyes of those who have gone before can pierce the little shadow that lies between, we know that the good knights of old look gladly down on these good knights of to-day. For it is good to be remembered. The tireless struggle for name and fame since the sunrise of history attests it; and the ancestry worship in the East and the world-wide hope of immortality show the fierce hunger in the human soul that the memory of it not only shall not perish from this earth, but that, across the Great Divide, it shall live on—neither forgetting nor forgotten. You are here in memory of those good knights to prove that the age of chivalry is not gone; that though their good swords are rust, the stainless soul of them still illumines every harmless spear point before me and makes it a torch that shall reveal, in your own hearts still aflame, their courage, their chivalry, their sense of protection for the weak, and the honor in which they held pure women, brave men, and almighty God.

"The tournament, some say, goes back to the walls of Troy. The form of it passed with the windmills that Don Quixote charged. It is with you to keep the high spirit of it an ever-burning vestal fire. It was a deadly play of old—it is a harmless play to you this day. But the prowess of the game is unchanged; for the skill to strike those pendent rings is no less than was the skill to strike armor-joint, visor, or plumèd crest. It was of old an exercise for deadly combat on the field of battle; it is no less an exercise now to you for the field of life—for the quick eye, the steady nerve, and the deft hand which shall help you strike the mark at which, outside these lists, you aim. And the crowning triumph is still just what it was of old—that to the victor the Rose of his world—made by him the Queen of Love and Beauty for us all—shall give her smile and with her own hands place on his brow a thornless crown."

Perfect silence honored the Hon. Samuel Budd. The Mayor was nodding vigorous approval, the jeering ones kept still, and when after the last deep-toned word passed like music from his lips the silence held sway for a little while before the burst of applause came. Every knight had straightened in his saddle and was looking very grave. Marston's eyes never left the speaker's face, except once, when they turned with an unconscious appeal, I thought, to the downcast face of Blight—whereat the sympathetic little sister seemed close to tears. The Knight of the Cumberland shifted in his saddle as though he did not quite understand what was going on, and once Mollie, seeing the eyes through the mask-holes fixed on her, blushed furiously, and little Buck grinned back a delighted recognition. The Hon. Sam sat down, visibly affected by his own eloquence; slowly he wiped his face and then he rose again.

"Your colors, Sir Knights," he said, with a commanding wave of his truncheon, and one by one the knights spurred forward and each held his lance into the grandstand that some fair one might tie thereon the colors he was to wear. Marston, without looking at the Blight, held his up to the little sister and the Blight carelessly turned her face while the demure sister was busy with her ribbons, but I noticed that the little ear next to me was tingling red for all her brave look of unconcern. Only the Knight of the Cumberland sat still.

"What!" said the Hon. Sam, rising to his feet, his eyes twinkling and his mask of humor on again; "sees this maskèd springal"—the Hon. Sam seemed much enamored of that ancient word—"no maid so fair that he will not beg from her the boon of colors gay that he may carry them to victory and receive from her hands a wreath therefor?" Again the Knight of the Cumberland seemed not to know that the Hon. Sam's winged words were meant for him, so the statesman translated them into a mutual vernacular.

"Remember what I told you, son," he said. "Hold up yo' spear here to some one of these gals jes' like the other fellows are doin'," and as he sat down he tried surreptitiously to indicate the Blight with his index finger. But the knight failed to see and the Blight's face was so indignant and she rebuked him with such a knife-like whisper that, humbled, the Hon. Sam collapsed in his seat, muttering:

"The fool don't know you—he don't know you."

For the Knight of the Cumberland had turned the black horse's head and was riding, like Ivanhoe, in front of the nobles and ladies, his eyes burning up at them through the holes in his white mask. Again he turned, his mask still uplifted, and the behavior of the beauties there, as on the field of Ashby, was no whit changed: "Some blushed, some assumed an air of pride and dignity, some looked straight forward and essayed to seem utterly unconscious of what was going on, some drew back in alarm which was perhaps affected, some endeavored to forbear smiling and there were two or three who laughed outright." Only none "dropped a veil over her charms" and thus none incurred the suspicion, as on that field of Ashby, that she was "a beauty of ten years' standing" whose motive, gallant Sir Walter supposes in defence, however, was doubtless "a surfeit of such vanities and a willingness to give a fair chance to the rising beauties of the age." But the most conscious of the fair was Mollie below, whose face was flushed and whose brown fingers were nervously twisting the ribbons in her lap, and I saw Buck nudge her and heard him whisper:

"Dave ain't going to pick *you* out, I tell ye. I heered Mr. Budd thar myself tell him he *had* to pick out some other gal."

"You hush!" said Mollie indignantly.

It looked as though the Knight of the Cumberland had grown rebellious and meant to choose whom he pleased, but on his way back the Hon. Sam must have given more surreptitious signs, for the Knight of the Cumberland reined in before the Blight and held up his lance to her. Straightway the colors that were meant for Marston fluttered from the Knight of the Cumberland's spear. I saw Marston bite his lips and I saw Mollie's face aflame with fury and her eyes darting lightning—no longer at Marston now, but at the Blight. The mountain girl held nothing against the city girl because of the Wild Dog's infatuation, but that her own lover, no matter what the Hon. Sam said, should give his homage also to the Blight, in her own presence, was too much. Mollie looked around no more. Again the Hon. Sam rose.

"Love of ladies," he shouted, "splintering of lances! Stand forth, gallant knights. Fair eyes look upon your deeds! Toot again, son!"

Now just opposite the grandstand was a post some ten feet high, with a small beam projecting from the top toward the spectators. From the end of this hung a wire, the end of which was slightly upturned in line with the course, and on the tip of this wire a steel ring about an inch in diameter hung lightly. Nearly forty yards below this was a similar ring similarly arranged; and at a similar distance below that was still another, and at the blast from the Hon. Sam's herald, the gallant knights rode slowly, two by two, down the lists to the western extremity—the Discarded Knight and the Knight of the Cumberland, stirrup to stirrup, riding last—where they all drew up in line, some fifty yards beyond the westernmost post. This distance they took, that full speed might be attained before jousting at the first ring, since the course—much over one hundred yards long—must be covered in seven seconds or less, which was no slow rate of speed. The Hon. Sam arose again:

"The Knight of the Holston!"

Farther down the lists a herald took up the same cry and the good knight of Athelstanic build backed his steed from the line and took his place at the head of the course.

With his hickory truncheon the Hon. Sam signed to his trumpeter to sound the onset.

"Now, son!" he said.

With the blare of the trumpet Athelstane sprang from his place and came up the course, his lance at rest; a tinkling sound and the first ring slipped down the knight's spear and when he swept past the last post there was a clapping of hands, for he held three rings triumphantly aloft. And thus they came, one by one, until each had run the course three times, the Discarded jousting next to the last and the Knight of the Cumberland, riding with a reckless *Cave, Adsum* air, the very last. At the second joust it was quite evident that the victory lay between these two, as they only had not lost a single ring, and when the black horse thundered by, the Hon. Sam shouted "Brave lance!" and jollied his betting enemies, while Buck hugged himself triumphantly and Mollie seemed temporarily to lose her chagrin and anger in pride of her lover, Dave. On the third running the Knight of the Cumberland excited a sensation by sitting upright, waving his lance up and down between the posts and lowering it only when the ring was within a few feet of its point. His recklessness cost him one ring, but as the Discarded had lost one, they were still tied, with eight rings to the credit of each, for the first prize. Only four others were left—the Knight of the Holston and the Knight of the Green Valley tying with seven rings for second prize, and the fat Maxwelton Braes and the Knight at Large tying with six rings for the third. The crowd was eager now and the Hon. Sam confident. On came the Knight at Large, his face a rainbow, his plume wilted and one red base-ball stocking slipped from its moorings

—two rings! On followed the fat Maxwelton, his plaid streaming and his kilts flapping about his fat legs—also two rings!

"Egad!" quoth the Hon. Sam. "Did yon lusty trencherman of Annie Laurie's but put a few more layers of goodly flesh about his ribs, thereby projecting more his frontal Falstaffian proportions, by my halidom, he would have to joust tandem!"

On came Athelstane and the Knight of the Green Valley, both with but two rings to their credit, and on followed the Discarded, riding easily, and the Knight of the Cumberland again waving his lance between the posts, each with three rings on his spear. At the end the Knight at Large stood third, Athelstane second, and the Discarded and the Knight of the Cumberland stood side by side at the head of the course, still even, and now ready to end the joust, for neither on the second trial had missed a ring.

The excitement was intense now. Many people seemed to know who the Knight of the Cumberland was, for there were shouts of "Go it, Dave!" from everywhere; the rivalry of class had entered the contest and now it was a conflict between native and "furriner." The Hon. Sam was almost beside himself with excitement; now and then some man with whom he had made a bet would shout jeeringly at him and the Hon. Sam would shout back defiance. But when the trumpet sounded he sat leaning forward with his brow wrinkled and his big hands clinched tight. Marston sped up the course first—three rings—and there was a chorus of applauding yells.

"His horse is gittin' tired," said the Hon. Sam jubilantly, and the Blight's face, I noticed, showed for the first time faint traces of indignation. The Knight of the Cumberland was taking no theatrical chances now and he came through the course with level spear and, with three rings on it, he shot by like a thunderbolt.

"Hooray!" shouted the Hon. Sam. "Lord, what a horse!" For the first time the Blight, I observed, failed to applaud, while Mollie was clapping her hands and Buck was giving out shrill yells of encouragement. At the next tilt the Hon. Sam had his watch in his hand and when he saw the Discarded digging in his spurs he began to smile and he was looking at his watch when the little tinkle in front told him that the course was run.

"Did he get 'em all?"

"Yes, he got 'em all," mimicked the Blight.

"Yes, an' he just did make it," chuckled the Hon. Sam. The Discarded had wheeled his horse aside from the course to watch his antagonist. He looked pale and tired—almost as tired as his foam-covered steed—but his teeth were set and his face was unmoved as the Knight of the Cumberland came on like a demon, sweeping off the last ring with a low, rasping oath of satisfaction.

"I never seed Dave ride that-a-way afore," said Mollie.

"Me, neither," chimed in Buck.

The nobles and ladies were waving handkerchiefs, clapping hands, and shouting. The spectators of better degree were throwing up their hats and from every part of the multitude the same hoarse shout of encouragement rose:

"Go it, Dave! Hooray for Dave!" while the boy on the telegraph-pole was seen to clutch wildly at the crossbar on which he sat —he had come near tumbling from his perch.

The two knights rode slowly back to the head of the lists, where the Discarded was seen to dismount and tighten his girth.

"He's tryin' to git time to rest," said the Hon. Sam. "Toot, son!"

"Shame!" said the little sister and the Blight both at once so severely that the Hon. Sam quickly raised his hand.

"Hold on," he said, and with hand still uplifted he waited till Marston was mounted again. "Now!"

The Discarded came on, using his spurs with every jump, the red of his horse's nostrils showing that far away, and he swept on, spearing off the rings with deadly accuracy and holding the three aloft, but having no need to pull in his panting steed, who stopped of his own accord. Up went a roar, but the Hon. Sam, covertly glancing at his watch, still smiled. That watch he pulled out when the Knight of the Cumberland started and he smiled still when he heard the black horse's swift, rhythmic beat and he looked up only when that knight, shouting to his horse, moved his lance up and down before coming to the last ring and, with a dare-devil yell, swept it from the wire.

"Tied—tied!" was the shout; "they've got to try it again! they've got to try it again!"

The Hon. Sam rose, with his watch in one hand and stilling the tumult with the other. Dead silence came at once.

"I fear me," he said, "that the good knight, the Discarded, has failed to make the course in the time required by the laws of the tournament." Bedlam broke loose again and the Hon. Sam waited, still gesturing for silence.

"Summon the time-keeper!" he said.

The time-keeper appeared from the middle of the field and nodded.

"Eight seconds!"

"The Knight of the Cumberland wins," said the Hon. Sam.

The little sister, unconscious of her own sad face, nudged me to look at the Blight—there were tears in her eyes.

Before the grandstand the knights slowly drew up again. Marston's horse was so lame and tired that he dismounted and let a darky boy lead him under the shade of the trees. Marston stood on foot among the other knights, his arms folded, worn out and vanquished, but taking his bitter medicine like a man. I thought the Blight's eyes looked pityingly upon him.

The Hon. Sam arose with a crown of laurel leaves in his hand:

"You have fairly and gallantly won, Sir Knight of the Cumberland, and it is now your right to claim and receive from the hands of the Queen of Love and Beauty the chaplet of honor which your skill has justly deserved. Advance, Sir Knight of the Cumberland, and dismount!"

The Knight of the Cumberland made no move nor sound.

"Get off yo' hoss, son," said the Hon. Sam kindly, "and get down on yo' knees at the feet of them steps. This fair young Queen is a-goin' to put this chaplet on your shinin' brow. That horse'll stand."

The Knight of the Cumberland, after a moment's hesitation, threw his leg over the saddle and came to the steps with a slouching gait and looking about him right and left. The Blight, blushing prettily, took the chaplet and went down the steps to meet him.

"Unmask!" I shouted.

"Yes, son," said the Hon. Sam, "take that rag off."

Then Mollie's voice, clear and loud, startled the crowd. "You better not, Dave Branham, fer if you do and this other gal puts that thing on you, you'll never—" What penalty she was going to inflict, I don't know, for the Knight of the Cumberland, half kneeling, sprang suddenly to his feet and interrupted her. "Wait a minute, will ye?" he said almost fiercely, and at the sound of his voice Mollie rose to her feet and her face blanched.

"Lord God!" she said almost in anguish, and then she dropped quickly to her seat again.

The Knight of the Cumberland had gone back to his horse as though to get something from his saddle. Like lightning he vaulted into the saddle, and as the black horse sprang toward the opening tore his mask from his face, turned in his stirrups, and brandished his spear with a yell of defiance, while a dozen voices shouted:

"The Wild Dog!" Then was there an uproar.

"Goddle mighty!" shouted the Hon. Sam. "I didn't do it, I swear I didn't know it. He's tricked me—he's tricked me! Don't shoot—you might hit that hoss!"

There was no doubt about the Hon. Sam's innocence. Instead of turning over an outlaw to the police, he had brought him into the inner shrine of law and order and he knew what a political asset for his enemies that insult would be. And there was no doubt of the innocence of Mollie and Buck as they stood, Mollie wringing her hands and Buck with open mouth and startled face. There was no doubt about the innocence of anybody other than Dave Branham and the dare-devil Knight of the Cumberland.

Marston had clutched at the Wild Dog's bridle and missed and the outlaw struck savagely at him with his spear. Nobody dared to shoot because of the scattering crowd, but every knight and every mounted policeman took out after the outlaw and the beating of hoofs pounded over the little mound and toward Poplar Hill. Marston ran to his horse at the upper end, threw his saddle on, and hesitated—there were enough after the Wild Dog and his horse was blown. He listened to the yells and sounds of the chase encircling Poplar Hill. The outlaw was making for Lee. All at once the yells and hoof-beats seemed to sound nearer and Marston listened, astonished. The Wild Dog had wheeled and was coming back; he was going to make for the Gap, where sure safety lay. Marston buckled his girth and as he sprang on his horse, unconsciously taking his spear with him, the Wild Dog dashed from the trees at the far end of the field. As Marston started the Wild Dog saw him, pulled something that flashed from under his coat of mail, thrust it back again, and brandishing his spear, he came, full speed and yelling, up the middle of the field. It was a strange thing to happen in these modern days, but Marston was an officer of the law and was between the Wild Dog and the ford and liberty through the Gap, into the hills. The Wild Dog was an outlaw. It was Marston's duty to take him.

The law does not prescribe with what weapon the lawless shall be subdued, and Marston's spear was the only weapon he had. Moreover, the Wild Dog's yell was a challenge that set his blood afire and the girl both loved was looking on. The crowd gathered the meaning of the joust—the knights were crashing toward each other with spears at rest. There were a few surprised oaths from men, a few low cries from women, and then dead silence in which the sound of hoofs on the hard turf was like thunder. The Blight's face was white and the little sister was gripping my arm with both hands. A third horseman shot into view out of the woods at right angles, to stop them, and it seemed that the three horses must crash together in a heap. With a moan the Blight buried her face on my shoulder. She shivered when the muffled thud of body against body and the splintering of wood rent the air; a chorus of shrieks arose about her, and when she lifted her frightened face Marston, the Discarded, was limp on the ground, his horse was staggering to his feet, and the Wild Dog was galloping past her, his helmet gleaming, his eyes ablaze, his teeth set, the handle of his broken spear clinched in his right hand, and blood streaming down the shoulder of the black horse. She heard the shots that were sent after him, she heard him plunge into the river, and then she saw and heard no more.

VIII

THE KNIGHT PASSES

A telegram summoned the Blight home next day. Marston was in bed with a ragged wound in the shoulder, and I took her to tell him good-by. I left the room for a few minutes, and when I came back their hands were unclasping, and for a Discarded Knight the engineer surely wore a happy though pallid face.

That afternoon the train on which we left the Gap was brought to a sudden halt in Wildcat Valley by a piece of red flannel tied to the end of a stick that was planted midway the track. Across the track, farther on, lay a heavy piece of timber, and it was plain that somebody meant that, just at that place, the train must stop. The Blight and I were seated on the rear platform and the Blight was taking a last look at her beloved hills. When the train started again, there was a cracking of twigs overhead and a shower of rhododendron leaves and flowers dropped from the air at the feet of the Blight. And when we pulled away from the high-walled cut we saw, motionless on a little mound, a black horse, and on him, motionless, the Knight of the Cumberland, the helmet on his head (that the Blight might know who he was, no doubt), and both hands clasping the broken handle of his spear, which rested across the pommel of his saddle. Impulsively the Blight waved her hand to him and I could not help waving my hat; but he sat like a statue and, like a statue, sat on, simply looking after us as we were hurried along, until horse, broken shaft, and shoulders sank out of sight. And thus passed the Knight of the Cumberland with the last gleam that struck his helmet, spear-like, from the slanting sun.

EDITH WHARTON

Madame De Treymes

Edith Wharton (1862–1937)

After a brief, unmerited eclipse, the reputation of this able social critic and mistress of the art of fiction is waxing once again. Better still, her work is receiving critical attention on its own merits and not as the work of a disciple of Henry James who had stumbled, somehow, into popularity. Mrs. Wharton's discipleship to James has been indeed overstressed. The author of The House of Mirth, Ethan Frome, The Custom of the Country, *and* The Age of Innocence *can stand on her own feet, and the public in its preference for her work has shown itself wiser than the critics. No careful reader will fail to recognize that while she rarely spread the analytical process over her pages, it had been performed in her mind and controls the movement of the story and the actions of the characters. She had a French devotion to clarity of expression and formal discipline, no matter how complicated the situations and psychologies with which she had to deal—an approach to fiction best expressed in her own words: "My last page is always latent in my first."*

Her work is often dismissed as limited in its range. "She was the gifted expositor of a small group in 19th Century New York society," says one critic; whereas in fact her best work is timeless, and her beautifully executed "period" backgrounds are incidental to the tragic human problems which are at the core of her books. Two of her finest achievements, Ethan Frome *(1911) and* Summer *(1917), have nothing to do with New York at all, or with society in the narrow sense. Mrs. Wharton, herself, was never happy with this tendency to type her work, and pointed out in a letter on the composition of* Ethan Frome *that her experience of life and range of interests inclined her as much to New England for the materials of her writing, as to New York.*

Madame de Treymes *is a short work but it deals brilliantly with a favorite situation of the author's—the heartbreak inevitable whenever an honest individual is pitted against the rigid conventions and collective strength of an alien group. It is essentially the same theme so beautifully handled in the later and better-known* The Age of Innocence, *and it exhibits another characteristic of Mrs. Wharton's which is rare in American fiction—an unsentimental and true spirit of compassion.*

MADAME DE TREYMES

I

JOHN DURHAM, while he waited for Madame de Malrive to draw on her gloves, stood in the hotel doorway looking out across the Rue de Rivoli at the afternoon brightness of the Tuileries gardens.

His European visits were infrequent enough to have kept unimpaired the freshness of his eye, and he was always struck anew by the vast and consummately ordered spectacle of Paris: by its look of having been boldly and deliberately planned as a background for the enjoyment of life, instead of being forced into grudging concessions to the festive instincts, or barricading itself against them in unenlightened ugliness, like his own lamentable New York.

But today, if the scene had never presented itself more alluringly, in that moist spring bloom between showers, when the horse-chestnuts dome themselves in unreal green against a gauzy sky, and the very dust of the pavement seems the fragrance of lilac made visible—today for the first time the sense of a personal stake in it all, of having to reckon individually with its effects and influences, kept Durham from an unrestrained yielding to the spell. Paris might still be—to the unimplicated it doubtless still was—the most beautiful city in the world; but whether it were the most lovable or the most detestable depended for him, in the last analysis, on the buttoning of the white glove over which Fanny de Malrive still lingered.

The mere fact of her having forgotten to draw on her gloves as they were descending in the hotel lift from his mother's drawing-room was, in this connection, charged with significance to Durham. She was the kind of woman who always presents herself to the mind's eye as completely equipped, as made up of exquisitely cared for and finely-related details; and that the heat of her parting with his family should have left her unconscious that she was emerging gloveless into Paris, seemed, on the whole, to speak hopefully for Durham's future opinion of the city.

Even now, he could detect a certain confusion, a desire to draw breath and catch up with life, in the way she dawdled over the last buttons in the dimness of the porte-cochère, while her footman, outside, hung on her retarded signal.

When at length they emerged, it was to learn from that functionary that Madame la Marquise's carriage had been obliged to yield its place at the door, but was at the moment in the act of regaining it. Madame de Malrive cut the explanation short. "I shall walk home. The carriage this evening at eight."

As the footman turned away, she raised her eyes for the first time to Durham's.

"Will you walk with me? Let us cross the Tuileries. I should like to sit a moment on the terrace."

She spoke quite easily and naturally, as if it were the most commonplace thing in the world for them to be straying afoot together over Paris; but even his vague knowledge of the world she lived in—a knowledge mainly acquired through the perusal of yellow-backed fiction—gave a thrilling significance to her naturalness. Durham, indeed, was beginning to find that one of the charms of a sophisticated society is that it lends point and perspective to the slightest contact between the sexes. If, in the old unrestricted New York days, Fanny Frisbee, from a brown stone door-step, had proposed that they should take a walk in the Park, the idea would have presented itself to her companion as agreeable but unimportant; whereas Fanny de Malrive's suggestion that they should stroll across the Tuileries was obviously fraught with unspecified possibilities.

He was so throbbing with the sense of these possibilities that he walked beside her without speaking down the length of the wide alley which follows the line of the Rue de Rivoli, suffering her even, when they reached its farthest end, to direct him in silence up the steps to the terrace of the Feuillants. For, after all, the possibilities were double-faced, and her bold departure from custom might simply mean that what she had to say was so dreadful that it needed all the tenderest mitigation of circumstance.

There was apparently nothing embarrassing to her in his silence: it was a part of her long European discipline that she had learned to manage pauses with ease. In her Frisbee days she might have packed this one with a random fluency; now she was content to let it widen slowly before them like the spacious prospect opening at their feet. The complicated beauty of this prospect, as they moved toward it between the symmetrically clipped limes of the lateral terrace, touched him anew through her nearness, as with the hint of some vast impersonal power, controlling and regulating her life in ways he could not guess, putting between himself and her the whole width of the civilization into which her marriage had absorbed her. And there was such fear in the thought—he read such derision of what he had to offer in the splendour of the great avenues tapering upward to the sunset glories of the Arch—that all he had meant to say when he finally spoke compressed itself at last into an abrupt unmitigated: "Well?"

She answered at once—as though she had only awaited the call of the national interrogation—"I don't know when I have been so happy."

"So happy?" The suddenness of his joy flushed up through his fair skin.

"As I was just now—taking tea with your mother and sisters."

Durham's "Oh!" of surprise betrayed also a note of disillusionment, which she met only by the reconciling murmur: "Shall we sit down?"

He found two of the springy yellow chairs indigenous to the spot, and placed them under the tree near which they had paused, saying reluctantly, as he did so: "Of course it was an immense pleasure to *them* to see you again."

"Oh, not in the same way. I mean—" she paused, sinking into the chair, and betraying, for the first time, a momentary inability to deal becomingly with the situation. "I mean," she resumed, smiling, "that it was not an event for them, as it was for me."

"An event?"—he caught her up again, eagerly; for what, in the language of any civilization, could that word mean but just the one thing he most wished it to?

"To be with dear, good, sweet, simple, real Americans again!" she burst out, heaping up her epithets with reckless prodigality.

Durham's smile once more faded to impersonality, as he rejoined, just a shade on the defensive: "If it's merely our Americanism you enjoyed—I've no doubt we can give you all you want in that line."

"Yes, it's just that! But if you knew what the word means to me! It means—it means—" she paused as if to assure herself that they were sufficiently isolated from the desultory groups beneath the other trees—"it means that I'm *safe* with them: as safe as in a bank!"

Durham felt a sudden warmth behind his eyes and in his throat. "I think I do know——"

"No, you don't, really; you can't know how dear and strange and familiar it all sounded: the old New York names that kept coming up in your mother's talk, and her charming quaint ideas about Europe—their all regarding it as a great big innocent pleasure ground and shop for Americans; and your mother's missing the home-made bread and preferring the American asparagus—I'm so tired of Americans who despise even their own asparagus! And then your married sister's spending her summers at—where is it?—the Kittawittany House on Lake Pohunk——"

A vision of earnest women in Shetland shawls, with spectacles and thin knobs of hair, eating blueberry-pie at unwholesome hours in a shingled dining-room on a bare New England hilltop, rose pallidly between Durham and the verdant brightness of the Champs Elysées, and he protested with a slight smile: "Oh, but my married sister is the black sheep of the family—the rest of us never sank as low as that."

"Low? I think it's beautiful—fresh and innocent and simple. I remember going to such a place once. They have early dinner—rather late—and go off in buckboards over terrible roads, and bring back goldenrod and autumn leaves, and read nature books aloud on the piazza; and there is always one shy young man in flannels—only one —who has come to see the prettiest girl (though how he can choose among so many!) and who takes her off in a buggy for hours and hours——" She paused and summed up with a long sigh: "It is fifteen years since I was in America."

"And you're still so good an American."

"Oh, a better and better one every day!"

He hesitated. "Then why did you never come back?"

Her face altered instantly, exchanging its retrospective light for the look of slightly shadowed watchfulness which he had known as most habitual to it.

"It was impossible—it has always been so. My husband would not go; and since—since our separation—there have been family reasons."

Durham sighed impatiently. "Why do you talk of reasons? The truth is, you have made your life here. You could never give all this up!" He made a discouraged gesture in the direction of the Place de la Concorde.

"Give it up! I would go tomorrow! But it could never, now, be for more than a visit. I must live in France on account of my boy."

Durham's heart gave a quick beat. At last the talk had neared the point toward which his whole mind was straining, and he began to feel a personal application in her words. But that made him all the more cautious about choosing his own.

"It is an agreement—about the boy?" he ventured.

"I gave my word. They knew that was enough," she said proudly; adding, as if to put him in full possession of her reasons: "It would have been much more difficult for me to obtain complete control of my son if it had not been understood that I was to live in France."

"That seems fair," Durham assented after a moment's reflection: it was his instinct, even in the heat of personal endeavour, to pause a moment on the question of "fairness." The personal claim reasserted itself as he added tentatively: "But when he *is* brought up—when he's grown up: then you would feel freer?"

She received this with a start, as a possibility too remote to have entered into her view of the future. "He is only eight years old!" she objected.

"Ah, of course it would be a long way off?"

"A long way off, thank heaven! French mothers part late with their sons, and in that one respect I mean to be a French mother."

"Of course—naturally—since he has only you," Durham again assented.

He was eager to show how fully he took her point of view, if only to dispose her to the reciprocal fairness of taking his when the time came to present it. And he began to think that the time had now come; that their walk would not have thus resolved itself, without excuse or pretext, into a tranquil session beneath the trees, for any purpose less important than that of giving him his opportunity.

He took it, characteristically, without seeking a transition. "When I spoke to you, the other day, about myself—about what I felt for you—I said nothing of the future, because, for the moment, my mind refused to travel beyond its immediate hope of happiness. But I felt, of course, even then, that the hope involved various difficulties—that we can't, as we might once have done, come together without any thought but for ourselves; and whatever your answer is to be, I want to tell you now that I am ready to accept my share of the difficulties." He paused, and then added explicitly: "If there's the least chance of your listening to me, I'm willing to live over here as long as you can keep your boy with you."

II

Whatever Madame de Malrive's answer was to be, there could be no doubt as to her readiness to listen. She received Durham's words without sign of resistance, and took time to ponder them gently before she answered, in a voice touched by emotion: "You are very generous—very unselfish; but when you fix a limit—no matter how remote—to my remaining here, I see how wrong it is to let myself consider for a moment such possibilities as we have been talking of."

"Wrong? Why should it be wrong?"

"Because I shall want to keep my boy always! Not, of course, in the sense of living with him, or even forming an important part of his life; I am not deluded enough to think that possible. But I do believe it possible never to pass wholly out of his life; and while there is a hope of that, how can I leave him?" She paused, and turned on him a new face, a face in which the past of which he was still so ignorant showed itself like a shadow suddenly darkening a clear pane. "How can I make you understand?" she went on urgently.

"It is not only because of my love for him—not only, I mean, because of my own happiness in being with him; that I can't, in imagination, surrender even the remotest hour of his future; it is because, the moment he passes out of my influence, he passes under that other—the influence I have been fighting against every hour since he was born!—I don't mean, you know," she added, as Durham, with bent head, continued to offer her the silent fixity of his attention, "I don't mean the special personal influence—except inasmuch as it represents something wider, more general, something that encloses and circulates through the whole world in which he belongs. That is what I meant when I said you could never understand! There is nothing in your experience—in any American experience—to correspond with that far-reaching family organization, which is itself a part of the larger system, and which encloses a young man of my son's position in a network of accepted prejudices and opinions. Everything is prepared in advance—his political and religious convictions, his judgements of people, his sense of honour, his ideas of women, his whole view of life. He is taught to see vileness and corruption in every one not of his own way of thinking, and in every idea that does not directly serve the religious and political purposes of his class. The truth isn't a fixed thing: it's not used to test actions by, it's tested by them, and made to fit in with them. And this forming of the mind begins with the child's first consciousness; it's in his nursery stories, his baby prayers, his very games with his playmates! Already he is only half mine, because the Church has the other half, and will be reaching out for my share as soon as his education begins. But that other half is still mine, and I mean to make it the strongest and most living half of the two, so that, when the inevitable conflict begins, the energy and the truth and the endurance shall be on my side and not on theirs!"

She paused, flushing with the repressed fervour of her utterance, though her voice had not been raised beyond its usual discreet modulations; and Durham felt himself tingling with the transmitted force of her resolve. Whatever shock her words brought to his personal hope, he was grateful to her for speaking them so clearly, for having so sure a grasp of her purpose.

Her decision strengthened his own, and after a pause of deliberation he said quietly: "There might be a good deal to urge on the other side—the ineffectualness of your sacrifice, the probability that when your son marries he will inevitably be absorbed back into the life of his class and his people; but I can't look at it in that way, because if I were in your place I believe I should feel just as you do about it. As long as there was a fighting chance I should want to keep hold of my half, no matter how much the struggle cost me. And one reason why I understand your feeling about your boy is that I have the same feeling about *you*: as long as there's a fighting chance of keeping my half of you—the half he is willing to spare me —I don't see how I can ever give it up." He waited again, and then brought out firmly: "If you'll marry me, I'll agree to live out here as long as you want, and we'll be two instead of one to keep hold of your half of him."

He raised his eyes as he ended, and saw that hers met them through a quick clouding of tears.

"Ah, I am glad to have had this said to me! But I could never accept such an offer."

He caught instantly at the distinction. "That doesn't mean that you could never accept *me*?"

"Under such conditions——"

"But if I am satisfied with the conditions? Don't think I am speaking rashly, under the influence of the moment. I have expected something of this sort, and I have thought out my side of the case. As far as material circumstances go, I have worked long enough and successfully enough to take my ease and take it where I choose. I mention that because the life I offer you is offered to your boy as well." He let this sink into her mind before summing up gravely: "The offer I make is made deliberately, and at least I have a right to a direct answer."

She was silent again, and then lifted a cleared gaze to his. "My direct answer then is: if I were still Fanny Frisbee I would marry you."

He bent toward her persuasively. "But you will be—when the divorce is pronounced."

"Ah, the divorce——" She flushed deeply, with an instinctive shrinking back of her whole person which made him straighten himself in his chair.

"Do you so dislike the idea?"

"The idea of divorce? No—not in my case. I should like anything that would do away with the past—obliterate it all—make everything new in my life!"

"Then what——?" he began again, waiting with the patience of a wooer on the uneasy circling of her tormented mind.

"Oh, don't ask me; I don't know; I am frightened."

Durham gave a deep sigh of discouragement. "I thought your coming here with me today—and above all your going with me just now to see my mother—was a sign that you were *not* frightened!"

"Well, I was not when I was with your mother. She made everything seem easy and natural. She took me back into that clear American air where there are no obscurities, no mysteries——"

"What obscurities, what mysteries, are you afraid of?"

She looked about her with a faint shiver. "I am afraid of everything!" she said.

"That's because you are alone; because you've no one to turn to. I'll clear the air for you fast enough if you'll let me."

He looked forth defiantly, as if flinging his challenge at the great city which had come to typify the powers contending with him for her possession.

"You say that so easily! But you don't know; none of you know."

"Know what?"

"The difficulties——"

"I told you I was ready to take my share of the difficulties—and my share naturally includes yours. You know Americans are great hands at getting over difficulties." He drew himsely up confidently. "Just leave that to me—only tell me exactly what you're afraid of."

She paused again, and then said: "The divorce, to begin with—they will never consent to it."

He noticed that she spoke as though the interests of the whole clan, rather than her husband's individual claim, were to be considered; and the use of the plural pronoun shocked his free individualism like a glimpse of some dark feudal survival.

"But you are absolutely certain of your divorce! I've consulted—of course without mentioning names——"

She interrupted him, with a melancholy smile: "Ah, so have I. The divorce would be easy enough to get, if they ever let it come into the courts."

"How on earth can they prevent that?"

"I don't know; my never knowing how they will do things is one of the secrets of their power."

"Their power? What power?" he broke in with irrepressible contempt. "Who are these bogeys whose machinations are going to arrest the course of justice in a—comparatively—civilized country? You've told me yourself that Monsieur de Malrive is the least likely to give you trouble; and the others are his uncle the abbé, his mother and sister. That kind of a syndicate doesn't scare me much. A priest and two women *contra mundum*!"

She shook her head. "Not *contra mundum*, but with it, their whole world is behind them. It's that mysterious solidarity that you can't understand. One doesn't know how far they may reach, or in how many directions. I have never known. They have always cropped up where I least expected them."

Before this persistency of negation Durham's buoyancy began to flag, but his determination grew the more fixed.

"Well, then, supposing them to possess these supernatural powers; do you think it's to people of that kind that I'll ever consent to give you up?"

She raised a half-smiling glance of protest. "Oh, they're not wantonly wicked. They'll leave me alone as long as——"

"As I do?" he interrupted. "Do you want me to leave you alone? Was that what you brought me here to tell me?"

The directness of the challenge seemed to gather up the scattered strands of her hesitation, and lifting her head she turned on him a look in which, but for its underlying shadow, he might have recovered the full free beam of Fanny Frisbee's gaze.

"I don't know why I brought you here," she said gently, "except from the wish to prolong a little the illusion of being once more an American among Americans. Just now, sitting there with your mother and Katy and Nannie, the difficulties seemed to vanish; the problems grew as trivial to me as they are to you. And I wanted them to remain so a little longer; I wanted to put off going back to them. But it was of no use—they were waiting for me here. They are over there now in that house across the river." She indicated the grey sky-line of the Faubourg, shining in the splintered radiance of the sunset beyond the long sweep of the quays. "They are a part of me—I belong to them. I must go back to them!" she sighed.

She rose slowly to her feet, as though her metaphor had expressed an actual fact and she felt herself bodily drawn from his side by the influences of which she spoke.

Durham had risen too. "Then I go back with you!" he exclaimed energetically; and as she paused, wavering a little under the shock of his resolve: "I don't mean into your house—but into your life!" he said.

She suffered him, at any rate, to accompany her to the door of the house, and allowed their debate to prolong itself through the almost monastic quiet of the quarter which led thither. On the way, he succeeded in wresting from her the confession that, if it were possible to ascertain in advance that her husband's family would not oppose her action, she might decide to apply for a divorce. Short of a positive assurance on this point, she made it clear that she would never move in the matter; there must be no scandal, no *retentissement*, nothing which her boy, necessarily brought up in the French tradition of scrupulously preserved appearances, could afterward regard as the faintest blur on his much-quartered escutcheon. But even this partial concession again raised fresh obstacles; for there seemed to be no one to whom she could entrust so delicate an investigation, and to apply directly to the Marquis de Malrive or his relatives appeared, in the light of her past experience, the last way of learning their intentions.

"But," Durham objected, beginning to suspect a morbid fixity of idea in her perpetual attitude of distrust—"but surely you have told me that your husband's sister—what is her name? Madame de

Treymes?—was the most powerful member of the group, and that she has always been on your side."

She hesitated. "Yes, Christiane has been on my side. She dislikes her brother. But it would not do to ask her."

"But could no one else ask her? Who are her friends?"

"She has a great many; and some, of course, are mine. But in a case like this they would be all hers; they wouldn't hesitate a moment between us."

"Why should it be necessary to hesitate between you? Suppose Madame de Treymes sees the reasonableness of what you ask; suppose, at any rate, she sees the hopelessness of opposing you? Why should she make a mystery of your opinion?"

"It's not that; it is that, if I went to her friends, I should never get real opinion from them. At least I should never know if it *was* her real opinion; and therefore I should be no farther advanced. Don't you see?"

Durham struggled between the sentimental impulse to soothe her, and the practical instinct that it was a moment for unmitigated frankness.

"I'm not sure that I do; but if you can't find out what Madame de Treymes thinks, I'll see what I can do myself."

"Oh—*you*!" broke from her in mingled terror and admiration; and pausing on her doorstep to lay her hand in his before she touched the bell, she added with a half-whimsical flash of regret: "Why didn't this happen to Fanny Frisbee?"

III

Why had it not happened to Fanny Frisbee?

Durham put the question to himself as he walked back along the quays, in a state of inner commotion which left him, for once, insensible to the ordered beauty of his surroundings. Propinquity had not been lacking: he had known Miss Frisbee since his college days. In unsophisticated circles, one family is apt to quote another; and the Durham ladies had always quoted the Frisbees. The Frisbees were bold, experienced, enterprising: they had what the novelists of the day called "dash." The beautiful Fanny was especially dashing; she had the showiest national attributes, tempered only by a native grace of softness, as the beam of her eyes was subdued by the length of their lashes. And yet young Durham, though not unsusceptible to such charms, had remained content to enjoy them from a safe distance of good-fellowship. If he had been asked why, he could not have told; but the Durham of forty understood. It was because there were, with minor modifications, many other Fanny Frisbees; whereas never before, within his ken, had there been a Fanny de Malrive.

He had felt it in a flash, when, the autumn before, he had run across her one evening in the dining-room of the Beaurivage at Ouchy; when, after a furtive exchange of glances, they had simultaneously arrived at recognition, followed by an eager pressure of hands, and a long evening of reminiscence on the starlit terrace. She was the same, but so mysteriously changed! And it was the mystery, the sense of unprobed depths of initiation, which drew him to her as her freshness had never drawn him. He had not hitherto attempted to define the nature of the change: it remained for his sister Nannie to do that when, on his return to the Rue de Rivoli, where the family were still sitting in conclave upon their recent visitor, Miss Durham summed up their groping comments in the phrase: "I never saw anything so French!"

Durham, understanding what his sister's use of the epithet implied, recognized it instantly as the explanation of his own feelings. Yes, it was the finish, the modelling, which Madame de Malrive's experience had given her that set her apart from the fresh uncomplicated personalities of which she had once been simply the most charming type. The influences that had lowered her voice, regulated her gestures, toned her down to harmony with the warm dim background of a long social past—these influences had lent to her natural fineness of perception a command of expression adapted to complex conditions. She had moved in surroundings through which one could hardly bounce and bang on the genial American plan without knocking the angles off a number of sacred institutions; and her acquired dexterity of movement seemed to Durham a crowning grace. It was a shock, now that he knew at what cost the dexterity had been acquired, to acknowledge this even to himself; he hated to think that she could owe anything to such conditions as she had been placed in. And it gave him a sense of the tremendous strength of the organization into which she had been absorbed, that in spite of her horror, her moral revolt, she had not reacted against its external forms. She might abhor her husband, her marriage, and the world to which it had introduced her, but she had become a product of that world in its outward expression, and no better proof of the fact was needed than her exotic enjoyment of Americanism.

The sense of the distance to which her American past had been removed was never more present to him than when, a day or two later, he went with his mother and sisters to return her visit. The region beyond the river existed, for the Durham ladies, only as the unmapped environment of the Bon Marché; and Nannie Durham's exclamation on the pokiness of the streets and the dulness of the houses showed Durham, with a start, how far he had already travelled from the family point of view.

"Well, if this is all she got by marrying a Marquis!" the young lady summed up as they paused before the small sober hotel in its high-walled court; and Katy, following her mother through the stone-vaulted and stone-floored vestibule, murmured: "It must be simply freezing in winter."

In the softly-faded drawing-room, with its old pastels in old frames, its windows looking on the damp green twilight of a garden sunk deep in blackened walls, the American ladies might have been even more conscious of the insufficiency of their friend's compensations, had not the warmth of her welcome precluded all other reflections. It was not till she had gathered them about her in the corner beside the tea-table, that Durham identified the slender dark lady loitering negligently in the background, and introduced in a comprehensive murmur to the American group, as the redoubtable sister-in-law to whom he had declared himself ready to throw down his challenge.

There was nothing very redoubtable about Madame de Treymes, except perhaps the kindly yet critical observation which she bestowed on her sister-in-law's visitors: the unblinking attention of a civilized spectator observing an encampment of aborigines. He had heard of her as a beauty, and was surprised to find her, as Nannie afterward put it, a mere stick to hang clothes on (but they *did* hang!), with a small brown glancing face, like that of a charming little inquisitive animal. Yet before she had addressed ten words to him—nibbling at the hard English consonants like nuts—he owned the justice of the epithet. She was a beauty, if beauty, instead of being restricted to the cast of the face, is a pervasive attribute informing the hands, the voice, the gestures, the very fall of a flounce and tilt of a feather. In this impalpable *aura* of grace Madame de Treymes' dark meagre presence unmistakably moved, like a thin flame in a wide quiver of light. And as he realized that she looked much handsomer than she was, so, while they talked, he felt that she understood a great deal more than she betrayed. It was not through the groping speech which formed their apparent medium of communication that she imbibed her information: she found it in the air, she extracted it from Durham's look and manner, she caught it in the turn of her sister-in-law's defenceless eyes—for in her presence Madame de Malrive became Fanny Frisbee again!—she put it together, in short, out of just such unconsidered indescribable trifles as differentiated the quiet felicity of her dress from Nannie and Katy's "handsome" haphazard clothes.

Her actual converse with Durham moved, meanwhile, strictly in the conventional ruts: had he been long in Paris, which of the new plays did he like best, was it true that American *jeunes filles* were sometimes taken to the Boulevard theatres? And she threw an interrogative glance at the young ladies beside the tea-table. To Durham's reply that it depended how much French they knew, she shrugged and smiled, replying that his compatriots all spoke French like Parisians, enquiring, after a moment's thought, if they learned it, *là bas, des nègres,* and laughing heartily when Durham's astonishment revealed her blunder.

When at length she had taken leave—enveloping the Durham ladies in a last puzzled penetrating look—Madame de Malrive turned to Mrs. Durham with a faintly embarrassed smile.

"My sister-in-law was much interested; I believe you are the first Americans she has ever known."

"Good gracious!" ejaculated Nannie, as though such social darkness required immediate missionary action on some one's part.

"Well, she knows *us*," said Durham, catching, in Madame de Malrive's rapid glance, a startled assent to his point.

"After all," reflected the accurate Katy, as though seeking an excuse for Madame de Treymes' unenlightenment, "*we* don't know many French people, either."

To which Nannie promptly if obscurely retorted: "Ah! but we couldn't and *she* could!"

IV

Madame de Treymes' friendly observation of her sister-in-law's visitors resulted in no expression on her part of a desire to renew her study of them. To all appearances, she passed out of their lives when Madame de Malrive's door closed on her; and Durham felt that the arduous task of making her acquaintance was still to be begun.

He felt also, more than ever, the necessity of attempting it; and in his determination to lose no time, and his perplexity how to set most speedily about the business, he bethought himself of applying to his cousin Mrs. Boykin.

Mrs. Elmer Boykin was a small plump woman, to whose vague prettiness the lines of middle age had given no meaning: as though whatever had happened to her had merely added to the sum total of her inexperience. After a Parisian residence of twenty-five years, spent in a state of feverish servitude to the great artists of the Rue de la Paix, her dress and hair still retained a certain rigidity in keeping with the directness of her gaze and the unmodulated candour of her voice. Her very drawing-room had the hard bright atmosphere of her native skies, and one felt that she was still true at heart to the national ideals in electric lighting and plumbing.

She and her husband had left America owing to the impossibility of living there with the finish and decorum which the Boykin standard demanded; but in the isolation of their exile they had created about them a kind of phantom America, where the national prejudices continued to flourish unchecked by the national progressiveness: a little world sparsely peopled by compatriots in the same attitude of chronic opposition toward a society chronically unaware of them. In this uncontaminated air Mr. and Mrs. Boykin had preserved the purity of simpler conditions, and Elmer Boykin, returning rakishly from a Sunday's racing at Chantilly, betrayed, under his "knowing" coat and the racing-glasses slung ostentatiously across his shoulder, the unmistakable cut of the American business man coming "up town" after a long day in the office.

It was a part of the Boykins' uncomfortable but determined attitude—and perhaps a last expression of their latent patriotism—to live in active disapproval of the world about them, fixing in memory with little stabs of reprobation innumerable instances of what the abominable foreigner was doing; so that they reminded Durham of persons peacefully following the course of a horrible war by pricking red pins in a map. To Mrs. Durham, with her gentle tourist's view of the European continent, as a vast Museum in which the human multitudes simply furnished the element of costume, the Boykins seemed abysmally instructed, and darkly expert in forbidden things; and her son, without sharing her simple faith in their omniscience, credited them with an ample supply of the kind of information of which he was in search.

Mrs. Boykin, from the corner of an intensely modern Gobelin sofa, studied her cousin as he balanced himself insecurely on one of the small gilt chairs which always look surprised at being sat in.

"Fanny de Malrive? Oh, of course: I remember you were all very intimate with the Frisbees when they lived in West Thirty-third Street. But she has dropped all her American friends since her marriage. The excuse was that de Malrive didn't like them; but as she's been separated for five or six years, I can't see—. You say she's been very nice to your mother and the girls? Well, I dare say she is beginning to feel the need of friends she can really trust; for as for her French relations——! That Malrive set is the worst in the Faubourg. Of course you know what *he* is; even the family, for decency's sake, had to back her up, and urge her to get a separation. And Christiane de Treymes——"

Durham seized his opportunity. "Is she so very reprehensible too?"

Mrs. Boykin pursed up her small colourless mouth. "I can't speak from personal experience. I know Madame de Treymes slightly—I have met her at Fanny's—but she never remembers the fact except when she wants me to go to one of her *ventes de charité*. They all remember us then; and some American women are silly enough to ruin themselves at the smart bazaars, and fancy they will get invitations in return. They say Mrs. Addison G. Pack followed Madame d'Alglade around for a whole winter, and spent a hundred thousand francs at her stalls; and at the end of the season Madame d'Alglade asked her to tea, and when she got there she found *that* was for a charity too, and she had to pay a hundred francs to get in."

Mrs. Boykin paused with a smile of compassion. "That is not *my* way," she continued. "Personally I have no desire to thrust myself into French society—I can't see how any American woman can do so without loss of self-respect. But any one can tell you about Madame de Treymes."

"I wish you would, then," Durham suggested.

"Well, I think Elmer had better," said his wife mysteriously, as Mr. Boykin, at this point, advanced across the wide expanse of Aubusson on which his wife and Durham were islanded in a state of propinquity without privacy.

"What's that, Bessy? Hah, Durham, how are you? Didn't see you at Auteuil this afternoon. You don't race? Busy sight-seeing, I suppose? What was that my wife was telling you? Oh, about Madame de Treymes."

He stroked his pepper-and-salt moustache with a gesture intended rather to indicate than to conceal the smile of experience beneath it. "Well, Madame de Treymes has not been like a happy country—she's had a history: several of 'em. Some one said she constituted the *feuilleton* of the Faubourg daily news. *La suite au prochain numéro*—you see the point? Not that I speak from personal knowledge. Bessy and I have never cared to force our way"——He paused, reflecting that his wife had probably anticipated him in the expression of this familiar sentiment, and added with a significant nod: "Of course you know the Prince d'Armillac by sight? No? I'm surprised at that.

Well, he's one of the choicest ornaments of the Jockey Club: very fascinating to the ladies, I believe, but the deuce and all at baccara. Ruined his mother and a couple of maiden aunts already—and now Madame de Treymes has put the family pearls up the spout, and is wearing imitation for love of him."

"I had that straight from my maid's cousin, who is employed by Madame d'Armillac's jeweller," said Mrs. Boykin with conscious pride.

"Oh, it's straight enough—more than *she* is!" retorted her husband, who was slightly jealous of having his facts reinforced by any information not of his own gleaning.

"Be careful of what you say, Elmer," Mrs. Boykin interposed with archness. "I suspect John of being seriously smitten by the lady."

Durham let this pass unchallenged, submitting with a good grace to his host's low whistle of amusement, and the sardonic enquiry: "Ever do anything with the foils? D'Armillac is what they call over here a *fine lame*."

"Oh, I don't mean to resort to bloodshed unless it's absolutely necessary; but I mean to make the lady's acquaintance," said Durham, falling into his key.

Mrs. Boykin's lips tightened to the vanishing point. "I am afraid you must apply for an introduction to more fashionable people than *we* are. Elmer and I so thoroughly disapprove of French society that we have always declined to take any part in it. But why should not Fanny de Malrive arrange a meeting for you?"

Durham hesitated. "I don't think she is on very intimate terms with her husband's family——"

"You mean that she's not allowed to introduce *her* friends to them," Mrs. Boykin interjected sarcastically; while her husband added, with an air of portentous initiation: "Ah, my dear fellow, the way they treat the Americans over here—that's another chapter, you know."

"How some people can *stand* it!" Mrs. Boykin chimed in; and as the footman, entering at that moment, tendered her a large coronetted envelope, she held it up as if in illustration of the indignities to which her countrymen were subjected.

"Look at that, my dear John," she exclaimed—"another card to one of their everlasting bazaars! Why, it's at Madame d'Armillac's, the Prince's mother. Madame de Treymes must have sent it, of course. The brazen way in which they combine religion and immorality! Fifty francs admission—*rien que cela*!—to see some of the most disreputable people in Europe. And if you're an American, you're expected to leave at least a thousand behind you. Their own people naturally get off cheaper." She tossed over the card to her cousin. "There's your opportunity to see Madame de Treymes."

"Make it two thousand, and she'll ask you to tea," Mr. Boykin scathingly added.

V

In the monumental drawing-room of the Hôtel de Malrive—it had been a surprise to the American to read the name of the house emblazoned on black marble over its still more monumental gateway—Durham found himself surrounded by a buzz of feminine teasipping oddly out of keeping with the wigged and cuirassed portraits frowning high on the walls, the majestic attitude of the furniture, the rigidity of great gilt consoles drawn up like lords-in-waiting against the tarnished panels.

It was the old Marquise de Malrive's "day," and Madame de Treymes, who lived with her mother, had admitted Durham to the heart of the enemy's country by inviting him, after his prodigal disbursements at the charity bazaar, to come in to tea on a Thursday. Whether, in thus fulfilling Mr. Boykin's prediction, she had been aware of Durham's purpose, and had her own reasons for falling in with it; or whether she simply wished to reward his lavishness at the fair, and permit herself another glimpse of an American so picturesquely embodying the type familiar to French fiction—on these points Durham was still in doubt.

Meanwhile, Madame de Treymes being engaged with a venerable Duchess in a black shawl—all the older ladies present had the sloping shoulders of a generation of shawl-wearers—her American visitor, left in the isolation of his unimportance, was using it as a shelter for a rapid survey of the scene.

He had begun his study of Fanny de Malrive's situation without any real understanding of her fears. He knew the repugnance to divorce existing in the French Catholic world, but since the French laws sanctioned it, and in a case so flagrant as his injured friend's, would inevitably accord it with the least possible delay and exposure, he could not take seriously any risk of opposition on the part of the husband's family. Madame de Malrive had not become a Catholic, and since her religious scruples could not be played on, the only weapon remaining to the enemy—the threat of fighting the divorce—was one they could not wield without self-injury. Certainly, if the chief object were to avoid scandal, common sense must counsel Monsieur de Malrive and his friends not to give the courts an opportunity of exploring his past; and since the echo of such explorations, and their ultimate transmission to her son, were what Madame de Malrive most dreaded, the opposing parties seemed to have a common ground for agreement, and Durham could not but regard his friend's fears as the result of over-taxed sensibilities. All this had seemed evident enough to him as he entered the austere portals of the Hôtel de Malrive and passed, between the faded liveries of old family servants, to the presence of the dreaded dowager above. But he had not been ten minutes in that presence before he had arrived at a faint intuition of what poor Fanny meant. It was not in the exquisite mildness of the old Marquise, a little grey-haired bunch of a woman in dowdy mourning, or in the small neat presence of the priestly uncle, the Abbé who had so obviously just stepped down from one of the picture-frames overhead: it was not in the aspect of these chief protagonists, so outwardly unformidable, that Durham read an occult danger to his friend. It was rather in their setting, their surroundings, the little company of elderly and dowdy persons—so uniformly clad in weeping blacks and purples that they might have been assembled for some mortuary anniversary—it was in the remoteness and the solidarity of this little group that Durham had his first glimpse of the social force of which Fanny de Malrive had spoken. All these amiably chatting visitors, who mostly bore the stamp of personal insignificance on their mildly sloping or aristocratically beaked faces, hung together in a visible closeness of tradition, dress, attitude and manner, as different as possible from the loose aggregation of a roomful of his own countrymen. Durham felt, as he observed them, that he had never before known what "society" meant; nor understood that, in an organized and inherited system, it exists full-fledged where two or three of its members are assembled.

Upon this state of bewilderment, this sense of having entered a room in which the lights had suddenly been turned out, even Madame de Treymes' intensely modern presence threw no illumination. He was conscious, as she smilingly rejoined him, not of her points of difference from the others, but of the myriad invisible threads by which she held to them; he even recognized the audacious slant of her little brown profile in the portrait of a powdered ancestress beneath which she had paused a moment in advancing. She was simply one particular facet of the solid, glittering, impenetrable body, which he had thought to turn in his hands and look through like a crystal; and when she said, in her clear staccato English, "Perhaps you will like to see the other rooms," he felt like crying out in his blindness: "If I could only be sure of seeing *anything* here!" Was she conscious of his blindness, and was he as remote and unintelligible to her as she was to him? This possibility, as he followed her through the nobly-unfolding rooms of the great house, gave him his first hope of recoverable advantage. For, after all, he had some vague traditional lights on her world and its antecedents; whereas to her he was a wholly new phenomenon, as unexplained as a fragment of meteorite dropped at her feet on the smooth gravel of the garden-path they were pacing.

She had led him down into the garden, in response to his admiring exclamation, and perhaps also because she was sure that, in the chill spring afternoon, they would have its embowered privacies to themselves. The garden was small, but intensely rich and deep—one of those wells of verdure and fragrance which everywhere sweeten the air of Paris by wafts blown above old walls on quiet streets; and as Madame de Treymes paused against the ivy bank masking its farther boundary, Durham felt more than ever removed from the normal bearings of life.

His sense of strangeness was increased by the surprise of his companion's next speech.

"You wish to marry my sister-in-law?" she asked abruptly; and

Durham's start of wonder was followed by an immediate feeling of relief. He had expected the preliminaries of their interview to be as complicated as the bargaining in an Eastern bazaar, and had feared to lose himself at the first turn in a labyrinth of "foreign" intrigue.

"Yes, I do," he said with equal directness; and they smiled together at the sharp report of question and answer.

The smile put Durham more completely at his ease, and after waiting for her to speak, he added with deliberation: "So far, however, the wishing is entirely on my side." His scrupulous conscience felt itself justified in this reserve by the conditional nature of Madame de Malrive's consent.

"I understand; but you have been given reason to hope——"

"Every man in my position gives himself his own reasons for hoping," he interposed with a smile.

"I understand that too," Madame de Treymes assented. "But still—you spent a great deal of money the other day at our bazaar."

"Yes: I wanted to have a talk with you, and it was the readiest—if not the most distinguished—means of attracting your attention."

"I understand," she once more reiterated, with a gleam of amusement.

"It is because I suspect you of understanding everything that I have been so anxious for this opportunity."

She bowed her acknowledgement, and said: "Shall we sit a moment?" adding, as he drew their chairs under a tree: "You permit me, then, to say that I believe I understand also a little of our good Fanny's mind?"

"On that point I have no authority to speak. I am here only to listen."

"Listen then: you have persuaded her that there would be no harm in divorcing my brother—since I believe your religion does not forbid divorce?"

"Madame de Malrive's religion sanctions divorce in such a case as——"

"As my brother has furnished? Yes, I have heard that your race is stricter in judging such *écarts*. But you must not think," she added, "that I defend my brother. Fanny must have told you that we have always given her our sympathy."

"She has let me infer it from her way of speaking of you."

Madame de Treymes arched her dramatic eyebrows. "How cautious you are! I am so straightforward that I shall have no chance with you.

"You will be quite safe, unless you are so straightforward that you put me on my guard."

She met this with a low note of amusement.

"At this rate we shall never get any farther; and in two minutes I must go back to my mother's visitors. Why should we go on fencing? The situation is really quite simple. Tell me just what you wish to know. I have always been Fanny's friend, and that disposes me to be yours."

Durham, during this appeal, had had time to steady his thoughts; and the result of his deliberation was that he said, with a return to his former directness: "Well, then, what I wish to know is, what position your family would take if Madame de Malrive should sue for a divorce." He added, without giving her time to reply: "I naturally wish to be clear on this point before urging my cause with your sister-in-law."

Madame de Treymes seemed in no haste to answer; but after a pause of reflection she said, not unkindly: "My poor Fanny might have asked me that herself."

"I beg you to believe that I am not acting as her spokesman," Durham hastily interposed. "I merely wish to clear up the situation before speaking to her in my own behalf."

"You are the most delicate of suitors! But I understand your feeling. Fanny also is extremely delicate: it was a great surprise to us at first. Still, in this case—" Madame de Treymes paused—"since she has no religious scruples, and she had no difficulty in obtaining a separation, why should she fear any in demanding a divorce?"

"I don't know that she does: but the mere fact of possible opposition might be enough to alarm the delicacy you have observed in her."

"Ah—yes: on her boy's account."

"Partly, doubtless, on her boy's account."

"So that, if my brother objects to a divorce, all he has to do is to announce his objection? But, my dear sir, you are giving your case into my hands!" She flashed an amused smile on him.

"Since you say you are Madame de Malrive's friend, could there be a better place for it?"

As she turned her eyes on him he seemed to see, under the flitting lightness of her glance, the sudden concentrated expression of the ancestral will. "I am Fanny's friend, certainly. But with us family considerations are paramount. And our religion forbids divorce."

"So that, inevitably, your brother will oppose it?"

She rose from her seat, and stood fretting with her slender boot-tip the minute red pebbles of the path.

"I must really go in: my mother will never forgive me for deserting her."

"But surely you owe me an answer?" Durham protested, rising also.

"In return for your purchases at my stall?"

"No: in return for the trust I have placed in you."

She mused on this, moving slowly a step or two toward the house.

"Certainly I wish to see you again; you interest me," she said smiling. "But it is so difficult to arrange. If I were to ask you to come here again, my mother and uncle would be surprised. And at Fanny's——"

"Oh, not there!" he exclaimed.

"Where then? Is there any other house where we are likely to meet?"

Durham hesitated; but he was goaded by the flight of the precious minutes. "Not unless you'll come and dine with me," he said boldly.

"Dine with you? *Au cabaret?* Ah, that would be diverting—but impossible!"

"Well, dine with my cousin, then—I have a cousin, an American lady, who lives here," said Durham, with suddenly-soaring audacity.

She paused with puzzled brows. "An American lady whom I know?"

"By name, at any rate. You send her cards for all your charity bazaars."

She received the thrust with a laugh. "We do exploit your compatriots."

"Oh, I don't think she has ever gone to the bazaars."

"But she might if I dined with her?"

"Still less, I imagine."

She reflected on this, and then said with acuteness: "I like that, and I accept—but what is the lady's name?"

VI

On the way home, in the first drop of his exaltation, Durham had said to himself: "But why on earth should Bessy invite her?"

He had, naturally, no very cogent reasons to give Mrs. Boykin in support of his astonishing request, and could only, marvelling at his own growth in duplicity, suffer her to infer that he was really, shamelessly "smitten" with the lady he thus proposed to thrust upon her hospitality. But, to his surprise, Mrs. Boykin hardly gave herself time to pause upon his reasons. They were swallowed up in the fact that Madame de Treymes wished to dine with her, as the lesser luminaries vanish in the blaze of the sun.

"I am not surprised," she declared, with a faint smile intended to check her husband's unruly wonder. "I wonder *you* are, Elmer. Didn't you tell me that Armillac went out of his way to speak to you the other day at the races? And at Madame d'Alglade's sale—yes, I went there after all, just for a minute, because I found Katy and Nannie were so anxious to be taken—well, that day I noticed that Madame de Treymes was quite *empressée* when we went up to her stall. Oh, I didn't buy anything: I merely waited while the girls chose some lampshades. They thought it would be interesting to take home something painted by a real Marquise, and of course I didn't tell them that those women *never* make the things they sell at their stalls. But I repeat I'm not surprised: I suspected that Madame de Treymes had heard of our little dinners. You know they're really horribly bored in that poky old Faubourg. My poor John, I see now why she's been making up to you! But on one point I am quite determined, Elmer; whatever you say, I shall *not* invite the Prince d'Armillac."

Elmer, as far as Durham could observe, did not say much; but, like his wife, he continued in a state of pleasantly agitated activity till the momentous evening of the dinner.

The festivity in question was restricted in numbers, either owing to the difficulty of securing suitable guests, or from a desire not to have it appear that Madame de Treymes' hosts attached any special importance to her presence; but the smallness of the company was counterbalanced by the multiplicity of the courses.

The national determination not to be "downed" by the despised foreigner, to show a wealth of material resource obscurely felt to compensate for the possible lack of other distinctions—this resolve had taken, in Mrs. Boykin's case, the shape—or rather the multiple shapes—of a series of culinary feats, of gastronomic combinations, which would have commanded her deep respect had she seen them on any other table, and which she naturally relied on to produce the same effect on her guest. Whether or not the desired result was achieved, Madame de Treymes' manner did not specifically declare; but it showed a general complaisance, a charming willingness to be amused, which made Mr. Boykin, for months afterward, allude to her among his compatriots as "an old friend of my wife's—takes pot-luck with us, you know. Of course there's not a word of truth in any of those ridiculous stories."

It was only when, to Durham's intense surprise, Mr. Boykin hazarded to his neighbour the regret that they had not been so lucky as to "secure the Prince"—it was then only that the lady showed, not indeed anything so simple and unprepared as embarrassment, but a faint play of wonder, an under-flicker of amusement, as though recognizing that, by some odd law of social compensation, the crudity of the talk might account for the complexity of the dishes.

But Mr. Boykin was tremulously alive to hints, and the conversation at once slid to safer topics, easy generalizations which left Madame de Treymes ample time to explore the table, to use her narrowed gaze like a knife slitting open the unsuspicious personalities about her. Nannie and Katy Durham, who, after much discussion (to which their hostess candidly admitted them), had been included in the feast, were the special objects of Madame de Treymes' observation. During dinner she ignored in their favour the other carefully-selected guests—the fashionable art-critic, the old Legitimist general, the beauty from the English Embassy, the whole impressive marshalling of Mrs. Boykin's social resources—and when the men returned to the drawing-room, Durham found her still fanning in his sisters the flame of an easily-kindled enthusiasm. Since she could hardly have been held by the intrinsic interest of their converse, the sight gave him another swift intuition of the working of those hidden forces with which Fanny de Malrive felt herself encompassed. But when Madame de Treymes, at his approach, let him see that it was for him she had been reserving herself, he felt that so graceful an impulse needed no special explanation. She had the art of making it seem quite natural that they should move away together to the remotest of Mrs. Boykin's far-drawn salons, and that there, in a glaring privacy of brocade and ormolu, she should turn to him with a smile which avowed her intentional quest of seclusion.

"Confess that I have done a great deal for you!" she exclaimed, making room for him on a sofa judiciously screened from the observation of the other rooms.

"In coming to dine with my cousin?" he enquired, answering her smile.

"Let us say, in giving you this half hour."

"For that I am duly grateful—and shall be still more so when I know what it contains for me."

"Ah, I am not sure. You will not like what I am going to say."

"Shall I not?" he rejoined, changing colour.

She raised her eyes from the thoughtful contemplation of her painted fan. "You appear to have no idea of the difficulties."

"Should I have asked your help if I had not had an idea of them?"

"But you are still confident that with my help you can surmount them?"

"I can't believe you have come here to take that confidence from me?"

She leaned back, smiling at him through her lashes. "And all this I am to do for your *beaux yeux?*"

"No—for your own: that you may see with them what happiness you are conferring."

"You are extremely clever, and I like you." She paused, and then brought out with lingering emphasis: "But my family will not hear of a divorce."

She threw into her voice such an accent of finality that Durham, for the moment, felt himself brought up against an insurmountable barrier, but, almost at once, his fear was mitigated by the conviction that she would not have put herself out so much to say so little.

"When you speak of your family, do you include yourself?" he suggested.

She threw a surprised glance at him. "I thought you understood that I am simply their mouthpiece."

At this he rose quietly to his feet with a gesture of acceptance. "I have only to thank you, then, for not keeping me longer in suspense."

His air of wishing to put an immediate end to the conversation seemed to surprise her. "Sit down a moment longer," she commanded him kindly; and as he leaned against the back of his chair, without appearing to hear her request, she added in a low voice: "I am very sorry for you and Fanny—but you are not the only persons to be pitied."

"The only persons?"

"In our unhappy family." She touched her breast with a sudden tragic gesture. "I, for instance, whose help you ask—if you could guess how I need help myself!"

She had dropped her light manner as she might have tossed aside her fan, and he was startled at the intimacy of misery to which her look and movement abruptly admitted him. Perhaps no Anglo-Saxon fully understands the fluency in self-revelation which centuries of the confessional have given to the Latin races, and to Durham, at any rate, Madame de Treymes' sudden avowal gave the shock of a physical abandonment.

"I am so sorry," he stammered—"is there any way in which I can be of use to you?"

She sat before him with her hands clasped, her eyes fixed on his in a terrible intensity of appeal. "If you would—if you would! Oh, there is nothing I would not do for you. I have still a great deal of influence with my mother, and what my mother commands we all do. I could help you—I am sure I could help you; but not if my own situation were known. And if nothing can be done it must be known in a few days."

Durham had reseated himself at her side. "Tell me what I can do," he said in a low tone, forgetting his own preoccupations in his genuine concern for her distress.

She looked up at him through tears. "How dare I? Your race is so cautious, so self-controlled—you have so little indulgence for the extravagances of the heart. And my folly has been incredible—and unrewarded." She paused, and as Durham waited in a silence which she guessed to be compassionate, she brought out below her breath: "I have lent money—my husband's, my brother's—money that was not mine, and now I have nothing to repay it with."

Durham gazed at her in genuine astonishment. The turn the conversation had taken led quite beyond his uncomplicated experiences with the other sex. She saw his surprise, and extended her hands in deprecation and entreaty. "Alas, what must you think of me? How can I explain my humiliating myself before a stranger? Only by telling you the whole truth—the fact that I am not alone in this disaster, that I could not confess my situation to my family without ruining myself, and involving in my ruin some one who, however undeservedly, has been as dear to me as—as you are to——"

Durham pushed his chair back with a sharp exclamation.

"Ah, even that does not move you!" she said.

The cry restored him to his senses by the long shaft of light it sent down the dark windings of the situation. He seemed suddenly to know Madame de Treymes as if he had been brought up with her in the inscrutable shades of the Hôtel de Malrive.

She, on her side, appeared to have a startled but uncomprehending sense of the fact that his silence was no longer completely sympathetic, that her touch called forth no answering vibration; and she made a desperate clutch of the one chord she could be certain of sounding.

"You have asked a great deal of me—much more than you can guess. Do you mean to give me nothing—not even your sympathy—in return? It is because you have heard horrors of me? When are they not said of a woman who is married unhappily? Perhaps not in your fortunate country, where she may seek liberation without dishonour. But here—! You who have seen the consequences of our disastrous marriages—you who may yet be the victim of our cruel and abominable system; have you not pity for one who has suffered in the same way, and without the possibility of release?" She paused, laying her hand on his arm with a smile of deprecating irony. "It is not because you are not rich. At such times the crudest way is the shortest, and I don't pretend to deny that I know I am asking you a trifle. You Americans, when you want a thing, always pay ten times what it is worth, and I am giving you the wonderful chance to get what you most want at a bargain."

Durham sat silent, her little gloved hand burning his coat-sleeve as if it had been a hot iron. His brain was tingling with the shock of her confession. She wanted money, a great deal of money: that was clear, but it was not the point. She was ready to sell her influence, and he fancied she could be counted on to fulfil her side of the bargain. The fact that he could so trust her seemed only to make her more terrible to him—more supernaturally dauntless and baleful. For what was it that she exacted of him? She had said she must have money to pay her debts; but he knew that was only a pretext which she scarcely expected him to believe. She wanted the money for some one else; that was what her allusion to a fellow-victim meant. She wanted it to pay the Prince's gambling debts—it was at that price that Durham was to buy the right to marry Fanny de Malrive.

Once the situation had worked itself out in his mind, he found himself unexpectedly relieved of the necessity of weighing the arguments for and against it. All the traditional forces of his blood were in revolt, and he could only surrender himself to their pressure, without thought of compromise or parley.

He stood up in silence, and the abruptness of his movement caused Madame de Treymes' hand to slip from his arm.

"You refuse?" she exclaimed; and he answered with a bow: "Only because of the return you propose to make me."

She stood staring at him, in a perplexity so genuine and profound that he could almost have smiled at it through his disgust.

"Ah, you are all incredible," she murmured at last, stooping to repossess herself of her fan; and as she moved past him to rejoin the group in the farther room, she added in an incisive undertone: "You are quite at liberty to repeat our conversation to your friend!"

VII

Durham did not take advantage of the permission thus strangely flung at him. Of his talk with her sister-in-law he gave to Madame de Malrive only that part which concerned her.

Presenting himself for this purpose, the day after Mrs. Boykin's dinner, he found his friend alone with her son; and the sight of the child had the effect of dispelling whatever illusive hopes had attended him to the threshold. Even after the governess's descent upon the scene had left Madame de Malrive and her visitor alone, the little boy's presence seemed to hover admonishingly between them, reducing to a bare statement of fact Durham's confession of the total failure of his errand.

Madame de Malrive heard the confession calmly; she had been too prepared for it not to have prepared a countenance to receive it. Her first comment was: "I have never known them to declare themselves so plainly——" and Durham's baffled hopes fastened themselves eagerly on the words. Had she not always warned him that there was nothing so misleading as their plainness? And might it not be that, in spite of his advisedness, he had suffered too easy a rebuff? But second thoughts reminded him that the refusal had not been as unconditional as his necessary reservations made it seem in the repetition; and that, furthermore, it was his own act, and not that of his opponents, which had determined it. The impossibility of revealing this to Madame de Malrive only made the difficulty shut in more darkly around him, and in the completeness of his discouragement he scarcely needed her reminder of his promise to regard the subject as closed when once the other side had defined its position.

He was secretly confirmed in this acceptance of his fate by the knowledge that it was really he who had defined the position. Even now that he was alone with Madame de Malrive, and subtly aware of the struggle under her composure, he felt no temptation to abate his stand by a jot. He had not yet formulated a reason for his resistance: he simply went on feeling, more and more strongly with every precious sign of her participation in his unhappiness, that he could neither owe his escape from it to such a transaction, nor suffer her, innocently, to owe hers.

The only mitigating effect of his determination was in an increase of helpless tenderness toward her; so that, when she exclaimed, in answer to his announcement that he meant to leave Paris the next night: "Oh, give me a day or two longer!" he at once resigned himself to saying: "If I can be of the least use, I'll give you a hundred."

She answered sadly that all he could do would be to let her feel that he was there—just for a day or two, till she had readjusted herself to the idea of going on in the old way; and on this note of renunciation they parted.

But Durham, however pledged to the passive part, could not long sustain it without rebellion. To "hang around" the shut door of his hopes seemed, after two long days, more than even his passion required of him; and on the third he despatched a note of good-bye to his friend. He was going off for a few weeks, he explained—his mother and sisters wished to be taken to the Italian lakes: but he would return to Paris, and say his real farewell to her, before sailing for America in July.

He had not intended his note to act as an ultimatum: he had no wish to surprise Madame de Malrive into unconsidered surrender. When, almost immediately, his own messenger returned with a reply from her, he even felt a pang of disappointment, a momentary fear lest she should have stooped a little from the high place where his passion had preferred to leave her; but her first words turned his fear into rejoicing.

"Let me see you before you go: something extraordinary has happened," she wrote.

What had happened, as he heard from her a few hours later—finding her in a tremor of frightened gladness, with her door boldly closed to all the world but himself—was nothing less extraordinary than a visit from Madame de Treymes, who had come, officially delegated by the family, to announce that Monsieur de Malrive had decided not to oppose his wife's suit for divorce. Durham, at the news, was almost afraid to show himself too amazed; but his small signs of alarm and wonder were swallowed up in the flush of Madame de Malrive's incredulous joy.

"It's the long habit, you know, of not believing them—of looking for the truth always in what they *don't* say. It took me hours and hours to convince myself that there's no trick under it, that there can't be any," she explained.

"Then you *are* convinced now?" escaped from Durham; but the shadow of his question lingered no more than the flit of a wing across her face.

"I am convinced because the facts are there to reassure me. Christiane tells me that Monsieur de Malrive has consulted his lawyers, and that they have advised him to free me. Maître Enguerrand has been instructed to see my lawyer whenever I wish it. They quite understand that I never should have taken the step in face of any opposition on their part—I am so thankful to you for making that perfectly clear to them!—and I suppose this is the return their pride makes to mine. For they *can* be proud collectively——" She broke off, and added, with happy hands outstretched: "And I owe it all to you—Christiane said it was your talk with her that had convinced them."

Durham, at this statement, had to repress a fresh sound of amazement; but with her hands in his, and, a moment after, her whole self drawn to him in the first yielding of her lips, doubt perforce gave way to the lover's happy conviction that such love was after all too strong for the powers of darkness.

It was only when they sat again in the blissful after-calm of their understanding, that he felt the pricking of an unappeased distrust.

"Did Madame de Treymes give you any reason for this change

of front?" he risked asking, when he found the distrust was not otherwise to be quelled.

"Oh, yes: just what I've said. It was really her admiration of *you*—of your attitude—your delicacy. She said that at first she hadn't believed in it: they're always looking for a hidden motive. And when she found that yours was staring at her in the actual words you said: that you really respected my scruples, and would never, never try to coerce or entrap me—something in her—poor Christiane!—answered to it, she told me, and she wanted to prove to us that she was capable of understanding us too. If you knew her history you'd find it wonderful and pathetic that she can!"

Durham thought he knew enough of it to infer that Madame de Treymes had not been the object of many conscientious scruples on the part of the opposite sex; but this increased rather his sense of the strangeness than of the pathos of her action. Yet Madame de Malrive, whom he had once inwardly taxed with the morbid raising of obstacles, seemed to see none now; and he could only infer that her sister-in-law's actual words had carried more conviction than reached him in the repetition of them. The mere fact that he had so much to gain by leaving his friend's faith undisturbed was no doubt stirring his own suspicions to unnatural activity; and this sense gradually reasoned him back into acceptance of her view, as the most normal as well as the pleasantest he could take.

VIII

The uneasiness thus temporarily repressed slipped into the final disguise of hoping he should not again meet Madame de Treymes; and in this wish he was seconded by the decision, in which Madame de Malrive concurred, that it would be well for him to leave Paris while the preliminary negotiations were going on. He committed her interests to the best professional care, and his mother, resigning her dream of the lakes, remained to fortify Madame de Malrive by her mild unimaginative view of the transaction, as an uncomfortable but commonplace necessity, like house-cleaning or dentistry. Mrs. Durham would doubtless have preferred that her only son, even with his hair turning grey, should have chosen a Fanny Frisbee rather than a Fanny de Malrive; but it was a part of her acceptance of life on a general basis of innocence and kindliness, that she entered generously into his dream of rescue and renewal, and devoted herself without after-thought to keeping up Fanny's courage with so little to spare for herself.

The process, the lawyers declared, would not be a long one, since Monsieur de Malrive's acquiescence reduced it to a formality; and when, at the end of June, Durham returned from Italy with Katy and Nannie, there seemed no reason why he should not stop in Paris long enough to learn what progress had been made.

But before he could learn this he was to hear, on entering Madame de Malrive's presence, news more immediate if less personal. He found her, in spite of her gladness in his return, so evidently preoccupied and distressed that his first thought was one of fear for their own future. But she read and dispelled this by saying, before he could put his question: "Poor Christiane is here. She is very unhappy. You have seen in the papers——?"

"I have seen no papers since we left Turin. What has happened?"

"The Prince d'Armillac has come to grief. There has been some terrible scandal about money and he has been obliged to leave France to escape arrest."

"And Madame de Treymes has left her husband?"

"Ah, no, poor creature: they don't leave their husbands—they can't. But de Treymes has gone down to their place in Brittany, and as my mother-in-law is with another daughter in Auvergne, Christiane came here for a few days. With me, you see, she need not pretend—she can cry her eyes out."

"And that is what she is doing?"

It was so unlike his conception of the way in which, under the most adverse circumstances, Madame de Treymes would be likely to occupy her time, that Durham was conscious of a note of scepticism in his query.

"Poor thing—if you saw her you would feel nothing but pity. She is suffering so horribly that I reproach myself for being happy under the same roof."

Durham met this with a tender pressure of her hand; then he said, after a pause of reflection: "I should like to see her."

He hardly knew what prompted him to utter the wish, unless it were a sudden stir of compunction at the memory of his own dealings with Madame de Treymes. Had he not sacrificed the poor creature to a purely fantastic conception of conduct? She had said that she knew she was asking a trifle of him; and the fact that, materially, it would have been a trifle, had seemed at the moment only an added reason for steeling himself in his moral resistance to it. But now that he had gained his point—and through her own generosity, as it still appeared—the largeness of her attitude made his own seem cramped and petty. Since conduct, in the last resort, must be judged by its enlarging or diminishing effect on character, might it not be that the zealous weighing of the moral anise and cummin was less important than the unconsidered lavishing of the precious ointment? At any rate, he could enjoy no peace of mind under the burden of Madame de Treymes' magnanimity, and when he had assured himself that his own affairs were progressing favourably, he once more, at the risk of surprising his betrothed, brought up the possibility of seeing her relative.

Madame de Malrive evinced no surprise. "It is natural, knowing what she has done for us, that you should want to show her your sympathy. The difficulty is that it is just the one thing you *can't* show her. You can thank her, of course, for ourselves, but even that at the moment——"

"Would seem brutal? Yes, I recognize that I should have to choose my words," he admitted, guiltily conscious that his capability of dealing with Madame de Treymes extended far beyond her sister-in-law's conjecture.

Madame de Malrive still hesitated. "I can tell her; and when you come back tomorrow——"

It had been decided that, in the interests of discretion—the interests, in other words, of the poor little future Marquis de Malrive—Durham was to remain but two days in Paris, withdrawing then with his family till the conclusion of the divorce proceedings permitted him to return in the acknowledged character of Madame de Malrive's future husband. Even on this occasion, he had not come to her alone; Nannie Durham, in the adjoining room, was chatting conspicuously with the little Marquis, whom she could with difficulty be restrained from teaching to call her "Aunt Nannie." Durham thought her voice had risen unduly once or twice during his visit, and when, on taking leave, he went to summon her from the inner room, he found the higher note of ecstasy had been evoked by the appearance of Madame de Treymes, and that the little boy, himself absorbed in a new toy of Durham's bringing, was being bent over by an actual as well as a potential aunt.

Madame de Treymes raised herself with a slight start at Durham's approach: she had her hat on, and had evidently paused a moment on her way out to speak with Nannie, without expecting to be surprised by her sister-in-law's other visitor. But her surprises never wore the awkward form of embarrassment, and she smiled beautifully on Durham as he took her extended hand.

The smile was made the more appealing by the way in which it lit up the ruin of her small dark face, which looked seared and hollowed as by a flame that might have spread over it from her fevered eyes. Durham, accustomed to the pale inward grief of the inexpressive races, was positively startled by the way in which she seemed to have been openly stretched on the pyre; he almost felt an indelicacy in the ravages so tragically confessed.

The sight caused an involuntary readjustment of his whole view of the situation, and made him, as far as his own share in it went, more than ever inclined to extremities of self-disgust. With him such sensations required, for his own relief, some immediate penitential escape, and as Madame de Treymes turned toward the door he addressed a glance of entreaty to his betrothed.

Madame de Malrive, whose intelligence could be counted on at such moments, responded by laying a detaining hand on her sister-in-law's arm.

"Dear Christiane, may I leave Mr. Durham in your charge for two minutes? I have promised Nannie that she shall see the boy put to bed."

Madame de Treymes made no audible response to this request, but when the door had closed on the other ladies she said, looking quietly at Durham: "I don't think that, in this house, your time will hang so heavy that you need my help in supporting it."

Durham met her glance frankly. "It was not for that reason that Madame de Malrive asked you to remain with me."

"Why, then? Surely not in the interest of preserving appearances, since she is safely upstairs with your sister?"

"No; but simply because I asked her to. I told her I wanted to speak to you."

"How you arrange things! And what reason can you have for wanting to speak to me?"

He paused a moment. "Can't you imagine? The desire to thank you for what you have done."

She stirred restlessly, turning to adjust her hat before the glass above the mantelpiece.

"Oh, as for what I have done——!"

"Don't speak as if you regretted it," he interposed.

She turned back to him with a flash of laughter lighting up the haggardness of her face. "Regret working for the happiness of two such excellent persons? Can't you fancy what a charming change it is for me to do something so innocent and beneficent?"

He moved across the room and went up to her, drawing down the hand which still flitted experimentally about her hat.

"Don't talk in that way, however much one of the persons of whom you speak may have deserved it."

"One of the persons? Do you mean me?"

He released her hand, but continued to face her resolutely. "I mean myself, as you know. You have been generous—extraordinarily generous."

"Ah, but I was doing good in a good cause. You have made me see that there is a distinction."

He flushed to the forehead. "I am here to let you say whatever you choose to me."

"Whatever I choose?" She made a slight gesture of deprecation. "Has it never occurred to you that I may conceivably choose to say nothing?"

Durham paused, conscious of the increasing difficulty of the advance. She met him, parried him, at every turn: he had to take his baffled purpose back to another point of attack.

"Quite conceivably," he said: "so much so that I am aware I must make the most of this opportunity, because I am not likely to get another."

"But what remains of your opportunity, if it isn't one to me?"

"It still remains, for me, an occasion to abase myself——" He broke off, conscious of a grossness of allusion that seemed, on a closer approach, the real obstacle to full expression. But the moments were flying, and for his self-esteem's sake he must find some way of making her share the burden of his repentance.

"There is only one thinkable pretext for detaining you: it is that I may still show my sense of what you have done for me."

Madame de Treymes, who had moved toward the door, paused at this and faced him, resting her thin brown hands on a slender sofa-back.

"How do you propose to show that sense?" she enquired.

Durham coloured still more deeply: he saw that she was determined to save her pride by making what he had to say of the utmost difficulty. Well! he would let his expiation take that form, then—it was as if her slender hands held out to him the fool's cap he was condemned to press down on his own ears.

"By offering in return—in any form, and to the utmost—any service you are forgiving enough to ask of me."

She received this with a low sound of laughter that scarcely rose to her lips. "You are princely. But, my dear sir, does it not occur to you that I may, meanwhile, have taken my own way of repaying myself for any service I have been fortunate enough to render you?"

Durham, at the question, or still more, perhaps, at the tone in which it was put, felt, through his compunction, a vague faint chill of apprehension. Was she threatening him or only mocking him? Or was this barbed swiftness of retort only the wounded creature's way of defending the privacy of her own pain? He looked at her again, and read his answer in the last conjecture.

"I don't know how you can have repaid yourself for anything so disinterested—but I am sure, at least, that you have given me no chance of recognizing, ever so slightly, what you have done."

She shook her head, with the flicker of a smile on her melancholy lips. "Don't be too sure! You have given me a chance and I have taken it—taken it to the full. So fully," she continued, keeping her eyes fixed on his, "that if I were to accept any farther service you might choose to offer, I should simply be robbing you—robbing you shamelessly." She paused, and added in an undefinable voice: "I was entitled, wasn't I, to take something in return for the service I had the happiness of doing you?"

Durham could not tell whether the irony of her tone was self-directed or addressed to himself—perhaps it comprehended them both. At any rate, he chose to overlook his own share in it in replying earnestly: "So much so, that I can't see how you can have left me nothing to add to what you say you have taken."

"Ah, but you don't know what that is!" She continued to smile, elusively, ambiguously. "And what's more, you wouldn't believe me if I told you."

"How do you know?" he rejoined.

"You didn't believe me once before; and this is so much more incredible."

He took the taunt full in the face. "I shall go away unhappy unless you tell me—but then perhaps I have deserved to," he confessed.

She shook her head again, advancing toward the door with the evident intention of bringing their conference to a close; but on the threshold she paused to launch her reply.

"I can't send you away unhappy, since it is in the contemplation of your happiness that I have found my reward."

IX

The next day Durham left with his family for England, with the intention of not returning till after the divorce should have been pronounced in September.

To say that he left with a quiet heart would be to overstate the case: the fact that he could not communicate to Madame de Malrive the substance of his talk with her sister-in-law still hung upon him uneasily. But of definite apprehensions the lapse of time gradually freed him, and Madame de Malrive's letters, addressed more frequently to his mother and sisters than to himself, reflected, in their reassuring serenity, the undisturbed course of events.

There was to Durham something peculiarly touching—as of an involuntary confession of almost unbearable loneliness—in the way she had regained, with her re-entry into the clear air of American associations, her own fresh trustfulness of view. Once she had accustomed herself to the surprise of finding her divorce unopposed, she had been, as it now seemed to Durham, in almost too great haste to renounce the habit of weighing motives and calculating chances. It was as though her coming liberation had already freed her from the garb of a mental slavery, as though she could not too soon or too conspicuously cast off the ugly badge of suspicion. The fact that Durham's cleverness had achieved so easy a victory over forces apparently impregnable, merely raised her estimate of that cleverness to the point of letting her feel that she could rest in it without farther demur. He had even noticed in her, during his few hours in Paris, a tendency to reproach herself for her lack of charity, and a desire, almost as fervent as his own, to expiate it by exaggerated recognition of the disinterestedness of her opponents—if opponents they could still be called. This sudden change in her attitude was peculiarly moving to Durham. He knew she would hazard herself lightly enough wherever her heart called her; but that, with the precious freight of her child's future weighing her down, she should commit herself so blindly to his hand stirred in him the depths of tenderness. Indeed, had the actual course of events been less auspiciously regular, Madame de Malrive's confidence would have gone far toward unsettling his own; but with the process of law going on unimpeded, and the other side making no sign of open or covert resistance, the fresh air of good faith gradually swept through the inmost recesses of his distrust.

It was expected that the decision in the suit would be reached by mid-September; and it was arranged that Durham and his family should remain in England till a decent interval after the conclusion of the proceedings. Early in the month, however, it became necessary for Durham to go to France to confer with a business associate who was in Paris for a few days, and on the point of sailing for Cherbourg. The most zealous observance of appearances could hardly forbid Durham's return for such a purpose; but it had been agreed between himself and Madame de Malrive—who had once more been left alone by Madame de Treymes' return to her family—that, so close to the fruition of their wishes, they would propitiate fate by a scrupulous adherence to usage, and communicate only, during his hasty visit, by a daily interchange of notes.

The ingenuity of Madame de Malrive's tenderness found, however, the day after his arrival, a means of tempering their privation. "Christiane," she wrote, "is passing through Paris on her way from Trouville, and has promised to see you for me if you will call on her today. She thinks there is no reason why you should not go to the Hôtel de Malrive, as you will find her there alone, the family having gone to Auvergne. She is really our friend and understands us."

In obedience to this request—though perhaps inwardly regretting that it should have been made—Durham that afternoon presented himself at the proud old house beyond the Seine. More than ever, in the semi-abandonment of the *morte saison*, with reduced service, and shutters closed to the silence of the high-walled court, did it strike the American as the incorruptible custodian of old prejudices and strange social survivals. The thought of what he must represent to the almost human consciousness which such old houses seem to possess, made him feel like a barbarian desecrating the silence of a temple of the earlier faith. Not that there was anything venerable in the attestations of the Hôtel de Malrive, except in so far as, to a sensitive imagination, every concrete embodiment of a past order of things testifies to real convictions once suffered for. Durham, at any rate, always alive in practical issues to the view of the other side, had enough sympathy left over to spend it sometimes, whimsically, on such perceptions of difference. Today, especially, the assurance of success—the sense of entering like a victorious beleaguerer receiving the keys of the stronghold—disposed him to a sentimental perception of what the other side might have to say for itself, in the language of old portraits, old relics, old usages dumbly outraged by his mere presence.

On the appearance of Madame de Treymes, however, such considerations gave way to the immediate act of wondering how she meant to carry off her share of the adventure. Durham had not forgotten the note on which their last conversation had closed: the lapse of time serving only to give more precision and perspective to the impression he had then received.

Madame de Treymes' first words implied a recognition of what was in his thoughts.

"It is extraordinary, my receiving you here; but *que voulez vous?* There was no other place, and I would do more than this for our dear Fanny."

Durham bowed. "It seems to me that you are also doing a great deal for me."

"Perhaps you will see later that I have my reasons," she returned, smiling. "But before speaking for myself I must speak for Fanny."

She signed to him to take a chair near the sofa-corner in which she had installed herself, and he listened in silence while she delivered Madame de Malrive's message, and her own report of the progress of affairs.

"You have put me still more deeply in your debt," he said as she concluded; "I wish you would make the expression of this feeling a large part of the message I send back to Madame de Malrive."

She brushed this aside with one of her light gestures of deprecation. "Oh, I told you I had my reasons. And since you are here—and the mere sight of you assures me that you are as well as Fanny charged me to find you—with all these preliminaries disposed of, I am going to relieve you, in a small measure, of the weight of your obligation."

Durham raised his head quickly. "By letting me do something in return?"

She made an assenting motion. "By asking you to answer a question."

"That seems very little to do."

"Don't be so sure! It is never very little to your race." She leaned back, studying him through half-dropped lids.

"Well, try me," he protested.

She did not immediately respond; and when she spoke, her first words were explanatory rather than interrogative.

"I want to begin by saying that I believe I once did you an

injustice, to the extent of misunderstanding your motive for a certain action."

Durham's uneasy flush confessed his recognition of her meaning. "Ah, if we must go back to *that*——"

"You withdraw your assent to my request?"

"By no means; but nothing consolatory you can find to say on that point can really make any difference."

"Will not the difference in my view of you perhaps make a difference in your own?"

She looked at him earnestly, without a trace of irony in her eyes or on her lips. "It is really I who have an *amende* to make, as I now understand the situation. I once turned to you for help in a painful extremity, and I have only now learned to understand your reasons for refusing to help me."

"Oh, my reasons——" groaned Durham.

"I have learned to understand them," she persisted, "by being so much, lately, with Fanny."

"But I never told her!" he broke in.

"Exactly. That was what told *me*. I understood you through her, and through your dealings with her. There she was—the woman you adored and longed to save; and you would not lift a finger to make her yours by means which would have seemed—I see it now—a desecration of your feeling for each other." She paused, as if to find the exact words for meanings she had never before had occasion to formulate. "It came to me first—a light on your attitude—when I found you had never breathed to her a word of our talk together. She had confidently commissioned you to find a way for her, as the mediaeval lady sent a prayer to her knight to deliver her from captivity, and you came back, confessing you had failed, but never justifying yourself by so much as a hint of the reason why. And when I had lived a little in Fanny's intimacy—at a moment when circumstances helped to bring us extraordinarily close—I understood why you had done this; why you had let her take what view she pleased of your failure, your passive acceptance of defeat, rather than let her suspect the alternative offered you. You couldn't, even with my permission, betray to any one a hint of my miserable secret, and you couldn't, for your life's happiness, pay the particular price that I asked." She leaned toward him in the intense, almost childlike, effort at full expression. "Oh, we are of different races, with a different point of honour; but I understand, I see, that you are good people—just simply, courageously *good!*"

She paused, and then said slowly: "Have I understood you? Have I put my hand on your motive?"

Durham sat speechless, subdued by the rush of emotion which her words set free.

"That, you understand, is my question," she concluded with a faint smile; and he answered hesitatingly: "What can it matter, when the upshot is something I infinitely regret?"

"Having refused me? Don't!" She spoke with deep seriousness, bending her eyes full on his: "Ah, I have suffered—suffered! But I have learned also—my life has been enlarged. You see how I have understood you both. And that is something I should have been incapable of a few months ago."

Durham returned her look. "I can't think that you can ever have been incapable of any generous interpretation."

She uttered a slight exclamation, which resolved itself into a laugh of self-directed irony.

"If you knew into what language I have always translated life! But that," she broke off, "is not what you are here to learn."

"I think," he returned gravely, "that I am here to learn the measure of Christian charity."

She threw him a new, odd look. "Ah, no—but to show it!" she exclaimed.

"To show it? And to whom?"

She paused for a moment, and then rejoined, instead of answering: "Do you remember that day I talked with you at Fanny's? The day after you came back from Italy?"

He made a motion of assent, and she went on: "You asked me then what return I expected for my service to you, as you called it; and I answered, the contemplation of your happiness. Well, do you know what that meant in my old language—the language I was still speaking then? It meant that I knew there was horrible misery in store for you, and that I was waiting to feast my eyes on it: that's all!"

She had flung out the words with one of her quick bursts of self-abandonment, like a fevered sufferer stripping the bandage from a wound. Durham received them with a face blanching to the pallor of her own.

"What misery do you mean?" he exclaimed.

She leaned forward, laying her hand on his with just such a gesture as she had used to enforce her appeal in Mrs. Boykin's boudoir. The remembrance made him shrink slightly from her touch, and she drew back with a smile.

"Have you never asked yourself," she enquired, "why our family consented so readily to a divorce?"

"Yes, often," he replied, all his unformed fears gathering in a dark throng about him. "But Fanny was so reassured, so convinced that we owed it to your good offices——"

She broke into a laugh. "My good offices! Will you never, you Americans, learn that we do not act individually in such cases? That we are all obedient to a common principle of authority?"

"Then it was not you——"

She made an impatient shrugging motion. "Oh, you are too confiding—it is the other side of your beautiful good faith!"

"The side you have taken advantage of, it appears?"

"I—we—all of us. I especially!" she confessed.

X

There was another pause, during which Durham tried to steady himself against the shock of the impending revelation. It was an odd circumstance of the case, that though Madame de Treymes' avowal of duplicity was fresh in his ears, he did not for a moment believe that she would deceive him again. Whatever passed between them now would go to the root of the matter.

The first thing that passed was the long look they exchanged: searching on his part, tender, sad, undefinable on hers. As the result of it he said: "Why, then, did you consent to the divorce?"

"To get the boy back," she answered instantly; and while he sat stunned by the unexpectedness of the retort, she went on: "Is it possible you never suspected? It has been our whole thought from the first. Everything was planned with that object."

He drew a sharp breath of alarm. "But the divorce—how could that give him back to you?"

"It was the only thing that could. We trembled lest the idea should occur to you. But we were reasonably safe, for there has only been one other case of the same kind before the courts." She leaned back, the sight of his perplexity checking her quick rush of words. "You didn't know," she began again, "that in that case, on the remarriage of the mother, the courts instantly restored the child to the father, though he had—well, given as much cause for divorce as my unfortunate brother?"

Durham gave an ironic laugh. "Your French justice takes a grammar and dictionary to understand."

She smiled. "*We* understand it—and it isn't necessary that you should."

"So it would appear!" he exclaimed bitterly.

"Don't judge us too harshly—or not, at least, till you have taken the trouble to learn our point of view. You consider the individual—we think only of the family."

"Why don't you take care to preserve it, then?"

"Ah, that's what we do; in spite of every aberration of the individual. And so, when we saw it was impossible that my brother and his wife should live together, we simply transferred our allegiance to the child—we constituted *him* the family."

"A precious kindness you did him! If the result is to give him back to his father."

"That, I admit, is to be deplored; but his father is only a fraction of the whole. What we really do is to give him back to his race, his religion, his true place in the order of things."

"His mother never tried to deprive him of any of those inestimable advantages!"

Madame de Treymes unclasped her hands with a slight gesture of deprecation.

"Not consciously, perhaps; but silences and reserves can teach so much. His mother has another point of view——"

"Thank heaven!" Durham interjected.

"Thank heaven for *her*—yes—perhaps; but it would not have done for the boy."

Durham squared his shoulders with the sudden resolve of a man breaking through a throng of ugly phantoms.

"You haven't yet convinced me that it won't have to do for him. At the time of Madame de Malrive's separation, the court made no difficulty about giving her the custody of her son; and you must pardon me for reminding you that the father's unfitness was the reason alleged."

Madame de Treymes shrugged her shoulders. "And my poor brother, you would add, has not changed; but the circumstances have, and that proves precisely what I have been trying to show you: that, in such cases, the general course of events is considered, rather than the action of any one person."

"Then why is Madame de Malrive's action to be considered?"

"Because it breaks up the unity of the family."

"*Unity——!*" broke from Durham; and Madame de Treymes gently suffered his smile.

"Of the family tradition, I mean: it introduces new elements. You are a new element."

"Thank heaven!" said Durham again.

She looked at him singularly. "Yes—you may thank heaven. Why isn't it enough to satisfy Fanny?"

"Why isn't what enough?"

"Your being, as I say, a new element; taking her so completely into a better air. Why shouldn't she be content to begin a new life with you, without wanting to keep the boy too?"

Durham stared at her dumbly. "I don't know what you mean," he said at length.

"I mean that in her place——" she broke off, dropping her eyes. "She may have another son—the son of the man she adores."

Durham rose from his seat and took a quick turn through the room. She sat motionless, following his steps through her lowered lashes, which she raised again slowly as he stood before her.

"Your idea, then, is that I should tell her nothing?" he said.

"Tell her *now*? But, my poor friend, you would be ruined!"

"Exactly." He paused. "Then why have you told *me*?"

Under her dark skin he saw the faint colour stealing. "We see things so differently—but can't you conceive that, after all that has passed, I felt it a kind of loyalty not to leave you in ignorance?"

"And you feel no such loyalty to her?"

"Ah, I leave her to you," she murmured, looking down again.

Durham continued to stand before her, grappling slowly with his perplexity, which loomed larger and darker as it closed in on him. "You don't leave her to me; you take her from me at a stroke! I suppose," he added painfully, "I ought to thank you for doing it before it's too late."

She stared. "I take her from you? I simply prevent your going to her unprepared. Knowing Fanny as I do, it seemed to me necessary that you should find a way in advance—a way of tiding over the first moment. That, of course, is what we had planned that you shouldn't have. We meant to let you marry, and then—. Oh, there is no question about the result: we are certain of our case—our measures have been taken *de loin*." She broke off, as if oppressed by his stricken silence. "You will think me stupid, but my warning you of this is the only return I know how to make for your generosity. I could not bear to have you say afterward that I had deceived you twice."

"Twice?" he looked at her perplexedly, and her colour rose.

"I deceived you once—that night at your cousin's, when I tried to get you to bribe me. Even then we meant to consent to the divorce—it was decided the first day that I saw you." He was silent, and she added, with one of her mocking gestures: "You see from what a *milieu* you are taking her!"

Durham groaned. "She will never give up her son!"

"How can she help it? After you are married there will be no choice."

"No—but there is one now."

"*Now?*" She sprang to her feet, clasping her hands in dismay. "Haven't I made it clear to you? Haven't I shown you your course?" She paused, and then brought out with emphasis: "I love Fanny, and I am ready to trust her happiness to you."

"I shall have nothing to do with her happiness," he repeated doggedly.

She stood close to him, with a look intently fixed on his face. "Are you afraid?" she asked with one of her mocking flashes.

"Afraid?"

"Of not being able to make it up to her——?"

Their eyes met, and he returned her look steadily.

"No; if I had the chance, I believe I could."

"I know you could!" she exclaimed.

"That's the worst of it," he said with a cheerless laugh.

"The worst——?"

"Don't you see that I can't deceive her? Can't trick her into marrying me now?"

Madame de Treymes continued to hold his eyes for a puzzled moment after he had spoken; then she broke out despairingly: "Is happiness never more to you, then, than this abstract standard of truth?"

Durham reflected. "I don't know—it's an instinct. There doesn't seem to be any choice."

"Then I am a miserable wretch for not holding my tongue!"

He shook his head sadly. "That would not have helped me; and it would have been a thousand times worse for her."

"Nothing can be as bad for her as losing you! Aren't you moved by seeing her need?"

"Horribly—are not *you*?" he said, lifting his eyes to hers suddenly.

She started under his look. "You mean, why don't I help you? Why don't I use my influence? Ah, if you knew how I have tried!"

"And you are sure that nothing can be done?"

"Nothing, nothing: what arguments can I use? We abhor divorce—we go against our religion in consenting to it—and nothing short of recovering the boy could possibly justify us."

Durham turned slowly away. "Then there is nothing to be done," he said, speaking more to himself than to her.

He felt her light touch on his arm. "Wait! There is one thing more——" She stood close to him, with entreaty written on her small passionate face. "There is one thing more," she repeated. "And that is, to believe that I am deceiving you again."

He stopped short with a bewildered stare. "That you are deceiving me—about the boy?"

"Yes—yes; why shouldn't I? You're so credulous—the temptation is irresistible."

"Ah, it would be too easy to find out—"

"Don't try, then! Go on as if nothing had happened. I have been lying to you," she declared with vehemence.

"Do you give me your word of honour?" he rejoined.

"A liar's? I haven't any! Take the logic of the facts instead. What reason have you to believe any good of me? And what reason have I to do any to you? Why on earth should I betray my family for your benefit? Ah, don't let yourself be deceived to the end!" She sparkled up at him, her eyes suffused with mockery; but on the lashes he saw a tear.

He shook his head sadly. "I should first have to find a reason for your deceiving me."

"Why, I gave it to you long ago. I wanted to punish you—and now I've punished you enough."

"Yes, you've punished me enough," he conceded.

The tear gathered and fell down her thin cheek. "It's you who are punishing me now. I tell you I'm false to the core. Look back and see what I've done to you!"

He stood silent, with his eyes fixed on the ground. Then he took one of her hands and raised it to his lips.

"You poor, good woman!" he said gravely.

Her hand trembled as she drew it away. "You're going to her—straight from here?"

"Yes—straight from here."

"To tell her everything—to renounce your hope?"

"That is what it amounts to, I suppose."

She watched him cross the room and lay his hand on the door.

"Ah, you poor, good man!" she said with a sob.

ROBERT HERRICK

The Master of the Inn

Robert Herrick (1868–1938)

THERE WAS a moral, reforming purpose behind all of Herrick's extensive work in fiction. He hoped to arouse in his fellow-Americans—and especially among professional people: lawyers, physicians, teachers and the like—a sense of their duty to society. They seemed to him, as a group intolerably self-satisfied and smug, and in permanent full cry after the wrong quarry. Over and over again he stressed by example the eroding effect of selfishness and foolish convention on human personality, but with such an effort at complete objectivity that the human values were sacrificed to the thesis. In his day, the women's clubs seethed with debate over the merits of his problem novels, but today's reader finds them cold and remote from reality, and begins to suspect that the writer moved through progressive disappointments in his species to a general quarrel with life itself. He posed problem after problem, but he offered no cures.

The Master of the Inn, however, is in another key. With this short and graceful work, Herrick touched a chord responsive in the minds and hearts of that vast, literate, but unliterary public which turns to books for help and inspiration. It is a small masterpiece of its kind.

THE MASTER OF THE INN

I

IT WAS a plain brick house, three full stories, with four broad chimneys, and overhanging eaves. The tradition was that it had been a colonial tavern—a dot among the fir-covered northern hills on the climbing post-road into Canada. The village scattered along the road below the inn was called Albany—and soon forgotten when the railroad sought an opening through a valley less rugged, eight miles to the west.

Rather more than thirty years ago the Doctor had arrived, one summer day, and opened all the doors and windows of the neglected old house, which he had bought from scattered heirs. He was a quiet man, the Doctor, in middle life then or nearly so; and he sank almost without remark into the world of Albany, where they raise hay and potatoes and still cut good white pine off the hills. Gradually the old brick tavern resumed the functions of life: many buildings were added to it as well as many acres of farm and forest to the Doctor's original purchase of intervale land. The new Master did not open his house to the public, yet he, too, kept a sort of Inn, where men came and stayed a long time. Although no sign now hung from the old elm tree in front of the house, nevertheless an ever-widening stream of humanity mounted the winding road from White River and passed through the doors of the Inn, seeking life. . . .

That first summer the Doctor brought with him Sam, the Chinaman, whom we all came to know and love, and also a young man, who loafed much while the Doctor worked, and occasionally fished. This was John Herring—now a famous architect—and it was from his designs, sketched those first idle summer days, that were built all the additions to the simple old house—the two low wings in the rear for the "cells," with the Italian garden between them; the marble seat curving around the pool that joined the wings on the west; also the substantial wall that hid the Inn, its terraced gardens and orchards, from Albanian curiosity. Herring found a store of red brick in some crumbling buildings in the neighborhood, and he discovered the quarry whence came those thick slabs of purple slate. The blue-veined marble was had from a fissure in the hills, and the Doctor's School made the tiles.

I think Herring never did better work than in the making over of this old tavern: he divined that subtle affinity which exists between north Italy, with all its art, and our bare New England; and he dared to graft boldly one to the other, having the rear of the Inn altogether Italian with its portico, its dainty colonnades, the garden and the fountain and the pool. From all this one looked down on the waving grass of the Intervale, which fell away gently to the turbulent White River, then rose again to the wooded hills that folded one upon another, with ever deepening blue, always upward and beyond.

Not all this building at once, to be sure, as the millionaire builds; but a gradual growth over a couple of decades; and all built lovingly by the "Brothers," stone on stone, brick and beam and tile—many a hand taking part in it that came weak to the task and left it sturdy. There was also the terraced arrangement of gardens and orchards on either side of the Inn, reaching to the farm buildings on the one side and to the village on the other. For a time Herring respected the quaint old tavern with its small rooms and pine wainscot; then he made a stately two-storied hall out of one half where we dined in bad weather, and a pleasant study for the Doctor from the rest. The doors east and west always stood open in the summer, giving the rare passer-by a glimpse of that radiant blue heaven among the hills, with the silver flash of the river in the middle distance, and a little square of peaceful garden close at hand. . . . The tough northern grasses rustled in the breezes that always played about Albany; and the scent of spruce drawn by the hot sun—the strong resinous breath of the north—was borne from the woods.

Thus it started, that household of men in the old Inn at the far end of Albany village among the northern hills, with the Doctor and Sam and Herring, who had been flung aside after his first skirmish with life and was picked up in pure kindness by the Doctor, as a bit of the broken waste of our modern world, and carried off with him out of the city. The young architect returning in due time to the fight—singing—naturally venerated the Doctor as a father; and when a dear friend stumbled and fell in the *via dura* of this life, he whispered to him word of the Inn and its Master—of the life up there among the hills where Man is little and God looks down on his earth. . . . "Oh, you'll understand when you put your eyes on White Face some morning! The Doctor? He heals both body and soul." And this one having heeded spoke the word in turn to others in need—"to the right sort, who would understand." Thus the custom grew like a faith, and a kind of brotherhood was formed, of those who had found more than health at the Inn—who had found themselves. The Doctor, ever busy about his farms and his woods, his building, and above all his School, soon had on his hands a dozen or more patients or guests, as you might call them, and he set them to work speedily. There was little medicine to be found in the Inn: the sick labored as they could and thus grew strong. . . .

And so, as one was added to another, they began to call themselves in joke "Brothers," and the Doctor, "Father." The older "Brothers" would return to the Inn from all parts of the land, for a few days or a few weeks, to grasp the Doctor's hand, to have a dip in the pool, to try the little brooks among the hills. Young men and middle-aged, and even the old, they came from the cities where the heat of living had scorched them, where they had faltered and doubted the goodness of life. In some way word of the Master had reached them, with this compelling advice—"Go! And tell him I sent you." So from the clinic or the lecture-room, from the office or the mill—wherever men labor with tightening nerves—the needy one started on his long journey. Toward evening he was set down before the plain red face of the Inn. And as the Stranger entered the old hall, a voice was sure to greet him from within somewhere, the deep voice of a hearty man, and presently the Master appeared to welcome the newcomer, resting one hand on his guest's shoulder perhaps, with a yearning affection that ran before knowledge.

"So you've come, my boy," he said. "Herring [or some one] wrote me to look for you."

And after a few more words of greeting, the Doctor beckoned to Sam, and gave the guest over to his hands. Thereupon the Chinaman slippered through tiled passageways to the court, where the Stranger, caught by the beauty and peace so well hidden, lingered a while. The little space within the wings was filled with flowers as far as the yellow water of the pool and the marble bench. In the centre of the court was an old gray fountain—sent from Verona by a Brother—from which the water dropped and ran away among the flower beds to the pool. A stately elm tree shaded this place, flecking the water below. The sun shot long rays beneath its branches into the court, and over all there was an odor of blossoming flowers and the murmur of bees.

"Bath!" Sam explained, grinning toward the pool.

With the trickle of the fountain in his ears the Stranger looked out across the ripening fields of the Intervale to the noble sky-line of the Stowe hills. Those little mountains of the north! Mere hills to all who know the giants of the earth—not mountains in the brotherhood of ice and snow and rock! But in form and color, in the lesser things that create the love of men for places, they rise nobly toward heaven, those little hills! On a summer day like this their broad breasts flutter with waving tree-tops, and at evening depth on depth of purple mist gathers over them, dropping into those soft curves where the little brooks flow, and mounting even to the sky-line. When the sun has fallen, there rests a band of pure saffron, and in the calm and perfect peace of evening there is a hint of coming moonlight. Ah, they are of the fellowship of mountains, those little hills of Stowe! And when in winter their flanks are jewelled with ice and snow, then they raise their heads proudly to the stars, calling across the frozen valleys to their greater brethren in the midriff of the continent—"Behold, we also are hills, in the sight of the Lord!" . . .

Meantime Sam, with Oriental ease, goes slipping along the arcade until he comes to a certain oak door, where he drops your bag, and disappears, having saluted. It is an ample and lofty room, and on the outer side of it hangs a little balcony above the orchard, from which there is a view of the valley and the woods beyond, and from somewhere in the fields the note of the thrush rises. The room itself is cool, of a gray tone, with a broad fireplace, a heavy table, and many books. Otherwise there are bed and chairs and dressing-table, the necessities of life austerely provided. And Peace! God, what Peace to him who has escaped from the furnace men make! It is as if he had come all the way to the end of the world, and found there a great still room of peace.

Soon a bell sounds—with a strange vibration as though in distant lands it had summoned many a body of men together—and the household assembles under the arcade. If it is fair and not cold, Sam and his helpers bring out the long narrow table and place it, as Veronese places his feasters, lengthwise beneath the colonnade, and thus the evening meal is served. A fresh, coarse napkin is laid on the bare board before each man, no more than enough for all those present, and the Doctor sits in the middle, serving all. There are few dishes, and for the most part such as may be got at home there in the hills. There is a pitcher of cider at one end and a pitcher of mild white wine at the other, and the men eat and drink, with jokes and talk—the laughter of the day. (The novice might feel only the harmony of it all, but later he will learn how many considered elements go to the making of Peace.) Afterward, when Sam has brought pipes and tobacco, the Master leads the way to the sweeping semicircle of marble seat around the pool with the leafy tree overhead; and there they sit into the soft night, talking of all things, with the glow of pipes, until one after another slips away to sleep. For as the Master said, "Talk among men in common softens the muscles of the mind and quickens the heart." Yet he loved most to hear the talk of others.

Thus insensibly for the Novice there begins the life of the place, opening in a gentle and persistent routine that takes him in its flow and carries him on with it. He finds Tradition and Habit all about him, in the ordered, unconscious life of the Inn, to which he yields without question. . . . Shortly after dawn the bell sounds, and then the men meet at the pool, where the Doctor is always first. A plunge into the yellow water which is flecked with the fallen leaves, and afterward to each man's room there is brought a large bowl of coffee and hot milk, with bread and eggs and fruit. What more he craves may be found in the hall.

Soon there is a tap on the newcomer's door, and a neighborly voice calls out—"We all go into the fields every morning, you know. You must earn your dinner, the Doctor says, or borrow it!" So the Novice goes forth to earn his first dinner with his hands. Beyond the gardens and the orchards are the barns and sheds, and a vista of level acres of hay and potatoes and rye, the bearing acres of the farm, and beyond these the woods on the hills. "Nearly a thousand acres, fields and woods," the neighbor explains. "Oh, there's plenty to do all times!" Meantime the Doctor strides ahead through the wet grass, his eyes roaming here and there, inquiring the state of his land. And watching him the newcomer believes that there is always much to be done wherever the Doctor leads.

It may be July and hay time—all the Intervale grass land is mowed by hand—there is a sweat-breaking task! Or it may be potatoes to hoe. Or later in the season the apples have to be gathered—a pleasant pungent job, filling the baskets and pouring them into the fat-bellied barrels. But whatever the work may be the Doctor keeps the Novice in his mind, and as the sun climbs high over the Stowe hills, he taps the new one on the shoulder—"Better stop here to-day, my boy! You'll find a good tree over there by the brook for a nap. . . ."

Under that particular tree in the tall timothy, there is the coolest spot, and the Novice drowses, thinking of those wonderful mowers in *Anna*, as he gazes at the marching files eating their way through the meadow until his eyelids fall and he sleeps, the ripple of waving timothy in ears. At noon the bell sounds again from the Inn, and the men come striding homeward wiping the sweat from their faces. They gather at the swimming pool, and still panting from their labor strip off their wet garments, then plunge one after another, like happy boys. From bath to room, and a few minutes for fresh clothes, and all troop into the hall, which is dark and cool. The old brick walls of the tavern never held a gayer lot of guests.

From this time on each one is his own master; there is no common toil. The farmer and his men take up the care of the farm, and the Master usually goes down to his School, in company with some of the Brothers. Each one finds his own way of spending the hours till sunset—some fishing or shooting, according to the season; others, in tennis or games with the boys of the School; and some reading or loafing—until the shadows begin to fall across the pool into the court, and Sam brings out the long table for dinner.

The seasons shading imperceptibly into one another vary the course of the day. Early in September the men begin to sit long about the hall-fire of an evening, and when the snow packs hard on the hills there is wood-cutting to be done, and in early spring it is the carpenter's shop. So the form alters, but the substance remains—work and play and rest. . . .

To each one a time will come when the Doctor speaks to him alone. At some hour, before many days have passed, the Novice will find himself with those large eyes resting on his face, searchingly. It may be in the study after the others have scattered, or at the pool where the Master loved to sit beneath the great tree and hear his "confessions," as the men called these talks. At such times, when the man came to remember it afterward, the Doctor asked few questions, said little, but listened. He had the confessing ear! And as if by chance his hand would rest on the man's arm or shoulder. For he said—"Touch speaks: soul flows through flesh into soul."

Thus he sat and confessed his patients one after another, and his dark eyes seemed familiar with all man's woes, as if he had listened always. Men said to him what they had never before let pass their lips to man or woman, what they themselves scarce looked at in the gloom of their souls. Unawares it slipped from them, the reason within the reason for their ill, the ultimate cause of sorrow. From the moment they had revealed to him this hidden thing—had slipped the leash on their tongues—it seemed no longer to be feared. "Trouble evaporates, being properly aired," said the Doctor. And already in the troubled one's mind the sense of the confused snarl of life began to lessen and veils began to descend between him and it. . . . "For you must learn to forget," counselled the Doctor, "forget day by day until the recording soul beneath your mind is clean. Therefore—work, forget, be new!" . . .

A self-important young man, much concerned with himself, once asked the Master:

"Doctor, what is the regimen that you would recommend to me?"

And we all heard him say in reply—

"The potatoes need hilling, and then you'll feel like having a dip in the pool."

The young man, it seems, wrote back to the friend in the city who had sent him—"This Doctor cannot understand my case: he tells me to dig potatoes and bathe in a swimming pool. That is all!

All!" But the friend, who was an old member of the Brotherhood, telegraphed back—"Dig and swim, you fool!" Sam took the message at the telephone while we were dining, and repeated it faithfully to the young man within the hearing of all. A laugh rose that was hard in dying, and I think the Doctor's lips wreathed in smile. . . . In the old days they say the Master gave medicine like other doctors. That was when he spent part of the year in the city and had an office there and believed in drugs. But as he gave up going to the city, the stock of drugs in the cabinet at the end of the study became exhausted, and was never renewed. All who needed medicine were sent to an old Brother, who had settled down the valley at Stowe. "He knows more about pills than I do," the Doctor said. "At least he can give you the stuff with confidence." Few of the inmates of the Inn ever went to Stowe, though Dr. Williams was an excellent physician. And it was from about this time that we began to drop the title of doctor, calling him instead the Master; and the younger men sometimes, Father. He seemed to like these new terms, as denoting affection and respect for his authority.

By the time that we called him Master, the Inn had come to its maturity. Altogether it could hold eighteen guests, and if more came, as in midsummer or autumn, they lived in tents in the orchard or in the hill camps. The Master was still adding to the forest land—fish and game preserve the village people called it; for the Master was a hunter and a fisherman. But up among those curving hills, when he looked out through the waving trees, measuring by eye a fir or a pine, he would say, nodding his head—"Boys, behold my heirs—from generation to generation!"

He was now fifty and had ceased altogether to go to the city. There were ripe men in the great hospitals that still remembered him as a young man in the medical school; but he had dropped out, they said—why? He might have answered that, instead of following the beaten path, he had spoken his word to the world through men—and spoken widely. For there was no break in the stream of life that flowed upward to the old Inn. The "cells" were always full, winter and summer. Now there were coming children of the older Brothers, and these, having learned the ways of the place from their fathers, were already house-broken, as we said, when they came.

They knew that no door was locked about the Inn, but that if they returned after ten it behooved them to come in by the pool and make no noise. They knew that when the first ice formed on the pool, then they were not expected to get out of bed for the morning plunge. They knew that there was an old custom which no one ever forgot, and that was to put money in the house-box behind the hall door on leaving, at least something for each day of the time spent, and as much more as one cared to give. For, as every one knew, all in the box beyond the daily expense went to maintain the School on the road below the village. So the books of the Inn were easy to keep—there was never a word about money in the place—but I know that many a large sum of money was found in this box, and the School never wanted means.

That I might tell more of what took place in the Inn, and what the Master said, and the sort of men one found there, and the talk we all had summer evenings beside the pool and winter nights in the hall! Winter, I think, was the best time of all the year, the greatest beauty and the greatest joy, from the first fall of the snow to the yellow brook water and the floating ice in White River. Then the broad velvety shadows lay on the hills between the stiff spruces, then came rosy mornings out of darkness when you knew that some good thing was waiting for you in the world. After you had drunk your bowl of coffee, you got your axe and followed the procession of choppers, who were carefully foresting the Doctor's woods. In the spring when the little brooks had begun to run down the slopes, there was road making and mending; for the Master kept in repair most of the roads about Albany, grinding the rock in his pit, saying that—"a good road is one sure blessing."

And the dusks I shall never forget—those gold and violet moments with the light of immortal heavens behind the rampart of hills; and the nights, so still, so still like everlasting death, each star set jewel-wise in a black sky above a white earth. How splendid it was to turn out of the warm hall where we had been reading and talking into the frosty court, with the thermometer at twenty below and still falling, and look down across the broad white valley, marked by the streak of bushy alders where the dumb river flowed, up to the little frozen water courses among the hills, up above where the stars glittered! You took your way to your room in the silence, rejoicing that it was all so, that somewhere in this tumultuous world of ours there was hidden all this beauty and the secret of living; and that you were of the brotherhood of those who had found it. . . .

Thus was the Inn and its Master in the year when he touched sixty, and his hair and beard were more white than gray.

II

Then there came to the Inn one day in the early part of the summer a new guest—a man about fifty, with an aging, worldly face. Bill, the Albany stage man, had brought him from Island Junction, and on the way had answered all his questions, discreetly, reckoning in his wisdom that his passenger was "one of those queer folks that went up to the old Doctor's place." For there was something smart and fashionable about the stranger's appearance that made Bill uncomfortable.

"There," he said, as he pulled up outside the red brick house and pointed over the wall into the garden, "mos' likely you'll find the man fussin' 'round somewheres inside there, if he hain't down to the School," and he drove off with the people's mail.

The stranger looked back through the village street, which was as silent as a village street should be at four o'clock on a summer day. Then he muttered to himself, whimsically, "Mos' likely you'll find the old man fussin' 'round somewheres inside!" Well, *what next?* And he glanced at the homely red brick building with the cold eye of one who has made many goings out and comings in, and to whom novelty offers little entertainment. As he stood there (thinking posisibly of that early train from the junction on the morrow) the hall door opened wide, and an oldish man with white eye-brows and black eyes appeared. He was dressed in a linen suit that deepened the dark tan of his face and hands. He said:

"You are Dr. Augustus Norton?"

"And you," the Stranger replied with a gracious smile, "are the Master—and this is the Inn!"

He had forgotten what Percival called the old boy—forgot everything these days—had tried to remember the name all the way up—nevertheless, he had turned it off well! So the two looked at each other—one a little younger as years go, but with lined face and shaking fingers; the other solid and self-contained, with less of that ready language which comes from always jostling with nimble wits. But as they stood there, each saw a Man and an Equal.

"The great surgeon of St. Jerome's," said our Master in further welcome.

"Honored by praise from your lips!" Thus the man of the city lightly turned the compliment, and extended his hand, which the Master took slowly, gazing meanwhile steadily at his guest.

"Pray come into my house," said the Master of the Inn, with more stateliness of manner than he usually had with a new Brother. But, it may be said, Dr. Augustus Norton had the most distinguished name of that day in his profession. He followed the Master to his study, with uncertain steps, and sinking into a deep chair before the smouldering ashes looked at his host with a sad grin—"Perhaps you'll give me something—the journey, you know? . . ."

Two years before the head surgeon of St. Jerome's had come to the hospital of a morning to perform some operation—one of those affairs for which he was known from coast to coast. As he entered the officers' room that day, with the arrogant eye of the commander-in-chief, one of his aides looked at him suspiciously, then glanced again—and the great surgeon felt those eyes upon him when he turned his back. And he knew why! Something was wrong with him. Nevertheless in glum silence he made ready to operate. But when the moment came, and he was about to take the part of God toward the piece of flesh lying in the ether sleep before him, he hesitated. Then, in the terrible recoil of Fear, he turned back.

"Macroe!" he cried to his assistant, "you will have to operate. I cannot—I am not well!"

There was almost panic, but Macroe was a man, too, and proceeded to do his work without a word. The great surgeon, his hands now trembling beyond disguise, went back to the officers' room, took off his white robes, and returned to his home. There he wrote his resignation to the directors of St. Jerome's, and his resignation from other offices of honor and responsibility. Then he sent for a medical man, an old friend, and held out his shaking hand to him:

"The damn thing won't go," he said, pointing also to his head.

"Too much work," the doctor replied, of course.

But the great surgeon, who was a man of clear views, added impersonally, "Too much everything, I guess!"

There followed the usual prescription, making the sick man a wanderer and pariah—first to Europe, "to get rid of me," the surgeon growled; then to Georgia for golf, to Montana for elk, to Canada for salmon, and so forth. Each time the sick man returned with a thin coat of tan that peeled off in a few days, and with those shaking hands that suggested immediately another journey to another climate. Until it happened finally that the men of St. Jerome's who had first talked of the date of their chief's return merely raised their eyebrows at the mention of his name.

"Done for, poor old boy!" and the great surgeon read it with his lynx eyes, in the faces of the men he met at his clubs. His mouth drew together sourly and his back sloped. "Fifty-two," he muttered. "God, this is too early—something ought to pull me together." So he went on trying this and that, while his friends said he was "resting," until he had slipped from men's thoughts.

One day Percival of St. Jerome's, one of those boys he had growled at and cursed in former times, met him crawling down the avenue to his quietest club, and the old surgeon took him by the arm—he was gray in face and his neck was wasting away—and told the story of his troubles—as he would to anyone these days. The young man listened respectfully. Then he spoke of the old Inn, of the Brotherhood, of the Master and what he had done for miserable men, who had despaired. The famous surgeon, shaking his head as one who has heard of these miracles many times and found them naught, was drinking it all in, nevertheless.

"He takes a man," said the young surgeon, "who doesn't want to live and makes him fall in love with life."

Dr. Augustus Norton sniffed.

"In love with life! That's good! If your Wonder of the Ages

can make a man of fifty fall in love with anything, I must try him." He laughed a sneering laugh, the feeble merriment of doubt.

"Ah, Doctor!" cried the young man, "you must go and live with the Master. And then come back to us at St. Jerome's: for we need you!"

And the great surgeon, touched to the heart by these last words, said:

"Well, what's the name of your miracle-worker, and where is he to be found? . . . I might as well try all the cures—write a book on 'em one of these days!" . . .

So he came by the stage to the gate of the old Inn, and the Master, who had been warned by a telegram from the young doctor only that morning, stood at his door to welcome his celebrated guest.

He put him in the room of state above the study, a great square room at the southwest, overlooking the wings and the flower-scented garden, the pool, and the waving grass fields beyond, dotted with tall elms—all freshly green.

"Not a bad sort of place," murmured the weary man, "and there must be trout in those brooks up yonder. Well, it will do for a week or two, if there's fishing." . . . Then the bell sounded for dinner which was served for the first time that season out of doors in the soft twilight. The Brothers had gathered in the court beside the fountain, young men and middle-aged—all having bent under some burden, which they were now learning to carry easily. They stood about the hall door until the distinguished Stranger appeared, and he walked between them to the place of honor at the Master's side. Every one at the long table was named to the great surgeon, and then with the coming of the soup he was promptly forgotten, while the talk of the day's work and the morrow's rose vigorously from all sides. It was a question of the old mill, which had given way. An engineer among the company described what would have to be done to get at the foundations. And a young man who happened to sit next to the surgeon explained that the Master had reopened an old mill above the Inn in the Intervale, where he ground corn and wheat and rye with the old water-wheel; for the country people, who had always got their grain ground there, complained when the mill had been closed. It seemed to the Stranger that the dark coarse bread which was served was extraordinarily good, and he wondered if the ancient process had anything to do with it and he resolved to see the old mill. Then the young man said something about bass: there was a cool lake up the valley, which had been stocked. The surgeon's eye gleamed. Did he know how to fish for bass! Why, before this boy—yes, he would go at five in the morning, sharp. . . . After the meal, while the blue wreaths of smoke floated across the flowers and the talk rose and fell in the court, the Master and his new guest were seated alone beneath the great elm. The surgeon could trace the Master's face in the still waters of the pool at their feet, and it seemed to him like a finely cut cameo, with gentle lines about the mouth and eyes that relieved the thick nose. Nevertheless he knew by certain instinct that they were not of the same kind. The Master was very silent this night, and his guest felt that some mystery, some vacuum existed between them, as he gazed on the face in the water. It was as if the old man were holding him off at arm's length while he looked into him. But the great surgeon, who was used to the amenities of city life, resolved to make his host talk:

"Extraordinary sort of place you have here! I don't know that I have ever seen anything just like it. And what is your System?"

"What is my System?" repeated the Master wonderingly.

"Yes! Your method of building these fellows up—electricity, diet, massage, baths—what is your line?" An urbane smile removed the offence of the banter.

"I have no System!" the Master replied thoughtfully. "I live my life here with my work, and those you see come and live with me as my friends."

"Ah, but you have ideas . . . extraordinary success . . . so many cases," the great man muttered, confused by the Master's steady gaze.

"You will learn more about us after you have been here a little time. You will see, and the others will help you to understand. To-morrow we work at the mill, and the next day we shall be in the gardens—but you may be too tired to join us. And we bathe here, morning and noon. Harvey will tell you all our customs."

The celebrated surgeon of St. Jerome's wrote that night to an old friend: "And the learned doctor's prescription seems to be to dig in the garden and bathe in a great pool! A daffy sort of place—

but I am going bass fishing to-morrow at five with a young man, who is just the right age for a son! So to bed, but I suspect that I shall see you soon—novelties wear out quickly at my years."

Just here there entered that lovely night wind, rising far away beyond the low lakes to the south—it soughed through the room, swaying the draperies, sighing, sighing, and it blew out the candle. The sick man looked down on the court below, white in the moonlight, and his eyes roved farther to the dark orchard, and the great barns and the huddled cattle.

"Quite a bit of country here!" the surgeon murmured. As he stood there looking into the misty light which covered the Intervale, up to the great hills above which floated luminous cloud banks, the chorus of an old song rose from below where the pipes gleamed in the dark about the pool. He leaned out into the air, filled with all the wild scent of green fields, and added under a sort of compulsion—"And a good place, enough!"

He went to bed to a deep sleep, and over his tired, worldly face the night wind passed gently, stripping leaf by leaf from his weary mind that heavy coating of care which he had wrapped about him in the course of many years.

Dr. Augustus Norton did not return at the end of one week, nor of two. The city saw him, indeed, no more that year. It was said that a frisky, rosy ghost of the great surgeon had slipped into St. Jerome's near Christmas—had skipped through a club or two and shaken hands about pretty generally—and disappeared. Sometimes letters came from him with an out-of-the-way postmark on them, saying in a jesting tone that he was studying the methods of an extraordinary country doctor, who seemed to cure men by touch. "He lives up here among the hills in forty degrees of frost, and if I am not mistaken he is nearer the Secret than all of you pill slingers"—(for he was writing a mere doctor of medicine!). "Anyhow I shall stay on until I learn the Secret—or my host turns me out; for life up here seems as good to me as ice-cream and kisses to a girl of sixteen. . . . Why should I go back mucking about with you fellows—just yet? I caught a five-pounder yesterday, and *ate* him!"

There are many stories of the great surgeon that have come to me from those days. He was much liked, especially by the younger men, after the first gloom had worn off, and he began to feel the blood run once more. He had a joking way with him that made him a good table companion, and the Brothers pretending that he would become the historian of the order taught him all the traditions of the place. "But the Secret, the Secret! Where is it?" he would demand jestingly. One night—it was at table and all were there—Harvey asked him:

"Has the Master confessed you?"

" 'Confessed me'?" repeated the surgeon. "What's that?"

A sudden silence fell on all, because this was the one thing never spoken of, at least in public. Then the Master, who had been silent all that evening, turned the talk to other matters.

The Master, to be sure, gave this distinguished guest all liberties, and they often talked together as men of the same profession. And the surgeon witnessed all—the mending of the mill, the planting and the hoeing and the harvesting, the preparations for the long winter, the chopping and the road-making—all, and he tested it with his hands. "Not bad sport," he would say, "with so many sick-well young men about to help!"

But meanwhile the "secret" escaped the keen mind, though he sought for it daily.

"You give no drugs, Doctor," he complained. "You're a scab on the profession!"

"The drugs gave out," the Master explained, "and I neglected to order more. . . . There's always Bert Williams at Stowe, who can give you anything you might want—shall I send for him, Doctor?"

There was laughter all about, and when it died down the great surgeon returned to the attack.

"Well, come, tell us now what you do believe in? Magic, the laying on of hands? Come, there are four doctors here, and we have the right to know—or we'll report you!"

"I believe," said the Master solemnly, in reply to the banter, "I believe in Man and in God." And there followed such talk as had never been in the old hall; for the surgeon was, after his kind, a materialist and pushed the Master for definition. The Master believed, as I recall it, that Disease could not be cured, for the most part. No chemistry would ever solve the mystery of pain! But Disease could be ignored, and the best way to forget pain was through labor. Not labor merely for oneself; but also something for others. Wherefore the School, around which the Inn and the farm and all had grown. For he told us then that he had bought the Inn as a home for his boys, the waste product of the city. Finding the old tavern too small for his purpose and seeing how he should need helpers, he had encouraged ailing men to come to live with him and to cure themselves by curing others. Without that School below in the valley, with its workshops and cottages, there would have been no Inn!

As for God—that night he would go no further, and the surgeon said rather flippantly, we all thought, that the Master had left little room in his world for God, anyhow—he had made man so large. It was a stormy August evening, I remember, when we had been forced to dine within on account of the gusty rain that had come after a still, hot day. The valley seemed filled with murk, which was momentarily torn by fire, revealing the trembling leaves upon the trees. When we passed through the arcade to reach our rooms, the surgeon pointed out into this sea of fire and darkness, and muttered with a touch of irony—

"HE seems to be talking for himself this evening!"

Just then a bolt shot downward, revealing with large exaggeration the hills, the folded valleys—the descents.

"It's like standing on a thin plank in a turbulent sea!" the surgeon remarked wryly. "Ah, my boy, Life's like that!" and he disappeared into his room.

Nevertheless, it was that night he wrote to his friend: "I am getting nearer this Mystery, which I take to be, the inner heart of it, a mixture of the Holy Ghost and Sweat—with a good bath afterward! But the old boy is the mixer of the Pills, mind you, and he *is* a Master! Most likely I shall never get hold of the heart of it; for somehow, yet with all courtesy, he keeps me at a distance. I have never been 'confessed,' whatever that may be—an experience that comes to the youngest boy among them! Perhaps the Doctor thinks that old fellows like you and me have only dead sins to confess, which would crumble to dust if exposed. But there is a sting in very old sins, I think—for instance—oh! if you were here tonight, I should be as foolish as a woman. . . ."

The storm that night struck one of the school buildings and killed a lad. In the morning the Master and the surgeon set out for the School Village, which was lower in the valley beyond Albany. It was warm and clear at the Inn; but thick mist wreaths still lay heavily over the Intervale. The hills all about glittered as in October, and there was in the air that laughing peace, that breath of sweet plenty which comes the morning after a storm. The two men followed the foot-path, which wound downward from the Inn across the Intervale. The sun filled the windless air, sucking up the spicy odors of the tangled path—fern and balsam and the mother scent of earth and rain and sun. The new green rioted over the dead leaves. . . . The Master, closely observing his guest, remarked:

"You seem quite well, Doctor. I suppose you will be leaving us soon?"

"Leaving?" the surgeon questioned slowly, as if a secret dread had risen at the Master's hint of departure. "Yes," he admitted, after a time, "I suppose I am what you would call well—well enough. But something still clogs within me. It may be the memory of Fear. I am afraid of myself!"

"Afraid? You need some test, perhaps. That will come sooner or later; we need not hurry it!"

"No, we need not hurry!"

Yet he knew well enough that the Inn never sheltered drones, and that many special indulgences had been granted him: he had borrowed freely from the younger Brothers—of their time and strength. He thought complacently of the large cheque which he should drop into the house-box on his departure. With it the Master would be able to build a new cottage or a small hospital for the School.

"Some of them," mused the Master, "never go back to the machine that once broke them. They stay about here and help me—buy a farm and revert! But for the most part they are keen to get back to the fight, as is right and best. Sometimes when they loiter too long, I shove them out of the nest!"

"And I am near the shoving point?" his companion retorted

quickly. "So I must leave all your dear boys and Peace and Fishing and *you*! Suppose so, suppose so! . . . Doctor, you've saved my life —oh, hang it, that doesn't tell the story. But even *I* can feel what it is to live at the Inn!"

Instinctively he grasped his host by the arm—he was an impulsive man. But the Master's arm did not respond to the clasp; indeed, a slight shiver seemed to shake it, so that the surgeon's hand fell away while the Master said:

"I am glad to have been of service—to you—yes, especially to *you*. . . ."

They came into the School Village, a tiny place of old white houses, very clean and trim, with a number of sweeping elms along the narrow road. A mountain brook turned an old water-wheel, supplying power for the workshops where the boys were trained. The great surgeon had visited the place many times in company with the Master, and though he admired the order and economy of the institution, and respected its purpose—that is, to create men out of the refuse of society—to tell the truth, the place bored him a trifle. This morning they went directly to the little cottage that served as infirmary, where the dead boy had been brought. He was a black-haired Italian, and his lips curved upward pleasantly. The Master putting his hand on the dead boy's brow as he might have done in life stood looking at the face.

"I've got a case in the next room, I'd like to have your opinion on, Doctor," the young physician said in a low tone to the surgeon, and the two crossed the passage into the neighboring room. The surgeon fastened his eyes on the sick lad's body: here was a case he understood, a problem with a solution. The old Master coming in from the dead stood behind the two.

"Williams," the surgeon said, "it's so, sure enough—you must operate—at once!"

"I was afraid it was that," the younger man replied. "But how can I operate here?"

The surgeon shrugged his shoulders— "He would never reach the city!"

"Then I must, you think——"

The shrewd surgeon recognized Fear in the young man's voice.

Quick the thrill shot through his nerves, and he cried, "I will operate *now*."

In half an hour it was over, and the Master and the surgeon were leaving the village, climbing up by the steep path under the blazing noon sun. The Master glanced at the man by his side, who strode along confidently, a trifle of a swagger in his buoyant steps. The Master remarked:

"The test came, and you took it—splendidly."

"Yes," the great surgeon replied, smiling happily, "it's all there, Doctor, the old power. I believe I am about ready to get into harness again!" After they had walked more of the way without speaking, the surgeon added, as to himself—"But there are other things to be feared!"

Though the Master looked at him closely he invited no explanation, and they finished their homeward walk without remark.

It soon got about among the inmates of the Inn what a wonderful operation the surgeon of St. Jerome's had performed, and it was rumored that at the beginning of autumn he would go back to his old position. Meantime the great surgeon enjoyed the homage that men always pay to power, the consideration of his fellows. He had been much liked; but now that the Brothers knew how soon he was to leave them, they surrounded him with those attentions that men most love, elevating him almost to the rank of the Master—and they feared him less. His fame spread, so that from some mill beyond Stowe they brought to the Inn a desperate case, and the surgeon operated again successfully, demonstrating that he was once more master of his art, and master of himself. So he stayed on merely to enjoy his triumph and escape the dull season in the city.

It was a wonderful summer, that! The fitful temper of the north played in all its moods. There were days when the sun shone tropically down into the valleys, without a breath of air, when the earthy, woodsy smells were strong—and the nights—perfect stillness and peace, as if some spirit of the air were listening for love words on the earth. The great elms along Albany road hung their branches motionless, and when the moon came over behind the house the great hills began to swim ghostly, vague—beyond, always beyond! . . .

And then there were the fierce storms that swept up the valley and hung growling along the hills for days, and afterward, sky-washed and clear, the westerly breeze would come tearing down the Intervale, drying the earth before it. . . . But each day there was a change in the sound and the smell of the fields and the woods—in the quick race of the northern summer—a change that the surgeon, fishing up the tiny streams, felt and noted. Each day, so radiant with its abundant life, sounded some under-note of fulfilment and change—speaking beforehand of death to come.

Toward the end of August a snap of cold drove us in-doors for the night meal. Then around the fire there was great talk between the Master and the surgeon, a sort of battle of the soul, to which we others paid silent attention. For wherever those nights the talk might rise, in the little rills of accidental words, it always flowed down to the deep underlying thoughts of men. And in those depths, as I said, these two wrestled with each other. The Master, who had grown silent of late years, woke once more with fire. The light, keen thrusts of the surgeon, who argued like a fencer, roused his whole being; and as day by day it went on we who watched saw that in a way the talk of these two men set forth the great conflict of conflicts, that deepest fissure of life and belief anent the Soul and the Body. And the Master, who had lived his faiths by his life before our eyes, was being worsted in the argument! The great surgeon had the better mind, and he had seen all of life that one may see with eyes. . . .

They were talking of the day of departure for the distinguished guest, and arranging for some kind of triumphal procession to escort him to White River. But he would not set the time, shrinking from this act, as if all were not yet done. There came a warm, glowing day early in September, and at night after the pipes were lighted the surgeon and the Master strolled off in the direction of the pool, arm in arm. There had been no talk that day, the surgeon apparently shrinking from coming to the last grapple with one whose faiths were so important to him as the Master's.

"The flowers are dying: they tell me it's time to move on," said the surgeon. "And yet, my dear host, I go without the Secret, without understanding All!"

"Perhaps there is no inner Secret," the Master smiled. "It is all here before you."

"I know that—you have been very good to me, shared everything. If I have not learned the Secret, it is my fault, my incapacity. But—" and the gay tone dropped quickly and a flash of bitterness succeeded— "I at least know that there *is* a Secret!"

They sat down on the marble bench and looked into the water, each thinking his thoughts. Suddenly the surgeon began to speak, hesitantly, as if there had long been something in his mind that he was compelled to say.

"My friend," he said, "I too have something to tell—the cause within the cause, the reason of the reason—at least, sometimes I think it is! The root reason for all—unhappiness, defeat, for the shaking hand and the jesting voice. And I want you to hear it—if you will."

The Master raised his face from the pool but said never a word. The surgeon continued, his voice trembling at times, though he spoke slowly evidently trying to banish all feeling.

"It is a common enough story at the start, at least among men of our kind. You know that I was trained largely in Europe. My father had the means to give me the best, and time to take it in. So I was over there, before I came back to St. Jerome's, three, four years at Paris, Munich, Vienna, all about. . . . While I was away I lived as the others, for the most part—you know our profession—and youth. The rascals are pretty much the same to-day, I judge from what my friends say of their sons! Well, at least I worked like the devil, and was decent. . . . Oh, it isn't for that I'm telling the tale! I was ambitious, then. And the time came to go back, as it does in the end, and I took a few weeks' run through Italy as a final taste of the lovely European thing, and came down to Naples to get the boat for New York. I've never been back to Naples since, and that was twenty-six years ago this autumn. But I can see the city always as it was then! The seething human hive—the fellows piling in the freight to the music of their songs—the fiery mouth of Vesuvius up above. And the soft, dark night with just a plash of waves on the quay!"

The Master listened, his eyes again buried in the water at their feet.

"Well, *she* was there on board, of course—looking out also into that warm dark night and sighing for all that was to be lost so soon. There were few passengers in those days. . . . She was my countrywoman, and beautiful, and there was something—at least so I thought then—of especial sweetness in her eyes, something strong in her heart. She was engaged to a man living somewhere in the States, and she was going back to marry him. Why she was over there then I forget, and it is of no importance. I think that the man was a doctor, too—in some small city. . . . I loved her!"

The Master raised his eyes from the pool and leaning on his folded arms looked into the surgeon's face.

"I am afraid I never thought much about that other fellow—never have to this day! That was part of the brute I am—to see only what is before my eyes. And I knew by the time we had swung into the Atlantic that I wanted that woman as I had never wanted things before. She stirred me, mind and all. Of course it might have been some one else—any one you will say—and if she had been an ordinary young girl, it might have gone differently? It is one of the things we can't tell in this life. There was something in that woman that was big all through and roused the spirit in me. I never knew man or woman who thirsted more for greatness, for accomplishment. Perhaps the man she was to marry gave her little to hope for—probably it was some raw boy-and-girl affair such as we have in America. . . . The days went by, and it was clearer to both of us what must be. But we didn't speak of it. She found in me, I suppose, the power, the sort of thing she had missed in the other. I was to do all those grand things she was so hot after. I have done some of them too. But that was when she had gone and I no longer needed her. . . . I needed her then, and I took her—that is all.

"The detail is old and dim—and what do you care to hear of a young man's loves! Before we reached port it was understood between us. I told her I wanted her to leave the other chap—he was never altogether clear to me—and to marry me as soon as she could. We did not stumble or slide into it, not in the least: we looked it through and through—that was her kind and mine. How she loved to look life in the face! I have found few women who like that. . . . In the end she asked me not to come near her the last day. She would write me the day after we had landed, either yes or no. So she kissed me, and we parted still out at sea."

All the Brothers had left the court and the arcades, where they had been strolling, and old Sam was putting out the Inn lights. But the two men beside the pool made no movement. The west wind still drew in down the valley with summer warmth and ruffled the water at their feet.

"My father met me at the dock—you know he was the first surgeon at St. Jerome's before me. My mother was with him. . . . But as she kissed me I was thinking of that letter. . . . I knew it would come. Some things must! Well, it came."

The silent listener bent his head, and the surgeon mused on his passionate memory. At last the Master whispered in a low voice that hardly reached into the night:

"Did you make her happy?"

The surgeon did not answer the question at once.

"Did you make her happy?" the old man demanded again, and his voice trembled this time with such intensity that his companion looked at him wonderingly. And in those dark eyes of the Master's he read something that made him shrink away. Then for the third time the old man demanded sternly:

"Tell me—did you make her happy?"

It was the voice of one who had a right to know, and the surgeon whispered back slowly:

"Happy? No, my God! Perhaps at first, in the struggle, a little. But afterward there was too much—too many things. It went, the inspiration and the love. I broke her heart—she left me! That—that is *my* Reason!"

"It *is* the Reason! For you took all, all—you let her give all, and you gave her—what?"

"Nothing—she died."

"I know—she died."

The Master had risen, and with folded arms faced his guest, a pitying look in his eyes. The surgeon covered his face with his hands, and after a long time said:

"So you knew this?"

"Yes, I knew!"

"And knowing you let me come here. You took me into your house, you healed me, you gave me back my life!"

And the Master replied with a firm voice:

"I knew, and I gave you back your life." In a little while he explained more softly: "You and I are no longer young men who feel hotly and settle such a matter with hate. We cannot quarrel now for the possession of a woman. . . . She chose: remember that! . . . It was twenty-six years this September. We have lived our lives, you and I; we have lived out our lives, the good and the evil. Why should we now for the second time add passion to sorrow?"

"And yet knowing all you took me in!"

"Yes!" the old man cried almost proudly. "And I have made you again what you once were. . . . What *she* loved as you," he added to himself, "a man full of Power."

Then they were speechless in face of the fact: the one had taken all and the sweet love turned to acid in his heart, and the other had lost and the bitter turned to sweet! When a long time had passed the surgeon spoke timidly:

"It might have been so different for her with you! You loved her—more."

There was the light of a compassionate smile on the Master's lips as he replied:

"Yes, I loved her, too."

"And it changed things—for you!"

"It changed things. There might have been my St. Jerome's—my fame also. Instead, I came here with my boys. And here I shall die, please God."

The old Master then became silent, his face set in a dream of life, as it was, as it would have been; while the great surgeon of St. Jerome's thought such thoughts as had never passed before into his mind. The night wind had died at this late hour, and in its place there was a coldness of the turning season. The stars shone near the earth and all was silent with the peace of mysteries. The Master looked at the man beside him and said calmly:

"It is well as it is—all well!"

At last the surgeon rose and stood before the Master.

"I have learned the Secret," he said, "and now it is time for me to go."

He went up to the house through the little court and disappeared within the Inn, while the Master sat by the pool, his face graven like the face of an old man, who has seen the circle of life and understands. . . . The next morning there was much talk about Dr. Norton's disappearance, until some one explained that the surgeon had been suddenly called back to the city.

The news spread through the Brotherhood one winter that the old Inn had been burned to the ground, a bitter December night when all the water-taps were frozen. And the Master, who had grown deaf of late, had been caught in his remote chamber, and burned or rather suffocated. There were few men in the Inn at the time, it being the holiday season, and when they had fought their way to the old man's room, they found him lying on the lounge by the window, the lids fallen over the dark eyes and his face placid with sleep or contemplation. . . . They sought in vain for the reason of the fire—but why search for causes?

All those beautiful hills that we loved to watch as the evening haze gathered, the Master left in trust for the people of the State—many acres of waving forests. And the School continued in its old place, the Brothers looking after its wants and supplying it with means to continue its work. But the Inn was never rebuilt. The blackened ruins of buildings were removed and the garden in the court extended so that it covered the whole space where the Inn had stood. This was enclosed with a thick plantation of firs on all sides but that one which looked westward across the Intervale. The spot can be seen for miles around on the Albany hill side.

And when it was ready—all fragrant and radiant with flowers—they placed the Master there beside the pool, where he had loved to sit, surrounded by men. On the sunken slab his title was engraved—

THE MASTER OF THE INN

RICHARD HARDING DAVIS

The Consul

THE CONSUL

FOR over forty years, in one part of the world or another, old man Marshall had served his country as a United States consul. He had been appointed by Lincoln. For a quarter of a century that fact was his distinction. It was now his epitaph. But in former years, as each new administration succeeded the old, it had again and again saved his official head. When victorious and voracious place-hunters, searching the map of the world for spoils, dug out his hiding-place and demanded his consular sign as a reward for a younger and more aggressive party worker, the ghost of the dead President protected him. In the State Department, Marshall had become a tradition. "You can't touch HIM!" the State Department would say; "why, HE was appointed by Lincoln!" Secretly, for this weapon against the hungry head-hunters, the department was infinitely grateful. Old Man Marshall was a consul after its own heart. Like a soldier, he was obedient, disciplined; wherever he was sent, there, without question, he would go. Never against exile, against ill-health, against climate did he make complaint. Nor when he was moved on and down to make way for some ne'er-do-well with influence, with a brother-in-law in the Senate, with a cousin owning a newspaper, with rich relatives who desired him to drink himself to death at the expense of the government rather than at their own, did old man Marshall point to his record as a claim for more just treatment.

And it had been an excellent record. His official reports, in a quaint, stately hand, were models of English; full of information, intelligent, valuable, well observed. And those few of his countrymen, who stumbled upon him in the out-of-the-world places to which of late he had been banished, wrote of him to the department in terms of admiration and awe. Never had he or his friends petitioned for promotion, until it was at last apparent that, save for his record and the memory of his dead patron, he had no friends. But, still in the department the tradition held and, though he was not advanced, he was not dismissed.

"If that old man's been feeding from the public trough ever since the Civil War," protested a "practical" politician, "it seems to me, Mr. Secretary, that he's about had his share. Ain't it time he give some one else a bite? Some of us that has done the work, that has borne the brunt——"

"This place he now holds," interrupted the Secretary of State suavely, "is one hardly commensurate with services like yours. I can't pronounce the name of it, and I'm not sure just where it is, but I see that, of the last six consuls we sent there, three resigned within a month and the other three died of yellow-fever. Still, if you insist——"

The practical politician reconsidered hastily. "I'm not the sort," he protested, "to turn out a man appointed by our martyred President. Besides, he's so old now, if the fever don't catch him, he'll die of old age, anyway."

The Secretary coughed uncomfortably. "And they say," he murmured, "republics are ungrateful."

"I don't quite get that," said the practical politician.

Of Porto Banos, of the Republic of Colombia, where as consul Mr. Marshall was upholding the dignity of the United States, little could be said except that it possessed a sure harbor. When driven from the Caribbean Sea by stress of weather, the largest of ocean tramps, and even battle-ships, could find in its protecting arms of coral a safe shelter. But, as young Mr. Aiken, the wireless operator, pointed out, unless driven by a hurricane and the fear of death, no one ever visited it. Back of the ancient wharfs, that dated from the days when Porto Banos was a receiver of stolen goods for buccaneers and pirates, were rows of thatched huts, streets, according to the season, of dust or mud, a few iron-barred, jail-like barracks, customhouses, municipal buildings, and the white-washed adobe houses of the consuls. The back yard of the town was a swamp. Through this at five each morning a rusty engine pulled a train of flat cars to the base of the mountains, and, if meanwhile the rails had not disappeared into the swamp, at five in the evening brought back the flat cars laden with odorous coffee-sacks.

In the daily life of Porto Banos, waiting for the return of the train, and betting if it would return, was the chief interest. Each night the consuls, the foreign residents, the wireless operator, the manager of the rusty railroad met for dinner. There at the head of the long table, by virtue of his years, of his courtesy and distinguished manner, of his office, Mr. Marshall presided. Of the little band of exiles he was the chosen ruler. His rule was gentle. By force of example he had made existence in Porto Banos more possible. For women and children Porto Banos was a death-trap, and before "old man Marshall" came there had been no influence to remind the enforced bachelors of other days. They had lost interest, had grown lax, irritable, morose. Their white duck was seldom white. Their cheeks were unshaven. When the sun sank into the swamp and the heat still turned Porto Banos into a Turkish bath, they threw dice on the greasy tables of the Café Bolivar for drinks. The petty gambling led to petty quarrels; the drinks to fever. The coming of Mr. Marshall changed that. His standard of life, his tact, his worldly wisdom, his cheerful courtesy, his fastidious personal neatness shamed the younger men; the desire to please him, to stand well in his good opinion, brought back pride and self-esteem.

The lieutenant of her Majesty's gun-boat *Plover* noted the change.

"Used to be," he exclaimed, "you couldn't get out of the Café Bolivar without some one sticking a knife in you; now it's a debating club. They all sit round a table and listen to an old gentleman talk world politics."

If Henry Marshall brought content to the exiles of Porto Banos, there was little in return that Porto Banos could give to him. Magazines and correspondents in six languages kept him in touch with those foreign lands in which he had represented his country, but of the country he had represented, newspapers and periodicals showed him only too clearly that in forty years it had grown away from him, had changed beyond recognition.

When last he had called at the State Department, he had been made to feel he was a man without a country, and when he visited his home town in Vermont, he was looked upon as a Rip Van

Winkle. Those of his boyhood friends who were not dead had long thought of him as dead. And the sleepy, pretty village had become a bustling commercial centre. In the lanes where as a young man, he had walked among wheatfields, trolley-cars whirled between rows of mills and factories. The children had grown to manhood with children of their own.

Like a ghost, he searched for house after house, where once he had been made welcome, only to find in its place a towering office building. "All had gone, the old familiar faces." In vain he scanned even the shop fronts for a friendly, homelike name. Whether the fault was his, whether he would better have served his own interests than those of his government, it now was too late to determine. In his own home, he was a stranger among strangers. In the service he had so faithfully followed, rank by rank, he had been dropped, until now he, who twice had been a consul-general, was an exile, banished to a fever swamp. The great Ship of State had dropped him overside, had "marooned" him, and sailed away.

Twice a day he walked along the shell road to the Café Bolivar, and back again to the consulate. There, as he entered the outer office, José, the Colombian clerk, would rise and bow profoundly.

"Any papers for me to sign, José?" the consul would ask.

"Not today, Excellency," the clerk would reply. Then José would return to writing a letter to his lady-love; not that there was anything to tell her, but because writing on the official paper of the consulate gave him importance in his eyes, and in hers. And in the inner office the consul would continue to gaze at the empty harbor, the empty coral reefs, the empty, burning sky.

The little band of exiles were at second breakfast when the wireless man came in late to announce that a Red D. boat and the island of Curaçoa had both reported a hurricane coming north. Also, that much concern was felt for the safety of the yacht *Serapis*. Three days before, in advance of her coming, she had sent a wireless to Wilhelmstad, asking the captain of the port to reserve a berth for her. She expected to arrive the following morning.

But for forty-eight hours nothing had been heard from her, and it was believed she had been overhauled by the hurricane. Owing to the presence on board of Senator Hanley, the closest friend of the new President, the man who had made him president, much concern was felt at Washington. To try to pick her up by wireless, the gunboat *Newark* had been ordered from Culebra, the cruiser *Raleigh*, with Admiral Hardy on board, from Colon. It was possible she would seek shelter at Porto Banos. The consul was ordered to report.

As Marshall wrote out his answer, the French consul exclaimed with interest:

"He is of importance, then, this senator?" he asked. "Is it that in your country ships of war are at the service of a senator?"

Aiken, the wireless operator, grinned derisively.

"At the service of *this* senator, they are!" he answered. "They call him the 'king-maker,' the man behind the throne."

"But in your country," protested the Frenchman, "there is no throne. I thought your president was elected by the people?"

"That's what the people think," answered Aiken. "In God's country," he explained, "the trusts want a rich man in the Senate, with the same interests as their own, to represent them. They chose Hanley. He picked out of the candidates for the presidency the man he thought would help the interests. He nominated him, and the people voted for him. Hanley is what we call a 'boss.' "

The Frenchman looked inquiringly at Marshall.

"The position of the boss is the more dangerous," said Marshall gravely, "because it is unofficial, because there are no laws to curtail his powers. Men like Senator Hanley are a menace to good government. They see in public office only a reward for party workers."

"That's right," assented Aiken. "Your forty years' service, Mr. Consul, wouldn't count with Hanley. If he wanted your job, he'd throw you out as quick as he would a drunken cook."

Mr. Marshall flushed painfully, and the French consul hastened to interrupt.

"Then, let us pray," he exclaimed, with fervor, "that the hurricane has sunk the *Serapis*, and all on board."

Two hours later, the *Serapis*, showing she had met the hurricane and had come out second best, steamed into the harbor.

Her owner was young Herbert Livingstone, of Washington. He

once had been in the diplomatic service, and, as minister to The Hague, wished to return to it. In order to bring this about he had subscribed liberally to the party campaign fund.

With him among other distinguished persons, was the all-powerful Hanley. The kidnapping of Hanley for the cruise, in itself, demonstrated the ability of Livingstone as a diplomat. It was the opinion of many that it would surely lead to his appointment as a minister plenipotentiary. Livingstone was of the same opinion. He had not lived long in the nation's capital without observing the value of propinquity. How many men he knew were now paymasters, and secretaries of legation, solely because those high in the government met them daily at the Metropolitan Club, and preferred them in almost any other place. And if, after three weeks as his guest on board what the newspapers called his floating palace, the senator could refuse him even the prize legation of Europe, there was no value in modest merit. As yet, Livingstone had not hinted at his ambition. There was no need. To a statesman of Hanley's astuteness, the largeness of Livingstone's contribution to the campaign fund was self-explanatory.

After her wrestling-match with the hurricane, all those on board the *Serapis* seemed to find in land, even in the swamp land of Porto Banos, a compelling attraction. Before the anchors hit the water, they were in the launch. On reaching shore, they made at once for the consulate. There were many cables they wished to start on their way by wireless; cables to friends, to newspapers, to the government.

José, the Colombian clerk, appalled by the unprecedented invasion of visitors, of visitors so distinguished, and Marshall, grateful for a chance to serve his fellow-countrymen, and especially his countrywomen, were ubiquitous, eager, indispensable. At José's desk the great senator, rolling his cigar between his teeth, was using, to José's ecstasy, José's own pen to write a reassuring message to the White House. At the consul's desk a beautiful creature, all in lace and pearls, was struggling to compress the very low opinion she held of a hurricane into ten words. On his knee, Henry Cairns, the banker, was inditing instructions to his Wall Street office, and upon himself Livingstone had taken the responsibility of replying to the inquiries heaped upon Marshall's desk, from many newspapers.

It was just before sunset, and Marshall produced his tea things, and the young person in pearls and lace, who was Miss Cairns, made tea for the women, and the men mixed gin and limes with tepid water. The consul apologized for proposing a toast in which they could not join. He begged to drink to those who had escaped the perils of the sea. Had they been his oldest and nearest friends, his little speech could not have been more heart-felt and sincere. To his distress, it moved one of the ladies to tears, and in embarrassment he turned to the men.

"I regret there is no ice," he said, "but you know the rule of the tropics; as soon as a ship enters port, the ice-machine bursts."

"I'll tell the steward to send you some, sir," said Livingstone, "and as long as we're here——"

The senator showed his concern.

"As long as we're here?" he gasped.

"Not over two days," answered the owner nervously. "The chief says it will take all of that to get her in shape. As you ought to know, Senator, she was pretty badly mauled."

The senator gazed blankly out of the window. Beyond it lay the naked coral reefs, the empty sky, and the ragged palms of Porto Banos.

Livingstone felt that his legation was slipping from him.

"That wireless operator," he continued hastily, "tells me there is a most amusing place a few miles down the coast, Las Bocas, a sort of Coney Island, where the government people go for the summer. There's surf bathing and roulette and cafés chantants. He says there's some Spanish dancers—"

The guests of the *Serapis* exclaimed with interest; the senator smiled. To Marshall the general enthusiasm over the thought of a ride on a merry-go-round suggested that the friends of Mr. Livingstone had found their own society far from satisfying.

Greatly encouraged, Livingstone continued, with enthusiasm:

"And that wireless man said," he added, "that with the launch we can get there in half an hour. We might run down after dinner."

He turned to Marshall.

"Will you join us, Mr. Consul?" he asked, "and dine with us, first?"

Marshall accepted with genuine pleasure. It had been many months since he had sat at table with his own people. But he shook his head doubtfully.

"I was wondering about Las Bocas," he explained, "if your going there might not get you in trouble at the next port. With a yacht, I think it is different, but Las Bocas is under quarantine——"

There was a chorus of exclamations.

"It's not serious," Marshall explained. "There was bubonic plague there, or something like it. You would be in no danger from that. It is only that you might be held up by the regulations. Passenger steamers can't land any one who has been there at any other port of the West Indies. The English are especially strict. The Royal Mail won't even receive any one on board here without a certificate from the English consul saying he has not visited Las Bocas. For an American they would require the same guarantee from me. But I don't think the regulations extend to yachts. I will inquire. I don't wish to deprive you of any of the many pleasures of Porto Banos," he added, smiling, "but if you were refused a landing at your next port I would blame myself."

"It's all right," declared Livingstone decidedly. "It's just as you say; yachts and war-ships are exempt. Besides, I carry my own doctor, and if he won't give us a clean bill of health, I'll make him walk the plank. At eight, then, at dinner. I'll send the cutter for you. I can't give you a salute, Mr. Consul, but you shall have all the side boys I can muster."

Those from the yacht parted from their consul in the most friendly spirit.

"I think he's charming!" exclaimed Miss Cairns. "And did you notice his novels? They were in every language. It must be terribly lonely down here, for a man like that."

"He's the first of our consuls we've met on this trip," growled her father, "that we've caught sober."

"Sober!" exclaimed his wife indignantly. "He's one of the Marshalls of Vermont. I asked him."

"I wonder," mused Hanley, "how much the place is worth? Hamilton, one of the new senators, has been deviling the life out of me to send his son somewhere. Says if he stays in Washington he'll disgrace the family. I should think this place would drive any man to drink himself to death in three months, and young Hamilton, from what I've seen of him, ought to be able to do it in a week. That would leave the place open for the next man."

"There's a postmaster in my State thinks he carried it." The senator smiled grimly. "He has consumption, and wants us to give him a consulship in the tropics. I'll tell him I've seen Porto Banos, and that it's just the place for him."

The senator's pleasantry was not well received. But Miss Cairns alone had the temerity to speak of what the others were thinking.

"What would become of Mr. Marshall?" she asked.

The senator smiled tolerantly.

"I don't know that I was thinking of Mr. Marshall," he said. "I can't recall anything he has done for this administration. You see, Miss Cairns," he explained, in the tone of one addressing a small child, "Marshall has been abroad now for forty years, at the expense of the taxpayers. Some of us think men who have lived that long on their fellow-countrymen had better come home and get to work."

Livingstone nodded solemnly in assent. He did not wish a post abroad at the expense of the taxpayers. He was willing to pay for it. And then, with "ex-Minister" on his visiting cards, and a sense of duty well perfomed, for the rest of his life he could join the other expatriates in Paris.

Just before dinner, the cruiser *Raleigh* having discovered the whereabouts of the *Serapis* by wireless, entered the harbor, and Admiral Hardy came to the yacht to call upon the senator, in whose behalf he had been scouring the Caribbean Seas. Having paid his respects to that personage, the admiral fell boisterously upon Marshall.

The two old gentlemen were friends of many years. They had met, officially and unofficially, in many strange parts of the world. To each the chance reunion was a piece of tremendous good fortune. And throughout dinner, the guests of Livingstone, already bored with each other, found in them and their talk of former days new and delightful entertainment. So much so that when, Marshall having assured them that the local quarantine regulations did not extend to a yacht, the men departed for Las Bocas, the women insisted that he and the admiral remain behind.

It was for Marshall a wondrous evening. To foregather with his old friend, whom he had known since Hardy was a mad midshipman, to sit at the feet of his own charming countrywomen, to listen to their soft, modulated laughter, to note how quickly they saw that to him the evening was a great event, and with what tact each contributed to make it the more memorable; all served to wipe out the months of bitter loneliness, the stigma of failure, the sense of undeserved neglect. In the moonlight, on the cool quarter-deck, they sat, in a half-circle, each of the two friends telling tales out of school, tales of which the other was the hero or the victim, "inside" stories of great occasions, ceremonies, bombardments, unrecorded "shirt-sleeve" diplomacy.

Hardy had helped to open the Suez Canal. Marshall had assisted the Queen of Madagascar to escape from the French invaders. On the Barbary Coast Hardy had chased pirates. In Edinburgh Marshall had played chess with Carlyle. He had seen Paris in mourning in the days of the siege, Paris in terror in the days of the Commune; he had known Garibaldi, Gambetta, the younger Dumas, the creator of Pickwick.

"Do you remember that time in Tangier," the admiral urged, "when I was a midshipman, and got into the bashaw's harem?"

"Do you remember how I got you out?" Marshall replied grimly.

"And," demanded Hardy, "do you remember when Adelina Patti paid a visit to the *Kearsarge* at Marseilles in '65—George Dewey was our second officer—and you were bowing and backing away from her, and you backed into an open hatch, and she said—my French isn't up to it—what was it she said?"

"I didn't hear it," said Marshall; "I was too far down the hatch."

"Do you mean the old *Kearsarge*?" asked Mrs. Cairns. "Were you in the service then, Mr. Marshall?"

With loyal pride in his friend, the admiral answered for him:

"He was our consul-general at Marseilles!"

There was an uncomfortable moment. Even those denied imagination could not escape the contrast, could see in their mind's eye the great harbor of Marseilles, crowded with the shipping of the world, surrounding it the beautiful city, the rival of Paris to the north, and on the battle-ship the young consul-general making his bow to the young Empress of Song. And now, before their actual eyes, they saw the village of Porto Banos, a black streak in the night, a row of mud shacks, at the end of the wharf a single lantern yellow in the clear moonlight.

Later in the evening Miss Cairns led the admiral to one side.

"Admiral," she began eagerly, "tell me about your friend. Why is he here? Why don't they give him a place worthy of him? I've seen many of our representatives abroad, and I know we cannot afford to waste men like that." The girl exclaimed indignantly: "He's one of the most interesting men I've ever met! He's lived everywhere, known every one. He's a distinguished man, a cultivated man; even I can see he knows his work, that he's a diplomat, born, trained, that he's——"

The admiral interrupted with a growl.

"You don't have to tell ME about Henry," he protested. "I've known Henry twenty-five years. If Henry got his deserts," he exclaimed hotly, "he wouldn't be a consul on this coral reef; he'd be a minister in Europe. Look at me! We're the same age. We started together. When Lincoln sent him to Morocco as consul, he signed my commission as a midshipman. Now I'm an admiral. Henry has twice my brains and he's been a consul-general, and he's *here*, back at the foot of the ladder!"

"Why?" demanded the girl.

"Because the navy is a service and the consular service isn't a service. Men like Senator Hanley use it to pay their debts. While Henry's been serving his country abroad, he's lost his friends, lost his 'pull.' Those politicians up at Washington have no use for him. They don't consider that a consul like Henry can make a million dollars for his countrymen. He can keep them from shipping goods where there's no market, show them where there is a market." The admiral snorted contemptuously. "You don't have to tell ME the value of a good consul. But those politicians don't consider that. They only see that he has a job worth a few hundred dollars, and they want it, and if he hasn't other politicians to protect him, they'll take it."

The girl raised her head.

"Why don't you speak to the senator?" she asked. "Tell him you've known him for years that——"

"Glad to do it!" exclaimed the admiral heartily. "It won't be the first time. But Henry mustn't know. He's too confoundedly touchy. He hates the *idea* of influence, hates men like Hanley, who abuse it. If he thought anything was given to him except on his merits, he wouldn't take it."

"Then we won't tell him," said the girl. For a moment she hesitated.

"If I spoke to Mr. Hanley," she asked, "told him what I learned to-night of Mr. Marshall, would it have any effect?"

"Don't know how it will affect Hanley," said the sailor, "but if you asked *me* to make anybody a consul-general, I'd make him an ambassador."

Later in the evening Hanley and Livingstone were seated alone on deck. The visit to Las Bocas had not proved amusing, but, much to Livingstone's relief, his honored guest was now in good-humor. He took his cigar from his lips, only to sip at a long cool drink. He was in a mood flatteringly confidential and communicative.

"People have the strangest idea of what I can do for them," he laughed. It was his pose to pretend he was without authority. "They believe I've only to wave a wand, and get them anything they want. I thought I'd be safe from them on board a yacht."

Livingstone, in ignorance of what was coming, squirmed apprehensively.

"But it seems," the senator went on, "I'm at the mercy of a conspiracy. The women folk want me to do something for this fellow Marshall. If they had their way, they'd send him to the Court of St. James. And old Hardy, too, tackled me about him. So did Miss Cairns. And then Marshall himself got me behind the wheel-house, and I thought he was going to tell me how good he was, too! But he didn't."

As though the joke were on himself, the senator laughed appreciatively.

"Told me, instead, that Hardy ought to be a vice-admiral."

Livingstone, also, laughed, with the satisfied air of one who cannot be tricked.

"They fixed it up between them," he explained, "each was to put in a good word for the other." He nodded eagerly. "That's what *I* think."

There were moments during the cruise when Senator Hanley would have found relief in dropping his host overboard. With mock deference, the older man inclined his head.

"That's what *you* think, is it?" he asked. "Livingstone," he added, "you certainly are a great judge of men!"

The next morning, old man Marshall woke with a lightness at his heart that had been long absent. For a moment, conscious only that he was happy, he lay between sleep and waking, frowning up at his canopy of mosquito net, trying to realize what change had come to him. Then he remembered. His old friend had returned. New friends had come into his life and welcomed him kindly. He was no longer lonely. As eager as a boy, he ran to the window. He had not been dreaming. In the harbor lay the pretty yacht, the stately, white-hulled war-ship. The flag that dropped from the stern of each caused his throat to tighten, brought warm tears to his eyes, fresh resolve to his discouraged, troubled spirit. When he knelt beside his bed, his heart poured out his thanks in gratitude and gladness.

While he was dressing, a blue-jacket brought a note from the admiral. It invited him to tea on board the war-ship, with the guests of the *Serapis*. His old friend added that he was coming to lunch with his consul, and wanted time reserved for a long talk. The consul agreed gladly. He was in holiday humor. The day promised to repeat the good moments of the night previous.

At nine o'clock, through the open door of the consulate, Marshall saw Aiken, the wireless operator, signalling from the wharf excitedly to the yacht, and a boat leave the ship and return. Almost immediately the launch, carrying several passengers, again made the trip shoreward.

Half an hour later, Senator Hanley, Miss Cairns, and Livingstone came up the water-front, and entering the consulate, seated themselves around Marshall's desk. Livingstone was sunk in melancholy. The senator, on the contrary, was smiling broadly. His manner was one of distinct relief. He greeted the consul with hearty good-humor.

"I'm ordered home!" he announced gleefully. Then, remembering the presence of Livingstone, he hastened to add: "I needn't say how sorry I am to give up my yachting trip, but orders are orders. The President," he explained to Marshall, "cables me this morning to come back and take my coat off."

The prospect, as a change from playing bridge on a pleasure boat, seemed far from depressing him.

"Those filibusters in the Senate," he continued genially, "are making trouble again. They think they've got me out of the way for another month, but they'll find they're wrong. When that bill comes up, they'll find me at the old stand and ready for business!" Marshall did not attempt to conceal his personal disappointment.

"I am so sorry you are leaving," he said; "selfishly sorry, I mean. I'd hoped you all would be here for several days."

He looked inquiringly toward Livingstone.

"I understood the *Serapis* was disabled," he explained.

"She is," answered Hanley. "So's the *Raleigh*. At a pinch, the admiral might have stretched the regulations and carried me to Jamaica, but the *Raleigh's* engines are knocked about too. I've *got* to reach Kingston Thursday. The German boat leaves there Thursday for New York. At first it looked as though I couldn't do it, but we find that the *Royal Mail* is due to-day, and she can get to Kingston Wednesday night. It's a great piece of luck. I wouldn't bother you with my troubles," the senator explained pleasantly, "but the agent of the *Royal Mail* here won't sell me a ticket until you've put your seal to this."

He extended a piece of printed paper.

As Hanley had been talking, the face of the consul had grown grave. He accepted the paper, but did not look at it. Instead, he regarded the senator with troubled eyes. When he spoke, his tone was one of genuine concern.

"It is most unfortunate," he said. "But I am afraid the *Royal Mail* will not take you on board. Because of Las Bocas," he explained. "If we had only known!" he added remorsefully. "It is *most* unfortunate."

"Because of Las Bocas?" echoed Hanley. "You don't mean they'll refuse to take me to Jamaica because I spent half an hour at the end of a wharf listening to a squeaky gramophone?"

"The trouble," explained Marshall, "is this: if they carried you, all the other passengers would be held in quarantine for ten days, and there are fines to pay, and there would be difficulties over the mails. But," he added hopefully, "maybe the regulations have been altered. I will see her captain, and tell him——"

"See her captain!" objected Hanley. "Why see the captain? He doesn't know I've been to that place. Why tell *him*? All I need is a clean bill of health from you. That's all HE wants. You have only to sign that paper."

Marshall regarded the senator with surprise.

"But I can't," he said.

"You can't? Why not?"

"Because it certifies to the fact that you have not visited Las Bocas. Unfortunately, you have visited Las Bocas."

The senator had been walking up and down the room. Now he seated himself, and stared at Marshall curiously.

"It's like this, Mr. Marshall," he began quietly. "The President desires my presence in Washington, thinks I can be of some use to him there in helping carry out certain party measures—measures to which he pledged himself before his election. Down here, a British steamship line has laid down local rules which, in my case anyway, are ridiculous. The question is, are you going to be bound by the red tape of a ha'penny British colony, or by your oath to the President of the United States?"

The sophistry amused Marshall. He smiled good-naturedly and shook his head.

"I'm afraid, Senator," he said, "that way of putting it is hardly fair. Unfortunately, the question is one of fact. I will explain to the captain——"

"You will explain nothing to the captain!" interrupted Hanley. "This is a matter which concerns no one but our two selves. I am not asking favors of steamboat captains. I am asking an American consul to assist an American citizen in trouble, and," he added, with heavy sarcasm, "incidentally, to carry out the wishes of his President."

Marshall regarded the senator with an expression of both surprise and disbelief.

"Are you asking me to put my name to what is not so?" he said. "Are you serious?"

"That paper, Mr. Marshall," returned Hanley steadily, "is a mere form, a piece of red tape. There's no more danger of my carrying the plague to Jamaica than of my carrying a dynamite bomb. You *know* that."

"I *do* know that," assented Marshall heartily. "I appreciate your position, and I regret it exceedingly. You are the innocent victim of a regulation which is a wise regulation, but which is most unfair to you. My own position," he added, "is not important, but you can believe me, it is not easy. It is certainly no pleasure for me to be unable to help you."

Hanley was leaning forward, his hands on his knees, his eyes watching Marshall closely.

"Then you refuse?" he said. "Why?"

Marshall regarded the senator steadily. His manner was untroubled. The look he turned upon Hanley was one of grave disapproval.

"You know why," he answered quietly. "It is impossible."

In sudden anger Hanley rose. Marshall, who had been seated behind his desk, also rose. For a moment, in silence, the two men confronted each other. Then Hanley spoke; his tone was harsh and threatening.

"Then I am to understand," he exclaimed, "that you refuse to carry out the wishes of a United States Senator and of the President of the United States?"

In front of Marshall, on his desk, was the little iron stamp of the consulate. Protectingly, almost caressingly, he laid his hand upon it.

"I refuse," he corrected, "to place the seal of this consulate on a lie."

There was a moment's pause. Miss Cairns, unwilling to remain, and unable to withdraw, clasped her hands unhappily and stared at the floor. Livingstone exclaimed in indignant protest. Hanley moved a step nearer and, to emphasize what he said, tapped his knuckles on the desk. With the air of one confident of his advantage, he spoke slowly and softly.

"Do you appreciate," he asked, "that, while you may be of some importance down here in this fever swamp, in Washington I am supposed to carry some weight? Do you appreciate that I am a senator from a State that numbers four millions of people, and that you are preventing me from serving those people?"

Marshall inclined his head gravely and politely.

"And I want you to appreciate," he said, "that while I have no weight at Washington, in this fever swamp I have the honor to represent eighty millions of people, and as long as that consular sign is over my door I don't intend to prostitute it for *you*, or the President of the United States, or any one of those eighty millions."

Of the two men, the first to lower his eyes was Hanley. He laughed shortly, and walked to the door. There he turned, and indifferently, as though the incident no longer interested him, drew out his watch.

"Mr. Marshall," he said, "if the cable is working, I'll take your tin sign away from you by sunset."

For one of Marshall's traditions, to such a speech there was no answer save silence. He bowed, and, apparently serene and undismayed, resumed his seat. From the contest, judging from the manner of each, it was Marshall, not Hanley, who had emerged victorious.

But Miss Cairns was not deceived. Under the unexpected blow, Marshall had turned older. His clear blue eyes had grown less alert, his broad shoulders seemed to stoop. In sympathy, her own eyes filled with sudden tears.

"What will you do?" she whispered.

"I don't know what I shall do," said Marshall simply. "I should have liked to have resigned. It's a prettier finish. After forty years—to be dismissed by cable is—it's a poor way of ending it."

Miss Cairns rose and walked to the door. There she turned and looked back.

"I am sorry," she said. And both understood that in saying no more than that she had best shown her sympathy.

An hour later the sympathy of Admiral Hardy was expressed more directly.

"If he comes on board my ship," roared that gentleman, "I'll push him down an ammunition hoist and break his damned neck!"

Marshall laughed delightedly. The loyalty of his old friend was never so welcome.

"You'll treat him with every courtesy," he said. "The only satisfaction he gets out of this is to see that he has hurt me. We will not give him that satisfaction."

But Marshall found that to conceal his wound was more difficult than he had anticipated. When, at tea time, on the deck of the war-ship, he again met Senator Hanley and the guests of the *Serapis*, he could not forget that his career had come to an end. There was much to remind him that this was so. He was made aware of it by the sad, sympathetic glances of the women; by their tactful courtesies; by the fact that Livingstone, anxious to propitiate Hanley, treated him rudely; by the sight of the young officers, each just starting upon a career of honor, and possible glory, as his career ended in humiliation; and by the big war-ship herself, that recalled certain crises when he had only to press a button and war-ships had come at his bidding.

At five o'clock there was an awkward moment. The Royal Mail boat, having taken on her cargo, passed out of the harbor on her way to Jamaica, and dipped her colors. Senator Hanley, abandoned to his fate, observed her departure in silence.

Livingstone, hovering at his side, asked sympathetically:

"Have they answered your cable, sir?"

"They have," said Hanley gruffly.

"Was it—was it satisfactory?" pursued the diplomat.

"It *was*," said the senator, with emphasis.

Far from discouraged, Livingstone continued his inquiries.

"And when," he asked eagerly, "are you going to tell him?"

"Now!" said the senator.

The guests were leaving the ship. When all were seated in the admiral's steam launch, the admiral descended the accommodation ladder and himself picked up the tiller ropes.

"Mr. Marshall," he called, "when I bring the launch broadside to the ship and stop her, you will stand ready to receive the consul's salute."

Involuntarily, Marshall uttered an exclamation of protest. He had forgotten that on leaving the war-ship, as consul, he was entitled to seven guns. Had he remembered, he would have insisted that the ceremony be omitted. He knew that the admiral wished to show his loyalty, knew that his old friend was now paying him this honor only as a rebuke to Hanley. But the ceremony was no longer an honor. Hanley had made of it a mockery. It served only to emphasize what had been taken from him. But, without a scene, it now was too late to avoid it. The first of the seven guns had roared from the bow, and, as often he had stood before, as never he would so stand again, Marshall took his place at the gangway of the launch. His eyes were fixed on the flag, his gray head was uncovered, his hat was pressed above his heart.

For the first time since Hanley had left the consulate, he fell into sudden terror lest he might give way to his emotions. Indignant at the thought, he held himself erect. His face was set like a mask, his eyes were untroubled. He was determined they should not see that he was suffering.

Another gun spat out a burst of white smoke, a stab of flame. There was an echoing roar. Another and another followed. Marshall counted seven, and then, with a bow to the admiral, backed from the gangway.

And then another gun shattered the hot, heavy silence. Marshall, confused, embarrassed, assuming he had counted wrong, hastily returned to his place. But again before he could leave it, in savage haste a ninth gun roared out its greeting. He could not still be mistaken. He turned appealingly to his friend. The eyes of the admiral were fixed upon the war-ship. Again a gun shattered the silence. Was it a jest? Were they laughing at him? Marshall flushed miserably. He gave a swift glance toward the others. They were smiling. Then it *was* a jest. Behind his back, something of which they all were cognizant was going forward. The face of Livingstone alone betrayed a like bewilderment to his own. But the others, who knew, were mocking him.

For the thirteenth time a gun shook the brooding swamp land of Porto Banos. And then, and not until then, did the flag crawl slowly from the mast-head. Mary Cairns broke the tenseness by bursting into tears. But Marshall saw that every one else, save she and Livingstone, were still smiling. Even the bluejackets in charge of the launch were grinning at him. He was beset by smiling faces. And then from the war-ship, unchecked, came, against all regulations, three long, splendid cheers.

Marshall felt his lips quivering, the warm tears forcing their way to his eyes. He turned beseechingly to his friend. His voice trembled.

"Charles," he begged, "are they laughing at me?"

Eagerly, before the other could answer, Senator Hanley tossed his cigar into the water and, scrambling forward, seized Marshall by the hand.

"Mr. Marshall," he cried, "our President has great faith in Abraham Lincoln's judgment of men. And this salute means that this morning he appointed you our new minister to The Hague. I'm one of those politicians who keeps his word. I told you I'd take your tin sign away from you by sunset. I've done it!"

MARY RAYMOND SHIPMAN ANDREWS

The Counsel Assigned

THE COUNSEL ASSIGNED

A VERY old man told the story. Some twenty years ago, on a night in March, he walked down the bright hallway of a hotel in Bermuda, a splendid old fellow, straight and tall; an old man of a haughty, high-bridged Roman nose, of hawklike, brilliant eyes, of a thick thatch of white hair; a distinguished person, a personage, to the least observing; not unconscious possibly, as he stalked serenely toward the office, of the eyes that followed. An American stood close as the older man lighted his cigar at the office lamp; a red book was in his hand.

"That's a pretty color," the old fellow said in the assured tone of one who had always found his smallest remarks worth while.

The American handed it to him. As he turned over the leaves he commented with the same free certainty of words, and then the two fell to talking. Cigars in hand they strolled out on the veranda hanging over the blue waters of the bay, which rolled up unceasing music. There was a dance; a band played in the ballroom; girls in light dresses and officers in the scarlet jackets or the blue and gold of the British army and navy poured past.

The old man gazed at them vaguely and smiled as one might at a field of wind-blown daisies, and talked on. He told of events, travels, adventures—experiences which had made up an important and interesting life—a life spent partly, it appeared, in the United States, partly in Canada, where he was now a member of the Dominion Parliament. His enthusiasm, it developed, was for his profession, the law. The hesitating, deep voice lost its weakness, the dark eyes flashed youthfully, as he spoke of great lawyers, of legal *esprit de corps.*

"It's nonsense"—the big, thin, scholarly fist banged the chair arm—"this theory that the law tends to make men sordid. I'm not denying that there are bad lawyers. The Lord has given into each man's hand the ultimate shaping of his career; whatever the work, he can grasp it by its bigness or its pettiness, according to his nature. Doctors look after men's bodies and parsons after their souls; there's an opinion that lawyers are created to keep an eye on the purses. But it seems to me"—the bright old eyes gazed off into the scented darkness of the southern night—"it seems to me otherwise. It seems to me that the right lawyer, with his mind trained into a clean, flexible instrument, as it should be, has his specialty in both fields. I am a very old man; I have seen many fine deeds done on the earth, and I can say that I have not known either heroic physicians or saintly ministers of God go beyond what I've known of men of my own calling. In fact——"

The bright end of the cigar burned a red hole in the velvet darkness, the old man's Roman profile cut against the lighted window, and he was silent. He went on in his slow, authoritative voice:

"In fact, I may say that the finest deed I've known was the performance of a lawyer acting in his professional capacity."

With that he told this story:

The chairman of the county committee stopped at the open door of the office. The nominee for Congress was deep in a letter, and, unpretentious as were the ways of the man, one considered his convenience; one did not interrupt. The chairman halted and, waiting, regarded at leisure the face frowning over the paper. A vision came to him, in a flash, of mountain cliffs he had seen—rocky, impregnable, unchangeable; seamed with lines of outer weather and inner torment; lonely and grim, yet lovely with gentle things that grow and bloom. This man's face was like that; it stood for stern uprightness; it shifted and changed as easily as the shadows change across ferns and young birches on a crag; deep within were mines of priceless things. Not so definitely, but yet so shaped, the simile came to the chairman; he had an admiration for his Congressional candidate.

The candidate folded the letter and put it in his pocket; he swung about in his office chair. "Sorry to keep you waiting, Tom. I was trying to figure out how a man can be in two places at once."

"If you get it, let me know," the other threw back. "We've a use for that trick right now. You're wanted to make another speech Friday night."

The big man in the chair crossed his long legs and looked at his manager meditatively. "I didn't get it quite figured," he said slowly. "That's my trouble. I can't make the speech here Friday."

"Can't make—your speech! You don't mean that. You're joking. Oh I see—of course you're joking."

The man in the chair shook his head. "Not a bit of it." He got up and began to stride about the room with long, lounging steps. The chairman, excited at the mere suggestion of failure in the much-advertised speech, flung remonstrances after him.

"Cartright is doing too well—he's giving deuced good talk, and he's at it every minute; he might beat us yet you know; it won't do to waste a chance—election's too near. Cartright's swearing that you're an atheist and an aristocrat—you've got to knock that out."

The large figure stopped short, and a queer smile twisted the big mouth and shone in the keen, visionary eyes. "An atheist and an aristocrat!" he repeated. "The Lord help me!"

Then he sat down and for ten minutes talked a vivid flood of words. At the end of ten minutes the listener had no doubts as to the nominee's interest in the fight, or his power to win it. The harsh, deep voice stopped; there was a pause which held, from some undercurrent of feeling, a dramatic quality.

"We'll win!" he cried. "We'll win, and without the Friday speech. I can't tell you why, Tom, and I'd rather not be asked, but I can't make that speech here Friday." The candidate had concluded—and it was concluded.

Travelling in those days was not a luxurious business. There were few railways; one drove or rode, or one walked. The candidate was poor, almost as day laborers are poor now. Friday morning at daybreak his tall figure stepped through the silent streets of the western city before the earliest risers were about. He swung along the roads, through woodland and open country, moving rapidly and with the tireless ease of strong, accustomed muscles. He went through villages. Once a woman busy with her cows gave him a cup of warm milk. Once he sat down on a log and ate food from a package wrapped in paper, which he took from his pocket. Except for those times he did not stop, and nine o'clock found him on the outskirts of a straggling town, twenty miles from his starting-point.

The court-house was a wooden building with a cupola, with a front veranda of Doric pillars. The door stood wide to the summer morning. Court was already in session. The place was crowded, for there was to be a murder trial to-day. The Congressional candidate, unnoticed, stepped inside and sat by the door in the last row of seats.

It was a crude interior of white walls, of unpainted woodwork, of pine floors and wooden benches. The Franklin stove which heated it in winter stood there yet, its open mouth showing dead ashes of the last March fire; its yards of stovepipe ran a zigzag overhead. The newcomer glanced about at this stage-setting as if familiar with the type. A larceny case was being tried. The man listened closely and seemed to study lawyers and Judge; he was interested in the comments of the people near him. The case being ended, another was called. A man was to be tried this time for assault; the stranger in the back seat missed no word. This case, too, came to a close. The District Attorney rose and moved the trial of John Wilson for murder.

There was a stir through the court-room, and people turned on the hard benches and faced toward the front door, the one entrance. In the doorway appeared the Sheriff leading a childish figure, a boy of fifteen dressed in poor, home-made clothes, with a conspicuous bright head of golden hair. He was pale, desperately frightened; his eyes gazed on the floor. Through the packed crowd the Sheriff brought this shrinking, halting creature till he stood before the Judge inside the bar. The Judge, a young man, faced the criminal, and there was a pause. It seemed to the stranger, watching from his seat by the door, that the Judge was steadying himself against a pitiful sight.

At length: "Have you counsel?" the Judge demanded.

A shudder shook the slim shoulders; there was no other answer.

The Judge repeated the question, in no unkind manner. "Have you a lawyer?" he asked.

The lad's lips moved a minute before one heard anything; then he brought out, "I dunno—what that is."

"A lawyer is a man to see that you get your rights. Have you a lawyer?"

The lad shook his unkempt yellow head. "No. I dunno—anybody. I hain't got—money—to pay."

"Do you wish the court to assign you counsel?" He was unconscious that the familiar technical terms were an unknown tongue to the lad gasping before him. With that, through the stillness came a sound of a boot that scraped the floor. The man in the back seat rose, slouched forward, stood before the Judge.

"May it please your Honor," he said, "I am a lawyer. I should be glad to act as counsel for the defence."

The Judge looked at him a moment; there was something uncommon in this loose-hung figure towering inches above six feet; there was power. The Judge looked at him. "What is your name?" he asked.

The man answered quietly: "Abraham Lincoln."

A few men here and there glanced at the big lawyer again; this was the person who was running for Congress. That was all. A tall, gaunt man, in common clothes gave his name. Frontier farmers and backwoodsmen in homespun jeans, some of them with buckskin breeches, most in their shirt-sleeves, women in calico and sunbonnets, sat about and listened. Nobody saw more. Nobody dreamed that the name spoken and heard was to fill one of the great places in history.

The Judge, who had lived in large towns and learned to classify humanity a bit, alone placed the lawyer as outside the endless procession of the average. Moreover, he had heard of him. "I know your name, Mr. Lincoln; I shall be glad to assign you to defend the prisoner," he answered.

The jury was drawn. Man after man, giving his name, and, being questioned by the District Attorney, came under the scrutiny of the deep eyes under the overhanging brows—eyes keen, dreamy, sad, humorous; man after man, those eyes of Lincoln's sought out the character of each. But he challenged no one. The District Attorney examined each. The lawyer for the defence examined none; he accepted them all. The hard-faced audience began to glance at him impatiently. The feeling was against the prisoner, yet they wished to see some fight made for him; they wanted a play of swords. There was no excitement in looking at a giant who sat still in his chair.

The District Attorney opened the case for the People. He told with few words the story of the murder. The prisoner had worked on the farm of one Amos Berry in the autumn before, in 1845. On this farm was an Irishman, Shaughnessy by name. He amused himself by worrying the boy, and the boy came to hate him. He kept out of his way, yet the older man continued to worry him. On the 28th of October the boy was to drive a wagon of hay to the next farm. At the gate of the barn-yard he met Shaughnessy with Berry and two other men. The boy asked Berry to open the gate, and Berry was about to do it when Shaughnessy spoke. The boy was lazy he said—let him get down and open the gate himself. Berry hesitated, laughing at Shaughnessy, and the Irishman caught the pitchfork which the lad held and pricked him with it and ordered him to get down. The lad sprang forward, and, snatching back the pitchfork, flew at the Irishman and ran one of the prongs into his skull. The man died in an hour. The boy had been thrown into jail and had lain there nine months awaiting trial. This was the story.

By now it was the dinner hour—twelve o'clock. The court adjourned and the Judge and the lawyers went across the street to the tavern, a two-story house with long verandas; the audience scattered to be fed, many dining on the grass from lunches brought with them, for a murder trial is a gala day in the backwoods, and people make long journeys to see the show.

One lawyer was missing at the tavern. The Judge and the attorneys wondered where he was, for though this was not the eighth circuit, where Abraham Lincoln practised, yet his name was known here. Lawyers of the eighth circuit had talked about his gift of story telling; these men wanted to hear him tell stories. But the big man had disappeared and nobody had been interested enough to notice as he passed down the shady street with a very little, faded woman in shabby clothes; a woman who had sat in a dark corner of the court-room crying silently, who had stolen forward and spoken a timid word to Lincoln. With her he turned into one of the poorest houses of the town and had dinner with her and her cousin, the carpenter, and his family.

"That's the prisoner's mother," a woman whispered when, an

hour later, court opened again, and the defendant's lawyer came up the steps with the forlorn little woman and seated her very carefully before he went forward to his place.

The District Attorney, in his shirt sleeves, in a chair tipped against the wall, called and examined witnesses. Proof was made of the location; the place was described; eye-witnesses testified to the details of the crime. There appeared to be no possible doubt of the criminal's guilt.

The lad sat huddled, colorless from his months in jail, sunk now in an apathy—a murderer at fifteen. Men on the jury who had hardy, honest boys of their own at home frowned at him, and more than one, it may be, considered that a monster of this sort would be well removed. Back in her dark corner the shabby woman sat quiet.

The sultry afternoon wore on. Outside the open windows a puff of wind moved branches of trees now and then, but hardly a breath came inside; it was hot, wearisome, but yet the crowd stayed. These were people who had no theatres; it was a play to listen to the District Attorney drawing from one witness after another the record of humiliation and rage, culminating in murder. It was excitement to watch the yellow-haired child on trial for his life; it was an added thrill for those who knew the significance of her presence, to turn and stare at the thin woman cowering in her seat, shaking with that continual repressed crying. All this was too good to lose, so the crowd stayed. Ignorant people are probably not wilfully cruel; probably they like to watch suffering as a small boy watches the animal he tortures—from curiosity, without a sense of its reality. The poor are notoriously kind to each other, yet it is the poor, the masses, who throng the murder trials and executions.

The afternoon wore on. The District Attorney's nasal voice rose and fell examining witnesses. But the big lawyer sitting there did not satisfy people. He did not cross-examine one witness, he did not make one objection even to statements very damaging to his client. He scrutinized the Judge and the jury. One might have said that he was studying the character of each man; till at length the afternoon had worn to an end, and the District Attorney had examined the last witness and had risen and said: "The People rest." That side of the case was finished, and court adjourned for supper, to reopen at 7.30 in the evening.

Before the hour the audience had gathered. It was commonly said that the boy was doomed; no lawyer, even a "smart" man, could get him off after such testimony, and the current opinion was that the big hulking fellow could not be a good lawyer or he would have put a spoke in the wheel for his client before this. The sentiment ran in favor of condemnation; to have killed a man at fifteen showed depravity which was best put out of the way. Stern, narrow—the hard-living men and women of the backwoods set their thin lips into this sentence; yet down inside each one beat a heart capable of generous warmth if only the way to it were found, if a finger with a sure touch might be laid on the sealed gentleness.

Court opened. Not a seat was empty. The small woman in her worn calico dress sat forward this time, close to the bar. A few feet separated her from her son. The lawyers took their places. The Sheriff had brought in the criminal. The Judge entered. And then Abraham Lincoln stalked slowly up through the silent benches, and paused as he came to the prisoner. He laid a big hand on the thin shoulder, and the lad started nervously. Lincoln bent from his great height.

"Don't you be scared, sonny," he said quietly, but yet everyone heard every word. "I'm going to pull you out of this hole. Try to be plucky for your mother's sake."

And the boy lifted his blue, young eyes for the first time and glanced over to the shabby woman, and she met his look with a difficult smile, and he tried to smile back. The audience saw the effort of each for the other; the Judge saw it; and the jury—and Lincoln's keen eyes, watching ever under the heavy brows, caught a spasm of pity in more than one face. He took off his coat and folded it on the back of his chair and stood in his shirt sleeves. He stood, a man of the people in look and manner; a comfortable sense pervaded the spectators that what he was going to say they were going to understand. The room was still.

"Gentlemen of the Jury," began Abraham Lincoln, standing in his shirt sleeves before the court, "I am going to try this case in a manner not customary in courts. I am not going to venture to cross the tracks of the gentleman who has tried it for the prosecution. I shall not call witnesses; the little prisoner over there is all the witness I want. I shall not argue; I shall beseech you to make the argument for yourselves. All I'm going to do is to tell you a story and show you how it connects with this case, and then leave the case in your hands."

There was a stir through the court-room. The voice, rasping, unpleasant at first, went on:

"You, Jim Beck—you, Jack Armstrong——"

People jumped; these were the names of neighbors and friends which this stranger used. His huge knotted forefinger singled out two in the jury.

"You two can remember—yes, and you as well, Luke Green—fifteen years back, in 1831, when a long, lank fellow in God-forsaken clothes came into this country from Indiana. His appearance, I dare to say, was so striking that those who saw him haven't forgotten him. He was dressed in blue homespun jeans. His feet were in rawhide boots, and the breeches were stuffed into the tops of them most of the time. He had a soft hat which had started life as black, but had sunburned till it was a combine of colors. Gentlemen of the Jury, I think some of you will remember those clothes and that young man. His name was Abraham Lincoln."

The gaunt speaker paused and pushed up his sleeves a bit, and the jurymen saw the hairy wrists and the muscles of hand and forearm. Yes, they remembered the young giant who had been champion in everything that meant physical strength. They sat tense.

"The better part of a man's life consists of his friendships," the strong voice went on, and the eyes softened as if looking back over a long road travelled. "There are good friends to be found in these parts; that young fellow in blue jeans had a few. It is about a family who befriended him that I am going to tell you. The boy Abraham Lincoln left his father, who was, as all know, a man in the humblest walk of life, and at twenty-two he undertook to shift for himself. There were pretty pinching times along then, and Abraham could not always get work. One fall afternoon, when he had been walking miles on a journey westward to look for a chance, it grew late, and he realized suddenly that unless he should run across a house he would have to sleep out. With that he heard an axe ring and came upon a cabin. It was a poor cabin even as settlers' cabins go. There was cloth over the windows instead of glass; there was only one room, and a little window above which told of a loft. Abraham strode on to the cabin hopefully. The owner, a strong fellow with yellow hair, came up, axe in hand, and of him the young man asked shelter." Again the voice paused and a smile flashed which told of a pleasant memory.

"Gentlemen of the Jury, no king ever met a fellow-monarch with a finer welcome. Everything he had, the wood-chopper told Abraham, was his. The man brought the tired boy inside. The door was only five feet high and the young fellow had to stoop some to get in. Two children of five or six were playing, and a little woman was singing the baby to sleep by the fire. The visitor climbed up a ladder to the loft after supper.

"He crawled down next morning, and when he had done a few chores to help, he bethought himself to take advice from the wood-chopper. He asked if there were jobs to be got. The man said yes; if he could chop and split rails there was enough to do. Now Abraham had had an axe put into his hands at eight years, and had dropped it since only long enough to eat meals. 'I can do that,' he said.

" 'Do you like to work?' the woodsman asked.

"Abraham had to tell him that he wasn't a hand to pitch into work like killing snakes, but yet—well, the outcome of it was that he stayed and proved that he could do a man's job."

A whispered word ran from one to another on the benches—they began to remember now the youngster who could outlift, outwork and outwrestle any man in the county. The big lawyer saw, and a gleam of gratification flashed; he was proud always of his physical strength. He went on:

"For five weeks Abraham lived in the cabin. The family character became as familiar to him as his own. He chopped with the father, did housework with the mother, and tended Sonny, the baby, many a time. To this day the man has a clear memory of that golden-haired baby laughing as the big lad rolled him about the uneven floor. He came to know the stock, root and branch, and can vouch for it.

"When he went away they refused to take money. No part of his life has ever been more light-hearted or happier. Does anybody here think that any sacrifice which Abraham Lincoln could make in after life would be too great to show his gratitude to those people?"

He shot the question at the jury, at the Judge, and, turning, brought the crowded court-room into its range. A dramatic silence answered. The tiny woman's dim eyes stared at him, dilated. The boy's bright, sunken head had lifted a little and his thin fingers had caught at a chair at arm's length, and clutched it. The lawyer picked up his coat from where he had laid it, and, while every eye in the court-room watched him, he fumbled in a pocket, unhurried, and brought out a bit of letter-paper. Holding it, he spoke again:

"The young man who had come under so large a weight of obligation prospered in later life. By hard work, by good fortune, by the blessing of God, he made for himself a certain place in the community. As much as might be, he has—I have—kept in touch with those old friends, yet in the stress of a very busy life I have not of late years heard from them. Till last Monday morning this"—he held up the letter—"this came to me in Springfield. It is a letter from the mother who sat by the fire in that humble cabin and gave a greeting to the wandering, obscure youth which Abraham Lincoln, please God, will not forget—not in this world, not when the hand of death has set his soul free of another. The woodsman died years ago, the two older children followed him. The mother who sang to her baby that afternoon"—he swept about and his long arm and knotted finger pointed, as he towered above the court-room, to the meek, small woman shrinking on the front seat—"the mother is there."

The arm dropped; his luminous eyes shone on the boy criminal's drooping golden head; in the court-room there was no one who did not hear each low syllable of the sentence which followed.

"The baby is the prisoner at the bar."

In the hot crowded place one caught a gasp from back by the

door; one heard a woman's dress rustle, and a man clear his throat—and that was all.

There was silence, and the counsel for the defence let it alone to do his work. From the figure which loomed above the rude company virtue went out and worked a magic. The silence which stretched from the falling of Lincoln's voice; which he let stretch on—and on; which he held to its insistent witchcraft when every soul in the court-room began to feel it as personally harassing; this long silence shaped the minds before him as words could not. Lincoln held the throng facing their own thoughts, facing the story he had told, till all over the room men and women were shuffling, sighing, distressed with the push and the ferment of that silence.

At the crucial moment the frayed ends of the nerves of the audience were gathered up as the driver of a four-in-hand gathers up the reins of his fractious horses. The voice of the defendant's lawyer sounded over the throng.

"Many times, as I have lain wakeful in the night," he spoke as if reflecting aloud, "many times I have remembered those weeks of unfailing kindness from those poor people, and have prayed God to give me a chance to show my gratefulness. When the letter came last Monday calling for help, I knew that God had answered. An answer to prayer comes sometimes with a demand for sacrifice. It was so. The culminating moment of years of ambition for me was to have been to-night. I was to have made to-night a speech which bore, it is likely, success or failure in a contest. I lay that ambition, that failure, if the event so prove it, gladly on the altar of this boy's safety. It is for you"—his strong glance swept the jury—"to give him that safety. Gentlemen of the Jury, I said when I began that I should try this case in a manner not customary. I said I had no argument to set before you. I believe, as you are all men with human hearts, as some of you are fathers with little fellows of your own at home—I believe that you need no argument. I have told the story; you know the stock of which the lad comes; you know that at an age when his hands should have held school-books or fishing-rod, they held—because he was working for his mother—the man's tool which was his undoing; you know now the child was goaded by a grown man till in desperation he used that tool at hand. You know these things as well as I do. All I ask is that you deal with the little fellow as you would have other men deal in such a case with those little fellows at home. I trust his life to that test. Gentlemen of the Jury, I rest my case."

And Abraham Lincoln sat down.

A little later, when the time came, the jury filed out and crossed to a room in the hotel opposite. The boy stayed. Some of the lawyers went to the hotel bar-room, some stood about on the ground under the trees; but many stayed in the court-room, and all were waiting, watching for a sound from the men shut up across the way. Then, half an hour had passed, and there was a bustle, and people who had gone out crowded back. The worn small woman in the front row clasped her thin hands tight together.

The jury filed in and sat down on the shaky benches, and answered as their names were called, and rose and stood.

"Gentlemen of the Jury," the clerk's voice spoke monotonously, "have you agreed upon a verdict?"

"We have," the foreman answered firmly, woodenly, and the men and women thrilled at the conventional two syllables. They meant life or death, those two syllables.

"What is your verdict, guilty or not guilty?"

For a second, perhaps, no one breathed in all that packed mass. The small woman glared palely at the foreman; every eye watched him. Did he hesitate? Only the boy, sitting with his golden head down, seemed not to listen.

"Not guilty," said the foreman.

With that there was pandemonium. Men shouted, stamped, waved, tossed up their hats; women sobbed; one or two screamed with wild joy. Abraham Lincoln saw the slim body of the prisoner fall forward; with two strides he had caught him up in his great arms, and, lifting him like a baby, passed him across the bar into the arms, into the lap, of the woman who caught him, rocked him, kissed him. They all saw that, and with instinctive, unthinking sympathy the whole room surged toward her; but Lincoln stood guard and pushed off the crowd.

"The boy's fainted," he said loudly. "Give him air." And then, with a smile that beamed over each one of them there, "She's got her baby—it's all right, friends. But somebody bring a drink of water for Sonny."

The American, holding a cigar that had gone out, was silent. The old man spoke again, as if vindicating himself, as if answering objections from the other.

"Of course such a thing could not happen to-day," he said. "It could not have happened then in eastern courts. Only a Lincoln could have carried it off anywhere, it may be. But he knew his audience and the jury, and his genius measured the character of the Judge. It happened. It is a fact."

The American drew a long breath. "I have not doubted you, sir," he said. "I could not speak because—because your story touched me. Lincoln is our hero. It goes deep to hear of a thing like that." He hesitated and glanced curiously at the old man. "May I ask how you came by the story? You told it with a touch of—intimacy—almost as if you had been there. Is it possible that you were in that court-room?"

The bright, dark eyes of the very old man flashed hawklike as he turned his aquiline, keen face toward the questioner; he smiled with an odd expression, only partly as if at the stalwart, up-to-date American before him, more as if smiling back half a century to faces long ago dust.

"I was the Judge," he said.

JAMES BRENDAN CONNOLLY

The Trawler

James Brendan Connolly (1868–)

THE AUTHOR OF Out of Gloucester *will always hold high rank in the select company who have written well of ships, the sea, and sailormen. His best stories have a powerful, emotional impact, but they are never sentimental; neither do they rely on intricacies of plot. Mr. Connolly's simplicity of technique is the simplicity of art. The enthusiastic critic who described J. B. Connolly as the "nearest thing to Homer in our time," may have been guilty of a little exaggeration but one gathers what he meant. The Gloucester stories sing of men, and the struggle of men against the elements. Their style is the grand style.*

It is not every writer whose spirit and skill have won the praises of Joseph Conrad, Theodore Roosevelt, Rudyard Kipling, and Booth Tarkington; and this is to cite only a few of Mr. Connolly's admirers. The reason is not far to seek, for no one can miss the integrity of the man, the accuracy of his impressions or the truth of his emotions, and it is these which lift his fiction out of the common class. He has fished off the Banks with the Gloucestermen; he has known the bleak North Sea and the Baltic, too; he has sailed in merchant ships and in ships of war. Possibly it was his Aran Islands ancestry which conditioned him to salt water, or possibly Boston port where he was born and bred. At all events, the sea has found a laureate in him.

Connolly is a man's writer, and The Trawler *is a man's story. It is truly representative of the writer's work, and the editors trust that those who like it will turn to* Gloucestermen, *or* The U-Boat Hunters *for further delights, or to* Sea-Borne, *the salty autobiography of a salty man.*

THE TRAWLER

I

TO JOHN Snow's home in Gloucester came the tale this night of how Arthur Snow was washed from the deck of Hugh Glynn's vessel and lost at sea; and it was Saul Haverick, his sea clothes still on him, who brought the word.

"I'm telling you, John Snow," said Saul—and he out of breath almost with the telling—"and others than me will by an' by be telling you, what a black night it was, with a high-running sea and wind to blow the last coat o' paint off the vessel, but o' course *he* had to be the first o' the fleet—nothing less would do *him*—to make the market with his big ketch. It was for others, not for him, to show the way to take in sail, he said, and not a full hour before it happened that was." Such was Saul Haverick's ending.

John Snow said nothing; Mrs. Snow said nothing. Saul looked to me, but I gave no sign that I had heard him. Only John Snow's niece, Mary, looking up from her hands folded in her lap, said: "Surely you must find it painful, Saul Haverick, to ship with such a wicked man and take the big shares of money that fall to his crew?"

"Eh!" said Saul, surprised like at her. "I'm not denying that he is a great fish killer, Mary Snow, and that we haven't shared some big trips with him; but it is like his religion, I'm telling you, to be able to say how he allowed no man ever he crossed tacks with to work to wind'ard of him. He's that vain he'd drive vessel, himself, and all hands to the bottom afore he'd let some folks think anything else of him."

"He lost my boy—we'll say no more of him," said John Snow.

"Aye," said Saul Haverick, "we'll speak no more of him. But I was Arthur's dory mate, John Snow, as you well know, and my heart is sick to think of it. I'll be going now," and go he did, softly, and by way of the back stairs; and he no more than gone when a knock came to the door.

After a time, the clock on the mantel ticking loud among us, John Snow called out: "Come in!"

II

I remember how Hugh Glynn stepped within the door of John Snow's kitchen that night, and how he bent his head to step within; and, bending his head, took off his cap; and how he bowed to John Snow, Mrs. Snow, and Mary Snow in turn, and, facing John Snow, made as if to speak; but how his voice would not come, not until he had lifted his head yet higher and cleared his throat. And beginning again, he took a step nearer the middle of the floor, to where the light of the bracket lamp above the kitchen table shone full on his face. He was a grand man to look at, not only his face, but the height and build of him, and he was fresh in from sea.

"John Snow—and you, Mrs. Snow—the *Arbiter's* to anchor in the stream, and her flag's to half-mast. And knowing that, maybe there's no need to say anything more."

Mrs. Snow said nothing, Mary Snow said nothing, but I remember how from under John Snow's brows the deep eyes glowed out.

"Go on," said John Snow at last.

Hugh Glynn went on. "Well, he was a good boy, your Arthur—maybe you'd like to be told that, even by me, though of course you that was his father, John Snow, and you that was his mother, Mrs. Snow, know better than anybody else what he was. Three nights ago it was, and we to the south'ard of Sable Island in as nasty a breeze as I'd been in for some time. A living gale it was, a November no'wester—you know what that is, John Snow—but I'd all night been telling the crew to be careful, for a sea there was to sweep to eternity whoever it could 've caught loose around the deck. I could 've hove her to and let her lay, but I was never one to heave to my vessel—not once I'd swung her off for home. And there, God help me, is maybe my weakness.

"She was under her gaff tops'l, but I see she couldn't stand it. 'Boys,' says I, 'clew up that tops'l.' Which they did, and put it in gaskets, and your Arthur, I mind, was one of the four men to go aloft to clew it up. Never a lad to shirk was Arthur. Well, a stouter craft of her tonnage than the *Arbiter* maybe never lived, nor no gear any sounder, but there are things o' God's that the things o' man were never meant to hold out against. Her jib flew to ribbons. 'Cut it clear!' I says, and nigh half the crew jumped for'ard. Half a dozen of the crew to once, but Arthur,—your Arthur, your boy, Mrs. Snow, your son, John Snow—he was quick enough to be among the half-dozen. Among a smart crew he was never left behind. It looked safe for us all then, coming on to morning, but who can ever tell? Fishermen's lives, they're expected to go fast, but they're men's lives for all that, and 'Have a care!' I called to them, myself to the wheel at the time, where, God knows, I was careful.

"Well, I saw this big fellow coming, a mountain of water with a snow-white top to it against the first light of the morning. And I made to meet it. A better vessel than the *Arbiter* the hand o' man never turned out—all Gloucester knows that—but, her best and my best, there was no lifting her out of it. Like great pipe-organs aroaring this sea came, and over we went. Over we went, and I heard myself saying: 'God in Heaven! You great old wagon, but are you gone at last?' And said it again when maybe there was a fathom of water over my head—her quarter was buried that deep and she that long coming up. Slow coming up she was, though up she came at last. But a man was gone."

He had stopped; but he went on.

"It was Arthur, John Snow, and you, Mrs. Snow, who was gone. The boy you were expecting to see in this very room by now, he was gone. Little Arthur that ten years ago, when first I saw him, I could've swung to the ceiling of this room with my one finger—little Arthur was gone. Well, 'Over with a dory!' I said. And, gale and all, we over with a dory, with three of us in it. We looked and looked in that terrible dawn, but no use—no man short o' the Son o' God himself could 'a' stayed afloat, oilskins and red jacks, in that sea. But we had to look, and coming aboard the dory was stove in—smashed like 'twas a china teacup and not a new banker's double dory, against the rail. And it was cold. Our frost-bitten fingers slipped from her ice-wrapped rail, and the three of us nigh came to joining Arthur, and Lord knows—a sin, maybe you'll say, to think it, John Snow—but

I felt then as if I'd just as soon, for it was a hard thing to see a man go down to his death, maybe through my foolishness. And to have the people that love him to face in the telling of it—that's hard, too."

He drew a great breath. "And"—again a deep breath and a deepened note of pain—"that's what I've come to tell you, John Snow, and you, Mrs. Snow—how your boy Arthur was lost."

John Snow, at the kitchen table, I remember, one finger still in the pages of the black-lettered Bible he had been reading when Hugh Glynn stepped in, dropped his head on his chest and there let it rest. Mrs. Snow was crying out loud. Mary Snow said nothing, nor made a move, except to sit in her chair by the window and look to where, in the light of the kitchen lamp, Hugh Glynn stood.

There was a long quiet. Hugh Glynn spoke again. "Twenty years, John Snow, and you, Mrs. Snow—twenty good years I've been fishing out o' Gloucester, and in that time not much this side the western ocean I haven't laid a vessel's keel over. From Greenland to Hatteras I've fished, and many smart seamen I've been shipmates with—dory, bunk, and watch mates with in days gone by—and many a grand one of 'em I've known to find his grave under the green-white ocean, but never a smarter, never an abler fisherman than your boy Arthur. Boy and man I knew him, and, boy and man, he did his work. I thought you might like to hear that from me, John Snow. And not much more than that can I say now, except to add, maybe, that when the Lord calls, John Snow, we must go, all of us. The Lord called and Arthur went. He had a good life before him—if he'd lived. He'd've had his own vessel soon—could've had one before this—if he'd wanted. But 'No,' he says, 'I'll stay with you yet a while, Captain Hugh.' He loved me and I loved him. 'I'll stay with you yet a while, Captain Hugh,' he says, but, staying with me, he was lost, and if I was old enough to have a grown son o' my own, if 'twas that little lad who lived only long enough to teach me what it is to have hope of a fine son and then to lose him, if 'twas that little lad o' mine grown up, I doubt could I feel it more, John Snow."

John Snow let slip his book and stood up, and for the first time looked fair at Hugh Glynn. "We know, Captain Glynn," John Snow said, "and I'm thanking you now. It's hard on me, hard on us all—

our only son, Captain—our only child. But, doubtless, it had to come. Some goes young and some goes old. It came to him maybe earlier than we ever thought for, or he thought for, no doubt, but—it come. And what you have told us, Captain, is something for a man to be hearing of his son—and to be hearing it from you. And only this very night, with the word of you come home, my mind was hardening against you, Captain Glynn, for no denying I've heard hard things even as I've heard great things of you. But now I've met you, I know they mixed lies in the telling, Captain Glynn. And as for Arthur—" John Snow stopped.

"As for Arthur"—'twas something to listen to, the voice of Hugh Glynn then, so soft there was almost no believing it—"as for Arthur, John Snow, he went as all of us will have to go if we stop long enough with the fishing."

"Aye, no doubt. As you may go yourself, Captain?"

"As I expect to go, John Snow. To be lost some day—what else should I look forward to?"

"A black outlook, Captain."

"Maybe, maybe. And yet a man's death at the last."

"So 'tis, Captain—so 'tis."

John Snow and Hugh Glynn gripped hands, looked into each other's eyes, and parted—Hugh Glynn out into the night again and John Snow, with Mrs. Snow, to their room, from where I could hear her sobbing. I almost wanted to cry myself, but Mary Snow was there. I went over and stood behind her. She was looking after some one through the window.

It was Hugh Glynn walking down the steep hill. Turning the corner below, I remember how he looked back and up at the window.

For a long silence Mary Snow sat there and looked out. When she looked up and noticed me, she said: "It's a hard life, the bank fishing, Simon. The long, long nights out to sea, the great gales; and when you come home, no face, it may be, at the door to greet you."

"That it is, Mary."

"I saw his wife one day, Simon," said Mary Snow softly, "and the little boy with her. But a week before they were killed together that was; six years ago, and he, the great, tall man, striding between them. A wonderful, lovely woman and a noble couple, I thought. And the grand boy! And I at that heedless age, Simon, it was a rare person, be it man or woman, I ran ahead to see again."

"Come from the window, Mary," I said to that, "and we'll talk of things more cheerful."

"No, no, Simon—don't ask me to talk of light matters to-night." With that and a "Good night" she left me for her room.

Out into the street I went. John Snow's house stood at the head of a street atop of a steep hill, and I remember how I stood on the steps of John Snow's house and looked down the slope of the hill, and below the hill to the harbor, and beyond the harbor to clear water. It was a cold winter moonlight, and under the moon the sea heaved and heaved and heaved. There was no break in the surface of that sea that night, but as it heaved, terribly slow and heavy, I thought I could feel the steps beneath me heaving with it.

III

All that night I walked the streets and roads of Cape Ann, walking where my eyes would lose no sight of that sea to which I had been born, and thinking, thinking, thinking always to the surge and roar of it; and in the morning I went down to where Hugh Glynn's vessel lay in dock; and Hugh Glynn himself I found standing on the string-piece, holding by the hand and feeding candy to the little son of one of his crew, the while half a dozen men were asking him, one after the other, for what I, too, had come to ask.

My turn came. "I never met you to speak to before, Captain Glynn," I began, "but I was a friend of Arthur Snow's, and I was hopeful for the chance to ship with you in Arthur's place."

"My name is Simon Kippen," I went on, when he made no answer. "I was in John Snow's kitchen when you came in last night."

"I know"—he waved the hand that wasn't holding the little boy—"I know. And"—he almost smiled—"you're not afraid to come to sea with me?"

"Why more afraid," I said, "than you to take me with you?"

"You were a great friend of Arthur's?"

"A friend to Arthur—and more if I could," I answered.

He had a way of throwing his head back and letting his eyes look out, as from a distance, or as if he would take the measure of a man. 'Twas so he looked out at me now.

"He's a hard case of a man, shouldn't you say, Simon Kippen, who would play a shipmate foul?"

I said nothing to that.

"And, master or hand, we're surely all shipmates," he added; to which again I said nothing.

"Will you take Saul Haverick for dory mate?" he said again.

"I bear Saul Haverick no great love," I said; "but I have never heard he wasn't a good fisherman, and who should ask more than that of his mate in a dory?"

He looked out at me once more from the eyes that seemed so far back in his head; and from me he looked to the flag that was still to the half-mast of his vessel for the loss of Arthur Snow.

"We might ask something more in a dory mate at times, but he is a good fisherman," he answered at last. "A good hand to the wheel of a vessel, too, a cool head in danger, and one of the best judges of weather ever I sailed with. We're putting out in the morning. You can have the chance."

As to what was in my heart when I chose to ship with Hugh Glynn, I cannot say. There are those who tell us how they can explain every heart-beat, quick or slow, when aught ails them. I never could. I only know that standing on the steps of Mary Snow's house the night before, all my thought was of Mary Snow sitting at the window and looking down the street after Hugh Glynn. And "God help you, Simon Kippen!" I found myself saying—"it's not you, nor Saul Haverick, nor any other living man will marry Mary Snow while Hugh Glynn lives, for there is no striving against the strength of the sea, and the strength of Hugh Glynn is the strength of the sea." But of what lay beyond that in my heart I could not say.

And now I was to sea with Hugh Glynn, and we not four days out of Gloucester when, as if but to show me the manner of man he was, he runs clear to the head of Placentia Bay, in Newfoundland, for a baiting on our way to the banks; and whoever knows Placentia Bay knows what that means, with the steam-cutters of the Crown patrolling, and their sleepless watches night and day aloft, to trap whoever would try to buy a baiting there against the law.

No harm fell to Hugh Glynn that time. No harm ever fell to him, fishermen said. Before ever the cutters could get sight of him he had sight of them; and his bait stowed below, safe away he came, driving wild-like past the islands of the bay, with never a side-light showing in the night, and not the first time he had done so.

"What d'y' say to that, Simon? Didn't we fool 'em good?" he asked, when once more we were on the high seas and laying a free course for the western banks.

"I'm grateful you did not ask me to go in any dory to bring the bait off," I answered.

"Why is that, Simon?" he asked, as one who has no suspicion.

"It was against the law, Captain Glynn."

"But a bad law, Simon?"

"Law is law," I answered to that.

He walked from the wheel, where I was, twice to the break of the vessel and back again and said, in a voice no louder than was needful to be heard above what loose water was splashing over her quarter to my feet: "Don't be put out with me for what I'll tell you now, Simon. You're a good lad, Simon, and come of good people, but of people that for hundreds o' years have thought but one way in the great matters of life. And when men have lived with their minds set in the one way so long, Simon, it comes hard for them to understand any other way. Such unfrequent ones as differed from your people, Simon, them they cast out from among them. I know, I know, Simon, because I come from people something like to them, only I escaped before it was too late to understand that people who split tacks with you do not always do it to fetch up on a lee shore."

"And from those other people, no doubt, Captain Glynn, you learned it was right to break a country's laws?"

"It wasn't breaking our country's law, Simon, nor any good man's law, to get a baiting last night. There are a lot of poor fishermen, Simon—as none know better than yourself—in Placentia Bay who have bait to sell, and there is a law which says they must not. But whose law? An American law? No. God's law? No. The law of those poor people in Placentia Bay? No. Some traders who have the making of the laws? Yes. And there you have it. If the Placentia Bay fishermen aren't allowed to sell bait to me, or the like of me, they will have to sell it to the traders themselves, but have to take their one dollar, where we of Gloucester would pay them five, and, paying it, would give some of them and their families a chance to live."

He stood there in his rubber boots to his hips and his long great-coat to his ankles—he was one who never wore oilskins aboard ship—swinging with the swing of the plunging vessel as if he was built into her, and with his head thrown back and a smile, it may be, that was not a smile at all, and kept looking at me from out of eyes that were changeable as the sea itself.

"Don't you be getting mad with me, Simon, because we don't think alike in some things. To the devil with what people think of you—I've said that often enough, Simon, but not when they're good people. If some people don't like us, Simon, there will come no nourishment to our souls. Some day you're going to come to my way o' thinking, Simon, because we two are alike underneath."

"Alike!" I smiled to myself.

"Ay, alike at heart, Simon. We may look to be sailing wide apart courses now, but maybe if our papers were examined 'twould be found we'd cleared for the same last port of call, Simon."

And no more talk of anything like that between us until the night before we were to leave the fishing grounds for home. In the afternoon we had set our trawls, and, leaving the vessel, the skipper had said, "Our last set, boys. Let 'em lay to-night, and in the morning we'll haul"; and, returning aboard after setting, we had our supper and were making ready, such as had no watch to stand, to turn in for a good, long sleep against the labor of the morrow.

It was an oily sea that evening—a black, oily-smooth surface, lifting heavy and slow to a long swell. A smooth, oily sea—there is never any good comes out of it; but a beautiful sea notwithstanding, with more curious patterns of shifting colors than a man could count in a year playing atop of it. The colors coming and going and rolling and squirming—no women's shop ashore ever held such colors under the bright night-lights as under the low sun we saw this night on the western banks. It was a most beautiful and a most wicked sea to stop and look at.

And the sun went down that evening on a banking of clouds no less beautiful; a copper-red sun, and after 'twas gone, in lovely massy forms and splendid colors, were piled the clouds in all the western quarter.

Such of the crew as stopped to speak of it did not like at all the look of that sea and sky, and some stopped beside the skipper to say it, he leaning against the main rigging in the way he had the while he would be studying the weather signs; but he made no answer to the crew, to that or any other word they had this evening—except to Saul Haverick, and to him only when he came up from supper complaining of not feeling well.

He was one could drive his crew till they could not see for very weariness; but he was one could nurse them, too. "Go below and turn in," was his word to Saul, "and stay there till you feel better. Call me, Simon, if I'm not up," he then said to me. "I'll stand Saul's watch with you, if Saul is no better."

It was yet black night when I was called to go on watch, and, Saul Haverick still complaining, I went to call the skipper. But he was already up and had been, the watch before me said, for the better part of the night. I found him leaning over the gunnels of the wind'ard nest of dories when I went on deck, gazing out on a sea that was no longer oily-smooth, though smooth enough, too, what was to be seen of it, under the stars of a winter night.

I stood on the break and likewise looked about me. To anchor, and alone, lay the vessel, with but her riding-light to mark her in the dark; alone and quiet, with never a neighbor to hail us, nor a sound from any living thing whatever. The very gulls themselves were asleep; only the fores'l swaying to a short sheet, would roll part way to wind'ard and back to loo'ard, but quiet as could be even then, except for the little tapping noises of the reef-points when in and out the belly of the canvas would puff full up and let down again to what little wind was stirring.

It was a perfect, calm night, but no calm day was to follow. "Wicked weather ahead," said Hugh Glynn, and came and stood beside me on the break. "A wicked day coming, but no help for it now till daylight comes to see our trawls to haul 'em." And, as one who had settled that in his mind, he said no more of it, but from mainm'st to weather rail he paced, and back again, and I took to pacing beside him.

A wonderful time, the night-watches at sea, for men to reveal themselves. Night and sky overhead and the wide ocean to your elbow—it drives men to thought of higher things. The wickedest of men—I have known them, with all manner of blasphemies befouling their lips by day, to become holy as little children in the watches of the night.

No blasphemer was Hugh Glynn, nor did the night hold terror for him; only as we paced the break together he spoke of matters that but himself and his God could know. It was hard to listen and be patient, though maybe it was as much of wonder as of impatience was taking hold of me as I listened.

"Do you never fear what men might come to think of you, Captain Glynn," I said, "confessing your very soul?"

"Ho, ho, that's it, is it?" He came to a sudden stop in our walking. "I should only confess the body—is that it, Simon Kippen? And, of course, when a man confesses to one thing of his own free will, you know there must be something worse behind? Is that it, Simon?" He chuckled beside me and, as if only to scandalize me, let his tongue run wilder yet.

His tales were of violations of laws such as it had been my religion to observe since I was a boy, and little except of the comic, ridiculous side of them all. The serious matters of life, if 'twas to judge by what he spoke to me that night, had small interest for him. But the queer power of the man! Had it been light where he could see me, I would have choked before ever I would let him hear me laugh; but he caught me smiling and straightened up, chuckling, to say: "Many other things you would smile at, too, Simon, if your bringing up would but allow the frost to thaw from your soul."

"And are reckless carryings-on and desperate chancing things to smile at?"

"O Simon, Simon, what a righteous man you're to be that never expects to see the day when no harbor this side of God's eternal sea will offer you the only safe and quiet mooring!"

Again I saw Mary Snow sitting at the window and looking down the street, and remembering how she had spoken of his lonely home,

I said: "No doubt a man, like a vessel, Captain Glynn, should have always a mooring somewhere. A wonder you never thought of marrying again?"

"I have thought of it."

"And with some one woman in mind?"

"It may be." He answered that, too, without a pause.

"And does she know?"

"It may be she knows. No knowing when they know, Simon. As men best understand the soul, so it is woman's best gift to understand the heart. But no fair play in me to ask her. I've had my great hour, and may not have it again with another. To offer the woman I have in mind anything less than a great love—it would be to cheat, Simon. No, no, no—it's not the kind of a man I am now, but the kind you are, Simon, should marry."

"It's not my kind that women like best, Captain," I said.

"There are women to like every kind, Simon, and almost any kind of a woman would like your kind, Simon, if you would only learn to be less ashamed of what should be no shame. And it is you, already in love, who——"

"Me—in love?" I was like a vessel luffing to escape a squall, he had come on me so quickly.

"There it is, Simon—the upbringing of you that would never own up to what you think only yourself know. Three weeks to sea now you've been with me, and never a gull you've seen skirling to the west'ard that your eyes haven't followed. By no mistake do you watch them flying easterly. And when last evening I said, 'To-morrow, boys, we'll swing her off and drive her to the west'ard—to the west'ard and Gloucester!' the leaping heart in you drove the blood to your very eyes. Surely that was not in sorrow, Simon?"

I made no answer.

Back and forth we paced, and talked as we paced, until the stars were dimming in the sky and the darkness fading from the sea. He stopped by the rail and stared, aweary-like, I thought, upon the waters.

"Simon, surely few men but would rather be themselves than anybody else that lives; but surely, too, no man sailing his own wide courses but comes to the day when he wishes he'd been less free in his navigation at times. You are honest and right, Simon. Even when you are wrong you are right, because for a man to do what he thinks is right, whether he be right or wrong, at the time, is to come to be surely right in the end. And it is the like of you, not yet aweary in soul or body, should mate with the women molded of God to be the great mothers."

"You have done much thinking of some matters, Captain," I said, not knowing what else to say.

"Alone at sea before the dawn—it is a wonderful hour for a man to cross-question himself, Simon; and not many nights of late years that I haven't seen the first light of dawn creeping up over the edge of the ocean. You marry Mary Snow, Simon."

He knew. What could I say? "I never thought to talk like this, Captain, to a living man." In the growing light we now stood plain to each other's sight. "I don't understand what made me," I said, and said it, doubtless, with a note of shame.

"It may be just as well at your age that you don't understand every feeling that drives you on, Simon. Our brains grow big with age, but not our hearts. No matter what made you talk to-night, Simon, you marry Mary Snow."

I shook my head, but opened my heart to him, nevertheless. "I haven't the clever ways of Saul Haverick."

"Simon, it's my judgment this night that Mary Snow will never marry Saul Haverick."

"I'm glad to hear you think that, Captain. 'Twould spoil her life—or any woman's."

"No, no," he said, quick-like. "Almost any woman's—yes; but not Mary Snow's—not altogether."

"And why?"

"Because she's too strong a soul to be spoiled of her life by any one man; because no matter what man she marries, in her heart will be the image, not of the man her husband is, but of the man she'd wish him to be, and in the image of that man of her fancy will her children be born. Women molded of God to be the mothers of great men are fashioned that way, Simon. They dream great dreams for their children's sake to come, and their hearts go out to the man who helps to make their dreams come true. If I've learned anything of good women in life, Simon, it is that. And, no saying, I may be wrong in that, too, Simon, but so far I've met no man who knows more of it than I to gainsay me. You marry Mary Snow, Simon, and she will bear you children who will bring new light to a darkening world."

The dawn was rolling up to us and the next on watch was on deck to relieve me; and the cook, too, with his head above the fo'c's'le hatch, was calling that breakfast was ready, and we said no more of that.

"Go for'ard, Simon," said Captain Glynn, "and have your breakfast. After breakfast we'll break out her anchor, and out dories and get that gear aboard afore it's too late. I'll go below and see how Saul's getting on."

With that he went into the cabin; but soon was back to take his seat at the breakfast table; but no word of Saul until we had done eating, and he standing to go up on deck. Then he said: "Saul says he is still too sick to go in the dory with you, Simon."

And to that I said: "Well, I've hauled a halibut trawl single-handed before, Captain Glynn, and I can do it again if need be."

He put on his woolen cap, and across the table he looked at me, and I looked hard at him.

"This will be no morning to go single-handed in a dory, Simon. Saul is not too sick, he says, to stand to the wheel and handle the vessel in my place. I will take his place along with you in the dory."

What he was thinking I could not say. His head was thrown back and his eyes looking out and down at me, as from the top of a far-away hill, and no more knowing what thoughts lay behind them than what ships lay beyond the horizon.

IV

It was a blood-red sunrise and a sea that was making when we left the vessel, but nothing to worry over in that. It might grow into a dory-killing day later, but so far it was only what all winter trawlers have faced more days than they can remember.

We picked up our nearest buoy, with its white-and-black flag floating high to mark it, and as we did, to wind'ard of us we could see, for five miles it might be, the twisted lines of the dories stretching. Rising to the top of a sea we could see them, sometimes one and sometimes another, lifting and falling, and the vessel lifting and falling to wind'ard of them all.

Hugh Glynn took the bow to do the hauling and myself the waist for coiling, and it was a grand sight to see him heave in on that heavy gear on that December morning. Many men follow the sea, but not many are born to it. Hugh Glynn was. Through the gurdy he hauled the heavy lines, swinging forward his shoulders, first one and then the other, swaying from his waist and all in time to the heave of the sea beneath him, and singing, as he heaved, the little snatches of songs that I believe he made up as he went along.

As he warmed to his work he stopped to draw off the heavy sweater that he wore over his woolen shirt, and made as if to throw it in the bow of the dory. "But, no," he said, "it will get wet there. You put it on you, Simon, and keep it dry for me." He was a full size bigger than me in every way, and I put it on, over my cardigan jacket and under my oil jacket, and it felt fine and comfortable on me.

It came time for me to spell him on the hauling, but he waved me back. "Let be, let be, Simon," he said, "it's fine, light exercise for a man of a brisk morning. It's reminding me of my hauling of my first trawl on the Banks. Looking back on it, now, Simon I mind how the bravest sight I thought I ever saw was our string of dories racing afore the tide in the sea of that sunny winter's morning, and the vessel, like a mother to her little boats, standing off and on to see that nothing happened the while we hauled and coiled and gaffed inboard the broad-backed halibut. All out of myself with pride I was—I that was no more than a lad, but hauling halibut trawls with full-grown Gloucester men on the Grand Banks! And the passage home that trip, Simon! Oh, boy, that passage home!"

Without even a halt in his heaving in of the trawls, he took to singing:

"It came one day, as it had to come—
I said to you 'Good-by.'
'Good luck,' said you, 'and a fair, fair wind'—
Though you cried as if to die;

Was all there was ahead of you
When we put out to sea;
But now, sweetheart, we're headed home
To the west'ard and to thee.

"So blow, ye devils, and walk her home—
For she's the able *Lucy Foster*.
The woman I love is waiting me,
So drive the *Lucy* home to Gloucester.
O ho ho for this heaven-sent breeze,
Straight from the east and all you please!
Come along now, ye whistling gales,
The harder ye blow the faster she sails—
O my soul, there's a girl in Gloucester!"

He stopped to look over his shoulder at me. "Simon, boy, I mind the days when there was no stopping the songs in me. Rolling to my lips o' themselves they would come, like foam to the crests of high seas. The days of a man's youth, Simon! All I knew of a gale of wind was that it stirred the fancies in me. It's the most wonderful thing will ever happen you, Simon."

"What is, skipper?"

"Why, the loving a woman and she loving you, and you neither knowing why, nor maybe caring."

"No woman loves me, skipper."

"She will, boy—never a fear."

He took to the hauling, and soon again to the singing:

"My lad comes running down the street,
And what says he to me?
Says he, 'O dadda, dadda,
And you're back again from sea!

" 'And did you ketch a great big fish
And bring him home to me?
O dadda, dadda, take me up
And toss me high!' says he.

"My love looks out on the stormy morn,
Her thoughts are on the sea.
She says, ' 'Tis wild upon the Banks,'
And kneels in prayer for me.

" 'O Father, hold him safe!' she prays,
'And——'

"There's one, Simon!" he called.

A bad sea he meant. They had been coming and going, coming and going, rolling under and past us, and so far no harm; but this was one more wicked to look at than its mates. So I dropped the coiling lines and, with the oar already to the becket in the stern, whirled the dory's bow head on. The sea carried us high and far and, passing, left the dory deep with water, but no harm in that so she was still right side up.

"A good job, Simon," said Hugh Glynn the while we were bailing. "Not too soon and not too late."

That was the first one. More followed in their turn; but always the oar was handy in the becket, and it was but to whirl bow or stern to it with the oar when it came, not too soon to waste time for the hauling but never, of course, too late to save capsizing; and bailing her out, if need be, when it was by.

Our trawl was in, our fish in the waist of the dory, and we lay to our roding line and second anchor, so we might not drift miles to loo'ard while waiting for the vessel to pick us up. We could see the vessel—to her hull, when to the top of a sea we rose together; but nothing of her at all when into the hollows we fell together.

She had picked up all but the dory next to wind'ard of us. We would be the last, but before long now she would be to us. "When you drop Simon and me, go to the other end of the line and work back. Pick Simon and me up last of all," Hugh Glynn had said to Saul, and I remember how Saul, standing to the wheel, looked down over the taffrail and said, "Simon and you last of all," and nodded his head as our dory fell away in the vessel's wake.

Tide and sea were such that there was no use trying to row against it, or we would not have waited at all; but we waited, and as we waited the wind, which had been southerly, went into the east and snow fell; but for not more than a half-hour, when it cleared. We stood up and looked about us. There was no vessel or other dory in sight.

We said no word to each other of it, but the while we waited further, all the while with a wind'ard eye to the bad little seas, we talked.

"Did you ever think of dying, Simon?" Hugh Glynn said after a time.

"Can a man follow the winter trawler long and not think of it at times?" I answered.

"And have you fear of it, Simon?"

"I know I have no love for it," I said. "But do you ever think of it, you?"

"I do—often. With the double tides working to draw me to it, it would be queer enough if now and again I did not think of it."

"And have you fear of it?"

"Of not going properly—I have, Simon." And after a little: "And I've often thought it a pity for a man to go and nothing come of his going. Would you like the sea for a grave, Simon?"

"I would not," I answered.

"Nor me, Simon. A grand, clean grave, the ocean, and there was a time I thought I would; but not now. The green grave ashore, with your own beside you—a man will feel less lonesome, or so I've often thought, Simon."

"I've often thought so," he went on, his eyes now on watch for the bad seas and again looking wistful-like at me. "I'd like to lie where my wife and boy lie, she to one side and the lad to the other, and rise with them on Judgment Day. I've a notion, Simon, that with them to bear me up I'd stand afore the Lord with greater courage. For if what some think is true—that it's those we've loved in this world will have the right to plead for us in the next—then, Simon, there will be two to plead for me as few can plead."

He stood up and looked around. "It is a bad sea now, but worse later, and a strong breeze brewing. Simon"; and drew from an inside pocket of his woolen shirt a small leather notebook. He held it up for me to see, with the slim little pencil held by little loops along the edges.

" 'Twas hers. I've a pocket put in every woolen shirt I wear to sea so 'twill be close to me. There's things in it she wrote of our little boy. And I'm writing here something I'd like you to be witness to, Simon."

He wrote a few lines. "There, Simon. I've thought often this trip how 'tis hard on John Snow at his age to have to take to fishing again. If I hadn't lost Arthur, he wouldn't have to. I'm willing my vessel to John Snow. Will you witness it, Simon?"

I signed my name below his; and he set the book back in his inside pocket.

"And you think our time is come, skipper?" I tried to speak quietly, too.

"I won't say that, Simon, but foolish not to make ready for it."

I looked about when we rose to the next sea for the vessel. But no vessel. I thought it hard. "Had you no distrust of Saul Haverick this morning?" I asked him.

"I had. And last night, too, Simon."

"And you trusted him?"

"A hard world if we didn't trust people, Simon. I thought it over again this morning and was ashamed, Simon, to think it in me to distrust a shipmate. I wouldn't have believed it of any man ever I sailed with. But no use to fool ourselves longer. Make ready. Over with the fish, over with the trawls, over with everything but thirty or forty fathom of that roding line, and the sail, and one anchor, and the two buoys."

It was hard to have to throw back in the sea the fine fish that we'd taken hours to set and haul for; hard, too, to heave over the stout gear that had taken so many long hours to rig. But there was no more time to waste—over they went. And we took the two buoys—light-made but sound and tight half-barrels they were—and we lashed them to the risings of the dory.

"And now the sail to her, Simon."

We put the sail to her.

"And stand by to cut clear our anchorage!" I stood by with my bait knife; and, when he called out, I cut, and away we went racing before wind and tide; me in the waist, on the buoy lashed to the wind'ard side to hold her down, and he on the wind'ard gunnel, too, but aft, with an oar in one hand and the sheet of the sail in the other.

"And where now?" I asked, when the wind would let me.

"The lee of Sable Island lies ahead."

The full gale was on us now—a living gale; and before the gale the sea ran higher than ever, and before the high seas the flying dory. Mountains of slate-blue water rolled down into valleys, and the valleys rolled up into mountains again, and all shifting so fast that no man might point a finger and say, "Here's one, there's one!" —quick and wild as that they were.

From one great hill we would tumble, only to fall into the next great hollow; and never did she make one of her wild plunges but the spume blew wide and high over her, and never did she check herself for even the quickest of breaths, striving the while to breast up the side of a mountain of water, but the sea would roll over her, and I'd say to myself once again: "Now at last we're gone!"

We tumbled into the hollows and a roaring wind would drive a boiling foam, white as milk, atop of us; we climbed up the hills and the roaring wind would drive the solid green water atop of us. Wind, sea, and milk-white foam between them—they seemed all of a mind to smother us. These things I saw in jumps-like. Lashed to the wind'ard buoy I was by a length of roding line, to my knees in water the better part of the time, and busy enough with the bailing. There was no steady looking to wind'ard, such was the weight of the bullets of water which the wild wind drove off the sea crests; but a flying glance now and again kept me in the run of it.

I would have wished to be able to do my share of the steering, but only Hugh Glynn could properly steer that dory that day. The dory would have sunk a hundred times only for the buoys in the waist; but she would have capsized more times than that again only for the hand of him in the stern. Steady he sat, a man of marble, his jaw like a cliff rising above the collar of his woolen shirt, his two eyes like two lights glowing out from under his cap brim.

And yet for all of him I couldn't see how we could live through it. Once we were so terribly beset that, "We'll be lost carrying sail like this, Hugh Glynn!" I called back to him.

And he answered: "I never could see any difference myself, Simon, between being lost carrying sail and being lost hove to."

After that I said no more.

And so, to what must have been the wonder of wind and sea that day, Hugh Glynn drove the little dory into the night and the lee of Sable Island.

V

We took in our sail and let go our anchor. Hugh Glynn looked long above and about him. "A clear night coming, Simon; and cold, with the wind backing into the no'west. We'll lay here, for big vessels will be running for this same lee to-night, and maybe a chance for us to be picked up with the daylight. Did I do well this day by you, Simon?"

"I'd be a lost man hours back but for you," I said, and was for saying more in praise of him, but he held up his hand.

"So you don't hold me a reckless, desperate sail carrier, Simon, never mind the rest." His eyes were shining. "But your voice is weary, Simon, and you're hungry, too, I know."

I was hungry and worn—terribly worn—after the day, and so told him.

"Then lie down and 'twill rest you, and for a time make you forget the hunger. And while you're lying down, Simon, I'll stand watch."

And I made ready to lie down, when I thought of his sweater I was wearing. I unbuttoned my oil jacket to get at it. "It's colder already, skipper, and you will be needing it."

"No, it is you will be needing it, Simon. Being on my feet, d'y see, I can thrash around and keep warm."

"But will you call me and take it if it grows too cold, skipper?"

"I'll call you when I want it—lie down now."

"A wonderful calm night, full as quiet as last, skipper," I said, "only no harm in this night—no gale before us on the morrow."

"No, Simon," he said—"naught but peace before us. But lie down you, boy."

"And you'll call me, skipper," I said, "when my watch comes?"

"I'll call you when I've stood my full watch. Lie down now."

I lay down, meaning to keep awake. But I fell asleep.

I thought I felt a hand wrapping something around me in the

night, and I made to sit up, but a voice said, "Lie down, boy," and I lay down and went to sleep again.

When I awoke it was to the voices of strange men, and one was saying: "He will be all right now."

I sat up. I was still in the dory, and saw men standing over me; and other men were looking down from a vessel's side. Ice was thick on the rail of the vessel.

It was piercing cold and I was weak with the fire of the pains running through my veins, but, remembering, I tried to stand up. "Hsh-h, boy!" they said, "you are all right," and would have held me down while they rubbed my feet and hands.

I stood up among them, nevertheless, and looked for Hugh Glynn. He was on the after thwart, his arms folded over the gunnel and his forehead resting on his arms. His woolen shirt was gone from him. I looked back and in the waist of the dory I saw it, where they had taken it off me; and the sail of the boat he had wrapped around me, too; and his woolen mitts.

I lifted his head to see his face. If ever a man smiled, 'twas he was smiling as I looked. "Skipper! O skipper!" I called out; and again: "O skipper!"

One of the men who had been rubbing my feet touched my shoulder. "Come away, boy; the voice o' God called him afore you."

And so Hugh Glynn came to his green grave ashore; and so I came home to marry Mary Snow; and in the end to father the children which may or may not grow great as he predicted. But great in the eyes of the world they could become, greater than all living men, it might be, and yet fall far short in our eyes of the stature of the man who thought that 'twas better for one to live than for two to die, and that one not to be himself.

Desperate he was and lawbreaking, for law is law, whosoever it bears hard upon; but the heart was warm within him. And if my children have naught else, and it is for their mother and me to say, the heart to feel for others they shall have; and having that, the rest may follow or not, as it will; which would be Hugh Glynn's way of it, too, I think.

RICHARD HARDING DAVIS

The Deserter

THE DESERTER

IN Salonika, the American consul, the Standard Oil man, and the war correspondents formed the American colony. The correspondents were waiting to go to the front. Incidentally, as we waited, the front was coming rapidly toward us. There was "Uncle" Jim, the veteran of many wars, and of all the correspondents, in experience the oldest and in spirit the youngest, and there was the Kid, and the Artist. The Kid jeered at us, and proudly described himself as the only Boy Reporter who jumped from a City Hall assignment to cover a European War. "I don't know strategy," he would boast; "neither does the Man at Home. He wants 'human interest' stuff, and I give him what he wants. I write exclusively for the subway guard and the farmers in the wheat belt. When you fellows write about the 'Situation,' they don't understand it. Neither do you. Neither does Venizelos or the King. I don't understand it myself. So, I write my people heart-to-heart talks about refugees and wounded, and what kind of ploughs the Servian peasants use, and that St. Paul wrote his letters to the Thessalonians from the same hotel where I write mine; and I tell 'em to pronounce Salonika 'eeka,' and *not* put the accent on the 'on.' This morning at the refugee camp I found all the little Servians of the Frothingham unit in American Boy Scout uniforms. That's my meat. That's 'home week' stuff. You fellows write for the editorial page; and nobody reads it. I write for the man that turns first to Mutt and Jeff, and then looks to see where they are running the new Charlie Chaplin release. When that man has to choose between 'our military correspondent' and the City Hall Reporter, he chooses me!"

The third man was John, "Our Special Artist." John could write a news story, too, but it was the cartoons that had made him famous. They were not comic page, but front page cartoons, and before making up their minds what they thought, people waited to see what their Artist thought. So, it was fortunate his thoughts were as brave and clean as they were clever. He was the original Little Brother to the Poor. He was always giving away money. When we caught him, he would prevaricate. He would say the man was a college chum, that he had borrowed the money from him, and that this was the first chance he had had to pay it back. The Kid suggested it was strange that so many of his college chums should at the same moment turn up, dead broke, in Salonika, and that half of them should be women.

John smiled disarmingly. "It was a large college," he explained, "and coeducational." There were other Americans; Red Cross doctors and nurses just escaped through the snow from the Bulgars, and hyphenated Americans who said they had taken out their first papers. They thought hyphenated citizens were so popular with us, that we would pay their passage to New York. In Salonika they were transients. They had no local standing. They had no local lying-down place, either, or place to eat, or to wash, although they did not look as though that worried them, or place to change their clothes. Or clothes to change. It was because we had clothes to change, and a hotel bedroom, instead of a bench in a café, that we were ranked as residents and from the Greek police held a "permission to sojourn." Our American colony was a very close corporation. We were only six Americans against 300,000 British, French, Greek, and Servian soldiers, and 120,000 civilian Turks, Spanish Jews, Armenians, Persians, Egyptians, Albanians, and Arabs, and some twenty more other races that are not listed. We had arrived in Salonika before the rush, and at the Hotel Hermes on the waterfront had secured a vast room. The edge of the stone quay was not forty feet from us, the only landing steps directly opposite our balcony. Everybody who arrived on the Greek passenger boats from Naples or the Piræus, or who had shore leave from a man-of-war, transport, or hospital ship, was raked by our cameras. There were four windows—one for each of us and his work table. It was not easy to work. What was the use? The pictures and stories outside the windows fascinated us, but when we sketched them or wrote about them, they only proved us inadequate. All day long the pinnaces, cutters, gigs, steam launches shoved and bumped against the stone steps, marines came ashore for the mail, stewards for fruit and fish, Red Cross nurses to shop, tiny midshipmen to visit the movies, and the sailors and officers of the Russian, French, British, Italian, and Greek war-ships to stretch their legs in the park of the Tour Blanche, or to cramp them under a café table. Sometimes the ambulances blocked the quay and the wounded and frost-bitten were lifted into the motor-boats, and sometimes a squad of marines lined the landing stage, and as a coffin under a French or English flag was borne up the stone steps stood at salute. So crowded was the harbor that the oars of the boatmen interlocked.

Close to the stone quay, stretched along the three-mile circle, were the fishing smacks, beyond them, so near that the anchor chains fouled, were the passenger ships with gigantic Greek flags painted on their sides, and beyond them transports from Marseilles, Malta, and Suvla Bay, black colliers, white hospital ships, burning green electric lights, red-bellied tramps and freighters, and, hemming them in, the grim, mouse-colored destroyers, submarines, cruisers, dreadnaughts. At times, like a wall, the cold fog rose between us and the harbor, and again the curtain would suddenly be ripped asunder, and the sun would flash on the brass work of the fleet, on the white wings of the aeroplanes, on the snow-draped shoulders of Mount Olympus. We often speculated as to how in the early days the gods and goddesses, dressed as they were, or as they were not, survived the snows of Mount Olympus. Or was it only their resort for the summer?

It got about that we had a vast room to ourselves, where one might obtain a drink, or a sofa for the night, or even money to cable for money. So, we had many strange visitors, some half starved, half frozen, with terrible tales of the Albanian trail, of the Austrian prisoners fallen by the wayside, of the mountain passes heaped with dead, of the doctors and nurses wading waist-high in snow-drifts and for food killing the ponies. Some of our visitors wanted to get their names in the American papers so that the folks at home would know they were still alive, others wanted us to keep their names out of the papers, hoping the police would think them dead; another, convinced it was of pressing news value, desired us to advertise the fact that he had invented a poisonous gas for use in the trenches. With difficulty we prevented him from casting it adrift in our room. Or, he had for sale a second-hand motor-cycle, or he would accept a position as barkeeper, or for five francs would sell a state secret that, once made public, in a month would end the war. It seemed cheap at the price.

Each of us had his "scouts" to bring him the bazaar rumor, the Turkish bath rumor, the café rumor. Some of our scouts journeyed as far afield as Monastir and Doiran, returning to drip snow on the floor, and to tell us tales, one-half of which we refused to believe, and the other half the censor refused to pass. With each other's visitors it was etiquette not to interfere. It would have been like tapping a private wire. When we found John sketching a giant stranger in a cap and coat of wolf skin we did not seek to know if he were an Albanian brigand, or a Servian prince *incognito*, and when a dark Levantine sat close to the Kid, whispering, and the Kid banged on his typewriter, we did not listen.

So, when I came in one afternoon and found a strange American youth writing at John's table, and no one introduced us, I took it for granted he had sold the Artist an "exclusive" story, and asked no questions. But I could not help hearing what they said. Even though I tried to drown their voices by beating on the Kid's typewriter. I was taking my third lesson, and I had printed, "I Amm 5w writjng This, 5wjth my own lilly w?ite handS," when I heard the Kid saying:

"You can beat the game this way. Let John buy you a ticket to the Piræus. If you go from one Greek port to another you don't need a visé. But, if you book from here to Italy, you must get a permit from the Italian consul, and our consul, and the police. The plot is to get out of the war zone, isn't it? Well, then, my dope is to get out quick, and map the rest of your trip when you're safe in Athens."

It was no business of mine, but I had to look up. The stranger was now pacing the floor. I noticed that while his face was almost black with tan, his upper lip was quite white. I noticed also that he had his hands in the pockets of one of John's blue serge suits, and that the pink silk shirt he wore was one that once had belonged to the Kid. Except for the pink shirt, in the appearance of the young man there was nothing unusual. He was of a familiar type. He looked like a young business man from our Middle West, matter-of-fact and unimaginative, but capable and self-reliant. If he had had a fountain pen in his upper waistcoat pocket, I would have guessed he was an insurance agent, or the publicity man for a new automobile. John picked up his hat, and said, "That's good advice. Give me your steamer ticket, Fred, and I'll have them change it." He went out; but he did not ask Fred to go with him.

Uncle Jim rose, and murmured something about the Café Roma, and tea. But neither did he invite Fred to go with him. Instead, he told him to make himself at home, and if he wanted anything the waiter would bring it from the café downstairs. Then the Kid, as though he also was uncomfortable at being left alone with us, hurried to the door. "Going to get you a suit-case," he explained. "Back in five minutes."

The stranger made no answer. Probably he did not hear him. Not a hundred feet from our windows three Greek steamers were huddled together, and the eyes of the American were fixed on them. The one for which John had gone to buy him a new ticket lay nearest. She was to sail in two hours. Impatiently, in short quick steps, the stranger paced the length of the room, but when he turned and so could see the harbor, he walked slowly, devouring it with his eyes. For some time, in silence, he repeated this manœuvre; and then the complaints of the typewriter disturbed him. He halted and observed my struggles. Under his scornful eye, in my embarrassment I frequently hit the right letter. "You a newspaper man, too?" he asked. I boasted I was, but begged not to be judged by my typewriting.

"I got some great stories to write when I get back to God's country," he announced. "I was a reporter for two years in Kansas City before the war, and now I'm going back to lecture and write. I got enough material to keep me at work for five years. All kinds of stuff—specials, fiction stories, personal experiences, maybe a novel."

I regarded him with envy. For the correspondents in the greatest of all wars the pickings had been meagre. "You are to be congratulated," I said. He brushed aside my congratulations. "For what?" he demanded. "I didn't go after the stories; they came to me. The things

I saw I had to see. Couldn't get away from them. I've been with the British, serving in the R. A. M. C. Been hospital steward, stretcher bearer, ambulance driver. I've been sixteen months at the front, and all the time on the firing-line. I was in the retreat from Mons, with French on the Marne, at Ypres, all through the winter fighting along the Canal, on the Gallipoli Peninsula, and, just lately, in Servia. I've seen more of this war than any soldier. Because, sometimes, they give the soldier a rest; they never give the medical corps a rest. The only rest I got was when I was wounded."

He seemed no worse for his wounds, so again I tendered congratulations. This time he accepted them. The recollection of the things he had seen, things incredible, terrible, unique in human experience, had stirred him. He talked on, not boastfully, but in a tone, rather, of awe and disbelief, as though assuring himself that it was really he to whom such things had happened.

"I don't believe there's any kind of fighting I haven't seen," he declared; "hand-to-hand fighting with bayonets, grenades, gun butts. I've seen 'em on their knees in the mud choking each other, beating each other with their bare fists. I've seen every kind of airship, bomb, shell, poison gas, every kind of wound. Seen whole villages turned into a brickyard in twenty minutes; in Servia seen bodies of women frozen to death, bodies of babies starved to death, seen men in Belgium swinging from trees; along the Yzer for three months I saw the bodies of men I'd known sticking out of the mud, or hung up on the barb wire, with the crows picking them.

"I've seen some of the nerviest stunts that ever were pulled off in history. I've seen *real* heroes. Time and time again I've seen a man throw away his life for his officer, or for a chap he didn't know, just as though it was a cigarette butt. I've seen the women nurses of our corps steer a car into a village and yank out a wounded man while shells were breaking under the wheels and the houses were pitching into the streets." He stopped and laughed consciously.

"Understand," he warned me, "I'm not talking about myself, only of things I've seen. The things I'm going to put in my book. It ought to be a pretty good book—what?"

My envy had been washed clean in admiration.

"It will make a wonderful book," I agreed. "Are you going to syndicate it first?"

Young Mr. Hamlin frowned importantly.

"I was thinking," he said, "of asking John for letters to the magazine editors. So they'll know I'm not faking, that I've really been through it all. Letters from John would help a lot." Then he asked anxiously: "They would, wouldn't they?"

I reassured him. Remembering the Kid's jibes at John and his numerous dependents, I said: "You another college chum of John's?" The young man answered my question quite seriously. "No," he said; "John graduated before I entered; but we belong to the same fraternity. It was the luckiest chance in the world my finding him here. There was a month-old copy of the *Balkan News* blowing around camp, and his name was in the list of arrivals. The moment I found he was in Salonika, I asked for twelve hours leave and came down in an ambulance. I made straight for John; gave him the grip, and put it up to him to help me."

"I don't understand," I said. "I thought you were sailing on the *Adriaticus*?"

The young man was again pacing the floor. He halted and faced the harbor.

"You bet I'm sailing on the *Adriaticus*," he said. He looked out at that vessel, at the Blue Peter flying from her foremast, and grinned. "In just two hours!"

It was stupid of me, but I still was unenlightened. "But your twelve hours' leave?" I asked.

The young man laughed. "They can take my twelve hours' leave," he said deliberately, "and feed it to the chickens. I'm beating it."

"What d'you mean, you're beating it?"

"What do you suppose I mean?" he demanded. "What do you suppose I'm doing out of uniform, what do you suppose I'm lying low in the room for? So's I won't catch cold?"

"If you're leaving the army without a discharge, and without permission," I said, "I suppose you know it's desertion."

Mr. Hamlin laughed easily. "It's not *my* army," he said. "I'm an American."

"It's your desertion," I suggested.

The door opened and closed noiselessly, and Billy, entering, placed a new traveling bag on the floor. He must have heard my last words, for he looked inquiringly at each of us. But he did not speak and, walking to the window, stood with his hands in his pockets, staring out at the harbor. His presence seemed to encourage the young man. "Who knows I'm deserting?" he demanded. "No one's ever seen me in Salonika before, and in these 'cits' I can get on board all right. And then they can't touch me. What do the folks at home care *how* I left the British army? They'll be so darned glad to get me back alive that they won't ask if I walked out or was kicked out. I should worry!"

"It's none of my business," I began, but I was interrupted. In his restless pacings the young man turned quickly.

"As you say," he remarked icily, "it *is* none of your business. It's none of your business whether I get shot as a deserter, or go home, or——"

"You can go to the devil for all I care," I assured him. "I wasn't considering you at all. I was only sorry that I'll never be able to read your book."

For a moment Mr. Hamlin remained silent, then he burst forth with a jeer.

"No British firing squad," he boasted, "will ever stand *me* up."

"Maybe not," I agreed, "but you will never write that book."

Again there was silence, and this time it was broken by the Kid. He turned from the window and looked toward Hamlin. "That's right!" he said.

He sat down on the edge of the table, and at the deserter pointed his forefinger.

"Son," he said, "this war is some war. It's the biggest war in history, and folks will be talking about nothing else for the next ninety years; folks that never were nearer it than Bay City, Mich. But you won't talk about it. And you've been all through it. You've been to hell and back again. Compared with what you know about hell, Dante is in the same class with Dr. Cook. But you won't be able to talk about this war, or lecture, or write a book about it."

"I won't?" demanded Hamlin. "And why won't I?"

"Because of what you're doing now," said Billy. "Because you're queering yourself. Now, you've got everything." The Kid was very much in earnest. His tone was intimate, kind, and friendly. "You've seen everything, done everything. We'd give our eye-teeth to see what you've seen, and to write the things you can write. You've got a record now that'll last you until you're dead, and your grandchildren are dead—and then some. When you talk the table will have to sit up and listen. You can say 'I was there.' 'I was in it.' 'I saw.' 'I know.' When this war is over you'll have everything out of it that's worth getting—all the experiences, all the inside knowledge, all the 'nose-bag' news; you'll have wounds, honors, medals, money, reputation. And you're throwing all that away!"

Mr. Hamlin interrupted savagely.

"To hell with their medals," he said. "They can take their medals and hang 'em on Christmas trees. I don't owe the British army anything. It owes me. I've done *my* bit. I've earned what I've got, and there's no one can take it away from me."

"*You* can," said the Kid. Before Hamlin could reply the door opened and John came in, followed by Uncle Jim. The older man was looking very grave, and John very unhappy. Hamlin turned quickly to John.

"I thought these men were friends of yours," he began, "and Americans. They're fine Americans. They're as full of human kindness and red blood as a kippered herring!"

John looked inquiringly at the Kid.

"He wants to hang himself," explained Billy, "and because we tried to cut him down, he's sore."

"They talked to me," protested Hamlin, "as though I was a yellow dog. As though I was a quitter. I'm no quitter! But, if I'm ready to quit, who's got a better right? I'm not an Englishman, but there are several million Englishmen haven't done as much for England in this war as I have. What do you fellows know about it? You *write* about it, about the 'brave lads in the trenches'; but what do you know about the trenches? What you've seen from automobiles. That's all. That's where *you* get off! I've *lived* in the trenches for fifteen months, froze in 'em, starved in 'em, risked my life in 'em, and I've saved other lives, too, by hauling men out of the trenches. And that's no airy persiflage, either!"

He ran to the wardrobe where John's clothes hung, and from the bottom of it dragged a khaki uniform. It was still so caked with mud and snow that when he flung it on the floor it splashed like a wet bathing suit. "How would you like to wear one of those?" he demanded. "Stinking with lice and sweat and blood; the blood of other men, the men you've helped off the field, and your own blood."

As though committing hara-kiri, he slashed his hand across his stomach, and then drew it up from his waist to his chin. "I'm scraped with shrapnel from there to there," said Mr. Hamlin. "And another time I got a ball in the shoulder. That would have been a 'blighty' for a fighting man—they're always giving *them* leave—but all I got was six weeks at Havre in hospital. Then it was the Dardanelles, and sunstroke and sand; sleeping in sand, eating sand, sand in your boots, sand in your teeth; hiding in holes in the sand like a dirty prairie dog. And then, 'Off to Servia!' And the next act opens in the snow and the mud! Cold? God, how cold it was! And most of us in sun helmets."

As though the cold still gnawed at his bones, he shivered.

"It isn't the danger," he protested. "It isn't *that* I'm getting away from. To hell with the danger! It's just the plain discomfort of it! It's the never being your own master, never being clean, never being warm." Again he shivered and rubbed one hand against the other. "There were no bridges over the streams," he went on, "and we had to break the ice and wade in, and then sleep in the open with the khaki frozen to us. There was no firewood; not enough to warm a pot of tea. There were no wounded; all our casualties were frost bite and pneumonia. When we take them out of the blankets their toes fall off. We've been in camp for a month now near Doiran, and it's worse there than on the march. It's a frozen swamp. You can't sleep for the cold; can't eat; the only ration we get is bully beef, and our insides are frozen so damn tight we can't digest it. The cold gets into your blood, gets into your brains. It won't let you think; or else, you think crazy things. It makes you afraid." He shook himself like a man coming out of a bad dream.

"So, I'm through," he said. In turn he scowled at each of us, as though defying us to contradict him. "That's why I'm quitting," he added. "Because I've done my bit. Because I'm damn well fed up on it." He kicked viciously at the water-logged uniform on the floor. "Any one who wants my job can have it!" He walked to the window, turned his back on us, and fixed his eyes hungrily on the *Adriaticus*. There was a long pause. For guidance we looked at John, but he was staring down at the desk blotter, scratching on it marks that he did not see.

Finally, where angels feared to tread, the Kid rushed in. "That's certainly a hard luck story," he said; "but," he added cheerfully, "it's nothing to the hard luck you'll strike when you can't tell why you left the army." Hamlin turned with an exclamation, but Billy held up his hand. "Now wait," he begged, "we haven't time to get mussy. At six o'clock your leave is up, and the troop train starts back to camp, and——"

Mr. Hamlin interrupted sharply. "And the *Adriaticus* starts at five."

Billy did not heed him. "You've got two hours to change your mind," he said. "That's better than being sorry you didn't the rest of your life."

Mr. Hamlin threw back his head and laughed. It was a most unpleasant laugh. "You're a fine body of men," he jeered. "America must be proud of you!"

"If we *weren't* Americans," explained Billy patiently, "we wouldn't give a damn whether you deserted or not. You're drowning and you don't know it, and we're throwing you a rope. Try to see it that way. We'll cut out the fact that you took an oath, and that you're breaking it. That's up to you. We'll get down to results. When you reach home, if you can't tell why you left the army, the folks will darned soon guess. And that will queer everything you've done. When you come to sell your stuff, it will queer you with the editors, queer you with the publishers. If they know you broke your word to the British army, how can they know you're keeping faith with them? How can they believe anything you tell them? Every 'story' you write, every statement of yours will make a noise like a fake. You won't come into court with clean hands. You'll be licked before you start.

"Of course, you're for the Allies. Well, all the Germans at home will fear that; and when you want to lecture on your 'Fifteen Months at the British Front,' they'll look up your record; and what will they do to you? This is what they'll do to you. When you've shown 'em your moving pictures and say, 'Does any gentleman in the audience want to ask a question?' a German agent will get up and say, 'Yes, I want to ask a question. Is it true that you deserted from the British army, and that if you return to it, they will shoot you?' "

I was scared. I expected the lean and muscular Mr. Hamlin to fall on Billy, and fling him where he had flung the soggy uniform. But instead he remained motionless, his arms pressed across his chest. His eyes, filled with anger and distress, returned to the *Adriaticus*.

"I'm sorry," muttered the Kid.

John rose and motioned to the door, and guiltily and only too gladly we escaped. John followed us into the hall. "Let *me* talk to him," he whispered. "The boat sails in an hour. Please don't come back until she's gone."

We went to the moving picture palace next door, but I doubt if the thoughts of any of us were on the pictures. For after an hour, when from across the quay there came the long-drawn warning of a steamer's whistle, we nudged each other and rose and went out.

Not a hundred yards from us the propeller blades of the *Adriaticus* were slowly churning, and the rowboats were falling away from her sides.

"Good-bye, Mr. Hamlin," called Billy. "You had everything and you chucked it away. I can spell your finish. It's 'check' for *yours*."

But when we entered our room, in the centre of it, under the bunch of electric lights, stood the deserter. He wore the water-logged uniform. The sun helmet was on his head.

"Good man!" shouted Billy.

He advanced, eagerly holding out his hand.

Mr. Hamlin brushed past him. At the door he turned and glared at us, even at John. He was not a good loser. "I hope you're satisfied," he snarled. He pointed at the four beds in a row. I felt guiltily conscious of them. At the moment they appeared so unnecessarily clean and warm and soft. The silk coverlets at the foot of each struck me as being disgracefully effeminate. They made me ashamed.

"I hope," said Mr. Hamlin, speaking slowly and picking his words, "when you turn into those beds to-night you'll think of me in the mud. I hope when you're having your five-course dinner, and your champagne you'll remember my bully beef. I hope when a shell or Mr. Pneumonia gets me, you'll write a nice little sob story about the 'brave lads in the trenches.' "

He looked at us, standing like schoolboys, sheepish, embarrassed, and silent, and then threw open the door. "I hope," he added, "you all choke!"

With an unconvincing imitation of the college chum manner, John cleared his throat and said: "Don't forget, Fred, if there's anything I can do——"

Hamlin stood in the doorway smiling at us.

"There's something you can all do," he said.

"Yes?" asked John heartily.

"You can all go to hell!" said Mr. Hamlin.

We heard the door slam, and his hobnailed boots pounding down the stairs. No one spoke. Instead, in unhappy silence, we stood staring at the floor. Where the uniform had lain was a pool of mud and melted snow and the darker stains of stale blood.

JOHN GALSWORTHY

The Apple Tree

John Galsworthy (1867–1933)

THE ARCHITECT OF The Forsyte Saga, *that vast monument to the virtues and fatal defects of the British upper-middle class, needs no advertisement in this place. It is proper to recall, however, that his talents were not always exerted to catch a moment in history and give it enduring substance. In several of his shorter works he put aside his explicit moral purpose, his epic scope, and his realistic technique, and wrote like a lyric poet; like a sensitive participant in individual tragedy.*

The Apple Tree *is such a work. It ranks with* The Indian Summer of a Forsyte *as an almost perfect performance, in which Galsworthy's mannerisms (so handsomely parodied in Max Beerbohm's* Christmas Garland) *become insignificant as he is carried away by his theme.*

The Apple Tree *is a tale of youth, spring, renunciation, and the break of a simple heart. It was written in 1916, at a time when Great Britain's fortunes were at low ebb and the much-prized British virtues of fortitude and courage were most earnestly called for. This story, with its loving memories of atmospheres and weather and of the countryside in rebirth, is as much a paean of love of one's native place in a moment of danger as Masefield's haunting poem,* August, 1914. *And it is more. It is Megan David's story, she who was "tu lovin' 'earted" and died in spring as did so many of Robin Herrick's fair maids; in its telling Galsworthy's prose rises to a Shakespearian grandeur, and Megan's sorrow becomes the sorrow of all those simply generous ones who are rejected and cannot understand.*

THE APPLE TREE

"The Apple-tree, the singing and the gold."
MURRAY'S "HIPPOLYTUS OF EURIPIDES."

ON their silver-wedding day Ashurst and his wife were motoring along the outskirts of the moor, intending to crown the festival by stopping the night at Torquay, where they had first met. This was the idea of Stella Ashurst, whose character contained a streak of sentiment. If she had long lost the blue-eyed, flower-like charm, the cool slim purity of face and form, the apple-blossom colouring, that had so swiftly and so oddly affected Ashurst twenty-six years ago, she was still at forty-three a comely and faithful companion, whose cheeks were faintly mottled, and whose grey-blue eyes had acquired a certain fullness.

It was she who had stopped the car where the common rose steeply to the left, and a narrow strip of larch and beech, with here and there a pine, stretched out to the right, towards the valley between the road and the first long high hill of the full moor. She was looking for a place where they might lunch, for Ashurst never looked for anything; and this, between the golden furze and the feathery green larches smelling of lemons in the last sun of April—this, with a view into the deep valley and up to the long moor heights, seemed fitting to the decisive nature of one who sketched in water-colours, and loved romantic spots. Grasping her paint box, she got out.

"Won't this do, Frank?"

Ashurst, rather like a bearded Schiller, grey in the wings, tall, long-legged, with large remote grey eyes that sometimes filled with meaning and became almost beautiful, with nose a little to one side, and bearded lips just open—Ashurst, forty-eight, and silent, grasped the luncheon basket, and got out too.

"Oh! Look, Frank! A grave!"

By the side of the road, where the track from the top of the common crossed it at right angles and ran through a gate past the narrow wood, was a thin mound of turf, six feet by one, with a moor-stone to the west, and on it someone had thrown a blackthorn spray and a handful of bluebells. Ashurst looked, and the poet in him moved. At cross-roads—a suicide's grave! Poor mortals with their superstitions! Whoever lay there, though, had the best of it—no clammy sepulchre among other hideous graves carved with futilities—just a rough stone, the wide sky, and wayside blessings! And, without comment, for he had learned not to be a philosopher in the bosom of his family, he strode away up on to the common, dropped the luncheon basket under a wall, spread a rug for his wife to sit on—she would turn up from her sketching when she was hungry—and took from his pocket Murray's translation of the "Hippolytus." He had soon finished reading of "The Cyprian" and her revenge, and looked at the sky instead. And watching the white clouds so bright against the intense blue, Ashurst, on his silver-wedding day, longed for—he knew not what. Maladjusted to life—man's organism! One's mode of life might be high and scrupulous, but there was always an undercurrent of greediness, a hankering, and sense of waste. Did women have it, too? Who could tell? And yet, men who gave vent to their appetites for novelty, their riotous longings for new adventures, new risks, new pleasures, these suffered, no doubt, from the reverse side of starvation, from surfeit. No getting out of it—a maladjusted animal, civilised man! There could be no garden of his choosing, of "the Apple-tree, the singing, and the gold," in the words of that lovely Greek chorus, no achievable elysium in life, or lasting haven of happiness for any man with a sense of beauty—nothing that could compare with the captured loveliness in a work of art, set down for ever, so that to look on it or read was always to have the same precious sense of exaltation and restful inebriety. Life no doubt had moments with that quality of beauty, of unbidden flying rapture, but the trouble was they lasted no longer than the span of a cloud's flight over the sun; impossible to keep them with you, as Art caught beauty and held it fast. They were as fleeting as one of the glimmering or golden visions one had of the soul in nature, glimpses of its remote and brooding spirit. Here, with the sun hot on his face, a cuckoo calling from a thorn tree, and in the air the honey savour of gorse—here among the little fronds of the young fern, the starry blackthorn, while the bright clouds drifted by high above the hills and dreamy valleys—here and now was such a glimpse. But in a moment it would pass—as the face of Pan, that looks round the corner of a rock, vanishes at your stare. And suddenly he sat up. Surely there was something familiar about this view, this bit of common, that ribbon of road, the old wall behind him. While they were driving he had not been taking notice—never did; thinking of far things or of nothing—but now he saw! Twenty-six years ago, just at this time of year, from the farmhouse within half a mile of this very spot he had started for that day in Torquay whence it might be said he had never returned. And a sudden ache beset his heart; he had stumbled on just one of those past moments in his life, whose beauty and rapture he had failed to arrest, whose wings had fluttered away into the unknown; he had stumbled on a buried memory, a wild sweet time, swiftly choked and ended. And, turning on his face, he rested his chin on his hands, and stared at the short grass where the little blue milkwort was growing. . . .

And this is what he remembered.

1 §

On the first of May, after their last year together at college, Frank Ashurst and his friend Robert Garton were on a tramp. They had walked that day from Brent, intending to make Chagford, but Ashurst's football knee had given out, and according to their map they had still some seven miles to go. They were sitting on a bank beside the road, where a track crossed alongside a wood, resting the knee and talking of the universe, as young men will. Both were over six feet, and as thin as rails; Ashurst pale, idealistic, full of absence; Garton queer, round-the-corner, knotted, curly, like some primeval beast. Both had a literary bent; neither wore a hat. Ashurst's hair was smooth, pale, wavy, and had a way of rising on either side of his brow, as if always being flung back; Garton's was a kind of dark unfathomed mop. They had not met a soul for miles.

"My dear fellow," Garton was saying, "pity's only the effect of self-consciousness; it's a disease of the last five thousand years. The world was happier without."

Ashurst, following the clouds with his eyes, answered:

"It's the pearl in the oyster, anyway."

"My dear chap, all our modern unhappiness comes from pity. Look at animals, and Red Indians, limited to feeling their own occasional misfortune; then look at ourselves—never free from feeling the toothaches of others. Let's get back to feeling for nobody, and have a better time."

"You'll never practise that."

Garton pensively stirred the hotch-potch of his hair.

"To attain full growth, one mustn't be squeamish. To starve oneself emotionally's a mistake. All emotion is to the good—enriches life."

"Yes, and when it runs up against chivalry?"

"Ah! That's so English! If you speak emotion the English always think you want something physical, and are shocked. They're afraid of passion, but not of lust—oh, no!—so long as they can keep it secret."

Ashurst did not answer; he had plucked a blue flowerlet, and was twiddling it against the sky. A cuckoo began calling from a thorn-tree. The sky, the flowers, the songs of birds! Robert was talking through his hat! And he said:

"Well, let's go on, and find some farm where we can put up." In uttering those words, he was conscious of a girl coming down from the common just above them. She was outlined against the sky, carrying a basket, and you could see that sky through the crook of her arm. And Ashurst, who saw beauty without wondering how it could advantage him, thought: 'How pretty!' The wind, blowing her frieze skirt against her legs, lifted her battered peacock tam-o'-shanter; her greyish blouse was worn and old, her shoes were split, her little hands rough and red, her neck browned. Her dark hair waved untidy across her broad forehead, her face was short, her upper lip short, showing a glint of teeth, her brows were straight and dark, her lashes long and dark, her nose straight; but her grey eyes were the wonder—as dewy as if opened for the first time that way. She looked at Ashurst—perhaps he struck her as strange, limping along without a hat, with his large eyes on her, and his hair flung back. He could not take off what was not on his head, but put up his hand in a salute, and said:

"Can you tell us if there's a farm near here where we could stay the night? I've gone lame."

"There's only our farm near, sir." She spoke without shyness, in a pretty soft crisp voice.

"And where is that?"

"Down here, sir."

"Would you put us up?"

"Oh! I think we would."

"Will you show us the way?"

"Yes, sir."

He limped on, silent, and Garton took up the catechism.

"Are you a Devonshire girl?"

"No, sir."

"What then?"

"From Wales."

"Ah! I *thought* you were a Celt; so it's not your farm?"

"My aunt's, sir."

"And your uncle's?"

"He is dead."

"Who farms it, then?"

"My aunt, and my three cousins."

"But your uncle was a Devonshire man?"

"Yes, sir."

"Have you lived here long?"

"Seven years."

"And how d'you like it after Wales?"

"I don't know, sir."

"I suppose you don't remember?"

"Oh, yes! But it is different."

"I believe you!"

Ashurst broke in suddenly:

"How old are you?"

"Seventeen, sir."

"And what's your name?"

"Megan David."

"This is Robert Garton, and I am Frank Ashurst. We wanted to get on to Chagford."

"It is a pity your leg is hurting you."

Ashurst smiled, and when he smiled his face was rather beautiful.

Descending past the narrow wood, they came on the farm suddenly—a long, slow, stone-built dwelling with casement windows, in a farmyard where pigs and fowls and an old mare were straying. A short steep-up grass hill behind was crowned with a few Scotch firs, and in front, an old orchard of apple trees, just breaking into flower, stretched down to the stream and a long wild meadow. A little boy with oblique dark eyes was shepherding a pig, and by the house door stood a woman, who came towards them. The girl said:

"It is Mrs. Narracombe, my aunt."

"Mrs. Narracombe, my aunt," had a quick dark eye, like a mother wild-duck's, and something of the same snaky turn about her neck.

"We met your niece on the road," said Ashurst; "she thought you might perhaps put us up for the night."

Mrs. Narracombe, taking them in from head to heel, answered:

"Well, I can, if you don't mind one room. Megan, get the spare room ready, and a bowl of cream. You'll be wanting tea, I suppose."

Passing through a sort of porch made by two yew trees and some flowering currant bushes, the girl disappeared into the house, her peacock tam-o'-shanter bright athwart that rosy-pink and the dark green of the yews.

"Will you come into the parlour and rest your leg? You'll be from college, perhaps?"

"We were, but we've gone down now."

Mrs. Narracombe nodded sagely.

The parlour, brick-floored, with bare table and shiny chairs and sofa stuffed with horsehair, seemed never to have been used, it was so terribly clean. Ashurst sat down at once on the sofa, holding his lame knee between his hands, and Mrs. Narracombe gazed at him. He was only the son of a late professor of chemistry, but people found a certain lordliness in one who was often sublimely unconscious of them.

"Is there a stream where we could bathe?"

"There's the stream at the bottom of the orchard, but sittin' down you'll not be covered!"

"How deep?"

"Well, 'tis about a foot and a half, maybe."

"Oh! That'll do fine. Which way?"

"Down the lane, through the second gate on the right, an' the pool's by the big apple tree that stands by itself. There's trout there, if you can tickle them."

"They're more likely to tickle us!"

Mrs. Narracombe smiled. "There'll be the tea ready when you come back."

The pool, formed by the damming of a rock, had a sandy bottom; and the big apple tree, lowest in the orchard, grew so close that its boughs almost overhung the water; it was in leaf, and all but in flower—its crimson buds just bursting. There was not room for more than one at a time in that narrow bath, and Ashurst waited his turn, rubbing his knee and gazing at the wild meadow, all rocks and thorn trees and field flowers, with a grove of beeches beyond, raised up on a flat mound. Every bough was swinging in the wind, every spring bird calling, and a slanting sunlight dappled the grass. He thought of Theocritus, and the river Cherwell, of the moon, and the maiden with the dewy eyes; of so many things that he seemed to think of nothing; and he felt absurdly happy.

2 §

During a late and sumptuous tea with eggs to it, cream and jam, and thin, fresh cakes touched with saffron, Garton descanted on the Celts. It was about the period of the Celtic awakening, and the discovery that there was Celtic blood about this family had excited one who believed that he was a Celt himself. Sprawling on a horsehair chair, with a hand-made cigarette dribbling from the corner of his curly lips, he had been plunging his cold pin-points of eyes into Ashurst's and praising the refinement of the Welsh. To come out of Wales into England was like the change from china to earthenware! Frank, as a d——d Englishman, had not of course perceived the exquisite refinement and emotional capacity of that Welsh girl! And, delicately stirring in the dark mat of his still wet hair, he explained how exactly she illustrated the writing of the Welsh bard Morgan-ap-Something in the twelfth century.

Ashurst, full length on the horsehair sofa, and jutting far beyond its end, smoked a deeply-coloured pipe, and did not listen, thinking of the girl's face when she brought in a relay of cakes. It had been exactly like looking at a flower, or some other pretty sight in Nature—till, with a funny little shiver, she had lowered her glance and gone out, quiet as a mouse.

"Let's go to the kitchen," said Garton, "and see some more of her."

The kitchen was a white-washed room with rafters, to which were attached smoked hams; there were flower-pots on the window-sill, and guns hanging on nails, queer mugs, china and pewter, and portraits of Queen Victoria. A long, narrow table of plain wood was set with bowls and spoons, under a string of high-hung onions; two sheepdogs and three cats lay here and there. On one side of the recessed fireplace sat two small boys, idle, and good as gold; on the other sat a stout, light-eyed, red-faced youth with hair and lashes the colour of the tow he was running through the barrel of a gun; between them Mrs. Narracombe dreamily stirred some savoury-scented stew in a large pot. Two other youths, oblique-eyed, dark-haired, rather sly-faced, like the two little boys, were talking together and lolling against the wall; and a short, elderly, clean-shaven man in corduroys, seated in the window, was conning a battered journal. The girl Megan seemed the only active creature—drawing cider and passing with the jugs from cask to table. Seeing them thus about to eat, Garton said:

"Ah! If you'll let us, we'll come back when supper's over," and without waiting for an answer they withdrew again to the parlour. But the colour in the kitchen, the warmth, the scents, and all those faces, heightened the bleakness of their shiny room, and they resumed their seats moodily.

"Regular gipsy type, those boys. There was only one Saxon—the fellow cleaning the gun. That girl is a very subtle study psychologically."

Ashurst's lips twitched. Garton seemed to him an ass just then. Subtle study! She was a wild flower. A creature it did you good to look at. Study!

Garton went on:

"Emotionally she would be wonderful. She wants awakening."

"Are you going to awaken her?"

Garton looked at him and smiled. "How coarse and English you are!" that curly smile seemed saying.

And Ashurst puffed his pipe. Awaken her! That fool had the best opinion of himself! He threw up the window and leaned out. Dusk had gathered thick. The farm buildings and the wheel-house were all dim and blueish, the apple trees but a blurred wilderness; the air smelled of wood-smoke from the kitchen fire. One bird going to bed later than the others was uttering a half-hearted twitter, as though surprised at the darkness. From the stable came the snuffle and stamp of a feeding horse. And away over there was the loom of the moor, and away and away the shy stars that had not as yet full light, pricking white through the deep blue heavens. A quavering owl hooted. Ashurst drew a deep breath. What a night to wander out in! A padding of unshod hoofs came up the lane, and three dim, dark shapes passed—ponies on an evening march. Their heads, black and fuzzy, showed above the gate. At the tap of his pipe, and a shower of little sparks, they shied round and scampered. A bat went fluttering past, uttering its almost inaudible "chip, chip." Ashurst held out his hand; on the upturned palm he could feel the dew. Suddenly from overhead he heard little burring boys' voices, little thumps of boots thrown down, and another voice, crisp and soft—the girl's, putting them to bed, no doubt; and nine clear words: "No, Rick, you can't have the cat in bed"; then came a skirmish of giggles and gurgles, a soft slap, a laugh so low and pretty that it made him shiver a little. A blowing sound, and the glim of the candle that was fingering the dusk above, went out; silence reigned. Ashurst withdrew into the room and sat down; his knee pained him, and his soul felt gloomy.

"You go to the kitchen," he said; "I'm going to bed."

3 §

For Ashurst the wheel of slumber was wont to turn noiseless and slick and swift, but though he seemed sunk in sleep when his companion came up, he was really wide awake; and long after Garton, smothered in the other bed of that low-roofed room, was worshipping darkness with his upturned nose, he heard the owls. Barring the discomfort of his knee, it was not unpleasant—the cares of life did not loom large in night watches for this young man. In fact he had none; just enrolled a barrister, with literary aspirations, the world before him, no father or mother, and four hundred a year of his own. Did it matter where he went, what he did, or when he did it? His bed, too, was hard, and this preserved him from fever. He lay, sniffing the scent of the night that drifted into the low room through the open casement close to his head. Except for a definite irritation with his friend, natural when you have tramped with a man for three days, Ashurst's memories and visions that sleepless night were kindly and wistful and exciting. One vision, specially clear and unreasonable, for he had not even been conscious of noting it, was the face of the youth cleaning the gun; its intent, stolid, yet startled uplook at the kitchen doorway, quickly shifted to the girl carrying the cider jug. This red, blue-eyed, light-lashed, tow-haired face struck as firmly in his memory as the girl's own face, so dewy and simple. But at last, in the square of darkness through the uncurtained casement, he saw day coming, and heard one hoarse and sleepy caw. Then followed silence, dead as ever, till the song of a blackbird, not properly awake, adventured into the hush. And, from staring at the framed brightening light, Ashurst fell asleep.

Next day his knee was badly swollen; the walking tour was obviously over. Garton, due back in London on the morrow, departed at midday with an ironical smile which left a scar of irritation—healed the moment his loping figure vanished round the corner of the steep lane. All day Ashurst rested his knee, in a green-painted wooden chair on the patch of grass by the yew-tree porch, where the sunlight distilled the scent of stocks and gilly-flowers, and a ghost of scent from the flowering currant bushes. Beatifically he smoked, dreamed, watched.

A farm in the spring is all birth—young things coming out of bud and shell, and human beings watching over the process with faint excitement, feeding and tending what has been born. So still the young man sat, that a mother-goose, with stately cross-footed waddle, brought her six yellow-necked grey-backed goslings to strop their little beaks against the grass blades at his feet. Now and again Mrs. Narracombe or the girl Megan would come and ask if he wanted anything, and he would smile and say: "Nothing, thanks. It's splendid here." Towards tea-time they came out together, bearing a long poultice of some dark stuff in a bowl, and after a long and solemn scrutiny of his swollen knee, bound it on. When they were gone, he thought of the girl's soft "Oh!"—of her pitying eyes, and the little wrinkle in her brow. And again he felt that unreasoning irritation against his departed friend, who had talked such rot about her. When she brought out his tea, he said:

"How did you like my friend, Megan?"

She forced down her upper lip, as if afraid that to smile was not polite. "He was a funny gentleman; he made us laugh. I think he is very clever."

"What did he say to make you laugh?"

"He said I was a daughter of the bards. What are they?"

"Welsh poets, who lived hundreds of years ago."

"Why am I their daughter, please?"

"He meant that you were the sort of girl they sang about."

She wrinkled her brows. "I think he likes to joke. Am I?"

"Would you believe me, if I told you?"

"Oh, yes!"

"Well, I think he was right."

She smiled.

And Ashurst thought: 'You *are* a pretty thing!'

"He said, too, that Joe was a Saxon type. What would that be?"

"Which is Joe? With the blue eyes and red face?"

"Yes. My uncle's nephew."

"Not your cousin, then?"

"No."

"Well, he meant that Joe was like the men who came over to England about fourteen hundred years ago, and conquered it."

"Oh! I know about them; but is he?"

"Garton's crazy about that sort of thing; but I must say Joe does look a bit Early Saxon."

"Yes."

That "Yes" tickled Ashurst. It was so crisp and graceful, so conclusive, and politely acquiescent in what was evidently Greek to her.

"He said that all the other boys were regular gipsies. He should not have said that. My aunt laughed, but she didn't like it, of course, and my cousins were angry. Uncle was a farmer—farmers are not gipsies. It is wrong to hurt people."

Ashurst wanted to take her hand and give it a squeeze, but he only answered:

"Quite right, Megan. By the way, I heard you putting the little ones to bed last night."

She flushed a little. "Please to drink your tea—it is getting cold. Shall I get you some fresh?"

"Do you ever have time to do anything for yourself?"

"Oh! Yes."

"I've been watching, but I haven't seen it yet."

She wrinkled her brows in a puzzled frown, and her colour deepened.

When she was gone, Ashurst thought: 'Did she think I was chaffing her? I wouldn't for the world!' He was at that age when to some men "Beauty's a flower," as the poet says, and inspires in them the thoughts of chivalry. Never very conscious of his surroundings, it was some time before he was aware that the youth whom Garton had called "a Saxon type" was standing outside the stable door; and a fine bit of colour he made in his soiled brown velvet-cords, muddy gaiters, and blue shirt; red-armed, red-faced, the sun turning his hair from tow to flax; immovably stolid, persistent, unsmiling he stood. Then, seeing Ashurst looking at him, he crossed the yard at that gait of the young countryman always ashamed not to be slow and heavy-dwelling on each leg, and disappeared round the end of the house towards the kitchen entrance. A chill came over Ashurst's mood. Clods? With all the good will in the world, how impossible to get on terms with them. And yet—see that girl! Her shoes were split, her hands rough; but—what was it? Was it really her Celtic blood, as Garton had said?—she was a lady born, a jewel, though probably she could do no more than just read and write!

The elderly, clean-shaved man he had seen last night in the kitchen had come into the yard with a dog, driving the cows to their milking. Ashurst saw that he was lame.

"You've got some good ones there!"

The lame man's face brightened. He had the upward look in his eyes that prolonged suffering often brings.

"Yeas; they'm praaper buties; gude milkers tu."

"I bet they are."

" 'Ope as yure leg's better, zurr."

"Thank you, it's getting on."

The lame man touched his own: "I know what 'tes meself; 'tes a main worritin' thing, the knee. I've a—'ad mine bad this ten year."

Ashurst made the sound of sympathy that comes so readily from those who have an independent income, and the lame man smiled again.

"Mustn't complain, though—they mighty near 'ad it off."

"Ho!"

"Yeas; an' compared with what 'twas, 'tes almost so gude as nu."

"They've put a bandage of splendid stuff on mine."

"The maid she picks et. She'm a gude maid wi' the flowers. There's folks zeem to know the healin' in things. My mother was a rare one for that. 'Ope as yu'll zune be better, zurr. Goo ahn, therr!"

Ashurst smiled. "Wi' the flowers!" A flower herself!

That evening, after his supper of cold duck, junket, and cider, the girl came in.

"Please, auntie says—will you try a piece of our Mayday cake?"

"If I may come to the kitchen for it."

"Oh, yes! You'll be missing your friend."

"Not I. But are you sure no one minds?"

"Who would mind? We shall be very pleased."

Ashurst rose too suddenly for his stiff knee, staggered, and subsided. The girl gave a little gasp, and held out her hands. Ashurst took them, small, rough, brown; checked his impulse to put them to his lips, and let her pull him up. She came close beside him, offering her shoulder. And leaning on her he walked across the room. That shoulder seemed quite the pleasantest thing he had ever touched. But he had presence of mind enough to catch his stick out of the rack, and withdraw his hand before arriving at the kitchen.

That night he slept like a top, and woke with his knee of almost normal size. He again spent the morning in his chair on the grass patch, scribbling down verses; but in the afternoon he wandered about with the two little boys Nick and Rick. It was Saturday, so they were early home from school; quick, shy, dark little rascals of seven and six, soon talkative, for Ashurst had a way with children. They had shown him all their methods of destroying life by four o'clock, except the tickling of trout; and with breeches tucked up, lay on their stomachs over the trout stream, pretending they had this accomplishment also. They tickled nothing, of course, for their giggling and shouting scared every spotted thing away. Ashurst, on a rock at the edge of the beech clump, watched them, and listened to the cuckoos, till Nick, the elder and less persevering came up and stood beside him.

"The gipsy bogle zets on that stone," he said.

"What gipsy bogle?"

"Dunno; never zeen 'e. Megan zays 'e zets there; an' old Jim zeed 'e once. 'E was zettin' there naight afore our pony kicked-in father's 'ead. 'E plays the viddle."

"What tune does he play?"

"Dunno."

"What's he like?"

" 'E's black. Old Jim zays 'e's all over 'air. 'E's a praaper bogle. 'E don' come only at naight." The little boy's oblique dark eyes slid round. "D'yu think 'e might want to take me away? Megan's feared of 'e."

"Has she seen him?"

"No. She's not afeared o' yu."

"I should think not. Why should she be?"

"She zays a prayer for yu."

"How do you know that, you little rascal?"

"When I was asleep, she said: 'God bless us all, an' Mr. Ashes.' I yeard 'er whisperin'."

"You're a little ruffian to tell what you hear when you're not meant to hear it!"

The little boy was silent. Then he said aggressively:

"I can skin rabbets. Megan, she can't bear skinnin' 'em. I like blood."

"Oh! you do; you little monster!"

"What's that?"

"A creature that likes hurting others."

The little boy scowled. "They'm only dead rabbets, what us eats."

"Quite right, Nick. I beg your pardon."

"I can skin frogs, tu."

But Ashurst had become absent. "God bless us all, and Mr. Ashes!" And puzzled by the sudden inaccessibility, Nick ran back to the stream, where the giggling and shouts again uprose at once.

When Megan brought his tea, he said:

"What's the gipsy bogle, Megan?"

She looked up, startled.

"He brings bad things."

"Surely you don't believe in ghosts?"

"I hope I will never see him."

"Of course you won't. There aren't such things. What old Jim saw was a pony."

"No! There are bogles in the rocks; they are the men that lived long ago."

"They aren't gipsies, anyway; those old men were dead long before gipsies came."

She said simply: "They are all bad."

"Why? If there are any, they're only wild, like the rabbits. The flowers aren't bad for being wild; the thorn trees were never planted—and you don't mind them. I shall go down at night and look for your bogle, and have a talk with him."

"Oh, no! Oh, no!"

"Oh, yes! I shall go and sit on his rock."

She clasped her hands together: "Oh, please!"

"Why! What does it matter if anything happens to me?"

She did not answer; and in a sort of pet he added:

"Well, I daresay I shan't see him, because I suppose I must be off soon."

"Soon?"

"Your aunt won't want to keep me here."

"Oh, yes! We always let lodgings in summer."

Fixing his eyes on her face, he asked:

"Would you like me to stay?"

"Yes."

"I'm going to say a prayer for *you* to-night!"

She flushed crimson, frowned, and went out of the room. He sat, cursing himself, till his tea was stewed. It was as if he had hacked with his thick boots at a clump of bluebells. Why had he said such a silly thing? Was he just a towny college ass like Robert Garton, as far from understanding this girl?

4 §

Ashurst spent the next week confirming the restoration of his leg, by exploration of the country within easy reach. Spring was a revelation to him this year. In a kind of intoxication he would watch the pink-white buds of some backward beech tree sprayed up in the sunlight against the deep blue sky, or the trunks and limbs of the few Scotch firs, tawny in violent light, or again, on the moor, the gale-bent larches that had such a look of life when the wind streamed in their young green, above the rusty black under-boughs. Or he would lie on the banks, gazing at the clusters of dog-violets, or up in the dead bracken, fingering the pink, transparent buds of the dewberry, while the cuckoos called and yaffles laughed, or a lark, from very high, dripped its beads of song. It was certainly different from any spring he had ever known, for spring was within him, not without. In the daytime he hardly saw the family; and when Megan brought in his meals she always seemed too busy in the house or among the young things in the yard to stay talking long. But in the evenings he installed himself in the window seat in the kitchen, smoking and chatting with the lame man Jim, or Mrs. Narracombe, while the girl sewed, or moved about, clearing the supper things away. And sometimes, with the sensation a cat must feel when it purrs, he would become conscious that Megan's eyes—those dew-grey eyes—were fixed on him with a sort of lingering soft look that was strangely flattering.

It was on Sunday week in the evening, when he was lying in the orchard listening to a blackbird and composing a love poem, that he heard the gate swing to, and saw the girl come running among the trees, with the red-cheeked, stolid Joe in swift pursuit. About twenty yards away the chase ended, and the two stood fronting each other, not noticing the stranger in the grass—the boy pressing on, the girl fending him off. Ashurst could see her face, angry, disturbed; and the youth's—who would have thought that red-faced yokel could look so distraught! And painfully affected by that sight, he jumped up. They saw him then. Megan dropped her hands, and shrunk behind a tree-trunk; the boy gave an angry grunt, rushed at the bank, scrambled over and vanished. Ashurst went slowly up to her. She was standing quite still, biting her lip—very pretty, with her fine, dark hair blown loose about her face, and her eyes cast down.

"I beg your pardon," he said.

She gave him one upward look, from eyes much dilated; then, catching her breath, turned away. Ashurst followed.

"Megan!"

But she went on; and taking hold of her arm, he turned her gently round to him.

"Stop and speak to me."

"Why do you beg my pardon? It is not to me you should do that."

"Well, then, to Joe."

"How dare he come after me?"

"In love with you, I suppose."

She stamped her foot.

Ashurst uttered a short laugh. "Would you like me to punch his head?"

She cried with sudden passion:

"You laugh at me—you laugh at us!"

He caught hold of her hands, but she shrank back, till her passionate little face and loose dark hair were caught among the pink clusters of the apple blossom. Ashurst raised one of her imprisoned hands and put his lips to it. He felt how chivalrous he was, and superior to that clod Joe—just brushing that small, rough hand with his mouth! Her shrinking ceased suddenly; she seemed to tremble towards him. A sweet warmth overtook Ashurst from top to toe. This slim maiden, so simple and fine and pretty, was pleased, then, at the touch of his lips! And, yielding to a swift impulse, he put his arms round her, pressed her to him, and kissed her forehead. Then he was frightened —she went so pale, closing her eyes, so that the long, dark lashes lay on her pale cheeks; her hands, too, lay inert at her sides. The touch of her breast sent a quiver through him. "Megan!" he sighed out, and let her go. In the utter silence a blackbird shouted. Then the girl seized his hand, put it to her cheek, her heart, her lips, kissed it passionately, and fled away among the mossy trunks of the apple trees, till they hid her from him.

Ashurst sat down on a twisted old tree that grew almost along the ground, and, all throbbing and bewildered, gazed vacantly at the blossom which had crowned her hair—those pink buds with one white open apple star. What had he done? How had he let himself be thus stampeded by beauty—pity—or—just the spring! He felt curiously happy, all the same; happy and triumphant, with shivers running through his limbs, and a vague alarm. This was the beginning of—what? The midges bit him, the dancing gnats tried to fly into his mouth, and all the spring around him seemed to grow more lovely and alive; the songs of the cuckoos and the blackbirds, the laughter of the yaffles, the level-slanting sunlight, the apple blossom that had crowned her head——! He got up from the old trunk and strode out of the orchard, wanting space, an open sky, to get on terms with these new sensations. He made for the moor, and from an ash tree in the hedge a magpie flew out to herald him.

Of man—at any age from five years on—who can saw he has never been in love? Ashurst had loved his partners at his dancing class; loved his nursery governess; girls in school-holidays; perhaps never been quite out of love, cherishing always some more or less remote admiration. But this was different, not remote at all. Quite a new sensation; terribly delightful, bringing a sense of completed manhood. To be holding in his fingers such a wild flower, to be able to put it to his lips, and feel it tremble with delight against them! What intoxication, and—embarrassment! What to do with it—how meet her next time? His first caress had been cool, pitiful; but the next could not be, now that, by her burning little kiss on his hand, by her pressure of it to her heart, he knew that she loved him. Some natures are coarsened by love bestowed on them; others, like Ashurst's, are swayed and drawn, warmed and softened, almost exalted, by what they feel to be a sort of miracle.

And up there among the tors he was torn between the passionate desire to revel in this new sensation of spring fulfilled within him, and a vague but very real uneasiness. At one moment he gave himself up completely to his pride at having captured this pretty, trustful, dewy-eyed thing! At the next he thought with factitious solemnity: 'Yes, my boy! But look out what you're doing! You know what comes of it!'

Dusk dropped down without his noticing—dusk on the carved, Assyrian-looking masses of the rocks. And the voice of Nature said: "This is a new world for you!" As when a man gets up at four o'clock and goes out into a summer morning, and beasts, birds, trees stare at him as if all had been made new.

He stayed up there for hours, till it grew cold, then groped his way down the stones and heather roots to the road, back into the lane, and came again past the wild meadow to the orchard. There he struck a match and looked at his watch. Nearly twelve! It was black and unstirring in there now, very different from the lingering, bird-befriended brightness of six hours ago! And suddenly he saw this idyll of his with the eyes of the outer world—had mental vision of Mrs. Narracombe's snake-like neck turned, her quick dark glance taking it all in, her shrewd face hardening; saw the gipsy-like cousins coarsely mocking and distrustful; Joe stolid and furious; only the lame man, Jim, with the suffering eyes, seemed tolerable to his mind. And the village pub!—the gossiping matrons he passed on his walks; and then—his own friends—Robert Garton's smile when he went off that morning ten days ago; so ironical and knowing! Disgusting! For a minute he literally hated this earthy, cynical world that one belonged to, willy-nilly. The gate where he was leaning grew grey, a sort of shimmer passed before him and spread into the blueish darkness. The moon! He could just see it over the bank behind; red, nearly round—a strange moon! And turning away, he went up the lane that smelled of the night and cow-dung and young leaves. In the strawyard he could see the dark shapes of cattle, broken by the pale sickles of their horns, like so many thin moons, fallen ends-up. He unlatched the farm gate stealthily. All was dark in the house. Muffling his footsteps, he gained the porch, and, blotted against one of the yew trees, looked up at Megan's window. It was open. Was she sleeping, or lying awake perhaps, disturbed—unhappy at his absence? An owl hooted while he stood there peering up, and the sound seemed to fill the whole night, so quiet was all else, save for the never-ending murmur of the stream running below the orchard. The cuckoos by day, and now the owls—how wonderfully they voiced this troubled ecstasy within him! And suddenly he saw her at her window, looking out. He moved a little from the yew tree, and whispered: "Megan!" She drew back, vanished, reappeared, leaning far down. He stole forward on the grass patch, hit his shin against the green-painted chair, and held his breath at the sound. The pale blur of her stretched-down arm and face did not stir; he moved the chair, and noiselessly mounted it. By stretching up his arms he could just reach. Her hand held the huge key of the front door, and he clasped that burning hand with the cold key in it. He could see her face, the glint of teeth between her lips, her tumbled hair. She was still dressed—poor child; sitting up for him, no doubt! "Pretty Megan!" Her hot, roughened fingers clung to his; her face had a strange, lost look. To have been able to reach it—even with his hand! The owl hooted, a scent of sweetbriar crept into his nostrils. Then one of the farm dogs barked; her grasp relaxed, she shrank back.

"Good-night, Megan!"

"Good-night, sir!" She was gone! With a sigh he dropped back to earth, and sitting on that chair, took off his boots. Nothing for it but to creep in and go to bed; yet for a long while he sat unmoving, his feet chilly in the dew, drunk on the memory of her lost, half-smiling face, and the clinging grip of her burning fingers, pressing the cold key into his hand.

5 §

He awoke feeling as if he had eaten heavily overnight, instead of having eaten nothing. And far off, unreal, seemed yesterday's romance! Yet it was a golden morning. Full spring had burst at last—in one night the "goldie-cups," as the little boys called them, seemed to have made the field their own, and from his window he could see apple blossom covering the orchard as with a rose and white quilt. He went down almost dreading to see Megan; and yet, when not she but Mrs. Narracombe brought in his breakfast, he felt vexed and disappointed. The woman's quick eye and snaky neck seemed to have a new alacrity this morning. Had she noticed?

"So you an' the moon went walkin' last night, Mr. Ashurst! Did ye have your supper anywheres?"

Ashurst shook his head.

"We kept it for you, but I suppose you was too busy in your brain to think o' such a thing as that?"

Was she mocking him, in that voice of hers, which still kept some Welsh crispness against the invading burr of the West Country? If she knew! And at that moment he thought: 'No, no; I'll clear out. I won't put myself in such a beastly false position.'

But, after breakfast, the longing to see Megan began and increased with every minute, together with fear lest something should have been said to her which had spoiled everything. Sinister that she had not appeared, not given him even a glimpse of her! And the love poem, whose manufacture had been so important and absorbing yesterday afternoon under the apple trees, now seemed so paltry that he tore it up and rolled it into pipe spills. What had he known of love, till she seized his hand and kissed it! And now—what did he not know? But to write of it seemed mere insipidity! He went up to his bedroom to get a book, and his heart began to beat violently, for she was in there making the bed. He stood in the doorway watching; and suddenly, with turbulent joy, he saw her stoop and kiss his pillow, just at the hollow made by his head last night. How let her know he had seen that pretty act of devotion? And yet, if she heard him stealing away, it would be even worse. She took the pillow up, holding it as if reluctant to shake out the impress of his cheek, dropped it, and turned round.

"Megan!"

She put her hands up to her cheeks, but her eyes seemed to look right into him. He had never before realised the depth and purity and touching faithfulness in those dew-bright eyes, and he stammered:

"It was sweet of you to wait up for me last night."

She still said nothing, and he stammered on:

"I was wandering about on the moor; it was such a jolly night. I—I've just come up for a book."

Then, the kiss he had seen her give the pillow afflicted him with sudden headiness, and he went up to her. Touching her eyes with his lips, he thought with queer excitement: 'I've done it! Yesterday all was sudden—anyhow; but now—I've done it!' The girl let her forehead rest against his lips, which moved downward till they reached hers. That first real lover's kiss—strange, wonderful, still almost innocent—in which heart did it make the most disturbance?

"Come to the big apple tree to-night, after they've gone to bed. Megan—promise!"

She whispered back: "I promise."

Then, scared at her white face, scared at everything, he let her go, and went downstairs again. Yes! he had done it now! Accepted her love, declared his own! He went out to the green chair as devoid of a book as ever; and there he sat staring vacantly before him, triumphant and remorseful, while under his nose and behind his back the work of the farm went on. How long he had been sitting in that curious state of vacancy he had no notion when he saw Joe standing a little behind him to the right. The youth had evidently come from hard work in the fields, and stood shifting his feet, breathing loudly, his face coloured like a setting sun, and his arms, below the rolled-up sleeves of his blue shirt, showing the hue and furry sheen of ripe peaches. His red lips were open, his blue eyes with their flaxen lashes stared fixedly at Ashurst, who said ironically:

"Well, Joe, anything I can do for you?"

"Yeas."

"What, then?"

"Yu can goo away from yere. Us don' want yu."

Ashurt's face, never too humble, assumed its most lordly look.

"Very good of you, but, do you know, I prefer the others should speak for themselves."

The youth moved a pace or two nearer, and the scent of his honest heat afflicted Ashurst's nostrils.

"What d'yu stay yere for?"

"Because it pleases me."

" 'Twon't please yu when I've bashed yure 'ead in!"

"Indeed! When would you like to begin that?"

Joe answered only with the loudness of his breathing, but his eyes looked like those of a young and angry bull. Then a sort of spasm seemed to convulse his face.

"Megan don' want yu."

A rush of jealousy, of contempt, and anger with this thick, loud-breathing rustic got the better of Ashurt's self-possession; he jumped up, and pushed back his chair.

"You can go to the devil!"

And as he said those simple words, he saw Megan in the doorway with a tiny brown puppy spaniel in her arms. She came up to him quickly.

"Its eyes are blue!" she said.

Joe turned away; the back of his neck was literally crimson.

Ashurst put his finger to the mouth of the tiny brown bull-frog of a creature in her arms. How cosy it looked against her!

"It's fond of you already. Ah! Megan, everything is fond of *you*."

"What was Joe saying to you, please?"

"Telling me to go away, because you didn't want me here."

She stamped her foot; then looked up at Ashurst. At that adoring look he felt his nerves quiver, just as if he had seen a moth scorching its wings.

"To-night!" he said. "Don't forget!"

"No." And smothering her face against the puppy's little fat, brown body, she slipped back into the house.

Ashurst wandered down the lane. And at the gate of the wild meadow he came on the lame man and his cows.

"Beautiful day, Jim!"

"Ah! 'Tes brave weather for the grass. The ashes be later than th' oaks this year. 'When th' oak before th' ash——' "

Ashurst said idly: "Where were you standing when you saw the gipsy bogle, Jim?"

"It might be under that big apple tree, as you might say."

"And you really do think it was there?"

The lame man answered cautiously:

"I shouldn't like to say rightly that 't *was* there. 'Twas in my mind as 'twas there."

"What do you make of it?"

The lame man lowered his voice.

"They du zay old master, Mist' Narracombe, come o' gipsy stock. But that's tellin'. They'm a wonderful people, yu know, for claimin' their own. Maybe they knu 'e was goin', an' sent this feller along for company. That's what I've a-thought about it."

"What was he like?"

" 'E 'ad 'air all over 'is face, an' goin' like this, he was, zame as if 'e 'ad a viddle. They zay there's no such thing as bogles, but I've a-zeen the 'air on this dog standin' up of a dark naight, when I couldn' zee nothin', meself."

"Was there a moon?"

"Yeas, very near full, but 'twas on'y just risen, gold-like be'ind them trees."

"And you think a ghost means trouble, do you?"

The lame man pushed his hat up; his aspiring eyes looked at Ashurst more earnestly than ever.

" 'Tes not for me to zay that—but 'tes they bein' so unrestin'-like. There's things us don' understand, that's zartin, for zure. There's people that zee things, tu, an' others that don' never zee nothin'. Now, our Joe—yu might putt anything under 'is eyes an' 'e'd never zee it; and them other boys, tu, they'm rattlin' fellers. But yu take an' putt our Megan where there's suthin', she'll zee it, an' more tu, or I'm mistaken."

"She's sensitive, that's why."

"What's that?"

"I mean, she feels everything."

"Ah! She'm very lovin'-'earted."

Ashurst, who felt colour coming into his cheeks, held out his tobacco pouch.

"Have a fill, Jim?"

"Thank 'ee, sir. She'm one in an 'underd, I think."

"I expect so," said Ashurst shortly, and folding up his pouch, walked on.

"Lovin'-'earted!" Yes! And what was he doing? What were his intentions—as they say—towards this loving-hearted girl? The thought dogged him, wandering through fields bright with buttercups, where the little red calves were feeding, and the swallows flying high. Yes, the oaks were before the ashes, brown-gold already; every tree in different stage and hue. The cuckoos and a thousand birds were singing; the little streams were very bright. The ancients believed in a Golden Age, in the garden of the Hesperides! . . . A queen wasp settled on his sleeve. Each queen wasp killed meant two thousand fewer wasps to thieve the apples that would grow from that blossom in the orchard; but who, with love in his heart, could kill anything on a day like this? He entered a field where a young red bull was feeding. It seemed to Ashurst that he looked like Joe. But the young bull took no notice of this visitor, a little drunk himself, perhaps, on the singing and the glamour of the golden pasture under his short legs. Ashurst crossed out unchallenged to the hillside above the stream. From that slope a tor mounted to its crown of rocks. The ground there was covered with a mist of bluebells, and nearly a score of crab-apple trees were in full bloom. He threw himself down on the grass. The change from the buttercup glory and oak-goldened glamour of the fields to this ethereal beauty under the grey tor filled him with a sort of wonder; nothing the same, save the sound of running water and the songs of the cuckoos. He lay there a long time, watching the sunlight wheel till the crab-trees threw shadows over the bluebells, his only companions a few wild bees. He was not quite sane, thinking of that morning's kiss, and of to-night under the apple tree. In such a spot as this, fauns and dryads surely lived; nymphs, white as the crab-apple blossom, retired within those trees; fauns, brown as the dead bracken, with pointed ears, lay in wait for them. The cuckoos were still calling when he woke, there was the sound of running water; but the sun had couched behind the tor, the hillside was cool, and some rabbits had come out. 'To-night!' he thought. Just as from the earth everything was pushing up, unfolding under the soft insistent fingers of an unseen hand, so were his heart and senses being pushed, unfolded. He got up and broke off a spray from a crab-apple tree. The buds were like Megan—shell-like, rose-pink, wild, and fresh; and so, too, the opening flowers, white and wild, and touching. He put the spray into his coat. And all the rush of the spring within him escaped in a triumphant sigh. But the rabbits scurried away.

6 §

It was nearly eleven that night when Ashurst put down the pocket "Odyssey" which for half an hour he had held in his hands without reading, and slipped through the yard down to the orchard. The moon had just risen, very golden, over the hill, and like a bright, powerful, watching spirit peered through the bars of an ash tree's half-naked boughs. In among the apple trees it was still dark, and he stood making sure of his direction, feeling the rough grass with his feet. A black mass close behind him stirred with a heavy grunting sound, and three large pigs settled down again close to each other, under the wall. He listened. There was no wind, but the stream's burbling whispering chuckle had gained twice its daytime strength. One bird, he could not tell what, cried "Pip—pip," "Pip—pip," with perfect monotony; he could hear a night-jar spinning very far off; an owl hooting. Ashurst moved a step or two, and again halted, aware of a dim living whiteness all round his head. On the dark unstirring trees innumerable flowers and buds all soft and blurred were being bewitched to life by the creeping moonlight. He had the oddest feeling of actual companionship, as if a million white moths or spirits had floated in and settled between dark sky and darker ground, and were opening and shutting their wings on a level with his eyes. In the bewildering, still, scentless beauty of that moment he almost lost memory of why he had come to the orchard. The flying glamour that had clothed the earth all day had not gone now that night had fallen, but only changed into this new form. He moved on through the thicket of stems and boughs covered with that live powdering whiteness, till he reached the big apple tree. No mistaking that, even in the dark; nearly twice the height and size of any other, and leaning out towards the open meadow and the stream. Under its thick branches he stood still again, to listen. The same sounds exactly, and a faint grunting from the sleepy pigs. He put his hands on the dry, almost warm tree trunk, whose rough mossy surface gave forth a peaty scent at his touch. Would she come—would she? And among these quivering, haunted, moon-witched trees he was seized with doubts of everything! All was other-worldly here, fit for no earthly lovers; fit only for god and goddess, faun and nymph—not for him and this little country girl. Would it not be almost a relief if she did not come? But all the time he was listening. And still that unknown bird went "Pip—pip," "Pip—pip," and there rose the busy chatter of the little trout stream, whereon the moon was flinging glances through the bars of her tree-prison. The blossom on a level with his eyes seemed to grow more living every moment, seemed with its mysterious white beauty more and more a part of his suspense. He plucked a fragment and held it close—three blossoms. Sacrilege to pluck fruit-tree blossom—soft, sacred, young blossom—and throw it away! Then suddenly he heard the gate close, the pigs stirring again and grunting; and leaning against the trunk, he pressed his hands to its mossy sides behind him, and held his breath. She might have been a spirit threading the trees, for all the noise she made! Then he saw her quite close—her dark form part of a little tree, her white face part of its blossom; so still, and peering towards him. He whispered: "Megan!" and held out his hands. She ran forward, straight to his breast. When he felt her heart beating against him, Ashurst knew to the full the sensations of chivalry and passion. Because she was not of his world, because she was so simple and young and headlong, adoring and defenceless, how could he be other than her protector, in the dark! Because she was all simple, loving nature and beauty, as much a part of this spring night as was the living blossom, how should he not take all that she would give him—how not fulfil the spring in her heart and his! And torn between these two emotions he clasped her close, and kissed her hair. How long they stood there without speaking he knew not. The stream went on chattering, the owls hooting, the moon kept stealing up and growing whiter; the blossom all round them and above brightened in suspense of living beauty. Their lips had sought each other's, and they did not speak. The moment speech began all would be unreal! Spring has no speech, nothing but rustling and whispering. Spring has so much more than speech in its unfolding flowers and leaves, and the coursing of its streams, and in its sweet restless seeking! And sometimes spring will come alive, and, like a mysterious Presence stand, encircling lovers with its arms, laying on them the fingers of enchantment, so that, standing lips to lips, they forget everything but just a kiss. While her heart beat against him, and her lips quivered on his, Ashurst felt nothing but simple rapture—Destiny meant her for his arms, Love could not be flouted! But when their lips parted for breath, division began again at once. Only, passion now was so much the stronger, and he sighed:

"Oh! Megan! Why did you come?"

She looked up, hurt, amazed.

"Sir, you asked me to."

"Don't call me 'sir,' my pretty sweet."

"What should I be callin' you?"

"Frank."

"I could not. Oh, no!"

"But you love me—don't you?"

"I could not help lovin' you. I want to be with you—that's all."

"All!"

So faint that he hardly heard, she whispered:

"I shall die if I can't be with you."

Ashurst took a mighty breath.

"Come and be with me, then!"

"Oh!"

Intoxicated by the awe and rapture in that "Oh!" he went on, whispering:

"We'll go to London. I'll show you the world. And I *will* take care of you, I promise, Megan. I won't be a brute to you!"

"If I can be with you—that is all."

He stroked her hair, and whispered on:

"To-morrow I'll go to Torquay and get some money, and get you some clothes that won't be noticed, and then we'll steal away. And when we get to London, soon perhaps, if you love me well enough, we'll be married."

He could feel her hair shiver with the shake of her head.

"Oh, no! I could not. I only want to be with you!"

Drunk on his own chivalry, Ashurst went on murmuring:

"It's I who am not good enough for you. Oh! Megan, when did you begin to love me?"

"When I saw you in the road, and you looked at me. The first night I loved you; but I never thought you would want me."

She slipped down suddenly to her knees, trying to kiss his feet.

A shiver of horror went through Ashurst; he lifted her up bodily and held her fast—too upset to speak.

She whispered: "Why won't you let me?"

"It's I who will kiss your feet!"

Her smile brought tears into his eyes. The whiteness of her moonlit face so close to his, the faint pink of her opened lips, had the living unearthly beauty of the apple blossom.

And then, suddenly, her eyes widened and stared past him painfully; she writhed out of his arms, and whispered: "Look!"

Ashurst saw nothing but the brightened stream, the furze faintly gilded, the beech trees glistening, and behind them all the wide loom of the moonlit hill. Behind him came her frozen whisper: "The gipsy bogle!"

"Where?"

"There—by the stone—under the trees!"

Exasperated, he leaned the stream, and strode towards the beech clump. Prank of the moonlight! Nothing! In and out of the boulders and thorn trees, muttering and cursing, yet with a kind of terror, he rushed and stumbled. Absurd! Silly! Then he went back to the apple tree. But she was gone; he could hear a rustle, the grunting of the pigs, the sound of a gate closing. Instead of her, only this old apple tree! He flung his arms round the trunk. What a substitute for her soft body; the rough moss against his face—what a substitute for her soft cheek; only the scent, as of the woods, a little the same! And above him, and around, the blossoms, more living, more moonlit than ever, seemed to glow and breathe.

7 §

Descending from the train at Torquay station, Ashurst wandered uncertainly along the front, for he did not know this particular queen of English watering places. Having little sense of what he had on, he was quite unconscious of being remarkable among its inhabitants, and strode along in his rough Norfolk jacket, dusty boots, and battered hat, without observing that people gazed at him rather blankly. He was seeking a branch of his London Bank, and having found one, found also the first obstacle to his mood. Did he know anyone in Torquay? No. In that case, if he would wire to his Bank in London, they would be happy to oblige him on receipt of the reply. That suspicious breath from the matter-of-fact world somewhat tarnished the brightness of his visions. But he sent the telegram.

Nearly opposite to the post office he saw a shop full of ladies' garments, and examined the window with strange sensations. To have to undertake the clothing of his rustic love was more than a little disturbing. He went in. A young woman came forward; she had blue eyes and a faintly puzzled forehead. Ashurst stared at her in silence.

"Yes, sir?"

"I want a dress for a young lady."

The young woman smiled. Ashurst frowned—the peculiarity of his request struck him with sudden force.

The young woman added hastily:

"What style would you like—something modish?"

"No. Simple."

"What figure would the young lady be?"

"I don't know; about two inches shorter than you, I should say."

"Could you give me her waist measurement?"

Megan's waist!

"Oh! anything usual!"

"Quite!"

While she was gone he stood disconsolately eyeing the models in the window, and suddenly it seemed to him incredible that Megan —his Megan—could ever be dressed save in the rough tweed skirt, coarse blouse, and tam-o'-shanter cap he was wont to see her in. The young woman had come back with several dresses in her arms, and Ashurst eyed her laying them against her own modish figure. There was one whose colour he liked, a dove-grey, but to imagine Megan clothed in it was beyond him. The young woman went away, and brought some more. But on Ashurst there had now come a feeling of paralysis. How choose? She would want a hat too, and shoes, and gloves; and, suppose, when he had got them all, they commonised her, as Sunday clothes always commonised village folk! Why should she not travel as she was? Ah! but conspicuousness would matter; this was a serious elopement. And, staring at the young woman, he thought: 'I wonder if she guesses, and thinks me a blackguard?'

"Do you mind putting aside that grey one for me?" he said desperately at last. "I can't decide now; I'll come in again this afternoon."

The young woman sighed.

"Oh! certainly. It's a very tasteful costume. I don't think you'll get anything that will suit your purpose better."

"I expect not," Ashurst murmured, and went out.

Freed again from the suspicious matter-of-factness of the world, he took a long breath, and went back to visions. In fancy he saw the trustful, pretty creature who was going to join her life to his; saw himself and her stealing forth at night, walking over the moor under the moon, he with his arm round her, and carrying her new garments, till, in some far-off wood, when dawn was coming, she would slip off her old things and put on these, and an early train at a distant station would bear them away on their honeymoon journey, till London swallowed them up, and the dreams of love came true.

"Frank Ashurst! Haven't seen you since Rugby, old chap!"

Ashurst's frown dissolved; the face, close to his own, was blue-eyed, suffused with sun—one of those faces where sun from within and without joins in a sort of lustre. And he answered:

"Phil Halliday, by Jove!"

"What are you doing here?"

"Oh! nothing. Just looking round, and getting some money. I'm staying on the moor."

"Are you lunching anywhere? Come and lunch with us; I'm here with my young sisters. They've had measles."

Hooked in by that friendly arm Ashurst went along, up a hill, down a hill, away out of the town, while the voice of Halliday, redolent of optimism as his face was of sun, explained how "in this mouldy place the only decent things were the bathing and boating," and so on, till presently they came to a crescent of houses a little above and back from the sea, and into the centre one—an hotel—made their way.

"Come up to my room and have a wash. Lunch'll be ready in a jiffy."

Ashurst contemplated his visage in a looking-glass. After his farm-house bedroom, the comb and one spare shirt *régime* of the last fortnight, this room littered with clothes and brushes was a sort of Capua; and he thought: 'Queer—one doesn't realise——" But what—he did not quite know.

When he followed Halliday into the sitting room for lunch, three faces, very fair and blue-eyed, were turned suddenly at the words: "This is Frank Ashurst—my young sisters."

Two were indeed young, about eleven and ten. The third was perhaps seventeen, tall and fair-haired too, with pink-and-white cheeks just touched by the sun, and eyebrows, rather darker than the hair, running a little upward from her nose to their outer points. The voices of all three were like Halliday's, high and cheerful; they stood up straight, shook hands with a quick movement, looked at Ashurst critically, away again at once, and began to talk of what they were going to do in the afternoon. A regular Diana and attendant nymphs! After the farm this crisp, slangy, eager talk, this cool, clean, off-hand refinement, was queer at first, and then so natural that what he had come from became suddenly remote. The names of the two little ones seemed to be Sabina and Freda; of the eldest, Stella.

Presently the one called Sabina turned to him and said:

"I say, will you come shrimping with us?—it's awful fun!"

Surprised by this unexpected friendliness, Ashurst murmured:

"I'm afraid I've got to get back this afternoon."

"Oh!"

"Can't you put it off?"

Ashurst turned to the new speaker, Stella, shook his head and smiled. She was very pretty! Sabina said regretfully: "You might!" Then the talk switched off to caves and swimming.

"Can you swim far?"

"About two miles."

"Oh!"

"I say!"

"How jolly!"

The three pairs of blue eyes, fixed on him, made him conscious of his new importance. The sensation was agreeable. Halliday said:

"I say, you simply must stop and have a bathe. You'd better stay the night."

"Yes, do!"

But again Ashurst smiled and shook his head. Then suddenly he found himself being catechised about his physical achievements. He had rowed—it seemed—in his college boat, played in his college football team, won his college mile; and he rose from table a sort of hero. The two little girls insisted that he must see "their" cave, and they set forth chattering like magpies, Ashurst between them, Stella and her brother a little behind. In the cave, damp and darkish like any other cave, the great feature was a pool with possibility of creatures that might be caught and put into bottles. Sabina and Freda, who wore no stockings on their shapely brown legs, exhorted Ashurst to join them in the middle of it, and help sieve the water. He too was soon bootless and sockless. Time goes fast for one who has a sense of beauty, when there are pretty children in a pool and a young Diana on the edge, to receive with wonder anything you can catch! Ashurst never had much sense of time. It was a shock when, pulling out his watch, he saw it was well past three. No cashing his cheque to-day—the Bank would be closed before he could get there. Watching his expression, the little girls cried out at once:

"Hurrah! Now you'll have to stay!"

Ashurst did not answer. He was seeing again Megan's face, when at breakfast time he had whispered: "I'm going to Torquay, darling, to get everything. I shall be back this evening. If it's fine we can go to-night. Be ready." He was seeing again how she quivered and hung on his words. What would she think? Then he pulled himself together, conscious suddenly of the calm scrutiny of this other young girl, so tall and fair and Diana-like, at the edge of the pool, of her wondering blue eyes under those brows that slanted up a little. If they knew what was in his mind—if they knew that this very night he had meant——! Well, there would be a little sound of disgust, and he would be alone in the cave. And with a curious mixture of anger, chagrin, and shame, he put his watch back into his pocket and said abruptly:

"Yes; I'm dished for to-day."

"Hurrah! Now you can bathe with us."

It was impossible not to succumb a little to the contentment of these pretty children, to the smile on Stella's lips, to Halliday's "Ripping, old chap! I can lend you things for the night!" But again a spasm of longing and remorse throbbed through Ashurst, and he said moodily:

"I must send a wire!"

The attractions of the pool palling, they went back to the hotel. Ashurst sent his wire, addressing it to Mrs. Narracombe: "Sorry, detained for the night, back to-morrow." Surely Megan would understand that he had too much to do; and his heart grew lighter. It was a lovely afternoon, warm, the sea calm and blue, and swimming his great passion; the favour of these pretty children flattered him, the pleasure of looking at them, at Stella, at Halliday's sunny face; the slight unreality, yet extreme naturalness of it all—as of a last peep at normality before he took this plunge with Megan! He got his borrowed bathing dress, and they all set forth. Halliday and he undressed behind one rock, the three girls behind another. He was first into the sea, and at once swam out with the bravado of justifying his self-given reputation. When he turned he could see Halliday swimming along shore, and the girls flopping and dipping, and riding the little waves, in the way he was accustomed to despise, but now thought pretty and sensible, since it gave him the distinction of the only deep-water fish. But drawing near, he wondered if they would like him, a stranger, to come into their splashing group; he felt shy, approaching that slim nymph. Then Sabina summoned him to teach her to float, and between them the little girls kept him so busy that he had no time even to notice whether Stella was accustomed to his presence, till suddenly he heard a startled sound from her. She was standing submerged to the waist, leaning a little forward, her slim white arms stretched out and pointing, her wet face puckered by the sun and an expression of fear.

"Look at Phil! Is he all right? Oh, look!"

Ashurst saw at once that Phil was not all right. He was splashing and struggling, out of his depth, perhaps a hundred yards away; suddenly he gave a cry, threw up his arms, and went down. Ashurst saw the girl launch herself towards him, and crying out: "Go back, Stella! Go back!" he dashed out. He had never swum so fast, and reached Halliday just as he was coming up a second time. It was a case of cramp, but to get him in was not difficult, for he did not struggle. The girl, who had stopped where Ashurst told her to, helped as soon as he was in his depth, and once on the beach they sat down one on each side of him to rub his limbs, while the little ones stood by with scared faces. Halliday was soon smiling. It was—he said—rotten of him, absolutely rotten! If Frank would give him an arm, he could get to his clothes all right now. Ashurst gave him the arm, and as he did so caught sight of Stella's face, wet and flushed and tearful, all broken up out of its calm; and he thought: 'I called her Stella! Wonder if she minded?'

While they were dressing, Halliday said quietly:

"You saved my life, old chap!"

"Rot!"

Clothed, but not quite in their right minds, they went up all together to the hotel and sat down to tea, except Halliday, who was lying down in his room. After some slices of bread and jam, Sabina said:

"I say, you know, you *are* a brick!" And Freda chimed in:

"Rather!"

Ashurst saw Stella looking down; he got up in confusion, and went to the window. From there he heard Sabina mutter: "I say, let's swear blood bond. Where's your knife, Freda?" and out of the corner of his eye could see each of them solemnly prick herself, squeeze out a drop of blood and dabble on a bit of paper. He turned and made for the door.

"Don't be a stoat! Come back!" His arms were seized; imprisoned between the little girls he was brought back to the table. On it lay a piece of paper with an effigy drawn in blood, and the three names Stella Halliday, Sabina Halliday, Freda Halliday—also in blood, running towards it like the rays of a star. Sabina said:

"That's you. We shall have to kiss you, you know."

And Freda echoed:

"Oh! Blow—Yes!"

Before Ashurst could escape, some wettish hair dangled against his face, something like a bite descended on his nose, he felt his left arm pinched, and other teeth softly searching his cheek. Then he was released, and Freda said:

"Now, Stella."

Ashurst, red and rigid, looked across the table at a red and rigid Stella. Sabina giggled; Freda cried:

"Buck up—it spoils everything!"

A queer, ashamed eagerness shot through Ashurst; then he said quietly:

"Shut up, you little demons!"

Again Sabina giggled.

"Well, then, she can kiss your hand, and you can put it against your nose. It *is* on one side!"

To his amazement the girl did kiss her hand and stretch it out. Solemnly he took that cool, slim hand and laid it to his cheek. The two little girls broke into clapping, and Freda said:

"Now, then, we shall have to save your life at any time; that's settled. Can I have another cup, Stella, not so beastly weak?"

Tea was resumed, and Ashurst, folding up the paper, put it in his pocket. The talk turned on the advantages of measles, tangerine oranges, honey in a spoon, no lessons, and so forth. Ashurst listened, silent, exchanging friendly looks with Stella, whose face was again of its normal sun-touched pink and white. It was soothing to be so taken to the heart of this jolly family, fascinating to watch their faces. And after tea, while the two little girls pressed seaweed, he talked to Stella in the window seat and looked at her watercolour sketches. The whole thing was like a pleasurable dream; time and incident hung up, importance and reality suspended. To-morrow he would go back to Megan, with nothing of all this left save the paper with the blood of these children, in his pocket. Children! Stella was not quite that—as old as Megan! Her talk—quick, rather hard and shy, yet friendly—seemed to flourish on his silences, and about her there was something cool and virginal—a maiden in a bower. At dinner, to which Halliday, who had swallowed too much sea-water, did not come, Sabina said:

"I'm going to call you Frank."

Freda echoed:

"Frank, Frank, Franky."

Ashurst grinned and bowed.

"Every time Stella calls you Mr. Ashurst, she's got to pay a forfeit. It's ridiculous."

Ashurst looked at Stella, who grew slowly red. Sabina giggled; Freda cried:

"She's 'smoking'—'smoking!'—Yah!"

Ashurst reached out to right and left, and grasped some fair hair in each hand.

"Look here," he said, "you two! Leave Stella alone, or I'll tie you together!"

Freda gurgled:

"Ouch! You *are* a beast!"

Sabina murmured cautiously:

"*You* call *her* Stella, you see!"

"Why shouldn't I? It's a jolly name!"

"All right; we give you leave to!"

Ashurst released the hair. Stella! What would she call him—after this? But she called him nothing; till at bedtime he said, deliberately:

"Good-night, Stella!"

"Good-night, Mr. —— Good-night, Frank! It *was* jolly of you, you know!"

"Oh—that! Bosh!"

Her quick, straight handshake tightened suddenly, and as suddenly became slack.

Ashurst stood motionless in the empty sitting-room. Only last night, under the apple tree and the living blossom, he had held Megan to him, kissing her eyes and lips. And he gasped, swept by that rush of remembrance. To-night it should have begun—his life with her who only wanted to be with him! And now, twenty-four hours and more must pass, because—of not looking at his watch! Why had he made friends with this family of innocents just when he was saying good-bye to innocence, and all the rest of it? 'But I mean to marry her,' he thought; 'I told her so!'

He took a candle, lighted it, and went to his bedroom, which was next to Halliday's. His friend's voice called, as he was passing:

"Is that you, old chap? I say, come in."

He was sitting up in bed, smoking a pipe and reading.

"Sit down a bit."

Ashurst sat down by the open window.

"I've been thinking about this afternoon, you know," said Halliday rather suddenly. "They say you go through all your past. I didn't. I suppose I wasn't far enough gone."

"What did you think of?"

Halliday was silent for a little, then said quietly:

"Well, I did think of one thing—rather odd—of a girl at Cambridge that I might have—you know; I was glad I hadn't got her on my mind. Anyhow, old chap, I owe it to you that I'm here; I should have been in the big dark by now. No more bed, or baccy; no more anything. I say, what d'you suppose happens to us?"

Ashurst murmured:

"Go out like flames, I expect."

"Phew!"

"We may flicker, and cling about a bit, perhaps."

"H'm! I think that's rather gloomy. I say, I hope my young sisters have been decent to you?"

"Awfully decent."

Halliday put his pipe down, crossed his hands behind his neck, and turned his face towards the window. "They're not bad kids!" he said.

Watching his friend, lying there, with that smile, and the candlelight on his face, Ashurst shuddered. Quite true! He might have been lying there with no smile, with all that sunny look gone out for ever! He might not have been lying there at all, but "sanded" at the bottom of the sea, waiting for resurrection on the—ninth day, was it? And that smile of Halliday's seemed to him suddenly something wonderful, as if in it were all the difference between life and death—the little flame—the all! He got up, and said softly:

"Well, you ought to sleep, I expect. Shall I blow out?"

Halliday caught his hand.

"I can't say it, you know; but it must be rotten to be dead. Good-night, old boy!"

Stirred and moved, Ashurst squeezed the hand, and went downstairs. The hall door was still open, and he passed out on to the lawn before the Crescent. The stars were bright in a very dark blue sky, and by their light some lilacs had that mysterious colour of flowers by night which no one can describe. Ashurst pressed his face against a spray; and before his closed eyes Megan started up, with the tiny brown spaniel pup against her breast. "I thought of a girl that I might have—you know. I was glad I hadn't got her on my mind!" He jerked his head away from the lilac, and began pacing up and down over the grass, a grey phantom coming to substance for a moment in the light from the lamp at either end. He was with her again under the living, breathing whiteness of the blossom, the stream chattering by, the moon glinting steel-blue on the bathing-pool; back in the rapture of his kisses on her upturned face of innocence and humble passion, back in the suspense and beauty of that pagan night. He stood still once more in the shadow of the lilacs. Here the sea, not the stream, was Night's voice; the sea with its sigh and rustle; no little bird, no owl, no night-jar called or spun; but a piano tinkled, and the white houses cut the sky with solid curve, and the scent from the lilacs filled the air. A window of the hotel, high up, was lighted; he saw a shadow move across the blind. And most queer sensations stirred within him, a sort of churning, and twining, and turning of a single emotion on itself, as though spring and love, bewildered and confused, seeking the way, were baffled. This girl, who had called him Frank, whose hand had given his that sudden little clutch, this girl so cool and pure—what would *she* think of such wild, unlawful loving? He sank down on the grass, sitting there cross-legged, with his back to the house, motionless as some carved Buddha. Was he really going to break through innocence, and steal? Sniff the scent out of a wild flower, and—perhaps—throw it away? "Of a girl at Cambridge that I might have—you know!" He put his hands to the grass, one on each side, palms downward, and pressed; it was just warm still—the grass, barely moist, soft and firm and friendly. 'What am I going to do?' he thought. Perhaps Megan was at her window, looking out at the blossom, thinking of him! Poor little Megan! 'Why not?' he thought. 'I love her! But do I—really love her? or do I only want her because she is so pretty, and loves me? What am I going to do?' The piano tinkled on, the stars winked; and Ashurst gazed out before him at the dark sea, as if spell-bound. He got up at last, cramped and rather chilly. There was no longer light in any window. And he went in to bed.

8 §

Out of a deep and dreamless sleep he was awakened by the sound of thumping on the door. A shrill voice called:

"Hi! Breakfast's ready."

He jumped up. Where was he——? Ah!

He found them already eating marmalade, and sat down in the empty place between Stella and Sabina, who, after watching him a little, said:

"I say, do buck up; we're going to start at half-past nine."

"We're going to Berry Head, old chap; you *must* come!"

Ashurst thought: 'Come! Impossible. I shall be getting things and going back.' He looked at Stella. She said quickly:

"Do come!"

Sabina chimed in:

"It'll be no fun without you."

Freda got up and stood behind his chair.

"You've got to come, or else I'll pull your hair!"

Ashurst thought: 'Well—one day more—to think it over! One day more!' And he said:

"All right! You needn't tweak my mane!"

"Hurrah!"

At the station he wrote a second telegram to the farm, and then—

tore it up; he could not have explained why. From Brixham they drove in a very little wagonette. There, squeezed between Sabina and Freda, with his knees touching Stella's, they played "Up, Jenkins"; and the gloom he was feeling gave way to frolic. In this one day more to think it over, he did not want to think! They ran races, wrestled, paddled—for to-day nobody wanted to bathe—they sang catches, played games, and ate all they had brought. The little girls fell asleep against him on the way back, and his knees still touched Stella's in the narrow wagonette. It seemed incredible that thirty hours ago he had never set eyes on any of those three flaxen heads. In the train he talked to Stella of poetry, discovering her favourites, and telling her his own with a pleasing sense of superiority; till suddenly she said, rather low:

"Phil says you don't believe in a future life, Frank. I think that's dreadful."

Disconcerted, Ashurst muttered:

"I don't either believe or not believe—I simply don't know."

She said quickly:

"I couldn't bear that. What would be the use of living?"

Watching the frown of those pretty oblique brows, Ashurst answered:

"I don't believe in believing things because one wants to."

"But why should one *wish* to live again, if one isn't going to?"

And she looked full at him.

He did not want to hurt her, but an itch to dominate pushed him on to say:

"While one's alive one naturally wants to go on living for ever; that's part of being alive. But it probably isn't anything more."

"Don't you believe in the Bible at all, then?"

Ashurst thought: 'Now I shall really hurt her!'

"I believe in the Sermon on the Mount, because it's beautiful and good for all time."

"But don't you believe Christ was divine?"

He shook his head.

She turned her face quickly to the window, and there sprang into his mind Megan's prayer, repeated by little Nick: "God bless us all, and Mr. Ashes!" Who else would ever say a prayer for him, like her who at this moment must be waiting—waiting to see him come down the lane? And he thought suddenly: 'What a scoundrel I am!'

All that evening this thought kept coming back; but, as is not unusual, each time with less poignancy, till it seemed almost a matter of course to be a scoundrel. And—strange!—he did not know whether he was a scoundrel if he meant to go back to Megan, or if he did not mean to go back to her.

They played cards till the children were sent off to bed; then Stella went to the piano. From over on the window seat, where it was nearly dark, Ashurst watched her between the candles—that fair head on the long, white neck bending to the movement of her hands. She played fluently, without much expression; but what a picture she made, the faint golden radiance, a sort of angelic atmosphere—hovering about her! Who could have passionate thoughts or wild desires in the presence of that swaying, white-clothed girl with the seraphic head? She played a thing of Schumann's called "*Warum?*" Then Halliday brought out a flute, and the spell was broken. After this they made Ashurst sing, Stella playing his accompaniments from a book of Schumann songs, till, in the middle of "*Ich grolle nicht,*" two small figures clad in blue dressing growns crept in and tried to conceal themselves beneath the piano. The evening broke up in confusion, and what Sabina called "a splendid rag."

That night Ashurst hardly slept at all. He was thinking, only too hard, and tossed and turned. The intense domestic intimacy of these last two days, the strength of this Halliday atmosphere, seemed to ring him round, and make the farm and Megan—even Megan—seem unreal. Had he really made love to her—really promised to take her away to live with him? He must have been bewitched by the spring, the night, the apple blossom! This May madness could not but destroy them both! The notion that he was going to make her his mistress—that simple child not yet eighteen—now filled him with a sort of horror, even while it still stung and whipped his blood. He muttered to himself: "It's awful, what I've done—awful!" And the sound of Schumann's music throbbed and mingled with his fevered thoughts, and he saw again Stella's cool, white, fair-haired figure and bending neck, the queer, angelic radiance about her. 'I must have been—I must be—mad!' he thought. 'What came into me? Poor little Megan! "God bless us all, and Mr. Ashes!" "I want to be with you—only to be with you!"' And burying his face in his pillow, he smothered down a fit of sobbing. Not to go back was awful! To go back—more awful still!

Emotion, when you are young, and give real vent to it, loses its power of torture. And he fell asleep, thinking: 'What was it—a few kisses—all forgotten in a month!'

Next morning he got his cheque cashed, but avoided the shop of the dove-grey dress like the plague; and, instead, bought himself some necessaries. He spent the whole day in a queer mood, cherishing a kind of sullenness against himself. Instead of the hankering of the last two days, he felt nothing but a blank—all passionate longing gone, as if quenched in that outburst of tears. After tea Stella put a book down beside him, and said shyly:

"Have you read that, Frank?"

It was Farrar's "Life of Christ." Ashurst smiled. Her anxiety about his beliefs seemed to him comic, but touching. Infectious too, perhaps, for he began to have an itch to justify himself, if not to convert her. And in the evening, when the children and Halliday were mending their shrimping nets, he said:

"At the back of orthodox religion, so far as I can see, there's always the idea of reward—what you can get for being good; a kind of begging for favours. I think it all starts in fear."

She was sitting on the sofa, making reefer knots with a bit of string. She looked up quickly:

"I think it's much deeper than that."

Ashurst felt again that wish to dominate.

"You think so," he said; "but wanting the '*quid pro quo*' is about the deepest thing in all of us! It's jolly hard to get to the bottom of it!"

She wrinkled her brows in a puzzled frown.

"I don't think I understand."

He went on obstinately:

"Well, think, and see if the most religious people aren't those who feel that this life doesn't give them all they want. I believe in being good because to be good is good in itself."

"Then you do believe in being good?"

How pretty she looked now—it was easy to be good with her! And he nodded and said:

"I say, show me how to make that knot!"

With her fingers touching his, in manœuvring of the bit of string, he felt soothed and happy. And when he went to bed he wilfully kept his thoughts on her, wrapping himself in her fair, cool sisterly radiance, as in some garment of protection.

Next day he found they had arranged to go by train to Totnes, and picnic at Berry Pomeroy Castle. Still in that resolute oblivion of the past, he took his place with them in the landau beside Halliday, back to the horses. And, then, along the sea front, nearly at the turning to the railway station, his heart almost leaped into his mouth. Megan—Megan herself—was walking on the far pathway, in her old skirt and jacket and her tam-o'-shanter, looking up into the faces of the passers-by. Instinctively he threw his hand up for cover, then made a feint of clearing dust out of his eyes; but between his fingers he could see her still, moving, not with her free country step, but wavering, lost-looking, pitiful—like some little dog that has missed its master and does not know whether to run on, to run back—where to run. How had she come like this?—what excuse had she found to get away?—what did she hope for? But with every turn of the wheels that bore him away from her, his heart revolted and cried to him to stop them, to get out, and go to her! When the landau turned the corner to the station he could bear no more, and opening the carriage door, muttered: "I've forgotten something! Go on—don't wait for me! I'll join you at the castle by the next train!" He jumped, stumbled, spun round, recovered his balance, and walked forward, while the carriage with the astonished Hallidays rolled on.

From the corner he could only just see Megan, a long way ahead now. He ran a few steps, checked himself, and dropped into a walk. With each step nearer to her, further from the Hallidays, he walked more and more slowly. How did it alter anything—this sight of her?

How make the going to her, and that which must come of it, less ugly? For there was no hiding it—since he had met the Hallidays he had become gradually sure that he would not marry Megan. It would only be a wild love-time, a troubled, remorseful, difficult time—and then—well, then he would get tired, just because she gave him everything, was so simple, and so trustful, so dewy. And dew—wears off! The little spot of faded colour, her tam-o'-shanter cap, wavered on far in front of him, as she looked up into every face, and at the house windows. Had any man ever such a cruel moment to go through? Whatever he did, he felt he would be a beast. And he uttered a groan that made a nursemaid turn and stare. He saw Megan stop and lean against the sea-wall, looking at the sea; and he too stopped. Quite likely she had never seen the sea before, and even in her distress could not resist that sight. 'Yes—she's at the threshold,' he thought; 'everything's before her. And just for a few weeks' passion, I shall be cutting her life to ribbons. I'd better go and hang myself rather than do it!' And suddenly he seemed to see Stella's calm eyes looking into his, the wave of fluffy hair on her forehead stirred by the wind. Ah! it would be madness, would mean giving up all that he respected, and his own self-respect. He turned and walked quickly back towards the station. But memory of that poor, bewildered little figure, those anxious eyes searching the passers-by, smote him too hard again, and once more he turned towards the sea. The cap was no longer visible; that little spot of colour had vanished in the stream of the noon promenaders. And impelled by the passion of longing, the dearth which comes on when life seems to be whirling something out of reach, he hurried forward. She was nowhere to be seen; for half an hour he looked for her; then on the beach flung himself face downward in the sand. To find her again he knew he had only to go to the station and wait till she returned from her fruitless quest, to take her train home; or to take train himself and go back to the farm, so that she found him there when she returned. But he lay inert in the sand, among the indifferent groups of children with their spades and buckets. Pity at her little figure wandering, seeking, was well-nigh merged in the spring-running of his blood; for it was all wild feeling now—the chivalrous part, what there had been of it, was gone. He wanted her again, wanted her kisses, her soft, little body, her abandonment, all her quick, warm, pagan emotion; wanted the wonderful feeling of that night under the moonlit apple boughs; wanted it all with a horrible intensity, as the faun wants the nymph. The quick chatter of the little bright trout-stream, the dazzle of the buttercups, the rocks of the old "wild men"; the calling of the cuckoos and yaffles, the hooting of the owls; and the red moon peeping out of the velvet dark at the living whiteness of the blossom; and her face just out of reach at her window, lost in its love-look; and her heart against his, her lips answering his, under the apple tree—all this besieged him. Yet he lay inert. What was it that struggled against pity and this feverish longing, and kept him there paralysed in the warm sand? Three flaxen heads—a fair face with friendly blue-grey eyes, a slim hand pressing his, a quick voice speaking his name—"So you do believe in being good?" Yes, and a sort of atmosphere as of some old walled-in English garden, with pinks, and cornflowers, and roses, and scents of lavender and lilac—cool and fair, untouched, almost holy—all that he had been brought up to feel was clean and good. And suddenly he thought: 'She might come along the front again and see me!' and he got up and made his way to the rock at the far end of the beach. There, with the spray lifting into his face, he could think more coolly. To go back to the farm and love Megan out in the woods, among the rocks, with everything around wild and fitting—that, he knew, was impossible, utterly. To transplant her to a great town, to keep in some little flat or rooms, one who belonged so wholly to Nature—the poet in him shrank from it. His passion would be a mere sensuous revel, soon gone; in London, her very simplicity, her lack of all intellectual quality, would make her his secret plaything—nothing else. The longer he sat on the rock, with his feet dangling over a greenish pool from which the sea was ebbing, the more clearly he saw this; but it was as if her arms and all of her were slipping slowly, slowly down from him, into the pool, to be carried away out to sea; and her face looking up, her lost face with beseeching eyes, and dark, wet hair—possessed, haunted, tortured him! He got up at last, scaled the low rock-cliff, and made his way down into a sheltered cove. Perhaps in the sea he could get back his control—lose this fever! And stripping off his clothes, he swam out. He wanted to tire himself so that nothing mattered, and swam recklessly, fast and far; then suddenly, for no reason, felt afraid. Suppose he could not reach shore again—suppose the current set him out—or he got cramp, like Halliday! He turned to swim in. The red cliffs looked a long way off. If he were drowned they would find his clothes. The Hallidays would know; but Megan perhaps never—they took no newspaper at the farm. And Phil Halliday's words came back to him again: "A girl at Cambridge I might have—— Glad I hadn't got her on my mind!" And in that moment of unreasoning fear he vowed he would not have her on his mind. Then his fear left him; he swam in easily enough, dried himself in the sun, and put on his clothes. His heart felt sore, but no longer ached; his body cool and refreshed.

When one is as young as Ashurst, pity is not a violent emotion. And, back in the Hallidays' sitting-room, ravenously eating, he felt much like a man recovered from fever. Everything seemed new and clear; the tea, the buttered toast and jam tasted absurdly good; tobacco had never smelt so nice. And walking up and down the empty room, he stopped here and there to touch or look. He took up Stella's work-basket, fingered the cotton reels and a gaily-coloured plait of sewing silks, smelt at the little bag filled with woodroffe she kept among them. He sat down at the piano, playing tunes with one finger, thinking: 'To-night she'll play; I shall watch her while she's playing; it does me good to watch her.' He took up the book, which still lay where she had placed it beside him, and tried to read. But Megan's little, sad figure began to haunt him at once, and he got up and leaned in the window, listening to the thrushes in the Crescent gardens, gazing at the sea, dreamy and blue below the trees. A servant came in and cleared the tea away, and he still stood, inhaling the evening air, trying not to think. Then he saw the Hallidays coming through the gate of the Crescent, Stella a little in front of Phil and the children, with their baskets, and instinctively he drew back. His heart, too sore and discomfited, shrank from this encounter, yet wanted its friendly solace—bore a grudge against this influence, yet craved its cool innocence, and the pleasure of watching Stella's face.

From against the wall behind the piano he saw her come in and stand looking a little blank as though disappointed; then she saw him and smiled, a swift, brilliant smile that warmed yet irritated Ashurst.

"You never came after us, Frank."

"No; I found I couldn't."

"Look! We picked such lovely late violets!" She held out a bunch. Ashurst put his nose to them, and there stirred within him vague longings, chilled instantly by a vision of Megan's anxious face lifted to the faces of the passers-by.

He said shortly: "How jolly!" and turned away. He went up to his room, and avoiding the children, who were coming up the stairs, threw himself on his bed, and lay there with his arms crossed over his face. Now that he felt the die really cast, and Megan given up, he hated himself, and almost hated the Hallidays and their atmosphere of healthy, happy English homes. Why should they have chanced here, to drive away first love—to show him that he was going to be no better than a common seducer? What right had Stella, with her fair, shy beauty, to make him know for certain that he would never marry Megan; and, tarnishing it all, bring him such bitterness of regretful longing and such pity? Megan would be back by now, worn out by her miserable seeking—poor little thing!—expecting, perhaps, to find him there when she reached home. Ashurst bit at his sleeve, to stifle a groan of remorseful longing. He went to dinner glum and silent, and his mood threw a dinge even over the children. It was a melancholy, rather ill-tempered evening, for they were all tired; several times he caught Stella looking at him with a hurt, puzzled expression, and this pleased his evil mood. He slept miserably; got up quite early, and wandered out. He went down to the beach. Alone there with the serene, the blue, the sunlit sea, his heart relaxed a little. Conceited fool—to think that Megan would take it so hard! In a week or two she would almost have forgotten! And he—well, he would have the reward of virtue! A good young man! If Stella knew, she would give him her blessing for resisting that devil she believed in; and he uttered a hard laugh. But slowly the peace and beauty of sea and sky, the flight of the lonely seagulls, made him feel ashamed. He bathed, and turned homeward.

In the Crescent gardens Stella herself was sitting on a camp stool, sketching. He stole up close behind. How fair and pretty she was, bent diligently, holding up her brush, measuring, wrinkling her brows.

He said gently:

"Sorry I was such a beast last night, Stella."

She turned round, startled, flushed very pink, and said in her quick way:

"It's all right. I knew there was something. Between friends it doesn't matter, does it?"

Ashurst answered:

"Between friends—and we are, aren't we?"

She looked up at him, nodded vehemently, and her upper teeth gleamed again in that swift, brilliant smile.

Three days later he went back to London, travelling with the Hallidays. He had not written to the farm. What was there he could say?

On the last day of April in the following year he and Stella were married. . . .

Such were Ashurst's memories, sitting against the wall among the gorse, on his silver-wedding day. At this very spot, where he had laid out the lunch, Megan must have stood outlined against the sky when he had first caught sight of her. Of all queer coincidences! And there moved in him a longing to go down and see again the farm and the orchard, and the meadow of the gipsy bogle. It would not take long; Stella would be an hour yet, perhaps.

How well he remembered it all—the little crowning group of pine trees, the steep-up grass hill behind! He paused at the farm gate. The low stone house, the yew-tree porch, the flowering currants—not changed a bit; even the old green chair was out there on the grass under the window, where he had reached up to her that night to take the key. Then he turned down the lane, and stood leaning on the orchard gate—grey skeleton of a gate, as then. A black pig even was wandering in there among the trees. Was it true that twenty-six years had passed, or had he dreamed and awakened to find Megan waiting for him by the big apple tree? Unconsciously he put up his hand to his grizzled beard and brought himself back to reality. Opening the gate, he made his way down through the docks and nettles till he came to the stream, and the old apple tree itself. Unchanged! A little more of the grey-green lichen, a dead branch or two, and for the rest it might have been only last night that he had embraced that mossy trunk after Megan's flight and inhaled its woody savour, while above his head the moonlit blossom had seemed to breathe and live. In that early spring a few buds were showing already; the blackbirds shouting their songs, a cuckoo calling, the sunlight bright and warm. Incredibly the same—the chattering trout-stream, the narrow pool he had lain in every morning, splashing the water over his flanks and chest; and out there in the wild meadow the beech clump and the stone where the gipsy bogle was supposed to sit. And an ache for lost youth, a hankering, a sense of wasted love and sweetness, gripped Ashurst by the throat. Surely, on this earth of such wild beauty, one was meant to hold rapture to one's heart, as this earth and sky held it! And yet, one could not!

He went to the edge of the stream, and looking down at the little pool, thought: 'Youth and spring! What has become of them all, I wonder?' And then, in sudden fear of having this memory jarred by human encounter, he went back to the lane, and pensively retraced his steps to the cross-roads.

Beside the car an old, grey-bearded labourer was leaning on a stick, talking to the chauffeur. He broke off at once, as though guilty of disrespect, and touching his hat, prepared to limp on down the lane.

Ashurst pointed to the narrow green mound. "Can you tell me what this is?"

The old fellow stopped; on his face had come a look as though he were thinking. 'You've come to the right shop, mister!'

" 'Tes a grave," he said.

"But why out here?"

The old man smiled. "That's a tale, as yu may say. An' not the first time as I've a-told et—there's plenty folks asks 'bout that bit o' turf. 'Maid's Grave' us calls et, 'ereabouts."

Ashurst held out his pouch. "Have a fill?"

The old man touched his hat again, and slowly filled an old clay pipe. His eyes, looking upward out of a mass of wrinkles and hair, were still quite bright.

"If yu don' mind, zurr, I'll zet down—my leg's 'urtin' a bit today." And he sat down on the mound of turf.

"There's always a vlower on this grave. An' 'tain't so very lonesome, neither; brave lot o' folks goes by now, in they new motor cars an' things—not as 'twas in th' old days. She've a got company up 'ere. 'Twas a poor soul killed 'erself."

"I see!" said Ashurst. "Cross-roads burial. I didn't know that custom was kept up."

"Ah! but 'twas a main long time ago. Us 'ad a parson as was very God-fearin' then. Let me see, I've a 'ad my pension six year come Michaelmas, an' I were just on fifty when t'appened. There's no one livin' knows more about et than I du. She belonged close 'ere; same farm as where I used to work along o' Mrs. Narracombe—'tes Nick Narracombe's now; I dus a bit for 'im still, odd times."

Ashurst, who was leaning against the gate, lighting his pipe, left his curved hands before his face for long after the flame of the match had gone out.

"Yes?" he said, and to himself his voice sounded hoarse and queer.

"She was one in an 'underd, poor maid! I puts a vlower 'ere every time I passes. Pretty maid an' gude maid she was, though they wouldn't burry 'er up tu th' church, nor where she wanted to be burried neither." The old labourer paused, and put his hairy, twisted hand flat down on the turf beside the bluebells.

"Yes?" said Ashurst.

"In a manner of speakin'," the old man went on, "I think as 'twas a love-story—though there's no one never knu for zartin. Yu can't tell what's in a maid's 'ead—but that's wot I think about it." He drew his hand along the turf. "I was fond o' that maid—don't know as there was anyone as wasn' fond of 'er. But she was tu lovin'-'earted—that's where 'twas, I think." He looked up. And Ashurst, whose lips were trembling in the cover of his beard, murmured again: "Yes?"

" 'Twas in the spring, 'bout now as 't might be, or a little later—blossom time—an' we 'ad one o' they young college gentlemen stayin' at the farm—nice feller tu, with 'is 'ead in the air. I liked 'e very well, an' I never see nothin' between 'em, but to my thinkin' 'e turned the maid's fancy." The old man took the pipe out of his mouth, spat, and went on:

"Yu see, 'e went away sudden one day, an' never come back. They got 'is knapsack and bits o' things down there still. That's what stuck in my mind—'is never sendin' for 'em. 'Is name was Ashes, or somethen' like that."

"Yes?" said Ashurst once more.

The old man licked his lips.

"'Er never said nothin', but from that day 'er went kind of dazed lukin'; didn't seem rightly therr at all. I never knu a 'uman creature so changed in me life—never. There was another young feller at the farm—Joe Biddaford 'is name wer', that was praaperly sweet on 'er, tu; I guess 'e used to plague 'er wi' 'is attentions. She got to luke quite wild. I'd zee her sometimes of an avenin' when I was bringin' up the calves; ther' she'd stand in th' orchard, under the big apple tree, lukin' straight before 'er. 'Well,' I used t' think, 'I dunno what 'tes that's the matter wi' yu, but yu'm lukin' pitiful, that yu are.' "

The old man relit his pipe, and sucked at it reflectively.

"Yes?" said Ashurst.

"I remembers one day I said to 'er: 'What's the matter, Megan?'—'er name was Megan David, she come from Wales same as 'er aunt, ol' Missis Narracombe. 'Yu'm frettin' about somethin', I says. 'No, Jim,' she says, 'I'm not frettin'.' 'Yes, yu are!' I says. 'No,' she says, and tu tears cam' rollin' out. 'Yu'm cryin'—what's that, then?' I says. She putts 'er 'and over 'er 'eart: 'It 'urts me,' she says; 'but 'twill sune be better,' she says. 'But if anything shude 'appen to me, Jim, I wants to be burried under this 'ere apple tree.' I laughed. 'What's goin' to 'appen to yu?' I says; 'don't 'ee be fulish.' 'No,' she says, 'I won't be fulish.' Well, I know what maids are, an' I never thought no more about et, till tu days arter that, 'bout six in the avenin' I was comin' up wi' the calves, when I see somethin' dark lying in the strame, close to that big apple tree. I says to meself: 'Is that a pig—funny place for a pig to get to!' an' I goes up to et, an' I see what 'twas."

The old man stopped; his eyes, turned upward, had a bright, suffering look.

" 'Twas the maid, in a little narrer pool ther' that's made by the stoppin' of a rock—where I see the young gentleman bathin' once or twice. 'Er was lyin' on 'er face in the watter. There was a plant o' goldie-cups growin' out o' the stone just above 'er 'ead. An' when I come to luke at 'er face, 'twas luvly, butiful, so calm's a baby's—wonderful butiful et was. When the doctor saw 'er, 'e said: 'She culdn' never a-done it in that little bit o' watter ef 'er 'adn't a-been in an extarsy.' Ah! an' judgin' from 'er face, that was just 'ow she was. Et made me cry praaper—butiful et was! 'Twas June then, but she'd a-found a little bit of apple blossom left over somewheres, and stuck et in 'er 'air. That's why I thinks 'er must a-been in an extarsy, to go to et gay, like that. Why! there wasn't more than a fute and a 'arf o' watter. But I tell 'ee one thing—that meadder's 'arnted; I knu et, an' she knu et; an' no one'll persuade me as 'tesn't. I told 'em what she said to me 'bout bein' burried under th' apple tree. But I think that turned 'em—made et luke tu much's ef she'd 'ad it in 'er mind deliberate; an' so they burried 'er up 'ere. Parson we 'ad then was very particular, 'e was."

Again the old man drew his hand over the turf.

" 'Tes wonderful, et seems," he added slowly, "what maids'll du for love. She 'ad a lovin' 'eart; I guess 'twas broken. But us never *knu* nothin'!"

He looked up as if for approval of his story, but Ashurst had walked past him as if he were not there.

Up on the top of the hill beyond where he had spread the lunch, over, out of sight, he lay down on his face. So had his virtue been rewarded, and "The Cyprian," goddess of love, taken her revenge! And before his eyes, dim with tears, came Megan's face with the sprig of apple blossom in her dark, wet hair. 'What did I do that was wrong?' he thought. 'What *did* I do?' But he could not answer. Spring, with its rush of passion, its flowers and song—the spring in his heart and Megan's! Was it just Love seeking a victim! The Greek was right, then—the words of the "Hippolytus" as true to-day!

"For mad is the heart of Love,
And gold the gleam of his wing;
And all to the spell thereof
Bend when he makes his spring.
All life that is wild and young
In mountain and wave and stream
All that of earth is sprung,
Or breathes in the red sunbeam;
Yea, and Mankind. O'er all a royal throne,
Cyprian, Cyprian, is thine alone!"

The Greek was right! Megan! Poor little Megan—coming over the hill! Megan under the old apple tree waiting and looking! Megan dead, with beauty printed on her! . . .

A voice said:

"Oh, there you are! Look!"

Ashurst rose, took his wife's sketch, and stared at in silence.

"Is the foreground right, Frank?"

"Yes."

"But there's something wanting, isn't there?"

Ashurst nodded. Wanting? The apple tree, the singing, and the gold!

And solemnly he put his lips to her forehead. It was his silver-wedding day.

RING LARDNER

The Golden Honeymoon

Ring Lardner (1885–1933)

AMONG THAT TALENTED GROUP of magazine-fiction writers who give the years 1914–1929 a special brilliance in the annals of American letters, there was no better story-teller than Lardner and none whose darts of satire struck deeper into the rhinoceros hide of a generation complacently devoted to mammon.

Up to the time of the publication of How To Write Short Stories (1924), his reputation had been that of a sports-writer with a difference—a man with the gift of vivid language, and an ear for the turns of common speech, and a refreshingly humorous approach to such ancient American sanctities as the game of baseball.

You Know Me Al (1916), and other successes in the same, broadly funny vein hardly prepared Lardner's readers for such a study in irony as The Golden Honeymoon. In this story, as in some others where the intent is satiric, the note of pity, though muted, is present. But for the cheater, the bully, the mean of spirit, Lardner had no pity. Champion, for example, or Haircut are triumphs of reporting; the characters are self-arraigned, judged and despatched. It was his way, apparently at least, to give his characters free rein; to let them babble on in the words and phrases they would themselves have used, so that the illusion of reality is complete. Lardner's stories are dramas without stage or setting, in which the hand of the puppet-master is unseen, and almost unsuspected. It is a pity they are so few.

THE GOLDEN HONEYMOON

MOTHER says that when I start talking I never know when to stop. But I tell her the only time I get a chance is when she ain't around, so I have to make the most of it. I guess the fact is neither one of us would be welcome in a Quaker meeting, but as I tell Mother, what did God give us tongues for if He didn't want we should use them? Only she says He didn't give them to us to say the same thing over and over again, like I do, and repeat myself. But I say:

"Well, Mother," I say, "when people is like you and I and been married fifty years, do you expect everything I say will be something you ain't heard me say before? But it may be new to others, as they ain't nobody else lived with me as long as you have."

So she says:

"You can bet they ain't, as they couldn't nobody else stand you that long."

"Well," I tell her, "you look pretty healthy."

"Maybe I do," she will say, "but I looked even healthier before I married you."

You can't get ahead of Mother.

Yes, sir, we was married just fifty years ago the seventeenth day of last December and my daughter and son-in-law was over from Trenton to help us celebrate the Golden Wedding. My son-in-law is John H. Kramer, the real estate man. He made $12,000 one year and is pretty well thought of around Trenton; a good, steady, hard worker. The Rotarians was after him a long time to join, but he kept telling them his home was his club. But Edie finally made him join. That's my daughter.

Well, anyway, they come over to help us celebrate the Golden Wedding and it was pretty crimpy weather and the furnace don't seem to heat up no more like it used to and Mother made the remark that she hoped this winter wouldn't be as cold as the last, referring to the winter previous. So Edie said if she was us, and nothing to keep us home, she certainly wouldn't spend no more winters up here and why didn't we just shut off the water and close up the house and go down to Tampa, Florida? You know we was there four winters ago and staid five weeks, but it cost us over three hundred and fifty dollars for hotel bill alone. So Mother said we wasn't going no place to be robbed. So my son-in-law spoke up and said that Tampa wasn't the only place in the South, and besides we didn't have to stop at no high price hotel but could rent us a couple rooms and board out somewheres, and he had heard that St. Petersburg, Florida, was *the* spot and if we said the word he would write down there and make inquiries.

Well, to make a long story short, we decided to do it and Edie said it would be our Golden Honeymoon and for a present my son-in-law paid the difference between a section and a compartment so as we could have a compartment and have more privatecy. In a compartment you have an upper and lower berth just like the regular sleeper, but it is a shut in room by itself and got a wash bowl. The car we went in was all compartments and no regular berths at all. It was all compartments.

We went to Trenton the night before and staid at my daughter and son-in-law and we left Trenton the next afternoon at 3.23 P.M.

This was the twelfth day of January. Mother set facing the front of the train, as it makes her giddy to ride backwards. I set facing her, which does not affect me. We reached North Philadelphia at 4.03 P.M. and we reached West Philadelphia at 4.14, but did not go into Broad Street. We reached Baltimore at 6.30 and Washington, D.C., at 7.25. Our train laid over in Washington two hours till another train come along to pick us up and I got out and strolled up the platform and into the Union Station. When I come back, our car had been switched on to another track, but I remembered the name of it, the La Belle, as I had once visited my aunt out in Oconomowoc, Wisconsin, where there was a lake of that name, so I had no difficulty in getting located. But Mother had nearly fretted herself sick for fear I would be left.

"Well," I said, "I would of followed you on the next train."

"You could of," said Mother, and she pointed out that she had the money.

"Well," I said, "we are in Washington and I could of borrowed from the United States Treasury. I would of pretended I was an Englishman."

Mother caught the point and laughed heartily.

Our train pulled out of Washington at 9.40 P.M. and Mother and I turned in early, I taking the upper. During the night we passed through the green fields of old Virginia, though it was too dark to tell if they was green or what color. When we got up in the morning, we was a Fayetteville, North Carolina. We had breakfast in the dining car and after breakfast I got in conversation with the man in the next compartment to ours. He was from Lebanon, New Hampshire, and a man about eighty years of age. His wife was with him, and two unmarried daughters and I made the remark that I should think the four of them would be crowded in one compartment, but he said they had made the trip every winter for fifteen years and knowed how to keep out of each other's way. He said they was bound for Tarpon Springs.

We reached Charleston, South Carolina, at 12.50 P.M. and arrived at Savannah, Georgia, at 4.20. We reached Jacksonville, Florida, at 8.45 P.M. and had an hour and a quarter to lay over there, but Mother made a fuss about me getting off the train, so we had the darky make up our berths and retired before we left Jacksonville. I didn't sleep good as the train done a lot of hemming and hawing, and Mother never sleeps good on a train as she says she is always worrying that I will fall out. She says she would rather have the upper herself, as then she would not have to worry about me, but I tell her I can't take the risk of having it get out that I allowed my wife to sleep in an upper berth. It would make talk.

We was up in the morning in time to see our friends from New Hampshire get off at Tarpon Springs, which we reached at 6.53 A.M.

Several of our fellow passengers got off at Clearwater and some at Belleair, where the train backs right up to the door of the mammoth hotel. Belleair is the winter headquarters for the golf dudes and everybody that got off there had their bag of sticks, as many as ten and twelve in a bag. Women and all. When I was a young man we called it shinny and only needed one club to play with and about one game of it would of been a-plenty for some of these dudes, the way we played it.

The train pulled into St. Petersburg at 8.20 and when we got off the train you would think they was a riot, what with all the darkies barking for the different hotels.

I said to Mother, I said:

"It is a good thing we have got a place picked out to go to and don't have to choose a hotel, as it would be hard to choose amongst them if every one of them is the best."

She laughed.

We found a jitney and I give him the address of the room my son-in-law had got for us and soon we was there and introduced ourselves to the lady that owns the house, a young widow about forty-eight years of age. She showed us our room, which was light and airy with a comfortable bed and bureau and washstand. It was twelve dollars a week, but the location was good, only three blocks from Williams Park.

St. Pete is what folks calls the town, though they also call it the Sunshine City, as they claim they's no other place in the country where they's fewer days when Old Sol don't smile down on Mother Earth, and one of the newspapers gives away all their copies free every day when the sun don't shine. They claim to of only give them away some sixty-odd times in the last eleven years. Another nickname they have got for the town is "the Poor Man's Palm Beach," but I guess they's men that comes there that could borrow as much from the bank as some of the Willie boys over to the other Palm Beach.

During our stay we paid a visit to the Lewis Tent City, which is the headquarters for the Tin Can Tourists. But may be you ain't heard about them. Well, they are an organization that takes their vacation trips by auto and carries everything with them. That is, they bring along their tents to sleep in and cook in and they don't patronize no hotels or cafeterias, but they have got to be bona fide auto campers or they can't belong to the organization.

They tell me they's over 200,000 members to it and they call themselves the Tin Canners on account of most of their food being put up in tin cans. One couple we seen in the Tent City was a couple from Brady, Texas, named Mr. and Mrs. Pence, which the old man is over eighty years of age and they had come in their auto all the way from home, a distance of 1,641 miles. They took five weeks for the trip, Mr. Pence driving the entire distance.

The Tin Canners hails from every State in the Union and in the summer time they visit places like New England and the Great Lakes region, but in the winter the most of them comes to Florida and scatters all over the State. While we was down there, they was a national convention of them at Gainesville, Florida, and they elected a Fredonia, New York, man as their president. His title is Royal Tin Can Opener of the World. They have got a song wrote up which everybody has got to learn it before they are a member:

"The tin can forever! Hurrah, boys! Hurrah!
Up with the tin can! Down with the foe!
We will rally round the campfire, we'll rally once again,
Shouting, 'We auto camp forever!' "

That is something like it. And the members has also got to have a tin can fastened on to the front of their machine.

I asked Mother how she would like to travel around that way and she said:

"Fine, but not with an old rattle brain like you driving."

"Well," I said, "I am eight years younger than this Mr. Pence who drove here from Texas."

"Yes," she said, "but he is old enough to not be skittish."

You can't get ahead of Mother.

Well, one of the first things we done in St. Petersburg was to go to the Chamber of Commerce and register our names and where we was from as they's great rivalry amongst the different States in regards to the number of their citizens visiting in town and of course our little State don't stand much of a show, but still every little bit helps, as the fella says. All and all, the man told us, they was eleven thousand names registered, Ohio leading with some fifteen hundred-odd and New York State next with twelve hundred. Then come

Michigan, Pennsylvania and so on down, with one man each from Cuba and Nevada.

The first night we was there, they was a meeting of the New York-New Jersey Society at the Congregational Church and a man from Ogdensburg, New York State, made the talk. His subject was Rainbow Chasing. He is a Rotarian and a very convicting speaker, though I forget his name.

Our first business, of course, was to find a place to eat and after trying several places we run on to a cafeteria on Central Avenue that suited us up and down. We eat pretty near all our meals there and it averaged about two dollars per day for the two of us, but the food was well cooked and everything nice and clean. A man don't mind paying the price if things is clean and well cooked.

On the third day of February, which is Mother's birthday, we spread ourselves and eat supper at the Poinsettia Hotel and they charged us seventy-five cents for a sirloin steak that wasn't hardly big enough for one.

I said to Mother: "Well," I said, "I guess it's a good thing every day ain't your birthday or we would be in the poorhouse."

"No," says Mother, "because if every day was my birthday, I would be old enough by this time to of been in my grave long ago."

You can't get ahead of Mother.

In the hotel they had a card-room where they was several men and ladies playing five hundred and this new fangled whist bridge. We also seen a place where they was dancing, so I asked Mother would she like to trip the light fantastic toe and she said no, she was too old to squirm like you have got to do now days. We watched some of the young folks at it awhile till Mother got disgusted and said we would have to see a good movie to take the taste out of our mouth. Mother is a great movie heroyne and we go twice a week here at home.

But I want to tell you about the Park. The second day we was there we visited the Park, which is a good deal like the one in Tampa, only bigger, and they's more fun goes on here every day than you could shake a stick at. In the middle they's a big bandstand and chairs for the folks to set and listen to the concerts, which they give you music for all tastes, from Dixie up to classical pieces like Hearts and Flowers.

Then all around they's places marked off for different sports and games—chess and checkers and dominoes for folks that enjoys those kind of games, and roque and horse-shoes for the nimbler ones. I used to pitch a pretty fair shoe myself, but ain't done much of it in the last twenty years.

Well, anyway, we bought a membership ticket in the club which costs one dollar for the season, and they tell me that up to a couple years ago it was fifty cents, but they had to raise it to keep out the riffraff.

Well, Mother and I put in a great day watching the pitchers and she wanted I should get in the game, but I told her I was all out of practice and would make a fool of myself, though I seen several men pitching who I guess I could take their measure without no practice. However, they was some good pitchers, too, and one boy from Akron, Ohio, who could certainly throw a pretty shoe. They told me it looked like he would win the championship of the United States in the February tournament. We come away a few days before they held that and I never did hear if he win. I forget his name, but he was a clean cut young fella and he has got a brother in Cleveland that's a Rotarian.

Well, we just stood around and watched the different games for two or three days and finally I set down in a checker game with a man named Weaver from Danville, Illinois. He was a pretty fair checker player, but he wasn't no match for me, and I hope that don't sound like bragging. But I always could hold my own on a checkerboard and the folks around here will tell you the same thing. I played with this Weaver pretty near all morning for two or three mornings and he beat me one game and the only other time it looked like he had a chance, the noon whistle blowed and we had to quit and go to dinner.

While I was playing checkers, Mother would set and listen to the band, as she loves music, classical or no matter what kind, but anyway she was setting there one day and between selections the woman next to her opened up a conversation. She was a woman about Mother's own age, seventy or seventy-one, and finally she asked Mother's name and Mother told her her name and where she was from and Mother asked her the same question, and who do you think the woman was?

Well, sir, it was the wife of Frank M. Hartsell, the man who was engaged to Mother till I stepped in and cut him out, fifty-two years ago!

Yes, sir!

You can imagine Mother's surprise! And Mrs. Hartsell was surprised, too, when Mother told her she had once been friends with her husband, though Mother didn't say how close friends they had been, or that Mother and I was the cause of Hartsell going out West. But that's what we was. Hartsell left his town a month after the engagement was broke off and ain't never been back since. He had went out to Michigan and become a veterinary, and that is where he had settled down, in Hillsdale, Michigan, and finally married his wife.

Well, Mother screwed up her courage to ask if Frank was still living and Mrs. Hartsell took her over to where they was pitching horse-shoes and there was old Frank, waiting his turn. And he knowed Mother as soon as he seen her, though it was over fifty years. He said he knowed her by her eyes.

"Why, it's Lucy Frost!" he says, and he throwed down his shoes and quit the game.

Then they come over and hunted me up and I will confess I wouldn't of knowed him. Him and I is the same age to the month, but he seems to show it more, some way. He is balder for one thing. And his beard is all white, where mine has still got a streak of brown in it. The very first thing I said to him, I said:

"Well, Frank, that beard of yours makes me feel like I was back north. It looks like a regular blizzard."

"Well," he said, "I guess yourn would be just as white if you had it dry cleaned."

But Mother wouldn't stand that.

"Is that so!" she said to Frank. "Well, Charley ain't had no tobacco in his mouth for over ten years!"

And I ain't!

Well, I excused myself from the checker game and it was pretty close to noon, so we decided to all have dinner together and they was nothing for it only we must try their cafeteria on Third Avenue. It was a little more expensive than ours and not near as good, I thought. I and Mother had about the same dinner we had been having every day and our bill was $1.10. Frank's check was $1.20 for he and his wife. The same meal wouldn't of cost them more than a dollar at our place.

After dinner we made them come up to our house and we all set in the parlor, which the young woman had give us the use of to entertain company. We begun talking over old times and Mother said she was a-scared Mrs. Hartsell would find it tiresome listening to we three talk over old times, but as it turned out they wasn't much chance for nobody else to talk with Mrs. Hartsell in the company. I have heard lots of women that could go it, but Hartsell's wife takes the cake of all the women I ever seen. She told us the family history of everybody in the State of Michigan and bragged for a half hour about her son, who she said is in the drug business in Grand Rapids, and a Rotarian.

When I and Hartsell could get a word in edgeways we joked one another back and forth and I chafed him about being a horse doctor.

"Well, Frank," I said, "you look pretty prosperous, so I suppose they's been plenty of glanders around Hillsdale."

"Well," he said, "I've managed to make more than a fair living. But I've worked pretty hard."

"Yes," I said, "and I suppose you get called out all hours of the night to attend births and so on."

Mother made me shut up.

Well, I thought they wouldn't never go home and I and Mother was in misery trying to keep awake, as the both of us generally always takes a nap after dinner. Finally they went, after we had made an engagement to meet them in the Park the next morning, and Mrs. Hartsell also invited us to come to their place the next night and play five hundred. But she had forgot that they was a meeting of the Michigan Society that evening, so it was not till two evenings later that we had our first card game.

Hartsell and his wife lived in a house on Third Avenue North and had a private setting room besides their bedroom. Mrs. Hartsell couldn't quit talking about their private setting room like it was something wonderful. We played cards with them, with Mother and Hartsell partners against his wife and I. Mrs. Hartsell is a miserable card player and we certainly got the worst of it.

After the game she brought out a dish of oranges and we had to pretend it was just what we wanted, though oranges down there is like a young man's whiskers; you enjoy them at first, but they get to be a pesky nuisance.

We played cards again the next night at our place with the same partners and I and Mrs. Hartsell was beat again. Mother and Hartsell was full of compliments for each other on what a good team they made, but the both of them knowed well enough where the secret of their success laid. I guess all and all we must of played ten different evenings and they was only one night when Mrs. Hartsell and I come out ahead. And that one night wasn't no fault of hern.

When we had been down there about two weeks, we spent one evening as their guest in the Congregational Church, at a social give by the Michigan Society. A talk was made by a man named Bitting of Detroit, Michigan, on How I was Cured of Story Telling. He is a big man in the Rotarians and give a witty talk.

A woman named Mrs. Oxford rendered some selections which Mrs. Hartsell said was grand opera music, but whatever they was my daughter Edie could of give her cards and spades and not made such a hullaballoo about it neither.

Then they was a ventriloquist from Grand Rapids and a young woman about forty-five years of age that mimicked different kinds of birds. I whispered to Mother that they all sounded like a chicken, but she nudged me to shut up.

After the show we stopped in a drug store and I set up the refreshments and it was pretty close to ten o'clock before we finally turned in. Mother and I would of preferred tending the movies, but Mother said we musn't offend Mrs. Hartsell, though I asked her had we came to Florida to enjoy ourselves or to just not offend an old chatter-box from Michigan.

I felt sorry for Hartsell one morning. The women folks both had an engagement down to the chiropodist's and I run across Hartsell in the Park and he foolishly offered to play me checkers.

It was him that suggested it, not me, and I guess he repented himself before we had played one game. But he was too stubborn to give up and set there while I beat him game after game and the worst part of it was that a crowd of folks had got in the habit of watching me play and there they all was, looking on, and finally they seen what a fool Frank was making of himself, and they began to chafe him and pass remarks. Like one of them said:

"Who ever told you you was a checker player!"

And:

"You might maybe be good for tiddle-de-winks, but not checkers!"

I almost felt like letting him beat me a couple games. But the crowd would of knowed it was a put up job.

Well, the women folks joined us in the Park and I wasn't going to mention our little game, but Hartsell told about it himself and admitted he wasn't no match for me.

"Well," said Mrs. Hartsell, "checkers ain't much of a game anyway, is it?" She said: "It's more of a children's game, ain't it? At least, I know my boy's children used to play it a good deal."

"Yes, ma'am," I said. "It's a children's game the way your husband plays it, too."

Mother wanted to smooth things over, so she said:

"Maybe they's other games where Frank can beat you."

"Yes," said Mrs. Hartsell, "and I bet he could beat you pitching horse-shoes."

"Well," I said, "I would give him a chance to try, only I ain't pitched a shoe in over sixteen years."

"Well," said Hartsell, "I ain't played checkers in twenty years."

"You ain't never played it," I said.

"Anyway," says Frank, "Lucy and I is your master at five hundred."

Well, I could of told him why that was, but had decency enough to hold my tongue.

It had got so now that he wanted to play cards every night and when I or Mother wanted to go to a movie, any one of us would have to pretend we had a headache and then trust to goodness that they wouldn't see us sneak into the theater. I don't mind playing cards when my partner keeps their mind on the game, but you take a woman like Hartsell's wife and how can they play cards when they have got to stop every couple seconds and brag about their son in Grand Rapids?

Well, the New York-New Jersey Society announced that they was goin to give a social evening too and I said to Mother, I said:

"Well, that is one evening when we will have an excuse not to play five hundred."

"Yes," she said, "but we will have to ask Frank and his wife to go to the social with us as they asked us to go to the Michigan social."

"Well," I said, "I had rather stay home than drag that chatter-box everywheres we go."

So Mother said:

"You are getting too cranky. Maybe she does talk a little too much but she is good hearted. And Frank is always good company."

So I said:

"I suppose if he is such good company you wished you had of married him."

Mother laughed and said I sounded like I was jealous. Jealous of a cow doctor!

Anyway we had to drag them along to the social and I will say that we give them a much better entertainment than they had given us.

Judge Lane of Paterson made a fine talk on business conditions and a Mrs. Newell of Westfield imitated birds, only you could really tell what they was the way she done it. Two young women from Red Bank sung a choral selection and we clapped them back and they gave us Home to Our Mountains and Mother and Mrs. Hartsell both had tears in their eyes. And Hartsell, too.

Well, some way or another the chairman got wind that I was there and asked me to make a talk and I wasn't even going to get up, but Mother made me, so I got up and said:

"Ladies and gentlemen," I said. "I didn't expect to be called on for a speech on an occasion like this or no other occasion as I do not set myself up as a speech maker, so will have to do the best I can, which I often say is the best anybody can do."

Then I told them the story about Pat and the motorcycle, using the brogue, and it seemed to tickle them and I told them one or two other stories, but altogether I wasn't on my feet more than twenty or twenty-five minutes and you ought to of heard the clapping and hollering when I set down. Even Mrs. Hartsell admitted that I am quite a speechifier and said if I ever went to Grand Rapids, Michigan, her son would make me talk to the Rotarians.

When it was over, Hartsell wanted we should go to their house and play cards, but his wife reminded him that it was after 9.30 P.M., rather a late hour to start a card game, but he had went crazy on the subject of cards, probably because he didn't have to play partners with his wife. Anyway, we got rid of them and went home to bed.

It was the next morning, when we met over to the Park, that Mrs. Hartsell made the remark that she wasn't getting no exercise so I suggested that why didn't she take part in the roque game.

She said she had not played a game of roque in twenty years, but if Mother would play she would play. Well, at first Mother wouldn't hear of it, but finally consented, more to please Mrs. Hartsell than anything else.

Well, they had a game with a Mrs. Ryan from Eagle, Nebraska, and a young Mrs. Morse from Rutland, Vermont, who Mother had met down to the chiropodist's. Well, Mother couldn't hit a flea and they all laughed at her and I couldn't help from laughing at her myself and finally she quit and said her back was too lame to stoop over. So they got another lady and kept on playing and soon Mrs. Hartsell was the one everybody was laughing at, as she had a long shot to hit the black ball, and as she made the effort her teeth fell out on to the court. I never seen a woman so flustered in my life. And I never heard so much laughing, only Mrs. Hartsell didn't join in and she was madder than a hornet and wouldn't play no more, so the game broke up.

Mrs. Hartsell went home without speaking to nobody, but Hartsell stayed around and finally he said to me, he said:

"Well, I played you checkers the other day and you beat me bad and now what do you say if you and me play a game of horseshoes?"

I told him I hadn't pitched a shoe in sixteen years, but Mother said:

"Go ahead and play. You used to be good at it and maybe it will come back to you."

Well, to make a long story short, I give in. I oughtn't to of never tried it, as I hadn't pitched a shoe in sixteen years, and I only done it to humor Hartsell.

Before we started, Mother patted me on the back and told me to do my best, so we started in and I seen right off that I was in for it, as I hadn't pitched a shoe in sixteen years and didn't have my distance. And besides, the plating had wore off the shoes so that they was points right where they stuck into my thumb and I hadn't throwed more than two or three times when my thumb was raw and it pretty near killed me to hang on to the shoe, let alone pitch it.

Well, Hartsell throws the awkwardest shoe I ever seen pitched and to see him pitch you wouldn't think he would ever come nowheres near, but he is also the luckiest pitcher I ever seen and he made some pitches where the shoe lit five and six feet short and then schoonered up and was a ringer. They's no use trying to beat that kind of luck.

They was a pretty fair sized crowd watching us and four or five other ladies besides Mother, and it seems like, when Hartsell pitches, he has got to chew and it kept the ladies on the anxious seat as he don't seem to care which way he is facing when he leaves go.

You would think a man as old as him would of learnt more manners.

Well, to make a long story short, I was just beginning to get my distance when I had to give up on account of my thumb, which I showed it to Hartsell and he seen I couldn't go on, as it was raw and bleeding. Even if I could of stood it to go on myself, Mother wouldn't of allowed it after she seen my thumb. So anyway I quit and Hartsell said the score was nineteen to six, but I don't know what it was. Or don't care, neither.

Well, Mother and I went home and I said I hoped we was through with the Hartsells as I was sick and tired of them, but it seemed like she had promised we would go over to their house that evening for another game of their everlasting cards.

Well, my thumb was giving me considerable pain and I felt kind of out of sorts and I guess maybe I forgot myself, but anyway, when we was about through playing Hartsell made the remark that he wouldn't never lose a game of cards if he could always have Mother for a partner.

So I said:

"Well, you had a chance fifty years ago to always have her for a partner, but you wasn't man enough to keep her."

I was sorry the minute I had said it and Hartsell didn't know what to say and for once his wife couldn't say nothing. Mother tried to smooth things over by making the remark that I must of had something stronger than tea or I wouldn't talk so silly. But Mrs. Hartsell had froze up like an iceberg and hardly said good night to us and I bet her and Frank put in a pleasant hour after we was gone.

As we was leaving, Mother said to him: "Never mind Charley's nonsense, Frank. He is just mad because you beat him all hollow pitching horseshoes and playing cards."

She said that to make up for my slip, but at the same time she certainly riled me. I tried to keep ahold of myself, but as soon as we was out of the house she had to open up the subject and begun to scold me for the break I had made.

Well, I wasn't in no mood to be scolded. So I said:

"I guess he is such a wonderful pitcher and card player that you wished you had married him."

"Well," she said, "at least he ain't a baby to give up pitching because his thumb has got a few scratches."

"And how about you," I said, "making a fool of yourself on the roque court and then pretending your back is lame and you can't play no more!"

"Yes," she said, "but when you hurt your thumb I didn't laugh at you, and why did you laugh at me when I sprained my back?"

"Who could help from laughing!" I said.

"Well," she said, "Frank Hartsell didn't laugh."

"Well," I said, "why didn't you marry him?"

"Well," said Mother, "I almost wished I had!"

"And I wished so, too!" I said.

"I'll remember that!" said Mother, and that's the last word she said to me for two days.

We seen the Hartsells the next day in the Park and I was willing to apologize, but they just nodded to us. And a couple days later we heard they had left for Orlando, where they have got relatives. I wished they had went there in the first place.

Mother and I made it up setting on a bench.

"Listen, Charley," she said. "This is our Golden Honeymoon and we don't want the whole thing spoilt with a silly old quarrel."

"Well," I said, "did you mean that about wishing you had married Hartsell?"

"Of course not," she said, "that is, if you didn't mean that you wished I had, too."

So I said:

"I was just tired and all wrought up. I thank God you chose me instead of him as they's no other woman in the world who I could of lived with all these years."

"How about Mrs. Hartsell?" says Mother.

"Good gracious!" I said. "Imagine being married to a woman that plays five hundred like she does and drops her teeth on the roque court!"

"Well," said Mother, "it wouldn't be no worse than being married to a man that expectorates towards ladies and is such a fool in a checker game."

So I put my arm around her shoulder and she stroked my hand and I guess we got kind of spoony.

They was two days left of our stay in St. Petersburg and the next to the last day Mother introduced me to a Mrs. Kendall from Kingston, Rhode Island, who she had met at the chiropodist's.

Mrs. Kendall made us acquainted with her husband, who is in the grocery business. They have got two sons and five grandchildren and one great-grandchild. One of their sons lives in Providence and is way up in the Elks as well as a Rotarian.

We found them very congenial people and we played cards with them the last two nights we was there. They was both experts and I only wished we had met them sooner instead of running into the Hartsells. But the Kendalls will be there again next winter and we will see more of them, that is, if we decide to make the trip again.

We left the Sunshine City on the eleventh day of February, at 11 A.M. This give us a day trip through Florida and we seen all the country we had passed through at night on the way down.

We reached Jacksonville at 7 P.M. and pulled out of there at 8.10 P.M. We reached Fayetteville, North Carolina, at nine o'clock the following morning, and reached Washington, D. C., at 6.30 P.M., laying over there half an hour.

We reached Trenton at 11.01 P.M. and had wired ahead to my daughter and son-in-law and they met us at the train and we went to their house and they put us up for the night. John would of made us stay up all night, telling about our trip, but Edie said we must be tired and made us go to bed. That's my daughter.

The next day we took our train for home and arrived safe and sound, having been gone just one month and a day.

Here comes Mother, so I guess I better shut up.

RING LARDNER

Haircut

HAIRCUT

I GOT another barber that comes over from Carterville and helps me out Saturdays, but the rest of the time I can get along all right alone. You can see for yourself that this ain't no New York City and besides that, the most of the boys works all day and don't have no leisure to drop in here and get themselves prettied up.

You're a newcomer, ain't you? I thought I hadn't seen you round before. I hope you like it good enough to stay. As I say, we ain't no New York City or Chicago, but we have pretty good times. Not as good, though, since Jim Kendall got killed. When he was alive, him and Hod Meyers used to keep this town in an uproar. I bet they was more laughin' done here than any town its size in America.

Jim was comical, and Hod was pretty near a match for him. Since Jim's gone, Hod tries to hold his end up just the same as ever, but it's tough goin' when you ain't got nobody to kind of work with.

They used to be plenty fun in here Saturdays. This place is jam-packed Saturdays, from four o'clock on. Jim and Hod would show up right after their supper, round six o'clock. Jim would set himself down in that big chair, nearest the blue spittoon. Whoever had been settin' in that chair, why they'd get up when Jim come in and give it to him.

You'd of thought it was a reserved seat like they have sometimes in a theayter. Hod would generally always stand or walk up and down, or some Saturdays, of course, he'd be settin' in this chair part of the time, gettin' a haircut.

Well, Jim would set there a w'ile without openin' his mouth only to spit, and then finally he'd say to me, "Whitey,"—my right name, that is, my right first name, is Dick, but everybody round here calls me Whitey—Jim would say, "Whitey, your nose looks like a rosebud tonight. You must of been drinkin' some of your aw de cologne."

So I'd say, "No, Jim, but you look like you'd been drinkin' somethin' of that kind or somethin' worse."

Jim would have to laugh at that, but then he'd speak up and say, "No, I ain't had nothin' to drink, but that ain't sayin' I wouldn't like somethin'. I wouldn't even mind if it was wood alcohol."

Then Hod Meyers would say, "Neither would your wife." That would set everybody to laughin' because Jim and his wife wasn't on very good terms. She'd of divorced him only they wasn't no chance to get alimony and she didn't have no way to take care of herself and the kids. She couldn't never understand Jim. He *was* kind of rough, but a good fella at heart.

Him and Hod had all kinds of sport with Milt Sheppard. I don't suppose you've seen Milt. Well, he's got an Adam's apple that looks more like a mushmelon. So I'd be shavin' Milt and when I'd start to shave down here on his neck, Hod would holler, "Hey, Whitey, wait a minute! Before you cut into it, let's make up a pool and see who can guess closest to the number of seeds."

And Jim would say, "If Milt hadn't of been so hoggish, he'd of ordered a half a cantaloupe instead of a whole one and it might not of stuck in his throat."

All the boys would roar at this and Milt himself would force a smile, though the joke was on him. Jim certainly was a card!

There's his shavin' mug, settin' on the shelf, right next to Charley Vail's. "Charles M. Vail." That's the druggist. He comes in regular for his shave, three times a week. And Jim's is the cup next to Charley's. "James H. Kendall." Jim won't need no shavin' mug no more, but I'll leave it there just the same for old time's sake. Jim certainly was a character!

Years ago, Jim used to travel for a canned goods concern over in Carterville. They sold canned goods. Jim had the whole northern half of the State and was on the road five days out of every week. He'd drop in here Saturdays and tell his experiences for that week. It was rich.

I guess he paid more attention to playin' jokes than makin' sales. Finally the concern let him out and he come right home here and told everybody he'd been fired instead of sayin' he'd resigned like most fellas would of.

It was a Saturday and the shop was full and Jim got up out of that chair and says, "Gentlemen, I got an important announcement to make. I been fired from my job."

Well, they asked him if he was in earnest and he said he was and nobody could think of nothin' to say till Jim finally broke the ice himself. He says, "I been sellin' canned goods and now I'm canned goods myself."

You see, the concern he'd been workin' for was a factory that made canned goods. Over in Carterville. And now Jim said he was canned himself. He was certainly a card!

Jim had a great trick that he used to play w'ile he was travelin'. For instance, he'd be ridin' on a train and they'd come to some little town like, well, like, we'll say, like Benton. Jim would look out the train window and read the signs on the stores.

For instance, they'd be a sign, "Henry Smith, Dry Goods." Well, Jim would write down the name and the name of the town and when he got to wherever he was goin' he'd mail back a postal card to Henry Smith at Benton and not sign no name to it, but he'd write on the card, well, somethin' like "Ask your wife about that book agent that spent the afternoon last week," or "Ask your Missus who kept her from gettin' lonesome the last time you was in Carterville." And he'd sign the card, "A Friend."

Of course, he never knew what really come of none of these jokes, but he could picture what *probably* happened and that was enough.

Jim didn't work very steady after he lost his position with the Carterville people. What he did earn, doin' odd jobs round town, why he spent pretty near all of it on gin and his family might of starved if the stores hadn't of carried them along. Jim's wife tried her hand at dressmakin', but they ain't nobody goin' to get rich makin' dresses in this town.

As I say, she'd of divorced Jim, only she seen that she couldn't support herself and the kids and she was always hopin' that some day Jim would cut out his habits and give her more than two or three dollars a week.

They was a time when she would go to whoever he was workin' for and ask them to give her his wages, but after she done this once or twice, he beat her to it by borrowin' most of his pay in advance. He told it all round town, how he had outfoxed his Missus. He certainly was a caution!

But he wasn't satisfied with just outwittin' her. He was sore the way she had acted, tryin' to grab off his pay. And he made up his mind he'd get even. Well, he waited till Evans's Circus was advertised to come to town. Then he told his wife and two kiddies that he was goin' to take them to the circus. The day of the circus, he told them he would get the tickets and meet them outside the entrance to the tent.

Well, he didn't have no intentions of bein' there or buyin' tickets or nothin'. He got full of gin and laid round Wright's poolroom all day. His wife and the kids waited and waited and of course he didn't show up. His wife didn't have a dime with her, or nowhere else, I guess. So she finally had to tell the kids it was all off and they cried like they wasn't never goin' to stop.

Well, it seems, w'ile they was cryin', Doc Stair came along and he asked what was the matter, but Mrs. Kendall was stubborn and wouldn't tell him, but the kids told him and he insisted on takin' them and their mother in the show. Jim found this out afterwards and it was one reason why he had it in for Doc Stair.

Doc Stair come here about a year and a half ago. He's a mighty handsome young fella and his clothes always look like he has them made to order. He goes to Detroit two or three times a year and w'ile he's there he must have a tailor take his measure and then make him a suit to order. They cost pretty near twice as much, but they fit a whole lot better than if you just bought them in a store.

For a w'ile everybody was wonderin' why a young doctor like Doc Stair should come to a town like this where we already got old Doc Gamble and Doc Foote that's both been here for years and all the practice in town was always divided between the two of them.

Then they was a story got round that Doc Stair's gal had throwed him over, a gal up in the Northern Peninsula somewheres, and the reason he come here was to hide himself away and forget it. He said himself that he thought they wasn't nothin' like general practice in a place like ours to fit a man to be a good all round doctor. And that's why he'd came.

Anyways, it wasn't long before he was makin' enough to live on, though they tell me that he never dunned nobody for what they owed him, and the folks here certainly has got the owin' habit, even in my business. If I had all that was comin' to me for just shaves alone, I could go to Carterville and put up at the Mercer for a week and see a different picture every night. For instance, they's old George Purdy —but I guess I shouldn't ought to be gossipin'.

Well, last year, our coroner died, died of the flu. Ken Beatty, that was his name. He was the coroner. So they had to choose another man to be coroner in his place and they picked Doc Stair. He laughed at first and said he didn't want it, but they made him take it. It ain't no job that anybody would fight for and what a man makes out of it in a year would just about buy seeds for their garden. Doc's the kind, though, that can't say no to nothin' if you keep at him long enough.

But I was goin' to tell you about a poor boy we got here in town—Paul Dickson. He fell out of a tree when he was about ten years old. Lit on his head and it done somethin' to him and he ain't never been right. No harm in him, but just silly. Jim Kendall used to call him cuckoo; that's a name Jim had for anybody that was off their head, only he called people's head their bean. That was another of his gags, callin' head bean and callin' crazy people cuckoo. Only poor Paul ain't crazy, but just silly.

You can imagine that Jim used to have all kinds of fun with Paul. He'd send him to the White Front Garage for a left-handed monkey wrench. Of course they ain't no such a thing as a left-handed monkey wrench.

And once we had a kind of a fair here and they was a baseball game between the fats and the leans and before the game started Jim called Paul over and sent him way down to Schrader's hardware store to get a key for the pitcher's box.

They wasn't nothin' in the way of gags that Jim couldn't think up, when he put his mind to it.

Poor Paul was always kind of suspicious of people, maybe on account of how Jim had kept foolin' him. Paul wouldn't have much to do with anybody only his own mother and Doc Stair and a girl here in town named Julie Gregg. That is, she ain't a girl no more, but pretty near thirty or over.

When Doc first come to town, Paul seemed to feel like here was a real friend and he hung round Doc's office most of the w'ile; the only time he wasn't there was when he'd go home to eat or sleep or when he seen Julie Gregg doin' her shoppin'.

When he looked out Doc's window and seen her, he'd run downstairs and join her and tag along with her to the different stores. The poor boy was crazy about Julie and she always treated him mighty nice and made him feel like he was welcome, though of course it wasn't nothin' but pity on her side.

Doc done all he could to improve Paul's mind and he told me once that he really thought the boy was gettin' better, that they was times when he was as bright and sensible as anybody else.

But I was goin' to tell you about Julie Gregg. Old Man Gregg was in the lumber business, but got to drinkin' and lost the most of his money and when he died, he didn't leave nothin' but the house and just enough insurance for the girl to skimp along on.

Her mother was a kind of a half invalid and didn't hardly ever leave the house. Julie wanted to sell the place and move somewheres else after the old man died, but the mother said she was born here and would die here. It was tough on Julie, as the young people round this town—well, she's too good for them.

She's been away to school and Chicago and New York and different places and they ain't no subject she can't talk on, where you take the rest of the young folks here and you mention anything to them outside of Gloria Swanson or Tommy Meighan and they think you're delirious. Did you see Gloria in Wages of Virtue? You missed somethin'!

Well, Doc Stair hadn't been here more than a week when he come in one day to get shaved and I recognized who he was as he had been pointed out to me, so I told him about my old lady. She's been ailin' for a couple years and either Doc Gamble or Doc Foote, neither one, seemed to be helpin' her. So he said he would come out and see her, but if she was able to get out herself, it would be better to bring her to his office where he could make a completer examination.

So I took her to his office and w'ile I was waitin' for her in the reception room, in come Julie Gregg. When somebody comes in Doc Stair's office, they's a bell that rings in his inside office so as he can tell they's somebody to see him.

So he left my old lady inside and come out to the front office and that's the first time him and Julie met and I guess it was what they call love at first sight. But it wasn't fifty-fifty. This young fella was the slickest lookin' fella she'd ever seen in this town and she went wild over him. To him she was just a young lady that wanted to see the doctor.

She'd come on about the same business I had. Her mother had been doctorin' for years with Doc Gamble and Doc Foote and without no results. So she'd heard they was a new doc in town and decided to give him a try. He promised to call and see her mother that same day.

I said a minute ago that it was love at first sight on her part. I'm not only judgin' by how she acted afterwards but how she looked at him that first day in his office. I ain't no mind reader, but it was wrote all over her face that she was gone.

Now Jim Kendall, besides bein' a jokesmith and a pretty good drinker, well, Jim was quite a lady-killer. I guess he run pretty wild durin' the time he was on the road for them Carterville people, and besides that, he'd had a couple little affairs of the heart right here in town. As I say, his wife could of divorced him, only she couldn't.

But Jim was like the majority of men, and women, too, I guess. He wanted what he couldn't get. He wanted Julie Gregg and worked his head off tryin' to land her. Only he'd of said bean instead of head.

Well, Jim's habits and his jokes didn't appeal to Julie and of course he was a married man, so he didn't have no more chance than, well, than a rabbit. That's an expression of Jim's himself. When somebody didn't have no chance to get elected or somethin', Jim would always say they didn't have no more chance than a rabbit.

He didn't make no bones about how he felt. Right in here, more than once, in front of the whole crowd, he said he was stuck on Julie and anybody that could get her for him was welcome to his house and his wife and kids included. But she wouldn't have nothin' to do with him; wouldn't even speak to him on the street. He finally seen he wasn't gettin' nowheres with his usual line so he decided to try the rough stuff. He went right up to her house one evenin' and when she opened the door he forced his way in and grabbed her. But she broke loose and before he could stop her, she run in the next room and locked the door and phoned to Joe Barnes. Joe's the marshal. Jim could hear who she was phonin' to and he beat it before Joe got there.

Joe was an old friend of Julie's pa. Joe went to Jim the next day and told him what would happen if he ever done it again.

I don't know how the news of this little affair leaked out. Chances is that Joe Barnes told his wife and she told somebody else's wife and they told their husband. Anyways, it did leak out and Hod Meyers had the nerve to kid Jim about it, right here in this shop. Jim didn't deny nothin' and kind of laughed it off and said for us all to wait; that lots of people had tried to make a monkey out of him, but he always got even.

Meanw'ile everybody in town was wise to Julie's bein' wild mad over the Doc. I don't suppose she had any idear how her face changed when him and her was together; of course she couldn't of, or she'd of kept away from him. And she didn't know that we was all noticin' how many times she made excuses to go up to his office or pass it on the other side of the street and look up in his wondow to see if he was there. I felt sorry for her and so did most other people.

Hod Meyers kept rubbin' it into Jim about how the Doc had cut him out. Jim didn't pay no attention to the kiddin' and you could see he was plannin' one of his jokes.

One trick Jim had was the knack of changin' his voice. He could make you think he was a girl talkin' and he could mimic any man's voice. To show you how good he was along this line, I'll tell you the joke he played on me once.

You know, in most towns of any size, when a man is dead and needs a shave, why the barber that shaves him soaks him five dollars for the job; that is, he don't soak *him*, but whoever ordered the shave. I just charge three dollars because personally I don't mind much shavin' a dead person. They lay a whole lot stiller than live customers. The only thing is that you don't feel like talkin' to them and you get kind of lonesome.

Well, about the coldest day we ever had here, two years ago last winter, the phone rung at the house w'ile I was home to dinner and I answered the phone and it was a woman's voice and she said she was Mrs. John Scott and her husband was dead and would I come out and shave him.

Old John had always been a good customer of mine. But they live seven miles out in the country, on the Streeter road. Still I didn't see how I could say no.

So I said I would be there, but would have to come in a jitney and it might cost three or four dollars besides the price of the shave. So she, or the voice, it said that was all right, so I got Frank Abbott to drive me out to the place and when I got there, who should open the door but old John himself! He wasn't no more dead than, well, than a rabbit.

It didn't take no private detective to figure out who had played me this little joke. Nobody could of thought it up but Jim Kendall. He certainly was a card!

I tell you this incident just to show you how he could disguise his voice and make you believe it was somebody else talkin'. I'd of swore it was Mrs. Scott had called me. Anyways, some woman.

Well, Jim waited till he had Doc Stair's voice down pat; then he went after revenge.

He called Julie up on a night when he knew Doc was over in Carterville. She never questioned but what it was Doc's voice. Jim said he must see her that night; he couldn't wait no longer to tell her somethin'. She was all excited and told him to come to the house. But he said he was expectin' an important long distance call and wouldn't she please forget her manners for once and come to his office. He said they couldn't nothin' hurt her and nobody would see her and he just *must* talk to her a little w'ile. Well, poor Julie fell for it.

Doc always keeps a night light in his office, so it looked to Julie like they was somebody there.

Meanw'ile Jim Kendall had went to Wright's poolroom, where they was a whole gang amusin' themselves. The most of them had drank plenty of gin, and they was a rough bunch even when sober. They was always strong for Jim's jokes and when he told them to come with him and see some fun they give up their card games and pool games and followed along.

Doc's office is on the second floor. Right outside his door they's a flight of stairs leadin' to the floor above. Jim and his gang hid in the dark behind these stairs.

Well, Julie come up to Doc's door and rung the bell and they was nothin' doin'. She rung it again and she rung it seven or eight times. Then she tried the door and found it locked. Then Jim made some kind of a noise and she heard it and waited a minute, and then she says, "Is that you, Ralph?" Ralph is Doc's first name.

They was no answer and it must of came to her all of a sudden that she'd been bunked. She pretty near fell downstairs and the whole gang after her. They chased her all the way home, hollerin', "Is that you, Ralph?" and "Oh, Ralphie, dear, is that you?" Jim says he couldn't holler it himself, as he was laughin' too hard.

Poor Julie! She didn't show up here on Main Street for a long, long time afterward.

And of course Jim and his gang told everybody in town, everybody but Doc Stair. They was scared to tell him, and he might of never knowed only for Paul Dickson. The poor cuckoo, as Jim called him, he was here in the shop one night when Jim was still gloatin' yet over what he'd done to Julie. And Paul took in as much of it as he could understand and he run to Doc with the story.

It's a cinch Doc went up in the air and swore he'd make Jim suffer. But it was a kind of a delicate thing, because if it got out that he had beat Jim up, Julie was bound to hear of it and then she'd know that Doc knew and of course knowin' that he knew would make it worse for her than ever. He was goin' to do somethin', but it took a lot of figurin'.

Well, it was a couple days later when Jim was here in the shop again, and so was the cuckoo. Jim was goin' duck-shootin' the next day and had came in lookin' for Hod Meyers to go with him. I happened to know that Hod had went over to Carterville and wouldn't be home till the end of the week. So Jim said he hated to go alone and he guessed he would call it off. Then poor Paul spoke up and said if Jim would take him he would go along. Jim thought a w'ile and then he said, well, he guessed a half-wit was better than nothin'.

I suppose he was plottin' to get Paul out in the boat and play some joke on him, like pushin' him in the water. Anyways, he said Paul could go. He asked him had he ever shot a duck and Paul said no, he'd never even had a gun in his hands. So Jim said he could set in the boat and watch him and if he behaved himself, he might lend him his gun for a couple of shots. They made a date to meet in the mornin' and that's the last I seen of Jim alive.

Next mornin', I hadn't been open more than ten minutes when Doc Stair come in. He looked kind of nervous. He asked me had I seen Paul Dickson. I said no, but I knew where he was, out duck-shootin' with Jim Kendall. So Doc says that's what he had heard, and he couldn't understand it because Paul had told him he wouldn't never have no more to do with Jim as long as he lived.

He said Paul had told him about the joke Jim had played on Julie. He said Paul had asked him what he thought of the joke and the Doc had told him that anybody that would do a thing like that ought not to be let live.

I said it had been a kind of a raw thing, but Jim just couldn't resist no kind of a joke, no matter how raw. I said I thought he was all right at heart, but just bubblin' over with mischief. Doc turned and walked out.

At noon he got a phone call from old John Scott. The lake where Jim and Paul had went shootin' is on John's place. Paul had come runnin' up to the house a few minutes before and said they'd been an accident. Jim had shot a few ducks and then give the gun to Paul and told him to try his luck. Paul hadn't never handled a gun and he was nervous. He was shakin' so hard that he couldn't control the gun. He let fire and Jim sunk back in the boat, dead.

Doc Stair, bein' the coroner, jumped in Frank Abbott's flivver and rushed out to Scott's farm. Paul and old John was down on the shore of the lake. Paul had rowed the boat to shore, but they'd left the body in it, waitin' for Doc to come.

Doc examined the body and said they might as well fetch it back to town. They was no use leavin' it there or callin' a jury, as it was a plain case of accidental shootin'.

Personally I wouldn't never leave a person shoot a gun in the same boat I was in unless I was sure they knew somethin' about guns. Jim was a sucker to leave a new beginner have his gun, let alone a half-wit. It probably served Jim right, what he got. But still we miss him round here. He certainly was a card!

Comb it wet or dry?

SIR JAMES BARRIE

Farewell Miss Julie Logan

Sir James Barrie (1860–1937)

BARRIE WAS WELL AWARE *that the spirit and manner of his writing did not please his younger contemporaries of the nineteen-twenties and 'thirties, but he was not a bit abashed by it. In a letter of comment on the critical reception given his play,* Mary Rose, *he remarked: "The only good thing I found was that what my work failed in was robustness . . . why can't I be more robust? You see how it rankles. Also, I am very distressed at the way our cricketers are doing in Australia. I almost weep over them, tho' not robustly."*

That atmosphere of "charm" which had so delighted two previous generations was quoted low on the literary exchange, post-1918. Barrie's thorough mastery of the journalist's craft, so ably exhibited in the Fleet Street passages of When A Man's Single*—the boyish, bubbling fun which animated many of the episodes of* Peter Pan*—the consummate sense of theater which has made his plays the delight of actors—all these positive virtues were lost sight of as the gavel came down and sentiment was exiled to the literary lumber-room.*

Barrie's reputation suffered for the same reason Kipling's did; he had been too long praised for a few accidental qualities of his work. The "charm," the manner had been exalted at the expense of the whole man. The social climate altered; the manner appeared outmoded; and to the chorus of malice which always accompanies the downfall of an old favorite, a writer of genius was written off.

There is a healthier critical attitude today; possibly we have grown up sufficiently to enjoy a story without trying it in terms of the latest literary orthodoxy. At all events, the editors make no excuse for including Farewell Miss Julie Logan *in* The Scribner Treasury. *It was Barrie's last considerable work and wrought with all his skill—not an ordinary ghost story, but something far more weird and impressive. "It's terribly elusive," said Barrie, after he'd finished it, "and perhaps mad; but was I not dogged to go through with it?"*

FAREWELL MISS JULIE LOGAN

I

THE ENGLISH

This is December One, 186—

I THINK it prudent to go no nearer to the date, in case what I am writing should take an ill turn or fall into curious hands. I need not be so guarded about the weather. It is a night of sudden blasts that half an hour ago threw my window at me. They went skirling from room to room, like officers of the law seeking to seize and deliver to justice the venturesome Scots minister who is sitting here ready to impeach all wraiths and warlocks. There was another blast the now. I believe I could rope the winds of the manse to my bidding to-night, and by running from door to door, opening and shutting, become the conductor of a gey sinister orchestra.

I am trying to make a start at the Diary the English have challenged me to write. There is no call to begin to-night, for as yet not a flake has fallen in this my first winter in the glen; and the Diary is to be a record of my life here during the weeks ('tis said it may be months) in which the glen is 'locked,' meaning it may be so happit in snow that no one who is in can get out of it, and no one who is out can get in. Then, according to the stories that crawl like mists among our hills, where the English must have picked them up, come forms called the 'Strangers.' You 'go queer' yourself without knowing it and walk and talk with these doolies, thinking they are of your world till maybe they have mischieved you.

It is all, of course, superstitious havers, bred of folk who are used to the travail of out of doors, and take ill with having to squat by the saut-bucket; but I have promised with a smile to keep my eyes and ears intent for tergiversations among my flock, and to record them for the benefit of the English when they come back next August.

My name is the Rev. Adam Yestreen; and to be candid I care

not for the Adam with its unfortunate associations. I am twenty-six years of age and, though long in the legs, look maybe younger than is seemly in my sacred calling, being clean-shaven without any need to use an implement; indeed I may say I have desisted for two years back.

I took a fair degree at St. Andrews, but my Intellectuals suffered from an addiction to putting away my books and playing on the fiddle. When I got my call to this place my proper course was to have got rid of the fiddle before I made my entry into the glen, which I did walking with affected humility behind three cart-loads of furniture all my own, and well aware, though I looked down, that I was being keeked at from every window, of which there are about two to the mile.

When the English discovered how ashamed I was of my old backsliding with the fiddle, they had the effrontery to prig with me to give them a tune, but I hope it is unnecessary for me to say that they had to retire discomfited. I have never once performed on the instrument here, though I may have taken it out of its case nows and nans to fondle the strings.

What I miss, when my unstable mind is on the things of this world, is less my own poor cajoling with the gut than not hearing the tunes from better hands; the more homely Scottish lilts, I mean, for of course the old reprehensible songs that kowtow to the Stewarts find no asylum with me.

Though but half a Highlander, I have the Gaelic sufficiently to be able to preach in it once every Sabbath, as enjoined; but the attendances are small, as, except for stravaigers, there are not so many pure Hielandmen nowadays in the glen.

My manse and kirk are isolated on one side of the burn, and the English call them cold as paddocks, but methinks a noble look falls on them when the Sabbath bell is ringing. My predecessor, Mr. Carluke, tore down the jargonelle tree, which used to cling to my gable-end, because he considered that, when in flourish (or as the English say, in blossom, a word with no gallantry intilt), it gave the manse the appearance of a light woman. The marks are still scarted on the wall. Round the manse, within a neat paling that encloses my demesne, there are grossart-bushes, rizers and rasps, a gean, beeskeps and the like, that in former hands were called the yard, but I call it the garden, and have made other improvements.

The gean is my only tree, but close by is a small wood of fir and birch with a path through it that since long before my time has been called the Thinking Path because so many ministers have walked up and down it before the diets of worship with their hands behind their backs. I try to emulate them, but they were deeper men than I am, and many a time I forget to think, though such had been my intention. In other days a squirrel frequented this wood, and as you might say adopted one minister after another, taking nuts from their hands, though scorning all overtures from the laity; but I have never seen it, and my detractors, of whom there are a flow (though I think I am well likit as a whole), say that it deserted the wood as a protest when it heard that I preached in a gown.

There is a deal of character about the manse, particularly, of course, in the study, which is also my living-room. It and my dining-room are the only two rooms in the glen (except at the Grand House) without a bed in them, and I mention this, not with complacence to show how I live nowadays, but as evidence that we are a thrifty people, though on Sabbath well put on. Some are also well plenished within; and to have their porridge with porter instead of milk is not an uncommon occurrence.

The finest of my gear, all the chairs in horse-hair, belong to the dining-room, which, however, is best fitted for stately occasions, and you would know it is seldom used by the way the fire smokes. I cannot say that I am at ease in it, while, on the other hand, I never enter my study up the stair without feeling we are sib; to which one might say it responds.

Never have I a greater drawing to my study than when the lamp is lit and the glow from the fire plays on my red curtains and the blue camstane and my clouty rug. It is an open fireplace without a grate, and I used to be shamed of its wood and peat scattering such a mess of ashes till the English told me that piles of ashes are a great adornment, since when I have conflict with my bit maid, because she wants to carry them away daily, not having the wit to know that they are an acquisition.

Most of my wall space and especially two presses are sternly lined with mighty books, such as have made some of my congregation thankful that they have never learned to read. Yet it is a room that says to any one of spirit, 'Come in by and take a chair, and not only a chair but the best chair,' which is the high-backed grandy, agreeably riven in the seat. I seldom occupy it myself, except at a by-time on a Sabbath afternoon when the two diets have exhausted me a wee, but Dr. John sinks into it as naturally as if he had bought it at the roup. This was the auction of such plenishing as Mr. Carluke did not take away with him, and in the inventory there was mentioned as part of the study furniture, 'servant's chair,' which puzzled some of the bidders, but I saw through it at once. It meant, not to his glorification, that a kitchen chair was kept here for the servant to sit on, and this meant that he held both morning and evening family exercise in the study, which meant again that he breakfasted and supped there; for he wouldna have two fires. It made me smile in a tolerant way, for one would have thought, on the night I spent with him, that the dining-room was his common resort.

On the other side of the burn, but so close that I can keep a vigilant eye on them, are the Five Houses in a Row, which the English say, incorrectly but with no evil design, contain all the congregation I can depend upon in a tack of wild weather. On the contrair, there is a hantle of small farms in the glen, forbye shepherds' shielings and bothies, and an occasional roadside bigging of clay and divot in which may be man or beast; truly, when I chap I am sometimes doubtful which will come to the door.

The English, who make play with many old words that even our Highlandmen have forgotten, call the Five Houses the 'clachan.' They are one-storey houses, white-washed and thacked, and every one of them (to the astonishment of the English) has a hallan to itself. We may be poor, say the Scottish, but we will not open into a room. The doors face the glen road, on which grows a coarse bent grass in lines as straight as potato drills, and carriage-folk who do not keep the ruts are shaken most terrible. One of the English told me that his machine sometimes threw him so high in the air that when he was up there he saw small lochs hitherto unknown to man, and stopped his beast and fished them. The English, however, who have many virtues, though not of a very solid kind, are great exaggerators.

The carriage-folk, except when she lets what is familiarly called the Grand House to the English, consist of Mistress Lindinnock alone, who is called (but never to her face) the Old Lady. She has two spirited ponies, but not so spirited as herself. She goes to Edinburgh while the Grand House is let, and, excepting myself (on account of my office), she is the chief person in the glen. She has been a fine friend to me, but I have sometimes to admonish her for a little coarseness in her language, which may escape from her even when she is most genteel. I grieve to say that this lady of many commendable parts plays cards, and I once saw her at it. Her adversary was a travelling watchmaker, one of those who traverse the whole land carrying a wooden box of watches on his back, with a dozen more tickling in his many waistcoat pockets. They were playing for high sums too, the Old Lady sitting inside one of her windows and the man outside it on his box. I think this is done to preserve the difference in rank; but when I called her before me for it she said the object was to make all right for her future, as the players being on different sides of the window took away the curse.

She is also at times overly sly for one so old and little, and I am now referring to my gown. Soon after my settlement the ladies of the congregation presented me with a gown, and she as the most well-to-pass was the monetary strength of the movement; but though I was proud to wear my gown (without vain glory), we had members who argued that it had a touch of Rome. One may say that the congregation was divided anent it, and some Sabbaths I was sore bested whether to put it on or not. Whiles the decision was even taken out of my hands, for the gown would disappear at the back-end of the week and be returned to its nail on the Monday morning, the work undoubtedly of the no-gown party. On those occasions, of course, I made shift without it, and feeling ran so high that I could not but be conscious as I ascended the pulpit that they were titting at one another's sleeves.

They invented the phrase 'a gown Sabbath.' I took to hiding it, but whoever were the miscreants (and well I knew they were in their pews in front of me, looking as if they had never heard the word gown), they usually found my hoddy place. I mind once sitting on it a long Saturday night when I was labouring at my sermon, the which incident got about among my people. The Old Lady was very sympathetic and pressed me to lay the trouble before the Session, which in fairness to her as the outstanding subscriber I ettled to do, until (could any one believe it?) I discovered that she was the miscreant herself. I sorted her for it.

She is back again now, for the English, of course, have departed long since, and will not be seen again in the glen till next year's shooting time comes round. On the day they left they crossed over to remind me that they were looking forward to the Diary, and when I protested that I did not even know how to begin they said in their audacious way, 'You could begin by writing about us.' I have taken them at their word, though they little understand that I may have been making a quiet study of them while they thought that I was the divert.

As I say, I have found them to be very pleasant persons, so long as you make allowances for them that one could not be expected to make for his own people. The bright array of their kilts is a pretty bit of colour to us, the trousered people of the glen. They have a happy knack of skimming life that has a sort of attraction for deeper but undoubtedly slower natures.

The way they riot with their pockets is beyond words; I am credibly informed by Posty that they even have worms sent to them by post in tins.

They are easy to exploit for gain, as Posty was quick to see, and many a glass of —— has he, to my grief (for I am a totaler), got from them by referring to himself as 'she.' I have written that word with a dash because, now I cast back, I believe I have never heard it spoken by the glen folk. One might say that it is thus, ——, pronounced by them. They invite you to partake, and you are dull in the uptake if you don't understand of what you are being asked to partake.

They make a complete sentence by saying of a friend, 'He is one who on a market day,' and leaving the rest to the listener's common sense.

Similarly they say, 'He never unless he is in company,' or, 'He just at a time because he is lonely like.'

Now the English in this matter as in many others are different, and they give the thing its name and boldly say, with pride in knowing the word, Usquebaugh. In this I hold that they come out of the murky affair with greater honesty but more shamelessly than we do.

They were hospitable to me, and had me up at the Grand House once, giving me the most attractive lady to take in on my arm to dinner, and putting the most popular man on the other side of her to make up for me. They are so well-meaning that it would have vexed them to know I noticed this, and of course I gave it the go-by; but there are few things that escape my observation. On the Sabbath there were always some of them in the kirk, where they were very kindly to the plate but lazy at turning up the chapters. When they had new arrivals these were always brought to see the shepherds' dogs in the pews; in fact, I have decided that the one thing the English know for certain about Scottish religion is that there are shepherds' dogs in the pews.

The English, how quick they are compared to a cautious Scot like myself. He may be far deeper in the fundamentals when there is time to take soundings; but they are so ready.

That time I dined with them the talk might be on subjects I was better versed in than any of them, but they would away to another topic before I could steady myself and give utterance. My most pitiful posture was when I was unable not only to say a thing worth while but to say anything at all, however superficial. Is man ever more lonely than in company when all language forsakes him and he would be thankful if he could cry out 'Agamemnon'? At that dinner I sometimes wished I could have had a dictionary on my knee so as to get hold of any word whatever.

The man on the other side of the lady I was in charge of made a flattering remark to her about her looking very pretty to-night (they stick at nothing), and said to me across her did I not agree with him. It may just have been a considerateness in him to bring the dumb into the talk, a meritorious quality they have; but to be approached in such a direct manner about a lady's looks before her face threw me off my balance, and all I could reply was that I had not given the subject sufficient consideration to be able to make a definite statement about it. She stooped quickly at that, like one looking for her feet, but on reflection I had a suspicion she was anxious not to let me see her making a mouth, at which they are great adepts; and she will never know now that I can say a neat thing myself if they will give me time.

The thoughtlessness of them is something grievous, but their manners make me wae for my own.

When they said good-bye to me at the Five Houses their departure was like a flight of birds. As the poet says, they seemed to take away the sun in their pockets.

At the manse I had shown them my study, this room I am now sitting in (with the wind still on the rampage), and especially I drew their attention to what I have called the finest plenishing thereof, the two presses containing theological and classical tomes of great girth, somewhat warped in the binding. My friends cried out at this being all the reading I had to carry me through the time when the glen may be locked, and they sniffed (but in a polite way) at the closeness of my cosy room, not understanding, as any Presbyterian would have done, that what they mistook for mustiness was the noble smell of learning.

The ladies said that what I needed to madden me pleasantly was not a Diary but a wife. They were at the Five Houses by this time, getting into their machines, and I countered them with 'Who would have me?' I was not putting them to the question, but all the ladies cried out, 'I will,' and made pretence to want to leap from their carriages. I can see now they were just getting after me.

Such are this strange race, the English, whose light-heartedness, as in this extraordinary scene, can rise to a pitch called by the French abandon. I dare say they had forgotten all about me before they were out of the glen, and will never have another thought of the Diary; indeed, now as I look at my shelves of massive volumes, which were not of my collecting, I wish I had not agreed to call it a Diary, for that is a word of ill omen in this manse.

II

SOMEONE WHO WAS WITH HIM

December Third

I have read the above more than once and then hid it away from Christily, because it is written on sermon paper.

Christily is a most faithful young woman with a face as red and lush as a rasp, who knows her carritches both ways, and has such a reverence for ministers that she looks upon me more as an edifice than a mortal. She has an almost equal pride in herself for being a minister's servant, and walks into the kirk in her cheeping lastic sides with an official genteelity that some consider offensive. She has also a provoking way of discussing me in my presence as if I was not there, telling visitors the most intimate things about me, such as the food I like but it does not like me, the while she stands in what is meant to be a respectiful attitude, neither inside nor outside the door.

My visitors are likely to be few for some time to come; neighbours from the Five Houses whiles, and I hope Mistress Lindinnock and Dr. John from Branders.

The smith at the Five Houses is my chief elder, and as his bairns are innumerable, the family in their two pews are a heartsome sight. A more cautious man in argument I have never known. About as far as he will go is, 'I agree with you to a certain extent,' or 'My answer to that is Yes and No.' Posty has a story that he made the second of these answers at his marriage when asked if he took this woman.

Posty is also at the Five Houses, and is the kind that bears ill-will to none, even if they catch him cheating at the dambrod, which he does with the elbow. He has the cheery face that so often goes with roguery and being good at orra jobs, but though I don't lippen to him in matters of import, I like to fall in with him more than with some better men. I sometimes play at the teetotum with the smith's bairns, when there is a prize of cracknuts, and undoubtedly on such occasions Posty's pranks add to the festive scene. He will walk miles, too, to tell any ill news.

His most valued possession is a velocipede, which has so often come to bits when he was on it that near every man in the glen has been at the repairing of it, including myself, or at least has contributed twine or iron girds. He brings the letters from Branders on this machine, and as it often runs away with him, we all, dogs, hens and humans, loup the dyke when we see him bearing down on us. He carries telegrams too, but there are so few of these, now the English have gone, that when we see him waving one we ask, 'Who is dead?'

My great friend is Dr. John, who is sometimes in the glen to succour us, though he lives at Branders, where he sits under Mr. Watery, with whom I sometimes niffer pulpits.

Branders is an overgrown place of five hundred inhabitants, and stands high near a loch, out of which two streams run in opposite directions, like parties to a family feud that can no longer be settled with the claymore. In a spate as many new burns come brawling into this loch as there are hairs on a woman's head, and then are gone before they can be counted. Branders is not in the glen but just at the head of it, and, according to Dr. John, it stopped there because it said to itself, 'Those who go farther will fare worse.' It is jimply six miles from my manse in summer weather, but seventeen from the nearest railway station and electric telegraph. Dr. John says that whether Branders is the beginning or end of desolation depends on your looking up or down the road.

A gnarled, perjink little figure of about fifty is Dr. John, grandly bearded, but for a man of larger size. His blue eyes are hod away in holes, sunken into them, I suppose, because he has looked so long on snow. He wears a plaid in all weathers and sometimes even in the house, for, as he says, before he has time to wap it off and find it again somebody on a cart-horse will be clattering to his door to hurry him to my glen. I have seen him, too, sitting behind on that clattering horse. Repute says that for humane ends he will get through when the glen is locked to all others, though his sole recompense may be a ham at the killing, or a kebbock or a keg of that drink I have spelt ——. Though I touch it not, I cannot deny that he partakes as if it were water, and is celebrated (and even condoled with) for never being the worse of it. He always takes it hot, which he calls never mixing his drinks, and I don't know a neater hand at squeezing down the sugar with the ladle.

If he is in the glen he sometimes puts up his shalt at the Five Houses and stays the night with me, when we have long cracks, the kettle-lid plopping while he smokes his pipe, grunting, which is the Scottish way of bringing out the flavour. Last night was such an occasion, and up here in the study as we sat into the fire we got on to the stories about 'Strangers,' of which he says humorously he has heard many clutters though he has never had the luck to encounter the carls themselves. He maintains that the origin of all the clavers and clecking of nowadays was that lamentable affair of the '45, which, among its misdeeds, for long gave an ill name to the tartan.

The glen had been a great hiding place of 'pretty men' of the period, and among its fearsome crags and waur cleughs, if ancient tales be true, those ill-gettit gentlemen had lurked for months and some of them for years.

It is said that forebears of folk still in the glen used to see them from below searching for roots atween the rocks, and so distraught with hunger that they went on searching openly while they were being shot at by the red-coats, who would not face the steel. When the glen was in a sink of snow, and pursuit for a time at an end, they sometimes lay at the Grand House (which was loyal to their dark cause), and held secret carouse there.

They were talked of with an intake of the breath by the glen folk, who liked best to be of no party unless they were of both, would not betray them to an enemy that hunted them with blood-hounds, yet would hold no intercourse with them willingly, and looked the other way if they came upon one of the gaunt red-shanks unexpectedly, as sometimes happened, carrying braxy mutton or venison to his lurking place, or a salmon that the otters had left by the burn after taking one nip from its neck.

Those glen folk were too mouse to call the fugitives Jacobites. 'The Strangers,' they said.

In one case they said 'Someone Who Was With Him,' as if that was as far as it was canny to go. The Him was the Stranger who is believed by the simple to have been the Chevalier himself. He is said to have lain in the glen for a time in July month, fevered and so hard pressed that no friends dared go nigh him with nourishment lest it led to his capture. I have not seen his hoddy place, but the doctor tells me it is still there and is no more than a lair beneath what we call a bield, a shelter for sheep. Very like, it began by being a tod's hole, and was torn bigger with dirks. If it ever existed, the lair has been long filled up with stones, which are all that remain to mark the royal residence.

Sheep again shelter in the bield, but there were none there in the time of the Prince, if it was he, nor, as I say the story goes, could food be passed to him. In his extremity he was saved by the mysterious Someone Who Was With Him.

Of course the legend has it that she was young and fair and of high degree, and that she loved much.

She fed him with the unwilling help of the eagles. The Eagles Rock, which is not far from the bield, is a mighty mass, said by the ghillies of to-day to be unscaleable by man because of what is called the Logan stone. No eagles build there now; they have fallen to the guns of their modern enemy, the keepers, who swear that one pair of eagles will carry a hundred grouse or more to their nest to feed their young.

At that time there was an eagle's nest on the top of the rock. The climb is a perilous one, but now and again hardy folk get up as far as the Logan stone, where they turn back. There are Logan stones, I am told, throughout the world, and they are rocking stones. It is said they may be seen rocking in the wind, and yet hold on for centuries. Such a monster hangs out from our Eagles Rock, and you cannot reach the top save by climbing over it, nor can you get on to it without leaping. Twice men of the glen have leapt and it threw them off. Natheless, the story is that this Someone Who Was With Him got through the searchers in the dark, reached the top of the rock by way of the Logan stone, and after sometimes fighting the parent eagles for possession, brought down young grouse for her lord.

By all kind accounts she was a maiden, and in our glen she is remembered by the white heather, which, never seen here till then, is said, nonsensically, to be the marks of her pretty naked feet.

The white heather brought her little luck. In a hurried and maybe bloody flitting she was left behind. Nothing more is recorded of her except that when her lord and master embarked for France he enjoined his Highlanders 'to feed her and honour her as she had fed and honoured him.' They were faithful though misguided, and I dare say they would have done it if they could. Some think that she is in the bield in the hole beneath the stones, still waiting. They say, maybe there was a promise.

Such was the doctor's tale as we sat over the fire. 'A wayward woman,' was how he summed her up, with a shake of the head.

III

THE SPECTRUM

December Third (Contd.)

'I am thinking,' Dr. John was saying when I caught up with him again, for my mind had been left behind with this woman, and I was wondering if she was 'wayward,' and what was wrong with it, for I liked the word, 'I am thinking that all the clash about folk of nowadays meeting "Strangers" when the glen is locked comes out of that troubled past. In a white winter, as you have jaloused yourself, there is ower little darg for a hardy race, and they hark back by the hearthstone to the forgotten, ay, and the forbidden. But I assure you, Mr. Yestreen, despite the whispers, the very name of the '45 is now buried in its own stour. Even Posty, though he is so gleg with the pipes, gets by himself if you press him about what his old ballants mean. Neither good luck nor mischief, so far as I can discover, comes to the havrels of nowadays who think they have talked or walked with a Stranger; unless indeed, as some say, it was one of them who mairtered poor Mr. H.; and I understand he, being a learned man, always called it a Spectrum.'

This set us talking of him of whom I may have already let out that he once kept a Diary in this manse. It was so far back as to be just hearsay even to Dr. John, and belongs to the days when there were no seats in my kirk and all stood on their shanks. Though I say we talked about him we really said very little, unless an occasional furtive glance be speech. All in these parts become furtive when a word, falling as meaningless you would say as a cinder from the fire, brings a sough of the old man back to mind.

Mr. H. was a distant predecessor of mine, and a scholar such as the manse is not likely to house again. It was he who collected the library of noble erudition that is in the presses of this room, many of the volumes bound by his own hands that may have dawted them as he bound. His Diary was written on the fly-leaves of a number of them.

I believe he thought in Latin and Greek quicker than in his own tongue, for his hurried notes are often in those languages and the more deliberate ones in ours. I am in a dunce's cap with the Greek, but I can plod along with a Latin dictionary, and his entries in the Latin have made me so uneasy that I have torn out the pages and burned them. Mr. Carluke, whom I succeeded, had to confine himself, having no Latin, to the English bits, and he treated some of them similarly, for as he said to me they were about things that will not do at all.

They appear suddenly amidst matter grandly set forth, as if a rat had got at the pages. Minute examination has made me question their being in the same handwrite, though an imitation. This tampering, if such it was, had got by Carluke's attention. 'You mean,' Dr. John said to me when I had let him study these bits of Diary (which he peered into with a magnifier the size of a thimble that he carries in his waistcoat pocket and is near as much dreaded by malingerers as he is himself), 'that it is the handwrite of the Spectrum?' If Dr. John has a failing it is that he hankers too much to tie one down to a statement, and of course I would not accept this interpretation, for I do not believe in Spectrums.

It is not known even by the credulous when, in Mr. H.'s distorted fancy, the Spectrum first came chapping softly at the manse door, and afterwards blattering on it, in a wicked desire to drive the lawful possessor out of the house and take his place. But it was while the glen was locked. Sometimes one of the twain was inside the house and sometimes the other. Sounds were heard, they say, coming from the study, of voices in conflict and blows struck. The dwellers of that time in the Five Houses, of whom two carlines are still alive, maintained that they had seen Mr. H. sitting on his dyke at night, because the other was in possession. By this time no servant would bide in the manse after gloaming; and yet, though Mr. H. was now the one chapping at the door, they said they could see a light being carried in the house from room to room, and hear something padding on the floors. He did not walk, they said, he padded.

'When they found the minister, according to the stories,' Dr. John said, 'his face was in an awful mess.'

What had caused that, I asked, and he said shortly that he supposed Spectrums had teeth.

It was eerie to reflect that to those two carlines, as we call ancient women, my study must still be more his than mine, and that they would not be taken aback if they came into it at that moment and found the old man in the grandy chair.

'The wayward woman was a better visitor to the glen than this other at any rate,' I ventured, and the answer he made I would as soon he had kept to himself. 'According to some of the ranters,' he said, with a sort of leer at me, 'they are the same person.'

We tried to get on to more comfortable subjects, but it was as if the scholar's story would not leave the room. 'I feel as if there were three of us here to-night,' I said to the doctor.

'Ay,' said he, 'and a fourth keeking in at the window.'

As usual, the old-wife gossip in which we had been luxuriating (for what more was it?) was interrupted by Christily coming in to announce that our sederunt was at an end. She did this, not in words, but by carrying away the kettle. This garr'd us to our beds, fuming at her as being one of those women, than whom there are few more exasperating, who think all men should do their bidding. I had to be up betimes this morning to see him take the gate.

IV

THE LOCKING OF THE GLEN

December Nineteenth

In this white wastrie of a world the dreariest moment is when custom makes you wind up your watch. Were it not for the Sabbath I would get lost in my dates. Not a word has gone into my Diary for a fortnight bypast. Now would be the time for it if there were anything to chronicle; but nothing happens, unless one counts as an event that I brought my hens into the manse on discovering that their toes were frozen to the perch (I had to bring the perch too). My two sheep are also in by, and yesterday my garden slithered off to the burn with me on it like a passenger. I have sat down at an antrin time to the Diary to try to fill up with an account such as this of the locking of the glen, and the result has been rather disquieting to me, as I will maybe tell farther on and maybe not.

The glen road, on which our intercourse with ourselves as well as with the world so largely depends, was among the first to disappear under the blankets. White hillocks of the shape of eggs have arisen here and there, and are dangerous too, for they wobble as though some great beast beneath were trying to turn round. The mountains are so bellied out that they have ceased to be landmarks. The farm-towns look to me to be smored. I pull down my blinds so that I may rest my eyes on my blues and reds indoors. Though the Five Houses are barely a hundred yards away I have to pick out signs of life with my spy-glass.

I am practically cut off from my kind. Even the few trees are bearing white ropes, thick as my wrist, instead of branches, and the only thing that is a bonny black is the burn, once a mere driblet but now deep, with a lash around at corners, and unchancey to risk. At times of ordinary wet they cross here to the kirk in two easy jumps on boulders placed there for the purpose, and called the brig, but the boulders are now like sunk boats, and of the sprinkling of members who reached the kirk on the 9th, one used a vaulting pole and lost it.

Last Sabbath I did not open the kirk but got down to the burn and preached to a handful standing on the other side. My heart melted for the smith's bairns, every one of whom was there, and I have cried a notice across the burn that next Sabbath the bell will ring as a solemn reminder, but the service will be in the smiddy, whether I find that man's pole or not.

Two or three times Posty, without his velocipede, has penetrated to Branders and delivered my letters and a newspaper to me by casting them over the burn tied to stones. There is no word of Dr. John. For nearly a week, except for an occasional shout, I have heard no voice but Christily's. I sit up here o'nights trying to get meanings out of Mr. H.'s Diary, and not so much finding them in the written books as thinking I hear them padding up the stair as a wayward woman might do. In the long days I go out and shule, and get dunted by slides from the roof.

Of an evening Posty struts up and down in front of the Five Houses, playing on his pipes. I can see him like a pendulum passing the glints of light. I can hear him from the manse, but still better from the burnside, if I slue down to listen in the dark. On one of those nights I got a dirl in the breast of me. It was when I went back to the manse after hearing him finish that Border boast, 'My name it is little Jock Elliot.' The glen was deserted by all other sound now, but as I birzed open the manse door (for the snow had got into the staples) I heard my fiddle playing 'My name it is little Jock Elliot.' For a moment I thought that Christily was at it, but then I knew she must be bedded, and she has no ear, and it was grander playing than Posty's though he is a kittle hand. I suppose I did not stand still in my darkened hallan for more than half a minute, and when I struck a light to get at a candle the music stopped. There is no denying that the stories about the Spectrum flitted through me, and it needed a shove from myself to take me up the stair. Of course there was nobody. I had come back with the tune in my ears, or it was caused by some vibration in the air. I found my fiddle in the locked press just as I had left it, except that it must have been leaning against the door, for it fell into my arms as I opened the press, and I had the queer notion that it clung to me. I could not compose myself till I had gone through my manse with the candle, and even after that I let the instrument sleep with me.

More reasonable fancies came to me in the morning, as that it might be hard on a fiddle never to be let do the one thing it can do; also that maybe, like the performers, they have a swelling to cry out to rivals, 'I can do better than that.' Any allure I may have felt, to take advantage of this mere fancy and put the neck-rest beneath my chin again, I suppressed; but I let Posty know he could have the loan of my instrument on condition that he got it across the burn dry. By the smith's connivance this was accomplished in a cart. It is now my fiddle Posty plays instead of his pipes, which are not in much better condition than his velocipede and are repaired in a similar manner. I extracted just one promise from him, that he would abstain from the baneful Jacobite lilts he was so fond of; but he sometimes forgets or excuses himself across the burn by saying, 'She likes that kind best, and she is ill to control once she's off.' It is pretty to hear him in the gloaming, letting the songs loose like pigeons.

To write this account of the glen when it is locked has been an effort, for the reason that I have done it twice already and in the morning it was not there. I sat down by lamplight on both occasions to write it and thought I had completed my task, but next morning I found just a few broken lines on otherwise blank pages. Some of them were repeated again and again like a cry, such as 'God help me,' as if I were a bird caught in a trap. I am not in any way disturbed of mind or body, at any rate in the morning. Yet this was what I had written. I am none so sure but what it may prove to be all I have written again.

I will now go and say good-night to the Old Lady, for though it is barely half nine on the clock, we keep early hours in the wilderness. This is a moment I owe to her ingenuity. The Grand House, which has of course a statelier name of its own, is a steep climb from here and is at present inaccessible, the approach having thrown in its lot with the fields, but it is visible, and at half nine o'clock she shoots her blind up and down twice, and I reply with mine. Hers, I am thankful to say, is red, or the lamp behind it has a red shade, and this shooting of the blinds is our way of saying good-night to each other. When she shoots hers three times it means something personal about my gown, and I make no answer. There is a warmth, however, in saying good-night to a living being when the glen is so still that I am thinking you could hear a whit-rit on the move. Sometimes I stand by my window long after hers is dumb, and I have felt that night was waiting, as it must have done once, for the first day. It is the stillness that is so terrible. If only something would crack the stillness.

V

THE STRANGER

December Twenty-first

For the first time since the glen was locked Dr. John 'threw in,' as we say, this morning.

He came straight to the study, where he found us at family exercise. I did not look up from my knees, but Christily whispered to me, 'Be short,' which I dare say made me in consequence a little longer. Yet I knew she would not have taken such a liberty unless there was something untoward with the man, and though I found when I rose that he was on his knees with us, I saw that he had gone to sleep on them. His face was so peaked that I sent Christily hurriedly for the bottle of brandy which has lain in the manse uncorked since I came here six months ago, and as soon as he had partaken she hauled off his boots and ran him on to the stairhead to wring and scrape him, for he was getting on to the carpet.

I saw he ettled to be rid of her before communicating something by-ordinar to me, and he took the best way to effect this by saying in a sentence that he had got through to Joanna Minch and it was a girl and both were doing well; whereupon Christily was off to cry the tidings across the burn.

He was nodding in the grandy with fatigue, so that it looked as if only by sudden jerks could he keep his head on, but he brought out the words, 'There is more in it than I told Christily. I have been to the shieling, but I did not get through in time. There were two lives saved in that bit house in the small hours; but don't be congratulating me, for I had naught to do with it.'

Having said this, he fell head foremost into sleep, and I had ill rousing him, which I was sweer to do, but he had made it plain that he wanted to say more.

'It's such a camsterie tale,' he told me, 'as might banish sleep in any man; but I am dog-tired and unless you keep pulling my beard with all the strength that is in you I'll be dovering again.'

I may say here that I had to do as he instructed me several times. We must have looked a strange pair, the doctor yawning and going off in the middle of sentences while I tugged fiercely at the beard.

I will put his bewildering tale together as best I can. He had forced his way last evening to the farm of the Whammle, where a herd was lying with two broken legs. While he was there Fargie Routh, the husband of Joanna, had tracked him down to say that she was terrible near her reckoning. The doctor started off with him rather anxious, for Fargie was 'throughither,' and it was Joanna's first. Dr. John had floundered into worse drifts, but a stour of snow was plastering his face and he lost Fargie at the sleugh crossing. He tumbled and rumbled down in a way at which he is a master-hand, and reached the shieling hours before the husband, who is a decent stock but very unusual in the legs. The distance is a short mile when the track is above-ground. Dr. John was relieved to smell smoke, for he feared to find he was on a sleeveless errand, and that the woman would be found frozen.

I told him I knew the house, which is a lonesome one-roomed cot of double stone and divot, with but a bole window. I asked if he had found Joanna alone, but he had taken the opportunity of my making a remark to fall asleep again.

I got his eyes open in the manner recommended by him, and he said with one of his little leers at me, 'She was not quite alone; but maybe you are one of those who do not count an infant till it be christened.'

'If there is any haste for that——' I cried, looking for my boots.

'There is none,' he said.

'But who had been with her? Was she in such a bad condition that she could give you no information about that?'

'She was in fine condition and she could and she did,' he said. 'I was with her till Fargie, who had gone back to the Whammle, brought down the gude-wife, and I have no doubt Joanna is now giving the particulars to them. They are such uncommon particulars,' he went on, taking a chew at them, 'that I can fancy even the proud infant sitting up to listen.'

Then who was it that had acted in his place, I enquired, not daring to be more prolix lest he should again be overtaken.

That, he said, was what he was asking me.

'Dr. John——'

'Be assured,' said he, 'that I am too dung ower with tire to be trifling with you; but this will become more your affair than mine. It is not to me they will look to be told who she was but to their minister.'

'I hope I shall not fail them,' I said loftily. Nevertheless I dreed what was coming, and I insisted on his keeping awake 'or I would lay a hot iron on the beard.'

He said he had found a kettle on a bright fire and Joanna in her bed with the child, who was fittingly swaddled in her best brot. He would not let her talk until he had satisfied himself that everything necessary had been done, and then (for the curiosity was mounting to his brain) he said with pretended casualness, 'I see you have been having a nice cup of tea.'

'And merry she was at the making of it,' replied Joanna, turning merry herself.

'I forget,' said he, 'if you mentioned who she was?'

'Of course it was one of the Strangers,' she said.

'Of course it would be one of those curiosities,' said he, 'but I never chanced to fall in with ane; what was she like?'

'Oh,' said Joanna, 'she was like the little gentleman that sits under his tail'—meaning a squirrel.

'I thought she would be something like that,' he said; 'but had you no fear of her?'

'Never,' said Joanna, 'till after the bairn was born, and then for just a short time, when she capered about mad-like with glee, holding it high in the air, and dressing and undressing it in the brot, so as to have another peep at it, and very proud of what she had done for me and it till a queer change came over her and I had a sinking that she was going to bite it. I nippit it from her.'

'To bite them is not my usual procedure at a birth,' the doctor had said, 'but we all have our different ways.'

Joanna gave him a fuller story of the night than, as he said, would be of any profit to a sumph of a bachelor like Adam Yestreen, but he told me some of its events.

The door had blown open soon after Fargie's departure, leaving naught but reek to heat her, and the bole closed, and when the fire went down she would have been glad to cry back the reek. She thought the cold candle of her life was at the flicker. The Stranger relit the fire, but there was no way she could conceive of heating that body on the box-bed. Then the thought came to her.

'She strippit herself naked,' Joanna said, 'and made me keep my feet on her, as if she was one of them pig bottles for toasting the feet of the gentry; and when my feet were warm, she lay close to me, first on one side and then on the other. She was as warm as a browning bannock when she began, but by the time the heat of her had passed into me I'se uphaud she was cold as a trout.'

As to the actual birth, though this was Joanna's first child, she knew more about the business than did her visitor, who seems to have been in a dither of importance over the novelty of the occasion. She was sometimes very daring and sometimes at such a loss that in Joanna's words, 'she could just pet me and kiss me and draw droll faces at me with the intent to help me through, and when she got me through she went skeer with triumph, crying out as she strutted up and down that we were the three wonders of the world.'

The whole affair, Dr. John decided, must have been strange enough 'to put the wits of any medical onlooker in a bucket,' and if he let his mind rest on it he would forget how to sleep as well as how to practise surgery; so in the name of Charity would I leave him in the land of Nod for an hour while I thought out some simple explanation for my glen folk.

He got his hour, though sorely did I grudge it, for I was in a bucket myself.

When he woke refreshed I was by his side to say at once, as if there had not been a moment's interruption, 'Of course she was some neighbour.'

There was a glint in his blue eyes now, but he said decisively, 'There is no way out by that road, my man; Joanna is acquaint with every neighbour in the glen.'

'An outside woman of flesh and blood,' I prigged with him, 'must have contrived to force the glen; as, after all, you did yourself.'

That, he maintained, was even less possible than the other.

I was stout for there being some natural explanation, and he reminded me unnecessarily that there was the one Joanna gave. At this I told him sternly to get behind me.

I could not forbear asking him if he had any witting of such stories being common to other lonely glens, and he shook his head, which made me the more desperate.

He saw in what a stramash I was, and, dropping his banter, came kindly to my relief. 'Do you really think,' he said, in his helpful confident way, 'that I have any more belief in warlocks and "Strangers" than you have yourself? I'll tell you my conclusion, which my sleep makes clearer. It is that Joanna did the whole thing by herself, as many a woman has done before her. She must at some time, though, have been in a trance, which are things I cannot pretend to fathom, and have thought a woman was about her who was not there. It cows to think of a practical kimmer like Joanna having, even in her hour of genius, such an imagination; that bit about nearly biting the bairn is worthy of Mr. H.'s Spectrum.'

'None of that,' I cried. 'She no doubt got that out of the old minister's story.'

'Ay,' he granted, 'let's say that accounts for it. I admit it is the one thing that has been worrying me. But at any rate it is of no importance, as we are both agreed that Joanna was by her lonesome. She had no joyous visitor, no. Heigh-ho, Mr. Yestreen, it's almost a pity to have to let such a pleasantly wayward woman go down the wind.'

It was far from a pity to me. I was so thankful to him for getting rid of her that I pressed his hand repeatedly. I was done with wayward women.

VI

SUPERSTITION AND ITS ANTIDOTE

December Twenty-sixth

I got as far as the shieling two days behind Joanna's story and held a kirstening, this being the first at which I have ever officiated.

The usual course is to have it in the kirk toward the end of a service, but in urgent cases it may be on the day of birth. There was maybe no reason for precipitancy in this case, the child being lusty, but in the peculiar circumstances I considered it my duty to make her safe. When I took her in my arms, by far the youngest I had ever meddled with, I was suddenly aware of my youthful presumption. I should have been warned beforehand about the beauty of their finger nails.

Yet I dared not let on that I was the most ignorant in the room, for I was the minister, and therefore to be looked up to. Also Joanna swore to her visit from the Stranger, with side-looks at me as if she had given birth to a quandary as well as to a litlun; and the lave of the party present were already familiar with her story and were all agog.

So, knowing how ill it fares with a minister's usefulness if he does not keep upside with his flock, I was bolder than I felt, and told them in a short exposition that there had been no 'Stranger' in the affair; otherwise some of them would certainly have seen her.

They all nodded their agreement and thanked me for making it so clear, but I knew in my bones that they did not accept one word of my redding up, though they regarded it as very proper for a minister, especially one who was new to the glen.

This way they have, of heartily accepting what you tell them and then going their own gate, is disheartening to me, and at one time I thought of making any dirdum about Strangers a subject of stern discipline from the pulpit. Fear did not enter into my reluctance, for I knew they would esteem me the more the harder I got at them, but I drew back from the ease of superiority toward men and women whose simple lives have been so often more grimly fought than my own. It relieves me, therefore, to have decided that I may get through their chinks more creditably in another manner.

The amelioration in the weather, which probably will not last, is what put the idea into my head. Some of us have been able to step about a little these last days. A curran herd, weary of bothy life, have made so bold as to find out where the glen road is. Of course they cannot shule down to it, but they have staked some of the worst bits, and several carts have passed along as if the proximity to it gave them courage. I saw from the manse the Old Lady's carriage trying for Branders. The smith's klink-klink from the smiddy, which is the most murie sound in a countryside next to a saw-mill, shows that he has had at least one to shod. Posty has ridden on his velocipede the length of the Five Houses and back, with the result that you can hardly see his face for the brown paper.

It is true that there is no possibility of opening the kirk on Sabbath, for though we have thrown planks across the burn, with a taut rope to hang on by, the place is too mortal cold for sitting in through a service. There is, however, the smiddy, which can be used for other purposes besides preaching.

All our large social events take place in the smiddy, and the grandest consist of Penny Weddings, when you are expected, if convenient, to bring, say, a hen or a small piece of plenishing to the happy pair. The actual marriage, of course, takes place in the bride's home, and not, in the queer English way, in the kirk. We have had no weddings since I came, but twice last month we had Friendlies, which we consider the next best thing.

Our Friendlies are always in two parts, the first part being devoted to a lecture by the minister or some other person of culture, who is usually another minister. This lecture is invariably of a bright, entertaining character, and some are greater adepts at unbending in this way than others, the best being Mr. Watery of Branders, whose smile is of such expansion that you might say it spreads over the company like honey. Laughter and the clapping of hands in moderation are not only permissible during the lectures but encouraged.

The second part of a Friendly is mostly musical with songs, and is provided by local talent, in which Posty takes too great a lead. There is an understanding that I remain for the first song or so, whether I am lecturing or in the Chair. This is to give a tone to the second part, and then I slip away, sometimes wishing I could bide to enjoy the mirth, but I know my presence casts a shadow on their ease. The time in which Friendlies would be most prized is when the glen is locked, but the difficulty for all except the Five Houses lies in getting to the smiddy.

Nevertheless we are to attempt a Friendly on Thursday, though Mr. Watery, who was to be the lecturer with a magic lantern, which of course is a great addition, has cried off on account of nervousness lest the weather should change before he gets home again. I have undertaken to fill his place to the best of my more limited ability, as indeed it is.

I am doing so the more readily because of this idea that came to me, which promises to be a felicitous one. It is to lecture to them on

Superstition, with some sly and yet shattering references to a recent so-called event in the glen, all to be done with a light touch, yet of course with a moral, which is that a sense of humour is the best antidote to credulity. There are few of the smaller subjects to which I have given greater thought than to Humour, its ramifications and idiosyncrasies, and I have a hope that I may not do so badly at this. I wish Mr. Watery could be present, for I think I can say that I know more about Humour than he does, though he is easier at it.

VII

MISS JULIE LOGAN

December Twenty-eighth

Hours have passed since I finished my lecture. I know not how many times I have sat down to write about her, and then taken to wandering the study floor instead. My mind goes back in search of every crumb of her, and I am thinking I could pick her up better on my fiddle than in written words.

My eyes never fell on her till I got to my peroration. This is no reflection on my sight, for all the company in the smiddy, and there were more than thirty, had to sit in darkness so that they could better watch my face between the two candles. She was with Mistress Lindinnock, who presented me to her, and they came over to the manse while the shelties were being yoked. I held her hand to guide her across the planks. She is the Old Lady's grandniece, and her name is Miss Julie Logan. I am glad of her Christian name, for it has always been my favourite.

In the past few years, up to this night, my lot had thrown me mostly among my seniors, and a glow that once I knew seemed to be just a memory warning me that ministers must be done quickly with the clutches of youth.

I am no hand at describing the garb of beauty, and the nearest I can get to her, after much communing, is that she is a long stalk of loveliness. She carried a muff of fur, and at times would raise it to her face as if she know no better than to think it was a scent-bottle, or peep over it like a sitting bird in the bole of a tree.

The upper part of her attire was black and the rest green.

There was a diverting mutch on her head which, for some reason I cannot as yet determine, you could have got on smiling terms with though you had met it hanging on a nob.

She is from Edinburgh, and it was to get her that I saw the Grand House carriage fighting its way to Branders yesterday.

I have only seen her for twenty minutes. There is such a beloved huskiness in her voice that she should be made to say everything twice. She glides up a manse stair with what I take to be the lithesomeness of a panther. I like her well when she is haughty, and even better when she is melting, and best of all when she is the two together, which she often is.

I was all throughither when she sat down on the one of my chairs that I have hitherto held to be of the least account. She looked as meek at that moment as if a dove was brooding in her face.

It is not beauty of person that I heed but internal beauty, which in her is as plain to read as if she wore it outside.

What I would last part with is the way her face sparkles, not just her eyes but her whole face. This comes and goes, and when it has gone there is left the sweet homeliness that is woman's surest promise to man. Fine I knew for ever that I needed none but her.

Fain would I have made observations to her that put a minister in a favourable light. I am thinking that the Old Lady spoke at times, for she is a masterpiece of conversation, but all I remember of her is that she soon fell asleep in the grandy chair, which is a sudden way she has. This disregard of her company has sometimes annoyed me at kirk meetings (where we have to pause till she wakes up), but not on this occasion.

In my lecture I had spoken about humour which is profound and humour which is shallow, such as pulling away your chair. Miss Julie Logan said to me in the manse that she was only interested in the profound kind, with its ramifications and idiosyncrasies. She said she found it a hard kind to detect, and wished she could be so instructed as to recognize profound humour, whether written or spoken.

When she said this there was something so pleading in her shining eyes that, instead of replying in a capable manner, I offered to explain the thing with a bit of paper and a pencil.

I drew a note of exclamation, and showed her how they were put into books, at the end of sentences, to indicate that the remark was of a humorous character. She got the loan of the pencil and practised making notes of exclamation under my instruction.

She said she questioned whether profound humour would not still baffle her in the spoken word, and I agreed that here it was more difficult, but told her that if you watched the speaker's face narrowly you could generally tell by a glint in it; and if there was no glint his was the mistake and not yours.

She asked me to say something humourous to her, the while she would watch for the glint, which I did, and she saw it.

She said she feared it would be a long time before she could do my glint, and asked me to watch her face while she practised it; and I was very willing.

She said she would like to have my opinion on the statement of an Englishman about the bagpipes, namely that they sound best if you are far away from them, and the farther away the better. Other people present had laughed at that, and could I tell her why?

I said that no doubt what they laughed at was at the man's forgetting that if you were too far away from the pipes you would not hear them at all.

Even in those moments I was not such a gowk as to be unaware that I was making a deplorable exhibition of myself. Whatever she seemed to want me to say I just had to say it, for the power had gone from me to show her that I was not mentally deficient. However, when it came to this about the pipes I broke up and laid my face on the table, and she raised my head, and was woebegone when she saw the ruin she had made.

'Have I hurt you?' she asked, and I could just nod. 'Why did you let me?' she said with every bit of her, and I answered darkly, 'I cannot help saying or doing whatever Miss Julie Logan wants.'

The wet glittered on her eyes in a sort of contest as you can sometimes hear them do on the strings.

I said, 'It is bitter mortifying to me to be seen in such disadvantageous circumstances by Miss Julie Logan at the very time of all others when I should have liked to be better than my best.'

I stroked her muff and, somehow, the action made me say, 'This is a very unhomely manse,' though I had never thought that before.

She held out her hand to me, with the palm upwards like one begging for forgiveness, and I have been wondering ever since what she meant me precisely to do with it. I pressed it on my heart, and I filled at long last with what becomes a man in his hour and I said, 'I love you, Miss Julie Logan,' and she said as soft as a snowflake, 'Yes, I know.' Then Christily came in with the blackberry wine on a server, and when Miss Julie Logan drank it I could see her throat flushing as it went down, which they say also happened with Mary Stewart. Then the Old Lady woke up and said that the ponies must be yoked by this time, so I took the ladies across to the carriage, Christily going in front with the lamp. I could hear Miss Julie Logan talking sweetly to her, though it was the Old Lady who was on my arm.

It is now on the chap of midnight, and since I wrote the above I have been down to my kirk and unlocked the door and lit a candle and stood looking for a long time at the manse pew. It is in a modest position on the right of the pulpit, disdaining to call attention to itself. For my part, I could never walk down the aisle of any kirk without being as conscious of which was the manse pew as of which was the pulpit. I do not look, I just feel it.

Usually there is only Christily in my pew, and she sits at the far end. Not all manse pews have a door, but mine has, and I would sit next it if I were out of the pulpit, which can only be if another minister is officiating for me. When a minister is a married man, as all ministers ought to be, it is the lawful right of his wife to sit next the door, with a long empty space between her and the servant, unless they be blessed with children. I stood by my manse pew picturing Miss Julie Logan sitting next the door. She is a tall lady, and I wondered whether the seat was too low for her; and such is my condition that, if I had brought nails and a hammer with me, I would have raised it there and then.

VIII

CHRISTILY GOES QUEER

December Thirtieth

In the midst of my exaltation come disquieting symptoms in Christily. I think, now I look back, that she has been unsettled these past few days and that occasionally she has glanced covertly at me as if she feared I suspected her of something. Whether this was so or not, she is in a bad state now, and I am very ravelled in my mind about her.

It showed itself this morning when I made a remark to her about Miss Julie Logan. I knew it would be more befitting not to bring that name into everyday conversation, but something within me hankered to hear how it sounded on other lips. Nothing could have been more carefully casual than the way I introduced the subject, and yet the dryness came into my mouth that makes it so desirable for a public speaker to have a glass of water handy.

'And so,' I said, 'there is a young lady at the Grand House now, Christily.'

'Is there?' said she, like one cheering up for a gossip.

'Did you not know,' I enquired, 'that it is there Miss Julie Logan is staying?'

'What Miss Julie Logan?' she asked.

'The young lady,' I said patiently, 'whom Mistress Lindinnock brought to the manse the night before last.'

'I saw no young lady,' she said; 'there was just the two of you came in, you and Mistress Lindinnock.'

'Is this temper, Christily,' I demanded, 'or what is it? You helped Miss Julie Logan to a glass of blackberry wine; also you carried the lantern when I escorted them back to the carriage, and you were in front conversing with her.'

Her eyes stood out as in some sudden affliction, and, when I stepped toward her, asking if she was ill, she cried 'God help me!' and rushed out of the study.

What did it portend? Had I unwittingly opened the door to some secret the poor soul had been keeping from me? I was very riven and I followed on her heels to the kitchen, but she had locked the door and no answer could I get when I spoke through the keyhole to her. This was very disturbing from such an excellent woman, and I went on my knees, with the door between us, and called in a loud voice to the malevolent one to come out of her. I could hear her wailing sore.

In much perturbation I got across to the Five Houses on the chance of finding Dr. John, as Posty's wife is down with a complaint that beats the skill of her neighbours; the silly tod has found out that she is four years older than she thought, and though until that moment in robust health she at once took to her bed.

Fortunately I got the doctor, and on our way across I told him of what had happened. I was relieved to find that he did not take the matter with my seriousness; indeed he was more interested in Miss Julie Logan, of whom he had not heard till now, than in Christily's case, which he foretold would turn out to be tantrums brought on by my writing so many love-letters. It seems, though news to me, that Christily is responsible for tattle about my sitting for hours writing love-letters, these being what she has made of my Diary. However meddlesome this is, it took a load from my mind, and I was feeling comfortable when he went off to the kitchen, grinning, and declaring that he would shake her like a doctor's bottle.

He was gone for a long time, and it was a very different Dr. John who came back. I have seen him worry his way through some rasping ordeals, but never showing the least emotion. Now, however, he was in such a throb that at sight of him I cried out, 'Is it as bad as that?'

'It's bad,' he said. 'Man, it is so bad and so unexpected that for the first time in my practice I cannot even pretend to know how to act; let me be for a minute.' He paced the floor, digging his gnarled fists into his eyes, a way he has when in pursuit of a problem, as if the blackness thus created helped him to see better.

'There is one of two things that must be done,' he said, 'and I have got to choose, but the responsibility is very terrible.'

I waited, thinking he was to take me into his confidence, but, instead, he just fell to staring in a kind of wonderment at me. I began to assure him that every help I could give would be forthcoming, and at that he gave a jarring laugh. I was offended, but he was at once contrite and asked for my advice.

'We could ask the young lady to come down with Mistress Lindinnock and show herself,' I suggested.

'No, we could not,' he said, so sharply that I got stiff again. He put the matter right, though, when he told me of the two courses he had to decide between, for, after all, what I had proposed was one of them; namely to confront the poor sufferer with the two ladies, which he called the kill or cure step. The second course was to go canny for a few days in the hope that the hallucination might pass of itself. She might even wake up on the morrow without it, which at the worst would be a more gentle wakening than the other.

He asked me, not like a consultant but as one who needed a stronger man to lean on, which line of action I would prefer to be taken if I was in Christily's place, and on consideration I admitted that the first one seemed to carry the more grievous shock.

After some discussion we decided to give the softer plan a short trial. I said there could be no harm in it at any rate.

He said, still very worried, indeed he was shaking, that there might be great harm in it, but that he would risk it.

We agreed that, as on all subjects save the one she was as right as I was, it would be best for me in our daily intercourse to be just my usual, but not to talk to her as if I knew she was possessed by an evil spirit.

As the doctor was anxious she should be kept from brooding I also agreed to a proposal from him that her brother, Laurie who is at present at a loose end in Branders, should pay a visit to the manse for a few days, ostensibly to brighten her, but really of course to watch her on the quiet.

This gives small promise for the time being of a comfortable manse; but what is running in my head even now is that to-morrow afternoon I go, be the weather what it likes, to the Grand House to see Miss Julie Logan again. It will be the last day of the year, but Laurie should be here by then, and Christily will be safe in his care.

To-day I am keeping an observant eye on her myself. She has brought up my meals in her old examplary way and we have exchanged a few cautious words about household affairs, but her face is sore begrutten, and if I try to be specially kind to her she knows the reason and there is more than a threatening of a breakdown.

Poor woman, it is like to be a sad New Year's Eve to her, and a heavy one too for Dr. John, who left the manse, very broken. As I let him out I said, 'It is as if the Spectrum had come back to this house.'

'Wheesht, man,' he said.

IX

THE END OF A SONG

December Thirty-first

I will try to put down the events of this terrible night with clearness and precision.

It was in the early afternoon, the snow shimmering like mica, which is sheeps-silver, that I set out for the Grand House, buttoned very thick. Despite the darkness that encompassed Christily I was in an awful and sublime state of happiness.

This may have got into my very appearance and made it unusual, for I met some of the smith's bairns, who generally run to me, but they hinted back, and when I asked what fleyed them one said, 'Your face has come so queer.' I could have danced to them in the snow from sheer joy. I am not sure but what I did dance, though I never learned it.

Some of the windows in the Five Houses already showed a glime of light, not that it was needed yet, but my folk were practising precautions against my seeing them presently, for it is always a night of solemn gallanting. These precautions largely consisted in hanging heavy cloths, such as human habiliments, behind the blinds, so as to deaden the light to me should I be watching from the manse. There was no music as yet, and I was wondering where Posty and my fiddle were, when I fell in with them on the way. Though he has forgotten who the broken men were about whom he likes to play, I notice that one little bit from his forebears, as I take it, still clings to him; he walks up and down, while he is playing the fiddle, as if it were the pipes. On this occasion, however, I expect he was on the march for seasonable largess at the Grand House, which I am sure he always receives with complete surprise.

A thing commonly said about the Grand House is that it should be called the Grand Houses, there being in a manner two of them: though the one is but a reflection of the other in a round of water close by.

This lochy is only a kitten in size but deep; and I know not whether its unusual reflective properties are accidental, or, as some say, were a device of olden times to confuse the enemy when in liquor. At any rate one cannot easily tell in certain lights, unless you are particular about things being upside down, which is the house and which the reflection.

There is an unacceptable tale of the lord of the glen having been tracked to the house after Culloden, and of the red-coats being lured by a faithful retainer into the water, where they tried doors and windows till they drowned, the lord and his faithful retainer keeking over the edge at them and crying 'Bo.'

The house is of many periods, but its wonder is the banqueting hall, or rather a window therein.

They never banquet now in the hall, not even the English, and indeed it is nigh empty of gear except for tapestries on the walls, which the ignorant take to be carpets damaged in the '45. The great bowed window is said by travelled persons to stand alone among windows, for it is twenty-eight feet in height and more than half as wide. All who come to look at it count its little lozens, as we call the panes, which are to the number of two hundred and sixteen. These panes are made of some rare glass that has a tint of yellow in it, so that, whatever the weather is, to any one inside the hall it looks to be a sunny day. In the glen this glass is not thought much of and they say it should be renewed. The house is a bit old and weary, and I dare say these lozens are the only part of it that would shame renewal.

It was not here but in a bien little chamber where however indiscriminately you sit down you sit soft, that Mistress Lindinnock received me. She was tatting (but that cannot be the right word) at a new tapestry, or mending an old one, which was so voluminous that she rose out of it as from the snow. She is such a little old person that when she stands up you may think she has sat down; nevertheless she is so gleg at coming to the boil that contradictious men have stepped back hurriedly from the loof of her hand, and yet not been quick enough. She has always, as I have said, been a fine friend to me till this unhappy day.

She was the same woman though unusual quiet while we were talking of the ravel Christily was in, which I did not have to stress, as I found Dr. John had obligingly gone straight to her with the story from the manse yesterday. I could not help enquiring, with all the look of its being an orra question, how he had taken to Miss Julie Logan.

Sharp I got the dreadful answer: 'He had no opportunity, for I had already packed the woman back to Edinburgh.'

I was to have worse blows than this to-night, though at the moment I could not have credited it; so I will only say that when I rallied I asked with cold politeness when the young lady was coming back.

Mistress Lindinnock, I could see, was eyeing me closely to find out how I stood the news, but she replied at once, like one prepared for war, 'Never, I hope; I don't like your Miss Julie Logan, my good sir.'

I will not say that even in that stern moment I got no gliff of pleasure out of hearing her called my Miss Julie Logan. Also it gave me an opportunity to reply with the thunderbolt, 'That is what I want her to be.'

She stamped her foot at me, but I never weakened. 'I demand her address,' I said. She refused it, and I replied loftily that it mattered not as I was confident she would write to me.

She raised her arms at that, like one appealing to a Higher Power, and said, 'If she writes to you I give the thing up.' Once she swung me round with a rage I could not construe and said on her tiptoes,

'I could tell you things about her any one of which would make you drop her in the burn, though you were standing in the middle of it with the jade in your arms.'

I replied in my stateliest, which has froze many, that I would stand defiant in the middle of the ocean with Miss Julie Logan on those terms; and I meant it too, though I am no swimmer.

I dare say I was a rather dignified spectacle towering there, very erect, with my arms folded: at any rate she shuddered like one cowed who had never been cowed before; or else she became cunning, for she prigged with me to do as she, my old friend, wanted, saying endearing things about how much she had liked me in the days when I was sensible, and that if I were not such a calf I would see she was now fonder of me in my imbecility. Her words were not all, as will be seen, fittingly chosen, nor did I like the pity with which she glowered at me, for she was the one in need of it.

Yet I had a melting for her at moments; especially as I was going away with but a scantling of courtesy. When she said that it would be the first time I had left her house (and she might have added any house in the glen) without calling for a benison on it, I stood rebuked. As we went on our knees she whispered rather tremulously, 'Pray, dear minister, for all who may be in trouble this night, and even danger,' and I did so, and it made the tangled woman greet.

Of course I presumed she meant Christily, but as I was shaking hands with her my mind took a shrewd turn and I said almost threateningly, 'You were not referring, were you, to Miss Julie Logan?' It spoilt the comparative friendliness of our parting, for she flared up again and said, ' 'Deed no; she is the only one that is in no need of those words to-night.'

Unfortunate being, she little knew, nor did I, the impiety of that remark.

When I got outside I was like one with no gate to go. The tae half of me was warring with the other half. I sat down very melancholic by the little round of water I have spoken of. The night was forlorn, with the merest rim of the moon in sight, and no reflection on the water beyond some misty stars. I don't know why I sat there. It was not to keep vigil; I am sure I had no suspicion that Miss Julie Logan was still in the house.

I may have been there a considerable time before I saw or heard anything. What I heard came first: distant music. It may just have been Posty playing far away the most reprehensible but the loveliest of all the Jacobite cries, 'Will you no come back again?' Soon after he finished, if it was mortal man who played, all was as still again as if the death-cart my folk tell about was nearing the glen to cart away the old year.

Candles to a great number, and very sly, were beginning to get lit in the water. I spied on them interestedly. The full moon was now out of the clouds, and it was one of those nights when she wanders. The big window nearly filled the pond, and through it I saw a throng of people in the hall. So long as my eyes were fixed on the water of course it was only their reflections I saw. I saw them on their heads as in an inverted mirror, and they looked just as agreeable as the other way; maybe Nature herself does things with a disordered mind in the last gasp of the year.

They were in the Highland dress of lang syne. I never saw them all at once, because if they came nearer they were lost in the weeds and if they went back they had a neat way of going through the walls. The older ladies were in fine head-dresses and others in their ringlets; they were more richly attired than the men, and yet the men made the finer show. I could see the trews and an occasional flashing silver button or a gleam of steel; but near all colour had been washed out of them, as if they had been ower long among the caves and the eagles.

There was plenty of food on a table that sometimes came forward, and they drank toasts thereat. I could not always put a meaning to what they did, but I saw them dancing and conversing, and though they were perhaps poor and desperate, they all, the gentlemen as much as the ladies, seemed to me to be of the great. They did rochly things as if they had fogotten the pretty ways, and next minute there would be a flourish in their manners that would have beat the pipes.

There was no music, though, and when this came to me I minded that I was not getting a sound across the water from the hall itself, though owing to the quietness of the night I heard in the open as infinitely small a thing as the letting-go of a twig. The company were as quiet as their reflections. This made me look across the pond at the window itself, which so far I had been jouking lest the company there should take tent of me. I had a mistrust they were up to ploys that were not for a minister to see, and would mischief me if they catched me spying. But that stealthy stillness garr'd me look up and I took a step or two to see better. They were all on the move, but at once stopped, hands on dirk, and I opined they suspected a watcher. I doukit, and after that, except for a wink now and again, I looked at nothing but the reflections. I knew I was in danger, but this did not greatly fash me so long as I was not catched.

I had never lost a feeling that there was an air of expectancy about them. I saw them backing against the walls to leave more space in the middle, and all eyes turned to the door, as if awaiting a great person. I suppose the tune was still swimming in my head, for I thought I knew who was coming in, he who was fed from the eagle's nest, and I had a sinking that it would be my duty to seize him and hand him over.

But it was a woman, it was Miss Julie Logan. She was not finely attired like the other ladies, but so poorly that her garments were in tatters. She would have made a braver show if each of the ladies had torn off an oddment and made a frock for her between them.

It was not, however, as one of little account that they treated her or she treated them. She was the one presence in the hall to them. They approached her only when she signed to them that she could do with it, and as if overpowered by the distinction that was befalling them. The men made profound obeisance, and the ladies sank in that lovely way to the floor. On some she smiled and let them salute her hand, and others she looked at in a way I did not see, but they backed from her as if she had put the fear of Death into them. She gave the back of her hand to Mistress Lindinnock, and I never saw an old woman look so gratified.

With a few she took a step or two in the dance, mayhap to make others glower, and soon something was taking place that I could not at first fathom.

It was clear she was about to leave them; for a ceremony similar in most respects to that with which she had been received was repeated and the doors thrown open for her passing. But then they all gathered in the far end of the hall, or sank through it, with their backs to her, which was baffling to me; for up to that moment you could see how carefully they gave her their faces. Yet they did it of set purpose, or possibly at her command, for she was watching them more haughtily than ever.

As soon as she was sure that every face was to the wall a complete change came over her. She hastened—she almost ran in her eagerness—to a corner of the window and lifted from the floor a good-sized basket that I dare say they had placed there for her. She lifted it like one who knew for certain it would be there. She filled it with viands from the table, picking and choosing them with affectionate interest.

I thought that, being in some way I had to grope for, the one they held highest, she was too proud to let them know how hungry she was, though that very knowledge was what had made them place the basket so handily and look the other way while she filled it.

I thought that, reckless of correct behaviour, as all on that side were, they were Strangers, come trailing back into the present day under a command to honour and feed one who had long ago been left behind.

While she had been lording it so imperiously in the hall, she was belike thinking more about the basket than that she was the last sough of a song.

A moment after she was gone from the hall, with a withering look for any peeping face, I heard the first sound that had reached me from the house since I took to looking in the water. It was the closing of the front door. I hurried forward, and was in time to meet Miss Julie Logan, no longer a reflection, coming down the steps with the basket.

She said, 'Carry the basket, Adam,' and I carried it, but first I put my top-coat on her, and she slipped my hand into one of the pockets along with her own.

I think it was snowing again, or a tempest or something of the kind, but we were not heeding.

She took me to a small ruin of a bield for sheltering sheep in, and in a corner of it where was a pile of stones, maybe to mark some old grave, we sat down on them and opened the basket. She was very hungry, and I myself was also slow to desist from eating. For drinking we ate the snow, against which I have warned my Sabbath School scholars. The basket was so crammed with food of an engaging nature that when we paused, replete, there was still near a basketful left. Never in my life was I so merry as sitting on those stones, and she was also very droll. She had a way of shining her face close into mine and showing her pretty teeth like a child. It was the gaiety of her, but I did not quite like it. When we wandered on I wanted to bring the basket, but she said that was the place to leave it.

We said the kind of things a man and woman never say till they know each other through and through. It was all about ourselves, and love was one of the words I did not scruple to handle.

We were not bothering about far-back times or Mistress Lindinnock; but when we came to the burn it minded me of what the Old Lady had said I woud do in a certain hap. Miss Julie Logan demanded of me to repeat to her the exact words, which I did, with one exception, namely, 'I could tell you things about her any one of which would make you drop her in the burn, though you were standing in the middle of it with the jade in your arms.' I omitted the word jade, so as not to lessen the Old Lady.

Miss Julie Logan was in a dance of delight and handed me back my coat, crying, 'Adam, let us try it!'

I said there was danger in it, and she said, 'I like danger fine,' and she coaxed me, saying, 'When you have got me there I'll tell you what the Old Lady meant, and then, if you don't drop me, belike I will be yours, Adam.' I lifted her in my arms, and in the exultation of my man's strength she was like one without weight. I carried her into the burn. It was deep and sucking. She rubbed her head on my shoulder in a way that would make a man think she liked to be where she was. She peeped up at me, and hod. I am thinking now she was wae for both of us, though she was glittering too.

She said, 'Kiss me first, Adam, in case you have to drop me.' I kissed her. 'Hold me closer,' she said, 'lest by some dread undoing you should let me slip.' I held her closer. 'Adam dear,' she said, 'it is this, I am a Papist.' At that awful word I dropped her in the burn.

That she is still there I do not doubt, though I suppose she will have been carried farther down.

I have written this clear statement in the study, to be shown by Laurie to Dr. John and by him to the Branders constabulary. I have put down everything exactly as it happened, and I swear to its accuracy.

I have refused to go to my bed this night, and I know that Laurie is sitting on a chair outside my door. I have told him none of the facts, but I can see that the man already suspects me.

I can remember nothing after I heard the splash, but he says he found me running up and down the water-side, and that he had to take a high hand with me to get me home. I would not change out of my wet things for all his blustering, but Christily, her face swollen with misery, came bursting in and tore them off me and put me into something dry. This is the last service she will ever render to me.

X

A QUARTER OF A CENTURY

It is a quarter of a century since I stopped writing this Diary and put the thing out of my sight.

Circumstances made me want to look through it again; and there it was in the garret, between the same two boards of waxcloth where I had kept it hidden from Christily in the days of my windy youth. I had forgotten that it was written on sermon paper, and such dereliction from propriety disturbs my conscience now even more than the vapours set down in it about the Roman woman.

Of course I am aware now that she never existed. I have been aware all these twenty-five years that I was the one who went queer, and not the self-sacrificing Christily, that it was to watch me that the man Laurie was brought to the manse, and that the story the Old Lady told me was invented for her by Dr. John. My two good friends had to work their way through thorns to clear my disordered mind, but they managed it by the time the glen road had come up again like a spring flower.

I was long pithless and bedded with fevers, for which the doctor blamed the burn, and in that quiet time I got rid of all my delusions; though once in the middle of my rally I escaped everybody and made for the sheep bield to decide for certain that the basket was not still there. I was perfectly sane, and yet I did that. The result of my escapade was to retard my recovery for another month.

I left the glen for good early in August, just before the return of the English, with whom, though I liked them well, I had no desire to have further discourse about Diaries or what may seem to happen when that glen is locked. I have had two charges since I gave up my first, and for eighteen years I have been minister in this flourishing place in a mining district. Two years after my call I married a lady of the neighbourhood and it has been a blessed union, for my Mima is one in a thousand and the children grow in grace. I tell Mima everything except about the Roman, that being a passage in my life that never took place, nor have I sufficient intellect to be able to speak about it without doing so as if it were real.

I am thankful to say that the Roman is to me as if she never had been (and of course she never was, that just being a slip of the pen). A Scottish minister has few top-coats in his life, and when any old clothes will suffice I sometimes wear the one that is in the Diary. Many a night in this part where the rain turns black as it alights, I have been out in the old top-coat without remembering how pretty she looked in it; and this is natural, for she never was in it.

I have only once revisited my first charge, and it was a month ago. I stayed a night at Branders with Dr. John, who has got a partner now. My old friend's hold on life has become little more than a bat's to a shutter, but he will still be at it, and some day I suppose he will be found among his own hills stiff and content.

I walked down the glen through the heather, a solitary, unless it may be said that in a sense the young Adam I had been walked with me. The English were on the hills, but they were not my English.

I lay for two nights in the old manse and preached twice. They were not great sermons, but are held by some to be my two best, and

I keep them for visits. The lad that once I was thought himself a gifted preacher, but the man he became knows better. That is nothing to boast of, for there is naught that houks the spirit from you so much as knowing better.

Mr. Gallacher, who is the new minister, the second in succession to me, was preaching at Branders, and his wife, a genteel thick lady, sat in my old pew, nearest the door. It gave me, may I be forgiven, a sort of scunner of her. Gallacher was very civil, but he is not the kind of man, I think, that the Old Lady would have waved good-night to with her window-blind. She of course has been away with it this many a year.

There is a new postman, who, 'tis said, has trudged a distance equal to round the world since the days of my Posty. Christily is married on a provision merchant in Ireland, and once a year sends me a present of eggs, with a letter enquiring very guardedly about my health. Joanna Minch and the lass have gone to some other glen. The only faces I could give a name to in the Five Houses are the smith and two of his sons. The once lusty man is now an old carl sitting on his dyke, having reached that terrible time for a Scotsman of knowing that he will never be allowed by his well-intentioned off-spring to do another day's work for ever and ever. Sometimes, to give him an hour's pride, they let him wheel a barrow. He will have to die gradual on a fine bed of straw, but he would rather be gotten with his hammer in his hands.

There have been great changes at the manse, inside and out. One hardly knows the study now, for there is a sofa fornent the fireplace. It has a grate. They burn coal. I had sold the grandy to Mr. Gallacher, and one could see by the look of it that it had never missed me. There is an erection containing a foreign plant on the identical spot where the Roman sat; but she never sat there.

Outside, the chief change in the manse is that Mr. Gallacher has lifted the hen-house to the gable-end, which I consider a great mistake. He has also cut down my gean tree.

The glen has not been what can be called locked for the last eight years, and Mr. Gallacher knows very little about the old superstitions that plagued young Adam. He had heard something nonsensical about a red-shanked man on a horse whose hoofs made no marks, a poor affair though unaccountable. Mr. Gallacher was very sound about the hallucinations all being clavers unworthy of investigation, and on that point at least we were in agreement. I asked him, just to keep the conversation going, if any Stranger woman had been seen, but he had heard of none, nor could he, for there never was one.

Of course I could not go for a walk on the Sabbath day; but as I was leaving for Branders on the Monday I got up betimes to have a last wander in the glen. I did not specially want to do this, and I prefer to put it that the fillip came from the Adam I had been. The sun soon got very masterly, though there was a nip in the air at first, and I made the mistake of wearing the old top-coat.

I sat for a time among the heather by the pond, where the reflection from the Grand House is still to be seen, but it is somewhat spoilt by a small windmill having been erected close by to provide the breeze in which, 'tis said, the trout rise best. I am told that this was Posty's last contrivance to make things easy for the English. I thought with little respect of the Jacobites and the '45, and a dog that may have been of old descent drove me away.

I went on to the bield, but nothing is left of it now except the pile of stones. I stood looking for a long time at the place where we had left the basket.

I went to Joanna's shieling, though I knew she was gone, and I found it gone too. I just went because I was sure that Joanna's visitor had been my visitor, though we were both in a dwam when we thought we saw her. I liked to mind the Roman's bonny act in making a pig of herself to heat the cold body of Joanna. I wished she had been given a chance to do this. She would have done it if she could.

I went to the Eagles Rock, and it looked the more sinister because there was a scarf of rime hiding the Logan stone. When the rime drifted I thought I could see the stone shogging.

I left my visit to the burn-side to the end. There is now a swinging bridge for the convenience of church-goers in the back-end of the year; but though little more than a wimple of water was running and sometimes coming to a standstill, I found the exact bend in the burn where I dropped her, if she had been there to drop. I stood, unruffled, keeping an iron grip on myself, my mind so rid of the old fash that I marvelled at my calm. It was not so, however, with my top-coat, which I found becoming clammy-cold, as if recalling another time by the burn and feeling we were again too near for safety. You might have said it tugged at me to come away, but that of course was just a vagary of my mind.

The young Adam in me must have had the upper hand, for looking back, I see it was to him rather than to me it happened. He thought he had catched into his arms something padding by, whose husky voice said 'Adam' lovingly, the while her glamorous face snuggled into his neck, the way a fiddle does. Next moment he gave a cry because he thought he was running with blood; and even I had a sinking till I tried my throat with my handkerchief. Whatever had been there was gone now; and I hurried away myself, for I was as shaken as if it had been the Spectrum.

I bided the night at Branders with Dr. John, to whom all my story was so familiar except just one happening that I had always sworn never to reveal even to him.

We sat long over his pipe talking about what he called the old dead-and-done affair. We were very intimate that night, the one of us an ancient and the other getting on.

'Let us be thankful,' the doctor said, 'that it can all be so easily construed, for the long and the short of it is that you were just away in your mind. Any other construing of it would be too uncomfortable to go to our beds on even now.'

I said, taking a higher line: 'It is not even allowable'; and yet we discussed the possibility of its having had any backing to it for, I suppose, the last time. This would have meant that the glen, instead of its minister, does sometimes go queer in the terrible stillness of the time when it is locked. 'We should have to think,' the doctor said, with the kettle in his hand, 'that it all depended on the stillness of the glen. If it got to be stiller than themselves it woke them up, and they were at their old ploys again.'

'I am not seeing,' I said, 'how even that could bring me into it.'

'Nor am I,' he agreed, pouring out cosily, 'but let us say that in such incredible circumstances you might by some untoward accident have got involved while the rest of us escaped.'

The word accident is not a friend of mine, and so, or for some other reason, I said, 'I would rather think she had picked me out.' He smiled at that, not grasping that I was speaking for young Adam.

'Maybe,' he said to make me laugh, but failing, 'it was her echo that was back in the glen, and by some mischance you got into the echo.'

Then he grew graver, and said he would have none of those superstitions; the affair could only be construed naturally so long as we accepted the experiences I once thought I had gone through as having been nothing but the fancies of a crazy man.

'All of them?' I could not help saying.

'Every one,' said he, clapping me confidently on the shoulder; 'do you not see, man, that if any one of them was arguable it would be less easy to dispose of the lave?'

'That day during my illness,' I said, 'when I was but three parts convinced by your construing, and slipped away from you all to the bield to make certain that the basket was not there——'

'Precisely,' said he, 'that would be a case in point. What strange ravels might we have got entangled in if you had found that basket!'

My many years' old resolution to keep the thing dark from all, even from him, broke down, and I spoke out the truth. 'Dr. John,' I told him, 'I did find the basket that day.'

For long he threepit with me that I was away in my mind again, but he had to listen to me while I let out the tale, which has ceased to perturb me, though I have a sort of a shiver at writing it down. I found the basket with its provender in the bield where we had left it, and at that the peace which had been coming to me threatened to go, and my soul was affrichted. I prayed long, and I took the basket down to the burn and coupit its sodden gear therein, and itself I tore to bits and scattered. It was far waur to me at that time to think that she had been than that she was just a figment of the brain.

I told all this to Dr. John, and at first he was for spurning it, nor can I say for certain that he believes it now. I leave it at that, but fine I know it would be like forsaking the callant that once I was to cast doubt on what lies folded up in his breast.

I am back now, secure and serene, in my mining town which, in many ways, with its enterprise and modern improvements, including gas and carts to carry away any fluff of snow that falls, is far superior to my first charge. I have a wider sphere of usefulness and a grand family life. As I become duller in the uptake, time will no doubt efface every memory of Miss Julie of the Logan; and of mornings I may be waking up without the thought that I have dropped her in the burn. Of course it is harder on young Adam. I have a greater drawing to the foolish youth that once I was than I have pretended. When I am gone it may be that he will away back to the glen.